# RICHARD BURTON
## *My Brother*

# RICHARD BURTON

*My Brother*

## GRAHAM JENKINS

### with Barry Turner

MICHAEL JOSEPH  LONDON

*To my brother Tom and*
*my adopted mother Cassie*

MICHAEL JOSEPH LTD

Published by the Penguin Group
27 Wrights Lane, London w8 5tz, England
Viking Penguin Inc., 40 West 23rd Street, New York, New York 10010, USA
Penguin Books Australia Ltd, Ringwood, Victoria, Australia
Penguin Books Canada Ltd, 2801 John Street, Markham, Ontario, Canada l3r 1b4
Penguin Books (NZ) Ltd, 182–190 Wairau Road, Auckland 10, New Zealand

Penguin Books Ltd, Registered Offices: Harmondsworth, Middlesex, England

First published in Great Britain in 1988
Second Impression February 1988

Made and printed in Great Britain by
Richard Clay Ltd, Bungay, Suffolk
Filmset in Monophoto Sabon

*British Library Cataloguing in Publication Data*

Jenkins, Graham
 Richard Burton: my brother.
 1. Burton, Richard *1925–1984*  2. Actors
 ———Great Britain———Biography
 I. Title
 791.43'028'0924   PN2598.B795
 ISBN 0-7181-3010-3

# Contents

# Acknowledgements

This book could not have been written without the assistance of a large number of people who gave freely and generously of their time and knowledge. So first of all I should like to thank: Ron Berkeley, Elizabeth Bush, Alexander Cohen, Dai Dwsh Davies, John Dexter, John Dolan, Daniel Dillon Evans, Leslie Evans, the late Trevor George, Robert Hardy, Richard Harris, Kitty Carlisle Hart, Frank Hauser, Marjorie Lee, Richard Leech, Andrew Leigh, Carol Martin, John Parry, Sir Anthony Quayle, Chen Sam, Peter Shaffer, William Squire and the Reverend Eric Williams.

I owe a very special vote of thanks to all my family and particularly to my sisters Cis and Hilda. Elizabeth Taylor and her agent Robert Lantz have been an inspiration to me throughout the preparation of this book.

Dr Sonia Robertson and Mary Fulton were a constant source of cheerful encouragement and hospitality, and my good friend Ian Robertson played a vital part in the early stages of researching the story of my brother's life and career. Without Ian's assistance from the very beginning and his continued support throughout, this story would not have been told.

My warm thanks, too, to Barry Turner for making the manuscript a reality and to my editor, Roger Houghton, for guiding the book through to publication.

Above all I would like to thank my wife Hilary for her patience and understanding during the three years that I have been working on this book.

Ti wyddost beth ddywed fy nghalon.

Graham Jenkins
*Porthcawl, Wales January 1988*

# Introduction

*I* cannot, nor will I try to, explain here what Richard was and still is to my life, it would take an entire book to say what I feel. One day I may write that book, but not now, it's still too soon for me.

I am delighted that his family, with Graham as their representative, have put together this book to share with you some of the aspects of what made Richard the most remarkable man I have ever known.

The love he and his family shared was beautiful, rare, volatile, tender and as strong and wild as the Welsh valleys he loved so well.

He lives on in the memory of everyone he touched – his family are his history and his living heritage, and only they can understand what made this man the son and soul of Wales (which is a state of being, not just a nationality). Maybe their reminiscences will bring you closer to understanding this magnificent enigma.

I hope that this book makes you smile and feel happy he was here, even if it was only for a short while.

Elizabeth Taylor
*New York January 1988*

# Chapter 1

Stumbling on the extraordinary, we lose faith in our senses.
Can this really be happening to me?

For most, this feeling of amazement, of being of the world while somehow rising above the world, comes rarely. For Richard Burton it was an experience so frequent and so intense that in the end it parted him from reality.

He demanded to be extraordinary but never came to terms with his talent or his luck.

He was forever saying, 'Is this really happening to me?'

We were met at Geneva airport by two black limousines. We saw them immediately we came out of customs, parked close up to the central doors where there were signs for taxis and buses.

In charge of transport was Brook Williams, long time companion and chief gofer in the Burton household. As we approached, he started apologising. 'It was such a shock . . . Bound to be a muddle . . . So many wanted to come . . . Hotels are overbooked in the season.'

'I can imagine,' I said, and left it at that.

Outside were photographers and a television crew. We paused for them to take pictures.

I went to the front car with two sisters, the eldest, Cis, then in her eightieth year, and Hilda. Brother Verdun, his wife, Betty and sister Cassie followed in the second car.

Barely a word was spoken on the twenty minute drive to Pays de Galles. It was a time for memories. Now Rich was dead, none of us

1

could expect to pass this way again.

My own feelings were a confusing mix of sadness, shock and anger.

Sadness for a brother gone and sadness for what might have been. Somewhere in my luggage was a copy of that morning's *Times*. The headline read, 'Career Madly Thrown Away'. Many others had made the same point, if perhaps less callously. But it was not the whole story. In the last few years Richard had exorcised a devil. He was off the booze and his work, once so fickle, was again attracting serious interest.

Maybe it was all too late. I know now that his memory was leaving him faster than water out a leaky bucket. But in the last weeks he had looked fit and well. He was more confident than for a decade past. And he talked a lot about the future.

This is where sadness overlapped with shock. Why *now*?

And where shock overlapped with anger. We were told so little of the circumstances of Rich's death. When the news came through it was no more than the bare details. Verdun was the first to know. He was telephoned at his home in Cwmafan from Los Angeles of all places by Valerie Douglas, Rich's personal secretary.

She told him Rich had become ill at home, had been rushed to a hospital in Geneva, but had died before the doctors could help him. Verdun's first thought was how to tell the rest of the family. Hilda and Cassie lived nearby but on a Sunday morning he knew they would be at chapel. He went to find them.

An hour or so later Hilda rang me in Hampshire.

'Have you heard?' she asked tentatively.

'Heard what?'

'Richard is dead.'

We both had to struggle to talk and there were long silences as we fought back tears.

'Does Cis know?'

Cis or Cecilia was closer to Rich than any of us. After our mother's death when Rich was only two, she brought him up as her own child. In her later years Cis gives every appearance of frailty. Small and slight with white wispy hair and a voice as gentle as a breeze, she is every child's idea of a perfect grandmother. But her authority is undiminished. The family love and revere her and would do anything to stop her being hurt.

But on that fifth day of August 1984, there was no way of shielding her. Hilda, the strongest of our breed, rang Cis at her home in Hadley Wood where she lives near her two daughters and their families.

Her response was so much in character I might have guessed it

2

before the words were spoken.

'Why couldn't it have been me?'

After the call from Hilda I sat quietly with my wife, Hilary, talking at random about the past and then, as the shock subsided, a little about the future.

Richard had made known his wish to be buried at Pontrhydyfen, his birthplace, and, for him, the heart of his beloved Wales. But I guessed there might be difficulties. There were too many vested interests at stake.

'Shouldn't you ring Sally?' Hilary suggested.

'No, I don't think so. At least, not yet.'

But should I have rung Sally? She was, after all, Rich's wife. Any plans we had for the next few days had to start with her.

The fact was, I wanted time to reflect. Sally was young, tough and reasonably resourceful and, in those characteristics at least, everything Richard had needed in his fight to regain his self respect. But Sally was also a woman made jealous by her late arrival on the Burton marital scene. After just two years of living with Rich she resented any assumptions of intimacy from family or friends which excluded her. Most particularly, she resented the enduring love of the woman who gave Rich his happiest years – Elizabeth Taylor.

A battle of wills seemed inevitable.

To step into that contest uninvited was to ask for trouble. Instead, I drove north to Hadley Wood to be with Cis. But no sooner had I walked in the door and into her arms than the phone rang. It was Sally and she wanted to talk to me.

I took a deep breath, not quite knowing what to expect. Her voice was steady and clinically precise. She skipped over the clichés. Then, 'I want to make it clear. I don't want Cis to be at the funeral. She'll only trigger me off.'

'Look,' I said, 'I know you're upset. It's a terrible time for all of us. Can't we leave ourselves a few hours to think? I need to talk with the family.'

'I've done my thinking. You know what I want.'

We talked for another five minutes but I was feeling numb. How was I to tell Cis?

I slept on it and the following morning I passed on the gist of the conversation. Cis said quietly, 'So the funeral is to be in Celigny, not in Pontrhydyfen.'

Curiously, the assumption built in to Sally's opening words had not occurred to me. Of course, she had already made up her mind. There was to be no discussion.

'Well, you tell her,' declared Cis, 'I will be in Celigny for the funeral. I will be at the service and I will be at the graveside to say goodbye to Richard. It is what Richard would have wanted and it is what I am going to do.'

'And that makes two of us,' I said.

It was for the rest of the family to make up their own minds.

But what of Elizabeth? That she too had been warned off was a near certainty. Her reaction was more difficult to surmise.

In fact, like the rest of us, she was thinking it over. I discovered this later in the day when she rang from Los Angeles.

'What do you suggest I should do?' she asked.

By now, my brain was working and I was ready with an answer.

'I might quarrel with Sally's motives, but I can understand the problem. The funeral will be front page news all over the world. If you put in an appearance, the press will really have a field day. We could end up with a riot on our hands. And none of us wants that. Why not leave it a few days until the fuss has died down and then come to the memorial service at Pontrhydyfen?'

'Sally is ahead of you,' said Elizabeth. 'She's already thought of the memorial service. She doesn't want me in Wales either.'

For the rest of the day and half the night, the phone rang incessantly. One journalist after another asked the same questions and got the same answers. 'Just a few words, Mr Jenkins; just a few words.'

The following morning there was another call from Celigny, not Sally this time but Valerie Douglas who had flown in from Los Angeles to take charge of the funeral arrangements. I have a respect for Valerie which stops short of affection though it's fair to say that she was very good at her job and Rich thought the world of her. A secretary cum manager of the crabapple school, she had been with Richard since his early days in Hollywood. But her proprietorial view of her duties did not endear her to Elizabeth. When Rich and Elizabeth married her star faded though it did not disappear completely. Now, in her late sixties, she was enjoying her comeback – every minute of it.

I had tangled with Valerie three years earlier. Richard had asked me to host a dinner for Elizabeth who was in London starring in *The Little Foxes*. The bill – a hefty Dorchester one – was duly sent on to Valerie as Richard had instructed. Back came a blistering reprimand for my extravagance. (Where was I supposed to take Elizabeth Taylor? McDonalds?) At the Pontrhydyfen memorial service Valerie told me, 'I know you won't believe me, but it was your brother who told me to write about overdoing the entertainment.'

She was right. I did not believe her.

When Valerie rang the day after Rich's death, it was to demand that we should all stay away from the funeral.

'It would be best for all of us,' she explained sweetly, 'if the whole affair was kept low key. Surely you can see that.'

The logic of the argument was lost on me.

'What are you frightened of?' I asked. 'Surely you can't object to close family. If we're not eligible to attend, who is?'

There was a long pause.

'Well, if you must, you must,' she said finally.

'Thank you,' I said, and put down the phone.

They had one more try. Next in line for the role of dissuader was Brook Williams. Brook is the son of Emlyn Williams. Mostly, Rich valued him as an amiable and amusing companion.

After a few drinks, Brook can be outrageously camp.

'Graham, love,' he began. 'You know what it's like at this time of year. I've been trying to book rooms for you and your family but all the hotels are packed out. It's the tourists; they're everywhere.'

Suddenly, I was on firm ground.

'Forget it, Brook. I'm sure you have other things to worry about. Perhaps you don't know but I am chairman of a travel firm. I can fix everything from this end.'

He interrupted. 'No, no. There's no need for that. We'll arrange something. It's just that, well, it's all very difficult.'

I wished him the best of luck.

So here we were, two days later, in plush Mercedes travelling the Lausanne road along Lake Geneva with a small procession of press cars closely in tow.

We came into the village of Celigny, past the station with its Café de la Gare where Rich could always be found if he was not at home, and down the road toward Pays de Galles, or 'Land of the Welsh'.

'If I should die think only this of me – there is some corner of a foreign field that is, for ever – Wales.'

The gates were shut and bolted.

Standing outside were a pack of security guards distinguished by their navy blue denims and dark glasses. They carried pistols and truncheons. We showed the identity cards (like calling-cards) which Brook Williams had given us at the airport. The gates opened and the limousines edged through, leaving the rest of the procession to park on the roadside.

I had seen Pays de Galles many times before but I never ceased to wonder at its ordinariness. It is a provincial villa of the sort to be

5

found in any suburb of any European city. Pale cement, on box style architecture. Where is the splendid luxury of the Hollywood superstar? Not here. But this is what Rich called home – the antidote perhaps to the lavish fantasy of acting out his life on screen.

Brook led us into the living room – all cosy chintz and thick carpet. Sally's mother was there with Doris, Yul Brynner's former wife. We were introduced and sat down. Valerie Douglas appeared.

'You'll be wondering about Sally,' she said. 'She's resting at the moment and is not to be disturbed. She'll join you shortly.'

We made safe, courteous conversation. I let my thoughts drift.

Do you remember, Rich, when you and I were boys?


There was a singing competition at a county Eisteddfod. Rich and I were entered for the junior section where I was expected to take first prize. I shared the confidence of my elders. Was I not known as the Wonder Boy Soprano? No one else came within miles of my natural talent now perfected, or so I thought, by the training of a retired tin miner, Johnny Jenkins, himself the champion of many an Eisteddfod.

Came the day, I marched on to the stage, took one look at the ranks of important faces, and felt my throat go dry.

My performance was no more than adequate. Next on was Rich. All of ten years old, he faced the audience like a champion gladiator. A moment or two of silence until the paper rustlers and apple eaters settled down and then he was off. His voice lacked a certain finesse, but he sang and acted with pure rapture. The applause followed him all the way to the winner's rostrum, leaving me to collect the prize for runner-up.

It was Rich all over. Talented, yes, but he had something more – the knowledge that winning has most to do with wanting. And he wanted to succeed very much indeed.

There was another side to his character revealed that day. When the audience had dispersed and we were getting ready to go home, he came up to me, put his hand in mine and left me holding – the winner's medal. 'You take it,' he said, 'I thought you were the best.'

The unpredictable act of great generosity was to be a recurring feature of his life.


Sally came in. She was wearing a bedrobe done up to the neck. Her hair was neatly arranged but her face was stone white. Her eyes stared as if she was in a trance. She did not say a word.

The dozen or so people in the room who had been speaking in

whispers were now silent. Cis made the first move. She went over to Sally and gave her a hug. She did not respond.

Then we all started talking again – a forced, embarrassed conversation half directed at Sally. 'Have you been able to rest, dear?' – 'She does look tired doesn't she?' – 'Come over here and sit down' – 'Now is there anything we can do?'

Sally found her voice.

'I suppose you want to know what happened?' We all nodded, as if one.

'I woke up at about seven. Richard was still in bed which was unusual for him. He liked getting up early. I went back to sleep. When I woke up again, Richard was making funny gurgling noises. I couldn't wake him. I rang Valerie.'

'You did what?' I could not hide my amazement.

'I rang Valerie.'

'Seven thousand miles away? In Los Angeles?'

'I told you. I was frightened.'

'And what did Valerie say?'

'She said to get a doctor.'

I murmured something but Cis and Hilda signalled me to be quiet.

Valerie Douglas chimed in.

'Isn't it time you checked in at the hotel? We're eating early this evening. Sally has arranged Richard's favourite meal. I'm sure you'll want to brush up.'

The cars were waiting to take us the mile down the road. I would have preferred to walk but to do so would have been to risk being hijacked by the reporters massing outside the gates.

The Hotel Port d'Elleves is a cosy Swiss chalet affair overlooking the lake. Contrary to Brook Williams' predictions, there seemed to be rooms to spare. A few puzzled tourists mingled uneasily with the press corps who knew enough about the district not to book in to the smart hotels in Geneva.

When I'd emptied my case, I went down to the bar. I needed a drink.

The conflict of emotions left me with a sense of painful bewilderment. To feel like a stranger at my own brother's funeral was bad enough, but there was more – the overwhelming sensation that everyone in the Burton entourage was determined to put on a great performance. This was to be the last Burton extravaganza. All that was missing was the star.

There were some journalists sitting at a table. One of them recognised me and invited me over. The last thing I wanted was to launch

7

into an introspection on the Burton tragedy. But the talk was of the early days. The promise of greatness to come.

I was asked, 'Have you seen the grave?'

'No,' I said, 'I'm not even sure where it is.'

'We'll show you if you like. But you won't be very impressed.'

'What's wrong with it?'

'It's so overgrown. The cemetery looks like a wilderness. Do you want to see it?'

I caught sight of Cis and the others coming down the stairs.

'Tomorrow,' I said. 'We'll go tomorrow morning.'

Dinner at Pays de Galles was less fraught than I had anticipated. Sally did not say very much but she warmed to Verdun who told her stories about Rich which made her smile. The rest of us had heard them a hundred times before, but we caught the mood of the occasion and kept the conversation to neutral topics. The only harsh note came from Valerie Douglas who, feeling out of it, brought us back to the business in hand with a sharp reminder – 'Don't forget I want to talk to you guys tomorrow. I have some news for you.'

We presumed she was talking about the will.

Later, I tried to have a private word with Valerie. She had set up office in the library, Rich's hideaway, a part conversion of the old stables which were some way back from the house. It was a long room with one side lined with overlapping shelves. The opposite wall and the beams were decorated with acting awards, hung up like hunting trophies.

Valerie sat at the far end from the door. She was behind a table swamped with papers. Beside her was a small desk similarly laden. Telephones were placed strategically. I walked the full length of the room.

'I'm still trying to understand,' I said.

'Understand what?'

'How, why, Rich died.'

'It was a colossal haemorrhage. There was nothing anyone could do.'

I thought, that was what they said about Dadi Ni. He had died the same way, but at eighty-one. Rich had not reached fifty-nine.

'It was just that when I last saw him, he was on top form.'

'He may have looked that way to you, but he'd taken a lot of punishment.'

I could hardly disagree. Anyway, she was not keen to continue the conversation.

'Let's go down,' she suggested. 'The others will be waiting.'

She let me go ahead. Turning back I saw her locking the door behind her.

The day before the funeral, more family and friends arrived. Staying at the hotel were brother Dai and Gareth, Hilda's eldest son, who cut short his holiday to be with us. Ron Berkeley with his wife and son flew in from Paris. Ron had worked with Rich as his hairdresser and make-up man on nearly all his big films. Like every survivor in the movie jungle, he developed a shrewd business sense which he now puts to good use as head of a multi-million dollar fashion business. I was delighted to see Ron, who always manages to impart a sense of confidence and well being however desperate the circumstances. I was not altogether surprised to hear that he had come of his own volition when the expected invitation failed to materialise. Ron had assumed what we had been told, that accommodation would be tight. But we noted that evening that despite the growing accumulation of mourners and reporters, our hotel still had vacancies.

The children of Richard's extended family stayed at Pays de Galles. There was Kate, his daughter by his first wife, and her future husband Christopher, Sybil, who was not invited or, at any rate, did not appear; Richard's stepchild from his marriage to Elizabeth Taylor, Liza Todd with her husband Hap (short for Happy); and then Maria Burton, the adopted daughter of Richard and Elizabeth, and her husband Steve Carson. Neither Christopher nor Michael Wilding put in an appearance, which surprised me.

All of us were to meet together for the first time that evening.

After lunch, I and my two brothers with Gareth went to the church to rehearse our part in the funeral service. We were followed by a swarm of reporters who occupied a nearby café while we tested our voices against the acoustics of domed arches and heavy stonework. We put a lot of emotion into our singing and it did us the world of good.

'What next?' Gareth asked as we came out of the church.

'Shouldn't we go to the cemetery?' I suggested.

'What for? To see the grave? Even if it is in a bit of a mess, there's nothing much we can do.'

'Anyway,' said Verdun, 'we don't know where it is.'

I pointed to the reporters who were gathering outside the café. 'They'll show us.'

So, for the first and last time that week, instead of the press following us, we followed the press.

That Catholicism is the dominant faith in this part of Switzerland is evident by the location of the Protestant cemetery, well away from the public gaze. We got there through a field on a long muddy track to what looked like a small copse. In amongst the trees were four or five headstones and an open grave.

9

'It doesn't look too bad,' said Verdun. 'A bit remote, but what can you expect?'

It was true, the scene was much neater than I had expected. From the smell of freshly-cut grass, I assumed the gardeners had been hard at work all morning.

The spot where Rich was to be buried held our gaze. We were quiet for a moment as we thought forward twenty-four hours. Verdun broke the spell. 'Come on,' he said. 'Let's get back to the hotel.'

When the cars delivered us at Pays de Galles later in the afternoon, I made a beeline for the garden. I was not keen on more intense family heart searching. But before I could get out of the house I was cornered by Valerie Douglas.

'I suppose you've heard, Elizabeth wants to come to the funeral.'

I said I had not heard, but I was hardly surprised.

'Her appearance here would be inappropriate,' Valerie went on. 'It might be different if the funeral was in Wales. But here! What does she think she's up to?'

'I don't see how you can blame Elizabeth for the funeral arrangements.'

'I've already told you,' said Valerie, 'the funeral has to be in Switzerland. For tax reasons.'

Cis was standing close by. I had not realised she was listening until she cut across the conversation. She spoke quietly but with great emphasis.

'For why do you say Rich is to be buried here? For reasons of tax? But Rich is not worried about tax. And we, his family, are not worried about tax.'

'That's not the point,' said Valerie, knowing full well she had made a tactical error. 'The point is, the funeral will be here and Elizabeth Taylor must be told not to come.'

I felt my temper stretch.

'It's not up to you or us to tell Elizabeth what to do. She'll make up her own mind.'

'Well, Sally's not going to like it,' retorted Valerie and stalked off.

It occurred to me that if Elizabeth did plan on coming – and judging by Valerie's outburst the odds looked in favour – there was precious little any of us could do because she would be on the plane. Unless, of course, she intended arriving after the service. That way she might fulfil her wish to be with us but avoid disrupting the ceremony.

I went into the living room where Sally was receiving her guests. Liza Todd was on the telephone, concentrating hard. But as I entered she looked up and said into the receiver, 'Uncle Graham's just come in, do you want a word with him?'

10

From this I gathered she was talking to her mother.

As I took over from Liza I kept my eye on Sally who was glaring at me with obvious disapproval.

Elizabeth said, 'I won't be at the funeral tomorrow, Graham. I'm sure that's best for everyone. But I haven't made up my mind about Wales. Does the family want me at the memorial service?'

'Of course,' I said. 'But it's just, just a bit difficult to go into right now.'

'Oh, I see. You're overheard?'

'You could say so.'

'OK, let's talk later.'

I put down the receiver.

Sally got up. 'Why did you do that?'

'What?' I could not think what she was talking about.

'Why did you ring off? I wanted to talk to Elizabeth.'

'I'm sorry. I've only just come in. I assumed you'd already spoken to her.'

'Well, I hadn't.'

Her sharp tone told me I was in for a row I did not want. I made another apology and retreated, but she followed me out into the hall. She spoke now in a clenched whisper.

'Can't you get it straight? I don't want Elizabeth Taylor here or at the service in Wales.'

'And can't you understand, you have no right to make demands of the family or of Elizabeth. We will do what we think best.'

She had a lot more to say, but fortunately we were interrupted by one of the girls telling us that dinner was ready. The conversation over the table was subdued. The hotel party did not stay long.

Afterwards, in the car, Cis wanted to know. 'What was that between you and Sally?'

'It was about Elizabeth. She wants to come to the service in Pontrhydyfen. And I think she should.'

Cis nodded. 'And so do I.'


The third day was the day of the funeral.

We went to Pays de Galles to be allocated places in the convoy of luminaries. I sat alongside Cis with Gareth in the front passenger seat. At six foot and seventeen stone, I reckoned that Gareth was our best protection against over-attentive photographers. How right I was.

The crowd filled the road and stopped our car some fifty yards short of the church. After that we were on our own with me holding

11

on to Cis while Gareth forced a way ahead. No doubt there were a few genuine mourners in attendance, but they were vastly outnumbered by the press. The cameras were pushed close in on our faces. Up ahead I could see a television crew on top of their van recording a panoramic view of the melée.

During our slow shoulder-to-shoulder progression, Cis remained tight-lipped. But when we reached the sanctuary of the church, and the noise subsided behind us, she allowed herself a little smile. 'Who would have thought that Rich would become so popular.'

Occupying two front rows of seats, the Jenkins family was to lead the singing, or rather to take over the singing because all the hymns were in Welsh. I am pleased to say that when it came to it we put on a performance of which our brother would have been proud. Those listening outside said later that it sounded as if we had smuggled in all of South Wales to swell the volume.

But it was a long wait before we got started. As the minutes ticked by, my worries intensified. Where was Sally? It was some comfort to know that Verdun was with her in the car immediately following the hearse. Even so . . . .

In fact, what had happened was that the crush beyond the church was so great, the undertakers had been unable to unload the coffin. Instead, the hearse had set off on another circle of the village, ending up outside the vicarage. There, the coffin was carried through the garden, over the back wall and into the church by a side entrance. Sally, Verdun and the others who filed in behind the coffin looked nervous and confused.

Then we had to stand for five minutes' silence. This was Sally's contribution to the proceedings which she insisted upon against all advice. The tension was barely tolerable. It was like being in a library with notices everywhere saying Quiet. I wanted to scream just to break the trance. When, mercifully, the service proper began, for at least half an hour everything went according to plan. The prayers and the short address by Pastor Arnold Mobbs, who had known Rich since he moved to Switzerland, were given in English and French. Richard's beloved Kate, in her soft American accent, read Dylan Thomas's 'Do Not Go Gentle Into That Good Night'.

'. . . old age should burn and rave at close of day
Rage, rage, against the dying of the light.
And you, my father, there on the sad height,
Curse, bless me now with your fierce tears I pray.
Do not go gentle into that good night.
Rage, rage against the dying of the light.'

My part was to read the lesson, Chapter 13 of the First Epistle to the Corinthians, in English and Welsh: 'Though I speak with the tongues of men and angels, I am become as sounding brass, or a tinkling cymbal.' It was a favourite, learnt by heart, in Welsh, when Rich was knee-high.

When I left my seat in the congregation to go to the lectern, I stood for the first time above the level of the coffin. The mass of red flowers on top now took on a discernable pattern. It made me stop and catch my breath. I was looking down at the fiery red dragon of Wales.

As we filed out of the church into bright sunlight it took a moment or two to find our bearings. The cars were parked close by but we could not see them for the crowd of onlookers. There was nothing for it but to push forward and hope for the best.

As it happened, it was easier getting out of the church than getting in. It was only when we reached the cemetery that I realised why. The press had moved ahead of us to take up positions around the grave. Perched on ladders up against trees and the dry stone wall which edged the cemetery, the photographers peered down at us. I guessed they sought a high position to snap the best overall view of the ceremony but afterwards I found out that they were all looking beyond the tiny group of mourners. There was a rumour that Elizabeth Taylor would turn up at the last minute and they wanted to be in the best position to record her arrival. One particularly keen member of the paparazzi was lodged in the highest branches of a tree, almost directly above our heads. The irreverent thought occurred to me, how would it be if we shook him out of his perch? With luck, he might plummet into the grave. Now that would be a story worth reporting.

The service was a gentle murmur from Pastor Arnold Mobbs who had known Rich since he first came to Celigny in 1955. The Presbyterian minister had christened Kate and her sister Jessica, a sad child who was autistic and lived in a special home. When the formalities were completed the Welsh contingent prepared to launch into 'Sospan Fach', the rugby anthem much loved by Rich. The tune is from the old Welsh hymnal but the words are sheer nonsense. Cis thought the song inappropriate but Rich had often said that he wanted it sung at his funeral and Sally strenuously approved.

I was grateful to her; grateful too when, as our voices lifted, she permitted herself a little smile. Only once did she come close to breaking down. This was when she moved forward to place a letter on top of the coffin.

When we dispersed, I said to the reporters, 'It was Welsh enough, wasn't it? There were only six of us singing 'Sospan Fach' but we made it sound like the national male voice choir.'

Someone asked, 'What was in the letter?'

I said I did not know, which was true.

'And what about the rose?'

'The rose?'

'Didn't you see? There was a single red rose among the tributes. Do you know who sent it?'

I said I did not know, which was true. But I could guess.

After the funeral there was a gathering of local people at the Café de la Gare. Sally backed off at the last minute and returned directly to the house. But the rest of us went along to make polite conversation. In fact, the occasion was not as heavy going as I expected. With so many happy memories of Rich who was a generous friend to the village, the conversation flowed. Just a few weeks earlier, I discovered, Rich had been due to preside at the celebrations for the Swiss national day. It was a function he had performed most years when he was in Celigny in August. As the party broke up I had a word with the owner of the Café de la Gare who prepared all the meals at the Pays de Galles throughout our stay.

'Don't take this wrongly,' I said, 'but do you mind telling me what we are eating tonight?'

'Fish,' he said.

'Fish? Again?'

And it was the same fish – a sprat-sized creature fried, with chips. It did not figure in my list of great meals of our time.

'Look,' I said, 'do me a favour, make me something simple. What about a steak, medium rare?'

Paul said he would be happy to oblige.

Back at the house, we gathered for an early dinner. Sally was quick to spot the change in the menu. It was almost as if she was spoiling for a fight.

'What the hell do you think you're up to? Don't you like fish? It was your brother's favourite meal.'

'Yes,' I said, 'I like fish, but not every night.'

There was an embarrassed silence. We ate quickly and made ready to return to the hotel. The cars were waiting. The idea was for everyone to gather back at the house an hour or two later for a farewell drink. I cannot say I was very keen. I would have been happier with a short leave-taking there and then. But the rest of the family was properly wary of upsetting the prescribed timetable.

In the hotel lobby I met up with John Parry, BBC arts correspondent whom I knew well from my days at Broadcasting House. We chatted about this and that while I waited for our drivers to appear. Eventually, just one turned up. He did not know where his colleague was; maybe he had misunderstood his instructions. John Parry broke in. 'Don't worry. I'll give you a lift. I was going up that way.'

John followed the official car through the gates of Pays de Galles to the top of the drive. As we all got out Sally, who was waiting for us, shouted from the steps. I went over to her.

'Who's that with you?'

I told her.

'Are you mad?' she shouted. 'Do you think I want the BBC here? I hate the lot of them. Get him out! Get him out!'

At her volume, it was unnecessary to relay the message to John Parry. At thirty paces he heard enough to know he was most definitely not welcome. I shrugged my shoulders in his direction, we gave each other a wave and he drove off. As we went into the house, Cis took hold of Sally's arm.

'What is the matter, now. What has Graham done?'

Sally shook herself free, while saying to me, 'What did I tell you? I warned you not to bring Cis. I told you she'd get uptight.'

Then she stormed off.

Sally was not alone in her anger. It was as much as I could do to stay in the house long enough for the briefest formalities. As soon as I could get away I walked to the hotel, trying to shake off an ill temper. It was not difficult to understand why Sally was as she was. She had known Richard for little more than two years; they had been married for half that time. From Rich's side it was a relationship founded on uncertainty, about his career and where it was taking him, but more importantly about what he needed for peace of mind. Part of him was always with Elizabeth Taylor. If Sally had any single purpose it was to shake off the other woman. But she was not quite given long enough to achieve her ambition. She had never possessed Rich in the way she wanted. Now she was doubly sad; for a lost love and for what might have been. Did she not then deserve sympathy? Of course, without question. But what I could not take was her assumption that, somehow, we were all locked in a conspiracy against her; that by claiming some part of the memory of Rich we were trying to steal what was rightfully hers.

I was sitting on the hotel verandah looking out over the water, when Ron Berkeley nudged my elbow.

'It doesn't look as if you're out of the wood yet,' he said. 'Sally's just come in.'

I glanced back towards the lobby where Sally was talking earnestly with Ron's wife. I thought it best to let events take their course.

'You know what she's worried about,' said Ron. 'She thinks you're trying to get Elizabeth Taylor to the memorial service in Wales.'

'But that's not true,' I said. 'I'm fed up with telling everybody. What Elizabeth decides to do is her own affair.'

'It looks as if you'll have to be more persuasive,' suggested Ron.

Sally came up to me. She was tight-lipped and clearly very angry.

'I want you to tell Elizabeth you've changed your mind; that you don't want her to come to Wales.'

I got out of my chair. 'Look, I'll say it one more time. If Elizabeth wants to come, she'll be welcome. But she has to make up her own mind.'

'You're doing this deliberately,' Sally shouted. 'You could help if you wanted to. Unless you ring the woman, I'll do something desperate.'

Suddenly I was very tired.

An hour or so later Elizabeth rang me at the hotel. I told her all that had happened in the day including my rows with Sally.

'I don't know what to do,' said Elizabeth. 'I want to be at the memorial service but I don't want a fight with Sally. Do you think she will do something stupid?'

'I wouldn't be surprised,' I admitted.

'Well, I can't wait much longer. If I'm coming I must get a flight tomorrow morning. But I don't want to cause a great upset.'

The following morning as we were about to leave for the airport, I talked with Kate.

'Will she come?' she wanted to know.

'Maybe,' I said, 'but I think it's less likely by the minute.'

'Did you invite her?'

'No, because it's not up to me to issue invitations.'

There was a peep from a car horn.

'You'd better go,' said Kate. 'You don't want to miss the plane. You have a lot to do back in Wales.'

I picked up my suitcase. 'A memorial service I can handle,' I said. 'What I can do without is a civil war.'

# Chapter 2

The person that was Richard Burton – or Richard Walter Jenkins as he was for the first seventeen years – was shaped by a succession of accidents, not all of them happy ones.

The first and most tragic was the death of our mother. It happened soon after I was born in 1927 when she was forty-four. By all accounts she was a most extraordinary woman. That she gave birth to thirteen children was not of itself unusual for those days, but her pains to keep the family in good health and spirits, free from want were greater than any of us had a right to expect.

We were born in a terraced cottage in Pontrhydyfen, a hillside village just off the road from Cymmer to Port Talbot. Pontrhydyfen means bridge over the ford across two rivers, and indeed from our back garden we looked down into the valley, where the old ford used to be. It crossed the River Afan (Yr Afon Afan), which is Welsh for river – an example of the often ludicrous results of two languages co-existing.

In my day the traffic moved not below but above – on a viaduct which shadows the entire village with its lofty stilts. Long since converted to a ramblers' footpath, the view from the top is of the entire length of the Afan valley.

Pontrhydyfen made its living from coal mining and smelting – and, in the twenties, a poor living it was. When my father, known to us as Dadi Ni, first went into the mines, well before the turn of the century, every male teenager in the district worked with coal or copper. It was a measure of the decay of heavy industry that of Dadi Ni's own boys only Tom followed in his footsteps.

Dadi Ni took an enormous pride in honest labour. Slight and little more than five feet tall, his strength was a wiry agility and prodigious energy which he fuelled with large quantities of beer. It was a huge shock to him when, after the General Strike, his colliery shut down and left him on the dole. Later, he took on a succession of casual jobs, including night watchman at Port Talbot docks until, at seventy-one, he achieved his heart's desire – another chance to go down the pit. At the Wern Dolu colliery he worked underground for four years – until the retirement regulations at last caught up with him.

When father was young and in work, Edith his wife organised the family timetable around him. The big meals of the day were early in the morning and late in the evening. In the winter months when he was out of the house by 6.30 and not back before 7.00, he saw daylight only on Sunday.

After the General Strike and in the depths of recession, much of the burden for keeping us all fed and clothed fell to our mother. She took in washing, made sweets and non-alcoholic 'small' beer which she sold to neighbours and even tried her hand at wallpapering and decorating.

When he was famous, Rich loved to tell stories of the terrible deprivations of his boyhood. But it was our parents who had the hard time, not us. We ate plentifully and with great gusto. The main diet was fresh fish but there was a joint once a week and on Saturday we had cockles and lava bread – a huge treat. Lava bread is the cream of boiled seaweed – not very appetising for the uninitiated particularly as, on the plate, it looks like a cow pat – but to those who are raised on lava bread, it is sheer delight, the 'Welshman's caviar', as Richard called it.

I am still amazed to think of the culinary splendours created from such simple ingredients. One of my choice delicacies was sîencyn which utilised the leftovers from the bread bin. With grated cheese, a deep soaking in boiling hot tea and milk produced a delicious mush which compared favourably to the English bread and butter pudding.

But if the Jenkins family did better than most, this is not to say that additions to the family were welcomed unreservedly. An hour or so after Rich was born, he was carried downstairs for a general inspection. Ivor was preparing for work.

'What do you think of him?' asked Cis, who was cradling the baby in her arms.

Ivor gave his new brother a long look. 'He's all right, I suppose,' he conceded. 'But he's another mouth to feed.' And he walked out of the house.

Knowing that Mam would be worried about what Ivor thought, Cis went back to her to report that Ivor was delighted with the child.

Rich was accommodated in his parents' bedroom, in a cot beside the big double bed. In the room next door were two double beds, side by side. Cis, Hilda, Cassie and Edie slept in one; Dai, Will and Verdun in the other. Ivor had the tiny box room at the top of the house, having recently taken it over from Tom, the eldest, who had married and set up his own home. No wonder we were a close-knit family.

On the day of my birth, Mam was up bright and early to tackle a pile of washing. When the children left for school she was already on to the ironing. Before the morning was out, the midwife had called and by mid-afternoon the Jenkins family had increased to eleven.

It is said that Mam, usually so calm and untroubled, was visibly worried by this latest pregnancy. Well into her forties, she was at an age when so much could, and often did, go wrong.

In the days following there was much to'ing and fro'ing by the doctor and by neighbours who helped out with meals and other chores. Everyone kept saying it would be all right. But as time went on, the older ones knew it was not all right.

On the sixth day, Hilda, on her way home from school, overheard two women gossiping. One was asking the latest news on Mrs Jenkins. The other shook her head and slowly waved a hand in front of her face. Hilda immediately guessed what had happened but tried not to think of the obvious truth as she ran the short distance to the house. On the way she met Verdun who had been giving Rich a piggyback along the grass verge of the cemetery. He too had heard the neighbours talking. When they stepped in at the front door, the sound of weeping left them without doubt.

Mam died of septicemia, a common infection after childbirth – and when antibiotics were unavailable, often fatal.

In those days, grief was unrestrained. There was no attempt to stiffen the upper lip, to put on a brave face or any of that nonsense. To let loose the emotion was to create an antidote to suffering. Opportunities to express mourning were sought and encouraged. Even so, viewed from this distance, it seems a little hard on Verdun that less than a week after the funeral he should have to sing at a concert in the Jerusalem Chapel. His solo was 'A Mother's Prayer'.

> I never can forget the day,
> I heard my mother kindly say,
> 'I'm leaving now your tender care,
> Remember, child, your mother's prayer.'

Sixty years on, Verdun has no doubt that the day Mam died and the day of the concert were the unhappiest of his life.

Dadi Ni suffered most of all. Half his life had disappeared. In less than eighteen months he had lost his wife and his livelihood. He was never quite the same man again. No one could ever replace his Maud. As a teenager I asked my father, 'What was Mam really like?' He answered, with tears in his eyes, 'As good as gold, the best in the world.' And with all the insensitivity of youth I felt embarrassed and left him alone to his memories.

Ivor took over as head of the house. He was barely twenty-one but he knew his own mind and was capable of bringing a sense of order to the family. His nearest contemporary, Cis, had married four months earlier leaving Hilda as the next girl in line. But Hilda was only nine, an age when, despite herself, she would be more of a hindrance than a help. Her attempts to bamboozle Ivor were to provide Rich the actor and raconteur with a profilic fund of stories. And what if they were exaggerated a little over the years? Rich cheerfully described himself as the 'master of the hyperbole'.

First off was the scandalous affair of the forged shopping list. Hilda was deputised to collect the groceries from the Co-op. Twice a week Ivor made out a list of purchases which Hilda dutifully read out to the shop assistant as tins and packets were gathered in from the shelves. There came the moment when Hilda realised the awful temptation of substituting an occasional purchase of her own choice. She succumbed. Instead of jam she asked for Cadbury's chocolate to the same value. The problem was what to say to Ivor when he asked for bread and jam for tea and found he had only bread. Never short of an answer, Hilda claimed she must have left the jam on the counter; she would collect it on her next visit. But then to buy jam she had to miss another item on the list. So for the next few days the family went short of tea – then butter – then sugar. Each time the discrepancy was spotted Hilda's excuses became more imaginative until, having bought yet more chocolate, she enjoyed one last fling. She told Ivor that by a dreadful accident, half the contents of the shopping basket had fallen over the side of the viaduct. What Ivor thought of that excuse was heard the full length of the street.

Hilda had better luck with the secret of the broken chair. It collapsed when, playing with her younger sisters, all three tried to sit on it simultaneously. With great care they refitted the pieces, then slipped the jacket of Verdun's suit over the back of the chair. They waited. Verdun came in, grabbed his jacket and watched in horror as the chair fell to bits. He was still staring when Ivor opened the door to investigate the noise. Poor Verdun was whacked all over the house for his clumsiness while the girls stood by wearing angelic smiles.

Rich and I were not witnesses to these adventures. We had our own quite different lives to lead. Soon after Mam's death, I was taken in by brother Tom and his wife Cassie who lived three miles away in Cwmafan. Rich went to Cis who had set up home with her husband Elfed in in Taibach, five miles to the sea side of Pontrhydyfen. Meeting regularly at weekends I thought of Rich as my best friend. But it took me some time to recognise a closer relationship. Just after my fourth birthday, Rich put me right. We were playing by the river one Sunday afternoon when suddenly he clutched my arm.

'You know we're brothers, don't you?' he declared solemnly.

I did not, but I was suitably overawed so I said nothing.

He gripped my arm harder. 'We must never let the distance from Cwmafan to Taibach come between us.'

What drama! I promised faithfully, of course.

But I still had not worked through all the family connections. Some time later I was asked to take some flowers to the cemetery. An old lady from the village came over to speak to me.

'You're Dic Jenkins' son, aren't you?'

I said I was not quite sure. 'I think he's my grandfather.'

'Oh, no, boy,' she said. 'You're his son all right. And that,' she added, pointing to where the flowers rested on a mound of earth, 'is your mother's grave.'

Of all the influences on young Rich none was more powerful or lasting than that of Cis – his mother in all but name. In later years he showed his gratitude in many ways, not least by naming her the most important woman in his life. She was the standard by which all others were judged. No one relished the comparison.

Rich moved in with Cis on 25 October 1927, a few months short of her twenty-second birthday and a mere four months after she married Elfed James. For Elfed, who was already burdened with the insecurity of a miner's life, the financial and emotional challenge of caring for an infant brother-in-law was difficult to accept. But Cis was determined to do her duty – by both of her men. When Elfed lost his temper or spoke out of turn Cis was quick to shield Rich. He was never smacked. This could make Elfed feel as if he were second fiddle. 'Nothing is good enough for that boy. Anything is good enough for me.'

This was not true. Cis put her heart and soul into making a decent home, getting up in the early hours to prepare breakfast and see Elfed off to work before knuckling down to the domestic chores. At the same time she helped out with the Jenkins' laundry. With Rich in a pram or on her shoulder, she would walk the six miles to Pontrhydyfen to collect the dirty clothes, traipse home to Taibach to do the washing and ironing and then return the following day.

Cis divided her time with scrupulous fairness. Where, as she now admits, she might have been less than even-handed was in her show of affection. When it came to a choice between Elfed and Rich, as it often did, Elfed lost out. This assumed injustice may well have determined his attitude when Rich came to the first great turning point in his life.

More responsibilities came for Cis with the birth of two daughters, Marian in 1928, and Rhianon in 1931. Around this time she and Elfed put down a small sum of money loaned from his mother for a house of their own. On a mortgage of ten shillings a week the family moved into 73 Caradoc Street, a three-bedroomed 1920s semi built on 'the Side', literally the side of the mountain. The back garden gave a complete view of Taibach – the Wesleyan chapel and the Eastern School facing each other just down the road, then the main street with the Co-op, more chapels and the library and, over the street, the steel mill which sent out showers of soot and metal splinters to blanket the town. A short walk from number 73 was a baker's shop run by the Hopkins family. In 1937 they had a son who, like Rich, was to become a fine actor. His name was Anthony.

Rich had his own bedroom which also accommodated a seafarer's trunk, a large black tin box handed down from Elfed's grandfather, who had taken it halfway around the world. It was used by all the children as a treasure house for their toys. One of the great treats at weekends was to embark on a ritual search of the box for toys which had passed unnoticed for so long they had regained their novelty. But Rich always ended up with his old favourites – a red and green railway engine, a Meccano set (from which nothing recognisable was ever made) and a set of skittles. The skittles were knocked down with a ball held to a pole by a length of string. Rich had great trouble finding a name for this game until a friend who was master at demolishing all the skittles in one, confided that older and more sophisticated players knew it as The Swinging Tit. Rich was delighted and lost no time in sharing his knowledge with the rest of the family. The reception was not what he expected. But undaunted by Cis's tut-tutting or Elfed's loud reproof, he and the girls referred ever after to The Swinging Tit, if always in hushed tones.

Rich's most treasured possession was a three-legged stool. It cost two and sixpence from Bendalls and from a week after it was bought it wobbled under the strain of its many duties. The stool was variously

22

a shop counter, the entrance to a mysterious cave, the steering wheel of a luxury car and, frequently, the platform for an impassioned oration on whatever subject happened to be uppermost in Rich's imagination.

Rich was quick to discover the power of language – the Welsh language to be precise since our patch of South Wales remained loyal to its mother tongue. Neither Rich nor I spoke a word of English until we were six and only then because we picked up odd words from the wireless.

The inspiration to stretch the use of language came from the chapel. Each Sunday along we trooped, spick and span, fresh from the zinc bath installed once a week in the kitchen for the highly organised routine of bath night. The chapel was our other world. Within that simple building we let our emotions rip. We sang lustily, prayed fervently and listened in awe to the thunderous declarations of moral judgement. A good preacher was a poet in action. He could spin words into a story of such power as to stop the mind.

Rich had a fancy to do the same. He had all the advantages – a fine, strong voice, a good memory and a sense of timing. With little encouragement he would give a front room sermon, declaring to the family, his congregation, the virtues of temperance and clean living. But he played for laughs, exaggerating the brimstone expressions of the inspired preacher and his readiness to point the finger – up towards heaven and down, down to everlasting damnation.

Once when we gathered to hear the self-styled paragon of virtue, we noticed that to one side of Rich was erected a pile of books. Their purpose was unclear until, at the climax of Joshua's triumph at Jericho, with a great crash, the books came tumbling down. The people of Jericho could not have been half as surprised at the collapse of their defences.

It was home entertainment of a high order and such was the demand – 'Come on, Rich, give us a sermon' – that he extended the act to take in the rest of the service, albeit a shortened version which disposed of a hymn, a prayer and a lesson in three minutes flat. And this is where Rich first showed his ability as a performer – not so much in presentation, but in his sensitivity to the audience. He knew what they wanted and what they could take. He could adapt his routine to suit the mood of the moment – collecting laughs where none had come before, he stretched the joke; if the response was half-hearted, he immediately changed tack. But, best of all, he never outstayed his welcome.

His first appearance in front of an impartial audience was at chapel where, from the age of seven, he made regular appearances at the lectern to deliver a Sunday lesson. The curiosity here was that he gave more of a recitation than a reading. Instead of standing head down, with his eyes fixed on the big print of the bible, he lifted his face to the congregation to hold forth as if the words were his very own. It was assumed, and with every indication of approval from the more pious worshippers, that Rich had gone to enormous trouble to learn the verses by heart – closeted in his room, no doubt, for all of Saturday while other small boys were wasting their energy playing in the street. They could not have been further from the mark. Rich practised, it is true, but after running through the verses a few times he had no difficulty in remembering the extract almost word for word. It was the same with stories and poetry. Whatever took his fancy on the classroom or library shelves he learned off by heart to add to his repertoire of home entertainment.

Weekends at Pontrhydyfen were not complete without the juvenile talent show – Rich leading with a tall tale or recitation and the rest of us following with songs to make the heart swell. But in the week, when he was with Cis, his best audience was his two nieces, Marian and Rhianon, who were in awe of the older boy. Rich took advantage of his seniority to impose his choice of entertainment. Fear and horror came top of the list.

There was the strange case of the locked room, as investigated by the master detective, Charlie Chan. Rich went through all the motions of a terrified man incarcerated alone in his house. As the girls sat together on the sofa, biting their nails, he struggled with the window and rattled the door as, with mounting hysteria, the dreadful fear took hold – there was no way out. But then – what was it? – the sound of a key turning. Someone, out there, was unlocking the door. As Rich spoke these thoughts, he edged across the room until with an agonising burst of courage he grasped the handle, turned it, opened the door and slowly, fearfully, stepped out, closing the door behind him.

The girls waited – and waited – until it was obvious that if they wanted to know the rest of the story they had to follow Rich into the hall. But it was a winter's evening and there was no gas light out there. The door edged open. On a small table by the hatstand was a candle. Its thin flame illuminated the stairs where stood – Charlie Chan.

It was Rich with his pyjama coat on back to front. The Chinese effect was achieved by stretching his eyes into slits. It was not an award-winning impersonation, but in poor light it was strong enough to inspire terror in poor Marian and Rhianon. As a compliment to the actor, their screams were accepted as applause.

The time came when Rich and the girls grew apart. They took to dolls and he discovered rugby. They still played together but the occasions were invariably cut short by Rich suggesting a game of hide and seek.

'You count up to one hundred and then find me.' When they opened their eyes, it was to find that he had gone off with the other boys to kick a football.

Rich was growing up.

# Chapter 3

*F*rom about the age of seven to when he joined the air force at the end of the war, Rich had two great passions – and neither of them was a woman. His first love was rugby – and who could blame him? Rugby is the highest expression of Welsh culture. It requires exceptional physical and mental skills, with a touch of ruthless cunning. Not a bad training for life. Rich was suited to the game by build and by temperament. He was not the canniest player but what he lacked in artistry he more than made up for with raw energy. His enthusiasm for the game stayed with him all his life.

Along with rugby went a passion for reading. Rich gobbled up any printed material – books, comics, papers – which came his way. He solemnly informed Hilda that reading was the source of all wisdom. Some of his favourite authors might have been surprised to hear their work being described so loftily, but if, at an early age, Rich was not the most discriminating of readers, the sheer quantity of books which came his way guaranteed at least a passing acquaintance with some of the better writers. Cis and Elfed did all they could to encourage him though buying books was a luxury they could ill afford. Fortunately, the Carnegie Library, just down the road, was sufficiently stocked to meet the demands of the most avid reader. Rich went there every day after school. It was to be his favourite retreat throughout his life in Taibach.

Rich adapted quickly to the English language and took huge delight in the discovery of new words. As his less well informed, younger brother, I was the first to hear of the latest acquisitions in his vocabulary. 'Sycophant,' he said to me one day. 'Do you know what a sycophant is?' I did not and he told me. But it was not so much the meaning of the word as its sound which fascinated him. With Welsh intonation, each syllable given its own emphasis, 'sycophant' was a cruel and terrible word. We tried it out on our friends with devastating results. They may not have understood but they knew an insult when they heard one.

The power of words stimulated the desire to perform. His favourite prop was a brass candlestick. This served very well as a telephone, an aid Rich used to bring in characters who were never actually seen. The minister at the chapel, his schoolmaster, the librarian, all came in for gentle but well observed parody. The opening line – 'This is Richard Jenkins speaking. Now, I want a few words with you.' – became so familiar to us all, it was, in itself, a guarantee of a laugh.

The candlestick also functioned as a microphone, carried by Rich as an intrepid BBC radio reporter, sending back news of great events. He delighted Dadi Ni with a full-length commentary on the world heavyweight fight between Joe Louis and the Welsh boy from Tonypandy, Tommy Farr. It was a meticulously researched entertainment. Blow by blow accounts of the match in the newspapers and on the radio were sifted for the most dramatic imagery. When he was ready, Rich gathered us together in the front room. He sat behind a small table with his candlestick and an empty glass tumbler. Then he began, in an impeccable English accent.

'Good evening, ladies and gentlemen. This is the BBC. We are now taking you over to New York for a live commentary for the boxing match of the century.'

Thereafter, it was a mix of Welsh and English, but all powerful stuff.

'And Tommy Farr has landed another blow to the jaw, and another. The champion is reeling, I can see blood streaming from his right eye. Can this be the end?'

Well, no it couldn't because there was the little difficulty of explaining how it was that Joe Louis snatched victory, albeit on points.

The glass tumbler was for sound effects. By pressing it against his mouth, Rich achieved the hollow atmospherics of a trans-Atlantic broadcast. Dadi Ni declared himself entirely convinced.

'Better than the real thing, boy,' he told Rich who basked in the uncustomary show of approval from his normally reticent father.

Maybe this encouraged him to try his hand at impressing a wider audience. Without telling anyone in the family he entered a verse-reading competition – and won. We heard the news from Hilda who was told by a friend. 'He has a beautiful voice,' reported the friend. 'They do say it's the best in the valley.'

As a junior at the Eastern School, Rich did just enough work to get by. Apart from his feel for language he was not exceptional in a way that automatically marked him out for scholastic success. But then, in his last year, he encountered Meredith Jones, the teacher responsible for training the brightest and the best to win places at Port Talbot Secondary School.

Meredith Jones was a man of great power. A signal of approval from him was the Taibach equivalent of the order of merit. More than prestige was at stake. Those who did so well in the exams as to be accepted for an academic education were virtually guaranteed a well paid and reputable job when they left school. And this at a time when jobs were hard to come by. For the lucky few there was the prospect of university and promotion to the ranks of the middle-class professions. Boys who defied the limitations of their environment to become doctors or lawyers were talked about in hushed tones of respect long after they had departed to make their fortune in Cardiff or the big cities across the border.

It was fortunate for Rich that Meredith Jones enjoyed talking. There were those who complained he did little else. Himself a scholarship boy, the son of a miner, he was passionate in his desire to awake the talent in young people. He achieved this by bombarding them with questions and arguments – anything to elicit a response that could be evidence of a lively mind. Facts took second place to imagery so that, reacting one with the other, Meredith Jones and his class would frequently launch off on some flight of rhetoric, far beyond the bounds of formal education. He had an opinion on every subject under the sun but best of all, he loved talking about his home and country.

'Gentlemen,' he would thunder through his thick ginger moustache, 'let no man despise Wales, her language or her literature. She has survived many storms; she has survived many empires. Her time will come. When the last truckload of coal reaches Cardiff, when the last black diamond is dug from the earth of Glamorgan, there will be men then digging gems of pure brilliance from the inexhaustible mines of the literature and language of Wales.'

His impact on the young Jenkins hardly needs to be emphasised. Rich loved the man. But others were not so enthusiastic. Less flamboyant personalities were easily overwhelmed. Meredith Jones was seen by many as a tyrant, dispensing favours only to those who sought and met with his approval. That he could be harsh and insensitive was undeniable.

'I am going to teach you something important,' he announced one day, 'and Danny here will help me.' Danny was the sort of boy who liked to stay hidden at the back of the class. For all I know he was able enough but he was made shy by a speech impediment which transformed every utterance into a high-pitched stutter. Meredith Jones led Danny out to the front and asked him to stand on a chair. 'Now, Danny, I want you to recite.'

Danny spluttered a few lines before surrendering to the barrage of laughter let loose by, among others, Rich and his friends. Meredith Jones rounded on them. 'How dare you mock the afflicted. Are you so selfish as to take pleasure in the misfortune of others? Come out here, all of you.' He then proceeded to give each of the miscreants a sound beating.

Long afterwards, Rich insisted that, for him, the experience was character forming, a lesson in humility. I did not doubt it. But I could not help wondering what Danny got out of it?

Rich took the scholarship exam in his stride and settled in at the Port Talbot Secondary School. But he did not lose contact with Meredith Jones. In 1940, his mentor left teaching to set up a youth club, the first to be sponsored by the local county council. Rich was one of the founding members. Provision for this venture was not exactly lavish. It was accommodated in a near derelict building on the edge of the Eastern School playground. It was gas lit and had a leaky roof. But the response from the youngsters was overwhelming. Suddenly, they had a place to call their own. It made a welcome contrast to evenings at home where every move was monitored by their elders.

The club had a drama group led by Leo Lloyd, a teacher of English who was a close associate of Meredith Jones. Rich was an eager participant, throwing himself wholeheartedly into any part which came his way. By professional standards he was hopelessly over-indulgent, giving all he had in every role, as if melodrama was the only bench mark. It was a mystery to me where he had picked up the exaggerated gestures, the staring eyes, the long pauses after every sentence – until I started going with him to the cinema.

The Taibach Picture Drome, known to its regular patrons as the

Cach, had not quite caught up with the times. Even in the early part of the war, it was still showing silent films. But Rich was captivated. With a change of programme mid-week and a special children's matinee on Saturdays (actually a re-run of films which had all but exhausted their box office appeal) it was theoretically possible to visit the Cach three times a week. But the pocket money did not allow for such extravagance. A way round the problem was provided by a close friend of Rich's. Trevor George had an after school job in a barber's shop where he performed the duties of 'wobbler'. These included lathering up the customers who were there for a shave and sweeping up the fallout from the short back and sides. As part payment Trevor collected the two free passes which the Cach awarded to the barber in return for displaying a window poster. Naturally, Rich was in on the deal.

One of the first films Rich and I saw together was Cecil B. De Mille's version of *Cleopatra*. It was billed as the most expensive film ever made. Who said that history never repeats itself?

A chance for Rich to demonstrate coarse acting as perfected by his silent screen heroes came when Leo Lloyd entered his drama group for Glamorgan's first Youth Eisteddfod. The production was a popular morality play of the time called *The Bishop's Candlesticks*, lifted from Victor Hugo's novel, *Les Misérables*. Rich had the meatiest role, that of the escaped convict intent on robbery who is transformed into a decent citizen by the artless generosity of his victim. Since the performance was in mime, Rich was able to concentrate all on body language, just like Rudolph Valentino. It was all there. The hand raised against the eye (fear), the arms outstretched (the appeal for mercy), the head bowed and shaking (guilt) and, finally, the eyes raised to heaven to signify the repentant sinner.

The club's supporters, a full bus-load of them, roared their approval. It was clear to them who deserved the first prize. The adjudicator was more difficult to please. He began by observing the virtue in restraint. A dramatic point, he argued, could sometimes be put across more effectively if it was implied rather than blazoned forth in a statement of the obvious. All this was too much for Leo Lloyd who interposed, in a loud voice, his own views on the quality of the adjudicator. 'The man is obviously biased. He has no sense at all.'

Thoroughly confused, the adjudicator hurried on to his conclusion which was really very favourable to the play and to Rich. The Taibach boys returned home in triumph.

Rich found in the activities of the youth club a stimulation which was absent in his formal education. Meredith Jones and Leo Lloyd treated him like an adult and he responded in a way which impressed them with his maturity.

'You have real talent in that boy,' they told Cis.

The talent showed most obviously in his study of literature of which acting was a crucial element. Only too well aware of his club's limitations as a centre of dramatic excellence, Meredith Jones encouraged Rich to branch out. He commended his protege to Philip Burton, an English teacher at the grammar school, but more importantly, a rising star of the local cultural establishment. Here was a drama enthusiast whose reputation was so far advanced as to bring him offers of work on Welsh radio. Philip Burton had even visited the United States. He was a man of the world; and still only in his thirties.

Rich was already on slight acquaintance with Philip Burton who taught him English from his first year at grammar school. But Rich had failed to make an impression. His single appearance in a Burton production – as Mr Vanbatten in *The Apple Cart* – had attracted criticism for his atrocious American accent. 'In any case,' said the director, drawing attention to a feature of the young man others were too polite to talk about, 'he has spots.' There was no denying the fact. Rich had a skin so ravaged by acne as to suggest trench warfare. In his late teens, the pimples subsided, but their battlefield remained for the rest of his life.

Those who had faith in Rich were not so easily deterred by the blemishes of puberty. But by 1941, when he was fifteen, argument as to his real abilities was academic. The family had decided. Rich must leave school to earn his living.

The break in his education was not sanctioned without much heart searching. Cis wanted him to stay on; the family was sympathetic. But where was the money to come from? Like the rest of us, Rich was eager to pay his way. His morning newspaper round was a steady if modest earner which he supplemented by instigating a collection as well as a delivery. The old newspapers he accumulated were sold as wrapping paper to a local fish and chip shop. But it was nowhere near enough. A growing boy with a healthy appetite and a tendency to punish his clothes into early patchwork was an expensive item on the household budget. These were hard times for Cis and Elfed, as for the rest of the family. Hilda, who had left school at thirteen to help out at home, was now married with a baby son. Her husband, Dai, was off at the war. Tom's Cassie had died but he still looked after me and his daughter Mair.

Verdun, also married, had been badly injured in a mining accident. He was mending a coal cutter when some fool threw the main switch. The machine cut off half his foot. A year later he was back down the pit but it was a long time before he was on to full earnings. His only solace was the compensation which he used to buy a piano for his daughter, Ann. She had a fine voice and later turned professional.

Ivor was still looking after our two younger sisters, Cassie and Edie, and Dadi Ni, a responsibility which forced him to postpone his own marriage until he was thirty-five – when he and Gwen had been engaged for twelve years.

Brothers Dai and Will were in regular employment, one in the police, the other in the army. Neither could be described as high earners. Nonetheless, Dai offered to help with Rich's schooling, as did brother Tom. His gesture was truly magnanimous since, as my foster parent, he was already paying for my education.

Perhaps with a little more effort a solution might have been found. Later Elfed was blamed for not trying quite hard enough, but it was asking a lot of him to continue supporting Rich into the years when the vast majority of young people were fending for themselves. It was not as if they got on particularly well. Elfed always harboured a resentment against his demanding and, in his view, disruptive brother-in-law. Unlike Rhianon and Marian who were polite and well behaved, Rich had a mischievous streak which put him at odds with all authority. Cis let him get away with it; Elfed was not so tolerant.

Only once as I recall was Elfed inspired to a burst of spontaneous praise for Rich. It happened on the day Rich went off to play his first game of cricket. He wore a pair of hand-me-down flannels which Cis had rooted from the bottom of the linen basket. They were baggy at the knees and thin on the rear, but Rich was delighted to have the conventional kit. Performer in the making he may have been, but in those days he was not that keen to be different.

Having made a few runs he returned in buoyant mood, tossing a coin. At first Cis imagined Rich had brought home a prize but when she saw it was a gold sovereign he treated so carelessly she had second thoughts.

'I found it in my pocket,' Rich explained. 'I guessed it might be worth something.'

Elfed was summoned. He stared hard at the coin for a moment, then burst out, 'My God, you've found it. This was my father's. He gave it to me when I was twenty-one. I thought I'd lost it.'

Rich was the hero. Some time later, Elfed asked, 'How did you know it was valuable?'

'That's easy,' said Rich. 'A man at the match offered me sixpence for it. I realised if he wanted to give me that much, it must be worth more.' Elfed was impressed. For a time thereafter he conceded credit where it was due. But Rich quickly got through the residue of goodwill, and none of us were too surprised when we were told that Rich had, after all, left school. 'He has a good job,' Cis told me. 'Mr Maynard's taking him on at the Co-op menswear.'

The Co-op was the biggest store in town which was not saying too much. In wartime, its normally austere appearance was made yet more forbidding by the walls of depleted shelves. But for want of a livelier alternative and for the sake of the divi, the customers remained loyal.

Rich and the retail trade were ill suited. He simply could not take it seriously. When Mrs Jones turned up at the shop wanting to buy her Gareth a new suit, but not having enough clothing coupons, Rich was quick to oblige. 'Don't you worry,' he assured his nervous customer, 'you can settle up next time.' It was not long before everyone in town knew that, for Co-op bargains, Rich was the boy to make for.

I remember an effusive greeting from a neighbour who, hitherto, had hardly acknowledged my existence.

'That brother of yours,' she confided, 'there's a real friend for you. He won't let you down.'

I found out later that Rich had supplied her husband and sons with a full stock of winter underwear, all off coupons.

When he was not needed behind the counter, Rich could be found in the library across the road. When he *was* needed behind the counter, Rich could be found in the library across the road.

Mr Maynard, who was a kindly man and not ill disposed towards his apprentice, gave a lack of progress report to Cis. 'He's a bright lad,' he told her. 'No doubt about it. But he's not – well, how can I put it? – he's not quite what we expected. Perhaps you could have a word with him?'

Cis did have a word with him. Elfed had several words with him. Their conflicting approach to the problem made it worse.

'He's not happy at the Co-op,' argued Cis.

'He's not paid to be happy,' said Elfed.

Encouraged by Cis to believe that, maybe, there was a life beyond the Co-op, Rich poured out his resentment to others who might support his break for freedom.

Sympathiser-in-chief was Ivor – on the face of it an unlikely candidate since it was entirely out of character for him to play the patient and understanding adviser. Ivor was the tough nut of the family. A face miner who was proud of his record for shifting more coal in a day than any of his mates, he brought into the home the same rigorous standards that governed his life in the pit. Stories abound of Ivor's exaggerated sense of fair play which he would defend against all comers.

There was the time when Verdun, still a boy and fresh into work, came home from the pit with his first trumps – the little extra paid by a miner to his young helper. Verdun put his week's wage – seven and sixpence – and his trumps – a threepenny bit – on the mantlepiece.

'What's this?' demanded Ivor.

'My pay,' said Verdun.

'No,' said Ivor, his voice getting louder, '*THIS!*' he pointed to the threepenny piece which Verdun had placed to one side.

'It's my trumps. Mr Davies gave it me.'

'He did, did he,' Ivor grabbed Verdun by the arm. 'Then we'll pay a call on Mr Davies.'

Together they marched out of the house and along the street to where the Davies family lived. Mrs Davies answered the door. She was a tiny woman, not given to resisting steamrollers.

'Is William there?' bellowed Ivor.

'I'll get him,' said Mrs Davies and disappeared.

A few moments later her husband was at the door.

'Is this the boy who's working with you?' Ivor demanded.

'It is,' said William, 'and he's the best I've ever had.'

'So is this his entitlement?' Ivor revealed the threepence in his hand. William became defensive. 'I've had a hard week, what with the Co-op to pay and so forth.'

'We've all had a hard week,' shouted Ivor. 'So you know what you can do with this.' He threw the coin into the hallway. 'Shove it up your arse.'

After that, Verdun worked with another miner and his trumps increased accordingly.

Ivor's conception of justice was not always favourable to those closest to him. When Hilda set her heart on buying a wristwatch, she calculated the only way she could do it was to save a little each week on the housekeeping to pay for the watch on the never-never. The plan worked perfectly until Hilda was rushed into hospital with acute appendicitis. Before she departed she gave her younger sister, Cassie, some rapid coaching in delaying tactics. 'All you have to say is . . .'

But Cassie got it wrong and Ivor found out. When Hilda came home from hospital it was to be told the watch had to go back. Years later when Hilda related the story to Rich, he made a shamefaced Ivor go straight out to buy her a splendid new gold watch. She wears it to this day.

From all this it can be gathered that Ivor was not an easy man to sway. No one certainly could describe him as a soft touch – except when it came to Rich.

For Rich he would do anything.

So when the novice shop assistant called round to his home to confess how unhappy he was at the Co-op and how he would do anything to get back to school, Ivor was angry on his behalf and promised he would do all he could to help.

Outside the family, Rich found his most powerful advocate in Meredith Jones. As a regular at the Youth Club, Rich had opportunities enough to persuade Meredith that he was in there fighting. His stage performances, though still a trifle over-dramatic, were a compelling display of individuality, a characteristic which he reinforced off stage by engaging in long, animated conversations on any subject under the sun.

Meredith was entranced.

When asked by Cis for an opinion on Rich, he answered promptly, 'The boy is wasted in that shop. He should be back at school, finishing his education.'

'Can you help?' asked Cis.

'I'm doing my damnedest,' Meredith assured her. 'But don't get your hopes up because it's not done yet.'

Meredith Jones went out of his way to recruit some powerful sponsors for Rich. 'What are strings for,' he asked, rhetorically, 'except to be pulled?'

Philip Burton was among the first to be roped in. He admitted he had been a little hasty in his assessment of Rich as a lightweight. A boy who was determined to break the mould – just as he and Meredith had defied the conventions of their upbringing – such a boy deserved support. Rich's former headmaster, Pop Reynolds, was sympathetic but saw difficulties. Teachers' recommendations alone would not work the magic. A reinstatement at the grammar school was a rare event. To achieve it, political muscle had to be exerted. Meredith Jones went to work on Councillor Llewellyn Heycock (later Lord Heycock), president of the youth club and a member of the Glamorgan Education Committee.

Every boy who made a success, argued Meredith, was a credit to the education service. Richard Jenkins had great promise, but it was likely to remain unfulfilled – unless he returned to school. Could the education committee, in all conscience, refuse the boy the opportunity to prove his talent? Councillor Heycock promised to speak to the school governors.

He encountered tough opposition from the chairman who did not like bending the rules. Heycock argued that Rich would take his school certificate within a year along with his contemporaries who had not missed out on their education. What could be fairer than that? Moreover, if Rich succeeded he was certain to go to college to train as a teacher. And teachers were in short supply.

A few days later, Meredith sent a boy to 73 Caradoc Street to ask Cis if she could call in at the school. When she hurried round – expecting the worst but hoping for the best – she was greeted by Meredith in his most expansive mood.

'Good news,' he boomed. 'The boy can return to his rightful place.'

Cis almost cried with relief and pleasure.

'But what about Elfed?' Meredith asked. 'How will you handle him? Do you want me to come and have a chat?'

'Don't worry,' said Cis, who feared that pressure from the short-tempered schoolmaster was more than likely to stiffen resistance, 'I'll think of something.'

But her hope of avoiding a row was misplaced because the only other advocate who could tackle Elfed head on was Ivor.

'Do try to keep your voice down,' begged Cis.

Ivor said he would do his best. The conversation started well.

'The boy deserves his chance,' they agreed.

'But there just isn't the money,' Elfed put in. 'It's all very well for you, Ivor, you're a face worker on piece rates. You earn good money, twice as much as me, I shouldn't wonder.'

That did it.

'And what about the sacrifices I've made and Tom has made?' roared Ivor. 'Don't you think we've done our bit?'

'He's your brother. He's not my son.'

By now the two men were standing glaring at each other. Cis tried a few soothing words.

36

'Very well, if that's the way it's to be, we'll all put our hands in our pockets.'

But that was not the end of the story. 'The strange thing is,' Cis recalls, 'that when it came to the point, Elfed would not accept a penny. He had his pride, you see.'

A formal letter inviting Rich to resume his studies followed shortly. Years on, when he counted his income in millions, he told me it was the most valuable offer he ever received.



After ten months out on his own, re-adapting to the school routine was a curious experience for Rich. Academically he was a model student who worked hard to make up for lost time. But socially he had advanced much faster than his classmates. His ebullient personality was, in any case, ill suited to the formal discipline of not speaking until spoken to and always staying in line. Egged on by his less resolute friends who enjoyed the spectacle of authority under attack as long as they were not in the firing line, Rich could be relied upon to challenge the powers.

'Where's your gas mask?' Pop Reynolds demanded to know when he spotted Rich at the school gate without the regulation pack.

'I left it at home, by mistake,' said Rich. 'Where's yours?'

Pop Reynolds had the grace to admit he was equally forgetful. The rudeness went unpunished.

It was a trivial offence and a minor triumph for Rich, but was so uncharacteristic of the school as a whole that it was blown out of proportion. Questions were asked about his seriousness of purpose. Was he not seen drinking in a pub and smoking in the street? And what about these stories of his fondness for girls? There was nothing wrong with polite conversation between the sexes. But in the woods?

Among those who felt that Rich might be in danger of squandering his opportunities was Phil Burton. From his first day back at school, Rich had seen a lot of the man who was to be his cultural and pro-fessional mentor. Phil Burton was his English teacher, his commanding officer in the Air Training Corps and, with increasing frequency, his director on stage. In November 1942, Rich played his first major role in a Burton production, that of Owen Brown, younger brother of John, in *Gallows Glorious*, an emotional tribute to the hero of the

American Civil War. In the closing minutes of the play Rich had a wonderful chance to grip the audience. Accompanied by an invisible choir celebrating victory over death 'His Soul Goes Marching On', Owen was to be blessed with a vision of John Brown leading his army across the sky. Rich made the most of it. Alone on stage, arms outstretched, eyes lifted, he proclaimed the glory of the Lord.

Phil Burton made his by now customary plea for restraint ('You don't have to use a sledgehammer. A gentle tap will do the trick') but he was sufficiently impressed to offer Rich another role, this time in his own play, *Youth at the Helm*, written for the BBC Welsh radio. Rich went to Cardiff for the recording. It was, he told me, like travelling to a new world. He was surrounded by people who were excited by what the BBC had to offer, the chance of reaching out to a whole population. The thrill of performing in a makeshift theatre to an audience of a hundred paled against the excitement of the studio and the hanging mike. There was no one to applaud but many to hear. Not having to act, physically, he concentrated on voice. And what a voice.

It was the first time I had heard the disembodied Rich. I was bowled over by the melodious, seductive tones of the Welsh Welsh, deeper and stronger than anything you will hear in the north.

Phil Burton too must have been impressed because it was after this that he began to take seriously Rich's now openly declared ambition to be a professional actor. The teacher was in need of a favourite, a young hopeful who could fulfil, by proxy, the dreams of a frustrated actor. His first protege, Thomas Owen Jones, was a clever young actor who had won a scholarship to RADA and appeared in West End plays and films before joining up as a fighter pilot. His death in the Battle of Britain came as a hammer blow to Phil whose sadness for a lost talent was compounded by a strong affection for the boy.

Rich appeared as a godsend. Here was the young Jones all over again, but with even greater potential. My brother had come a long way since the day Phil Burton had reported unfavourably upon his complexion. At seventeen, Rich had more than sufficient qualities to compensate for the after effects of acne. He had the rough good looks of a warrior, a stubborn jaw and compelling blue eyes. He was strong and intelligent and he could act. Phil knew that Richard Jenkins was capable of great things – just as long as he kept his mind on his ambitions and was not diverted by idle pursuits.

How could this be achieved? Phil called on Cis to talk about the future. He was worried, he said, that the education Rich was enjoying was not sufficiently intensive to bring him up to standard in the short time left to him at school. He needed extra tuition from someone who appreciated his abilities and was dedicated to his success.

Cis knew that anything she had to say was bound to be unhelpful. Ah yes, her Rich deserved the best but it was pie in the sky even to think about paying out for private schooling. The family budget was already stretched to its limit.

Phil reassured her. Money was not the obstacle. He, Philip Burton, would provide. But if he was to act as patron for Rich he had to be confident that his sacrifice was appreciated. It was necessary for Rich to live in an intellectually lively environment.

And where would that be? Cis wanted to know.

Well, as it happened, there was a spare room in the house in Port Talbot where Phil Burton had his own lodgings. If Rich moved in there, Phil could give him all the help he needed to achieve scholastic excellence while keeping a watchful eye on his protege. In short, Phil was offering himself as benefactor and mentor.

The proposition was enormously attractive. Cis was proud to think that a celebrity, respected throughout South Wales, should be prepared to put himself out for her Rich. And it was not as if he was about to leave the country. He would still be close at hand, she would still see a lot of him.

Others in the family were less inclined to take the offer at face value. Could it be that Phil Burton was attracted by more than intellectual qualities?

A bachelor in his early forties, he had led a protected life. After the death of his father when Phil was just fourteen, the prevailing influence of his formative years had been a strong-willed mother whose ambitions for her son were rewarded by a good honours degree at the University of Wales. That a career in teaching was not all he wanted was made evident by his dogged pursuit of a reputation as a writer and director. He never showed any inclination to marry. He used to say that his drama groups were his family.

As the youngest, my view on Rich's future was neither sought nor given. But looking back I can understand why my brothers were worried. Anyway, it was not as if Rich would be unchaperoned. Phil Burton's lodgings in Connaught Street were part of the household of a middle-aged widow and her two daughters. A pillar of the chapel, Mrs

Smith was scrupulous in the management of her affairs. She was not the sort to tolerate any hanky panky.

Rich moved in with Phil Burton at the start of the Easter term in 1943.

The question must be asked. In that curious, close relationship between Phil Burton and Richard Jenkins, who led whom? On the face of it, Phil was the originator of ideas, the creator of opportunities and the master of technique. He worked Rich hard, teaching him all he knew of literature and drama, pointing the way to great writers. He showed by rigorous elocution training how English vowels could hone down the Welsh accent and make yet more memorable an already splendid voice.

But Rich too was demanding. He knew that he had a short time in which to prove himself. His final school exams were just months away. In other schools, in other parts of the country those of his contemporaries who hankered after an acting career were already planning their applications to RADA.

The change in Rich in the first months of his life with Phil Burton was apparent to everyone. Intellectually and socially he acquired a confidence which quite overawed the younger members of the family. He dressed well, at Phil's expense, adopted manners which some miners might have thought a trifle fussy and talked fluently on topics outside the normal run of conversation.

Phil Burton had a document drawn up assigning him as Rich's legal guardian. When he first raised the subject with the family, the word 'adoption' was used but no one took kindly to this and, anyway, the point became academic when it was realised that Phil was too young to meet the legal requirements. A guardianship seemed not so drastic but, still, some justification was needed. It was not good enough to say that it merely formalised what already existed. In that case, why bother?

Phil tried hard to persuade Cis, because he knew the rest of the family would listen to her, and Hilda who was also influential but for a different reason. It was she who looked after Dadi Ni and it was Dadi Ni who had to make the final decision. Phil told the sisters that he would be in a much better position to go on helping Rich if he became the boy's guardian. For example, he could use his influence to secure for him a decent higher education. Richard Burton, the foster son of a middle-class teacher, was more likely to be accepted than Richard Jenkins, true son of a retired coalminer.

Ideas on post-school education were already well advanced. Phil had looked into a scheme whereby volunteers for officer rank in the RAF could, at government expense, spend a preliminary six months at Oxford. Then after doing their time in the forces they could return to university to complete their degrees.

'I have every confidence,' said Phil, 'that with my support and recommendation as his teacher *and* guardian, Richard will be chosen.'

It all seemed reasonable enough at the time, though in retrospect I do wonder if the social distinctions were quite as vital as he suggested. I have to say that Rich himself was dubious on this point – he had no great wish to fit in with middle class conventions. But he did go along with Phil's plans for him. And he was not at all averse to changing his name. As he subsequently admitted to any journalist who cared to ask: 'Phil Burton didn't adopt me, I adopted Phil Burton.'

But this did not mean that Rich was eager to walk out on the family. On the contrary, his lack of sentimentality on matters of appearance contrasted with his enthusiasm for holding on to the reality of family ties. To me, his younger brother, he gave generously of his time and attention. In the air training corps, where I was two years behind him, he taught me the Morse code and the rudiments of navigation. I remember listening with rapt attention as he explained the theory of flight, making an apparently complex subject appear ludicrously simple. He stimulated my interest in rugby, encouraged me in my reading and taught me to be loyal to my own. After a welcome favour, he turned away my thanks. 'We have to look after each other. You would do the same for me.'

On that clause of the family creed Rich and Dadi Ni were as one. But our father was of a more conservative generation. However often the advantages of the Burton connection were explained to him, he could never quite reconcile himself to Rich assuming another name. To him, it was a renunciation of a birthright. And the Welsh miners of the old school were very strong on birthright.

A meeting was arranged between Dadi Ni and Phil Burton. It was to take place at Hilda's cottage in Pontrhydyfen where Dadi Ni could at least feel he was on home ground. Phil was to bring the documents which Dadi Ni had to sign to make the guardianship official. But when Phil arrived, Dadi Ni was not to be found. He had popped out for a drink at the Miners Arms and was last seen heading in the direction of the British Lion. Along the way were several other pubs where he might have stopped off.

So Dadi Ni and Phil Burton never did get to talk to each other. The legend, repeated in so many books and articles, that Rich was signed away by his father, is utterly untrue. Instead, in December 1943, the family as a whole decided that Richard Jenkins should become Richard Burton. All it needed to work this transformation was an ad in the local newspaper. For us it was a small thing. For Philip Burton, as much as for Rich, it was a first claim to fame.

# Chapter 4

My born-again brother sailed through his higher school certificate and was duly awarded a place at Exeter College, Oxford. His last stage performance as a schoolboy was in the unlikely role of Professor Henry Higgins in Shaw's *Pygmalion*. He tackled the part as an exercise in elocution for himself as well as for the hapless Eliza. There was a gap now before Rich could resume his studies. He needed a temporary job. But not any job would do. On the lookout for a suitable enterprise for his prodigy, Phil Burton spotted an ad in the *Western Mail* inviting young Welsh actors to audition for a new Emlyn Williams play called *The Druids Rest*. The engagement almost exactly matched the time Rich had to work before starting at University. More to the point it was difficult to think of a better launching pad for the professional career.

Not yet forty, Emlyn Williams, actor, writer and director was recognised as a famous son of Wales. Two of his plays, *Night Must Fall* and *The Corn is Green* were in the front rank of popular quality theatre, attracting queues at the box office and praise from the critics. Like Terence Rattigan, he had a sixth sense for what the audience would like. *The Druids Rest*, a modest little comedy, was expected to make a decent profit on tour, but not to achieve a lengthy West End run. The story was of a Welsh family – Mum, Dad and their two boys – who were persuaded by the youngest son, Tomas, that the lodger they harboured under their roof was in fact a notorious murderer on the run. Rich had his sights on the Tomas role but this went to Brynmor Thomas who was the right age, almost fourteen, and already known to Welsh audiences as a cute boy actor. But Rich's journey to

43

Cardiff was not in vain. For a start he met Emlyn Williams and Daphne Rye, the formidable casting director for H. M. Tennent, the leading West End theatre management. Both thought Rich had the voice and the presence to make a good actor. They were also impressed by Phil Burton – a restrained, sensible man, thought Emlyn, quite a change from the usual run of over protective and over indulgent parents, who filled the audition rooms with their nervous chatter.

The combined impact of the young actor and his guardian ensured that Rich did not come away empty handed. He was offered the part of Glen, the older brother. It was a minor role calling for a lot of standing about listening to the other actors. But Rich was over the moon. It was his first chance to test himself against the expectations of an audience of total strangers who were in the theatre because they had paid to be there and not because they were friends of the family. Rehearsals started in London in early November, 1943. The war battered city was not the most comfortable place to be but with the odds on an Allied victory shortening every week, there was a mood of optimism which favoured all types of entertainment. This counted two ways for Rich – the prospect of a receptive audience for *The Druids Rest* and the promise of a right-roaring time when he was not working. With his stand in, a fellow Welshman by name of Stanley Baker, Rich explored the pubs, the clubs and the dance halls. They made an exuberant pair, eager to lose their innocence and surrounded by girls who were really only too pleased to help.

But mostly the time was spent on hard work with rehearsals continuing late into the evening, with maybe supper afterwards to talk on about the play and to dream about the wider shores of acting. It was during one of these late-night sessions that Rich introduced Emlyn Williams to the words of Dylan Thomas. They were walking through darkest Soho (the blackout was still enforced) when Rich launched into an imaginative poetry recital right there in the middle of the street. It was a declaration of love for Welsh melody which Dylan Thomas could write better than any other and Richard could speak better than most. Emlyn knew then that this would not be the last time he and Rich would work together; not if he could help it.

*The Druids Rest* opened in Liverpool at the Royal Court. The furthest stop was the Prince of Wales in Cardiff. This called for a family outing but none of us had a car and anyway, petrol was in short supply. The train was ruled out because there were no connections late at night. Eventually, Ivor persuaded our local doctor to let us have use of his big black Riley and enough petrol for the sixty mile return journey.

What a night to remember. That the play was a sell-out was entirely attributed by us to the crowd appeal of Richard Burton. We said as much to all our fellow playgoers who showed an interest and to quite a few who did not. I sat with Tom, Ivor and his wife Gwen, a few rows from the front of the dress circle. We spent what was left of our sweet ration on a small box of chocolates which Gwen held in her lap and passed round during the interval. I read the programme six times. In bold type dwarfing all else except the name of the play was a warning of what to do in the event of an air raid. The nearest shelter, I recall, was in Wood Street. But I also remember thinking it would take more than a few German bombs to get the Jenkins family out of the theatre in the middle of the performance.

For those of us who were there for partisan reasons, the play was something of a confusion. By concentrating so hard on Rich, who had the least demanding role in the entire production, we lost track of what else was going on. We were nervous too. I suppose that stage fright is a common enough experience but surely not for the audience. We sat with hands clenched willing Rich not to forget a word or fluff a line.

After the show we found our way backstage for a small celebration. When Rich came over to give Cis a great big hug and kiss, the tears of joy and pride rolled down her cheeks. I met Stanley Baker who, responding politely to the question of a none too sophisticated man of the theatre, said that, yes, he would quite like to be an actor and that, no, he did not intend to be Rich's stand in for the rest of his career.

In the second week of January the play transferred to Swansea. A record family excursion was led by Dadi Ni whose experience of the theatre was slight but who appreciated, as he said, a good story. That he sat still throughout and not once asked the way to the bar suggested he was not disappointed. Then for Rich, it was off to London again, this time for the opening of *The Druids Rest* at the St Martin's Theatre off Shaftesbury Avenue. Just down the road at the Empire Leicester Square, an eleven-year-old Elizabeth Taylor was making her debut in a weepie called *Lassie Come Home*.

The notices for *The Druids Rest* were at best lukewarm. One critic said it was less of a play than a number of amusing sketches of the Welsh character. Everyone agreed that Brynmor Thomas stole the show and there were a few kind words for the stars – Michael Shepley, who specialised in peppery colonel types (he once described himself as the last of the gentlemen actors) and Gladys Henson, the archetypal working class housewife. Rich had to be consoled by a paragraph in the *New Statesman* where he was described as showing 'exceptional ability' in his struggle to play 'a wretched part'. There was praise too from Daphne Rye and her boss at H. M. Tennent, Hugh 'Binkie' Beaumont, whose eye for a handsome young actor was not entirely ruled by hedonism.

*The Druids Rest* was taken off after two months. Before coming home, Rich saw Robert Helpmann's *Hamlet* at the New Theatre but missed out on the Gielgud version which opened at the Haymarket later in the year. By then he too was in Shakespeare – with the Oxford University Drama Society.

In the last month before Oxford, Rich did another radio play for Phil Burton, now a part-time contract producer for the BBC Wales. Rich was cast in the title role of Dic Penderym, a hero of the early Welsh labour movement who in addition to his other misfortunes (he was unjustly accused of murdering a policeman) had a bad stammer which the actor was called upon to reproduce. The day after the broadcast, Cis's daughter Marian was accosted in the street by a friend. 'I heard your Rich on the wireless,' said the girl. 'Very good he was. But with a stammer like that' (she sucked in her breath) 'he can't have much of a future in the theatre.'

Six months at Oxford was not long enough for Rich to achieve all that he wanted. So he took it at a rush, packing activity into all hours of the day and most of the night. If his exertions were largely outside the formal curriculum, this suited his RAF sponsors who were looking to their trainee officers to acquire social maturity more than academic excellence. But Rich was ahead of them. What with Phil Burton's tuition and his acting experience he was already possessed of enough maturity for a forty-year-old. Free from the doubts and inhibitions which usually afflict a teenager as he emerges into the wide world, Rich pursued his interests with single-minded determination.

The first objective was to gain a foothold in the Drama Society. In a sense this was easier than he could have imagined because his tutor, Nevill Coghill, was also director of OUDS. Coghill was a divided character. On one side was the brilliant teacher whose proudest work was to be a bestseller translation into modern English of Chaucer's *Canterbury Tales*. On the other side was the man of the theatre. Happy memories of his childhood games of charades spilled over into his adult life when the excitement of one of the great challenges, holding the attention of a live audience for two hours or more, was satisfied by staging high-calibre student productions. He was much respected in the professional theatre and later collaborated on a long running musical of the *Canterbury Tales*. But he never strayed so far towards the West End as to cut loose from academia.

Coghill was immediately impressed by Rich who, thanks to Phil Burton, knew the power of great literature. And he had the voice to match the words, as the professor discovered at their first meeting when Rich launched into Hamlet's famous soliloquy.

'I want to act,' explained Rich.

His tutor made encouraging noises.

'No I mean here, at Oxford. I want to act with the Drama Society.'

It was the moment for restraint. 'I don't see how that is possible. You are here for just six months. In that time we have only one production which is already cast and into rehearsals.'

'You've cast every part?'

'Every part, I'm afraid.'

Rich went away disappointed. But by their next meeting Professor Coghill had thought of a consolation prize. 'Why not understudy? I know it's not like the real thing but at least you would be involved.'

The play was *Measure for Measure*, one of Shakespeare's least successful comedies. Intriguingly, Emlyn Williams had tried and failed to bring it to life in an Old Vic production in 1937. Now, Rich went for the Williams role, that of the sanctimonious Angelo, master of Vienna, who condemns a man to death for the crime of lechery only to fall victim to the same temptations. His rival for the part, because from the very beginning this is how Rich saw him, was Halham Fordham who, post university, was to make a fine reputation as a radio actor.

Rich took to understudying in a way that was unsettling for his principal. By putting up suggestions as to how the role should be played, he invited comparisons that favoured his own interpretation. This and the constant enquiries as to the state of Halham Fordham's health brought an unaccustomed tension to what, after all, was an amateur production. Years on, Rich created some highly romanticised stories of how he got to play his first Shakespearian role. In one version Halham Fordham was taken ill on the first night just before curtain up: in another the unfortunate actor broke down in dismay when he realised he would not aspire to the Burton heights. Reality was a call up paper. Halham Fordham went off to fight the Germans leaving Rich to conquer the stage.

Playing in the open air, in and among the cloisters, Rich needed all his energy and passion to bring Angelo to life. Once, he overdid it. When Angelo comes to realise his quandary he suffers an agony of indecision:

'What dost thou, or what art thou, Angelo? Dost thou desire her foully for those things that make her good? Oh, let her brother live!

Thieves for their robbery have authority when judges steal themselves.'

At this point Rich cracked his fist against an ancient pillar which retaliated by shooting a stone splinter into his eye. When first I heard this story I was properly sympathetic but with repetition and embellishment ('I'm telling you Graham, it was a lump of rock as big as my hand') I descended to sarcasm. ('So you were blinded for the rest of the performance were you? That must have been very confusing for the other actors.')

Only brief notices of *Measure for Measure* appeared in the quality nationals but there were fulsome reviews in magazines favoured by the Oxford establishment such as *The Tatler* and *Horse and Hound*. At Nevill Coghill's invitation, Binkie Beaumont turned up and stayed long enough to congratulate Rich. 'If after the war, you still want to be a professional actor,' he told him, 'come and see me. We should be able to find you something.'

Another guest was Phil Burton who was enjoying his own run of success with the BBC. Having accepted an offer to take up a permanent job as a drama producer he was in the process of moving to Cardiff. Maybe with both in a state of high excitement they expected too much of the evening. Or perhaps Phil was heavy-handed in his detailed criticism of Rich's performance. In any event, there was some tension between them which led Rich to cut short their dinner and go on alone to a student party.

It was insensitive of Rich but it was symptomatic of his refusal to be held to account – by anyone. In the company of friends, Rich was generous in his praise of Phil Burton who, he maintained, was a superb director. He even tried to involve him in student productions. But he did not take kindly to the suggestions that he might in any way be dependent on the man he called father.

Of course it was out of the question that any of Rich's true family should visit him in Oxford. The indulgence would have been as excessive as it was inappropriate. We acknowledged, more readily than Phil Burton I believe, that like every youngster Rich needed the chance to find his own way. But there is no denying, social embarrassment played a part. None of us then would have felt comfortable in the tight little world of university manners. At the same time we feared that Rich might choose to disregard the family. It was a natural but unjustified anxiety. True, Rich did play the Phil Burton card when he wanted to impress the public school contingent but with those who were closest to him he never made any attempt to disguise his origins. Friends like Tim Hardy, better known as the actor Robert Hardy, who came from a prosperous, middle class background, knew all about us before we had even heard his name.

Rich's skill in playing the social conventions was more apparent in his eagerness to adapt to the interests of his companions. When he was with Tim Hardy, for whom rugby held no appeal, the talk was of great plays and the roles they were planning for themselves. But in the rugby pubs, with his own team, the University Second XV, known as the Greyhounds, it was all raucous songs and ribald stories. Rich liked to be liked.

Departure from Oxford to take up full time residence with the RAF was an occasion of great heart searching. Like everyone else on the brief journey into higher education, Rich pledged to return to Oxford after the war. For the rest of his life he regretted not sticking to his word.

But while there was no degree or any other formal recognition of achievement, he did not come away entirely empty-handed. Nevill Coghill predicted that Rich would be a successful, maybe even a great actor. For his private records, as Rich later discovered, his tutor was yet more fulsome. 'This boy is a genius,' he wrote, adding later, 'I have had only two men of genius to teach – W. H. Auden and Richard Burton. When they happen one cannot mistake them.'

After two short hops to the West Country and to Lancashire, Rich was posted to Winnipeg in Canada. If it was not exactly the centre of the war zone, remember, the worst of the fighting was over. Rich saw his period in uniform merely as an exercise in marking time. He would not be long for civvy street. But it was not as simple as that. International tensions in peace time meant that the numbers in the British forces had to be kept up. This was achieved by adopting a policy of last in, last out. Rich had to wait nearly three years, until November 1947, for his freedom.

For the most part he kept his distance from forces' entertainment. Occupying his skills as a raconteur to gather a crowd in a pub was one thing but high jinks on stage in the tatty productions favoured by the ENSA (Entertainment National Service Association) were not to his liking. He was at one with the disgruntled trooper who jumped on stage at the end of an ENSA play shouting, 'Three cheers for the audience'.

Marking time for Rich was reading, rugby and riotous behaviour – usually in that order. When he left the RAF Rich was word perfect in all of the great Shakespearian roles. He was also a promising wing-forward. So much was declared by Bleddyn Williams who was soon to reach the glorious heights of a Cardiff and Wales and British Lions centre-three-quarter. With another rugby friend Dai, or Dinger Evans, a rock of a man, Rich toured the local bars. I cannot imagine that the landlords regarded them as a welcome sight. What profits they created in the consumption of beer they wiped out in damage to property and people. Fights with servicemen who were not RAF, or not Welsh, or even on occasion, not from the same part of Wales were the cause of frequent detentions. But Rich enjoyed his reputation as a jovial mixer. He had long since given up any idea of trying for a commission.

Serious theatre was a world away. He enjoyed talking about it to the interested friends like Mick Misell who had a hankering to act (and one day would come into his own as Warren Mitchell). And when he returned to Britain in late 1945 he was quick to renew contact with Tim Hardy whose enquiring mind was a spur to ambition. But the little I saw of Rich at this period made me think that, as an actor, he had lost his sense of purpose.

He told me about a fantastic hitchhike from Winnipeg to New York, one thousand miles on less than two dollars. 'It was easy in uniform,' he told me. 'Every motorist thought he owed us something for helping to win the war.'

American hospitality carried him along in New York. There were parties galore and an abundance of generous hearted girls eager to show him the city, and a lot else besides. As Rich talked, my teenage imagination, already made hyperactive by a chance adventure in the back row of the cinema, nearly cracked under the strain.

'And what about Broadway?'

'Broadway?'

'Yes, what about the theatres?'

Notwithstanding Rich's lavish descriptions of the good life I had assumed that it was the chance to see good acting which had principally attracted him to New York. But not a bit of it.

'Oh I got some free tickets. I went to see *Oklahoma*.'

A light musical? Nothing else? Surely this was not the same Rich who had impressed Emlyn Williams and Nevill Coghill with his single minded devotion to the classics.

If I was surprised, Phil Burton was worried. He could see his prize slipping away from his grasp. When Rich had settled into his penultimate posting at Bircham Newton, in the remotest part of Norfolk, Phil made strenuous efforts to restore his protegé to the front rank of radio drama. But Cardiff, where Phil's influence was greatest, was too far from RAF Docking for the lifeline to hold for very long.

Fortunately, Rich had other friends who wanted him to succeed. In early 1947 Emlyn Williams asked him to play Morgan Evans in his television production of *The Corn is Green*. This was interesting on two counts. As the study of a young Welshman of poor background marked out for a brilliant career by a dedicated teacher, *The Corn is Green* had an obvious biographical significance for Rich as well as for the author. That the play was to be performed live on television was an added inducement.

Though still in its infancy and somewhat retarded by a wartime ban on output, BBC television was eager to test its appeal against other forms of popular entertainment. But confined to the studio with static cameras and set, it was natural for television drama producers to look to the stage for their inspiration. Plays which had done well in London were the first choice for adaptation to the small screen. At the same time stage actors who had to know all their lines on opening night were more likely to get work on live television than film actors who could mug up on their parts from day to day.

Though over-age for the part, Rich was one of the few actors around who had the experience and the ability to play Morgan Evans on television. He grabbed the chance to do something new and exciting. What he made of it remains a matter of conjecture. There were very few television sets in those days, certainly in our part of the country, and I have yet to come across anyone out of the potential audience of several thousand who actually saw the play. But the effect on Rich was undeniable. He was back in business and he was enjoying every minute of it.

He was also in love. The cause was a vivacious young lady who shared his television debut. Her name was Eleanor Summerfield. An independent spirit of great character, as her subsequent career as an actress and comedienne was to prove, she was attracted to Rich without allowing herself to be overwhelmed by him. After *The Corn is Green*, Eleanor went on tour with a company which seemed to take perverse delight in putting the greatest possible distance between her and Rich. He used up his quota of weekend passes hitchhiking to far flung outposts of the theatre circuit. Occasionally he wrote home.

'He'll not be here for Christmas,' reported Cis. 'He says he's spending his leave in Scotland. What do you think that means?'

Her brothers knew very well what it meant but thought it polite to remain silent.

'He's twenty-one,' said Ivor. 'He's old enough to look after himself.'

The affair lasted eight months. Rich never told me why it ended but I suspect that Eleanor was too self-willed to make an ideal partner for Rich at this period in his life. Having recovered his ambition he, like all successful actors, wanted all the attention focused on him. Eleanor was not prepared for that. Rich had to wait another eighteen months for someone who was.

# Chapter 5

Within hours of his release from the military, Rich joined the queue of young hopefuls outside the offices of H. M. Tennent. It was, he told me, a spur of the moment decision. Having handed in his kit, and been given a rail warrant to take him home to Wales, he realised he had to change trains in London. Why not take the opportunity, he reasoned, to find out if Binkie Beaumont remembered him from Oxford days? He did and, more to the point, so did Daphne Rye who immediately offered to sign up Rich at ten pounds a week (a fortune for anyone used to RAF pay). As events were to show, she was also prepared to help his career in other ways. It was as if she and her boss, who could be equally attentive, were in friendly rivalry for the attentions of the curiously handsome young actor. I say 'curiously' because Rich was not at all in the mould of the traditional matinee idol. There was nothing of the finely chiselled profile so beloved by the stage photographers. Rather, he had a puggish look – tough but at the same time warm and inviting. 'The face of a boxing poet,' said Emlyn Williams.

It was a first impression which could puzzle and disarm the competition. Richard Leech, also a contract player with Tennent who was to be a great friend, remembers the first time he set eyes on the much heralded discovery from the valleys.

'When he came in I thought, who is this? He's not an actor. He's just a squat Welsh rugby player. I won't have any trouble here. But I was wrong. Oh boy, was I wrong.'

Tennent's unwillingness to pay ready money extinguished any dream Rich had of returning to Oxford. Years on when he was disillusioned with blockbuster movies and disgusted with the inanities of the publicity circuit, he spoke lovingly of what he imagined he had missed. But at the time he poured scorn on Tim Hardy who went back to finish his degree, and on Warren Mitchell who won a place at the Royal Academy of Dramatic Art.

The family did not quite know what to think. The high value put on education caused regret for the opportunities Rich was passing up. But there was respect for his earning power.

'Ten quid a week, is ten quid a week, there's no denying it,' said Ivor in the tautology of bar room conversation. 'And he gets it whether he's working or not.' For miners who had laboured a lifetime for less it sounded like a dream come true.

Rich's first Tennent role was little more than a walk on in an inconsequential play called *Castle Anna* at the Lyric, Hammersmith. But he also understudied the lead which gave him the chance in rehearsals to show what he could do. I missed this and his next play, *Dark Summer*, which went on tour in early 1948, because I was taking my turn in the forces, as a naval rating in the Far East. But I was home in time for the opening of Rich's first film, *The Last Days of Dolwyn*.

This was an Emlyn Williams project in every sense. He was the writer, director and the star with the meatiest role, that of an upstart bureaucrat who returns to Wales to execute a scheme to flood his native valley to make a reservoir. Out to thwart his plans is an old lady, played by Edith Evans, and her foster son, Gareth, who in the last scene accidentally kills the villain. Rich was cast as Gareth.

Viewed today, it must be said that Emlyn Williams let his sense of melodrama run away with him. *The Last Days of Dolwyn* did not measure up to Carol Reed's *The Fallen Idol* or *The Third Man* or Anthony Asquith's *The Winslow Boy*, all of which were made by London Films at about this time. But it brought in the audiences in Britain and in the States where, as *Woman of Dolwyn*, it appealed to the stereotyped image of the Welsh as a race of starry-eyed sentimentalists.

For Rich, *The Last Days of Dolwyn* was the luckiest of breaks, though as his acting friends observed, he behaved as if it were his due. The fact was that after six months on a Tennent salary he was impatient for action. Everybody told him he was good, so why could he not have the opportunity to show it? A camera test for a minor role in a film yet to be guaranteed a production date, was not what he had in mind. Rich was still very much a man of the theatre. The film business was a grey area for him. He did not doubt that he could make an impact on the screen, but was it worth the effort? He never did get to answer the question.

Emlyn Williams sought to allay his fears. The camera test was not the usual chaotic affair overseen by trainees. The legendary Otto Heller, director of photography on the film, was there alongside the director who gave Rich careful instructions on what to do and how to do it. A few days later, Emlyn Williams sent a telegram to the provincial theatre where Rich was appearing in *Dark Summer*. It read, 'You have won the scholarship', a quote from *The Corn is Green* which needed no interpretation.

Rich was in. But still he did not realise what he was into. The backer for *The Last Days of Dolwyn* was Sir Alexander Korda, the great impresario of the British film industry and the only film maker on this side of the Atlantic who understood the American market. For part of the war, he had headed the British end of the MGM operation and though now running his own studios at Shepperton, he kept up his links with the US including a valuable distribution arrangement with Twentieth Century-Fox. Korda did things the American way which included generous budgets (he was often accused of extravagance) and big publicity billings for his actors. For the first time, the press was encouraged to show an interest in Richard Burton. Who was he? What did he want to do with his life?

Except in the barest detail Rich seemed unable to decide the answers to these questions. Take background. He was from the South Wales mining community, of that there was no doubt. But thereafter he could be working class and proud of it, or (courtesy of Phil Burton) middle class and equally proud of it. It all depended on the circumstances of the interview and what he thought the journalist wanted to hear.

In the early days, he tended to give Phil Burton more than his due asserting, for instance, that a formal adoption order had been agreed when he was only twelve. In fact, there was no adoption order and Rich was well past his seventeenth birthday when he moved in with his guardian. The glorification of Phil Burton meant a corresponding downgrading of the family. It was said that Rich spent his early years in penury, which was totally untrue, or that Dadi Ni was too fond of the booze to know what was going on. No one could deny that our father was a keen supporter of the local brewery, but then, it was difficult to find a miner who was anything else. But he was never roaring drunk and never lost control of his temper as Rich and Ivor were liable to do. Even when an overwrought friend pushed Dadi Ni into the canal, he emerged in a forgiving mood. If the same thing had happened to Rich he would not have felt peace of mind until he had flung the other man off the top of the viaduct.

The worst that could be said of Dadi Ni's drinking is that he used it as an excuse for avoiding unpleasant decisions. This is far short of the reports, often started by Rich in his jokiest revelations, of having to carry the old man home from the pub or of him finishing a session by sliding under the table.

No doubt it is unfair to blame Rich for all the misinformation and downright lies about the family which rolled off the presses over the years. But, at the same time, I cannot entirely blame the press. As Emlyn Williams often said to Richard: 'You certainly gave them plenty of copy.'

By the standards of Richard Burton's Hollywood debut, now a mere three years ahead, the promotion associated with his appearance in *The Last Days of Dolwyn* was modest indeed. But he was flattered by the attention of Korda's publicists who were far more adventurous than their colleagues in the theatre. Instead of relying on the critics for their press coverage they went out to create news and feature articles. Even before the film was released, Bill O'Bryen, casting director, nominated Rich as one of the ten likeliest stars of the future. For the record the other nine were: Jack Hawkins, Norman Wooland, Michael Gough, Jack Watling, Moira Lister, Honor Blackman, Sarah Churchill, Faith Brook and Rona Anderson.

I was back in Britain for the première of *The Last Days of Dolwyn*. It was an excuse for another family outing to Cardiff. Even to my untrained eye, Rich had what they called 'screen presence'. In a secondary role he held the attention wonderfully against such practised scene stealers as Edith Evans and Emlyn Williams. But for me seeing him on the screen larger than life was less of a surprise than hearing him sing. He had to get through a Welsh love ballad, 'Ar Lan Y Mor', which was not at all his style of music. I heard he needed several takes to get it right but he remembered the words for ever afterwards. When I last heard him singing it, it was in duet with Elizabeth Taylor who adopted the song as her Welsh party piece.

Rich's leave of absence from Tennent to film *The Last Days of Dolwyn* was extended a month to allow him to play his most challenging theatre role to date – that of Constantine in *The Seagull*. For this opportunity he had to thank the actor and director Clifford Evans, who had persuaded the Arts Council to support a new season of fortnightly repertory at Swansea's Grand Theatre. Rich was heavily feted by the Welsh papers as a national celebrity. But unlike the London papers which quickly caught on to the mischief in Richard Burton, our own press portrayed him as a high-minded young man who spent his free time reading scripts and contemplating his next contribution to the living arts. Maybe on home ground Rich was more cautious about what he said to reporters but, with hindsight, his unnatural reserve probably had more to do with the fact that he was in love again – and did not yet want to admit it.

The girl was Sybil Williams, she was Welsh, nineteen and an actress who had played a bit part in *The Last Days of Dolwyn*. That much we were allowed to know before Rich returned to London. A few days later, on 5 February 1949, he sent a telegram: 'Married this morning. Pity Wales.'

The second sentence was not, as I first thought, a lament for all the single girls in the kingdom who now had to make do with second best, but a genuine cry from the heart for the Welsh XV who had unexpectedly lost against Scotland at Murrayfield.

Sybil and Rich had a lot in common. She too was from South Wales; she too had been brought up by an older sister, both her parents having died young. Much of her early life was in Northampton but her roots were in the Rhondda Valley where her father had been a pit manager. Like Rich, Sybil took to acting as an escape from the nine to five routine. She went to the London Academy of Music and Dramatic Art. But there the parallel ended for, whatever her qualities, Sybil was not a great actress. That she landed a bit part in *The Last Days of Dolwyn* was more a tribute to Emlyn Williams's generosity than to her raw talent. Yet, when she was herself, her personality sparkled. Sybil was the sort of person who would liven up a gathering just by walking in the door. She was ever cheerful, sympathetic and loyal. Add to this a period beauty which favoured the wholesome, good time girl and it was hardly surprising that Rich was hooked.

Though he never said as much, at least not to me, I feel certain that for Rich, marriage was a quick dash for security. Caught up in the swirl of celebrity games he needed a fixed point, a base where he could put up the shutters and feel secure. Just like Cis before her, Sybil was the ideal homemaker.

There was only one small problem. They had nowhere to start a home. This time the guardian angel in Rich's life (an overworked benefactor if ever there was one) materialised in the shape of Daphne Rye. At a nominal rent, she let the couple a small furnished flat at the top of her house in the Fulham Road. For good measure she threw in a champagne reception.

Chelsea in the fifties was the place to be for a rising young actor. Famous names of the profession were well represented in the smart Georgian and Victorian terraces. Just down the road from the Burtons lived the Williamses, Emlyn and Molly with their children Alan and Brook. In the belief that it was time for Rich to settle down, Emlyn had encouraged the relationship with Sybil. Now he was happy to use his influence to introduce Rich to powerful friends in the theatre and film. There were parties galore. They were great fun, if not always as useful as Rich hoped. He was still at the stage when he was prepared to sit at the feet of the great to hear words of wisdom. So often he was disappointed.

On the evening he met Terence Rattigan, the writer was seated room centre surrounded by young admirers. Rich was propelled forward by his host and introduced to him. Rattigan extended a gentle hand. 'I was just saying,' he confided to Rich who was anticipating a gem on stage technique, 'I was just saying, when I was at Oxford I was quite the prettiest thing of my year.'

The Rattigan connection was a disappointment in another context. In March 1949 Rich landed a small role in a new Rattigan play, *Adventure Story*, about Alexander the Great. The lead was Paul Scofield. Three years older than Rich and already a veteran of Stratford, he was well established in the public mind as one of the most exciting actors of his generation. For Rich, the temptation to challenge and thus over-act in what was essentially a submissive role was irresistible. After three days' rehearsal he was summarily replaced by Robert Flemying, a quieter and more amenable actor, who, as it happened, was also blessed with a wonderfully deep, resonant voice.

Rich was furious, the more so because he genuinely admired Scofield and badly wanted to share success with him. He was angry too because he knew he was at fault. After a few drinks he would even admit the fact, though formally his excuse was that he was too young to play Paul Scofield's older brother. When, in all innocence, I suggested that he might have used heavier make-up I was rewarded by an icy silence.

Fortunately for Rich there were early compensations which soon wiped clean the memory of his humbling experience. His second film, *Now Barabbas . . .*, was an adaptation of a William Douglas Home play, his third for the West End and the first to be counted a success. The theme (uncharacteristically for a writer more at home with light comedy) was the destructive force of prison life on inmates and workers alike. Rich played an IRA saboteur, so convincingly as to come out best in the reviews, which were otherwise politely dismissive of the efforts of a distinguished cast led by Cedric Hardwicke. The trouble with the film was that it turned out to be such a lukewarm version of the play, which had some painful things to say about the inhumanity of prison life. The theatre of the forties was not all French windows and swinging tennis racquets.

Praise for his work on the film set raised the standing of Richard Burton as a Tennent contract player. Soon after his departure from *Adventure Story*, Rich was signed up for the John Gielgud production of Christopher Fry's verse drama *The Lady's not for Burning*. With hindsight it is easy to see this as the chance of a lifetime. But in fairness to Rich, who to begin with was thoroughly dismissive of the entire project, the golden prospects were not immediately apparent. Fry was new to the West End where verse drama, unless it was by T. S. Eliot, was generally assumed to be commercially unviable. As star and co-director, Gielgud was the natural choice to give the play a distinctive style; who better to handle the author's verbal pyrotechnics? But this was a period when the Gielgud magic was thought to be fading. His name alone was no longer a guarantee of success.

Still, the role was bigger than any previously offered him and Binkie Beaumont was so enthusiastic on the actor's behalf, Rich thought it was about time he put in for a rise. Offered £15 a week he pressed for £20. Finally Beaumont compromised – £17.10s. Delighted with his negotiating skills Rich splashed out on a taxi all the way back to Fulham Crescent. As he got out he met Emlyn Williams who was the first to hear of the Burton triumph. He was not impressed.

'Go back and ask for £30,' he ordered.

With enormous reluctance Rich did as he was told, pausing on the way to build up his courage in the only way he knew. The interview was long and heated but Beaumont gave way. As Rich left his manager fired a parting shot, 'I suppose that old Welsh pit pony put you up to this.'

*The Lady's not for Burning* was a triumph. The critics were full of praise for a play in which author and actors revelled in the joy of imaginative language. 'An exciting night out for the brain' was a front-of-house review quote which, for once, accurately depicted the consensus view. Christopher Fry was proclaimed theatre personality of the year. Everybody in the cast had their share of praise though given the range of talent on parade, Rich was delighted to be hailed, yet again, as 'an exciting new discovery'. There was a scene in which all he had to do was to scrub the floor while John Gielgud and his co-star, Pamela Brown, for whom the play was specially written, worked with the dialogue. Rich was said by one critic to perform this dramatic task 'convincingly'. 'So convincingly,' added John Gielgud, 'he attracted all the attention. The audience couldn't take their eyes off him.'

The company was an extraordinary mix of ages with the senior level represented by Harcourt Williams, Eliot Makeham and Esme Percy, all in their seventies, and the junior by Claire Bloom, then just seventeen. Of Rich's generation were Peter Bull, who looked like a friendly version of his own name, and Richard Leech. Both liked playing jokes. A week before opening Peter Bull asked Rich if he had seen his front-of-house picture. Rich found himself looking at a middle aged stranger wearing a beret at a jaunty angle. The picture stayed put for the first month. So often was a story told of Esme Percy losing his glass eye, that he felt compelled to put out a statement that he was not inclined to divert the audience's attention by rolling a marble across the stage.

It was in rehearsal for *The Lady's not for Burning* that John Gielgud congratulated Rich on his radio portrayal of Shakespeare's Henry V. 'So talented,' he murmured. Rich was delighted. 'And so like dear Larry,' added Gielgud in one of his deflating asides.

Rich treasured the back-handed compliment. 'It makes a better story. If he'd just said "Well Done", there wouldn't be anything to tell.'

The BBC *Henry V* was another project which, in the long-running mood of ill temper following his dismissal from *Adventure Story*, Rich was inclined to reject as an unworthy crumb of comfort. It originated with Frank Hauser, then a young director with radio drama who was commissioned to produce a celebratory offering for Shakespeare's birthday. Having chosen to present *Henry V*, albeit in a shortened version, it was simply a question of finding a suitably commanding voice to fill the leading role. Re-enter Tim Hardy who knew Frank Hauser from post war Oxford when both were finishing their degrees. He set up a meeting between Frank and Rich.

It was a boisterous evening with the three of them arguing like mad about how best to convey Shakespeare to a living-room audience. With the Rattigan lost opportunity fresh in his mind, Rich was over sensitive to criticism and angrily dismissed any opinion which did not coincide with his own. As the dinner progressed and the drinks bill lengthened Rich got louder and more aggressive. Frank Hauser might reasonably have called a stop there and then but, a Cardiff man himself, he knew a thing or two about the contentious Welsh and was not deterred. After departing the restaurant (to the plain delight of the other patrons) they collected Sybil from the Prince of Wales Theatre, where she was an assistant stage manager, and went on to the Burton flat to continue their debate.

'It was difficult,' said Frank Hauser, 'not to be won over by the Burton personality. It was a curious mixture of aggression and collusion. He was his own man and stood up for what he believed, which you couldn't help but admire. Yet at the same time he made you feel that if anyone was going to influence him it would be you alone – that you above all were so fascinating and stimulating, as to be worth his attention.'

That Rich was not a beginner in radio weighed heavily in his favour. The rigorous apprenticeship with Phil Burton had taught him how to cope with the limitations of the sound studio such as the static mike. To shout a speech, as Shakespearian kings were wont to do, usually required the actor to stand well back from the mike. If he retreated too far he was liable to sound as if he were yodelling from a mountain top. Rich could magnify his voice without hollering, a skill which made his performance all the more convincing.

Still, it was a big role to entrust to a relative newcomer and it was a tribute to Frank Hauser's powers of persuasion that his BBC seniors allowed him to get away with it. The gamble paid off. *Henry V* was transmitted to an appreciative audience. What adverse criticism there was fastened on the BBC efforts to squeeze a quart into a pint pot — three hours of stage drama into a mere ninety minutes.

The West End run of *The Lady's not for Burning* brought a succession of Welsh visitors to London. I have to say that the play was not well liked by many of us because, for all its cleverness, it failed to grab the emotions. The comedy of manners had an underlying tension but it was difficult to work up any interest in the leading characters or in what happened to them. But it was Rich, not the play, we really came to see. And after Rich, who did all that his fan club could expect of him, including handing out drinks as if there was no tomorrow, we were eager to meet Sybil.

That she was the ideal choice for Rich no one had any doubt. She was pretty and astute and amusing and she knew how to handle him. Whether Rich knew how to handle Sybil was another matter. When he leaned heavily on her loyalty and patience in small matters, like turning up late at a restaurant or not turning up at all, we could not help wondering if sometimes he made more serious demands on her sensitivity.

Maybe it is always the same with successful people. Dedication to winning precludes many of the ordinary domestic civilities. Certainly Rich showed all the signs of a man working to get to the top. His workload was prodigious. When he was not at the theatre performing or rehearsing, he was to be found at Broadcasting House recording another play or at the film studios where he was now pretty well constantly in demand. For weeks on end his working day would begin at seven in the make-up room at Pinewood and end at ten-thirty as the audience filed out of the Globe Theatre. I know that stories abound of Rich's extra-marital affairs but, while I am the last to claim that fidelity was his strongest suit, I do wish that those who profess such close knowledge of his romantic exploits would explain where he found the time to satisfy so many demands.

Once or twice Rich and Sybil spent weekends with the family. The local feeling was that they made the ideal couple, not at all spoilt by success. Rich responded cheerfully to the inevitable ribbing from friends and neighbours who had known him since childhood. One old boy who called him Douglas Fairbanks and thought he was cracking the most hilarious joke of all time, repeated the line often enough to be insulting. But Rich took it all in good part. He went to the same pubs he had known as a boy, sat talking in the same front rooms and went with the same crowd to the Saturday match. When he and Sybil were the guests of honour at a dinner dance in Margam, he told his hosts that 'since he did not own a dinner jacket they would have to accept him in an ordinary suit'. This went down well with those who were not invited. 'He's genuine enough is our Rich,' they told each other.

Professionally, Rich could do no wrong. His films were low budget affairs destined for screening as second feature. But so consistently good were his reviews that Korda put him under contract at a princely £100 a week. True to his central casting image as an actor of many accents, he played successively a Liverpudlian sailor, a Norwegian fighter pilot and a Romany smuggler. The first of these films, a docklands saga called *Waterfront*, was directed by a youthful Michael Anderson, who was just starting out on a career which would encompass *The Dam Busters* and Mike Todd's *Round the World in Eighty Days*. But *Waterfront*, his first solo effort, was not a success. What should have been an exciting adventure somehow turned out as a dreary melodrama which even Robert Newton at his villainous best could not save.

In *The Woman with No Name*, Rich had the chance to play opposite Phyllis Calvert, one of the most popular British stars of the period. Their on-screen love affair was brief (Rich's character was killed off in the first reel) but memorable, not least for Cis who flooded out a Cardiff cinema with her tears. When Rich rang the following day to find out how she liked the film, Cis told him she had not cried so much in years.

'I'm sorry about that,' said Rich assuming the worst.

'Yes,' she sighed, 'it was lovely.'

Rich's next film appearance was in a light comedy which he hated. *Green Grow the Rushes*, an everyday story of smuggling folk, was not his style. A blatant attempt to cash in on the popularity of *Whisky*

*Galore* (before its rapid descent into oblivion the film was actually renamed *Brandy Ashore*), everyone involved in the project suffered from an excess of good intentions. The money was put up by the film technicians' union, the ACT, whose members were made nervous by the apparent failure of the British film industry to fight on two flanks – against Hollywood on one side and BBC television on the other. It was a sign of the times that cinema attendance was dipping and famous studios were being sold off for development or commercial television. *Green Grow the Rushes* did nothing to reverse the trend. But for one rising young actor, it did help to concentrate his thoughts on his long term future. For the real money it looked very much as if America was the place to be.

Meanwhile, the Burton income was of a size to bring a smile to the face of his bank manager. Each film made him at least a thousand pounds for, at most, six weeks' work. I was staying with Rich when the cheque for *Green Grow the Rushes* was delivered. It was two thousand pounds. As a recruit to local government on three hundred a year with luncheon vouchers, I was wide eyed with admiration.

In early 1950 Rich and Sybil moved out of Daphne Rye's apartment into a house of their own. The Hampstead address – 6 Lyndhurst Road – sounded very grand but in fact, it was a bomb damaged property with only one habitable floor. The builders were told to start on the roof and then work their way down. Rich would probably have paid for the entire renovation out of his own pocket but Sybil was smart enough to know that there were generous grants for war repairs. Thanks to her, they created a very presentable home at modest cost. But they were not there long enough to enjoy it. Within a year they had decided to build a new house which became 10 Squire's Mount, also in Hampstead. Before it was half finished, Rich had departed for New York to appear with John Gielgud in the Broadway production of *The Lady's not for Burning*.

The offer came through when Rich was appearing in another Christopher Fry play, *The Boy with a Cart*, at the Lyric, Hammersmith. Written twelve years earlier for a Sussex Festival, this simple mystery play might never have got to London had it not been for the success of *The Lady's not for Burning*. When Gielgud had to withdraw from that play, so in effect closing it, to join Anthony Quayle for a Stratford season, he urged Rich to consider *The Boy with a Cart* as his next stage undertaking. If he, Rich, could persuade Binkie Beaumont to put up the money, Gielgud was prepared to come in as director.

It was a heaven-sent opportunity for Rich who recognised the value of playing his first stage lead under the guidance of one of the theatrical greats. But not for the first time the problem was in making the figures add up to a sensible business proposition. By no stretch of imagination could the play qualify for Shaftesbury Avenue. The prospective audience was limited to the intellectual side of the cultural establishment which reduced the likely box office take from the thousands to hundreds. If the prospect was to break even, a short run at a theatre outside the West End was called for. The Lyric was ideal. Moreover, it was available. *The Boy with the Cart* was booked in for six weeks.

I was there for the opening night and for the emotional scenes backstage after the final curtain. For the first time Rich felt like a star and he loved it. John Gielgud told him he had just given one of the most delightful performances he had ever seen in the theatre. Christopher Fry thought the part could not be better played. The feelings of gratitude were mutual. There and then Rich promised to appear in yet another Fry revival, *A Phoenix too Frequent*, for a short out of town season. With Gielgud about to take the London cast of *The Lady's not for Burning* to Broadway and Laurence Olivier playing in *Venus Observed* at the St James', Fry was at the summit of his popularity. Sadly for him the fashion for verse drama soon passed. Within four years Osborne, Pinter and Wesker were leading the way towards a realism in the theatre that precluded the high flown sentiments of poetic imagery. By then, Rich too was out of harmony with live theatre but for somewhat different reasons.

Towards the end of the second week of *The Boy with a Cart*, one of the company spotted Anthony Quayle in the audience. The significance of his visit was not lost on Rich. Quayle had lately taken over the direction of the Memorial Theatre at Stratford-upon-Avon where he had brought in star names such as John Gielgud and Peggy Ashcroft to rival the Old Vic in the quality of Shakespearian productions. Quayle was a man of enormous energy (which he attributed in part to the frustrations of time serving in the army), a gifted actor and director and an able administrator, a combination of qualities which immediately put him ahead of the game. But he had another quality, as important as all the rest put together. He was a great talent spotter. His entire repertory was blessed by a company of actors whose holding power could not be bettered anywhere in the country.

Anthony Quayle's third season at the Memorial coincided with the Festival of Britain, the year in which a war weary nation, brought lower still by years of economic austerity, was supposed to show the world that it could still measure up to the finest. From a leading classical theatre – Quayle himself would no doubt have said, *the* leading classical theatre – an extra special effort was called for. The decision was to put on four of Shakespeare's history plays – *Richard II*, the two parts of *Henry IV*, and *Henry V* – and present them as a continuing story. Curiously, this had never been tried before. Tradition held that each play was a distinct entity and so logically it must have seemed with the star roles in the Henries clearly identified as Falstaff and Hotspur. With Hal relegated to the second league of characters, it was not surprising that his advance to power, the crucial unifying factor, should have been neglected.

Quayle's idea was to bring a new understanding to Shakespeare's history cycle by restoring Hal to the centre of the action. But not everyone believed this was desirable or even possible. He needed an actor for Hal who had faith in the director's intentions and the power to realise them.

Having made his choice (when he saw Rich in *The Boy with a Cart* he said to himself 'That's it. Let's do it'), there remained the problem of persuading the actor that it was in his best interest to spend a season at Stratford. For Rich the advantages were not clear cut. Against the prestige of the Memorial Theatre had to be set the glamour of an American debut and the opportunities that were likely to come from his Broadway appearance in *The Lady's not for Burning*. Rich was notoriously unsentimental in his attitude to Shakespeare. He had a hankering for the great roles but a nightly appearance in doublet and hose did not of itself appeal. Nor did he like competition when the odds were stacked against him. If he was to play Hal he would be up against the Hotspur of Michael Redgrave, an acclaimed Shakespearian actor and an established favourite with Old Vic and Stratford audiences. There was a risk that his inexperience might show.

The objections were anticipated by Anthony Quayle who thought of a nimble way around them. Instead of contacting Rich direct, he rang Sybil. Would she be interested in taking the minor role of the Welsh princess in the first part of *Henry IV*? Sybil, of course, was delighted. There was, said Anthony Quayle, just one other thing. He was thinking of Richard to play Hal. Perhaps Sybil would like to sound him out. Quayle himself had no doubt that the move to Stratford would give a mighty lift to Rich's career. But given that the money was not too exciting, persuasion might be easier if Sybil put in a good word as a preliminary to a formal offer.

Rich guessed immediately what Quayle was up to. But he was tempted almost in spite of himself. The challenge was formidable and he had no idea if he could bring it off but, he knew also, sooner or later he would have to try. Sybil was not alone in urging him to take the plunge. John Gielgud, who had spent two successful seasons at the

Memorial, was strongly in favour. So too was fellow Welshman, Hugh Griffith, a larger than life character actor who had appeared with Rich in *The Last Days of Dolwyn* and in numerous radio plays. Griffith was already cast as John of Gaunt in *Richard II* and as Owen Glendower in the final part of *Henry IV*.

And then there was Tim Hardy who had been recruited to Stratford direct from RADA. In his case, it was not Anthony Quayle but his wife Dorothy who had acted as talent spotter. Having seen Tim and Robert Shaw in a student production she urged her husband to snap them up. Tim took great delight in proclaiming the Quayles' ability to pick out a winner. It was a gentle reminder of Rich's early judgement which he was now embarrassed to recall, that Tim did not have the steel in his character to fight his way to the top.

The deal taking Rich to Stratford was clinched when Hugh Griffith and his wife offered to share with the Burtons their rented manor house at Oxhill, just outside Stratford.

'We'll set up a little Wales in Warwickshire,' promised Griffith. 'What do you think of that, boyo?'

Rich liked the idea very much.

With their future settled for the year ahead, Rich and Sybil set sail for America. With minor exceptions the cast for *The Lady's not for Burning* was the same for New York as for London. This meant that Rich could be reunited with Peter Bull and Richard Leech, both first class actors who, refusing to take themselves too seriously, could always be relied upon to bring a sense of fun to the proceedings. Nor was there any shortage of amusement in New York. After the tension of the first night and the relief of the next day's enthusiastic reviews, came a succession of extravagant parties which had Rich trying to prove that when it came to hard drinking, he was Welsh champion and a world competitor.

I cannot say that in all this Rich gave much thought to Sybil. They were together for much of the day but at night after the show, Rich usually set off on his own, to return in the small hours. If there were no professional claims on his time, he slept through until lunch. Inevitably, there were rumours of an affair. Rich was strenuous in his denials. When the rumours persisted he had a talk with Richard Leech whose training as a doctor made him company friend, counsellor and father confessor rolled into one.

'You've heard what they're saying?' asked Rich.

The doctor confessed that he had overheard a word or two.

'Well it's not true. I may have a bit of fun but I'm not stupid. Why are they doing it? They're ruining everything, not just for me but for Sybil. She's no fool you know!'

Richard Leech agreed that Sybil was indeed highly perceptive.

'She's very upset. I don't think she can take much more of this. Will you help?'

'Of course,' said his friend. 'But what can I do?'

'I want you to stand up for me, boyo. When you hear gossip, tell them it's all lies. Just show a bit of faith in me, that's all it needs.'

True to his word, Richard Leech dived in to defend his maligned colleague. 'How dare you say that – what evidence do you have? Just think how hurtful this is to Sybil!'

A few weeks later on when Rich had left the cast to start rehearsals at Stratford, the girl linked with Rich ('Why are they doing this to me? Why?') took Richard Leech on one side.

'I need your help.'

'Now if it's about those rumours,' Richard assured her, 'you needn't worry. I don't think anyone takes them seriously any more!'

Her distress mounted. 'Do you think I worry about what people say? Anyway, the rumours were true. We *were* having an affair.'

Richard thought he must have misheard. 'What are you saying?'

'He lied to you for Sybil. He said everyone would listen to what you told them, but first you had to believe what *you* were told.'

Richard was angry, then amused. He had fallen for the Welsh charm. He had no one to blame. But there was still a question. 'So what do you want to see me about?'

The girl hesitated just for a moment. 'Ah well. That's a bit more difficult. It's like this. Well, you see . . .' And then in a rush. 'I think I'm pregnant.'

When that little matter was finally cleared up, Richard Leech thought back to a conversation with Sybil. It was late at night when Richard and his wife were returning from a party to their hotel. Sybil, who was in a room down the corridor, was standing in the doorway.

'I thought Rich might be with you,' she said.

Her friends made comforting noises. 'Don't worry, he'll be back soon. He's probably been held up by some Hollywood mogul.'

'Oh, I'm not worried,' said Sybil. 'I know Rich. I can take most things. It's just that I couldn't bear it if I believed he was unfaithful.'

# Chapter 6

Stratford was make or break for Richard Burton.

The advance notices showed that Anthony Quayle had put together a roll call of talent calculated to impress the most seasoned theatregoer. Rich was to invite comparison with Michael Redgrave as Richard II, Harry Andrews as Henry IV and Anthony Quayle himself as Falstaff. Backing them were a group of younger actors – Alan Badel, William Fox, Richard Wordsworth, Barbara Jefford, William Squire, Duncan Lamont, Robert Hardy and Geoffrey Balydon among them – all of whom could so highlight a secondary role as to magnify any inadequacies of the star performers.

Expectations were high all round. It was not just the regular theatre public who took an interest. Encouraged by the Festival of Britain to think proudly, the country demanded its heroes, in the arts as much as in sport and politics. With his much touted promise of greatness, Rich was a prime candidate for elevation.

The reinterpretation of the history plays as laid down by Quayle, favoured Rich in his now eager desire to attract a popular following. He was under orders to build up the role of Hal whereas Quayle and Redgrave were making a self-conscious effort to tone down their parts, a much riskier undertaking. It said much for the dedication of these actors who, incidentally, were also jointly responsible for directing the plays, that they stuck to their guns even when some notable critics accused them of perversely misunderstanding Shakespeare's intentions. Thus, Anthony Quayle was not greatly thanked for giving Falstaff some depth of character instead of simply portraying him as a merry old soul. And Michael Redgrave was told that his Hotspur was

67

'overshadowed' by Hal, as if this was a self evident fault in his performance.

For his contribution to the *Henry IV* double bill, Rich walked away with the lion's share of the plaudits. From Harold Hobson who, as the recent successor of the great James Agate at the *Sunday Times*, assumed the mantle of senior critic, there was embarrassingly extravagant praise, but so overwritten as to be virtually incomprehensible to the ordinary reader. 'Instead of a light hearted rapscallion,' said Hobson, 'Mr Burton offers a young knight keeping a long vigil in the cathedral of his own mind.' By which I think he meant that Rich fulfilled Hazlitt's definition of a great actor as 'the man who can master stillness'.

'Your eye picks him out and refuses to leave him,' wrote Philip Hope Wallace. This ability to compel attention even when appearing to do very little, fascinated the young Kenneth Tynan, then critic for the *Spectator* and not, as Rich's other biographers seem to imagine, *The Observer*, a paper he did not join for another three years.

'His Prince Hal,' observed Tynan, 'is never a roaming boy; he sits, hunched or sprawled with dark, unwinking eyes; he hopes to be amused by his bully companions, but the eyes constantly move beyond them into a time when he must steady himself for the crown . . . Fluent and sparing of gesture, compact and spruce of build, Burton smiles where other Hals have guffawed; relaxes where they have strained; and Falstaff must work hard to divert him.'

Looking back after nearly forty years, Anthony Quayle believes that Hal remains in the front rank of Richard Burton performances. It was not just an actor's ability – though he had plenty of that; he also had a lively mind, a feeling for verse and what Quayle describes as the 'heaven sent actor's mask', which derives in some mysterious way from the spacing of the eyes and the balance of the cheek bones and jaw. The extra quality which made for an exceptional performance was his intuitive understanding of the contradictions and conflicting emotions in Hal's character. 'They were something of his own,' says Anthony Quayle. 'Like Hal he was not sure who he was or what he wanted to be.'

This explains why Rich was less satisfactory as Henry V – a man who had come to terms with his own destiny. Rich, the private person, was very far from that idyllic state.

If his Henry V was not quite what the critics expected (it was too restrained for conventional taste) and if his last Stratford engagement as the lover Ferdinand in *The Tempest* was near disaster (Rich was entirely out of sympathy with the soppy youth), the wonderful and original portrayal of Hal entitled him, as Kenneth Tynan put it, 'to swell the thin company of living actors who have shown us the mystery and the power of which heroes are capable'.

But if his admirers in the quality press erected the pedestal for Richard Burton, it was their colleagues in the mass circulation dailies who gave him the lift which put him on top. Papers like the *Mirror*, the *Express* and the dear old *Daily Herald* were ecstatic in their praise. 'If the entire Festival of Britain can even approach this standard,' said a *Daily Mirror* reporter, 'the triumph over the moaners will be complete.'

The other Welsh players at Stratford took pleasure in the reflected glory and used their advantage, in ways that could sometimes irritate the rest of the company, to promote the idea of a Welsh enclave responsible only to itself. The leading dissident was Hugh Griffith, whose house Rich and Sybil shared for the entire seven month season. Famed for his stage and film image as a wicked old man, Hugh Griffith tried for the same level of eccentricity in real life. In the Griffith household everything was Welsh including the three corgis – Branwen, Olwen and Matholwch. The Welsh dragon was on display in every room.

At his worst, Griffith would encourage the rebel in his young friend – 'Go on boyo, you tell them' – so that Rich often made a fool of himself over silly misunderstandings. At best, he could think up a neat trick for showing that the Welsh – the masters of poetry – could bring something new to Shakespeare. There is a moment in the first part of *Henry V* when the chieftain Glendower (Hugh Griffith) and his daughter have a private chat. Shakespeare does not provide any dialogue, merely a stage instruction. Hugh Griffith thought he would try for a little variety in the proceedings by creating some lines in his native language. The actress who played opposite him fell in with the ploy. Her husband was appalled.

'Sybil may be Welsh,' said Rich, 'but she doesn't speak the language. The only word she knows is "bach" and she can't even pronounce that properly.' But never one to let the team down Rich laid on a course of what he claimed were superb elocution lessons. On the night, Sybil was word perfect. 'The publicity,' conceded Anthony Quayle, 'was not unwelcome.'

Rich made friends as well as admirers in his stint at the Memorial Theatre. Among them were several Americans and American based actors who journeyed to Stratford solely to witness the Burton phenomenon. When Rich had advance notice he sent out invitations to stay overnight at Oxhill. This made for some interesting and unusual parties. One weekend when Hilary, my wife, and I came to Oxhill,

Rich said casually, 'You'll have to watch yourself this evening. Humphrey Bogart is coming to dinner.'

'Bogart? Are you serious?'

'You bet. And I'd be careful what you say if I were you. He can turn nasty when he doesn't like someone.'

He gave no hint that he was anything but serious – and who was I to disbelieve him? Having sat through *Casablanca* and *The Maltese Falcon* I had a clear image of Bogart as a man not to be trifled with. So, playing for safety I was unusually quiet throughout the meal. I just sat there with damp palms, like Peter Lorre or Elisha Cook hoping to avoid a sock in the teeth.

Rich, I noticed, was not under the same compulsion to exercise restraint. He argued away on all manner of subjects, even banging his fist on the table to emphasise a point. Bogart gave as good as he got but not once did he lose his calm. I was impressed. Obviously, Rich had a way with this difficult character.

After the meal, Rich took me to one side.

'There's no need to overdo it,' he said. 'If you don't join in soon, I'm going to run out of things to say.'

All right, I was only twenty-four and still mother green. How was I to know that, in reality, Humphrey Bogart was just like any other successful actor – fifty per cent charm (rough or smooth, it still adds up the same) and fifty per cent insecurity. As the evening went on I realised he was not happy with what he was or what he had accomplished. He wanted more but had no idea how to achieve it.

'Have you ever heard of an American actor called Edwin Booth?'

'Wasn't he the man who shot President Lincoln?'

'No,' said Bogart, 'that was his brother James Wilkes Booth. Up to the time of the assassination Edwin Booth was one of the leading classical actors in the States. He travelled coast to coast playing all the great Shakespearian roles. Wherever he went he pulled in the crowds. And this was in the days when a theatre could be just a circle of lamps in the town square.'

'And is that what you'd have wanted to do?'

'Hell,' shouted Bogart. 'It's what I want to do now. Play Shakespeare, I mean. I can do without the lamps in the square.'

I was amazed. 'You, play Shakespeare?'

'And why not?' growled the actor.

Suddenly I was under threat again. 'Oh, no reason. No reason at all,' I mumbled. I was back in the Peter Lorre part. 'Can I get you another drink?'

Rich broke in. He sounded determined. 'Well, now I'll tell you something. I'd give up Shakespeare tomorrow to play decent parts in films like *The Treasure of the Sierra Madre* and *Key Largo*.' (These were two of Bogart's latest.) 'We're all in a rut but yours is more comfortable than most. You're a lucky man.'

But he did not mean all that he said.

'The problem for Bogie,' he told me later, 'is that like all American stars, he's typecast. His fans don't want to see him as anything but the all-American tough guy. Well, they're not going to do that to me. I want to be free to take any part I fancy.'

Curiously it was not long afterwards that Rich was offered a film role he fancied very much indeed. He played Edwin Booth in the Twentieth Century-Fox production, *The Prince of Players*. The film was not a box office success but it gave Rich a lot of satisfaction and it remains one of the best testimonies to the Burton versatility in Shakespeare.

After seeing the film Bogart phoned his congratulations. 'You were good,' he said.

'Thank you,' said Rich.

'Mind you,' said Bogart, 'I'm not saying I wouldn't have done better!'


Triumph at Stratford was followed by disaster on Broadway. To appear in Jean Anouilh's *Legend of Lovers* (called *Point of Departure* in London) must have seemed a good idea at the time. Anouilh was a distinguished and fashionable writer. Richard Burton was up in lights together with Dorothy McGuire whose theatre and film success in the matinee romance, *Claudia*, had brought her a popular following.

Heading the supporting cast was Hugh Griffith who could be relied upon to liven up rehearsal, usually at the expense of the director. Once, after numerous requests to repeat a scene, Griffith stormed out of the theatre.

'I will stay no longer,' he bellowed as he marched up the central aisle. 'I am going home.'

Ten minutes later he was back. 'I tried,' he announced grandly, 'but I found I could not walk the ocean.'

Sadly, *Legend of Lovers*, an update of the fable of Orpheus and Eurydice, did not appeal to the critics who found it pretentious and wordy. The play opened at the Plymouth Theater on Boxing Day 1951. It closed on 12 January.

Rich came home to an offer to star in *Montserrat*, a Lillian Hellman drama with a capital *D*. It centred on Rich as a Spanish Army officer in Central America caught up in a rebellion. Six hostages are to be killed, if the whereabouts of the rebel leader are not revealed. The secret is kept, the hostages shot and the officer is left with a bad conscience. The play opened in Brighton, transferred to the Lyric, Hammersmith and closed, all within three weeks.

It was now about six months since Rich had taken Stratford by storm. In that time there had been no shortage of work or promise of work. But the results were a sad disappointment, even though Richard Burton the actor emerged from two theatrical flops with good personal notices. What was missing was the excitement of moving on and up in the world. It was all sub-standard Shakespeare.

The dull period came to an end with a summons to a meeting with Alexander Korda.

'I want you to go to Hollywood,' boomed the producer.

'For what?'

Korda waved a fat cigar. 'To be a star. A great star.'

The intention was welcome but the details of how it was to be achieved remained hazy. What did soon become clear was that Korda, to whom Rich was still under contract, had made a lucrative sub-letting deal with Darryl Zanuck, production boss of Twentieth Century-Fox. For appearing in three films, Rich was to be paid £100,000, of which twenty per cent was to go to Korda. It was a staggering amount of money – one million pounds in today's currency – and even allowing for Korda's share, Rich was set to become a very wealthy man. Korda's American contacts had paid off in a big way.

'But what parts are they offering me?' Rich wanted to know. The question was put many times and the response from Korda was always the same.

'Don't worry. Relax. They'll think of something.'

The Burtons were packed and ready to sail when Rich discovered not from Korda but from a news item that his first Hollywood film was to be an adaptation of the Daphne du Maurier bestseller *My Cousin Rachel*. Rich did not need reminding that it was in another du Maurier film, *Rebecca*, that Laurence Olivier had consolidated his screen reputation. But that was ten years earlier. There had been a lot of changes in the film industry since then and Rich was not convinced that an old fashioned costume melodrama could still pull in the crowds.

Having decided to keep his thoughts to himself until he had seen a script, Rich waited for word from Korda. When it came it was to invite the Burtons to a grand send-off party.

'But what about the script?' pleaded Rich.

'Don't worry,' said Korda and put down the phone.

The day of the party came and still there was no script. Rich began to feel the first pangs of desperation. The flow of drinks had a calming effect but as Korda shook hands to say goodbye, Rich made one last effort.

'Is there any chance of getting a script before we sail?'

'A script? A script?' Korda declaimed in his thick Hungarian accent. 'The boy wants a script?' Then turning to an assistant, 'You heard him. Give him a script.'

The assistant rummaged in his briefcase and handed over a weighty manuscript. Rich was delighted and relieved. It was only later, at home, when he turned to the title page that he found he was looking at a well thumbed copy of *The Four Feathers* – a Korda production from 1939.

Without any lines to study, Rich spent the Atlantic crossing reading and thinking about his future. He knew enough about himself to recognise that while he could be a shrewd manipulator he was no businessman. Nor did he understand the subtleties of film contracts which could run to several pages of close typed gobbledygook. He needed someone to manage his legal and financial affairs.

He met the answer to his problem as soon as he got off the boat. Aaron Frosch was a young lawyer working his way up the hierarchy of Twentieth Century-Fox. His job when he first met Rich was to act as the official reception for visiting British actors.

That Aaron Frosch could go far soon became apparent to Rich. On the journey west aboard the Express Super Chief (this was in the days when to travel coast to coast by rail was to travel in style), they talked of little else except the intricacies of film finance with Aaron Frosch throwing out gems of advice on how to space out his earnings to minimise tax and increase income by taking advantage of studio perks such as chauffeur driven cars and five star hotels. For someone who knew what they were doing the possibilities seemed endless. Before they reached Los Angeles, Rich had made up his mind.

'I want you to represent me,' he told Aaron Frosch.

'Fine,' said Aaron. 'But there are just two problems. The first is that to work for you I would have to set up my own office. This would cost a lot of money and I don't have a lot of money. The second problem is that I already have an employer – Twentieth Century-Fox.'

Rich thought for a moment.

'If I solve the first of the problems can you handle the second?'

Aaron thought he could. And this is how my brother helped to set up a show business law firm which turned out to be the best of its kind. It was a partnership which, early on, made them both millionaires.

Rich was bemused by Hollywood. The flamboyant wealth, the wild parties, the sheer outrageousness delighted him. All these famous names! In a quick succession of handshakes one evening he met Elizabeth Taylor who was pregnant. Afterwards, he had to be told who she was. But despite the lavish hospitality, Rich was not yet a Hollywood convert. He was careful with his money (he and Sybil rented a modest house on the unfashionable side of town) and he was not taken in by the insincerity of so many he had to work with.

'They will say or do anything to protect themselves,' he wrote. 'They're all so bloody frightened.'

In another letter a single sentence sprang out like a punch to the jaw. 'To hell with all the sycophants.'

Every way he turned there was someone waiting to tell him what a brilliant actor he was. This might have been encouraging (no one is averse to compliments) if Rich's self professed admirers had actually seen any of his performances. But all they were doing, as Rich knew only too well, was to respond to the signals sent out by the studio publicists. Their bosses had decided Richard Burton was classed with Marlon Brando as a star in the making. And heaven help any one who wanted to argue.

'They flatter me rapaciously and obscenely,' he told Richard Leech. 'I am so great, great, great. It's like a new drink – Brando and Burton – guaranteed to go to your head if you stay too long in this town.'

*My Cousin Rachel* did not get off to a good start. Rich's apprehension about the script – or lack of it – was endorsed by the director, George Cukor. When at last the screenplay was delivered, but without an ending, Cukor had more harsh words for the writer. He was not convinced by Nunnally Johnson's argument that there was time enough to settle on a denouement once they were into shooting. Cukor was a methodical director who liked to see his way ahead. He said as much to the producer who also happened to be Nunnally Johnson. Johnson immediately went to a higher authority who decided in his favour. Cukor was replaced by Henry Koster, the German-born director who was known more for his reliability in turning in a serviceable product than for imaginative award-winning film making.

Predictably, *My Cousin Rachel* joined the long line of torrid romances aimed at middle aged mums hot in pursuit of vicarious excitement. It was part of the film market which remained strong despite television. Early indications of a box office hit spurred the gossip and feature writers into action. As a du Maurier hero, Rich was said to be a worthy successor to the fiery young Laurence Olivier. Even the *New Yorker* commended his sex appeal – 'lean, handsome, troubled and upstanding'.

74

Rich was grateful to Henry Koster who was patient and considerate with the fledgling star. There was less understanding from Rich's partner in lust, Olivia de Havilland. Already an established Hollywood name (she had two Oscars and three nominations to her credit), Miss de Havilland was disinclined to share the limelight. But what she knew about playing to the camera Rich was able to match with an understanding of the mechanics of acting which came from his theatre experience.

'There was a scene,' he told me, 'where I had to run up a staircase, turn back at the top and then speak my lines. I did all this and when Henry said "cut", the studio crew gave me a round of applause. I didn't know what it was all about until Henry let slip that most film actors couldn't do so many moves in one take. For a stage actor, it was the easiest thing in the world.'

When the film was released Olivia de Havilland was asked what she thought of Rich.

'There is not another leading man like him,' she said, just a trifle ambiguously. But in a magazine interview she, or her public relations counsellor, declared that 'there was no limit to the fame awaiting Richard Burton'. Privately, she could not stand the sight of him, an antipathy no doubt reinforced by the indelible memory of being on the wrong side of a block of scenery when Rich had a temper tantrum. He kicked it down on top of her.

For his part in *My Cousin Rachel*, Rich gained his first Oscar nomination, as best supporting actor. He lost out to Anthony Quinn (*Viva Zapata*) which was nothing to be ashamed about. Other trophies did come his way including a press award for the most promising newcomer to Hollywood. It was a sculpture about nine inches high showing a 35mm film encircling a globe. When he came back to Hampstead he used it as a doorstop in the lavatory.

'Can't you think of a better place to put it?' I asked him.

He shook his head. 'You've got the wrong idea,' he said. 'I want people to see and admire it. Now what chance is there of that if I put it up on the mantelpiece with the other ornaments? But in the loo, what else have they got to look at?' I could not fault his logic.


The Welsh premiere of *My Cousin Rachel* caused great excitement and not a little patriotic fervour.

'It's a great day when a son of Wales conquers Hollywood,' proclaimed the doyen of Cardiff cinema managers. 'Something special is called for.'

The 'something special' required a telegram to Rich asking him to despatch a suit of clothes he had worn in the film. On the first night, some fifteen minutes before the end of the credits, I went backstage at the Capital and changed into the hero's costume. With the help of a full length mirror I hunched my shoulders and jutted my chin in a way that I hoped resembled a typical Burton stance. Then, holding that position, I made my way to the wings to hear the manager announce to the audience the arrival of an honoured guest. I walked on.

The applause was tumultuous. My first reaction was relief and delight that the impersonation had been so successful. But as the clapping continued I could not help wondering if this audience could take a joke. I had not wished to be hounded off stage by a fusillade of well aimed ice cream cartons. I held up my hands to beg silence.

'Ladies and gentleman,' I began, 'I am not Richard Burton.'

But the trouble was, by projecting my voice, I even sounded like Richard Burton.

'Who are you then?' shouted someone. 'Olivia de Havilland?'

That broke the ice.

'Truthfully,' I said, 'I am not Richard. He is working in Hollywood and cannot be here. But he has sent me along, his brother Graham, to thank you for this wonderful reception.'

There was silence for a moment but as I turned to walk off, the applause was renewed. I breathed a sigh of relief.

Dadi Ni waited to see the film until it came to the Odeon at Port Talbot. Afterwards, Hilda asked him what he thought of it. He put on a glum expression. 'Well I'm not sure I liked all that kissing and cuddling. It wasn't decent. What will Sybil say?'

Hilda tried to reassure him. 'It's a film, Dad. It's only acting.'

'Acting is it?' shrugged Dadi Ni. 'Well, all I can say is, it looked real enough to me.'

After *My Cousin Rachel* there was talk of Rich coming home for a spell to make a picture for Korda. The subject was the true life story of Richard Hillary, a Battle of Britain pilot who was hideously burned when his plane caught fire and crashed. Hillary's fight for recovery over a long painful succession of operations and an equally painful attempt to come to terms with his terrible scars, were recorded in a diary which became a bestselling biography, *The Last Enemy*. While the author was at the height of his fame and against all medical advice, he went back to the RAF and was killed on a routine training flight. It was the stuff of which legends are made.

Rich was fascinated by the inner man, a personality coming to terms with a new body which had none of the grace and beauty of its former self. But this was a theme which scared the film makers. We were still at a time when war stories were mostly about clean limbed heroes who fought and died without allowing too much introspection to interfere with the action.

So, instead of *The Last Enemy*, Rich made *The Desert Rats*, a war story in the traditional mould, for Twentieth Century-Fox. Later, he convinced himself that, in fact, Korda never intended *The Last Enemy* to go beyond a script outline. It was simply a ruse to force Darryl Zanuck to offer more to keep Richard Burton on his side of the Atlantic. When I showed surprise at this revelation, Rich persisted. 'Korda never made *The Last Enemy*, did he? How do you explain that? If he had really wanted to do the film, there were plenty of other actors ready to play Hillary.'

In the film industry, the cynical view was usually right.

*The Desert Rats* was a highly profitable enterprise for Rich – it brought him in over ninety thousand dollars for just seven weeks' work. There were other compensations, not least the opportunity of playing opposite James Mason who was repeating his now famous impersonation of Rommel, a role he had performed to great acclaim in *The Desert Fox*, released two years earlier. But though Mason gave the film a stature it might not otherwise have obtained it was Rich who indisputedly was the star. His soldier hero may not have had the depth of character of a Richard Hillary but there was no denying his appeal to audiences hungry for adventure.

There was a third name above the title – that of Robert Newton. His career had dived since he had appeared with Rich in *Waterfront* and it was as much for old times' sake as anything that he was still given star treatment. The problem was drink.

'I've told him,' said Rich. 'We've all told him. If he doesn't lay off, it'll kill him.'

Twenty years on, many were to say precisely the same to Richard Burton.

Rich was less than halfway through shooting *The Desert Rats* when he clinched a deal on his third Fox film. *The Robe* was a biblical blockbuster, quite the most important Burton film thus far. But more was at stake than Rich's acting reputation.

Like every other Hollywood studio, Fox was suffering the pain of competition from the small screen. Between 1946 and 1951, five thousand cinemas closed in the US while ticket sales dropped by almost a half. It was the same story in Britain. Unkind critics joked that the trans-Atlantic film industry was kept going only by the sale of popcorn in one country and ice cream in the other. New ideas were needed to put life into the cinema. But instead of thinking about new creative ideas – putting the emphasis on quality – the narrow minds of the money men concentrated on technological wizardry to save their investments. First it was 3D, the process by which audiences could feel they were part of the action. But to experience the three-dimensional effect you had to wear coloured glasses, an encumberance which punters and management came to dislike once the novelty had worn off.

The next gimmick to astonish the public was Cinemascope. There was never any logical reason for the cinema screen to be square, argued the innovators. So why not widen the field of vision, allow the eye to wander over the panorama in a way that was quite impossible with television. The idea took hold but there was still much boardroom agonising before a script and a star were selected to launch the counter attack on home viewing. With an eye to the respectable middle-of-the-road audience – the former bedrock of the cinema – the choice fell on a simplistic religious fable which had already made millions for the book stores. *The Robe*, by Lloyd C. Douglas, was the story of Mercellus, a Roman tribune who carried out the execution of Jesus but who himself was martyred when he converted to Christianity.

To play Marcellus, an actor was needed who had a strong romantic image but who would not appear out of place in a religious epic. Vibrant young heroes who were following in the wake of Errol Flynn and John Wayne were not encouraged to apply. Richard Burton, on the other hand, might have been tailor-made for the part. That he had romantic appeal was undeniable. He also had what one critic described as a 'rough sensuality' which made him believable as a Roman soldier caught up in a personal struggle between duty and conscience. But it was his acting experience which counted more in his favour. From the bewildered young lover in *The Lady's not for Burning* to the troubled Hal to brave Desert Rat, his work combined star quality with seriousness of purpose. It was not a feature of his career that was to last much longer but for now it was his strongest card and he played it for all it was worth, which by today's values was close to one million dollars.

His director from *My Cousin Rachel*, Henry Koster, who was also to direct *The Robe*, spoke up strongly in Rich's favour. Nonetheless the offer took a long time in coming. Tyrone Power and Laurence Olivier were among several possible contenders who were sounded out and declined. Darryl Zanuck could be forgiven for wondering if a relative newcomer to films, with only two Hollywood roles behind him, was capable of leading the recovery of the entire industry. There was a lot of money at stake. It was not only the five million dollar production budget at risk but also the many additional millions needed to convert cinemas to Cinemascope. If the wide screen went the way of 3D, there might be nothing left of Hollywood except deserted back lots.

When, at last, Rich signed to play Marcellus, he was described by the formidable Louella Parsons as the 'hottest thing in Hollywood'. The other gossip columnists followed with ever more extravagant praise for the Welsh wonderboy.

Rich had another group of admirers – in their way more powerful than any press lobby. These were the self-appointed moralists for whom a religious film of such magnificent dimensions was the equivalent of a second coming. Rich did not welcome their attention. For one thing, he despised their cloying hypocrisy. He was, after all, acting in a film about Christ which was restrained by daft censorship laws from portraying the Saviour as a real person. Any attempt to introduce a note of realism into the proceedings was viewed with suspicion.

'I was told,' said Rich, '"When in doubt, look towards heaven. Be pious." There were times when I wanted to throw up.'

But if he had to do what he was told on set, he insisted on playing his own game away from the studio. He drank copiously, smoked heavily and fell in love with his leading lady. Sybil was tolerant of two vices and kept silent about the third. I fancy that by now she had settled on the philosophy of marriage that was to sustain her for the next ten years. This was to accept that Rich might wander but that sooner or later he would come home. Other women were an inconvenience to the smooth running of the Burton marriage but they were not a threat, least of all Jean Simmons, Rich's co-star in *The Robe*, who was only recently married to Stewart Granger.

Understanding as much about the film business as her husband, Sybil almost certainly took the view put to me years later by a very famous actress.

'You can't act falling in love without really falling in love – if just a little. There's no harm in it.'

Ironically though this was said by the only woman who did threaten Sybil – and who finally defeated her – Elizabeth Taylor.

If I knew my brother, he treated his indiscretions as a game. Like Sybil, he did not think of them as a hazard to marriage, except in so far as he had to keep silent about his many escapades. He told me, as he told many friends, that his involvement with a certain actress led him to a nasty encounter with the husband.

'He invited me over for a drink. When we were alone he told me he had something important to say. Then he went behind a desk, opened a drawer and took out a gun. He put it down in front of him, all the

79

time talking about me and his wife, accusing me of forcing her into an affair. He wanted me to swear on the Bible that I would never see her again!'

'And did you?'

'Of course. What do you think I am?'

'And did you keep your word?'

'Ah well . . . you know what they say about a promise made under duress, don't you? It's not really a promise at all. Still, I was more careful, I didn't want my head blown off.'

True or false? Movie buffs will know that his story bears a close resemblance to a scene in *The VIPs*, when Rich, playing a super-rich businessman, accuses Louis Jourdan of stealing his wife. All I can say is that Rich told me the story many years before the film was made. Perhaps he also passed it on to Terence Rattigan who built it in to his script.

Rich was quickly bored by *The Robe*. 'It is,' he wrote, 'like all epics; indifferent.'

That his frustration did not often spill over into ill temper ('I've had only four screaming fits in this picture') was entirely to the credit of Victor Mature, a veteran of Hollywood potboilers who refused to take himself or anyone else on the set too seriously.

Some of Rich's favourite anecdotes featured Victor Mature. Legend had it that this muscle-bound man, described by studio publicity as 'a beautiful hunk', would never take a risk which might lead to physical injury, however minor. Rich asked him if the story was true.

'You'd better believe it,' said Mature. 'I think twice before walking up a wet step.'

When he starred in *Samson and Delilah*, he was asked to wrestle with a lion.

'No way,' he told the director.

'But Victor, this is a very old lion.'

'No way.'

'But Victor this is tame; it's so gentle it wouldn't harm a baby.'

'No way.'

'But Victor, this lion has no teeth.'

'So what do you want, for me to be gummed to death?'

Another story from *Samson and Delilah*. When, in the famous dinner scene, they brought on the head of John the Baptist, Victor Mature ruined the take by shouting out, 'Dig that crazy dessert.'

Rich was intrigued by the sheer professionalism of Mature. The temptation was to underrate this self depreciating performer.

'But when it came to cinematic technique,' said Rich, 'he knew the business from A to Z. I learned a lot from him.'

When filming started on *The Robe*, no one quite knew what to expect. They simply hoped for the best and worried incessantly about not getting it. After the first rushes were viewed by the production chiefs, there were murmurs that Rich was too wooden (a criticism that was to dog his film career) and that there was not enough action. Rich was understandably nervous. He knew that his future was riding on the audience reaction to this film. Seeking reassurance he took advantage of a party invitation to approach Spyros Skouras, Greek-American president of Twentieth Century-Fox and the chief instigator of Cinemascope.

'What will you do,' asked Rich, 'if *The Robe* is not a success?'

Skouras was thoughtful. After a pause he growled, 'We start by hanging you by your thumbs.'

But as the production advanced with all the actors doing their best with a limp script, studio opinion shifted towards Rich in a big way. The word was out that Richard Burton was turning in a magnificent performance which would make Fox a killing at the box office. Without waiting for solid evidence of achievement, Darryl Zanuck decided he wanted Rich on a studio property – before anyone else tried to cash in. He offered Rich a ten-year contract worth something over one million dollars. This was in 1953, remember, when you could buy a fine out-of-town house in its own grounds for less than twenty thousand dollars and a luxury Cadillac for eight hundred dollars. With Rich's approval Aaron Frosch tried for better terms, and got them.

'It's fantastic,' he wrote home. 'They are offering as much as fifty thousand sterling per picture and are absolutely convinced when I turn them down that I'm a clever boy after more money.'

But Rich was serious. He had every intention of rejecting the offer. Even Aaron Frosch could not believe it. So confident was he of settling a deal, he encouraged the Fox lawyers to draw up a contract. When they realised a signature from Burton was not theirs for the asking, the recalcitrant actor was summoned before Zanuck to explain himself.

Zanuck was used to getting his own way. A favourite Hollywood story had him shouting at an assistant who was careless enough to interrupt him, 'Don't say yes until I've finished talking.'

But Rich was not to be bullied. He wanted to make films but at the same time he was determined to shape his own career. For a man of just twenty-seven it was asking too much to sign over the next decade to one studio, however prestigious. As Rich was leaving the meeting, Zanuck warned him, 'You know I could stop you working in Hollywood. But for me, you might never make another picture.'

'I believe you,' said Rich. 'But I can go back to the theatre. I have an offer from London. I might very well take it. You can't stop that, can you?'

What Rich did not point out was the value of the offer – a mere fifty pounds a week. Still, it came from the Old Vic, a world centre of artistic excellence, and from Michael Benthall, one of the best directors of his day, who had worked with Richard at Stratford.

Benthall rang the Burton home from New York where he was visiting Katherine Hepburn. She was sitting by his side when he made the call.

'I think it's time you tried Hamlet,' said the director.

Rich was cautious.

'Oh, I don't know about that. I'm not sure I'm ready for it.'

Katherine Hepburn snatched the phone from her guest.

'Now look here. You are going to play Hamlet. And that's final.'

It was an order so compelling as to be almost certainly the determining factor in Rich's decision to reject Twentieth Century-Fox.

But his career was not all that concerned him. After a year in Hollywood, he was homesick, Sybil likewise. They were longing to get back to London and to Wales. When after fifty-eight days shooting, *The Robe* was completed, he could not wait to escape to New York and on to the first boat to Southampton. Sadly, it was not as easy as that. He had to wait for at least a month while the film was edited, in case any retakes were needed. Rich and Sybil decided to make the best of it by renting a beach house in Santa Monica. They felt they could both do with a rest, lounging and swimming and frying in the sun.

In the evenings they set off on the social round or entertained visitors, one of whom was Emlyn Williams.

'He was in great form,' Rich reported to a friend, 'and made me more homesick than ever. He played the part of the eternal Welsh lodger, sly and odiously polite and agreeing, and always trying to create trouble between husband and wife: "Never mind Mrs Burton bach, your husband may be late coming home and perhaps with spirits on his breath but I'll be here, Mrs Burton bach. There! There! There!"'

But they had fun together.

'We went out almost every night and escorted the master to parties at one of which I had to be left the night. To Emlyn's delight.'

As the time for departure approached so Rich became more nervous and difficult to live with.

'I'm looking forward to the Old Vic with a kind of belligerent apprehension,' he wrote. 'I wake up sweating with fear in the middle of the night and smoke and walk myself and mutter myself back into some semblance of confidence. Hamlet is the mischief, of course!'

There was another cause for apprehension. With a release date for *The Robe* still to be agreed, no one was eager to pre-empt the critics' verdict. In fact, Rich had to wait until he was back in London before he knew the fate of Hollywood's 'most ambitious picture in the fourteen years since *Gone With the Wind*'.

The verdict was to become tiresomely familiar over the years. The critics on the tabloids liked the film and liked Richard Burton. The critics on the heavyweight papers liked Richard Burton but disliked the film. It 'contains more piety than wit and more spectacle than humanity,' said *Time*, but 'it is ably served by a competent cast, headed by Richard Burton'. C. A. Lejeune, writing in *The Observer*, praised Rich's 'attempt to put some real character into the tribune', adding, 'If his attempt is not crowned with very great success, it is not the fault of the actor who does his best with the material.'

Happily for all concerned the studio bosses were more at home reading the box office returns than press reviews. The popularity of *The Robe* was undeniable. This was partly thanks to Cinemascope which on the whole was favourably received and which gave the film a curiosity value. But Richard Burton was the star they all came to see. In one hundred and thirty-five minutes running time, he was scarcely off the screen. Someone calculated that of seven hundred speeches, Rich had to deliver three hundred and thirteen.

Hardly surprisingly, most of the publicity for the film centred on Rich. It did him no harm at all when he reopened negotiations with Fox (he eventually settled for a non-exclusive contract for seven films at a base fee of one hundred thousand dollars a picture plus a share of the profits). And the almost daily press coverage boosted the appeal of the Old Vic company and filled the home of Shakespeare with audiences who might not otherwise have been attracted to the classics.

But Rich still had mixed feelings about Hollywood. When he felt low he talked about the 'mean time' he had there. But it was his own character, not that of his American hosts, which disturbed him.

'I didn't do many favours,' he told me. And then brightening up. 'Oh yes, there was one. A stuntman who was getting on a bit came to me one day to talk about a scene we were doing together. We had to fight our way up a flight of steps so that he could fall off the top of the battlements. "It's simple," he said, "but please make it look difficult." I asked him why. "Because I get a hundred bucks for every retake and I could do with the money."

'So on the first take I dropped my sword; on the second I had a sneezing fit and on the third I was the one who nearly fell over the side. After that I couldn't think what else to do except get it right. So my friend walked off with four hundred dollars. He was very grateful. It was my one good turn at Hollywood.'

It is true that in this period of his life Rich could be enormously self-centred. His reputation for selfishness was reinforced by a tendency to keep a tight hold on his pocketbook. Maybe it was insecurity, the fear that what he had gained so early in life he could just as easily lose.

But signs of the later extravagantly generous Burton were beginning to appear. On her birthday, Sybil woke up to find a red ribbon in her hand. It stretched off the bed, across the floor and out of the door. She followed it – down the stairs, across the living room, into the hall and out through the front door. There she found her present, tied with a bow of red ribbon – a red MG sports car.

This story came to me by Rich's friend and fellow actor William Squire and I cannot resist adding his postscript. Having told his wife about Sybil's present he awoke on his own birthday to find a red ribbon leading down the stairs and out the front door. At the end of it was a red MG – the Dinky toy version.

# Chapter 7

As soon as they were back from America, Rich and Sybil spent a week with the family. It could so easily have been a disaster. As the local boy made good in wicked Hollywood Rich was a prime target for gossipmongers and fortune hunters. But he was so unlike what everyone imagined a star to be. He stayed with Hilda (not in a fine hotel), he visited the pubs he had known since he was a boy (not the country club) and he enjoyed the company of old friends (instead of making a beeline for the nobs). Even if there was a certain amount of calculation in this playing the ordinary boy from the valley, it worked a treat. The bores were seen off before they had a chance to get in on the act, leaving the rest of us to enjoy the rare chance of a family reunion.

Every evening there was a gathering in the Miners Arms or the Copper House, both just a short walk from where Hilda and Tom lived. Both pubs did good business that week. Rich had to put up with a lot of ribbing but he took it all in good part. There was a worrying moment when he was approached by a young miner who had had one pint too many.

'I want you to come outside.'

Rich himself was too high to refuse. In the cold air, he asked, 'What's all this about?'

'Over here,' asked the miner pointing to the gents. Rich followed him in. They stood side by side at the strip of guttering which served for a latrine.

'Well?'

'Nothing,' said the miner. 'It's just that I wanted to tell my friends that I've had a piss with Richard Burton.'

At the end of a glorious seven-day celebration, Rich and Sybil returned to London, he to start rehearsals for *Hamlet*. Notwithstanding the challenge of Anthony Quayle, the Old Vic was still the most famous Shakespearian theatre in the world, with a long list of triumphs and honourable defeats to back its claims. Edith Evans, the first West End star to perform in the Waterloo Road, went there, she said, to learn how to play Shakespeare. That was in the mid thirties when Laurence Olivier, Ralph Richardson and John Gielgud were asserting their talents.

Rich was determined to join the elect. But there was a division of opinion as to whether Hamlet was the best way to start. For the convention of the time, Rich at twenty-seven was thought by some to be a little young to tackle the role. Olivier had been thirty and Robert Helpmann thirty-five before they had taken up the challenge. A student of Old Vic history had wickedly pointed out that Frank Benson, a doyen of the pre First World War theatre, was over seventy when, by his own estimate, he got the true measure of the part. But Gielgud had done it at twenty-six and Alec Guinness, in a modern dress production at the Old Vic, at twenty-four.

A more serious objection to the prospect of a Burton Hamlet was his well known impatience with the surly Dane. There was too much posturing to suit his restrained style of acting. And yet the great soliloquies appealed to his reflective nature. As Richard Harris, a great friend of later years, has said of my brother, 'He was always Hamlet. He became a middle aged Hamlet, ever introspective, easily disillusioned.'

In the cast were Claire Bloom, whom Rich had got to know when they were together in *The Lady's not for Burning*, Robert Hardy whose meticulously practised skill as a sword fighter was to be put to good use and other friends like Michael Hordern and William Squire who made good company on and off stage. Wendy Hiller played Emilia and Rosemary Harris, Desdemona.

The only slight tension was between Rich and Claire Bloom. Though an actress of enviable experience she was a mere twenty-two, a reserved young lady who was naturally wary of playing opposite a man whose slaphappy ways with women she had witnessed at first hand. She confessed her fears to William Squire.

'You should have seen him in New York. He's a terrible man. Will you protect me?'

William said he would be delighted. With the two of them seen together so much the rest of the cast made the obvious deduction. In his usual blunt way, Rich put the question to William.

'Is there something between you two?'

He was rewarded by a suitable shocked reaction.

'There's nothing between us. Nothing at all.'

'Well it bloody well looks as if there is,' said Rich.

In the following weeks, William fulfilled his pledge and stuck close. Until the day when he was sitting in the stalls with Claire Bloom while Rich was rehearsing on stage. After listening for a while in awed silence, Claire whispered, 'He is wonderful, isn't he?'

William leaned over to give her a kiss on the cheek.

'Goodbye Claire,' he said, and departed.

It was, he claims now, his best exit line ever.

*Hamlet* opened at the Edinburgh Festival in August 1953. The critics were kind but not wildly enthusiastic. It was said that Rich gobbled his words as if he was in a hurry to finish the play. Robert Hardy was among those who missed the feel for the great poetry while admitting that Rich brought dash and energy to the role. Part of the difficulty was the venue, a theatre created within the Assembly Hall, an imposing manorial style Church of Scotland edifice just below Edinburgh Castle. Less from choice than from the need to accommodate the perimeter columns blocking the view, the actors' space was a platform stage, with the audience on three sides. There was little in the way of scenery. Michael Benthall hung the fourth side of the hall with looped curtains but otherwise there were just a few heraldic shields dotted about. The main entrance to the stage was a broad flight of stairs which also served to carry the actors out into the audience. J. C. Trewin of the *Illustrated London News* who was seated at the end of a row, recalls how 'courtiers might brush past you, or Ophelia would dart out in her madness, or you would turn to find their Majesties of Denmark coming down behind the bier'.

There were moments too of dire peril. A critic sitting beside J. C. Trewin was all but impaled on a sword. When he came to write his review he began, 'Last night I sat transfixed . . .'

Rich found the setting and the style of production disconcerting and was unable to disguise his uneasiness. Phil Burton made the pilgrimage to Edinburgh to reinforce Michael Benthall's plea for a more measured performance. Once he had an idea fixed in his head, Rich did not take easily to directions but the old magic of Phil Burton, even though it had not been much in evidence in the last year or two, seemed as powerful as ever. By the time *Hamlet* opened at the Old Vic where Rich felt much more at home, he had tempered the pace of his delivery but without losing any of the passion or excitement of the role.

But the critics were still not entirely happy. While praising a performance which, to quote Harold Hobson, 'was as satisfying as any that memory can recall for a good many years', they pointed out the 'lack of subtlety and even variety' which stopped it short of a triumph. Rich was left with a nagging worry that he had not quite cracked the part. It was the reason he came back to it fifteen years later when he was invited to try his luck on Broadway.

When a reviewer described Rich as a 'rugger playing Hamlet', he was closer than he might have imagined. It was at this time that my brother made his last appearance on the muddy turf. In defiance of his contract which quite sensibly ruled against parachuting, big game hunting, mountain climbing and rugby football as unreasonable insurance risks, he rose to the challenge of a local game. After his muscle-building course of weight lifting, decreed by the producers of *The Robe*, he was confident he could put on a decent show. But he reckoned without his celebrity status which, to the opposing team, was like a red rag to a bull.

'I knew I was in trouble,' said Rich, 'when I was in mid scrum and I heard someone shout, "Never mind the bloody ball, where's the bloody actor?!"'

He emerged with multiple bruises to his pride. His body suffered less even if he did claim to spend the next week at the Old Vic playing Hamlet like Richard III. He was certainly in good enough shape to lead the post-match celebrations with favourite stories of great rugby characters like Annie Mort from Taibach who before a home match at Aberavon would drop goals from around forty yards with either foot to entertain the crowd. Annie, explained Rich, wore what we used to call 'sensible' shoes. Then there was Five-Cush Cannon who won the sixth replay of a cup final (the previous five encounters having ended with scores 0–0, 0–0, 0–0, 0–0, 0–0 with extra time) by throwing the ball over the bar from a scrum ten yards out in a deep fog and claiming a dropped goal. And getting it.

But the most unlikely hero ('It's all as true as I stand here,' protested Rich) was Jimmy One Arm who, despite his affliction suffered in the First World War, played for Cwmavon in the 1920s.

'He was clever, you see. He used the misplaced sympathy of innocent visiting players who didn't go at him with the same delivery as they would against a two-armed man. How were they to know it was just a ploy to lure them on to concussion or other organic damage? I tell you, going easy on Jimmy One Arm was first cousin to stepping into a grave and waiting for the shovels to start.'

By happy accident Rich's early appearances at the Old Vic coincided with the British premieres of *The Desert Rats* and *The Robe*. It was an impresario's dream. While the press lined up for interviews, the fans

1. Richard as a baby near the house where he was born. (*Graham Jenkins*)   2. Richard as a young boy. (*Graham Jenkins*)   3. Graham with one of his many prizes for singing. (*Graham Jenkins*)   4. The house, No 2. Dan-y-bont, in Pontrhydyfen where Richard was born. The porch was built later to deter souvenir hunters from stealing the commemorative plaque. (*Topham*)

5. Richard out walking with his father. (*BBC Hulton Picture Library*)

6. *From left to right* Cis, Hilda, Richard and Elfed. 1947. (*Graham Jenkins*)

7. Richard signing autographs in Pontrhydyfen. (*BBC Hulton Picture Library*)

8. *From left to right* Sybil, Ivor, Ivor's wife Gwen, Richard and Philip Burton in New York for the production of *The Lady's not for Burning*. 1951. (*J. Bess Studios*)

9. Richard and Sybil off to New York to film *The Robe*. 1952. (*BBC Hulton Picture Library*)

10. Richard in *Alexander the Great*. (*Topham*)

11. Richard and Sybil with their first daughter Kate in Pays de Galles, Switzerland. 1958. (*Rex Features*)

12. Richard as King Arthur in
*Camelot.* (*Rex Features*)

13. The photograph which
revealed to the world that Richard
and Elizabeth were having an
affair. 1962. (*Rex Features*)

14. An intimate portrait of Richard and Elizabeth taken during their first few months together. (*Marjorie Lee*)

15. Elizabeth and Richard during the filming of *Cleopatra*. (*Rex Features*)

16. Richard as Hamlet, George Rose as the First Gravedigger in the modern-dress production of *Hamlet*. 1964. (*Rex Features*)

17. Elizabeth Taylor helping offstage in *Hamlet*. (*Rex Features*)

18. *From left to right* Michael Wilding Jr., Maria, Richard, Elizabeth, Liza Todd and Gaston the chauffeur. (*Rex Features*)

19. Richard and Elizabeth with their adopted daughter Maria. 1967. (*Rex Features*)

blockaded the box office. The gallery at the Old Vic, where a perch on a wooden bench could be had for two shillings, was packed night after night with youngsters out to catch a glimpse of the real Richard Burton. Not that he had it all his own way. Playing opposite Rich was a contemporary whose build up as a potential theatrical great made him a close rival for the victor's crown. John Neville had much in common with Richard Burton. Born into a working class family he came to drama encouraged by an older friend, not quite a Phil Burton figure, but one who was sufficiently appreciative of the living arts to take John on frequent visits to Stratford. Instead of Oxford and the RAF, John Neville chose the Navy and RADA followed by an intensive apprenticeship at the Birmingham Rep. and the Briston Old Vic where he attracted respectful notices and popular acclaim. His was the more conventional route to the Shakespearian summit, as mapped out by John Gielgud with whom he was often favourably compared.

So it was that having started from much the same point, John Neville and Richard Burton ended up as contrasting actors – the one classical and melodic, the other brooding and dangerous, more in the fashion of the young Olivier. As the season progressed and John Neville came into his own with a stunning performance in *Richard II*, the fans divided, Burton versus Neville. It was not the way the elders in the stalls liked to judge their Shakespeare but they could hardly deny that teenage hero worship had its commercial compensations. Michael Benthall was among the first to see the possibilities. For the third year of his five-year plan, he pencilled in Burton and Neville to alternate as Othello and Iago. It was an audacious scheme which neither actor could resist.

'It's mad,' said Rich. 'Let's do it.'

Meanwhile, they had to get through the current season. For Rich who began and ended with *Hamlet*, there were three other major roles to confront – Coriolanus, Caliban and Sir Toby Belch. He was also cast as Philip the Bastard in *King John*. For this he had little to say but was on stage a lot, a feature of the production which delighted his teenage followers but disconcerted the rest of the cast who had to work overtime to hold the attention of the audience.

As Caliban, the 'savage and deformed slave' of *The Tempest*, the miracle was in the make-up. It took over two hours to transform Rich into a hideous beast, an endurance test which caused him great anguish because it was virtually impossible for him to lift a glass. It was worth the effort. His descent into bestiality was acclaimed as further evidence of what one critic described as his 'vigorous versatility'. But there were some doubters who, knowing Rich's dislike for dressing up, judged that he was leaning too far toward farce. Their opinion gathered strength when Rich tried out his Sir Toby Belch, a padded and painted freak with a stick-on bald pate who looked less out of Shakespeare than a refugee from Bertram Mills' Circus with a slapstick talent to match.

But all was forgiven for his Coriolanus, by far his greatest contribution to Shakespearian acting. It was a role wished on him by Phil Burton who knew that his Richard was one of the few young actors capable of portraying the divided personality that was Coriolanus, not as a savage thug, but as a tragic hero. The production owed much to Laurence Olivier's interpretation, also seen at the Old Vic, which was the talk of the theatre year in 1939. Taking his cue from Lewis Casson, his director, Olivier had revealed his patrician as a victim of arrested development. Here was a mother's boy who, damned by his insufferable snobbery, arrogance and pride, had enough in him of loyalty and even generosity to hint at unfulfilled greatness. The testing moment is the final death scene when Coriolanus is roused to a suicidal frenzy by Arfidius' gibe – 'thou boy of tears'. The long remembered climax as performed by Olivier had him shrieking his rage as he ran a flight full of stairs to a platform there to meet his assassins' spears. A pause, and then he toppled backwards to be caught and held by his ankles, like a carcass above the stage. Curtain. It was a difficult act to follow but Rich managed it. As Harold Hobson said of his Coriolanus: 'Nothing in his life becomes him like the leaving of it . . . Mr Burton has this foul mouthed Roman traitor clad in a great scarlet cloak, that is like a splash of blood on the world's face, stand with arms outstretched in front of the dark city doors of Corioli and, in the attitude of a priest celebrating some tremendous ritual, is stabbed to death by his envious enemies. He falls with a crash of an empire.'

The ambiguity of the character entranced audiences. Again, from Harold Hobson, 'Mr Burton tries to soften Coriolanus, not in his voice which has the authoritarian ring all right, but in his face, which is frequently suffused with a smile of singular sweetness altogether belying the savagery and insolence of what he was to say.'

Olivier himself was full of praise. It was, he said, the best Coriolanus he had seen, a compliment which, strictly interpreted, excluded his own performance. And rightly so.

The catalogue of backstage visitors was heavily weighted towards the great and the good. His peers he recognised but even with advanced warning from the stage door and introductions from those in the know it was impossible for Rich to keep track of the politicians, business tycoons, ambassadors and other dignitaries who came to shake his hand and wish him luck.

One visitor who did not require an announcement was Winston Churchill who came to see *Hamlet*. Rich was bowled over. He could be naively susceptible to flattery from those he regarded as giants in their craft. And the Prime Minister was undoubtedly of that category. After the event Rich wove a thick web of fantasy round the evening. Stories of what Churchill said or did were a regular part of his bar room entertainment and not to be taken too seriously. There is little doubt that Churchill congratulated Rich on showing him a 'very fine, virile prince' or that they managed a rapport which, unexpectedly for Rich, was to serve him well in his subsequent career. But the often repeated anecdote of Churchill going into competition with Rich by audibly mumbling Hamlet's lines from the front stalls, must be counted as pure fancy. As told by Rich after a few drinks it sounded convincing enough. But judged in cold print, was it even remotely feasible?

Humphrey Bogart and his wife Lauren Bacall came to see *Hamlet*. Afterwards they took Rich and Sybil back to their Dorchester suite for dinner. It was the first time Rich had been into the hotel. Within years it was to become a second home to him. William Squire also went along that evening. As a young man he attracted the visitors' admiration for his ability to age so convincingly on stage.

'And without make-up,' exclaimed Bogart. 'Would you believe it?'

Embarrassed by so much attention from the great man, and scrabbling for nice things to say in return, William let slip that he thought Bogart's pyjamas, flung over a chair, were splendid, quite the most luxurious he had ever seen.

'Take them,' said Bogart. 'They're yours.'

Which is how William Squire came into possession of blue silk night attire monogrammed HB. It was an act of spontaneous generosity which made its impact on Rich as well as on the recipient of the gift. It surprised, it impressed, it left a lasting memory; it was the way for a star to behave.

'You like it? Take it. It's yours,' was to symbolise Burton's hospitality to family, friends and not a few passing acquaintances.

# Chapter 8

*I*n between rehearsals and performances at the Old Vic, the likeliest place to find Rich was Broadcasting House where his distinctive voice was much in demand. A drama producer once told me, 'Richard can bring out a depth of meaning that even a writer doesn't suspect.' Another said, 'He speaks the English language better than almost anybody else.'

The admiration was mutual. Rich loved radio. It gave him enormous opportunity to create imagery outside the close confines of stage or film. The disembodied voice could take its listeners anywhere, do anything. Then again, radio had its practical virtues. It slotted in conveniently to the life of a stage actor and it did not overstate its claims on time or effort. Radio could be hard work but the labour came in short, intensive bursts and when one job was finished, there was always something new to enliven the spirit.

Actors whom Rich admired but might never otherwise have encountered – like Donald Wolfit – felt the same way. Radio was fun and even if it did not pay very much it was a great boost to education and experience. I was often surprised at the names Rich associated with great acting. One such was Ernest Thesiger, a veteran of stage and screen, whom I first saw as the elderly Emperor Tiberius in *The Robe*. A shrunken skeletal figure, he wore a blond wig which made everyone laugh every time he walked on the set. But he overcame the indignity to turn in a convincing performance. To this day, it is memorable against a parade of excellent cameos. But Ernest Thesiger did not steal the picture as he did twenty years earlier as the effeminate mad scientist Dr Praetorious in *The Bride of Frankenstein*. From then on he was unrivalled as the elderly eccentric, ever threatening to surprise or shock. It was a role he relished in real life as much as in fiction. Rich told me that when Thesiger was invited back to his school, Marlborough College, as a guest of honour he enlivened a dinner with the senior master by casting a lascivious eye on some of the senior boys. After taking a more than usual pleasure in a close conversation with a well built sixth former, he turned to his host to express his admiration: 'I'd give *anything* to be that boy's mother.'

On radio, his spindly voice was much in demand to represent frailty – usually with a strong measure of deviousness.

'He was always around somewhere,' said Rich. 'Everybody made jokes about how tiny and shrivelled he was. I was in a studio once when an actor was playing about with an umbrella, trying to furl it properly. As he opened it someone shouted, "Don't do that, Ernest Thesiger might pop out."'

The danger of radio for Richard Burton was the tendency of some producers to let him get away with second best. The younger ones, particularly, could be slightly in awe of the Shakespearian wonder boy and disinclined to put him right when he really needed it. But Rich knew when he was being lazy and, despite his reputation for stubborness, was ready to accept direction. Frank Hauser, who had introduced him to radio, knew this only too well. When Rich sat down to record a selection of the work of the First World War poet Edward Thomas, it was immediately clear to Frank Hauser that he had not done his homework. The verses, of elaborate construction, were read without understanding or true feeling. To make matters worse, sitting next to Frank Hauser, listening with embarrassment, was the poet's widow. Ten minutes in, Frank stopped the recording, took Rich aside and give him a piece of his mind. My chastened brother went away to study the script, returning several hours later to give a near perfect performance.

'He always respected those who stood up to him,' said Frank Hauser. To which I might have added, 'Well, nearly always.'

The radio production which brought out the best in Richard Burton, and a host of other Welsh actors, was *Under Milk Wood*. The starting point for Rich's involvement was the death of Dylan Thomas at the ludicrously early age of thirty-nine. It happened in New York where Dylan had stopped off on the way to Hollywood where he was to complete work on a film script. Rich was saddened but not surprised by the news. He loved Dylan for what he was, a writer of genius and a Welsh writer at that. Though he did not speak the language, Dylan possessed a full measure of that peculiar Welsh literary talent, described by James Agate as 'putting the truth of its own imagination higher than other, more easily recognisable forms of truth'. The power of words, their imagery, counted for all, which led to curious syntax and to unforgettable art.

But however much Rich admired Dylan as a writer, as a private person he found him all but overwhelming. His personality was on automatic pilot to self destruction. He lived to excess in a way that Rich might have found curiously familiar if he had been able to look into the future. But at that period of his life, while he lived boldly and was just discovering the joys of extravagance, he was still young enough and ambitious enough to fear going over the top. Dylan had long since made the jump and was off and away into his own world.

Rich was one of the last people here to see Dylan alive. He stayed with Rich and Sybil in Hampstead a few days before leaving for America.

'He was on the cadge,' he told me. 'But then, he was always on the cadge.'

They had drunk heavily and invented wild schemes for combining their talents.

When I talked to Rich about the tragedy he rejected my synonym for wasted opportunities.

'He sought his own death and found it. I don't call that a tragedy.'

The script for *Under Milk Wood* – 'a play for voices' – was delivered to the BBC a few days before Dylan Thomas left for America. Elements of the play were known to Rich who had seen earlier versions and had been sufficiently impressed to incorporate extracts into his impromptu Dylan Thomas recital which he would give at the drop of a hat. The complete *Under Milk Wood* was delivered to the Old Vic by the producer Douglas Clevedon who was charged with the awesome responsibility of making radio history. Rich agreed immediately to head the cast. He took over First Voice (originally intended for the author), allowing the Second Voice (originally intended for Rich) to go to Richard Bebb.

'In fact,' said Rich, 'Dylan wrote the whole damn thing for himself.'

Just about everybody who was anybody in Welsh acting was roped in to play the other sixty-seven parts. Hugh Griffith appeared as Captain Cat, Meredith Edwards as Second Drowned, Mr Waldo, Utah Watkins and Butcher Benyon, and Rachel Roberts as Mae Rose Cottage, Mrs Dai Bread Two and sundry other parts. For anyone who does not know *Under Milk Wood*, the very names of the characters must give a fair idea of the richness of the dialogue. Sybil was in there, as Miss Myfanwy Price among others and so was Phil Burton who was the Preacher and Fourth Drowned. It was all great fun and it was a resounding success. *Under Milk Wood* was repeated endlessly (quite unlike any other radio play) and praised extravagantly. It was said by Watford Davies in his retrospective study of Dylan Thomas, to be 'quite simply, the best radio play ever written'. Interestingly, he stopped short of calling it a work of literature. Apparently such a grandiose term was inappropriate for a play which had no plot and reduced 'a view of life to immediately entertaining details'. Ah, well, the Dylan Thomas devotees could live with that. Having heard the broadcast they rushed out to buy the book and next to see the stage production and eventually the film starring Richard Burton, which opened the 1971 Venice Film Festival.

*Under Milk Wood* was thought by Rich to be one of the best things he did on radio though, that year, he was equally proud of his voice-over for a documentary feature. *Thursday's Children* was a government information film on the teaching of deaf children to speak. It won an Oscar and Rich could not have been better pleased if he had taken off the best actor award.

For sheer fun Rich appeared in 'The Frankie Howerd Show'. As nearly always in broad comedy he was stilted and uncomfortable, winning laughs simply as a good sport, willing to play the idiot. But he came away with a huge admiration for Frankie Howerd, a funny man who did not need a book of jokes to hold an audience. He did it all on nods, winks and innuendo.

'If I had his talent,' said Rich, 'I'd drop Shakespeare tomorrow.'

I have never asked Frankie Howerd but I rather suspect he would have reversed the compliment.

1953 ended with *Hamlet*'s traditional excursion to Elsinore where, said Shakespeare, the real history book prince plotted to kill the wretch who murdered his father. Rich was not in the best of health. The workload in London had been a strain, he was drinking too much and was nervous about his imminent return to Hollywood. On the boat he was at the centre of a drunken scene when he accused Michael Hordern of consorting with the critics. 'Traitor,' he shouted across the bar. 'The man's a traitor.'

The idea that Michael Hordern could not have a drink with journalist friends without betraying the cause was patently ludicrous and afterwards Rich apologised profusely. But his display of bad behaviour set the nerve endings tingling. How would he perform in a role in which he knew success had so far eluded him? In the event he performed wonderfully. Before the crowned heads of Denmark, Sweden and Norway he discovered another side to Hamlet's character.

*The Times* critic said it all. At Edinburgh and the Old Vic, he wrote, 'Richard Burton appeared to have selected from Hamlet all the most unsympathetic traits he could find. His playing had power, but it was curiously without charm. He has since come by a charm which sits extremely well on youthful melancholy; and in gaining charm, the performance has lost none of its original power.' Rich came back to London feeling more confident. He was determined that one day he would have another crack at the elusive Royal.

From the Old Vic, Rich went off on his one-year tour of duty on behalf of Twentieth Century-Fox. In every way except financial the experience was infinitely depressing but it had a lasting influence on him and, in my view, marked a turning point in his career.

The first of three successive films, *Prince of Players*, was thrown together round the life of Edwin Booth, the nineteenth-century American actor whom Rich had first heard of in conversation with Humphrey Bogart. The studio must have thought of it as a great opportunity to exploit Richard Burton's upmarket appeal as a leading Shakespearian actor while holding to a familiar story line of the single-minded fighter snatching victory from the jaws of defeat. (For Edwin to make a comeback after his brother had shot the president was, after all, quite an achievement. 'Almost,' said Rich, 'as remarkable as surviving a bad review in *The New York Times*.') But trying to have it both ways was a recipe for disaster. The Shakespearian extracts were pitched in like songs in a musical (Shakespeare's Greatest Hits) but without the same appeal. It was not entirely the director's fault. Rich as Edwin Booth on stage put on his best Stratford and Old Vic manner – restrained, thoughtful, pent up. The style simply did not come across on the big screen which needed an actor of the old school, with booming voice and violent histrionics, to make an impact. Rich knew he had got it wrong. On one of his brief visits to London when we met for a drink he ended up slamming his fist on the table in sheer frustration.

'I'd give anything to do the whole bloody thing again!' he shouted.

A few weeks later when I saw *Prince of Players* in a near deserted Aberavon cinema, I realised what he meant. The film was just dull. The critics tried hard to be kind though C. A. Lejeune delivered a hefty backhander when she said of Rich that he portrayed Edwin Booth 'as a plausible understudy for the young Laurence Olivier'. The general view was that more Booth and less bard would have done the film a lot of good.

The mood of dark depression soon passed. When Rich and Sybil came home for Christmas 1954, all the talk was of a new blockbuster movie which was to repeat the success of *The Robe*. Rich had been handed the title role in *Alexander the Great*. The budget was enormous, the attention to detail meticulously strict and the dedication to a high standard of acting and direction made evident by the choice of Robert Rossen to oversee the project. The location was to be the rolling sierras outside Madrid where the Spanish army was ready to fight Alexander's wars with the Persians as part of their training to defend the fatherland.

'Believe me, Graham,' said my brother, 'we're on to a winner. Hollywood history is crap but I've got a feeling this once could be different.'

He was wrong.

'Why?' I asked when he came back to admit another disaster. 'What happened?'

Unless you take the view that all epics are doomed by the weight of their own pretensions (and I would have thought David Lean has proved this not to be so), the likeliest explanation for the failure of *Alexander the Great* was the inability of the screenwriter, producer and director to hold the story together. Robert Rossen, who did all three jobs, was a gifted director of social dramas with a well deserved Oscar to his credit (*All the King's Men*). But a historical saga was not his element. He did his best to prove otherwise but though he professed great interest his attention wandered and he soon lost grasp of events. A large part of the reason was back in Hollywood where Rossen had lately come through a gruelling interrogation by the infamous House Committee on Un-American Activities. A self-confessed former Communist who had long since severed his links with the Party, Rossen had backtracked on his earlier refusal to name names. Consequently, he was ostracised by former friends on both sides of the political divide.

'He was a troubled man,' said Rich. 'He would say one thing and mean another. After the first few weeks he seemed to lose heart in the film.'

Rich took the easy way out. He did what he was told when he was told but otherwise played the game for laughs. Stanley Baker, one of his closest friends, kept the humour bubbling and Claire Bloom was there to provide excitement of a different sort. When he was not needed on set, Rich set off on the tourist trail, followed by a bevy of autograph hunters. Sometimes Sybil went with him; sometimes not.

*Alexander the Great* became Alexander the Bore. Three hours of closely studied military history was too much for audiences, let alone the critics. The best notices went to the Spanish cavalry and lancers who, with Cinemascope to help them, managed to hold attention while they engaged in pitched battle.

By now Rich had not too much faith in the artistic judgement of his Hollywood masters. But by his own estimation there was little he could do about it. The money was good – too good to pass up on a matter of principle when no immediate alternative was to hand. He might have tried to change studios but it was foolish to imagine that as an easy option. *Alexander the Great* was, after all, the responsibility of United Artists who had Rich on loan from Fox. One seemed to be as bad as another.

He could find refuge in the theatre. In fact, he would find a refuge there; he was booked to reappear at the Old Vic for the 1955–56 season. But he did not fancy a lifetime stint at perhaps one hundred pounds a week. The Burton problem, as described by Richard Harris after Rich's death, was already in evidence. 'Half of him wanted to be the best actor in the world. The other half didn't care enough.'

His third film of the year was the most desperate of the trio. *The Rains of Ranchipur* was a remake of the 1939 Tyrone Power vehicle, *The Rains Came*. The excuse for its revival was the impact of nature taking its revenge in the form of a massive tidal wave, massive flood and general mayhem blown up to Cinemascope proportions. It was difficult to understand why actors were needed at all except as endorsement for the technical wizardry. Incredibly, Rich was cast as an Indian doctor. Not even the make-up was convincing. They imported an elocution expert to help him with his accent but after a couple of lessons they agreed his case was hopeless. Dr Safti, as portrayed by Rich, must be the only Indian doctor on screen to sound as if he came from Cardiff.

Co-starring was Lana Turner, the original Sweater Girl pin-up of the war years, who thrived on romantic melodrama. Miss Turner overplayed her role while Mr Burton underplayed his, a combination which led to a less than satisfactory relationship on and off the screen.

When Rich came home he needed the rest. His moods were unpredictable, veering from undisguised glee at his financial success to weary contempt for the film industry for its apparent inability to deliver worthwhile parts.

'They can do it for Alec Guinness and James Mason,' he complained. 'Why not me?'

There was an easy answer often given as a compliment. Richard Burton was one of the small group of actors who possessed all the qualities of the screen hero. The strength of Guinness and Mason was in their talent for character acting. This gave them a wider choice of

98

roles including, in the case of James Mason, some wonderfully villainous parts, but it reduced their star rating and earning power below that of Richard Burton.

I do not believe for a moment that Rich needed me or anyone else to spell this out to him. He had a shrewd idea of the way Hollywood was moulding his career and though he had a desire to be trusted as a more versatile actor the will to fight for a change in the rules was fast receding.

For one thing he was beginning to enjoy the privileges of wealth. Who could blame him? It was quite something for a miner's son to return to the valley in a smart new Jaguar and with a roll of banknotes thick enough to buy out every beer cellar in the country. If he was looking for signs of approval from those who gave him his start, the show of wealth, solid proof of success, was more important than flattering reviews in the smart papers.

But to the extent that he also needed the approval of his peers, he calculated that it was possible to work a compromise which would give him the best of both worlds. To limit himself to one film a year in Hollywood would bring him in at least fifty thousand pounds, enough to meet all the demands on his pocketbook. Therefore, he could afford to live in Hampstead and play at Stratford or the Old Vic as the fancy took him.

It was a pipedream, as he was soon to discover, but while he played his second season at the Old Vic, the prospect looked real enough. He was to open in *Henry V*, a role he had not quite made his own four years earlier at Stratford. To be offered another crack at the elusive monarch was an exciting prospect.

When rehearsals started in late November, three of the six productions planned for the season had already been seen by the critics. Their comments did not inspire excitement at the box office. John Neville was praised for his Mark Antony but otherwise *Julius Caesar* was greeted with polite reserve. *The Merry Wives of Windsor* provided a jolly evening but was thought by many to deserve more respect than a knockabout farce. It was withdrawn prematurely just before Christmas, As for *The Winter's Tale*, no one could find a good word for it. The play was said to be the nearest to a complete failure the Old Vic had known in five years.

Stratford too was going through a dull patch. 'It is all so deadeningly anonymous,' wrote Kenneth Tynan. 'What Stratford needs again is an actor or director to set the tune for it, to bang a tuning fork against the text as Richard Burton did four years ago.'

Well, this time it was the Old Vic which revived on a strong dose of the Burton magic. Opening on 13 December, *Henry V* ran to full houses for seventy-one performances. The critics were ecstatic. 'It was,' said Philip Hope Wallace, 'the turning of the Old Vic's long run of ill luck.'

On one level it was old-fashioned performance with Rich giving full measure to the patriotic speeches. But he also managed to convey the brutal ruthlessness of the ambitious monarch, refusing to dilute the character with false charm.

'He gives a cunning warrior, stocky and astute, unafraid of harshness or of curling the royal lip,' declared Kenneth Tynan. 'The gallery gets no smiles from him, and the soldiery none but the scantiest commiseration.'

With Richard Burton's return to the Old Vic, the rivalry with John Neville was immediately reasserted. Those who favoured John Neville as the consistent star of the Old Vic (he was there for the full five-year cycle of history plays) felt that the title role in *Henry V* was rightfully his. Richard Burton was the usurper. But in making do with secondary billing as Chorus, John Neville turned in an extraordinary virtuoso performance which delighted his fans. Sadly, it also rocked the centre of the play. As Kenneth Tynan pointed out, 'The compere who steals the show is by definition a bad compere.'

Rich took it all as a great joke believing, with every justification, that if anyone was trying to upstage, it was the bobby soxers in the gallery who roared their approval whenever their favourite actor made a move.

The Burton–Neville duel of talents reached its climax with the Michael Benthall production of *Othello* in which the two actors alternated the leading roles. The press needed little encouragement to write up this contest in terms more appropriate to a wrestling match. 'The Fans make it Fight Night at the Vic' and 'Bobby-sox War over the Moor' were typical headlines. Rich was described as 'the Pontrhydyfen Profile'; Neville as 'the Barnet Barrymore'. Publicity of this order naturally provoked the teenagers towards greater excesses. There were evenings in the Old Vic when the roars of encouragement and approval from the gallery drowned out what was happening on stage. You needed a copy of the text to follow what was going on.

The strain on all the actors, but on Rich and John Neville in particular, was tremendous. To play Othello one night and Iago (the largest part in all of Shakespeare) the next was bad enough, but to perform in circumstances more appropriate to a rock concert could bring on a state of nervous exhaustion. On more than one occasion I discovered Rich slumped in a chair in his dressing room, drained of all energy, unable to move. I would help him out of his costume, clean off the greasepaint, load him into the car and drive him to Hampstead, all without a single word spoken.

Of all the many times I saw Rich as Othello and Iago, I cannot recall a single disaster of confused speeches or scrambled lines. The odd misplaced word, maybe, but never anything serious. However, there was one night when he suffered an identity crisis. We arrived late at the theatre. As Rich crashed in through the stage door he shouted to one of the other actors to ask what part he was playing. Either he misheard or the information was wrong because ten minutes before curtain up two Othellos appeared in the wings. There followed a frantic cleansing operation as various ladies with little sponges tried to get the black off Rich's face. They were not entirely successful. This Iago was not exactly coloured but he did look as if he had spent too long in the sun.

Possibly irritated by the hooray style of theatre promotion, the critics were not greatly impressed by the production. Mostly, they took the line that the exchange of roles was nothing but a publicity stunt to disguise the fact that neither actor was ready to play Othello. There was some justice in this. At thirty, Rich and John Neville were the youngest actors in living memory to attempt a role demanding, in the words of Kenneth Tynan, 'that unfeignable quality which some call weight and others majesty, and which comes only with age'.

But Rich as Iago won many plaudits. The calculated holding back of energy and emotion in a way that suggested a scheming mind in overdrive, building up to a climatic eruption, served him well as the treacherous lieutenant to Othello, as it had when he played Hal at Stratford. Whatever their differences both characters were enticed by power, wanting it for its own sake.

Friendly or no, the critics made little difference to the box office appeal of *Othello*. Every performance was a sell-out. The play was withdrawn on 12 May 1956 after Rich had played Othello twenty-four times. Had he stayed with the company the play could have continued its run for a year at least.

In fact, Rich departed the Old Vic earlier than originally planned. The reason was partly exhaustion with the sheer drudgery of theatre work. (Rich was not one of those who enjoyed the security of the routine; once he had mastered a role he was eager to get on to the next challenge.) But there was also an unhappy interlude when, for the first time, Rich came under the direction of Tyrone Guthrie. It was for a production of *Troilus and Cressida* which Guthrie, ever the seeker after novelty, set in the world of Ruritanian costumes and manners. Guthrie had a great admiration for Rich, describing him as 'one of the six gentlemen who mean anything in the box office and also can even begin to make a showing in the great parts'. But he was not at all sensitive to the delicate matter of actor's status. For Guthrie there was no such thing as a star, only bigger or smaller roles.

From the word go Rich was out of sorts with his part and with his director. As Thersites, 'a rascal; a scurvy railing knave; a very filthy rogue', Rich was asked to dress up like a bookie's runner which made him look more foolish than devilish. After a day or two of rehearsal, he backed off pleading doctor's orders.

He took his final bow at the Old Vic as Henry V, a suitable gesture of farewell since it was for this part that Rich won the prestigious *Evening Standard* award for best actor. It was, said the judges, an easy choice, quite unlike the play of the year which turned on a long drawn-out debate over the relative merits of *Waiting for Godot* and a piece by Jean Giraudoux called *Tiger at the Gate*. The fact that Samuel Beckett lost out to the now-forgotten Giraudoux should tell us something about the value of show business awards.


Holding to his conviction that it would not be long before he returned to the London stage, Rich used the break before his next film commitment to sort out his finances to his own and his family's best advantage. Some time earlier, at the instigation of Aaron Frosch, he had made himself into a company known as Atlantic Productions. Among the shareholders were all the senior members of the family who, twice a year, were given a gift – £750 in August and £250 just before Christmas. These were known as our 'fotos', the Welsh slang for cheque, and they arrived punctually right up to the year of Rich's death. (Incidentally, the last foto I received was accompanied by a note from Valerie Douglas saying that because the bank transaction had actually taken place a day or two after Rich had died, the value of the cheque would be deducted from any gain I might make under Rich's will.)

There were other outgoings which he claimed against tax but at a time when tax rates were steeply progressive Rich was keen to find ways of holding on to a higher proportion of his earnings.

'As it is,' he said, 'it's not worth bothering after the first fifteen thousand. Most of it goes straight to the Inland Revenue.'

The obvious solution, the one adopted by so many other high earners in the entertainment industry, was to become a tax exile.

'Look at it this way,' he said. 'As a resident abroad I can work three months a year in this country without getting into trouble with the

Inland Revenue. That gives me plenty of time for stage acting. The rest of the time I would probably want to be abroad, anyway, in Hollywood or on film location. So why don't I make the best of it?'

It was then only a question of finding a place to live where the authorities were amenable and the surroundings tolerable. The offshore islands were immediately discounted. 'I would feel cut off,' said Rich.

This left Switzerland as the likeliest prospect. It was close, convenient and offered a secure and unfussy style of living which appealed to Rich and Sybil.

They made their first sortie in early 1957 when they rented a small villa at Celigny. Within weeks they had bought Pays de Galles with its view of Mont Blanc. Their neighbours included the Aga Khan, Charles Chaplin, Peter Ustinov and Jean Anouilh. Rich opened his first Swiss bank account with the proceeds from *The Rains of Ranchipur* and *Alexander the Great* – it added up to close on one hundred thousand pounds.

With the move to Switzerland, Rich set up a family trust fund from which all of us benefited at one time or another. That we were able to buy our own homes when none of us were particularly well-off, was thanks entirely to our brother's generosity.

Just before he left to film in Jamaica he offered me use of his Jaguar.

'You've need of a car,' he said. 'Why not take this one?'

'No,' I said, 'it's a bit too grand for me, especially with petrol at three shillings a gallon. But I tell you what. Since you're offering, I wouldn't mind driving the MG.'

He laughed. 'I don't care what you do. But you'd better ask Sybil; it's her car.'

I drove it for a full year and cared for it like a baby. I have never had a better car since.

Whenever any one of us hit a bad patch, Rich was the first to help out. It was always done in a jokey way, almost as if he sought to deflect a show of gratitude.

A long letter to brother Tom, at a time when life was showing its rough side, had buried within it this short paragraph:

'Enclosed is a little cheque. I hope you will accept it. I know how a few weeks' unemployment cripples your finances, and I don't want you to scrape through Christmas. You can pay me back sixpence a week out of your old age pension! If Wales beat the All Blacks I'll give it to you as a present.'

Rich took a lot for granted but he was never crude in his giving. He recognised and respected working class pride.

In between thinking about Switzerland and actually moving there, Rich went off to make two modest films. The first, *Sea Wife*, was yet another of those ventures which must have looked all right on paper. It was a wartime love story of a shipwrecked sailor who falls in love with another survivor who just happens to be a nun. Despite exotic locations (the filming was in Jamaica) the story was made weak by the absence of any real passion and the perverse casting of Joan Collins as the religious novice. Already enjoying a reputation as a wicked lady, Miss Collins needed strong direction to steer her away from her self-imposed image. She might have got it from the first choice director, Roberto Rossellini, the leader of the Italian new wave, but with the break-up of his marriage to Ingrid Bergman and hotly publicised affair with an Indian screenwriter, he had too many problems on his mind to give much attention to the picture. Barely had filming started than Rossellini walked off the set, not to return. After that it was downhill all the way.

Joan Collins is on record as having livened up the proceedings by virtuously rejecting the advances of her co-star. But Rich denied he ever made the effort.

'She had a much exaggerated view of her own importance,' he said. 'But so did everybody else on the picture, including me. We deserved our disaster.'

The other film was *Bitter Victory* with Curt Jungens and Ruth Roman. For Rich it was a return to the desert war, with a love interest thrown in. So adverse was its reception that Columbia withdrew the film before it went out on general release.

Rich returned to Switzerland to lick his wounds. On a visit to Wales he told me he thought his film career might be finished. The disappointment of his latest venture was compounded by the knowledge that he had thrown away at least two good chances to make amends. Yet neither was rejected heedlessly. *Reach for the Sky*, the story of the legless war hero, Douglas Bader, looked set to be a re-run of the disappointment over *The Last Enemy* which Korda had promised but failed to produce. In the event *Reach for the Sky* was a box office hit and a triumph for Kenneth More who played the indomitable flyer with style.

Even more of a heartbreak was losing out to Peter O'Toole, then a virtual beginner in films, on the casting for *Lawrence of Arabia*. In the critical week or so when the part was his for the asking, Rich could not bring himself to sign away a year of his life on another historical epic. The torture of *Alexander the Great*, not to mention *The Robe*, was too fresh in his memory.

It was some time before he could bring himself to see the film which made Peter O'Toole an international star. When he did, his verdict was characteristic.

'Peter has a streak of wildness that makes him entirely believable as a mad genius. It is, in itself, a sort of genius. I don't know that I can match it.'

He was soon to find out. But for the moment Rich was content to distance himself from the movies. 'They sure to hell don't want me. And I sure to hell don't need them.'

The spur to his reviving confidence was the offers coming in to tempt him back to the stage. It was an exciting time in the British theatre with a new generation of writers led by John Osborne, Harold Pinter and Arnold Wesker leading the attack on conventional middle-of-the-road drama. Hardly a day passed without the delivery of a script that was worth the effort of reading. The welcome mat was out at Stratford and at the Old Vic and at other theatres like the Royal Court and the Oxford Playhouse (Frank Hauser's latest venture) where the sparks of originality were flying. But Rich was in no hurry to commit himself. For a while I assumed it was his artistic judgement which was running on slow time but various comments he let drop soon led me to realise that financial considerations were uppermost in his mind.

'When there's a lot of money going out,' he told me, 'you need a lot of money coming in.'

The tautology was not without force. Rich was beginning to take on the style and extravagances of a big star. Apart from an agent and financial adviser, he needed at least one secretary and a manager to handle his day-to-day arrangements.

Into this last role stepped brother Ivor. It was one way of keeping the money in the family but otherwise I was not over the moon about the appointment. My reservations were chiefly personal. While I admired Ivor as the driving force in the Jenkins family in the years after our mother's death, I was never able to get close to him, at least not until the last months of his life when circumstances dictated a dramatic change in our relationship.

Ivor was the strong man of the family – tall, powerfully built and something of a fitness freak. He was always immaculate. Even in his working clothes – after being invalided out of the army, he made a living as a bricklayer – his trousers had a razor edge crease and his shoes were sparkling. As a child I lived in awe of him.

That he could be a steadying force in Rich's life was undeniable. His down to earth talent for practicalities was bound to ease the running of the household while his common sense might help to put a

105

brake on some of Rich's wilder flights of fancy. But Ivor was not one to admire or argue on professional matters. Though an intelligent man he knew little of the theatre or films. For him, Rich was the creative genius who could do no wrong.

By mid summer 1957 Rich had decided on his next engagement. He was to return to the stage, after all, but not in London. The charms of the West End stage paled to a shadow against the bright inducements offered by Broadway. *Time Remembered* was another overweight fable from the pen of Jean Anouilh. No matter. Bolstered by Richard Burton and Helen Hayes, one of the grand dames of American theatre, the production brought in advance sales of six hundred thousand dollars, a record for a straight play in New York. The critics were polite without getting over-excited. Normally, they would have damned with their faint praise but this time they were overruled by ordinary theatregoers who were drawn less by the show than by the desire to find out what this young Richard Burton was all about.

Rich was thrilled by his reception and comforted by the feeling that, on stage, he was back on home ground. When I met him for dinner late one evening, I was amazed at the transformation from the restless and nervous character I had known in Wales not two months earlier to the assured and contented star performer, seemingly at the height of his powers.

After a few drinks he leaned across the table and tapped me on the arm. 'Gray,' he said, 'remember when we were boys? From the very first day I kicked a rugby ball, I had two ambitions: to play for Wales at Cardiff Arms Park and to play against England at Twickenham. Well, it hasn't worked out that way. But why should I worry? Stratford and the Old Vic have been my Cardiff Arms Park and Broadway my Twickenham. I haven't a complaint or care in the world. Life has been good to me.'

# Chapter 9

As a family, the year started sadly with the death of Dadi Ni and ended happily with the birth of Kate Burton, named after Katherine Hepburn. Rich declared total delight with his daughter but this did not stop him launching into an affair which proved to be a near fatal hazard to his marriage.

Dadi Ni died at eighty-one. The event should not have been unexpected yet he had come through so much it was difficult to accept that he was no longer with us. The news was cabled to Rich in Switzerland. Ivor was with him. We assumed they would come back for the funeral but they decided against it. Their absence naturally created some gossip locally and in the press, which thankfully was treated lightly by Rich. He told reporters that Dadi Ni would never have approved the extravagance of a plane ticket – just to attend a burial.

But there was more to it than that. All his life, Rich tried to keep his distance from suffering and grief. I do not mean by this that he did not care. When sympathy and help was needed, he was quick to offer both, whatever the cost. But you were not likely to see Rich at the side of a hospital bed or at a funeral. It was almost as if he was frightened of letting himself go, of revealing too much. For all his build-up as the indomitable hero, Richard Burton was very easily moved to tears.

There was something else with Dadi Ni. Rich was never altogether sure what his father thought about him. As he wrote to me, 'I didn't know Dadi Ni very well – he was always an enigma to me – but blood is blood and I feel very empty today. Ivor has been hit much harder of course, but is as taciturn as a rock. Feels a lot, says nothing.'

It occurred to me then that Ivor and Dadi Ni had much in common.

It was in the character of Dadi Ni to play his cards close to his chest. Compliments did not come easily from him. Yet Rich lived in a world where everybody told everybody, 'You were wonderful, darling'. He did not want or respect such effusiveness, least of all at home, but the contrast between all embracing warmth and what seemed to him to be chilly incomprehension made it difficult for him to get close to Dadi Ni. He assumed, wrongly, that Dadi Ni took no interest in his work. Certainly, the old man stayed away from Stratford and the Old Vic (at his age he could be forgiven for his dislike of long journeys) but he went to most of Rich's films.

When we were a lot older, stories about Dadi Ni often came into our conversation. Rich was surprised when I told him how our parent had enjoyed *The Robe*.

'He never even saw the film,' Rich protested.

'He did so. I should know, I took him. We went by bus to Swansea and stood in the queue. As we came up to the ticket counter, the cinema manager recognised me or Dadi Ni. He said it was a huge privilege to see us there and offered us the best seats, free of charge. But Dadi Ni wouldn't have it. "Oh no," he said, his eyes twinkling, "I couldn't accept. It would be like taking money out of my son's pocket."'

I was laughing all through this but Rich listened in silence. When I had finished, Rich thought for a moment. Then he said quietly, 'I didn't know,' and I could see there was a tear in his eye.

Early 1957 brought a summons to another funeral. It was for his friend Humphrey Bogart who was killed by throat cancer at fifty-eight. Again, Rich declined. But the memories stayed on.

'Can you believe it? The tough guy gone. He came from such a posh family. There was nothing tough about his upbringing. We used to joke about it. He said I had to give him lessons on how to look poor.'

I murmured something about how sorry I was.

'It was his real name, you know, Humphrey Bogart. But he had a middle name. DeForest. Imagine it. *Casablanca* starring Ingrid Bergman and Humphrey DeForest Bogart. I told him, with a name like that, you could make a career in soap opera.'

His favourite story of Bogart was of a party which had Cole Porter and Jack Buchanan among the guests. Each provided a little entertainment before Bogie turned to Rich.

'Spout some Shakespeare, kid!'

He did so and as he went into full voice, Cole Porter improvised an accompaniment and Jack Buchanan swept into a dance. What an act!

The following morning, Bogie was on the phone.

'I've just had a call from an agent,' he told Rich. 'He can get you eighteen thousand dollars a week if you do your act in front of a paying audience.'

'Great,' said Rich, 'what's the catch?'

'He wants Cole and Jack too.'

Kate was born on 11 September, weighing in at 6lb 4oz. She arrived a week prematurely which pleased Rich enormously because he was able to see her before flying to New York where he was to start rehearsals for *Time Remembered*. Playing opposite him in romantic mood was Susan Strasburg, at nineteen a seasoned Broadway actress who had earned her launch in *The Diary of Anne Frank*. Temporarily unaccompanied in New York, Rich took to inviting Miss Strasburg to parties and restaurants.

It was an exhilarating time on Broadway. Peter Ustinov was there with his play *Romanoff and Juliet*; Rex Harrison and Julie Andrews were appearing in *My Fair Lady*; and Laurence Olivier was startling his admirers as *The Entertainer*. Other party companions like Hugh Griffith and Donald Houston were in frequent attendance. Even Phil Burton was in town, pursuing his vocation as a guru of acting skills.

Pitched into this heady environment, my brother parted himself from any remaining vestiges of discretion. Susan Strasburg followed in his wake while creating a few waves of her own. She was no stranger to the bright lights. As the daughter of Lee Strasburg, founder and director of the Actors Studio and a titanic influence on American theatre and cinema, she had enjoyed an advanced upbringing and the company of lively minds. But she was still a girl with all the emotional extravagances of her age. Her affair with Rich was, for her, a matter of deadly seriousness. Rich was warned of this, by Ivor among others, but he ignored all the danger signals until it was too late to disentangle without great distress all round.

The arrival of Sybil and Kate allowed Rich the chance to play the devoted husband and father but by then he found it all but impossible to switch roles convincingly. The gossip writers simply did not believe him, Susan Strasburg likewise.

Of all the principals in this sad saga, Sybil alone retained her dignity. This she achieved by flatly refusing to believe that anything untoward was happening. She even had the courage to return to Switzerland before the end of the run, leaving Rich in New York to sort out the problems of his own making.

Immediately Sybil was out of the way, Susan Strasburg moved in for the kill. There are many versions of what happened but my conviction is that Rich stalled to prevent a crisis. He had no intention of running off with Susan Strasburg (as he repeatedly told any of us who asked) but he held back from saying anything quite so emphatic to the lady for fear that she might throw a fit in front of the paparazzi. When she saw him off at the airport, it was in the fair hope that before many days had passed he would be back waving his divorce papers in one hand and a shiny new wedding ring in the other.

The reality was a sailor's farewell – passionate and permanent. Whatever he promised to the contrary, after his departure from *Time Remembered*, Rich made no effort to make contact with Susan Strasburg. A few months later when he was filming in London, Susan came to see him but was turned away. The panic was over. I assumed, too readily, that Rich had learned his lesson. He was at the end of one sad little affair. But the tragic love story of his life had yet to begin.

The success of *Time Remembered* and the renewed press interest in Richard Burton as a box office star, gave the film producers something to talk about. Maybe his screen career was not finished, after all. One offer Rich liked the look of very much indeed. It was to appear in the film version of John Osborne's play, *Look Back In Anger*. When it was first put on at the Royal Court in 1956, *Look Back In Anger* created more interest – and controversy – than any other new play since the war. By exposing the savage frustration of a young intellectual caught up in the web of British class values, Osborne departed radically from tried West End conventions of what made a good play. The critics welcomed an entertainment which struck close to the core of British political malaise and young audiences responded vigorously to a writer who could demonstrate their grievances.

On the crest of *Look Back In Anger* and his next play, *The Entertainer*, which introduced Laurence Olivier to the new drama, John Osborne joined with his director, Tony Richardson, to set up Woodfall, an independent film company, as the vehicle for carrying their revolution to the cinema.

Rich was by no means a political animal. Though vaguely socialist by tradition, he had no difficulty in reconciling ideals of equality with great personal wealth because, in truth, he did not think about it a lot. But he was attracted to originality of ideas and when these coincided with the opportunity to test his range as an actor, the bait was irresistible. Well, maybe only when the money was right. *Look Back In Anger* on screen paid so much better than *Look Back In Anger* on stage.

A fine cast was assembled to match the quality of the product. Along with Rich as the anti-hero Jimmy Porter, were Mary Ure as his wife

Alison (the only survivor from the Royal Court production), Claire Bloom as Helena and Edith Evans, who gave one of her most moving performances, as Ma Tanner, a character referred to but never actually seen in the stage version.

At thirty-three, Rich was thought by some to be too old for his part (the American critics were particularly strong on this), but for me his age counted in his favour because it made the character more vulnerable. The callow Jimmy Porter of the theatre, ever whining about injustice, made you want to scream in frustration. If he felt that strongly about social inequality why didn't he get off his arse to do something about it? But in the film, Rich played a more mature and thoughtful Jimmy Porter whose anger drew sympathy because it conveyed a sense of time passing and opportunities lost. It was the first time I had seen Rich expose weakness and emotional inadequacy. *Look Back In Anger* was, for my money, the best thing he had done on stage or screen. The pity was that because the film was not a financial hit he failed to recognise the importance of what he had achieved.

I saw a lot of Rich during the filming of *Look Back In Anger*. He seemed to want family and friends around him. It was as if he was making an deliberate attempt to reinforce the domestic security he had so nearly lost over the affair with Susan Strasburg. When she appeared on the set at Elstree, the lack of warmth would not have shamed a November morning. Claire Bloom was also given the cold treatment which, I suspect, made the film an unhappy experience she felt she had done nothing to deserve.

Less easily deterred was Mary Ure, whose undisguised determination to get Rich into bed was all the more embarrassing because she was married to John Osborne. More than once I heard her proposition Rich in a way few men could have resisted.

'It's an occupational hazard,' he told me.

For the first time I could see that the problems were not all one way.

After *Look Back In Anger*, the fortunes of Richard Burton went down and up like a yo-yo, and just as fast. Two bad movies followed in quick succession. The first, *The Bramble Bush*, was a low grade soap opera about a doctor involved in the mercy killing of his best friend; the second, *Ice Palace*, took Rich to Alaska for a tepid yarn about fishing against the elements. According to him the dip in the reputation was more than compensated for by the lift in his bank balance. When shooting overran on *Ice Palace*, the fee to Rich, set at a basic fifty thousand pounds, more than doubled.

The upturn started with the first ever production of the John

Osborne play, *A Subject of Scandal and Concern*. Directed by Tony Richardson, it was shown on BBC television in 1960, three years before the play was adapted to the stage. Once again, Rich proved that he could show vulnerability without losing his grip of the role.

He went on to another television venture, this time a collaboration between the BBC and ABC to record a twenty-six-part documentary on the life and times of Winston Churchill. It was called *The Valiant Years*. As the off-screeen narrator, Rich had to be Churchill. But to imitate that distinctive voice was to invite ridicule as a second-rate impersonator. Instead Rich allowed his own deep mellow delivery to suggest the Churchill style while at the same time sticking close to the Churchill rhythm of pauses and inflexions. It was a superb display of acting which viewers on both sides of the Atlantic found entirely convincing. Churchill himself gave his unqualified approval.

'The actor and the politician have a lot in common,' said Rich. 'It takes one to know one. I was successful with Churchill because I knew his secret. He was the greatest actor of them all.'

With that thought in mind and knowing what was to come next for Rich, I could not help wondering how Churchill, in his prime, would have fared in a Broadway musical. Rich, I have to say, took it in his stride.

The idea was put to him by Moss Hart, one of the legendary Broadway writers and directors, who had worked with Rich on *Prince of Players*. Higher on his credits was the direction of Lerner and Loewe's *My Fair Lady* for which he had picked up an Tony award. After the triumph of *My Fair Lady*, Alan Jay Lerner and Frederick (Fritz) Loewe had followed up with the equally successful film musical, *Gigi*, which won ten Oscars, the largest number ever received by any film in the history of Academy Awards. Now they were back with the live theatre and reunited with Moss Hart for a muscial adaptation of the story of King Arthur (he of the Round Table), his marriage to Guinevere and Guinevere's romance with Lancelot.

It was a tall order because the hero had to win sympathy while losing his wife, which was not the usual way of doing things on the musical stage. But the team who could win over middle America to a Parisian man-about-town who falls in love with a pubescent schoolgirl (Gigi) was not easily constrained by tradition.

Even so, Rich thought long and hard about *Camelot*. Was he really the sort of actor who could feel comfortable trilling pretty lyrics across the footlights? He put his fears to Alan Lerner and Fritz Loewe who assumed he was worried about his singing ability.

Alan Lerner was encouraging. 'We had the same problem with Rex Harrison in *My Fair Lady*. Rex said he couldn't sing. But he learned to talk in tune and everyone thought he had a wonderful voice.'

Rich was appalled. 'But I can't do that. What would they say at home to a Welshman who was in a musical and wasn't allowed to sing? I'd be classed as a traitor.'

His prospective employers were not convinced.

'But do you have a singing voice?' they asked dubiously.

Rich cleared his throat.

'Listen to this,' he said and launched into a sturdy rendering of 'A Cry in the Wilderness' – in Welsh.

At that point it was still open to the producers to say 'Thank you' and 'Next please'. But instead they told Rich they wanted to go ahead, while reserving judgement on the musical virtues of the Welsh Presbyterian hymnal. For his part, Rich had built himself up to a level of enthusiasm where all his earlier worries were forgotten. He would play King Arthur and he would damn well make a success of it.

Rich quickly developed an affection for the triumvirate. Moss Hart he had got to know quite well over the years but he soon came to realise why this bubbly, talented man enjoyed working with Alan Lerner and Fritz Loewe. They had great style and humour.

I would love to believe Rich's version of the Rolls-Royce story.

'On a stayover in London, Alan, who had this great passion to own a Rolls-Royce, dragged Fritz along to a Bond Street showroom. "Which do you want?" Alan asked Fritz. "But I'm not buying," said Fritz. "You're the customer." "Don't be silly," said Alan. "Now you're here you might as well get one. You'll regret it if you don't." "OK," said Fritz warily, "I'll take that beauty." "Good," said Alan, "I'll have that one. Now we'd better find out what we do about paying." Fritz put a hand on his friend's shoulder. "Don't worry," he said, lifting his cheque book from his pocket, "I'll get this. You bought lunch."'

Honesty compels me to add that Alan denied the last part of the story though he did buy a Rolls-Royce and he did persuade Fritz to follow his example.

Good humour and singleness of purpose were at a premium on Camelot's run up to Broadway. The chapter of accidents would have stopped any other show in its tracks. Alan Lerner, whose third marriage had just broken up, suffered a haemorrhage brought on by depression and overwork. No sooner was he out of hospital than Moss Hart had a heart attack. Meanwhile, frantic efforts were being made to reduce Camelot to a presentable length. When it opened at the new O'Keefe Center in Toronto, the final act was still in full swing at midnight. One critic praised the show for 'helping considerably to shorten the winter'.

Cuts and further cuts were made. By the time the show reached Boston it was down to four hours – manageable but still overlong. Throughout these tribulations Rich, by common consent, gave magnificent support.

'God knows what would have happened had it not been for Richard Burton,' wrote Alan Lerner. 'If ever a star behaved like a star in every sense of the word, it was he.'

Rich led by example, learning new lines without complaint (before New York he had to rehearse what was virtually a rewritten second act) and offering encouragement to the rest of the cast. When there was time to spare he gave Shakespearian classes which became so popular as to attract recruits from outside the *Camelot* circle of actors. With Rich about, the inevitable moods of depression did not last very long. He had faith in the show and in the ability of the company to turn it round.

And he loved the challenge. 'It sounds perverse,' he admitted, 'but when you're given a perfectly written part, like Hamlet, there's not much you can do with it after the first few performances. The Burton Hamlet is the Burton Hamlet and that's that. But in a show like *Camelot* when the changes are coming thick and fast, all things are possible. You can make something of the part that is yours and yours alone.'

His co-star, Julie Andrews, though less of an extrovert, was equally supportive. She remained calm even when asked to learn a new song – one day before the first New York preview.

If they were looking for reasons to be optimistic, the strongest was the advance booking. It was phenomenal. Even lurid press stories of disasters out of town could not stem the queue at the box office.

But the opening at the Majestic Theater in New York was another matter. All the celebrities in the world – and most of them seemed to be gathered there – and all the glitter of first night razzamatazz could not disguise the fact that, even now, all was not well. The show was still too long and too heavy. It also suffered by comparison with *My Fair Lady* which was in its fifth year on Broadway. There were more joyous, hummable tunes to be had in the company of Professor Higgins and Eliza Doolittle.

A quick glance at the reviews suggested that *Camelot* would close in six months, after it had exhausted its advance booking. But this was to fail to take account of the persistence of Alan Lerner and Moss Hart, who was now back in action as director. Once more the surgical knife was brought out. Twenty minutes was lopped off the running time.

Then came the big break. 'The Ed Sullivan Show', the most popular on American television, devoted a whole hour to the music of Lerner and Loewe. No doubt the network expected a reworking of old favourites from *My Fair Lady* and *Gigi*. What it got was all the best from *Camelot* – 'If Ever I Would Leave You', and 'Where are the Simple Joys of Maidenhood?' , Rich singing 'Camelot' and Rich and Julie together singing 'What do the Single Folk Do?'.

The following morning the bandwagon started rolling. It was helped on its way by President Kennedy who declared *Camelot* to be his favourite musical. Earlier hostilities were forgotten. Everyone in the know said that *Camelot* was set for a very long run indeed.

I went out to New York for the opening of *Camelot*. It should have been one of the great moments of my life but no sooner had I arrived than I went down with 'flu which turned to pneumonia. I was promptly rushed off to Mount Sinai Hospital which can only be described as a luxury hotel for invalids. After I had been tucked up in bed by a pretty nurse and visited by a succession of doctors who looked as if they specialised in diseases of the rich, I fell to wondering about my health insurance.

The limit I could claim was two hundred and fifty pounds which, on a rough calculation of the value of my surroundings, meant that I had to recover by nightfall. In fact I was in Mount Sinai for three weeks. I never even saw the bill. Rich paid it on my behalf telling me that when I got home I had to claim the insurance and use it for a family holiday. I must have been the first patient to come out of Mount Sinai at a profit.

From hospital I was taken to the Burton apartment on Central Park West, a palatial residence with as many rooms as a whole street of houses in Port Talbot. On the mat outside the front door was printed a large B which I thought was just a touch ostentatious for short-term residents. Sybil explained.

'It's not us. This is the Bogart apartment. Lauren Bacall has let us have the place for as long as we're in New York.'

My hosts were under strict orders not to let me out of bed but I was desperate to see *Camelot* and threatened to be a difficult patient unless my wish was granted. So after a few evenings of frustrating inactivity, Sybil took me to the theatre. No effort was called for on my part. I did not even have to press the elevator button. Bob Wilson, a charming and gentle black American who was the latest addition to the Burton entourage, helped me in and out of the car, up and down steps and virtually lifted me into my seat in the centre stalls.

It was a magical evening. As the severest critic of my brother's singing I have to say that he confounded all my fears. His voice came across magnificently. But he was so much more than a singing actor. He had to impart love, joy, sadness and in the end, hope and strength of spirit. It was all very sentimental but none the worse for that. Lavished on the audience as only the American theatre knows how, the splendour of *Camelot* was, as a critic put it, 'the timeless dream of Broadway'.

Rich was so much at home in his portrayal of Arthur that he could work the audience as he wished. T. H. White, the author of *The Once and Future King*, on which *Camelot* was based, told me how Rich had proved to him his command of the script.

'In the speech about how he became a king while still a boy, he talked about the sword in the stone and how he thought it was a war memorial. It was, I thought, a hushed speech but Richard played it for a laugh. I objected to the treatment in a mild way saying, "Why break the pathos?" Richard said, "Very well, Tim; tonight just for you I'll play it straight." And he did. Until then, I didn't know an actor could compel an audience to laugh or not, as the fancy took him.'

I had my own evidence for Rich's ability to ring the changes. On that first evening, I was startled almost out of my seat when I heard King Arthur greet his crusty old friend Pellinore with the question,

'How goes it with my kinsman, Sir Graham? Word comes to me that he was gravely ill. I trust he is now in better health.'

Pellinore, played by Robert Coote, an actor of military style and bearing who did not welcome any departure from the rules, blustered a response. From where I was sitting it sounded like a vague indication that poor Sir Graham was on his way out. But on stage, the words of Pellinore came over with stark clarity.

'What the bloody hell are you talking about?'

Rich threw an arm around Robert's shoulder and boomed with laughter.

'No matter, no matter. We will talk of this again later.'

Pellinore looked understandably nervous.

In the weeks I stayed with Rich and Sybil, the routine was for me to drive with Rich to the theatre and stay with him in the dressing room until curtain up. Then I would watch the show from the wings.

Each day the car was ordered for just after five, earlier than was strictly necessary but Rich hated sitting in the rush hour traffic. Once at the theatre and having bounced our way through the crowd of autograph hunters, Rich did the round of the dressing rooms greeting the rest of the company. This was not just friendliness on his part. He liked to be sure there were no problems like an unexpected sickness before he started his own preparations for the show.

Rich never ate before going on stage but he drank copiously, starting with vodka and ending with a can or two or three of Budweiser beer. This was in the days when my brother's drinking was treated as a joke. Because however much booze he got through it never seemed to affect his performance, colleagues who might otherwise have delivered a friendly warning indulged his choice of relaxation. I remember someone telling me, 'For Richard the bottle is like a second wife; and who wants to break up a happy marriage?'

While his dresser bustled around, Rich and I filled the hour before curtain up with talk about family and rugby, anything but show business chatter. In the last moments he went over the opening scene in his mind while humming a couple of lines from the first song. But even in the early weeks of the show he never rehearsed in his dressing room.

'If I don't know it now,' he said, 'I never will.'

After a good show, Rich was in high spirits, eager to go out on the town. It was not at all like Stratford or the Old Vic where often he was too exhausted to change out of his costume. Standing ovations were not uncommon and when the cheering was loud and strong, Rich would come out with a phrase we had heard from our brother Tom.

'I reckon I've filled my ten drams today.'

Ten drams, or trucks, of coal justified a bonus.

Dinner with Sybil or some of the cast or with visiting celebrities seldom ended before two or three in the morning. But Rich was no longer a late riser. He was usually up at seven, planning a morning in the recording studios (he was still working on *The Valiant Years*) or meetings with producers and agents.

It was a hectic year, one in which he never missed a single performance and which culminated in a Tony award for best actor in a musical.

If, professionally, Rich was enjoying one of the best periods of his life, on the domestic front all was not well. It was difficult to understand why. If he had been a faithful husband it might have been said of Rich that he was suffering the seven-year-itch. But Sybil was reconciled to his philandering which he no longer sought to disguise. I suppose they both thought that after the Susan Strasburg affair any lesser indiscretion could be treated as incidental.

Drink was more of a problem in so far as Rich in his own home was liable to become argumentative and abusive. It was a side of him that most of his friends in the theatre had yet to see, though from comments made to me I suspect they guessed what Sybil had to put up with. That she did tolerate wild bouts of temper and even excused them says much for her.

Sybil, said Tim Hardy, 'was born to flower with Richard'. How true. She never did anything that was not with his interests in mind, but in a curious sort of way she gained strength from giving so much.

Rich was a lucky man and I told him so, adding, 'What did you use to say? You hadn't a care in the world. So what's happened to you?'

He hunched his shoulders and lowered his head as if he was about to wrap himself into a ball.

'I don't know, Gray, I don't know. It's just that, well, all this, it's not what I expected.'

He stopped there. There was nothing further to get out of him. It was clear that he had not yet found contentment. Why, I could only guess.

One possibility was the tragedy of his second daughter. Born on 26 November 1959, Jessica was a pretty dark-haired baby. Outwardly she appeared a normal, healthy child, if somewhat withdrawn. She never smiled or showed pleasure in the silly games children enjoy. In New York she spent all her waking hours staring, uncomprehending, at the flicker of the television screen. Rich was incensed.

'Why does she do that? It's not natural.' And to Sybil, 'Why the hell doesn't she do something, say something?'

Just before I returned home, they discovered the answer. Jessica was autistic.

When Sybil told me the medical verdict, I was lost for anything constructive to say.

'What does it mean?' I asked. 'Can she be helped?'

Sybil was tired and, unusually for her, clearly depressed.

'Nobody knows what autism really is. That's the hell of it. It's a sort of mental illness, I suppose. Jessica lives in a world of her own. She doesn't recognise me or Rich or anybody. There's no way of telling just how much she understands.'

Rich turned for advice to doctors and psychiatrists. The answer was always the same. There was very little that medical science could do. The only hope was that Jessica would eventually respond to the unselfish and undemanding love of those around her.

It did not have to be spelt out to Rich that the home of a busy actor who was out at odd times and travelling a lot was not best suited to the needs of an autistic child. Except in one respect. Ivor and his wife Gwen were on hand.

Not having any children of their own, Ivor and Gwen doted on the young Burtons. Nothing was too much trouble. I cannot say if Jessica might in the end have acknowledged their unstinting devotion. When Rich and Sybil parted, there were hints of possible breakthrough.

Gwen, who was the most gentle and motherly of women, told everybody she was making headway and was devastated when Jessica was taken away. The break with Kate was equally hard to bear though here it was Ivor who took the hardest knock.

Kate could not pronounce Ivor so she called him Eye-Eye and she wrote a poem saying how much she loved him. Ivor had the poem framed and kept it by his bed. It stayed there all his life.

Jessica was eventually put into a special home where she remains to this day. Sybil and Rich often went to see her until the doctors advised against any more visits. It was too upsetting for the girl, they said. As part of the divorce settlement with Sybil, Rich set up a trust fund which guarantees proper care for Jessica as long as she lives.

But this is to jump ahead in the story. When I left New York in early 1961, there was no thought in Rich's mind of breaking up the family. He was restless and discontented; maybe even feeling a little guilty now that he knew the seriousness of Jessica's illness and how little he could do to help her. But what he wanted was a distraction, not a disruption in his life.

The opportunity came with a phone call from producer Walter Wanger. He had seen *Camelot* and had enjoyed the show enormously. He wanted to have lunch with Rich to put an idea to him. Rich said he would be delighted. He hoped the idea was an exciting one. Oh yes, said Mr Wanger, he could be sure of that.

When they met, the producer lost no time in getting to the point. The offer was for Richard Burton to co-star, on second billing, with Elizabeth Taylor in the Twentieth Century-Fox blockbuster, *Cleopatra*. Perhaps, suggested Walter Wanger, Rich had heard a thing or two about the film. He was indulging in irony. Not to have heard of *Cleopatra* was akin to saying you lived on the moon.

Already a year into production, *Cleopatra* was less a tragedy than a disaster. No sooner had shooting commenced than the picture was deprived of its major asset. Elizabeth Taylor was rushed into hospital with a near fatal bout of pneumonia. Studio politics caused the resignation of the director and contractual limitations led to the premature departure of leading actors. Peter Finch who was to have been Caesar and Stephen Boyd, cast as Antony, dropped out to pursue other less stressful roles. The budget debit stood at five million dollars with nothing to show for it. Meanwhile, it had been decided to abandon filming in England where, belatedly, it was discovered that the climate was ill-suited to the recreation of ancient Egypt. Not for nothing was *Cleopatra* known as the film that fell flat on its asp.

But the latest news, insisted Wanger, was more encouraging.

Elizabeth Taylor had all but recovered and was ready to begin work, Joseph Mankiewicz, installed as a director of calming influence and sensitive touch, was heavily into rewriting the script, Rex Harrison looked set to play Caesar and the budget had been replenished. In fact, so much money was swishing around that it was possible to advance highly attractive terms; like a quarter of a million dollars plus generous living expenses including a family villa outside Rome (the latest choice for the location) and two chauffeur-driven cars on permanent call plus a share of the profits.

As an exciting diversion, *Cleopatra* was irresistible. The film took Rich into a higher earning bracket, which was success of a sort, it offered another chance to conquer the big screen and it was a way out of family preoccupations.

'Anyway,' he told me, 'I've always wanted to play Antony. This is maybe not quite what I had in mind but it's a good second best.'

There was one problem. Rich still had three months to go on his *Camelot* contract. Walter Wanger thought the matter could be settled amicably. Recognising someone who was determined to get what he wanted (Wanger, who was not a fit man, saw *Cleopatra* as a final glorious chapter in his career) Rich advised Alan Lerner to demand of Twentieth Century-Fox what he thought his star was worth. Alan conjured up a figure and put on a percentage to allow for bargaining. Fifty thousand dollars was what Alan Lerner suggested by way of compensation and that was precisely what he got. It was, he said, an easier way of making money than writing musicals.

As the outgoing star of *Camelot*, Rich had the biggest say in choosing his successor. He put forward the name of William Squire, fellow Welshman and Shakespearian actor whose career had spanned all the leading classical companies.

'But a musical,' queried Moss Hart, 'can he play in a musical?'

'If I can, he can,' declared Rich. There was really no answer to that.

William came over to New York and was given the full treatment. Rich took him to meet the cast, ending up at his own dressing room.

'And this,' he boomed, waving expressively, 'is all yours.' Shell-shocked by hospitality, William took in what was by far the most spacious and comfortable dressing room he had so far encountered. He was impressed but also a little bemused at a style of living to which few serious actors ever aspired. 'Richard had moved out of reach. We couldn't quite get to him any more.'

But there was a single welcome note of normality. After the show, Richard and William had dinner at Sardis. William spent some time studying the five-star menu, eventually coming up with a choice exotic enough to suit the occasion.

'And what are you going to have?' he asked Rich.

'Me?' said Rich, having thrown the menu aside without giving it a glance. 'Oh, I'll have a plate of chips.'

The waiter took the order without a blink. William half wondered if the man knew he was one of the few remaining links between Richard Burton and ordinary life.

I went to New York for Rich's final night in *Camelot*. It was an extraordinary experience which had me in tears when, after a dozen curtain calls, the company disappeared into the wings to leave the king alone on stage to abdicate his throne. At the farewell party, Moss Hart led the toast to the future of Richard Burton.

'Great actors like you,' he said, addressing himself to Rich, 'are born once in a lifetime. You are as big a personality off the stage as on the stage and you are, in every sense, larger than life.' He paused to raise his glass but instead of finishing on that high note he continued in softer voice, 'I beg you not to waste your wonderful gifts. You must know you have it in you to be one of the greatest stage actors of this century.'

Sadly, this plea was only heard. It was not understood.

# Chapter 10

And so to Elizabeth Taylor, alias Cleopatra.

At twenty-eight she was the nearest America had to a princess. She was photographed whenever she stepped out and quoted whenever she opened her mouth in public.

Her film career went far enough back into childhood for the entire country to have witnessed her maturity from winsome juvenile to stunning beauty. Devoid of privacy, her every action was open to public judgement. The devastation she suffered when her third husband, producer Mike Todd, died in a plane crash set off a tidal wave of sympathy which promptly receded when the tabloids blazoned the love of Elizabeth Taylor for the singer Eddie Fisher, her late husband's best friend.

The preliminary to their marriage was Eddie Fisher's much publicised divorce from Debbie Reynolds, whose prim ways made her favourite of the bible belt. Elizabeth was blamed, unjustly, for wrecking a partnership which was already heading for the rocks.

Elizabeth married Eddie Fisher in May 1959. By then she had completed her best film to date, *Cat on a Hot Tin Roof*, and had embarked on another sweaty piece from Tennessee Williams, *Suddenly Last Summer*. Her director, Joseph Mankiewicz, not one to dispense compliments lightly, described her as 'close to being the greatest actress in the world.'

Back on her pedestal as America's favourite actress, Elizabeth saw off the competition for Cleopatra with a deal which promised her one million dollars, ten per cent of the gross and a small army of paid servants. Meanwhile, she collected an Oscar for her latest film,

*Butterfield 8.* Elizabeth Taylor was at the height of her very considerable powers. She had much to lose.

Her long illness and slow recovery put a strain on the Twentieth Century-Fox accountants but they were up against the publicity people who could produce a mileage of press coverage to show how their girl would, to the benefit of all, shine at the box office. The more money poured into *Cleopatra*, it was argued, the more would eventually come out. The budget was reworked to add up to a staggering one hundred and twenty-four million dollars.

Enter Richard Burton. Plucked from *Camelot* where he had ruled as undisputed star he was now part of a film package in which the only vital constituent was Elizabeth Taylor. However generous the rewards to Rich or to Rex Harrison or to anyone else who appeared in *Cleopatra*, it was clear that their contribution was secondary to the overriding need to maximise Elizabeth's earning capacity.

Rich's place in the pecking order was confirmed by the casual way in which he and Sybil and the family were installed in their villa and then left to kick their heels for three months until he was wanted on set. (Wanger might have saved his money.) He made light of the experience – he wrote home letters saying how much he appreciated the enforced rest – but the idleness had more than a recuperative effect. The frustration of waiting rekindled his ambition. He was determined to win.

So it was that in the first scene with Elizabeth, shot in January 1962, he came almost as an adversary, an actor possessed with the desire to dominate. The effect was electrifying. Among those who crowded the set that day was Ron Berkeley who, as make-up artist for Elizabeth on most of her films, had seen her capitulate, on screen, to a succession of leading men. But this was new.

'Elizabeth was not used to assertive men. Oh, they might put on an act for a while but they nearly all ended up showing love by deference, paying tribute to her beauty. Only one other man had taken her by sheer force of personality. When she encountered Richard Burton it must have seemed to her that she had rediscovered Mike Todd.'

There were striking similarities between Richard Burton and the flamboyant showman producer. Both had tough, sometimes aggressive personalities, both enjoyed the pleasures of wealth and both were capable of phenomenal extravagance. But more to the immediate point, both had it in them to face Elizabeth on equal terms.

From their first meeting (excluding the early chance encounter at the Hollywood party when he was over for *The Robe*) Rich was neither frightened nor overawed by Elizabeth. This in itself must have come as a surprise to the lady. But he was also attentive and intrigued. How could he not have been? Elizabeth was, after all, a fascinating woman.

One reason why film production is so expensive is that it requires a lot of skilled people sitting around doing nothing, waiting for their turn to work. Not only is this method of organisation costly; it also creates an environment in which gossip thrives. Much of it is good humoured tittle-tattle about who is sharing a bed with whom and goes no further than the well stocked dinner table. But when the film is a projected world beater, the stars are front page favourites and rumours abound as to the unsatisfactory state of their current marriages, that is where the trouble starts. It quickly gathers pace if the location happens to be on the home ground of some of the sharpest, hardest and most cruelly devious scandal writers and photographers in the business. It was thus with *Cleopatra*.

One week after the first clinch, director and producer were discussing the probability of a Burton–Taylor affair and its likely impact in terms of adverse publicity. One week after that there were nudge nudge stories and suggestive pictures in every show business column at home and abroad.

In our little enclave in Wales, the rumours were greeted with disbelief and anger. But as the rumours persisted, anger turned to fear that after all, something was seriously wrong.

Many years afterwards Rich told me that he and Elizabeth had been thrown together by events. I knew then what he meant though if the comment had been made much earlier I might have dismissed it as an easy excuse for adultery.

The problem for them both was to do what they were paid to do – which was to fall in love on screen – and yet to keep their distance away from the set. With an actor of more celibate reputation and an actress of less obvious charms, this might have been possible. But they weren't and it wasn't.

And so what started as a harmless – or more or less harmless – flirtation soon became a matter of public concern. Sybil behaved with her customary dignity. She refused to panic and stayed loyal to Rich, but after many inconclusive challenges which showed her husband to be troubled and confused, she departed with the children to Switzerland.

'It is best,' she said, 'for Rich to be free to work out his own future.'

As Sybil flew out, Eddie Fisher flew in. Already made insecure by the challenge of trying to be something more than Elizabeth Taylor's husband, he made the fatal mistake of presenting himself too obviously as the aggrieved party. From the popular press he got the sympathy he expected but couched in such patronising terms as to make him look foolish. Elizabeth was privately furious at his anguished protestations while publicly asserting her determination to hold together her marriage. Likewise, Rich declared his love for Sybil and a refusal to countenance a break-up of his family.

Under some pressure from my relatives I tried to put through a call to Rich but either he was not available or he refused to speak to me – I suspect the latter. Whenever Rich was in trouble his first inclination was to try to ignore it. Instead I spoke to Ivor.

'What's going on, then?'

'What do you mean?'

'Oh, come on, Ivor. You know what I'm talking about.'

'If it's those newspaper stories, there's no truth in them.'

'Are you sure?'

'Would I be telling you otherwise?'

'It's just that it's difficult to believe they make it all up.'

'Well, they do. There was an article last week. It said that Rich had been to Elizabeth Taylor's villa a dozen times. But I know for a fact, he was there just once and that was to tell her it was all over.'

So there *was* an affair. What else was going on? I knew Ivor well enough to realise that he had two priorities – to protect Rich and to shield the family, expecially Cis, from hurtful news. He was not going to make it easy for me to find out the truth.

In another phonecall, I got out of him that he had persuaded Sybil to return to Rome to talk over the future with Rich. Leaving the two of them alone in the villa, Ivor and Gwen had taken a long weekend in Naples. That was in early February. On the same weekend, Elizabeth and Eddie Fisher met in Paris to try to sort out their lives.

From all that I discovered subsequently I do believe that Rich wanted to save his marriage but could not bring himself to cut away cleanly from Elizabeth. Anyway, given that they had a picture to make, his problem could not be solved by a straight choice.

Elizabeth argued much the same with Eddie Fisher. But neither he nor Sybil were prepared to accept half measures. Why, they must have asked, should we make sacrifices?

Sick to death of the humiliation piled on him by the press, Eddie Fisher retreated to Switzerland to the house he and Elizabeth had bought recently at Gstaad. Sybil decided to go to New York. She did not tell Rich of her plans but left Ivor to break the news after she had gone.

Rich, meanwhile, had some travelling of his own to do. He was to spend two days in Paris filming a cameo role for a star-spangled chronicle of the 1944 D-Day landings called *The Longest Day*. It was more than two years before I saw this film and, my, how it brought back memories of the turmoil of his private life. He played an RAF pilot as if the character was suffering from more than battle fatigue. In the scene where he and Donald Houston crouch over their drinks lamenting the friend who did not return, the pauses are so long as to suggest either that Rich had his mind elsewhere or the director of an otherwise very noisy film had suddenly been converted to the dramatic effect of the extended silence. I take the former to be the likeliest explanation.

I know that Rich intended flying the long route to Rome via New York where he hoped to persuade Sybil that their marriage could yet be saved. But the pulling power of Elizabeth Taylor proved too strong.

On 18 February, the world press carried the story of Elizabeth's attempted suicide.

Rich caught the first plane direct to Rome. So did Eddie Fisher.

The truth, as they discovered soon after landing, was not quite as dramatic as the morning's headlines. Elizabeth had indeed been taking sleeping tablets, but with the innocent intention of getting some sleep. No doubt she was piling on the agony as the misjudged victim of a romantic tug of war. But those around her heightened the tension by their cloying concern and melodramatic gestures. So when Elizabeth's hairdresser, Vivian Zavits, took her some sandwiches and milk, saw her stretched out on the bed and screamed 'Oh, my God, she's taken pills', it was simple reflex for one or other of the staff to summon an ambulance, doctors and the US cavalry.

While the ambulance roared across town to the Salvator Mundi Hospital another friend obligingly rang the press and told them where to wait to get the best pictures. Poor Elizabeth, befuddled by sleep, hardly knew what was going on. It took less than an hour for the doctors to report there was nothing at all wrong with Elizabeth Taylor but by then the press was in no mood for good news. They wanted to hear the worst and when they did not get it they suspected a cover up.

Support for this jaundiced view came when Walter Wanger put out a barely plausible story of how he and Elizabeth, having shared lunch, had eaten something which disagreed with them. This begged the question as to why Wanger was not also in hospital. Why he had to lie when he could just as easily have told the truth I cannot say, but the effect was to cause further confusion. Rich flew in to a barrage of reporters demanding to know his version of the story. When he said he did not have one, they shouted their disbelief. Rich was furious.

As his press agent, Chris Hoffa, hurried him out to his car, Rich heard for the first time that Elizabeth was all right.

'So what the hell else is going on?'

Chris Hoffa had no idea. The studio was refusing to make any statements, assuming, with scant regard for the perseverence of bloodhounds, that silence would end speculation. Predictably the reverse happened. Readers of the popular press had a wider choice of contradictory stories than at any time since the first day's shoot.

Rich determined that if no one else was willing to act, he would. On the journey from the airport, he and Chris Hoffa worked out a statement. It began:

> 'For the past several days uncontrolled rumours have been growing about Elizabeth and myself. Statements attributed to me have been distorted out of proportion, and a series of coincidences has lent plausibility to a situation which has become damaging to Elizabeth.'

There was more on the same lines, all well intentioned but too vague to achieve the aim of cutting out rumour and speculation.

Sadly, Rich did not consult the studio before issuing his statement so that the first Walter Wanger knew of it was when the press started bombarding him with telephone calls. Totally at a loss as to how to respond, he fell back on a straight refusal to believe that Rich had said anything at all. He even tried to persuade Rich to deny he ever made his statement.

The chaos off the *Cleopatra* set was matched by the chaos on the set. With thousands of extras milling about, it was virtually impossible to film any scenes with Elizabeth and Rich without someone smuggling out an unauthorised picture. Large sums of money were offered for the most intimate shot of the two stars together. One woman who was keen to make a fortune and her career in photojournalism, constructed an elaborate, fluffy hairpiece which served as a nest for a miniature camera. She was caught when a crew member noticed her predilection for manipulating her left breast like a bell push. The control mechanism was strapped to her bra.

With the entire Twentieth Century-Fox production terrified of adding fuel to what was obviously a blazing fire, Joe Mankiewicz was asked to postpone filming any scenes which might be judged controversial. This left Rich and Elizabeth little to do except concentrate on avoiding the press and sorting out their private lives.

The first rule, they decided, was to stay well away from each other. Leaving Elizabeth in Rome to celebrate her thirtieth birthday with her long suffering husband, Rich set off for Pays de Galles for a family conference. Ivor and Gwen were there; so too were our second eldest brother Tom and his wife, who went along to represent the views of the home base. If this sounds as if we were pushing our noses into affairs that did not concern us, I can only re-emphasise that we were all touched by Richard Burton's notoriety. There was no intention of giving uninvited advice but we did feel we had a right to know from Rich what was going on and to explain to him the upset and wrong caused by the sensationalist press.

By all accounts Rich put on his best act of contrition. He admitted an affair with Elizabeth but claimed it was a passing fancy common enough in the film business, which the press had exaggerated out of all proportion.

'I don't want to break up my marriage,' he insisted. 'I don't want to leave Sybil. Everything will be all right if only she'll listen to reason.'

A clear impression brought away by Tom was that Rich was actually frightened of what he had started. For the first time the prospect of losing Sybil was real. And not just Sybil. With her would go his confidence and his stability.

'He won't take the risk,' said Tom. 'He's not that much of a fool.'

But we reckoned without Elizabeth Taylor. She was a tough young lady who was not easily deflected. I guess that at this point she had still to fasten on Richard Burton as the man for her. But she had made another decision which was every bit as significant. She had decided that her marriage to Eddie Fisher was over.

When Rich arrived back in Rome he found a changed Elizabeth. The heartache she had been carrying around had disappeared. She was a lighter, happier Elizabeth, beautiful and great fun to be with. Rich soon caught the mood. Even the paparazzi seemed less threatening.

'Why should we hide away?' Rich demanded to know. 'What have we to be ashamed of?'

Elizabeth came up with a plan for thwarting their pursuers.

'They want pictures, so let's give them pictures. Let's give them more pictures than they expect, more pictures than they could ever want. Let's give them so many pictures, they'll never want to point a camera at us again.'

The idea appealed to Rich. It was outrageous, it was a laugh and it might just have worked. Never once did it occur to him that Sybil or anyone else in the family would misinterpret the rush of scurrilous publicity. They would know it was just good old Rich having his game. Wouldn't they?

On the evening of 31 March Rich and Elizabeth went out on the town. Forewarned, the photographers turned up in force. The couple was photographed hand in hand, joking and laughing. Short of a lingering embrace, whatever they were asked to do, they did.

The gossip writers claimed that Richard Burton and Elizabeth Taylor were in love. Now, they had the pictures to prove it.

The following day, the story made the front pages round the world.

The studio bosses did not know whether to laugh or cry. The Burton–Taylor affair was creating vast publicity for *Cleopatra*, more than any previous film had ever enjoyed. But was it good publicity? Among those who thought not was the Pope. A bulletin from the Vatican condemned the 'caprices of adult children' which were said to 'offend the nobility of the heart which millions of married couples judge to be a beautiful and holy thing.'

For a Presbyterian, causing offence in Rome was not such a dreadful thing. When it came up in a phone conversation, Rich was dismissive. 'He's never been on my party list.' Even so, the dishonourable mention from the Pope made its impact on public opinion, especially in the States where, once again, the moral minority turned against Elizabeth. Wagging tongues kept up a chorus of disapproval which hit a crescendo of absurdity when an eccentric far-right Democrat tried to persuade his colleagues in the House of Representatives to support a banning order on Richard Burton's entry into the United States. Backed by a weird assemblage of campaigners for righteousness, Congressman Feighan, who was not used to being taken seriously, fed the neurosis at Twentieth Century-Fox. Trembling for their jobs, the studio executives talked of nothing else but *Cleopatra*. Had they got a sellable film? If yes, would 'The Scandal' help or harm its prospects?

The fact was, nobody knew. But that did not deter speculation. Rich and Elizabeth tried to block their minds to what was going on around them. This was easier for Elizabeth who was more in control of herself and less inclined to take kindly to moral platitudes. Rich was at the other extreme – confused and, out of deference to Sybil, feeling that he had to listen to everyone. He was not short of choice. When the family had done with him – and we were all adamant in our desire to see him make a clean and final break with Elizabeth – the heavy guns such as Emlyn Williams were hauled to the front. He flew to Rome to urge his young friend to return to Sybil. Rich listened politely, agreed that Emlyn was talking good sense and said he would think about it. He told us all he would think about it.

I have no doubt he kept his promise. But he was a prisoner of his own emotions. He loved Sybil and was spellbound by Elizabeth. To act decisively was beyond him. He lived from day to day hoping decisions would be made for him, willing the fates to direct him. He was confused, uncharacteristically obtuse and contradictory, all without appearing to notice the change in his own character.

Just how muddled he had become was revealed to me a few months later when Rich was interviewed by Kenneth Tynan for *Playboy* magazine. By now filming on *Cleopatra* was finished and Rich and Elizabeth were in London working on their second film together, *The VIPs*. As a general rule, Rich was refusing press interviews but Tynan, who had sought him out for stardom and more than once had nominated him as Laurence Olivier's successor, was an obvious exception. The meeting was at the Dorchester where Rich and Elizabeth had adjoining suites overlooking Hyde Park. Possibly anticipating misunderstandings, Kenneth Tynan sensibly took along a tape recorder.

The talk began with a re-run of Burton the stage actor with some neat jibes at his eminent rivals ('Olivier frequently dries up; John Gielgud never stops drying up') and a bilious attack on modern playwrights. Of Samuel Beckett – '*Waiting for Godot* is playable, I suppose; it doesn't make sense, but it's playable'; of Arthur Miller – 'totally humourless'; of Tennessee Williams – 'There is only one line in all his plays that I consider memorable' (it was a stage direction in *A Streetcar Named Desire*); and of Eugene O'Neill – 'Hopeless. No good. The phoniest playwright I've ever read.' Only John Osborne escaped unscathed.

After this warming up session during which, no doubt, a fair amount of alcohol was consumed, Tynan steered the discussion towards personal matters.

'What,' he asked, 'are your views on the sanctity of marriage?'

Rich took the bait and was soon floundering in shallow waters.

'Monogamy is absolutely imperative.' (Yes, he really did say this.) 'The minute you start fiddling around outside the idea of monogamy, nothing satisfies anymore. Suppose you make love to an exciting woman other than your wife. It can't remain enough to go to bed with her; there must be something else, something more than the absolute compulsion of the body. But if there is something more, it will eventually destroy either you or your marriage.'

As I was soon to find out, this view was strictly in accord with the thinking of Elizabeth Taylor. Coming from her, it made sense. She had always stuck to the view that sex on its own was utterly meaningless. But from Rich? Who could blame Kenneth Tynan for not believing his ears. He posed the obvious follow up. How could Rich square his philosophy of marriage in general with his own in particular?

'Speaking for myself,' said Rich, 'I couldn't be unfaithful to my wife without feeling a profound sense of guilt.'

Well, that was good to know. But what about Elizabeth? Presumably he felt guilty about her.

'Absolutely not. I'm not unfaithful to my wife. I never have been, not for a moment.'

Tynan gave him a way out.

'Physically or spiritually?'

Rich spurned the offer.

'Neither. It's wrong to assume I've been unfaithful simply because I happen to live in the same hotel as another woman.' He went on, 'What I have done is to move outside the accepted idea of monogamy without investing the other person with anything that makes me feel guilty. So that I remain inviolate, untouched.'

There was more nonsense of this sort before Tynan mercifully let his victim off the hook. In reply to the last question, Rich confessed that he was 'a mass of contradictions'. To which we could all respond, 'You can say that again.'

I have quoted at length from this interview without the intention of showing that my brother was capable of making a fool of himself. That he did appear foolish was undeniable, but there was more to it than that. Rich was a deeply troubled man, possibly close to breakdown. The pressures were too many and too heavy for him to take.

Soon after he and Elizabeth departed Rome, the rumour went round that *Cleopatra* was, to put it mildly, an unmanageable film. Before its release, two hours had to be cut from the original running time. Even so, the story line was tediously protracted. Awesome spectacle there was in plenty but it could not compensate for lack of pace.

Depression settled on Twentieth Century-Fox. For weeks, it was said, the only sound to be heard at the studio was of senior staff clearing their desks. After the first shock of failure came the witch hunt. Who was to blame? The prime candidates were Richard Burton and Elizabeth Taylor. However competent as performers, their personal shenanigans had distracted producer and director from their professional responsibilities. Another version of the charge sheet held that while the film was good, if not brilliant, family entertainment, the stars' behaviour destroyed its appeal at the box office. At least four major US distributors took this view. So strongly did they feel about it they sued Fox for eight million dollars as compensation for loss of revenue.

Because of bad reviews and all the recriminations, it is usually assumed that *Cleopatra* was a financial disaster. I am not sure that anyone outside the boardroom of Fox has ever seen the true figures but from what Elizabeth has told me about her earnings from the picture (she was on a share of the gross) it must, in the end, have broken even. Certainly Rich emerged with a much healthier bank balance. It was his professional esteem that was on the sick list.

131

Despite all the traumas of *Cleopatra*, Rich and Elizabeth immediately decided to do another film together. From Rich's point of view it was a way of putting off the time when he would have to make a clear-cut decision about his marriage. For Elizabeth, it was a step in the right direction. But making the film was torment for both.

Written by Terence Rattigan, *The VIPs* was an attempt to cash in on the glamour of the jet set. Various important persons gathered at Heathrow for a New York flight. Among them was an enormously wealthy businessman (Rich), his glamorous jewel-decked wife (Elizabeth) and her lover (Louis Jourdan) who was plotting to steal her away. Stranded at the airport by fog these and other characters who were in no way connected except by the coincidence of their flight bookings, were able to act out their little dramas in and around the VIP lounge.

What should have been a modest production was elevated far above its station by producer Anatole de Grunwald, whose idea it was to hire Burton and Taylor for roles that were perilously close to recent experience. Having produced several of Rich's earlier films he had a direct line to the now infamous actor. His backers urged him to make use of it.

I worked alongside Rich for several weeks on the making of *The VIPs*. As his near double, except for about an inch in height, I was the natural choice for stand in. There was some difficulty in getting away from my regular job but by combining back leave with that year's entitlement I managed to achieve the equation. Hilary, my wife, was not best pleased at losing her holiday but we agreed the extra money would come in useful.

Long periods of waiting around gave me the rare opportunity of observing my brother, the film star, at close range. Part of what I saw distressed me enormously and made me think he had shrugged off any chance of returning to the heights of his profession. Hard drinking started with breakfast as Rich knocked back a tomato juice heavily laced with vodka, followed by another, followed by another.

If still the hard liquor had no obvious effect on his performance, it was, I concluded, more than a lucky chance that he had to play a morose, introspective character who spent much of his time comtemplating a wasted life. But there was a happier, more open and naturally relaxed side to Rich. It showed itself when he was off the set, in the company of Elizabeth.

I had decided not to like Elizabeth Taylor. But the resolution went by the board almost as soon as I met her. She was, more than I could ever have imagined, a natural woman. That she was naturally beautiful any fool could see though, for me, she was less the pin-up model than I expected. There was none of the passive, laidback 'look at me, aren't I the greatest' manner about her. Hers was a personality and a strong intelligence which demanded attention and respect. Twice in a week we went out to dinner together. (It was a sign of the times that on both occasions Rich was too drunk to accompany us.)

The conversation took the inevitable turn.

'Will you marry Richard?'

'What do you think?'

'I think he's a troubled man.'

'He needs someone to look after him.'

'Isn't Sybil supposed to do that?'

She laughed. 'Sybil was yesterday.'

Later, I was asked, 'Should I go to Wales?'

For a moment I was lost for a reply.

'It'll be difficult.'

This brought a snapped response.

'I never imagined it would be easy.'

'You really want to meet the family?'

'I have to, don't I? It might as well be soon.'

What could I say? I just shrugged.

'I suppose so.'

I realised then I was just a little frightened of Elizabeth. To stand in her way was to risk being hit by an avalanche. At the same time I could see very clearly how she captivated Rich. If Sybil stood for security, Elizabeth was excitement. She made you feel that life was interesting because it was unpredictable and dangerous. More than anyone I have ever known she could lift Rich out of his deep moods of depression. That was her great gift to him. What she could not do was to manage his life. That was one of the penalties of losing Sybil.

Before Elizabeth's visit to Wales (who could doubt it would happen?) Rich made his own exploratory trip. It was when filming on *The VIPs* was mainly long shots. For these I was indistinguishable from my brother. So, while I played Rich, he went off to give a more penetrating performance as the celebrated lover at odds with himself. I anticipated a huge row but the occasion passed off without a single cross word.

'How could we be angry with him?' Cis told me. 'He looked so sad.'

Tom put it another way.

'His coming home. It was like a cry for help.'

Elizabeth was not mentioned until the last day when Rich was saying goodbye to Cis.

'Do you want to meet Elizabeth?' he asked her.

133

'You must do what you think best,' said Cis in a tone of voice which implied, yes.

'I know you'll like her,' said Rich.

This line, 'I know you'll like her,' was used to good effect on friends and relatives alike. Elizabeth never let him down.

When Rich got on the phone to one of his closest friends, the response was cautious. Tim Hardy could scarcely reject an evening with Elizabeth Taylor but he felt a loyalty towards Sybil. A few days earlier she had called by for a long and tearful session of times remembered. Driving her back to Hampstead in his battered shooting brake, they chuntered up Park Lane, past the Dorchester. Sybil had a quiet sob.

'Do you still want him back?' asked Tim.

'I do,' wailed Sybil.

'Then you shall have him.'

Tim pulled hard down on the steering wheel, roared into the forecourt of the hotel and braked outside the revolving door. Then, made brave by good wine, he stomped up to the reception and demanded to speak to Richard Burton.

The desk clerk was understandably nervous. He was not used to paging important guests in the middle of the night to tell them a visitor had just walked in off the street. He summoned the duty manager, a tall, dignified figure, Tim recalls, resplendent in white tie and tails. Tim's confidence was fast ebbing but he repeated his demand.

The manager spoke as to a small child, explaining with great care why Mr Burton could not be disturbed. As he talked, Tim was made aware that his dog, a playful labrador who had followed him in from the car, was taking a more than passing interest in a large potted plant. Mumbling apologies he backed away leaving the Dorchester night staff to contemplate a lengthening trickle across the parquet floor.

The evening with Elizabeth Taylor was less traumatic.

'She was natural and charming and interested; not at all the big star straining to make an impression. When we said goodbye, she gave me a huge kiss. I was captivated.'

Other of Rich's friends were quick to agree. Elizabeth was rather special.

It was the same in Wales. When the couple turned up in a pale grey Daimler with Elizabeth looking like a million dollars, the gasp of wonder could be heard the length of the valley. But she was not seeking reverence. She wanted friends and she went all out to win them by launching what I can only describe as an electioneering campaign. When anyone wanted to shake hands, she shook hands; when anyone asked a question, she answered them. She asked quite a few questions of her own but none so simple as to suggest she had not done her homework.

Where Rich led, she followed, apparently happy to defer to the social pattern we had known since childhood but which must, to her, have seemed very strange indeed. The tiny houses and narrow streets; the pubs with their back room talk of victories on the rugby field; the family reunion with too many relatives arguing against each other.

They stayed with Hilda and slept in the small, spare room. It was a long trek down to the lavatory. Elizabeth asked for, and got, the only luxury of the week – a chamber pot under the bed.

The contrast with life at the Dorchester could not have been greater. There they occupied two roof-garden suites – the Harlequin Suite for Elizabeth and the Terrace Suite for Richard, and another corridor of rooms for Elizabeth's children, nannies, secretaries and personal assistants. Heading the administration, a full time job and no mistake, was Elizabeth's chief of staff, Dick Hanley, a gentle, unruffled character who started his career as secretary to Louis B. Mayer, the legendary boss of Metro-Goldwyn-Mayer. At that time, Elizabeth had been an MGM child star, one of the Mayer front runners in his unashamed pursuit of wholesome, escapist family entertainment.

When Elizabeth was on her travels, Dick Hanley led the advance party. At the Dorchester his first point of contact was Marjorie Lee, head of public relations, who knew all the celebrities. Then he would gladhand a procession of porters, waiters and barmen. While Dick was in town, a table close to the bar was put on permanent reserve. It was here, at what was known as The Office, that he entertained journalists, producers, directors and actors – a tightly controlled selection process which determined the lucky few who would eventually be summoned to the presence.

Rich was not too fussy about decorations or furniture. If it was comfortable, that was fine by him. If it was sumptuous, as at the Dorchester, even better. But familiarity with the good life made Elizabeth choosy. Chairs and tables had to be shifted about or replaced to suit her mood. During the filming of The VIPs she turned up at the Dorchester with a Van Gogh landscape which she had spotted in an auctioneer's catalogue. An interior designer was summoned to advise on the hanging of this latest acquisition.

Then there was the jewellery. Lots of it. Security demanded that it should be kept in a safe to which Dick Hanley alone had access. Each morning Elizabeth made a selection of the baubles she needed for the studio (she always wore her own jewellery on set) and each night they went back under lock and key.

Rich quickly got into the habit of adding to the collection. One Saturday morning Dick Hanley was summoned by telephone to meet Rich in a pub just off Piccadilly.

'And I want you to bring some cash.'

'How much?'

'Five thousand should do it.'

It was a lot of money to raise when the banks were closed but Dick Hanley had the best connections. Within an hour he was back; mission accomplished. Now he had to cope with Elizabeth.

'Where is he? What's he doing? Why does he want the money? Who's he with?'

Dick Hanley made soothing noises. 'There's no one with him. I met him in a bar. I gave him the money. He asked me if I wanted a beer and I said, no thanks.'

Elizabeth would not be pacified. For some reason she was terrified that Rich was up to no good. Not for the first time I wondered who was the dominant partner.

Just before lunch the errant lover returned, apparently unaware that he had caused any upset. He greeted a tight-lipped Elizabeth, gave her an enthusiastic kiss, turned her round and fastened a string of rubies round her neck.

It was more than a gift. It was a declaration.

'I often wondered if they would take ready money in the Burlington Arcade,' he said. 'Well, today I found out. And what's more, for cash, they give a discount.'

The life that Rich and Elizabeth started together was nothing if not stylish. In a party thank-you note, Tim Hardy remarked that the Burton–Taylor assemblage in full swing made him think of a minor court of Imperial Germany. Back came the reply: 'Bugger "minor"'.

But this idol of the screen never lost his fondness for the simpler pleasures. Once, after a hard week's filming, he contemplated the perfect relaxation.

'Do you know what I really want to do? I want to see the Welsh–Scottish match, tomorrow. Can you get tickets?'

I thought it might be arranged. We took the morning train to Cardiff and the early train back. The conversation flowed but not as fast as the drink. On the return journey the bar was packed with London-based Welsh supporters, everyone wanting to tell his pals that he had clicked glasses with Richard Burton. As we fell off the train at Paddington, the call went out for a last round to cement lasting friendships. A cheerful pub across the road looked ideal for the purpose.

But once in we realised our mistake. The place was packed with young toughs who looked as if they might have a cruel idea of fun. The appearance of a glamorous film actor fuelled what was already an aggressive mood. Rich did not seem to notice at first or chose to ignore the comments. But then they started in on Elizabeth. Rich was leaning against the bar facing me. I saw his face redden and I could guess what he had heard behind his back. Abruptly, he straightened, turned and hit the man full in the mouth.

After that, the pace of life accelerated alarmingly. The man with a swollen lip fell back over a three-legged stool. Grabbing at the bar for support but not quite making it, he took with him on his descent several glasses and assorted drinks. Rich stepped back clenching his fists as if to make ready for a return match. I grabbed him by the shoulder.

'Let's get out of here.'

Rich tried to shake me off.

'Don't be stupid,' I shouted. 'This could be real trouble.'

I pushed him into the crowd of spectators who were pressing forward to see the fun. I was not quite fast enough. The yob who had pulled himself up from the floor, was propelled forward by his friends. He butted Rich in the small of the back. Both of them stumbled forward and collapsed, Rich catching his head on the side of a table. I gripped his arm and made one last heave for the door.

There was a taxi parked just down the road. We made a run for it. If I had been the driver I would have set off in a hurry to look for a more respectable fare. But he was evidently unshockable because he took us on board, Rich spilling blood from his face, and did not even turn a hair when we told him to make for the Dorchester.

As we turned into Park Lane, the cabbie spoke for the first time.

'Are you Richard Burton?'

Rich admitted that he was. The driver glanced in the mirror to observe the two of us nursing our wounds.

'Is this for real?'

'How do you mean?' I asked.

'Well, I just wondered. Are we in a film?'

'No, no,' said Rich. 'This is for real.'

We stopped at the Dorchester and got out. I searched my pocket for change.

Rich bent down to talk to the cabbie through the driver's window.

'Now you know,' he said. 'Truth is stranger than fiction.'

'That's as maybe,' said the cabbie. 'It's cheaper as well. If you had been filming, I'd have charged you double.'

We were left standing on the pavement. With the excitement wearing off, Rich was contrite.

'I can't go in like this.'

I could see what he meant. With his torn jacket, a gash on his cheek and ripening black eye, the lobby of the Dorchester was the last place he wanted to be seen.

'Isn't there a side entrance?'

Rich was suitably grateful. 'Of course there is. Come on.'

We ran out into Park Lane and along to the far end of the hotel. 'This is it,' said Rich. He pushed into the revolving door, stepped smartly across a small foyer, through another set of doors and into – the ballroom. At least two hundred people were gathered for a formal dinner dance. Nobody called for the police but we did attract some shocked stares as, heads held high, we made the long march to our exit.

The following morning, the story of the pub fight was reported, more or less accurately, in all the popular Sunday papers. Rich was philosophical.

'It could have been worse,' he said, 'I might have spilled my drink.'

If *The VIPs* added nothing to the reputation of either of its leading actors, it did get them through an agonising period of indecision. Five weeks into shooting Rich told me he had asked Elizabeth to marry him. I knew she had said yes when she appeared on set sporting her engagement present – a large emerald and diamond brooch.

Sybil was invited to start divorce proceedings, on the understanding that Rich would not contest a generous financial settlement.

When Sybil recognised there was no going back, she rediscovered her energy for living. A lady of independent means (she could expect at least one million dollars from Rich) she wanted a fresh start. In April 1963 she set up home in New York. She knew and liked the city and after the year of *Camelot* she had more friends there than in London. But there was something else about New York. It had an infectious enthusiasm. Ideas were welcome; all things were possible.

'I knew if I came here, I'd be all right,' Sybil told a journalist. 'If New York had failed, I'd have been in real trouble.'

Making best use of her talents – wit, an ability to get on and a first hand knowledge of the entertainment business, she bought a partnership in a production company. A year later she took over the Strollers Club, renamed it Arthur's and turned it into one of New York's most fashionable discos.

Among those who played at Arthur's was a twenty-four-year-old rock musician, Jordan Christopher, one of a group called The Wild Ones. The gossip writers reported that he and Sybil, who was twelve years older, spent a lot of time with each other. Will they; won't they?

asked the prurient who were eventually answered by the glimpse of a wedding ring. Sybil was happy again.

We all sent our love while speculating how long it would last. It was brother Tom who settled our doubts.

'You don't have to worry about Sybil,' he said. 'She's not a girl to make the same mistake twice.'

More than twenty years on it looks as if he was right.

Rich, meanwhile, was enjoying, if that is quite the word, his own full measure of excitement. The trauma of *The VIPs* was followed by two good films which did wonders for the Burton reputation and self confidence. In *Becket*, a straight reworking of the Jean Anouilh play, Rich played the title role against Peter O'Toole as Henry II. The project worried him for a whole number of reasons.

'Can you imagine me as a saint? The critics will die laughing.'

I told him he would be mad to reject the part.

'I'd be better as the king,' he insisted.

What I think he meant was that it would be easier to play the king. Between Becket the saint and Becket the insufferable prig was a narrow line. Rich was not sure he could tread it without too many steps on the wrong side.

Another fear was the inevitable comparison with Peter O'Toole. Seven years younger than Rich and an international star by virtue of *Lawrence of Arabia*, Peter too was blessed with that promise of greatness. For both actors to share the screen was for Rich to risk being toppled by the newcomer. But it was not like Rich to think in this way. His normal attitude was to welcome talent in others.

'To work with clever people,' he used to say, 'is not only a pleasure; it's a necessity. You can't win against fools.'

That he started *Becket* wishing that Peter O'Toole was just a little less gifted was a measure of his confused thinking, the self-inflicted turmoil.

Another cause of nervousness was the director. Rich still recalled the spot of difficulty when Peter Glanville disposed of his services to the West End production of *Adventure Story*. Was there more conflict in store? Altogether it was a fraught time.

To hold back the panic, Rich drank more. It is usually said that my brother did not surrender to alcoholism for another five years. But if an alcoholic is one who cannot do without his daily booze then, in 1963, Rich was an alcoholic.

Beer was no longer the staple diet. After the breakfast vodka came the whisky pick-me-up for lunch and great quantities of wine followed by more whiskies in the afternoon and on, late on, into the evening.

To be in his company during these marathon sessions was to play life dangerously. When he was feeling good he could engulf you in a marvellous sensation of well-being. I loved him then and felt as close to him as any brother could be. But the fun times were interrupted by terrifying bouts of depression and ill temper when he became a stranger to us all. No one could tell when the storm would break.

At Rich's invitation, I turned up at Shepperton one day with a painter friend. When Rich came off the set we went to the King's Head, a genuine English oak-beamed pub in the heart of the village from which the film studio took its name. The small talk was about the skill, and cost, of recreating history for the screen. We had just seen Rich as Becket filmed against a façade of Canterbury Cathedral. What looked as imposing and solid as the real thing was, in fact, constructed entirely of papier-mâché over a steel scaffold. When told this, I was suitably amazed.

'You could have fooled me,' I said, 'I thought it was there for good.'

It was a lead in for Rich to tell one of his stories about falling through the scenery. Instead he just grunted.

'Don't be a bloody fool, Gray. You know better than that.'

I should have realised then we were in for trouble but for my friend's sake, I persevered. We had a few drinks chatting about this and that with Rich throwing in the occasional sour comment. Suddenly, he cut across the conversation.

'Well, let's get on with it. What do you want?'

The question was to my friend who was understandably lost for an answer. Stupidly, I tried to joke.

'Another drink,' I suggested.

Rich gave me a black look.

'Don't muck about,' he growled. I could almost hear the anger mounting. 'You're here,' (he pointed to my friend) 'and you want something. What is it?'

My friend cracked out a denial.

'I wanted nothing from you,' he said, 'except the pleasure of your company. It seems I'm to be disappointed.'

He put down his glass and walked out. Now I was furious.

'What the hell are you on about?'

Rich sneered, 'Don't tell me he wasn't trying to sell me a picture.'

'I don't think the idea even crossed his mind.'

'So you say.'

He turned away and I left him to sink deeper into his own foul mood. For a week afterwards I felt angry and depressed.

In fairness to Rich and to be honest about myself there were occasions (this last was not one of them) when an over-trusting nature led me into bad company. Shortly before the release of *Becket* I was telephoned by a journalist who asked if I could help with an article on Rich for a woman's magazine. We met over lunch and got on well together. I agreed to an interview. I was even to be paid for my trouble; not much, it was true, but the thought was welcome.

A week or two later, I had a call from Rich.

'Have you been talking to the papers?'

I told him about the magazine article.

'I don't know anything about that,' he said. 'But you might just go out and buy a copy of the *News of the World*. Then ring me back and we'll decide what to do.'

I did not have to open the paper to know I was in trouble. There, slapped across the centre spread was the Richard Burton story as told by Graham Jenkins. It was not greatly sensational but more was promised for the following week and the week after that. I started worrying about how much I had said or hinted at. It took me a little time to pluck up courage to get back to Rich. After a tirade which did not allow for interruptions, he asked, 'Did they pay you?'

I admitted to receiving two hundred pounds.

'Is that all?' he shouted. 'I can just about understand you wanting to sell your brother. What I can't forgive is selling me off so cheaply.' And he slammed down the phone.

This can only get worse, I thought, as I waited on tenterhooks for the next edition of the *News of the World*. But when it appeared there was no mention of Richard Burton. The lawyers had been at work, particularly my own lawyer and good friend Dai Morris.

When, some time later, I dared to ask Rich how he had managed to blow the whistle, he was reticent. All he would say was, 'It cost me more to get them to stop writing than it cost them to start you talking.'


*Becket* was greeted respectfully in Britain and enthusiastically in the United States. There was some reservation here as to the accuracy of the setting. It was all too clean, neat and tidy, like the story book portrayal of Merrie England. This did not worry the Americans who were less concerned with the historical niceties than with the quality of the acting. In this respect, Rich emerged with honour. He gave a sensitive and entirely convincing performance as the cynical, self-seeking courtier turned turbulent priest. The mantle of holiness was not the awkward fit he had anticipated.

In fact, all Rich's fears about taking on *Becket* proved to be unwarranted. His relationship with Peter O'Toole was close and convivial. Rivalry over the bottle appeared to be of greater moment than rivalry for the attention of the camera. Gleefully, they played up to their proud boast to be the only drinkers left standing at the last round. When Paramount trouble shooters flew in to assess the chances of ever getting their money back, the stars put on a convincing display of helpless inebriation. While they were rolling about the set acting drunk (in reality both were stone cold sober) one of the grey suits was heard to come up with an idea for a salvage operation.

'Maybe we can turn it into a comedy. Those two get more laughs than Laurel and Hardy.'

Throughout the filming of *Becket*, Elizabeth stayed on at the Dorchester. I have no doubt she turned down lucrative offers to be with Rich though she did manage to fill in time and make some money narrating a CBS documentary on London. She continued to play second fiddle in Rich's next film, a steamy drama filmed in Mexico called *Night of the Iguana*. Rich played a disgraced priest clapped out by booze who scraped a living as a tour guide.

Director John Huston described the character as 'a broken man, drinking heavily, and at the end of his tether,' adding, 'Ray Stark (the producer) and I agreed that Richard Burton was ideal for this role.' A few years later we might have called it typecasting.

Rich's co-stars were Ava Gardner, Deborah Kerr and the nubile Sue Lyon. Unkind gossips claimed that Elizabeth tagged along to keep a watch on her future husband, as the proximity of so many attractive women was thought to put too much of a strain on his fidelity. I believe that to be nonsense. Elizabeth went to Mexico for two reasons. She wanted to be with Rich but also by showing that his career came first, she hoped to overcome his sense of inferiority. Elizabeth knew well enough how Rich smarted at the cheap jibes. In public he joked about his junior status in the partnership.

'My sole ambition is to earn as much as Elizabeth and her only ambition is to play Hamlet.'

But in private his anger at journalists who called him Mr Cleopatra was terrible to behold. Elizabeth did not escape the lash. When he wanted to prove his superiority, usually after heavy drinking had made him rancorous, he baited her on her lack of formal education.

'Give me a line from Shakespeare, any line you can think of. I'll tell you the rest of the speech.'

'To be or not to be.'

'That's too easy. Come on, think of another one.'

Knowing what was coming, Elizabeth tried to divert the attack.

'This is silly. Let's talk about something else.'

But Rich stayed dead on course.

'Oh yes,' he sneered, 'I forgot. You don't know any Shakespeare, do you? Not one bloody word that doesn't come out of the dictionary of clichés.'

'Well, love. We can't all be geniuses.'

Elizabeth was at her best when she kept calm. As a shouter and furniture thrower she just added fuel to Rich's temper. But she had a way of delivering a gentle rebuke which could stifle an argument and turn Rich from anger to remorse.

Once, after listening impassively to a long, loud diatribe she got up and went to the door. Rich was about to start again when she said, very softly, 'You should be careful, love. One day you might harm more than yourself.'

When she left the room, Rich was close to tears.

In sober state he welcomed Elizabeth's knack for diffusing an argument. 'She makes me less volatile,' he told friends. But Elizabeth was closer to the truth when she responded, 'He's not less volatile. He just chooses when and where to be volatile with more discrimination.'

One of the bonuses of filming in Mexico was the discovery of Puerto Vallarta, a small fishing village on the Bay of Banderas. Rich and Elizabeth fell in love with the long and, in those days, empty beaches, warm and snug in the arms of a green mountain. It was here that they made their first home together, a tiled villa straddling two sides of a narrow street by way of a Bridge of Sighs, an exact replica of the original in Venice. For the next ten years it was to be their refuge, a place where they could be themselves. They called it Casa Kimberley.

Filming *Night of the Iguana* was in itself an escape. Though not exactly alone in Mexico – even when they were off the set they were always followed by a small crowd of staff and hangers-on – the couple did enjoy each other's company without the constant pressure of having to behave like stars.

In letters home, Rich talked openly for the first time of his love for Elizabeth. Long afterwards, when I could see their lives in some sort of perspective, I came to the view that it was in Mexico that Rich discovered how much he really needed her. Up to then he had worried incessantly about his own capacity for easy infatuation. What made Elizabeth different from any of the others? Was it just that she was a big star, a princess of the cinema? Or was there more to it? In Mexico he finally decided there *was* more, much more to it. His surrender to Elizabeth was total. Once he had come to terms with this, the sheer joy of knowing spilled over into every other part of his life. There were still rows, of course. With two such mercurial people, it could not have been otherwise. But taking a wider view, I could see that in his love for Elizabeth, Rich was at last beginning to understand his own character which in turn gave him a sense of contentment he had never known before. Where I was wrong was in believing it would last.

# Chapter 11

More evidence of the changed Richard Burton came in a short book called *A Christmas Story*. It was a journey down memory land to his early boyhood in Wales; days remembered with affection and gratitude. The style owed much to Dylan Thomas but the characters were true to the life of Richard Jenkins with, of course, Cis in pride of place.

'She was naive to the point of saintliness, and wept a lot at the misery of others. She felt all tragedies except her own . . . I knew that I had a bounden duty to protect her above all other creatures. It wasn't until thirty years later, when I saw her in another woman, that I realised I had been searching for her all my life.'

I found it hard to believe that Elizabeth had such a great need of protection but the sentiment was happily in tune with childhood fantasy.

I was one of the many who read *A Christmas Story* in manuscript and who urged him to get it published. His reluctance was less to do with false modesty than with the desire to be taken seriously as a writer. He knew that the book would sell on his name, but popularity alone was not his objective.

'It's just a first effort,' he told me. 'I know I can do much better than this.'

Privately I agreed but I could see no reason why he should not have the encouragement of seeing his first book in print. It would stimulate him to try again which is really what he wanted to do. This came across very clearly in a note to his one-time tutor, Nevill Coghill. It accompanied one of the first copies of *A Christmas Story* to arrive from the printers.

145

'If I can persuade Elizabeth to keep me free for three months,' he said, 'I'll write a book of bulk and prove, I hope, that actors can be literate.'

This was the period (the mid-sixties) when, more and more, Rich seriously contemplated a move away from films back to the theatre but, more particularly, to writing and teaching. He knew he had talents which were not stretched even in the best movies and with youth turning to middle age (he was forty in 1965) he felt a genuine desire to use his time, that most valuable commodity, to better advantage. Without knowing it, I suspect, Elizabeth encouraged his deliberations. Confident in his love for her, he found the strength to think beyond tomorrow. Elizabeth's influence was not always for the good, as we shall see, but in the early years of their relationship she above all others helped him to make sense of what was churning around in his mind.

Another important influence for good was Nevill Coghill whom Rich called his 'wise counsel'. They met infrequently but in correspondence Nevill was always ready to advise his protege and to help him achieve his ambitions. In many ways he was the natural successor to Phil Burton who, in Rich's view, lost his claim to offer objective guidance when he started inflating his reputation as a talent spotter ('I discovered Richard Burton') to boost his own flagging career.

As early as 1961 when Rich was in *Camelot*, Nevill was writing to urge his return to Shakespearian theatre. A specific project, a new production of *The Winter's Tale*, was mentioned. But Rich was already mesmerised by the prospect of donning a toga in *Cleopatra*. He sent his regrets.

'I'm afraid that with modern actors, especially if they combine film work with the stage, the idea of accepting an attractive offer spontaneously is dead. My commitments loom for years. In fact, the only free time I shall have in the next couple of years will come about only if the next play I do on Broadway fails quickly.'

Three years on, having emerged from his trial by media to discover some peace of mind, Rich was more disposed to listen to Nevill and to think about renewing his links with Oxford. One much discussed idea was for Rich to play Dr Faustus, a role he had always coveted.

Meanwhile, on the strength of the critical and financial success of *Becket* and *The Night of the Iguana*, Rich was buoyed up for one of the greatest theatrical challenges of his career. He was to play Hamlet on Broadway. This daunting prospect originated with a between-scenes chat with John Gielgud on the set of *Becket* in which John played the King of France. It was coming up to the year of Shakespeare's quatercentenary and both agreed thay had to do something to mark the occasion. To miss out was the equivalent of resigning from the best club in town. With both of them, though for critically different reasons, feeling that Rich had not quite mastered Hamlet at the Old Vic, John struck a chord when he suggested a second attempt. The thought had already occurred to Rich a few weeks earlier but such then was his lack of confidence that when Peter O'Toole said he was lobbying to play Hamlet at the National, Rich had quickly backed off. Now with encouragement from Gielgud his interest revived. But the problem of the O'Toole Hamlet remained.

'We can't run in tandem,' said Rich.

Gielgud waved a delicate hand. 'You could if you played Broadway.'

Rich was dubious. After the *Cleopatra* debacle he was not quite sure how he would be received in the United States. In any case, Shakespeare on Broadway was a rarity; profitable Shakespeare even more so.

Again, John Gielgud was reassuring. He had just returned from a successful New York run of his 'solo Shakespeare recital', *Ages of Man*.

'Do remember, dear boy,' he purred, 'the Americans are the most dreadful snobs. They only appreciate Shakespeare when it is spoken in pure English.'

The dragon bristled.

'John, you may have forgotten. I am Welsh.'

Gielgud was unabashed. 'Oh very well,' he responded sweetly, 'it is *almost* the same thing.'

They shifted to less sensitive matters. The producer for *Ages of Man* had been Alexander Cohen who was well versed in presenting the classics to American audiences. It was left that Rich would sound him out on the prospect of a Burton Hamlet.

But Rich was still not sure of himself. So instead of contacting Alex Cohen direct he asked his friend John Heyman, a young British film producer who worked on both sides of the Atlantic, to get a reaction.

It did not take long to come through. Cohen was enthusiastic and wanted a meeting. Now, Rich felt he was on secure ground. Soon he was telling everyone that after *Night of the Iguana*, he was Broadway bound. But by the time Cohen arrived in London, several other producers were trying to get in on the act while Rich was happily raising the stakes.

At their first meeting, over dinner, Rich told Alex Cohen that he wanted John Gielgud to direct him. 'Do you think he'll agree?'

Cohen was sure he would though privately he felt that the two greats were not an ideal match. Gielgud's style was to let the poetry carry the plot, to create what a critic described as 'vocalised word music'. The younger actor was more interested in discovering meaning, in putting across a convincing story even when this meant occasionally sacrificing the lyrical splendour of Shakespeare's verse.

But Gielgud himself did not seem to anticipate any difficulty – even though Rich's earlier version of Hamlet had wounded his poetical sensitivity. He told Cohen he had a notion to stage *Hamlet* in modern dress. Would Rich go along with that? Since my brother's concept of heaven was never again to be asked to put on costume, his acceptance was immediate. The show was on the road.

And what a show! Even before casting, media interest was vigorous, bordering on the frantic. After the sojourn in Mexico when the Burton–Taylor affair lost a little of its novelty value, Rich looked forward to publicity tempered by discretion. No chance.

With two divorces imminent and the certainty of a marriage to follow to make all come right (at least in the eyes of the popular press) his Hamlet became a sideshow to the continuing marital drama. The effect on Rich was to bring on a severe attack of the jitters. Though polite and outwardly cheerful in rehearsals he easily lost his concentration and had trouble remembering his lines, a problem which was still in evidence when the play opened its pre-Broadway tour at the O'Keefe Center in Toronto.

It was not the only fault with the production. There was a feeling among the critics that director and star were somehow at odds with each other, the Burton energy and passion trying to escape from the restraints of Gielgud's agonising, introspective version of *Hamlet* – and not quite making it. There is no doubt they had trouble in agreeing an interpretation of *Hamlet*. Though he took guidance from the director when it suited him, Rich was determined to go his own way. Sadly it was in a direction where Gielgud was unable to help him. The result was an undisciplined and unpredictable Hamlet who, at times, had the rest of the cast running round in circles.

The other curiosity of the production was the use of modern dress. It was an interesting if not entirely original idea to give the play a contemporary feel but Gielgud decided he could best do this by having his actors appear in rehearsal clothes. He told everyone to go out shopping for the sort of casual clothes they would wear for a cold day in Toronto or New York. Naturally, when they reappeared they looked ready not so much for rehearsal (a comfortable, rather shabby look) as for a smart weekend in the country. A fancy dress weekend, perhaps, what with those swords and scabbards and long flowing capes.

The audience was not quite sure how to take it and those who were unfamiliar with *Hamlet* were thoroughly confused when actors doubled on some parts. But then, as David Dillon Evans who played Osric and Reynaldo was heard to point out, Gielgud assumed that everybody knew *Hamlet*, line by line.

Whatever the faults on stage at that first night at the O'Keefe Center, they were obliterated from the public memory by the performance at the King Edward Sheraton where a crowd gathered at the elevators to see 'Liz and Dick' leave for the theatre and in the O'Keefe auditorium where the audience concentrated its attention on the seat in the front stalls reserved for Elizabeth. When the curtain rose and she had still not appeared, some of those to the rear kept standing up in the hope of spotting her. When she did slip in, soon after the beginning of the second act (for once, the delayed entrance was scheduled) there was a buzz of appreciation which, on stage, must have sounded like the warning of an earthquake. In a sense, I suppose it was.

Despite several hostile reviews, advance sales on a three-week run were at such a level as to justify an extra week. But Rich had no illusions as to the reason for the box office bonanza. After a party in which he and Elizabeth spent most of the time surrounded by security guards, he complained bitterly, 'People just stare at us as if we're prize animals.'

Interest in the Burton affair climbed again when it was announced that divorce proceedings on both sides were finalised and that the couple were free to marry. In fact, it was not as easy as that. Elizabeth's divorce from Eddie Fisher was hedged by legal niceties which advisers thought best not to challenge by remarrying within American jurisdiction. The answer was to take advantage of the more liberal Mexican marriage law which Alex Cohen, in his capacity as producer and father confessor contrived to do by arranging for a ceremony in the grounds of the Mexican embassy in Montreal. It took place on Sunday 15 March, 1964. Bob Wilson was best man. Hume Cronyn (Polonius), one of the best of actors and kindliest of men, was there as a witness. Less than an hour later there was a repeat performance conducted by a Unitarian minister on the eighth floor of the Ritz Carlton hotel. After which, the party flew back to Toronto to find a dressing room full of useful kitchen utensils – presents from the cast. Among sundry pots and pans the bride noticed, with appreciation, two rolling pins.

After the final curtain call at Monday's performance, Rich presented his wife 'for the first time on any stage'. As Elizabeth joined him to receive tumultuous applause, Rich spoke Hamlet's line to Ophelia in the nunnery scene, 'I say we will have no more marriages.' In response to our cable of congratulations he wired back, 'And they said it wouldn't last.'

Chaos in Toronto was followed by hysteria in Boston where the play was booked for a two-week run at the Schubert Theater immediately prior to its Broadway opening. When their plane touched down a crowd of some five thousand was waiting at Logan airport. It did not wait for long. As the pilot taxied towards the reception area, the fans broke through the police barriers and rushed on to the tarmac, bringing the aircraft to an abrupt halt. Very sensibly, the pilot refused to budge until his way was cleared. This took an hour at least by which time airport control had figured the best way of having their visitors disembark without causing a riot was to tug the aircraft into one of the maintenance hangers. There, a limousine was waiting to ferry the Burtons via the freight terminal to their hotel. But the excitement was not over yet. Another crowd, mostly fans but with a heavy contingent of press photographers, refused to clear a way through the lobby. In the melée Elizabeth was pushed up hard against a wall and hurt her back. Rich had his jacket torn and lost some hair to a maniac souvenir hunter.

Knowing what it was to be like for the rest of the run, Alex Cohen took over all the rooms on the Burton floor. It was the only way of retaining a little privacy.

Boston audiences enjoyed a Burton who had come to terms with his role. Or perhaps the role had come to terms with him because what we saw on stage was Richard Burton playing Richard Burton playing Hamlet. It was a commanding performance which delighted audiences and most of the critics for its power and excitement.

By now, Rich had settled into a routine. Maybe the life of a super celebrity was not so bad after all. He was friends once more with the press who clearly had decided that his rightful place was on the front page. He enjoyed the crowd of convivial acquaintances who gathered every time he showed his face, though afterwards when the barroom haze had cleared he was hard put to it to remember anyone's name.

And then there was the money to be made – lots of it. When *Hamlet* finished its record-breaking run on Broadway (four more performances than Gielgud had achieved when he was the prince), the gross was close to two million dollars. A dreadful film version made with the new 'electronic-optical process of Electronominium Theatrofilm' and inadequate lighting (Rich, dressed in black, seemed to disappear for large parts of his performance) brought in almost as much again before it was consigned to the archives. No wonder thoughts of retiring to Oxford were temporarily forgotten.

Elizabeth too was content to jolly along for a while – in her own laidback style. Opening night in Boston found her in her hotel enjoying a TV re-run of *How Green Was My Valley*, the 1941 Welsh weepie in which her friend Roddy McDowell played the juvenile lead. When Alex Cohen called for her at 6.45, fifteen minutes before curtain up, she was still glued to the set and had not even changed out of her bath robe.

Alex tried the gentle touch. 'Elizabeth, please, it's time to go. Do you think you might dress?'

Elizabeth glanced up. 'Not before the movie's over,' she declared firmly.

They arrived an hour late.

Rich was surprisingly tolerant of his wife's inadequate time-keeping. He saw it as all part of her act which he treated as a huge joke. He told friends, 'Elizabeth is one of those women who thinks if she's fifteen minutes late she's half an hour early.' Or, 'Elizabeth will be late for the Last Judgement – without an excuse.'

The build-up for New York was stupendous. The play was on the way to a sell-out a month before the critics came in and by opening night tickets were changing hands at four or five times their face value.

In the event, the reviews justified the euphoria. Rich was praised for his 'thinking man's Hamlet', more heroic than tragic, while John Gielgud was congratulated for 'pitching the performance to match Mr Burton's range and intensity'. In other words, the critics did not resent the play being adapted to suit the Burton style though *Time* pointed out that Hamlet portrayed as a hero 'can scarcely evoke the torment of a man who is to be overmastered by fortune and by fate'. I fancy London critics, ever the purists, might have made the same point, but much more forcefully.

With all the signals out for an extended run, the publicity machine went into overdrive. Every night crowds of sightseers blocked Forty-Sixth Street in front of the Lunt-Fontanne Theater. At about nine the police turned up with barriers to create a path from the stage door to the limousine parked in the road. At nine-thirty Elizabeth arrived to collect Rich who by then was well into his last act. An hour or so later, the couple appeared at the stage door. To make sure everybody got a good view they stood for a few moments in a spotlight beamed from an opposite building. They then hurried to the car which had to edge its way through the screaming multitude into Eighth Avenue.

None of this was strictly necessary. As someone on the production side said to me, it would have been a simple matter to avoid the mob by taking the fire exit and flagging down a passing taxi. But this was just too boring. Rich was not prepared to miss out on the chance to be the centre of attention. No longer Mr Cleopatra, he was Mr Burton in the company of Mrs Burton. For the first time in their marriage he was seen to be more newsworthy than his wife.

His drinking capacity continued to amaze. When I was with him he always managed three or four powerful martinis before going on stage and these were just a top-up on the day's intake. Alex Cohen remembers the evening Rich finished a bottle of bourbon – a half at each interval. Yet despite some stresses in the company, occasioned by inadequate playing by one of the principals, Rich was the model of consideration and good humour. And always, he was strictly the professional. He was there, on time, for every performance.

Only once did he show any signs of nervousness. It was when a party from a German adoption society turned up to meet Rich and Elizabeth. Their visit was to check out Eddie Fisher's successor as a suitable father for Maria, a four-year-old German girl whom Elizabeth planned to adopt. On his best behaviour, Rich ended a lengthy meeting with the delegation by offering them tickets for that night's performance. But he felt something more was needed to impress. It was not until he was on stage that he realised how he might pay a very special compliment. This is how Rich told the story.

'It suddenly came to me. Why not do a speech in German? Of course, if I'd have had any sense I would have chosen one of the lesser speeches but then – who would have noticed? So I roared into "To be or not to be" in my best Teutonic. The audience was a bit uneasy, nothing more, and the Germans were pleased. But all hell broke loose behind the clothesrack stage left where Polonius and Claudius were eavesdropping on Hamlet. "Sein oder nicht sein: das ist die Frage" was the last thing they expected to hear at the Lunt-Fontanne.'

The adoption order for Maria was confirmed soon afterwards. A pretty little four-year-old, she had a deformed leg which Elizabeth was determined to correct. A series of operations performed by the best surgeons justified her faith. Before she was much older Maria was able to walk normally.

After playing Hamlet for 136 performances in succession, Rich departed for Paris, taking Elizabeth, the children (Michael Wilding, aged eleven, Christoper Wilding, aged nine, Liza Todd, aged six and Maria) and sundry attendants and court jesters including Brook Williams, Bob Wilson and Ivor. The exodus was signalled by Aaron Frosch

20. Richard, Elizabeth and daughter Kate. (*Rex Features*)

21. Richard in middle age. (*Rex Features*)

22. Richard was always an avid reader. (*Rex Features*)

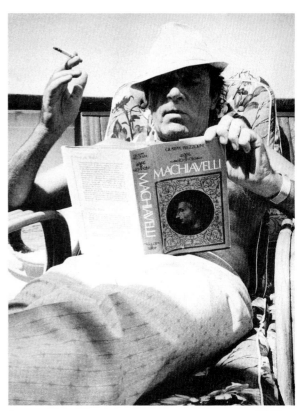

23. Richard talking to students at Oxford. (*BBC Hulton Picture Library*)

24. Richard and his third wife, Susan. (*BBC Hulton Picture Library*)

25. Richard arriving at Elizabeth Taylor's fiftieth birthday party – wearing the mink jacket she had bought him. 1982. (*Topham*)

26. *and* 27. Richard's lifestyle begins to take its toll. (*Rex Features*)

28. Richard with his last wife Sally soon after their marriage. 1983. (*Topham*)

29. Sally in 1986. (*Topham*)

30. 31. *and* 32. Three portrayals: Richard as Wagner (*Rex Features*), Trotsky (*Rex Features*) and O'Brien in 1984 (*Topham*)

33. Richard with his daughter Kate in *Ellis Island*, Richard's last film. (*Rex Features*)
34. Richard towards the end of his life. 1984. (*Rex Features*)
35. Graham and his wife Hilary at the London memorial service with brother Verdun and his wife Betty. (*Topham*)

36. The funeral in Celigny, Switzerland. *From left to right* 1. Brook Williams
2. Valerie Douglas   3. Dai   4. Cassie   5. Graham   6. Hilda   7. Betty, Verdun's
wife   8. Verdun   9. Sally   10. Maria   11. Steve Carson, Maria's husband
12. Ron Berkeley   13. Cis (*Rex Features*)

37. Sally at the London memorial service. (*Topham*)

38. Elizabeth and Cis at a private service at the house in Pontryhydyfen. The service, performed by the Reverend Eric Williams, followed closely the pattern of the service held for Richard's father years before. (*Topham*)

39. Family and friends gather to pay their last tributes outside the chapel at the memorial service in Pontryhydyfen. (*Topham*)

who warned that dallying on Broadway, or anywhere else in the States, could soon attract a hefty demand for back taxes.

The attraction of Paris was the opportunity for Elizabeth to get back into movies. For over a year she had limited herself to playing Mrs Burton, a part she enjoyed but one which did not make any money. Moreover, there was the risk that a longer absence from the set could adversely affect her earning power. So when an offer came from MGM with the customary one-million-dollar fee attached, Elizabeth was hooked. The touchy problem of what Rich would do for three months was solved, to Elizabeth's satisfaction, by inviting him to co-star, albeit at half her rate for the job.

That a Californian setting was recreated in France was one of the least bizarre features of the movie. If Rich and Elizabeth were keen to escape the grip of the taxman, MGM was happy to take advantage of lower operating costs. Given a highly favourable exchange rate there was plenty of scope in the budget for the stars to enjoy a majestic lifestyle.

All this was on the plus side. The minus was the story line and the script which were, to put it mildly, banal to the point of incredulity. *The Sandpiper* was the story of an affair between a bohemian artist and a lapsed Episcopalian minister.

'It was,' said Rich, 'pure soap opera but without the subtlety.'

Elizabeth was more circumspect. 'We never thought it would be an artistic masterpiece.'

Allowed a free choice I believe Rich would have turned down *The Sandpiper*. He told me more than once he was worried about the script which reminded him uncomfortably of the potboilers of his earlier career. But as he told me when he rang to suggest a visit to Paris, 'It is Elizabeth's turn, you know. She's done a lot for me. She can't just go on following me around.'

They both kept alive the hope that dross would turn to gold. They were disappointed. Rich comforted himself that, at least, they had done their best.

'There's not much you can do with a bad film. With a play you can tickle it, coax it into life. But when a film is dead, it stays dead.'

The compensation was the scale of creature comforts – more lavish than anything he had previously encountered. At the studios in Boulogne-sur-Seine he and Elizabeth shared a caravan about the size of a small hotel. They were ferried around in a Rolls-Royce which had a little red dragon engraved on the nearside door. The booze flowed as from a ruptured brewery and the parties were open-ended.

I sampled the VIP treatment at first hand when Rich asked me to go to Los Angeles to collect Elizabeth's mother and bring her to Paris. Normally such a task would have been totally unnecessary. Mrs Taylor was quite capable of looking after herself. But not long before Elizabeth's father had suffered a stroke from which he never recovered. The shock of his death was still very much in all our minds and Elizabeth spared no effort in trying to make life tolerable for her mother. In this latest instance, the best service was on offer at every stage of the journey. I felt guilty for those who were travelling economy.

Though he never made a show of planning ahead Rich must have been giving thought to his future because early on in the filming of *The Sandpiper* I saw a pile of well thumbed scripts in his hotel suite. I can't imagine when he found the time to read them.

On a weekend trip to Wales he talked enthusiastically of John Le Carré whose excursion into the seamier aspects of cold war espionage were judged by Rich to be a healthy antidote to the whizz bang heroics of the Bond movies. He had seen a treatment for the third and most cleverly constructed of the Le Carré novels, *The Spy Who Came in from the Cold*. I read the book and wondered how he could possibly make it work for him. The part of Leamas, the weary and expendable agent who engages blindly in one last game of double double dealing behind the Iron Curtain, called for low-key acting of a style that was certainly foreign to Rich. Hitherto when he had played the victim he went down bellowing defiance. Yet Leamas, the bewildered innocent who discovered too late how he had been manipulated, made his exit on a feeble whisper.

Maybe Rich imagined that he could keep up the part. Or perhaps he really did want to try something new although he gave no hint he was about to show us an unexpected side to his talent. My belief is that the director, Martin Ritt, who had taught at the Actors Studio and was known for his ability to extract strong performances from his actors, persuaded Rich that his character had great inner strength which, to be credible, must be kept below the surface.

The result was the best Burton film to date and probably the best he ever made. Disobeying all the rules for contemporary spy drama, Ritt filmed in black and white creating images said by Le Carré to be as 'factual and clinical as a street accident'.

*The Spy Who Came in from the Cold* was given a rapturous send-off by the critics. Leonard Mosley of the *Daily Express*, who had had some harsh things to say about Rich in the past, thought that Leamas compensated 'for every bad part he has ever played and every indiscretion he has ever committed off the screen or on'. He added, 'If he doesn't win an Oscar for it this year, there is not only no justice left in Hollywood but no judgement either.'

Mosley might have tempered his view if he had known what the competition was to be. Rich was indeed nominated for an Oscar but then so was Laurence Olivier for *Othello*, Rod Steiger for *The Pawnbroker* and Oscar Werner (who was also in *The Spy Who Came in from the Cold*) for *Ship of Fools*. In the event, they all lost out to Lee Marvin for his marvellously comic portrayal of the inebriated gunslinger in *Cat Ballou*.

Rich took his defeat in good part though on his fourth Oscar nomination, his expectations had been high.

'What do you think they are trying to tell me?' he asked rhetorically. 'That Lee Marvin is a better class of drunk?'

Filming *The Spy* was a pleasure and a profit. Rich set himself a new market value with his three-quarter-million-dollar fee from Paramount. At the same time he was working with people he respected and whose company he enjoyed, including old friends like Tim, alias Robert Hardy, and Warren Mitchell. At his best, he was warm and expansive. With Claire Bloom, cast as his girlfriend, he was edgy and nervous. Thoughts about what might have been disturbed him. He tried to keep his mind on the present.

'I know just the part for you,' he announced to Tim Hardy when they were talking about another film just about to go into production. 'It'll only take you a few days. I'll talk to the director.'

Tim was grateful but felt bound to decline. 'I'm off on holiday. I promised my wife months ago we would have this break. If I went back on my word, she'd never forgive me.'

Rich had the answer. 'Don't worry. You can follow on in our plane.'

Elizabeth thought this an excellent idea. 'It just sits there at Geneva. It's about time it paid its way.'

But Tim was adamant. 'All right,' said Rich, 'use the plane anyway.' And he went off to pour another drink. When he came back, Elizabeth was showing signs of impatience.

'Well, go on, love. Get on the phone. Tim wants to leave tomorrow.' Which is how Tim Hardy and his wife came to travel to the sun in real style.

There was a memorable weekend when, on an impulse, Rich and Elizabeth flew in from location in Dublin for the last occasion to date that England beat Wales at Cardiff Arms Park. In case there was any doubt as to her loyalty, Elizabeth wore a red bowler which, in moments of elation, she waved above her head, shouting and singing with the most raucous of our party. After the match we went to the Queen's Hotel along with several thousand other Welsh supporters.

Elizabeth seemed to be taking it all in good part, though filtered through the roar of the crowd I doubt she understood most of what was said to her. I worried more about the risk of her being trampled underfoot.

I leaned close to Rich. 'Let's find a way out of here.'

'Any ideas?' he shouted back.

We were squashed against the bar. I looked over to the door where thirsty fans trying to get in were holding back those who were trying to get out. There was no escape that way.

'It looks like the back door for us,' I roared.

We took hold of Elizabeth, one on each arm, and hoisted her up and over the bar. As we scrambled after her there was a moment when Elizabeth, red bowler still in place, stood in magnificent isolation behind the beer pumps. A customer surveyed her with interest.

'About time too,' he slurred. 'I want two Guinnesses, a gin and tonic and a pint of bitter.' He looked at her more closely. 'Here, haven't I seen you somewhere before?'

Rich grabbed Elizabeth and pushed her towards the kitchens.

'Hang on, hang on,' pleaded the customer, as we made our exit, 'what about my drinks.'

But making *The Spy* was perhaps more of a struggle for the Burtons than any of us realised at the time. To play Leamas convincingly Rich had to look bloated and tired and to feel despair, a mood from which it was not easy to break out, particularly when there were two bottles of vodka inside him. He drank heavily, he joked, because it was one of the terms of his contract. Leamas had to be convincing as a downhill boozer.

'Why act it,' asked Rich, 'when I can do it for real?'

Elizabeth, I suspect, was not entirely at home in her role as the Good Samaritan. She travelled around more on her own, always with a good reason (a visit to her mother in Los Angeles, a trip to Paris to console one of her staff whose teenage son had been killed in a shooting accident) but partly to escape the claustrophobia of someone else's film set.

The tensions surfaced easily. When *The Sandpiper* was released to a universal panning Elizabeth had to endure a chorus of 'I told you so,' from Rich. She got her own back a few months later when the box office returns showed an indecent profit.

Meanwhile, Maria went down with a bad attack of measles, valuable jewellery disappeared from Elizabeth's hotel suite in Dublin and Sybil remarried. This last item overlapped bad and good news. The first reaction from her former husband was 'Good luck to her, she deserves it.' But then, in his cups, he could be vicious about the younger man who had replaced him. Rich was just forty and was feeling his age. He did not like to be reminded of the competition close behind him.

After *The Spy* it was time for another joint effort. Both realised the financial clout they could muster when they appeared together. At the same time, neither wanted to gamble on another *Sandpiper*.

'It was our notoriety that sold that film,' Rich declared. 'It's a trick you can play only once.'

There was no shortage of offers. One that looked interesting but impracticable was a screen treatment of an Edward Albee play, *Who's Afraid of Virginia Woolf?* Among the most exciting of the younger playwrights, Albee had hit the jackpot with *Virginia Woolf*. A withering exposure of a certain type of middle class family, recognisable on both sides of the Atlantic, the play caught the popular mood of rebellion against domestic hypocrisy. But the storyline seemed ill-suited to the screen. There was not much the camera could do with a savage verbal punch-up except record it straight which meant putting an awful trust in the quality of dialogue and acting. A cynical producer might have asked, 'How many punters will pay good money to be depressed?'

Albee was fortunate in attracting a producer who could see the possibilities. Ernest Lehman was better known as a script writer and in this capacity had a number of successful social dramas to his credit such as *Executive Suite* and *Sweet Smell of Success*. But while both these were unconventional for their time, they depended on all-star casts to start them on their way. The same was needed for *Virginia Woolf* which was why the script turned up in Elizabeth's mail.

Legend has it that when Elizabeth was asked if she wanted to play Martha no one had any idea of suggesting Rich for the opposing role. I suppose it is just possible but Rich himself never believed it for a moment. It was standard practice to send a script to one of them in the hope that they might, of their own volition, come up with a joint proposal. That way it was likely to be cheaper for the studio.

The theory was, catch Elizabeth first and Richard Burton will not be far behind. But with *Virginia Woolf*, it almost didn't work. Elizabeth, who had seen rehearsals of the play in Paris, took an abiding dislike to Martha. And who could blame her? Elizabeth was thirty-five, very attractive and best known for her sympathetic roles. Martha was fifty-three, fat, loud-mouthed and a slut. The part, she decided, was not for her.

Rich was less hasty. He was attracted by the dialogue, some of the finest he had ever seen.

'You've only to read the first lines and you know this is a great play.'

So what if Elizabeth had to play against type. Wasn't that what acting was all about? 'I've just proved it with *The Spy*, haven't I?' he argued.

'Okay, so why don't you play George?' Elizabeth demanded to know.

The other part of the equation was filled in when Mike Nichols, whose Broadway reputation endeared him to Rich, signed as director. Warner Bros. had themselves a deal.

*Who's Afraid of Virginia Woolf?* was a professional commitment to a three month slanging match in front of the cameras. It took its toll on Rich and Elizabeth as it did on George Segal and Sandy Dennis, the other pair of fine actors who were the butt of George and Martha's cruel games. But they did not have to live together.

Professionally, the film was a triumph. Rich turned in the second best performance of his career and Elizabeth, by far the best of her career. The prize was an Oscar for Elizabeth, her second, and yet another near miss for Rich who lost out to his old rival Paul Scofield for his Thomas More in a worthy rendering of *A Man for All Seasons*.

*Virginia Woolf* shocked many including the puritan diehards in our family who thought that husband and wife behaving in such a way on screen was too degrading for words. But if a play or film is supposed to make you sit up and take notice then *Virginia Woolf* achieved its objective ten times over.

The cost, to Rich and Elizabeth, was the illusion that they could fight without getting hurt.

# Chapter 12

Over-running on *Virginia Woolf* and the subsequent cancellation of another film allowed Rich to fulfil his promise to Nevill Coghill to perform at Oxford on behalf of the appeal to build a new theatre in Oxford. One hundred thousand pounds was needed. Rich determined to raise every penny.

So it was that in February 1966, just over twenty-one years after his departure from Oxford for the RAF, Rich made his pilgrimage back to academia. It could so easily have been a disaster. A different type of actor might have lorded it over the students, expecting obeisance when vigorous debate on equal terms was more in order. But whatever his faults, the need for unmerited devotion, least of all from the young, was not among them. Rich threw himself in at the deep end, accepting every invitation to talk and argue about the business of acting. His audience, mostly of the university dramatic society (OUDS), were enthralled. However long the seminar and however late the hour, they wanted more. Nevill Coghill suggested half jokingly, that Rich should set aside a few weeks each year to lecture at the university.

'You are a natural teacher,' he told his former student. 'We could do with you here.'

Rich said he would think about it.

The rehearsal period for *Dr Faustus* was dangerously short. Rich had just ten days to fashion a complex role. Nevill, who directed, assumed that his star knew his lines before he set foot on stage. He was wrong. Rich could recite the big speeches but for the rest of the play he wandered like a lost man, groping for Marlowe's words and, when they would not come, throwing in a few of his own. The supporting actors, OUDS members who had mugged up on their parts weeks earlier, were understandably confused. Not experienced enough to be spontaneous on stage, they were easily thrown by a missed or mistimed cue. They had my sympathy. I recalled the sheer terror Rich engendered in the cast of *Hamlet* when in the first previews in Toronto he was clearly floundering. True professionals, masters of their craft, were made as fearful as a first night understudy who learns that the star has a sore throat. *Hamlet* was a Broadway triumph. But the transformation took weeks to achieve. For *Dr Faustus*, there were only hours for Rich to bring off the trick.

He did not make it. The first night was a classic of theatrical confusion. What should have been treated as a dress rehearsal or, at best, a cheap price preview, was mounted as a full scale charity premiere. Welcoming all the pre-publicity he could get for what, after all, was a money raising event, Nevill rather naively assumed that the critics would be tolerant of the imperfections. Instead they, and their editors, accepted the Burton hype at its face value. They anticipated great things and when they suffered disappointment, they let it show.

The evening started badly with a misallocation of tickets which had some eminent critics walking up and down the side aisles looking for spare seats. The confusion was made worse by the late arrival of a section of the audience who appeared to be misinformed on the time of curtain up. That they saw the entire play was thanks, if that is the word, to the technical difficulties backstage and a subsequent delayed start. The inadequacy of behind-the-scenes support showed throughout the production but most obviously when Elizabeth made her entrance in the non-speaking role of Helen of Troy (her first part in a stage play). The billow of dry ice from which she was intended to emerge was so thick as to mask her from the first dozen rows of the stalls. For some minutes those who had paid most for their tickets saw nothing except Elizabeth's feet. With their attention thus directed they could hardly fail to notice that below her period robes, she was wearing Gucci shoes.

Rich looked nervous and distressed. The more charitable observers pointed out that for much of the play Dr Faustus is nervous and distressed. Furthermore, it was a largely amateur production for which the Burtons had given their valuable time. It was not as if either of them were aiming at a top award.

But the London critics were not easily swayed by sentiment. They found the direction fussy, the humour misplaced and the acting lamentable. Leading the attack, *The Times* declared *Faustus* 'a sad example of university drama at its worst'. The other papers were hardly less vitriolic.

The pity of it was that after two or three nights, Rich settled into the role while the other actors took strength from his gain in confidence. By the end of the week, he was turning in a performance which satisfied him and pleased his audience. Those who enjoyed the final product, as it were, fought back against the critics and their hasty denunciations. Francis Warner, a fellow of St Peter's College, and an enthusiastic friend of the Burtons, told readers of the *Western Mail* that Faustus was 'the greatest performance' of Rich's career. 'As the last words faded . . . we were aware not only that this Faustus was Everyman but that the rendering was that of a great actor at the full, majestic stretch of his powers.'

Other defenders of OUDS leapt into that familiar battleground of literary discourse, the letters column of *The Times*. Praising Rich's 'electrifying performance', the writer Wolf Mankowitz accused the theatre reviewers of missing the real significance of the production. 'It is, surely, that by contributing his superb talent and incredibly valuable and highly sought after time to a student production, Mr Burton has made it possible for several generations of young theatrical talent to work with greater freedom and in better circumstances. By the gift to the Oxford University Dramatic Society of not only his services in the live theatre, but also of the total ownership of the projected film which he and Miss Taylor are to make with Mr Nevill Coghill, the Burtons' contribution to this Oxford nursery of the theatrical future is likely to be in the neighbourhood of £250,000 to £500,000.'

Unfortunately the appeal income from *Dr Faustus* was far below expectations. The stage production made just £3,000 while the film, financed by Rich to the tune of over £300,000, was a disaster at the box office and returned a loss.

As Elizabeth was heard to comment, 'We might as well have played Hollywood and let the profs have whatever we earned.'

But Rich did not see it in such cut and dried terms. His willingness to appear in *Faustus* and, with Nevill Coghill, to co-direct the film had less to do with the theatre appeal than with his perception of how his career should be developing. With the exception of *The Sandpiper* he had enjoyed a fair run of good work which had re-established him as as an actor to rank with the best. He had also made money which suggested that it was not only the junk which could command record fees. It was now that he began to think that maybe his highly bankable name could be used to best purpose by participating in film reconstructions of the classics. *Dr Faustus*, which came at the end of 1966, fell well short of every target – artistic and financial. But between the stage and the screen versions of *Dr Faustus*, he scored a palpable hit with the filming of *The Taming of the Shrew*.

The idea sprang from the fertile imagination of Franco Zeffirelli, the cosmopolitan Italian-born director who was best known for his operatic extravaganzas and, in Britain, as the instigator of two Old Vic productions, a joyously memorable *Romeo and Juliet* and a totally misconceived *Othello* with John Gielgud.

Having made up his mind to break into films, it was natural for Zeffirelli to choose a story which lent itself to colour and excitement. *The Taming of the Shrew* was ideal. It had been filmed only once before, with Douglas Fairbanks and Mary Pickford in 1928. That version had not been a success but it had opened up one or two interesting ideas, such as livening up the domestic conflict with an infusion of slapstick and of casting a husband and wife team as Petruchio and Katherine. (The earlier film had seen out the last years of the Fairbanks–Pickford marriage.)

Rich had first met Zeffirelli in Paris when he and Elizabeth were going through the torture of filming *The Sandpiper* while the director was enjoying the triumph of his stage version of *Who's Afraid of Virginia Woolf?*

Zeffirelli came back into their lives when Rich was filming *The Spy Who Came in from the Cold*. By then Rich and Elizabeth had decided on a team effort to translate *Virginia Woolf* to the screen though Elizabeth was still uncertain about her role and what it might do to her fan mail. The thought of another rough edged part was, for the moment, more than she dared contemplate. While Rich enthused at the prospect of working with Zeffirelli to popularise Shakespeare, Elizabeth stonewalled.

'Why can't we take one death defying risk at a time?'

But when they were into *Virginia Woolf*, knowing they had a winner, and Columbia had come up with a generous budget which was to gross the couple close on four million dollars, Elizabeth surrendered.

'Hell, why not? After this lot, it could even be fun.'

The location for *Taming of the Shrew* was Rome, a city which brought back not entirely happy memories for Rich and Elizabeth.

The paparazzi was out in force. Setting up camp outside the Burtons' villa, Ivan Kroscenko, the self-styled leader of the pack, threatened a battle royal.

'You'll notice I'm wearing my leather combat jacket,' he told a television interviewer.

At first, there was little to report. Though it was Zeffirelli's first major film, his experience in coping with temperamental opera singers made him a perfect master of ceremonies. The only serious problem was trying to match the work patterns of the two stars. Rich liked to start early in the morning to dispose of the main business of the day before settling down to a long, liquid lunch. If he reappeared at all in the afternoon, Zeffirelli could count himself lucky. Elizabeth on the other hand needed the hours before noon for dressing and make-up. It was, after all, a lavish costume production – a contrast to *Virginia Woolf* where she could just slip into something slovenly.

The logistics would have been simpler had Elizabeth and Rich not shared so many scenes. But unless there was to be a wholly original interpretation of *The Shrew* with Petruchio and Katherine barely meeting, the film depended on one of the stars accepting a radical change of lifestyle.

It was Elizabeth who gave way. She did not like it but she came on set every morning without complaint. Her conversion said a lot for Zeffirelli's powers of persuasion.

The only disaster was when the paparazzi, deprived for too long of sour gossip, staged a horrendous spectacle. Rich and Elizabeth were in the hotel lobby with Maria when they were confronted with a strange couple who wanted to pose with them for pictures. As the camera bulbs flashed, Rich was suddenly aware of what was happening. They were standing side by side with Maria's real parents who had been flown in from Germany by courtesy of the gutter press. Maria screamed, Rich lashed out and the photographers went away complaining that the Burtons were so uncooperative.

Aside from this unpleasant memory *The Taming of the Shrew* was a joyous romp. Some of the London critics were a bit sniffy about the play, seeing it as substandard Shakespeare out of tune with modern feminist ideas, and were dismissive of the Zeffirelli treatment which played up the comedy to the hysteria of knockabout farce. But where reviewers were able to cut themselves free from conventions, the praise was ecstatic. Picking up on the Zeffirelli sense of fun, the American press vied with each other to create the most outrageous puns.

Acclaiming the Burton Petruchio as 'the lusty, magisterial master Shakespeare meant him to be,' *Time* magazine depicted the film as 'a perfectly matched battle of the sexes in which the male of the species proves deadlier than the moll.' *Newsweek* countered with praise for Elizabeth as the 'sharp tongued tigress' who 'makes Kate seem the ideal bawd of Avon'.

For my money, Elizabeth pulled off the extraordinary trick of making attractive an otherwise irritating woman. Her Kate was a tough cookie, but she never lost her spark of femininity. A wonderful cast which boasted Michael York, Michael Hordern, Cyril Cusack and

Victor Spinetti caught the mood perfectly and stopped just short of playing over the top.

I loved the film and so did everyone in my circle. Of great pride to Rich was the knowledge that he was reaching a public not otherwise attracted to Shakespeare. Success here spurred his ambition to film more of the classics.

The London premiere was a rollicking West End beano with the added glitter of a royal guest. Princess Margaret was in attendance with her husband, Lord Snowdon, formerly Anthony Armstrong-Jones. This allowed Rich to make jokes about 'keeping up with the Joneses', a feat he achieved with masterly ease by taking twenty rooms at the Dorchester and inviting his entire family to spend a long weekend in London.

We arrived Friday evening, a party of three dozen or more, to a sumptuous dinner hosted by Rich and Elizabeth. The next day, after a late start, the men departed to Twickenham to see England play Scotland in the Calcutta Cup while their wives bought up Harrods. Another splendid feast was followed on Sunday by a party which went on for most of the night. And none of us had yet seen the film.

That was on Monday. To accommodate his personal guests at the Odeon, Leicester Square, the flagship of the Rank circuit (it really did have the look and style of a cruise liner) Rich paid charity prices for 150 seats. When the first of our convoy of chauffeur driven Daimlers pulled up alongside the red carpet, the last car still had not left the Dorchester.

Arriving early, I readily admit to the pleasure of vicarious fame when, as a Richard Burton lookalike, I caught the attention of on-lookers. Autograph books were pushed under my nose. I tried to wave them away but this did not go down too well and since easy explanations were not in order (just try shouting against a concert of admiring fans) I signed anything and everything with an indecipherable scrawl. I like to think there are still a few ageing romantics who hold dear the memory of Graham Jenkins masquerading as his brother.

The evident pleasure of the audience – laughter, applause and loud cheers – put us in fine mood for the big party, star night at the Dorchester's Terrace Room which was booked through until ten the next morning.

I had no idea I knew so many famous people though here again, the Burton looks made for easy identification.

'Who was that you were talking to?' asked Hilda.

'Sophia Loren,' I said, firmly.

'Don't be silly,' said Dai, 'that was Gina Lollobrigida.'

164

I was on safer ground with long standing friends of Rich such as Stanley Baker and Emlyn Williams though I did have some trouble remembering Laurence Harvey. Evidently, Princess Margaret had the same problem because when she asked what he was doing and he said he was working in dockland (where he happened to be filming) she must have assumed the worst.

'I see,' she murmured sweetly. 'Well, never mind. I do hear there are some divine little places down there.'

By the early hours the Jenkins family was in the ascendancy. There was plenty to celebrate – the film, Elizabeth's thirty-fifth birthday, our togetherness. We all did our party pieces.

Verdun told a couple of exaggerated stories abut our early childhood which Rich loved to hear over and over again. Hilda sang. I did my special solo which was to sing 'Sorrento' in three languages, accompanied at the piano by a rather tipsy Christopher Plummer. We finished up with the whole family ensemble performing as a massed choir. That included Cis, who had a superb soprano voice, her children, Marian and Rhianon, Verdun and Hilda and their children, Megan and Sian, and the rest of the clan. Rich and Elizabeth joined in, and we made music until the first shafts of light filtered through the curtains.

The sad moment was when we sang for Edie, the youngest of our sisters, who had died a few months earlier. Only forty-two, she was the first of our generation to go. And because it was so sudden, the loss was all the more traumatic. I could not help falling back on the old banality, 'It's later than we think.'

At breakfast we were all still in formal dress; a trifle jaded except for Elizabeth who sat there, radiant as ever, carrying enough jewellery to open a branch of Tiffanys.

Hilda leaned over towards me.

'What do you think that little lot is worth?' she asked.

Elizabeth must have overheard.

'Do you mean me or the trinkets?' she wanted to know.

Richard interrupted. 'It's the jewels she's talking about,' he said. 'She knows you're priceless.'

Elizabeth threw a bread roll at his head. He threw one back.

Judging by that day's papers a lot more than bread rolls was exchanged between Rich and Elizabeth. But I must say if there were any rows they passed me by. Could it have been that our friends in the press wanted to keep alive the titillating notion of real life copying fiction? In writing up *The Taming of the Shrew*, Donald Zec of the *Daily Mirror* gave as his subtitle, A Day in the Life of the Burtons. From this time it was a favourite with show business writers to relay every incident in the Burton relationship which seemed to re-enact scenes from *Virginia Woolf* or *The Shrew*.

Before returning home I went to see the latest acquisition – an ocean-going gin palace called *Kalizma* after three top girls, Kate, Liza and Maria. I did not have far to go. The yacht was moored on the Thames Embankment, just below Tower Bridge. But why, you might ask? Was there not enough room at the Dorchester? For humans, yes, but there was a problem with animals which were restricted from entering the country on short visits by the quarantine regulations. Since Elizabeth would not go anywhere without a small zoo, the yacht was there to accommodate her four-legged friends. In her absence two French poodles, O'Fie and E'en So, were left in charge. There was also a captain and crew of nine, but they did as they were told. No wonder the *Kalizma* was known alternatively as Noah's Ark without the flood or, less respectfully, as the most expensive dog kennel in the world.

It was, in fact, a fine craft; 147 feet of best oak fashioned at the turn of the century. Rich and Elizabeth bought it for £80,000 and spent more than twice that sum on a refitting. The stereo equipment alone cost more than my house. Among the little extras that make the lives of the super rich worth living was a 'mini moke', a vehicle designed like a jeep, which could be taken ashore to visit the sights wherever the yacht was berthed.

Mine was a fleeting visit, conducted in the glazed aftermath of a gargantuan party. I saw little. More observant, by nature and circumstances, was a friend of my younger days, Gladys Williams, who encountered the *Kalizma* a few weeks later when she was leading a group of fifty or more on a tour of the Italian lakes. Having lived most of her married life in the south of England, she had achieved a certain notoriety as the girl who went to school with Richard Burton. So, when the coach pulled into Portofino and the Italian guide announced that the splendid craft in the harbour belonged to the Burtons, the cry went up for Gladys to renew acquaintanceship with her old classmate.

'Come on love, now's your chance!'

Gladys was understandably nervous.

'Oh, I don't think I could. Anyway, they're probably not there.'

But the guide made sure she would not get away as easily as that.

'The whole town knows they are on board. I have seen them.'

By now the coach was on the jetty, just a few yards from the *Kalizma*. Gladys had no choice. She edged along the gangplank and spoke to the bearded Sicilian who stood on deck barring her way. That Rich and Elizabeth were not keen on uninvited guests was made plain by the sight of a gun slung over his shoulder.

'Can I speak to Mr Burton, please?'

'Who wants him?'

She said her name but the guard did not seem inclined to move. Then an unmistakable voice boomed out from the lower deck.

'Is that Gladys then?'

Rich appeared and threw his arms round his visitor. It was a great reunion, performed under the appreciative gaze of all the coach passengers who crowded against the nearside windows.

'Stay to lunch,' commanded Rich.

'I can't do that,' said Gladys. 'I've got all this lot to look after.'

Rich surveyed the crowd scene.

'Everybody stays for lunch,' he decided.

It was an afternoon to remember – four hours of champagne and caviar. Thereafter, fifty-three holidaymakers associated the *Kalizma* with three stars – Rich, Elizabeth and Gladys.

One of the best holidays of my life was enjoyed on the *Kalizma*. With Hilary, our two boys Richard and Alun, and Hilda, we spent two weeks cruising the Mediterranean. I remember having to persuade Hilda that it was not just tomato juice Rich was imbibing by serving her an equivalent drink. It laid her out for two hours.

The last I heard of the *Kalizma* it was owned by the financier, Peter de Savary. He had it redecorated but I am pleased to think he left in place the little brass plaque marking the spot where Rich presented Elizabeth with one of the biggest cut diamonds in the world. Elizabeth had bid for the Cartier diamond when it was put up for auction in New York but had dropped out at one million dollars. Rich tried harder and bought the elusive jewel in a private transaction.

I am told it costs £4,000 a day to hire the *Kalizma*. Cheap at the price, I would say.

# Chapter 13

*I*f *The Taming of the Shrew* was a high point in the Burton career, the film of *Dr Faustus* touched the depths. From the outset, Rich knew that it could not be a world beater. Everything about it was too modest. But he did hope for a quality picture which would enhance his reputation as a serious artist. Instead, he created a mess, with more special effects, as a technician pointed out, than fifty average films. And this time the responsibility was his alone. Rich put up the money, got in formidable talents such as Gabor Pogany as director of photography and John de Cuir as production designer, and co-directed.

But though the disappointment was chastening, it did not deter him from working again with Nevill Coghill. Among the ideas mooted was a film of *'Tis a Pity She's a Whore* – thought eminently suitable by Rich and Nevill because, like them, John Ford was an Exeter man. *The Duchess of Malfi* was also a lead candidate for adaptation to the screen. But the plan which travelled furthest was a film version of *The Tempest* for which Nevill hoped to re-enact the partnership of Richard Burton and John Gielgud.

For almost six months the triumvirate debated the question of a suitable location. The decision was critical because most of the scenes were exteriors of an unusual nature.

'We need,' wrote Gielgud, 'landscape that is remote, dreamy. Sometimes sand beach, sometimes rocks, with strange tracts of deserted scrub inland, with shadowy woods and jungles, changing to marshes and dangerous pools – strange animals and insects.'

The Coghill vote was for Tobago.

'It is a fantastic island, with rockiness as well as yellow sands and tropical, wooded vegetation; it is not heavily populated like parts of Jamaica, so it should not be hard to pick places where there is no sign of habitation.'

But this was not quite what Gielgud had in mind.

'My fear is that it is too conventionally tropical for *The Tempest*. Palm trees and lushness are all right for certain scenes. But I also crave for mists, silver birches and pools.' He thought Japan might suit. 'I do wish you could visit that country and see for yourself. Their films have such a unique and original quality, so much more poetic than the Bahamas.'

Rich gradually distanced himself from this esoteric discussion. The shock of a nearly complete write-off on *Dr Faustus* brought home the perils of independent production. Critical rejection was one thing, but a big financial loss was more difficult to take. Around this time, the easiest way to get on the wrong side of Rich was to point out that his *Faustus* was tax deductible.

'I've spent all these years trying not to pay tax,' he growled. 'Now you tell me I should have stayed at home and made nothing.'

Like others from a poor background, Rich was frightened of losing everything. Possessions were important to him. He gave away a lot of money, to family, friends and to causes that stirred his interest. But straight gifts were containable, while investment in high risk film production was open ended, and liable to be horribly expensive if plans did not work out.

In April 1967, a further missive from Nevill on the charms of Tobago brought back a cable, '*Tempest* could not possibly begin for at least a year and a half or two years because of other commitments.'

These other commitments amounted to a succession of lacklustre movies, starting with *The Comedians*, in which Elizabeth also starred. Rich has often been criticised for the rubbish he turned out over the next few years but while he never shirked his portion of the blame, it is crassly unfair to suggest that he wilfully sought mediocrity. *The Comedians*, for example, had the hallmarks of a quality product. Based on a Graham Greene novel, it dealt with a topical subject of wide interest, the tyrannical and corrupt dictatorship of Haiti in the days of Papa Doc. A strong cast of supporting actors was led by Alec Guinness and Peter Ustinov, both of whom turned in magnificent performances.

But somehow the film did not hang together as a convincing story. Part of the trouble was the mismatch of Rich and Elizabeth. This might seem unlikely after the success of *Virginia Woolf* and *The Shrew* but in both these earlier films they were playing on equal terms. In *The Comedians* there was a huge difference in style between the down-at-heel owner of an empty hotel and his mistress, the glamorous wife of a German diplomat. Try as they might, they did not even begin to look as if they were made for each other. While Rich was believable in his now familiar guise as a noble washout, Elizabeth was too strong for her role, too obviously in control of events which should have been beyond her comprehension.

But if Elizabeth was miscast in *The Comedians*, it was Rich who was sadly out of place in *Boom*, a film adaptation of the Tennessee Williams' play, *The Milk Train Doesn't Stop Here Any More*. As the mysterious young stranger who creates emotional havoc in the community, everything, including his age, was against him. Even a director as brilliant as Joseph Losey could do nothing to save him. The film was a write-off – hardly suitable nowadays for off-peak television.

If these films proved anything it was that Rich and Elizabeth were straining too hard after shared credits. They were equally responsible. For *The Comedians* it was Rich who insisted on casting his wife (she accepted at half her usual fee – an offer the producers could not refuse); for *Boom*, Elizabeth was the power broker. They recognised the error of their ways – neither was too proud to admit mistakes – but still they refused to work at a distance.

The compromise was to sign for different pictures on the same location. This is what happened when Rich made *Where Eagles Dare* at Elstree. Elizabeth was just down the road making *Secret Ceremony*.

*Where Eagles Dare* was the brainchild of an independent producer, Elliot Kastner, whose great skill was to put together an alluring package – scripts, stars, director – and then sell it on to one of the big studios. When he first made his approach to Rich, all he had was a draft script, based on Alistair MacLean's bestselling novel and a formula which was to earn a huge amount of money. On top of a one-million-pound fee (at last, the barrier was broken), Rich was on ten per cent of the gross – a deal which was to relegate all his earlier films into the league of minor earners.

It was a film without pretensions. But then, so much else of what he had been doing of late had ended up that way. If he was destined to be stuck with the mediocre, he reasoned, he might as well take the biggest reward for his time.

Five years on, I was with him when he received a financial update on *Where Eagles Dare*. He glanced at the paper then pushed it over to me with his finger pointing to the bottom line. His earnings were in excess of eight million pounds.

Nobody, least of all Elliot Kastner, suggested that this *Boys' Own* adventure was likely to win prizes for originality, but thought was given to developing a convincing storyline. The three double agents who were central to the convoluted plot but were also the weakest link were made plausible by showing how they were brainwashed with fanatical ideology. All this was eventually cut to make way for more death-defying hand-to-hand combat, a decision which explains why such cerebral actors as Peter Barkworth, Donald Houston and William Squire were to be seen hanging off mountains and fighting for their lives on runaway cable cars.

When I saw the rough cut I was sitting behind Clint Eastwood who was watching himself in what must have been his last supporting role before he achieved superstardom. As the lights went up, he turned to me. 'They've got the wrong title for this movie,' he drawled. 'They should have called it, "Where Doubles Dare".'

For the snowy mountain sequences, the location moved to Switzerland, home ground for Rich and Elizabeth who used their connections to get the best of everything. As the partner who was not working, Elizabeth put herself in charge of the good things in life – like champagne picnics brought up the slopes by a procession of hotel waiters.

'Isn't she beautiful?' murmured Rich when he caught sight of his wife, wrapped in a sable fur at the head of one of these processions. 'Isn't she just the most beautiful thing in the world?'

There was no one to disagree.

*Where Eagles Dare* was an old fashioned adventure – Bond without the sex and fast cars – which met the ever present demand for escapist entertainment. It satisfied the fantasy we all share of battling successfully against overwhelming odds. The critics hated it but, for once, their view was irrelevant.

Rich was on top form throughout the making of *Where Eagles Dare*. He was, to use his own phrase, 'supremely famous' and living life to the full. In London, it was one party after another, either at the Dorchester which the Burtons now regarded as a second home or on the yacht somewhere on the Thames. When the *Kalizma* had to go off for a refit, a slightly smaller vessel called the *Beatrice* (it slept only ten) was hired as a substitute. It cost a thousand pounds a week for fifteen weeks. Animals collected along the way – and Elizabeth was forever gathering to her small cuddly creatures in search of a home – stayed at the hotel until it was time to leave town when they were incorporated into the sailing menagerie. Elizabeth was extraordinarily tolerant of her pets. One interviewer who spent hours waiting to meet his dream heroine complained afterwards that his only lasting impression was of a squeaky little dog that peed on the carpet.

171

While Elizabeth fussed over her extended family, Rich brooded on the future. When their preoccupations clashed, usually over some domestic crisis, Rich would back away, if necessary locking himself in the bedroom. This is precisely what happened when we met for a brotherly chinwag at the Dorchester at the time when Elizabeth was proudly displaying her latest gift from an admirer – a pearl grey kitten with, as it turned out, an advanced sense of the ridiculous.

Lunch came up on two trolleys – one for the smoked salmon, the other for wine and beer. Rich started drinking and talking, leaving me to the eating.

'How do you see me as Simon Bolivar?' Rich wanted to know.

'Who?'

He was incredulous.

'You don't know Bolivar? One of the great South American heroes?'

I had to confirm my ignorance.

'It's just the part for me. It has everything. . . .'

I settled down for a short history lecture but Rich was suddenly interrupted by a squeal from Elizabeth. He turned to where she was standing by the window.

'What's the matter, luv?'

'It's the little kitten,' she screamed, 'it's out on the terrace.'

As we were six floors up with a drop straight down to Park Lane, this was not good news. But there was worse to come. Understandably terrified by the sight of three grim-faced humans slowly advancing on it with hands outstretched ('Here, kitty,' Rich boomed, 'come to daddy you little bugger before I tear you apart') the feline sought the only refuge to hand. It shot across to the far side of the terrace, climbed into the spout of a lead drainpipe and disappeared.

'Thank you,' said Elizabeth bitterly. 'Thank you so much for your help. Now, what the hell am I supposed to do?'

Rich was not in the least perturbed.

'Only one thing for it,' he said. 'Tell the engineer.' Then to me, 'Come on Gray, let's find somewhere quiet to talk.'

I followed him into the bedroom leaving Elizabeth shouting into the phone. Five minutes later, when Rich went back for the drinks trolley, the Dorchester rescue service had already swung into action. Two men in blue overalls were out in the terrace carefully dismantling the drainpipe.

'Best leave them to it,' said Rich as he came back to the bedroom and closed the door. 'They seem to know what they're doing.'

I don't know what happened to the Bolivar project except that it never got further than the talking stage. Presumably, the studio bosses did not share my brother's enthusiasm for rebel causes.

But there was no scarcity of options. Even the filming of *The Tempest* came back into the realm of practicalities. In May 1968 Nevill Coghill wrote, 'in great excitement' to announce that he had found a Prospero's island which would meet all the possible demands of Burton and Gielgud. The idyllic spot was Garnish Island off the Irish coast in Bantry Bay.

'It has everything. Cliffs, rocks, bogs, mountains in the near neighbourhood of incredible romantic beauty and wildness. Many sweeping landscapes with no sign of habitation. Marvellous lights and cloud effects, due to Atlantic weather conditions. The island itself is a paradise of flowers, the most gorgeous garden in Ireland; every sort of rhododendron, from white to crimson, and brilliant azaleas in wild effect, all sorts of trees, some flowering just now. Grassy glades, abundance of flowers; the whole planted so as to seem growing wild, and yet with the feeling of some overall magical control. Believe it or not, there is also a rustic Italianate palace at the centre of the island (habitable) which is just what I imagine Prospero would have conjured up for himself and described as "my poor cell". There would be no need to build a single set. It's all there already, flights of steps, a tower or two, a lily-pool, lawns, crags, groves. I can hardly wait to show it to you.'

The suggestion was for Richard and Elizabeth to take time off in the summer to sail the *Kalizma* to Bantry Bay. A week was duly set aside in August.

Meanwhile, Nevill had other excitements to occupy him. His translation of *The Canterbury Tales* into modern English, an unexpected bestseller which brought Chaucerian verse into popular currency, was now ready for what surely was its final manifestation – as a musical. When *The Canterbury Tales* opened at the Phoenix in London's West End, Rich and Elizabeth were in attendance. Everybody was nervous, except for Elizabeth who went about giving words of comfort and encouragement for all the world like Florence Nightingale at the front. Otherwise mature men wilted before her and afterwards, in proud recollection, fell to disputing her allocation of favours.

'My fondest love to Elizabeth,' wrote Nevill. 'I think of her always with happy memories, especially the memory of her presence and hands holding mine on the terrible night of the opening of *Canterbury Tales*.' He added, 'Eric Starkie [the director] claims she held his hands too, but I put that down to jealousy.'

This was the night on which Nevill made peace with the critics – or rather, they made peace with him. With a pocketful of ecstatic reviews and the assurance of a long run, later to be repeated on Broadway, he had finally made the leap to professional theatre. It is curious that in this transition, the relationship between Nevill and Rich underwent a sea change. Hitherto, the student had paid homage to the professor. Now the role of mentor shifted to the younger man, just as it had with Phil Burton. Nevill paid tribute to Rich for pushing him towards the full enjoyment of creative enterprises. It was a compliment Rich was unwilling to accept. He believed his own debt had still to be paid. For him, Phil Burton had started the ball rolling, Nevill had given it a powerful kick and Rich had simply kept it moving along. His gratitude to Nevill was such that when *Dr Faustus* brought disappointment he sent his friend a cheque for £15,000, a tidy sum in those days, in recognition of all that he had done to nurture young talent. Later, much larger sums were subscribed by Rich to the Oxford theatre appeal.

If helping Oxford was a pleasure worth savouring, so too was the opportunity to promote the culture of his beloved Wales. At the behest of many friends but notably John Morgan, a broadcaster Rich much admired, he and Elizabeth put £100,000 into Harlech, a consortium of business and the arts which aimed to secure the commercial television franchise for Wales and the West Country.

Rich was suspicious of television. He thought of it as an intrusive art form.

'If I made a bad film, people don't have to come to see it. But if I'm bad on television, people will still watch because it's so easy to switch on and so hard to switch off!'

His decision to back Harlech was made with the genuine hope that the new talent coming in to television would raise standards.

With the help of the Burton name, Harlech won its bid and was a great financial success. But Rich was never entirely happy with his investment. It did not achieve what he and, he assumed, his fellow directors had hoped for. The failure was all the more frustrating because, as we shall see, his own involvement did nothing to help his cause.


In mid-1968 Rich went to Celigny for the first time in more than two years. It was not a happy occasion. The caretaker at Pays de Galles, one of the longest serving members of the Burton household, had killed himself. Rich decided to go to the funeral. There was nothing directly he could do to help but he felt badly that he so rarely visited the home he had shared with Sybil. This was chiefly in deference to Elizabeth who naturally had an emotive objection to the place but who also preferred her own home at Gstaad, a magnificent chalet perched on the mountainside overlooking the famous ski slopes. It was the more impressive residence in every way though, perversely, Rich could never be persuaded to recognise its virtues.

Elizabeth was not pleased when Rich told her of his plans. She was booked to go into hospital for a few days and while it was nothing serious she felt the least he could do was to be close at hand. She knew also that his motives for travelling were not entirely altruistic. Rich had just finished a short and entirely satisfying piece of work (a recording of *The Rhyme of the Ancient Mariner* which, against all expectations, was to break into the charts with sales of over half a million copies) and was now at a loose end. A trip down memory lane appealed to his sentimental nature. He was supported by Ivor and Gwen who had their own fond recollections of Pays de Galles and indeed went back there periodically as part of their domestic round. Rich suggested they should accompany him.

So it was agreed, though Elizabeth remained unhappy. She acceded only on condition that they stayed at Gstaad, driving from there to Celigny for the funeral.

The story of the next three days has to be pieced together from snippets of information from many sources. No one knows the whole truth. What is beyond question is that events in Celigny that July left their mark on Rich for the rest of his life.

After the funeral, Rich and Ivor went to the Café de la Gare for a simple meal and a few drinks. Gwen said she would follow on; she wanted to visit some friends. When eventually she called by, the two brothers were well away, swopping old stories over large glasses of lager. Ivor complained that if he drank much more he would not be able to drive but Rich was in a talking mood and showed no signs of letting up. Leaving them to it, Gwen went off to find the wife of the proprietor, who, she knew, would keep her busy with a feast of village gossip.

It was late evening when Ivor rose unsteadily to announce that he was fetching the car. Rich pushed him back into his seat.

'We're not driving anywhere. We'll stay here. In my home.'

Gwen was secretly relieved though she knew that if Elizabeth found out they would all be in trouble. There was another problem. Pays de Galles had been empty for a long time. Obeying the instinct of a professional housewife, Gwen declared that the place needed a thorough airing before it was fit for habitation. She would go on ahead, she told them, to open up the house.

It was at least another two hours before Rich and Ivor decided to

175

call it a day. By then it was dusk but they saw, as they trudged their way up the road to Pays de Galles, there were no lights on in any of the rooms.

Gwen met them at the door. 'The electricity is off,' she said, 'and I can't find the main switch.'

Still merry on beer and, Gwen guessed, a more than generous quota of chasers, the men held each other in uproarious laughter at the thought of Gwen scrabbling around in the darkness. She was not amused.

'You're such children,' she complained. 'Just get those lights turned on, will you?'

Ivor stepped back. 'Oh, very well; very well.'

He held a finger to his lips. 'I am the only one who knows the secret of the lost switch.'

And still laughing he moved off towards the garage. Gwen went back into the house and Rich followed her. A few minutes later, the lights came on.

A few minutes after that, Rich announced he was going to bed.

'But where's Ivor?' Gwen wanted to know.

'Probably walking off a hangover,' said Rich. 'Sensible man. I'll join him.'

Gwen went on pottering for a while until she was ready for bed. As she came out of the kitchen she heard the front door bang and caught a glimpse of Rich hurrying towards the phone. As she came up to him he was lifting the receiver and dialling furiously. He was breathing heavily.

'Ivor's hurt. But don't worry. I'm getting an ambulance. Don't worry.'

It was two days before I knew there was something badly wrong. The news came to me by a circuitous route. Hilda's daughter Sian, who was in London, had a chance meeting with Jim Benton, one of Rich's many assistants, who was then staying at 11 Squires Mount. In casual conversation Sian asked after Ivor.

'How is he these days? I haven't seen him in ages.'

Jim went into his conspiratorial pose.

'Well, he's ill, very ill. But you're not supposed to know. So don't tell Gwen I said anything.'

Sian could understand that news like this was not to be bandied about but she did take for granted that her mother had been told. Yet, when she rang home that evening, Hilda was mystified.

'Maybe Graham knows.'

I was just as much in the dark but I knew what to do to find out what was going on. Or I thought I knew.

176

I rang Pays de Galles. No answer. I rang again and again and again. Still no answer. Finally, I got through to someone who announced herself as 'Mr Burton's secretary'. I asked for Rich but was told he was not available; likewise Gwen. When she asked if there was anything she could do to help, I put the question bluntly.

'Has my brother had an accident?'

There was a short pause. Then she said, 'It's true. He has been hurt. He's in hospital at Geneva. We think he has a broken neck. But the doctors will know more in a day or two. Please be patient. He is well looked after.'

A few days later Gwen rang.

'We're flying home,' she said. 'Ivor needs specialist treatment. He'll be in Stoke Mandeville hospital and I'll stay in a hotel.'

'Can he have visitors?'

'Yes, but I'm not sure he wants to see anyone. Not yet.'

I took a chance and drove to Stoke Mandeville a day after Ivor was brought in. When I arrived at the hospital I was told that Gwen was with him. I was shown to a waiting room. I read all the magazines without taking in a single word.

Gwen came in and I gave her a hug. Her eyes were red but otherwise she was her old self; capable and in control.

'He won't see you,' she said. 'I did warn you. Most of the time he just wants to be alone.'

I sat her down.

'I don't understand. Why does he want to keep me away? Is there something I haven't been told? What sort of shape is he in?'

She looked surprised. 'I thought you knew. Ivor is paralysed from the neck down. He'll never walk again.'

I said nothing for a while. I could only think of my elder brother as the tough guy, the fitness freak who had lived by muscle power. The idea of him bound to a bed or to a wheelchair was beyond comprehension.

'What happened?'

'He tripped on a grid. One of those things you use to scrape mud off your boots. He must have fallen badly. When Rich found him, he couldn't move.'

The next morning Gwen rang me in my hotel room.

'Ivor will see you. Just for a few minutes. Can you come over now?'

I sat by his bed for twenty minutes and exchanged as many words. As I got up to leave he said, 'You shouldn't have come.'

'I wanted to,' I said.

He was tight-lipped but there were tears in his eyes. Never before in my entire life had I seen my brother cry. I took hold of his hand.

177

'You'll be all right. Up and about in no time, eh?'

He gripped me hard.

'Oh yes, boyo. You wait. I'll be up and about.'

We both knew we were lying.

On the way home I stopped off to see Elizabeth. I had assumed she was still in the London Clinic but she was already back at the Dorchester, fighting fit and spoiling for a row. She knew about Ivor, that much was clear. Also, that she held Rich responsible for what had happened.

'Hell, I told him not to go to Celigny. Why does he always have to do such damn fool things?'

I considered the question.

'Where is Rich?' I asked. 'I thought he might be here.'

Elizabeth's voice sharpened.

'Don't ask me where he is. How should I know? He's not in Celigny. He's not in Gstaad. Maybe he's run away from home.'

It was a week before I heard from Rich. We had a brief telephone conversation during which he steadfastly refused to discuss the accident. And he never did talk about it in any logical way, at least not to me, or to anyone else in the family.

But the tragedy stayed with him. More than that it came to dominate his waking hours. For the rest of his life he was preoccupied with a sense of guilt which could be relieved only by heavier and heavier doses of alcohol. On many a drunken evening when I helped him to bed he would talk to me as if I was Ivor. When I stayed with him in Rome, sharing a room, he woke in the middle of the night calling out for Ivor. Yet he stayed away from the hospital. He hated sickness and, as I came to discover, he feared death – not as much his own as the death of others. He had a deep horror of annihilation.

Why did he feel responsibility for what happened at Celigny so keenly? The clue is, 'if only'.

If only they had stayed away from the funeral. If only Rich had not encouraged Ivor to drink. If only they had driven back to Gstaad instead of lodging overnight at Pays de Galles.

But there is something more. Rich and Ivor were both in drunken, boisterous mood. If they behaved to pattern, and from what Gwen told me, I have no doubt they did, it is quite easy to imagine them in horseplay, pushing and shoving each other about, throwing punches, wrestling, running and tripping. If the accident was not a simple fall but part of a silly game which went terribly wrong – an explanation which rings true for me – I can quite understand why Rich saddled himself with the blame and suffered the remorse.

When Rich talked about the family he was always open about his favourites. 'After Cis,' he told me, 'I loved Ivor the best. He was the nearest to a father to me.'

In the years ahead Rich and I were not always on the best of terms. Once or twice we had rows which got near to violence. After one of these bouts, by way of explanation, he invoked Oscar Wilde:

> 'Yet each man kills the thing he loves,
> By each let this be heard,
> Some do it with a bitter look,
> Some with a flattering word,
> The coward does it with a kiss,
> The brave man with a sword.'

The note was addressed to me but I remember thinking it could more suitably have gone to Ivor.

When it was plain that Ivor was not responding to treatment, he and Gwen went back to Switzerland to live at Gstaad. Two nurses joined the staff so that Ivor had whatever he needed, day or night. Cassie too had devoted herself to nursing him with loving care. The last time I saw him was in February 1972, less than a month before he died. I sat by his bed and we talked. We must have said more to each other in those three days than in the previous thirty years. For the first time I felt close to Ivor, realising that what I had always believed to be an unfeeling nature was in reality a barrier against genuine emotion which he feared as weakness. And living as he had as a young man when, against the odds, he had kept us together as a family, weakness was a luxury he felt he could never afford.

On the last night, he refused to let me go to bed. We talked on right the way through to breakfast when I drank a pint of coffee to keep me awake for the drive to Cherbourg. It was a stupid thing to do but for some reason, vital at the time but now long forgotten, I had to be on the Channel ferry by evening. I nearly did not make it. Driving on the wrong side of the road round a steep corner I was saved by a French truck driver who was doing the same in the opposite direction.

When at last I was allowed to sleep, my last waking thought was of Ivor. How curious it was. He had revealed so much of himself, but not once in our long exorcising sessions had he said a single word about the accident that was to be the death of him.

# Chapter 14

The turn of fortune for Rich showed first in his dealing with Woodfall Films, the company which had produced *Look Back in Anger*. The director from that film, Tony Richardson, offered him the lead in *Laughter in the Dark*, a thriller of sorts in which a wealthy art dealer, blinded in a car crash, takes revenge on his persecutors.

But after a few days' work or rather lack of work, Rich was thrown off the set. The statement put out by the company, that he was 'unpunctual and unprofessional', wounded him greatly but he could hardly deny that his initial enthusiasm for a tight budget film had waned considerably when he was told he had to put in an appearance on Sunday and after lunch.

A young Nicol Williamson took over his role (the competition was coming up fast) leaving Rich free to go off on a three-day binge. Elizabeth was furious. There was an angry exchange in the bar at the Dorchester which ended up with Elizabeth tipping her Jack Daniels over Richard's head. Rich took it in good part.

'Imagine what she could have done with a Bloody Mary.'

In his less endearing moods he was capable of goading Elizabeth into a terrible anger. If he was bored he would pitch in an unprovoked and outrageous opinion, just to get a reaction. Like,

'There can be too many Jews.'

'There can be too many Welsh.'

'There are more Jews than Welsh.'

'But it feels like there are more Welsh. They make so much noise. Talk, talk, talk.'

'They have a lot to talk about.'

'Oh no. They just take longer saying it!'

'I don't!'

'Sshmuck!'

It was a game for children and like all children's games it could end in tears, even when or especially when there was no serious content to the argument. The racial insult was a case in point. Of all people, Rich had an abiding detestation of racial prejudice and would jump to defend anyone he thought was the victim of discrimination. Bob Wilson, one of his closest companions, was unmistakably black.

Yet on a visit to Africa he caused a major upset with a response to a simple question. He was asked to name his favourite confectionery.

'Niggerheads,' he declared.

There was an awful silence. Rich was unperturbed.

'They're marshmallows with chocolate topping,' he explained innocently. 'They're called niggerheads.'

Suddenly, everybody was talking to change the conversation. Days later, Rich was at a dinner party hosted by a black politician. As the coffee was handed round, a delectable sight appeared centre table. In a voice that could always be heard above the competition, Rich boomed his appreciation: 'Niggerheads.'

There is no point in my arguing that it was all harmless fun. Rich could be thoroughly offensive, even when relatively sober. What I would say in his defence is that in his frequent verbal assaults on pretentious fools, he did us all a favour. I recall an awful meal when a well-known show business writer (one who had it in his power to do Rich and Elizabeth a lot of harm) bored us rigid with a diatribe of misinformed Hollywood gossip. When he could take no more, Rich leaned towards the speaker.

'I want you to know,' he declared, 'you really are the most disgusting little shit.'

Then, to an accompanying murmur of 'Hear, hear,' he got up from the table and weaved his way out of the room.

If in this first phase of the downturn of his career, Rich upset a lot of people, not least his wife, he always tried to keep on good terms with the children. They in turn gave him unstinting love. Not that Rich was what you might call an active father. It was Elizabeth who suggested things to do and places to go and who involved herself with the children.

Rich was just there. If the children wanted him he gave himself freely. And if he was not in the mood, Elizabeth was usually on hand to take the strain. As she described the relationship: 'The children have fun with Richard. As a family we have a sense of the ridiculous – way out ridiculous. We laugh at the same things and it's Richard who makes us laugh – by being himself – great, charming, rough with the kids as with everyone else. He may say to them, "Get a bloody move on" when they're wasting time or late and they'll accept it. But if he's in a really black mood, one of those melancholy Welsh moods, the word gets around, "Cool it". The children will warn me, "Watch it, Mom", or I'll give them the nod.'

To spend time with the family Rich and Elizabeth tried to adapt their work schedules to suit the school vacations of England, where Michael and Christopher were at Millfield, and Switzerland where Liza and Maria were at school. (Kate was at school in America and for most of the year lived with her mother.)

The holiday logistics were formidable. Gathering everyone at Puerto Vallarta, that most attractive hideaway, often entailed loss of school time for one or more of the children. This disturbed Rich who kept a close watch on educational standards. Tutors were employed to supplement what the regular teachers were able to provide. When Christopher had problems at Millfield, Rich promptly withdrew him from the school and turned to Nevill Coghill for advice.

'Do you, by any chance, know an able chap who would like to do a little globe-trotting for six or eight months and keep the boy up to the mark for entrance into school next autumn . . . ? Be sure that I do not want a crammer but somebody who will keep his mind working . . . I would like his mind to be ticking over at this terribly important time of his life and not atrophying in this land of comic-cuts.'

Nevill duly came up with a suitable candidate to instil an element of s... ility in the erratic world of the Burtons. John David Morley adapted easily to his curious job though registered with surprise the quantity of liquor Rich could take on without losing his senses and equally the unpredictable moments when his employer could slip from apparently sober conversation to an incomprehensible slur – 'as if he had fallen off a cliff'.

After the false start with Woodfall Films, Rich chose to wait for an offer that would attract Elizabeth. He was confident that the work would come in, despite the shaky fortunes of the film industry.

Twentieth Century-Fox was the first to put together an attractive package. For Elizabeth there was *The Only Girl in Town* with Warren Beatty. For Rich, an extraordinary caper called *Staircase*.

In this he was called upon to camp it up as a gay hairdresser trying to come to terms with middle age and a deteriorating relationship with his partner, played by Rex Harrison. The story goes that both actors thought the idea so outrageous they just had to say yes. But Rich at least took it all very earnestly. It was, he said, an important film about the pain of loneliness made more acute by a defiance of convention. The association of Burton and Harrison, both obviously, some might say notoriously, heterosexual in real life, would, it was hoped, command respect for the story and its message.

The plan misfired. Critics and public alike failed to detect the underlying seriousness of what looked curiously like a burlesque. Audiences either laughed in the wrong places or cringed with embarrassment as the two stars cavorted through every cliché known to gay life.

Rich was for ever loyal to the film claiming that it was one of his best efforts which would eventually be reassessed in a more favourable light. 'This is a great love story,' he wrote. And later, 'It is a kick against the system.'

If that was true, he might have thought of his next film as the system kicking back. *Anne of a Thousand Days* gave Rich the opportunity to show what he could do with Henry VIII. The answer, given the banality of the script, was not much, though the film was quite well received in America. Incredibly Rich landed an Oscar nomination, his sixth, but was not in the least surprised that it did not lead to the actual award. The fact was, the film bored him out of his mind. He agreed with a London reviewer who described it as 'a plod through Tudor history' which should be retitled *Anne of a Thousand Hours*.

Warned that his reputation for boozing was beginning to worry producers, he made a resolution to cut back. But it did not last. Given the dreadful scripts that were for ever being thrown his way, he could not bring himself to believe that his drinking made any difference one way or the other. It was the easy way out. What he should have been asking himself was why the good scripts were going elsewhere.

The best moments for Rich in the making of *Anne of a Thousand Days* were in his caravan talking with old friends who remembered the great days – Anthony Quayle, Michael Hordern, William Squire. One afternoon, when I called to see him, I was told to approach warily because the order had been posted, Mr Burton is not to be disturbed. I feared the worst. But when at last I was ushered in I found my brother surrounded by a group of distinguished character actors, all in Tudor costume, engaged in a heavy discussion on the mysteries of county cricket. Interestingly, there was not a drink in sight.

The natural, spontaneous side to Rich showed up again when he heard from a classmate he had last seen when they were together at Port Talbot Grammar. Thirty years on, Trevor George was a headmaster in the West Country. He wrote asking if Rich would mind if he brought a party of children to the studios. The reply was by return.

'Mind? Why should I mind? Bring them all.'

He laid on a guided tour which ended up with Rich leading a debate on the art of film making. Then there was tea on the lawn and a group photograph with Rich at centre in his Henry VIII costume.

A week later each of his guests received a signed picture. It was a small gesture but the children loved him for it.

After his excursion into sanitised history, Elizabeth suggested a break. Rich agreed. It was time to take stock. The movie industry was in poor shape. In the days when television was still the enemy and before video had come along to give home viewing a boost, the studios could think only of trying to hold audiences by appealing to the lowest common denominator. The Burtons followed the trend, hoping it was a short run.

'I've done the most awful rubbish,' Rich admitted to a journalist, 'just for somewhere to go in the morning.'

But it was not simply that bad movies predominated. There had been times like that before. What was worrying was the clearly perceptible slide in the popularity of the Taylor–Burton partnership. Younger audiences, on whom the industry increasingly depended, were no longer transfixed by the *Cleopatra* love story. It was so tame by the standards of the swinging sixties. What place was there for the Burtons in the age of the Beatles?

As always, Elizabeth took the knocks more easily than Rich. It was not that she was less sensitive, simply more realistic. Having experienced the vagaries of public opinion she knew how to work events in her favour. And if she failed? Well, there was a strong impression that Elizabeth didn't give a damn. With Rich, it was quite different. His insecurity surfaced very quickly and the future troubled him.

A little time on when arguments with Rich were commonplace, he told me, 'I drink to drown fear.' I could understand that. Depression was a pervasive enemy which had gathered strength from Ivor's tragedy and the guilt Rich carried with him. Now he was haunted by the prospect of a career trailing away into mediocrity. He needed somewhere he could feel safe. And when the real world had nothing to offer he sought refuge in fantasy.

For six months in 1969 and the early part of 1970 Rich and Elizabeth drifted from Switzerland to Mexico to Botswana in Southern Africa. This last trip started with a children's hospital appeal and ended with Elizabeth satisfying a long felt wish to go on safari. It was a nerve-racking time for their guides who failed conspicuously in their efforts to persuade Elizabeth that some animals could be dangerous.

Having made friends with a young leopard, described by Rich as her feline psychopath, she declared her intention of studying at close hand a dangerous breed of wild monkeys. Tales of severed limbs and blood all over the floor did nothing to deter her. She set out a trail of nuts and fruit from the trees where the monkeys lived right up and onto her veranda. There she placed a large bowl filled to the brim with the sort of goodies monkeys appreciate. In no time at all she had these apparently savage beasts climbing over the furniture and generally behaving as if they were part of the family.

'The one thing you must not do,' warned an attendant who spoke to Elizabeth from the far side of the room, 'is to let them eat from your hand. A false move and. . . .' He clawed the air in a way that left no room for misunderstanding.

The next day the same attendant nervously amended his advice. 'Okay, if you *must* let them feed out of your hand, try to keep very still.' Elizabeth turned her head sharply.

'What's that you say?'

The man fled.

For Rich the holiday was cut short by a severe bout of malaria. Apart from occasional back pains this was the first sign that his much abused constitution was not, as he loved to believe, invincible. His frailty angered him and he was not the easiest patient. But, at least, for seven weeks he was off the drink.

His nurse for all this time was Chen Sam, a remarkable young lady whose unabbreviated name confounded the assumption that she must be Chinese. In fact, her early years were spent in the Middle East, the child of an Egyptian father and an Italian mother who was sent to Britain as a teenager. A failed marriage later she was in Africa making a living as a pharmacist. She had a son in Paris.

It was not just her knowledge of pills and injections that qualified Chen for the job of restoring my brother. It was her refusal to be overawed by a loud voice and a dictatorial tone which really tipped the balance. An unconventional upbringing had made Chen self-reliant. She did not expect anything from the Burtons and so was not afraid to say what she thought. She told Rich plainly that if he wanted to recover he had to come off alcohol.

'For how long?' he demanded to know.

'For as long as it takes.'

As the fever mounted Rich gave away more of himself than at any other time in his life. Delirium stripped him of his actor's disguise. In the middle of the night, in a half sleep he talked of Ivor as the father he had always wanted. It had been such fun with Ivor, the straight talking, hard drinking man who was never afraid of trouble and who always gave straight advice. And where was he now, this father of his dreams? In a terrible half-life from which all the money in the world could not release him. Just like Jessica, the daughter he had loved. When he had last seen her she had screamed at him as a stranger to be feared. He had never gone back to the hospital. He would never see her again. But the memory of an eleven-year-old girl, locked away in an institution, stayed with him. And always there was the question. Am I to blame?

Recovery left Rich with a powerful awareness of time passing. If there was also a tinge of self pity – 'if only, if only' – it was wiped out by an event on the flight back from Botswana. It concerned Chen Sam who, recognised as a valued friend by Rich and Elizabeth, had been persuaded to join the Burton staff. This had not been achieved without some argument. More than once she had asked Rich, 'But what am I supposed to do?' and more than once Rich had responded, 'We'll think of something. Eventually.' His only insistence was on a change of name. The Welsh intonation of Chen Sam was not to his liking. As he emerged from convalescence he came up with an alternative.

'I will call you Zen Bhudda.'

So it was that Zen Bhudda alias Chen Sam was on the private jet with Rich and Elizabeth for their journey home. On landing, they were met by the usual bevy of photographers and reporters who caught everyone by surprise by making straight for Chen. Over the glare of the flashbulbs they shouted questions she could barely interpret. What was it they were trying to say? Something about her son? Had she heard about her son? Her son had pneumonia? Her son was dead?

The nightmare of coming to terms was for Chen a private matter. She did not want intruders, however well meaning. Elizabeth knew this and after the first awkward attempt to give comfort allowed Chen the freedom of her own thoughts. But Rich had difficulty in understanding the need to be alone. Grief had to be shared to be bearable. Always, Rich sought company. When Chen told him gently he could not help, he reverted to his own sadness.

'Right, then. I'm off for a drink.'


In the weeks following Rich turned again to Oxford, the perfect refuge even if made so by nostalgia posing as reality.

After *Dr Faustus* the Oxford fund had suffered a relapse. Where Burton had failed others refrained from trying their luck. Rich decided to mount a rescue operation with an outright gift of one hundred thousand pounds.

'Obviously it will not be enough,' he wrote to Nevill Coghill, 'but with a certain amount of brainwashing we will, hopefully, be able to get a lot more from the Gettys and Onassises of this world. The latter is a warm friend of ours and I'm sure that if he were given the right kind of publicity (which he loves) he might write us a splendid little cheque. On the other side of the Atlantic Aaron is in touch with all kinds of people whose wealth is awesome. So one way or another we might be able to multiply the original £100,000.'

In his letter of thanks ('it is a dream of a lifetime made real') Nevill returned to the idea of Rich spending a year's sabbatical at Oxford.

'I am excited to hear you are already finding an idea on which to ground your lectures. I am confident you could give us a great series if you can steadily explore this idea in the light of your experience and imagination. You have so many approaches that no one else has.'

To Aaron Frosch, Nevill wrote, 'I look forward to Richard making a big hit in the world of university teaching, as Granville Barker did a generation or so ago.'

Why did it not happen? It is too easy to suggest that Rich was tied to a style of living which precluded Oxford. He and Elizabeth had enough money to live how they wanted and where they wanted for the rest of their lives. But while it was quite possible to think of Rich bumbling round the cloisters, matching every eccentricity known to academic life, it was not so easy to imagine how Elizabeth might adapt. On brief acquaintance, she found Oxford amusing, but not compelling. To give it a year was asking a lot of a child of Hollywood, as Rich knew perfectly well.

The other difficulty for Rich was matching performance with promise. However much he told himself he wanted to write and to lecture, he found it hard to sustain a theme. He would start well only to be distracted by irrelevant and disconnected arguments. He was best at delivering ideas when he spoke other people's words or when he spoke his own spontaneously, as in a free-for-all debate.

At Puerto Vallarta or on board the *Kalizma*, Rich methodically set aside two or three hours a day for writing but rarely turned out anything substantial. He was only forty-four and had achieved more than most artists could claim for an entire career, yet he was burdened by the fear that somehow life had passed him by. Maybe it was too late for Oxford; maybe it was too late for anything except what he knew he could do – with one hand tied behind his back.

It was no surprise to me when, after months of introspection, the offer that tempted a return to work was top billing in a second-rate war movie. That *Raid on Rommel* ever got beyond the first planning meeting was entirely thanks to a cost-saving idea for recycling action footage from *Tobruk*, a Rock Hudson adventure yarn, made four years earlier. The fee was modest by Burton standards but it was only three weeks' work and the Mexican location was within easy reach of Puerto Vallarta. Rich excused the inevitably poor reviews by saying it was his way of getting back into the swing of things. There was one encouraging sign. He stayed on the wagon for the duration.

Towards the end of 1970 Rich came back to London to make another film for Elliot Kastner. But this was quite different from *Where Eagles Dare*. In *Villain*, Rich was, for the first time, the out-and-out nasty, a sadistic East End gang leader who murdered for fun. He had always wanted to play the master criminal, to let himself go in a role that was as outrageously evil as anything in Elizabethan drama. He had tried for it two years earlier when his own production company had put together a treatment for *The Greatest Train Robbery in the World*. But it was not just the title that was altogether too grandiose. In the end, the project and the part Rich fancied for himself went to his friend, Stanley Baker, who was practised at turning out workable films on a tight budget.

Not that there was anything excessive about *Villain*, except perhaps the acting. Rich went way over the top with a performance that was pure ham. But it was a conscious decision, reflecting with unnerving accuracy the public image of any number of London heavies who made their mark on police files in the late sixties. Grotesque to the point of hilarity they could choke laughter with a vicious twist.

*Villain* upset some of the older generation of fans who refused to accept a Burton without any redeeming features. Possibly for this reason the film came in for more flack than it deserved. Even today it is sadly underrated. I still believe it was a chilling commentary on its time with a stronger regard for authenticity than most of its kind.

Rich was hurt in two ways; financially, because he waived his fee in return for a percentage on gross which turned out to be very modest; and professionally because instead of giving his career a lift, as he had intended, *Villain* left producers with the impression that he was desperate for parts, however inapt.

The consolation was a visit to Buckingham Palace to receive the CBE. This was his only public honour and I often wondered if he was a little envious of those actor luminaries who were able to put 'Sir' before their names.

In conversation, he affected not to be worried by such trifles but he was too ready with excuses to make me believe he was entirely unconcerned.

'The Inland Revenue won't have it,' he confided. 'How can they give a knighthood to someone who doesn't pay taxes?'

'What about Noel Coward?'

Rich thought for a moment.

'True. But then he's much older. Maybe they have an amnesty for septuagenarians.'

He chose not to take into account, or at least to talk about, his failure to come to terms with respectability. To appear high up on the honours' list it was necessary either to be pure (a rarity) or to sin discreetly. Rich was disqualified on the first rule and congenitally incapable of obeying the second. I don't think he ever did anything discreetly in his entire life.

Still, he made great show of his CBE – Commander of the Most Excellent Order of the British Empire. He went to the Palace with the two women who meant most to him – Elizabeth and Cis. The pictures of the three of them, all smiling proudly, are among the happiest in the family album.

Before returning to Mexico (partly for a rest, mostly to avoid the attentions of the taxman) there was just time to fulfil a long standing ambition to film *Under Milk Wood*, a lasting homage to the memory of Dylan Thomas. Financed by Rich, it was a superior home movie put together without the help of a director by an extraordinary cast who did it for love. Elizabeth was there, so were Peter O'Toole, Glynis Johns, Vivien Merchant, Sian Phillips, Victor Spinetti and Ryan Davies. If the film proved anything it was the difficulty of translating poetry into pictures. But the words came across beautifully. As Rich commented after the press show, 'You can always close your eyes and think of Dylan.'

By now he was back on the drink. Interminable sessions of boozy reminiscences were interspersed by bouts of foul temper which Elizabeth alone was able to contain. Considering her own run of ill health, I wondered at her capacity for taking so much.

Elizabeth was good for Rich in every way, domestically. Professionally, I was not so sure. When it came to choosing scripts she nearly always deferred to Rich. Sometimes he was right; more often he was wrong. In the confusion of his middle years (a familiar crisis even to those outside the movie industry) he needed someone close to him who could say where he was going wrong. Elizabeth was unable to oblige because she did not know the answer.

With Hollywood in the doldrums and the British studios virtually out of business, offers of work popped up from the unlikeliest sources. After the disappointment of *Villain*, Rich was open to any suggestion as long as it was made to sound big and exciting.

'I can add up the money. The rest is luck.'

He knew it was not so but lacked the will to argue on matters that were central to his life. He went on with films which appalled him for the same reason that he went on drinking – to hold off the day when he had to make critical decisions.

His biggest fear was ending up on television – 'the little box' as he called it. Though a major shareholder in Harlech television he seldom put in an appearance or responded to calls for ideas. His only suggestion for a drama series, an adaptation of Richard Llewellyn's novel *How Green Was My Valley*, was received politely but, as he might have expected, it did not appeal to the young turks who rejected the cosy, sentimental interpretation of Welsh culture.

Lord Harlech, chairman of the company, admitted his frustration to a journalist.

'The truth is, whenever we approach Richard to do something specific he is never available. His approach to everything is wholly emotional, so that, although he appears willing, whenever we try to get down to details we run into a complete fog.'

Ah, little did the noble gentleman realise how frightened Rich was of compromising himself. Olivier, Richardson, Gielgud – what need had they of television? Mitchum, Lancaster, Grant, Douglas – when were they seen on the small screen except on chat shows or in re-runs of old movies? Television was for the fading stars. That was how Rich saw himself when at last, he agreed to perform for the audience in the living room. He anticipated disaster. And, for once, he was right.

# Chapter 15

Meanwhile, he had a quartet of embarrassing films to complete. The first, *Hammersmith is Out*, was financed by J. Cornelius Crean, a wealthy building contractor in search of glitter. What he found was an easy way of losing money. Rich was called upon to play a certified lunatic who escapes from an asylum to roam across America in lustful pursuit of wealth and power. Along the way he teams up with Elizabeth, cast as a fast-food waitress (can you believe this?) who falls for his psychotic charms.

There was a hope that, as director, Peter Ustinov might use his undoubted talents to lift the stars above their material. But miracles were not in his line. Came the day when Rich could say to David Blewitt, editor on the film, 'Well, we blew it, Blewitt.' It was not a very good joke but it afforded one of the few laughs of the month.

Soon after the wrap on *Hammersmith* the Burton entourage migrated to Yugoslavia where Rich was under contract to the Ministry of Culture. This improbable alliance came about with an offer to play the country's president, Marshal Tito, in a reconstruction of his days as a freedom fighter against the German invaders. It was inspired casting. Rich assumed an uncanny resemblance to the young Tito, a leader for whom he professed a great admiration. But everything else about the film spelt disaster. A bad script was rejuvenated by Wolf Mankowitz (brought in at Rich's insistence) who then had to stand by while every semblance of originality was squeezed out by the official guardians of ideological purity.

It was impossible to be angry. Rich and Elizabeth were treated with great ceremony, enjoying a level of hospitality reserved for visiting world leaders. While the personal staff (now over thirty strong including the aircrew for the private jet) were installed in a plush hotel, Rich and Elizabeth stayed at the presidential palace. There they enjoyed a standard of luxury which put their own trappings of wealth into the minor league.

'Whatever Marx said about egalitarianism,' observed Rich, 'it certainly didn't extend to politicians.'

Summoned to Belgrade for a family discussion, I looked forward to sampling Yugoslavian largesse. But the palace was denied to me. Security forbade me or anyone else not of the elect to step beyond the stout iron gates which separated ordinary mortals from the president.

My first sight of Rich after an interval of several weeks disturbed me profoundly. He looked tired and sounded exhausted. The drinking was steady and relentless. By lunch he had put back more than I could take in a week. It did nothing to improve his mood which veered from the sullen to the brutally argumentative.

I took it as a blessing when work on the film was postponed while the Yugoslavian exchequer tried to grapple with an inflated budget. It took them three years to sort out the mess and to summon the nerve to finish the job.

Meanwhile, the Burtons and company proceeded on their Cook's tour of Europe. Next stop was Rome, the location for the reconstruction of *The Assassination of Trotsky*. Rich perked up a little at the prospect of a second chance for getting it right with the legendary Joseph Losey. Even the script looked good.

'For one thing, the lines I have to speak are Trotsky's own. That is a decided advantage.'

But it was one of those films put together by an international consortium with an international cast (Alain Delon was the assassin) which foundered on mutual misunderstanding. Rich remained outwardly confident that Trotsky was a cut above his other recent portrayals. But the tension was missing. It was almost as if the story was being played as a documentary – worthy but uninspiring. When in the weeks ahead Rich spoke hopefully of *Trotsky* he was praying for a miracle in the cutting room. It did not happen and the film was panned. One critic suggested it should be sold as a cure for insomnia.

The fourth shot at giving new meaning to the phrase 'disaster movie' centred on Budapest. Hungarian and Italian money was solicited to make *Bluebeard*, the sort of film Rich always swore he would never get into. In this blatant attempt to cash in on the soft porn market, Rich was the nutty Baron von Sapper who compensated for impotence by murdering a succession of beautiful wives. His acting in bed was convincing enough to cause Elizabeth some irritation but to those who lacked a personal interest the sequence of attempted couplings was hilarious. The last pretence of any seriousness of purpose was abandoned when Raquel Welch appeared as a nun. In real life, her cleavage would have threatened another dissolution of the monasteries.

Rich liked to think he was immune to press jibes but the rush of stories accompanying *Bluebeard* hurt him greatly. For the first time he felt the world was treating him like a fool – and a pathetic one at that. He needed to show he still had fight in him, that he was a force to be reckoned with.

There are no prizes for guessing what he did to proclaim his comeback. He threw a party – the wildest, most extravagant party of his career. The excuse was Elizabeth's fortieth birthday but, from the day the news broke, no one doubted that the celebration had an ulterior motive. The message was clear: We're still around, we're still on top and we're still in command of the headlines.

The invitations went out by cable – the Burtons' favourite means of communication and, given the antiquated postal service in Hungary, the one most likely to get through.

COME TO BUDAPEST FOR THE WEEKEND OF FEBRUARY 26 AND 27 TO HELP ELIZABETH CELEBRATE HER BIG 40 STOP YOU WILL BE OUR GUESTS FROM ARRIVAL TO DEPARTURE STOP THE HOTEL IS VERY HILTON BUT THERE ARE FUN PLACES TO GO STOP DRESS INFORMAL FOR SATURDAY NIGHT IN SOME DARK CELLAR STOP DARK SUIT OR DINNER JACKET FOR SUNDAY STOP DARK GLASSES FOR HANGOVER

Who could resist?

Replies from the British contingent were channelled through Marjorie Lee at the Dorchester. As a guest herself, her assumption of the work of chief organiser was a noble act of self-sacrifice.

The family was well represented – seven of us with partners travelling together to London. Our holiday weekend started on Thursday at the Dorchester where we had our own private party. The following morning we were shepherded by Marjorie to Heathrow where Rich had chartered a 150-seater Trident to ferry his pleasure seekers into central Europe. Among those linking up with us from the States were Elizabeth's brother Howard, who could be relied upon to keep his head whatever the circumstances, his wife Mara and their children.

Budapest was not the most cheerful of cities in those days but we did our best to liven it up. The welcome laid on for us by Rich and Elizabeth gave us a flying start. We were installed at the Intercontinental, better known as the Duna Hotel, where our hosts had the penthouse suite. To give us all a good view of the Danube, Rich booked the entire top floor. In each room we found a huge bouquet of out of season blooms, champagne on ice and a bar stocked with best wine and spirits. Cards identifying us as belonging to the Burton party entitled holders to free access to all the hotel services. Elizabeth even arranged for the hairdresser to stay open on Sunday so that the ladies could look their best for the big night.

The first of what turned out to be a succession of lavish celebrations was held in the hotel's wine cellars, the only surviving part of the old Duna which had thrived in the days of the Empire. To recreate what it must have been like when dress-suited flunkies sought out the finest vintages, Rich insisted on candlelight and cobwebs, the latter ingeniously created by the designers from the film studios. Their cleverness did not impress Cis whose housewifely instincts reacted against dirt of any kind. She was seen flitting about with a pocket handkerchief dusting away the offending draperies.

'Do you mind?' said Rich coming up to her. 'Those cobwebs cost a dollar a time to put up.'

The guests were a curious mix of friends and colleagues from both sides of the Burton partnership, representing an extraordinary range of interest. I listened in on a lively conversation between an international pop artist (Ringo Starr) and a man of letters (Stephen Spender) in the full knowledge that neither had any idea of the other's identity. Nevill Coghill talked to Frankie Howerd, a favourite comedian since 1955 when Rich had seen him as Charley's Aunt – one of the funniest performances, Rich claimed, on any stage at any time. As a young actor, not yet a star, Rich had sought and achieved a guest appearance on Frankie Howerd's radio show.

'I wasn't much of a comedian,' Rich admitted, 'but I learned one hell of a lot about timing.'

The press corps was not specifically invited but neither was it discouraged from looking in. The publicity, Rich calculated, was bound to have a sharp edge (it always did when the Burtons were involved) but there was nothing outrageous to be heard or photographed and so no point in trying to impose restrictions. He reckoned without Alun Williams, the older son of Emlyn who was there with his father and Brook Williams. Why Alun bothered to come I cannot imagine because in the course of the evening he made it abundantly clear that he strongly disapproved of all this junketing. In a voice which could be overheard the other side of the Danube he demanded to know why so much money should be wasted in idle frivolity when, out there, ordinary, decent Hungarians were wondering where to find their next crust?

There were several good answers to this question. For a start, party-giving was a perfectly legitimate feature of the star system. If you've got it, flaunt it, was the first rule for getting to the top in Hollywood. No doubt there were better ways of managing an industry but the Burtons could hardly be blamed for following custom. For them to have stopped giving parties would have been the equivalent of a resignation from the league of top earners.

Then again, the fifty thousand pounds it cost to set up the Budapest jamboree was money earned and spent in Hungary, with obvious benefits to local employment on both sides of the equation. It would have been easier for Rich to take the money and run though what good this would have achieved (except for easing Alun Williams' conscience) I found it difficult to imagine. Needless to say, the press was not too interested in the subtler arguments. The following day, the papers reported Alun's outburst as the central attraction of the party. Rich was pressed for a response. What did he intend doing about it?

Fighting down the urge to deliver some apposite comments on the abuse of hospitality, Rich stopped the affair in its tracks and saved the weekend by announcing that whatever the cost of the party, a corresponding sum would be donated to charity. Subsequently, a cheque was handed over to the United Nations' Children's Fund.

Weekend sightseeing took us to the old part of the city (really two cities, Buda and Pest, separated by the Danube). The museums and art galleries were less fun than wandering the streets which, to our amazement, were a happy release from the formality of state-organised leisure. People stared at us as if we were prize exhibits but once we made the effort to start conversation we were beset by friendly strangers eager to try out their halting English.

On the Saturday afternoon the men divided between those who wanted to enjoy the sweaty pleasures of the Turkish baths (there was a wide choice of establishments on the banks of the river) and the rest who were happier watching others sweat on the rugby field. Rich had asked me to bring a video of the British Lions triumphant tour of New Zealand. An appreciative audience joined him in his suite to watch the re-run on television. There followed a small dinner party, mostly family but with one or two special guests. Verdun found himself next to Princess Grace of Monaco, an opportunity he relished but one which he thought he would have to forgo when his new shirt threatened to strangle him.

'I can't understand it,' he apologised when his attempts to release the pressure on his windpipe became too obvious to ignore. 'I know I asked for the right size.'

The princess was understanding. 'You must change. You can't sit there all evening looking as if you're about to have a seizure.'

With many apologies, Verdun departed the table. Ten minutes later he was back, looking much happier but with the same shirt.

'There was nothing wrong with the size,' he confessed sheepishly. 'It was just that I'd forgotten to take out the cardboard stiffeners.'

He expected and got a ribbing from us all but his humiliation was short-lived. Within hours the target for jokes had shifted from Verdun to Tom who was found by Rich contemplating a mound of Beluga caviar.

'What is it? What does it taste like?' he wanted to know.

Thinking carefully for a comparison that would make sense, Rich fastened on the Welsh delicacy made from seaweed.

'It's a bit like lava bread,' he told his brother. Tom relaxed. 'Oh, that's all right, then.' And taking hold of a piece of bread, he ladled on enough caviar to satisfy a royal banquet. At about thirty pounds a bite it was, thought Rich, a sandwich so expensive as to qualify for the *Guinness Book of Records*.

The big party was on the Sunday evening. For this we went up in the world, from the cellars of the Duna to the rooftop nightclub which was specially decorated with thousands of gold balloons and masses of white lilacs and red tulips.

'Madam's done it quite well, hasn't she?' observed Frankie Howerd.

Everything about the evening was magnificently and extravagantly grand including the thirty-piece orchestra, a distinct improvement on the Hungarian pop group from the Friday session, whose favourite number, 'I Left My Heart In San Francisco', was repeated to the point of insanity.

Since this was the birthday party proper, Elizabeth wore her present from Rich, a heart-shaped pendant that once belonged to Shah Jehan who built the Taj Mahal. Valued then at over one hundred thousand dollars it was inscribed 'Eternal love till death'. Obviously, we could not match such largesse but I think we acquitted ourselves handsomely with a presentation of an engraved plate crafted from finest Welsh steel.

The journey home was one long delicious round of anecdotes. How, on encountering Raquel Welch with her arm in plaster, one of my brothers, who must be nameless to protect him from his wife, asked if he could help put on her bra. How we all danced wth Princess Grace and how Rich, in a delightful impromptu speech, nominated her

Princess of Gwalia (an old name for Wales). And how Hilda on meeting Michael Caine told him how much she enjoyed *The Man Between*, only realising afterwards that she had been thinking of James Mason.

Staying overnight at the Dorchester we were invited to the BBC Lime Grove studios for a group interview. I was asked about Elizabeth's presents and mentioned that she had been given yet another dog, a large Hungarian hound of indeterminate breed. What I did not know then was that the beast had turned out to be a fast worker with the ladies. Left alone for a few minutes with the treasured Shih Tzu, he had worked his wicked way on the innocent poodle. Well, not so innocent according to Rich, who thereafter called her the French tart.

Back home we suffered the inevitable anticlimax. Brother-in-law Dai spoke for us all when, resuming work as a carpenter on the new M4 motorway, he told a friend, 'I feel like a multi-millionaire who's just gone bust.'

Thinking back on the Budapest party my only sadness was in noticing the change in Rich from the rock-like hero I had known most of my life to the tired, middle-aged celebrity who was feeling the days getting shorter. Caught off guard he looked in poor health. His back was playing him up (an inherited problem shared by all the Jenkins children) but more serious, or so it seemed then, were the after-effects of his bout of malaria. Elizabeth told me of at least two seizures, almost like epileptic fits, which had come upon Rich with terrifying suddenness. On the second of these, but for the presence of Chen Sam who turned in some nifty first aid, he might easily have choked on his own tongue.

For someone who needed to take better care of himself, Rich showed no sign of letting up on the harmful pleasures. The drinking bouts were sporadic but they still added up to a formidable consumption. And because the drinking was so obviously a problem it was easy to forget smoking – at least a hundred cigarettes a day – and the inadequacy of his diet. Fried chips were still his staple food. It was almost as if he was defying the fates to do their worst.

I checked with friends that it was not just my imagination. The consensus held that Rich was playing a dangerous game, putting himself and his marriage at risk. An actor who had worked with Rich on and off for over a decade told me that Elizabeth, who was no mean drinker herself, found it difficult to understand the total loss of control which could turn a loving husband into a raging brute. Maybe, it was suggested, she might decide to take it personally. If Rich was indeed fighting against something she did not have to look very far for an obvious target.

In seeking out opinions I tried to distinguish between sympathetic concern and malicious, often wishful, gossip. But it was not that easy. There was no denying that Rich had troubles; what was less obvious was the extent to which Elizabeth and Rich himself, thought of the troubles as self created. Who, in all this, was the real victim?

The opportunity to find out more came later in the year with an invitation to Munich where Rich was filming. He was coming up for his forty-seventh birthday and he wanted one member of the family to be with him on 10 November. He was fitter than when I had seen him in Budapest and when I said how well he looked, Elizabeth chimed in with the proud boast that he had been on the wagon for six months.

'But tonight,' declared Rich expansively, 'we celebrate.' Elizabeth was understandably cautious.

'I wouldn't have too much if I were you, love. Why don't we order a beer each to give you a toast?'

The drinks were brought up; good German lagers, ice cold. While I sipped mine I watched Rich fill his glass. With an almost malicious grin of satisfaction, he contemplated the light froth. Then he put the glass to his lips, tipped it back and swallowed the contents in one long gulp. Elizabeth looked on in near despair.

'That was a bit silly, wasn't it love?'

A still playful Rich answered. 'It's my birthday, isn't it? Surely I can do something special on my birthday.'

A little later he cut across a conversation I was having with Elizabeth.

'I am mindful of another drink,' he bellowed. 'And why am I drinking beer when I can afford champagne?'

The waiter came in so fast he might have been listening at the keyhole.

'If it's champagne,' said Elizabeth grimly, 'you two are on your own.' She got up.

'You stay where you are,' Rich shouted but without another word she turned and left the room.

Rich transferred his attention to the waiter who was standing by.

'Champagne! Champagne! Champagne!' he roared, banging his fist on a small table like a child demanding a toy.

The waiter hurried away. I sat tight, not quite knowing what to say or do. Rich had his head down, his elbows on his knees. He showed no inclination to talk and did not even look my way until there was an open bottle of Dom Perignon and a glass by his side. Then he started in on me.

'Well, young Gray. What are we going to do with you?'

His question surprised me. 'I don't think you have to do anything.'

'So you're happy. Contented with your lot. Is that it?'

'I wouldn't say so.'

'No, I didn't think you would. It can't be much of a life. Measuring out your days in a council office. With your intelligence you could be something better than, what do you call yourself? A chief clerk?'

The sneer in his voice was unmistakable. I bridled.

'I don't know what you're trying to say. It's not like that and you know it.'

But Rich had touched a sensitive nerve. By most standards I had done reasonably well. I had gone into local government as a late teenager and had risen through the ranks to become manager of the Afan Lido in Port Talbot, the biggest sports and entertainment complex in Britain. My other job, as a rugby reporter on Welsh radio, was essentially part time but it gave me huge pleasure. I had a lovely wife who knew me better than I knew myself and two fine youngsters. Not much to complain about there.

And yet. And yet. I was in the sort of job where the pressure to conform led to petty jealousies and vindictive backbiting. I was sick to death of having to justify any success I enjoyed by arguing my own merits against the implied advantages of starting as Richard Burton's brother. At forty-five I was thinking seriously of a change.

Rich interrupted my thoughts by slapping me hard on the knee.

'It's obvious. There's only one answer. You've got to work for me.'

The suggestion came as such a surprise, my response must have sounded ungracious.

'Oh no. You've got me wrong. That's not what I want at all.'

Now it was Rich's turn to bridle.

'And what the hell's wrong with working for me?'

I pointed to the now empty champagne bottle and to the replacement he had put on ice.

'It's not my sort of life.'

'You enjoy it when you're here.'

'But I'm only here for a while. Full time would kill me. Anyway, I wouldn't want to watch you destroying yourself.'

Rich stood up. He was shaking, though from anger or alcohol, I could not tell.

'You little bastard,' he shouted. 'How dare you tell me how to behave. Who do you think you are?'

There was a lot more of this. The two of us standing face to face, trading insults, mostly in Welsh, until we were too tired to go on.

The next morning at breakfast no one talked. After his second coffee Rich got up and went into his bedroom. We heard the soft tap of his portable typewriter.

'What are you writing?' Elizabeth called out.

'A letter,' said Rich.

'Who to?'

'My brother.'

After a few minutes he came out and handed me an envelope.

'Don't open it until you're on the plane,' he ordered.

Fastened into my seat with the air hostess hovering with a drink, I stared at the envelope a long time before lifting the flap. The letter read:

The first day of my forty-eighth year.

Dearest Graham,

Thank you for tolerating my blown mind yesterday. There is an element of schizophrenia in everybody's make-up (not done by Ron Berkeley) and peculiarly so in our family's and fine honed to a razor's edge in mine. My chief and most vicious faculty when I lose my balance on the tight-rope is to attack with malicious venom the people I love most. Towards the apathetic, I am apathetic. I don't bother to attack Harry John Doe Jones because he is not worth my attention, but show me a loved one and the bludgeon and sabre and épée and foil are out with lips curled the wrong way and my name is 'fang'.

Anyway, you are a fine and splendid man and I am proud to tell people so and the job and the jobs you have done are truly remarkable. With very few of my advantages you succeeded beyond the dreams of envy. Keep it up and – here comes the pot advising the kettle – watch the booze.

The letter confused me. It was a handsome apology; more, perhaps, than I deserved. But was it reasonable to see in it any hint of redemption? I was sufficiently encouraged to put the row behind me and not to talk about it with the family.

Good news followed in a day or two when I heard of a move forward in Rich's long promised intention to do more at Oxford. His election as an honorary fellow of St Peter's College required him to appear for the occasional lecture or seminar but not to live in Oxford for any length of time. It was, I thought, the perfect compromise. But contrary to the impression given by the papers, the honour was not entirely unsolicited. Engineered by Francis Warner, his lobbying was undoubtedly helped by Rich's promise to raise his contributions to the theatre appeal.

Nevill Coghill was delighted. Now well into his seventies he knew that time was short to achieve his ambition of a fine new theatre for Oxford. His sense of urgency heightened a few months later when he suffered a stroke. He wrote with typical lack of self-pity of his slow recovery and of his wish to get plans underway, 'before my time runs out'.

The problem seemed to be a lack of communication between Rich and those who looked after his affairs. Nevill tried to spell out what was wrong. On the plus side was a letter from Aaron Frosch: 'I am informed by telephone that Mr and Mrs Burton have indeed stated they are prepared to increase their gift and that the plans presented by Professor Coghill are acceptable to them. . . . I note that the plan is to commence building next March. We are scheduling a substantial payment on account of the said gift prior to that time.'

But March came and went without any transfer of funds. Nevill appealed directly to Rich.

'Do you think Aaron could be authorised by you to let us have the payments he mentions?'

As far as I know he never received a satisfactory response. Consequently building was postponed indefinitely. Rich, meanwhile, was still bubbling on about how he was planning to take Oxford by storm. He told a friend of his meeting the economist Kenneth Galbraith.

'I asked him the secrets of being a successful lecturer and he said, "You have to mumble so they can't hear anything you say and be as obscure as possible so they'll go out and buy the books."'

He reassured a journalist who asked him if he was really made out to be a teacher. 'Oh yes. I'll wear a rotting cap and a rugger scarf and say, "Good morning, Jones Minor. Never mind your tutorial. Send your sister up with the essay."'

I could not help wondering if Oxford was truly ready for him. Perhaps it was just as well we never found out. Still, my sympathy went out to Nevill Coghill and his friends who were victims of the very peculiar circumstances of the Burtons' lifestyle. These arose because there were too many self-interested people involved in their affairs. Letters did not get to Rich, telephone calls were not put through and meetings were cancelled at the last moment. All this was done, so it was said, to protect him from unnecessary pressures. But I suspect other motives, not least the desire by some of his employees to monopolise a valuable property. Aaron Frosch most definitely did not fall within this category. But he was made frail by the mounting torment of muscular sclerosis and was beginning to lose out to less scrupulous members of the household.

The position was made more complex by the changes in Rich's

character which made him altogether less predictable and by the deteriorating relationship with Elizabeth.

I realised all this at first hand when, after the Munich incident, I was encouraged by Rich to think again about a change of job. I made it clear that under no circumstances could I join the Burton staff. 'All right,' said Rich, 'what do you want to do?'

'If I was to resign my job and if we could afford it, we'd live in the Channel Islands, Guernsey probably. It's what we've always wanted to do.'

'Then what's the problem? Just do it. I've got some money there. You could look after it for me. You wouldn't make a fortune but with commissions and such you could bring in twenty or thirty thousand a year.'

It sounded like a fortune to me.

'Are you serious?'

'Never more so. Have you ever heard me joke about money?'

Well, that was true at least. After talking it over with Hilary, I decided on a break for freedom. But, sadly, like Nevill Coghill, I pitched my expectations too high. After the first flush of excitement at handing in my resignation accompanied by a few choice words on my reasons for leaving, I spent some anxious weeks trying to persuade Rich to advance beyond vague promises. By the time we came to move to Guernsey, there was still nothing in writing though Aaron assured me he could work out some sort of deal. It didn't happen. Instead we made our own way, me in property development, Hilary in the hotel business.

Looking back, I am profoundly grateful to Rich for giving me the push towards a new life. Returning from Guernsey I landed a job doing what I always wanted to do – sports organiser for the BBC. But for Rich telling me to get off my backside, it would never have happened. And if, along the way, I voiced my resentment at what I believed to be his lack of consideration or decent regard for business courtesies, I must now temper my views with the knowledge that he had more than enough problems of his own to occupy him.

# Chapter 16

After Budapest came the time for Rich and Elizabeth to fulfil their long-standing promise to do something for Harlech Television. Dozens of scripts were considered and pushed aside before one was found to satisfy the stars, the company and the money men who spoke for American interests. The writer was John Hopkins whose pedigree led with *Talking to a Stranger*, one of the most powerful domestic dramas ever to appear on British television. In this quartet of plays he looked at a family crisis from the point of view of four of the participants. Now he was called upon to try a similar technique with *Divorce His, Divorce Hers*, a study of a marriage break-up as seen by both partners.

But the idea was horribly misconceived. In trying for a re-run of *Who's Afraid of Virginia Woolf?*, Rich and Elizabeth were playing dangerously close to home. The rows they were having on set were so overlapping the rows they had in private, there were times when they hardly knew whose lives they were talking about. Professionally this might have worked, if the stars had been forced to submit to a higher discipline – an Edward Albee dialogue, for instance, or a Mike Nichols direction. But neither the writer nor director had that sort of power. In *Divorce His, Divorce Hers*, whatever Burton and Taylor wanted, Burton and Taylor got. And since they were in such turmoil they could not even begin to impose a sense of unity on what turned out to be a long-winded discourse of marital platitudes.

By now, Rich was well on the way to an emotional collapse brought on by excessive alcoholism. Elizabeth too, was hitting the Jack Daniels. What angered me so much was that no one, not even Elizabeth, seemed capable of spelling out to him the terrible dangers he was running. It took Rich himself to prove to me that you can't just tell an alcoholic to give up or die. He knows the choice is not so stark. He will tell you of a half world he has shaped from his own fantasies, somewhere between life and death. It is here that he can come to terms with his own troubled nature, where all questions are answered and all responsibilities lifted. But this half world has no permanence. It has to be recreated day after day while the fear of being left alone in the real world grows ever more painful.

Poor Rich. The passer-by would have said he had everything. If contentment was not his, then contentment was not to be had. To which my brother would reply,

'To have everything is to lose everything. The dread of losing is the greatest dread of all.'

And Rich was losing. He had already lost Ivor who had died three weeks after the Budapest party. He was losing his career to the inanities of the film industry, he was losing his mind to the mediocre film opportunities offered him and he was losing his wife to the anger of his failure. It was full circle.

Early in 1973 he admitted to me for the first time that he was an alcoholic. Confession frightened him. He made me promise not to say a word to Cis. He said she would worry more than was good for her but while this was true, he was really more concerned to sidestep her disapproval.

'I need all the help I can get,' he told me. 'I'm talking to doctors who know about this sort of thing. They say I can pull round.'

A few weeks later he submitted to a rigorous diet which excluded hard spirits and permitted only occasional glasses of wine.

The experience was terrifying.

'You shake, you sweat, you can't read. You can't pick anything up because your hands shake so much.'

But no sooner was he over the first horror than he went back on drink. A mutual friend said of him, 'He sees too many others who need their daily fix.'

In mid 1973 the Burton circus was back in Rome – Rich to play a Gestapo officer in a Carlo Ponti production, *Massacre in Rome*, and Elizabeth to play the older woman in a mawkish love story called *Ash Wednesday*.

They raved about their films (each thought the other was in a degrading role), about the people they worked for and about the people who worked for them. Of the joint staff only Chen Sam, Bob Wilson and Ron Berkeley inspired the trust of both employers. For the rest there were accusations of plotting and double dealing which, if half true, would have done credit to the Borgias.

Rich looked dreadful – his face loose and puffy, his arms hanging loosely, he shuffled about like a tired old man. Elizabeth hid weary eyes behind dark glasses. Billowing dresses could not disguise her excess weight. Though more obviously in command of herself than Rich, she was not easy to talk to. Quick to misinterpret, she could turn a kind word with a stinging rebuke.

The press reported every angry exchange, every traded insult, real or rumoured. Those of us who loved them both went through agonies of frustrating inactivity. What could we do to help? Telephone calls were refused, letters unanswered (I suspect Rich never even saw most of them). One letter was actually returned unopened.

In over a month there was just one communication, a cable to brother Tom. It read, 'Worry not. All is well between us.'

A few days later, Elizabeth flew to California. Officially it was put out that having finished work on *Ash Wednesday* she was travelling ahead of Rich who would join her when he was free to do so. Unofficially, it was an open secret that Elizabeth wanted to get away.

Recalling this time, she told me, 'We were killing each other. And for why? I couldn't just sit there and let it happen.'

Rich was befuddled, not knowing what to do next. After a week he was mooching about his hotel suite when he found his daughter Maria, now aged twelve, packing a suitcase.

'What are you up to, love?'

'I'm going to New York to be with Mommy.'

'Are you packing for me too?'

'No.'

They said goodbye and Maria left with her nanny.

From Elizabeth he heard not a word. When there was nothing else to do, Rich joined the trek to America. In New York he went to the Long Island home of Aaron Frosch and from there he rang Elizabeth in California, asking her to join him. Contrary to the usual story he did not rant or rave. According to Elizabeth he was almost plaintive, begging her to come back. She agreed as long as he would keep sober. He promised.

They met at Kennedy Airport. Rich was waiting for her in the back of a chauffeur-driven limousine. Elizabeth knew immediately he had been drinking. She sat tight-lipped as Rich embraced her and as they drove away her head drooped.

There followed the inevitable row. Rich tried to pre-empt his wife's justifiable anger by accusing her of being unfaithful. Harsh words were said of businessman Henry Wynberg who had been seen with Elizabeth; 'that second-hand car salesman', as Rich contemptuously described him. It was an epithet which stuck even though cars were only a small part of his business interests.

The shouting lasted all of two hours and at the end of it Elizabeth ordered the car for the drive back to Kennedy.

The formal announcement of a separation came from John Springer, Elizabeth's press secretary. By way of explanation Elizabeth spoke of 'loving each other too much' and of having 'been in each other's pockets constantly'. The statement ended a trifle dramatically. 'Pray for us.'

Aaron was told to work out the financial arrangement.

'It'll be very complex,' he warned.

'Just do whatever she wants,' said Rich.

Sensibly, Aaron went about his business cautiously. Like everyone else he hoped for a reconciliation. The signs were not entirely unhopeful.

Self-disgust and the shock of knowing Elizabeth was no longer in thrall to him sent Rich back to his booze-free diet. He hired a doctor and a nurse to make sure he stuck to it.

In August, he returned to Rome for another Carlo Ponti production, *The Voyage*, for which his co-star was Ponti's wife, Sophia Loren. These two were incredibly kind to Rich. Carlo Ponti believed in his talent and Sophia Loren in his humanity and though both had their faith strained to breaking point, they remained loyal. To stay on the wagon he needed someone near him who was witty, diverting and extremely patient. It had to be a woman, and a beautiful woman at that. Sophia Loren, unpaid and unthanked, accepted the role.

I spent several weekends with them. The call from Rich would come late in the week. 'Can you get over here, I want to talk?' It was always about Elizabeth; how life was joyless without her, how he wanted so much to recapture her love.

We slept in the same room, the conversation, often disjointed and always circuitous, going on late into the night. His last words before he went to sleep were ever the same, delivered in a deep growl.

'Another day, yr uffern, you hell; another day, drink, you devil. I've beaten you.'

I was intrigued to find that women still flocked round him. If they were seeking some advantage, financial or professional, I could understand but if they wanted more, I seriously doubted that Rich could deliver. One of them certainly had intimations of bliss. I was fast asleep one night when I felt a tug at my arm. I came round, hearing a whispered plea close to my ear.

'Reechard, Reechard. I am here. I love you. Take me. Take me.'

'Sorry love,' I said, lifting my head, 'the man you want is in the next bed.'

I was in Palermo with Rich when word came through that Elizabeth had been rushed to hospital. It sounded bad. Whoever rang from Los Angeles mentioned the probability of cancer. Rich went immediately to Carlo Ponti who gave him time off to fly to California. Before leaving Rich asked me to go to Naples in the *Kalizma*. I sailed in lonely state wondering how much more drama could be packed into two lives.

On arriving I was told to expect to see Rich before the end of the day. And not only Rich. Elizabeth was with him. It appeared she was not desperately ill, after all. Maybe, just desperately in love. When they came aboard the *Kalizma* I had never seen them look happier. We had a wonderful meal together, joking and laughing about old times. Hardly able to believe what I was witnessing, I wished them all the joy in the world.

'Tell them at home,' said Rich. 'The bad times are over.'

The good times lasted until Christmas when 'just to celebrate' Rich had a little drink. They were in Gstaad. There had been some thought of a family reunion in Wales but when nothing further was heard from Rich, we assumed he and Elizabeth wanted to be alone. In fact, Elizabeth was not even there. On the first appearance of a bottle she had packed her bags. When the bottle was replaced she booked a flight. And when the third bottle was emptied, she left.

They met up again briefly in Puerto Vallarta and in Oroville in northern California where, in March 1974, Rich went to co-star with Lee Marvin in *The Klansman*. A more inappropriate alliance it was difficult to imagine. If Rich was the reformed drinker who had lapsed, Lee Marvin was the unrepentant drinker who was still far short of his limit. The two got on famously but brought everyone else on the film to the edge of a nervous breakdown. More than once, the director, Terence Young, thought of abandoning the project.

Elizabeth came and went. She was on set just long enough to know there was nothing she could say to bring Rich to his senses. Just before leaving she urged Valerie Douglas, who now handled Rich's domestic affairs, to book him into St John's Hospital in Santa Monica.

'Either that,' she said, 'or he's a dead man.'

By all accounts it was a close run thing. The doctors told him if he continued to drink, he had less than a month to live. He submitted to treatment and suffered the torture. One of his lines from *The Comedians* came back to me: 'I've always wanted to know the worst about

207

myself; to feel the bottom of the gutter with my toes.' Now he knew. He could hardly walk without someone holding him up; he could hardly talk without someone finishing his sentences and he could not sleep without someone handing him the glass and the tablets.

The tumbril moved on. Rich was in hospital for about ten weeks. When he came out, divorce papers had been filed. The formalities took another six months to complete.

'I wonder,' mused Emlyn Williams, 'who will get custody of Brook?'

The first of many Burton comebacks started promisingly. At a time when not one of the big studios would invest a penny in him, Rich had one of the best offers for many a year. The BBC wanted him to play Churchill in *A Walk with Destiny*, a ninety-minute dramatised documentary co-produced with Hallmark. Based on Churchill's memoirs, the programme was to cover the period 1934 to 1940 when Sir Winston became prime minister. The producer, Jack Le Vein, had worked with Rich on *The Valiant Years*. It all looked very promising. There was just one problem. The deal was linked to a remake of *Brief Encounter*, the Trevor Howard and Celia Johnson classic which came out in 1945.

To this second, riskier enterprise Rich made token resistance. He enjoyed being told by people who should have known better that he was not too old or too world weary for the part. Then there was the touchy question of precedence. It was no secret Rich was second choice to Robert Shaw who was held up on other film commitments. But as Rich graciously put it, when he knew that Sophia Loren was to co-star and he heard 'her gently imperious voice which turns my stomach into a bag of butterflies', he was persuaded.

Now it was the turn of the BBC to need some persuading – that Rich was, indeed, fit for work. I can't say I blamed them. Superficially, he was a reformed character. He looked fitter and leaner. He dressed with care. Some of the old sparkle was back. He was able to laugh his booming laugh without sounding like a cracked bell.

But his mind was in uproar. He told me he felt as if he were coming out of a nightmare and still half asleep. He said the strangest things at the strangest times. Strolling the promenade in Nice he stopped an attractive woman, a perfect stranger, fixed her with his eyes and said, 'If I should go away, beloved, do not say he has forgotten me. Forever you abide a singing rib within my dreaming side.' Then he walked on. I often wonder how the story went down in some quiet French home above the town. 'I met this loony today who called me beloved . . .' No doubt it was put down to the effect of the sun.

Also in Nice, in a packed bar, observing three nuns come in carrying charity boxes, Rich thunderously ordered everybody to 'kneel and pray'. 'And do you know,' he later ruminated, 'some besotted bastards actually went down on the floor.'

But there was not much to laugh about. He talked a lot of Elizabeth. It was almost as if she was in the next room. Further away, perhaps, when he growled, 'She's better off without me.'

His temper was edgy. He could be cruel without provocation. We had a lot of this; the sneering dismissal of old friends, the snide remarks to create mischief.

When he saw Valerie Douglas quizzing one of his companions he shouted at her across a crowded table.

'I know what you're trying to find out. You want to know if I've slept with her.'

The assembly laughed dutifully.

Occasionally, the public was permitted a glimpse of the black side of Rich's character. A week before the American TV premiere of *A Walk With Destiny*, Rich was asked to write an article about Churchill for the arts section of the *New York Times*. They expected a laudatory piece on the great war leader. Instead, they were treated to a vitriolic assault on Churchill the right-wing politician, of whom Rich declared, 'to know him is to hate him'.

In other circumstances much of his argument might have been judged a useful corrective to the mythology of Churchill as the hero who could do no wrong. But having just played the man in a favourable light, after seeking extensive help from the Churchill family, his attack was in bad taste to say the least. To say the worst, it was way over the top, a catalogue of violent histrionics and gross inaccuracies. (Churchill did not order the shooting of Welsh strikers in the labour troubles of the 1920s.) The wild flights of prose indicated to some an unbalanced mind, though, in my view, allowance must always be made for Rich's lifelong desire to emulate Dylan Thomas.

The producers were appalled and made haste to disassociate themselves from the Burton thesis. Ironically, the publicity achieved a higher American rating for the play. But in Britain, the unfavourable press cut a swathe through the ranks of the Burton fan club.

Rich maintained his reputation for being accident prone in print when Stanley Baker, his friend and fellow countryman, died of cancer in 1976. The editor of the *Observer* had the bright idea of asking Rich to write an obituary. He responded with a rough, rambling piece which filled the front page of the review section. It was written with love, no one could doubt it, but graphic references to youthful indiscretions – 'we fought, we smashed windows and broke trains and lusted after the same women and drove through the Continent, pustular and acne'd and angry and madly in love with the earth and all its riches' – though liable to thrill the breakfast readers of a Sunday paper did not please the Baker family or some of the actor's straight-laced admirers.

*A Walk With Destiny* was greeted respectfully; *Brief Encounter* was dismissed as an absurdity.

'Where else,' asked Clive James in the *Observer*, 'would an Italian beauty queen with a wardrobe of exotic if badly chosen clothes pretend to be the humdrum wife of a British solicitor and make goo goo eyes at a raddled Welsh thespian trying to pass himself off as a promising physician by dyeing his hair with black boot-polish?'

He did colour his hair, not with boot polish but with a dye so strong that it would not come out by washing. It took him a year to get back to his natural grey.

'There,' he said when the last traces of black had disappeared. 'I feel old again. But still incredibly gifted.'

After *Brief Encounter*; nothing. Rich whiled away his time in a hotel suite waiting for a promised deal from one of those European film consortia where there are more accountants than actors. It didn't come.

Elizabeth, meanwhile, was back with Henry Wynberg who helped to keep her in the public eye. Rich too had his much publicised diversions – Princess Elizabeth of Yugoslavia, and Jeanne Bell, a striking beauty whose claim to fame was to feature as the first black girl in a *Playboy* centrefold. The rest of the household was much reduced. Bob Wilson was still there, so was Brook Williams (who kept a lower profile when Elizabeth was around) and Valerie Douglas. Otherwise there were just two secretaries and Rich's favourite pet, a one-eyed pekinese.

Much effort went into persuading the press that Rich was teetotal. But the evidence of long evenings in dark bars counted against him.

Among those who were not deluded were the members of the Council of Oxford University who, in late 1975, finally rejected the appeal of Nevill Coghill to award Rich an honorary degree.

'This is a great blow which I know you will feel as sharply as I do,' wrote Nevill to Aaron Frosch. 'I had secured all the support I could find, including a unanimous petition from the Curators of the University Theatre. . . . However, our hopes have been dashed and there is nothing more I can do about it except to record my disappointment and disgust at this fresh example of the hostility of the University to the Drama, against which I have striven for most of my life.'

But it was not the Drama that defeated Rich so much as the slightly

210

tatty image that now accompanied him. You could imagine that common-room conversation, 'This chap, Burton, not quite our sort, do you think?'

Nevill had another disappointment. His new theatre was not built. He had to make do with a rehearsal room tacked on to the existing Oxford Playhouse. It was called the Burton Beckett annexe.

To break the run of inactivity, Rich decided on a change of management. He called Robert Lantz, a top agent whose deceptive dry humour and gentle manner disguised one of the shrewdest brains in film and theatre. Rich was taking a chance. Years earlier he and Elizabeth had made a joint approach to Lantz. He agreed in principle to represent them.

'There's just one thing,' concluded Rich, 'we don't pay ten per cent. Five is our top.'

'I quite understand,' said Robby, smiling sweetly as he rose from the table. 'Why don't you come back when you can afford me.'

This time there was no quibbling over figures. Rich asked bluntly, 'Are you interested in representing a drunken, clapped-out old actor?'

Robby said he thought he could cope. 'But this must not hurt Elizabeth. I love her very much and would not do anything to upset her.'

Rich answered, 'Who does not love Elizabeth?'

With a career so obviously shaking on the edge, Robby decided there was no time to mount a gradual recovery. The rescue had to be bold and decisive. Another of the Lantz clients was the dramatist Peter Shaffer whose latest play, *Equus*, was enjoying a successful Broadway run. Heading the cast as the psychiatrist, Dysart, was Anthony Perkins who was on contract until the end of the year. A replacement was needed. Why not Burton?

John Dexter, who directed *Equus* in London and New York, was not immediately taken with the idea. He pointed out that Dysart is a dry-as-dust character, an unassertive middle-of-the-road professional who discovers his own emotional inadequacies through the investigation of a shocking crime. Dexter worried that Rich was too strong an actor to show Dysart's vulnerability. The counter view held that his troubles had softened up Rich. He *was* vulnerable.

It was worth a try. A meeting was fixed in London, at Squire's Mount where Gwen, Ivor's widow, had settled. The guests were to be Robby Lantz and Alex Cohen, producer of the Burton–Gielgud *Hamlet* and of several Shaffer plays on Broadway. When they arrived Gwen was bustling about preparing lunch. Rich would be down shortly, she said. After an hour, they heard a grunting outside the door. The handle was turned and in walked Rich looking as if he had lost his way.

His movements were clumsy, his speech slurred. He was, quite obviously, sloshed out of his mind.

The lunch was a nightmare of social ineptitude. At one point, leaning aside for a dish, Rich fell on the floor. It took one guest on each arm to get him to his feet.

Agent and producer were appalled but not defeated. Fortunately for Rich, they decided to try again another day. He was signed up for *Equus*.

In his dealings with friends and relatives, Rich was equally unpredictable. From being sober and sensible he could veer off on some fantastical argument which left us all gasping. He longed to see Elizabeth again. I felt that in this tumultuous period of his life she, more than anyone, represented self-control and stability – much as Sybil had done when the *Cleopatra* saga was at its peak.

He took to telephoning his ex-wife, sometimes more than once in a day. They continued to meet, I assume without the knowledge of their regular escorts. When the press stole a picture of them arm in arm it was explained away by an accidental overlap in their schedules. But when this happened twice in a month, a likelier explanation circulated. It gained currency when the two spent a short holiday at Gstaad. They looked so happy together.

It is true that Rich gloried in the rediscovered delights of a familiar partner. He was at home. This, he enthused, is how it always should be. As for Elizabeth, I am not so sure. There was, I know, a hope that Rich had, at last, taken hold of himself. But was it conceivable that she would gamble on recapturing the old magic? Evidently, yes, because two months later they were remarried. The ceremony took place in a village in northern Botswana.

On the face of it, a more unlikely setting could not be imagined. But it was remote and romantic and they loved the place. Rich said afterwards that it had all happened in a dream world. To which I could only respond that I and the rest of the family were part of it. We really believed the miracle had happened.

Elizabeth was the first to hit reality. On the very day of the wedding she found Rich so overloaded with vodka he could barely walk.

'I led the lad back to bed and suggested he tried to get a couple of hours' sleep so that his eyeballs could change from magenta to at least a pretty conjunctivitis pink.'

It was a brave attempt to laugh off what she must then have known to be a terrible mistake.

'How can you get mad at anyone so utterly outrageous? I love him deeply and truly and forever but I do recognise one or two flaws in the immense personage.'

Our first chance to congratulate the couple came in November. With Rich due to stay over in London for his fiftieth birthday, Elizabeth rang ahead to ask Marjorie Lee to organise a splendid party of the style only the Dorchester knows how to lay on.

Mindful of Rich's simple culinary taste, the designers chose what I can only describe as an upmarket Cockney theme. To carry the buffet of sausage and mash, tripe and onions, ham, turkey, pork and, of course, chips, the Orchid Room was occupied by a fleet of multi-coloured coster barrows. These were given a suitably luxurious setting by the addition of gold hangings and tablecloths.

Rich was surprised and pleased to see so many of his friends and family gathered to celebrate his birthday. Carrying a glass of wine which he sipped rarely he kept sober on into the early hours when he led the community singing in as fine a rendering of the Welsh language as to be heard outside the valleys.

But it was a different story when Rich and Elizabeth came to Pontrhydyfen to spend a few days with Hilda. Rich was in terrible shape, drawn and haggard. I asked Elizabeth what was wrong.

'It's what happens when he's been off the booze for a few days. Withdrawal symptoms. If he could stay off for a few more weeks, he'd be all right.'

Just like smoking, I thought. In the first stage of giving up smoking you actually feel much worse. Not that Rich had ever had that experience. For as long as I could remember he had been a hundred a day man. And he had no intention of giving up. Not yet, anyway.

'One of these days,' he used to say, 'I'll stop and suffer and be killed by a falling tree while walking the dog.'

This was always his excuse for not holding to his word. At the critical point he would tell himself he might as well go back to the bottle because if he didn't, something worse was just as likely to happen. Nonsense, of course, but no one has ever claimed a link between alcoholism and rational thinking.

Back in Switzerland, Elizabeth relived the indignities of living with an alcoholic The rows were long and painful, extending from one day to the next, picking up in the morning where they had stopped, exhausted, the night before.

Rich claimed he was bored. Having restored the old routine, he now found it wanting. But he was not so much bored as nervous. In a few weeks he would be back on Broadway, after a stage absence of more than twelve years. The challenge was almost more than he could bear to contemplate.

He sought reassurance in a way that was second nature to him – by

213

testing the strength of his personality on a new admirer, someone who could tell him he was still the best without making it sound like a cracked record. Among those favoured for this role was a twenty-seven-year-old blonde he spotted on the ski slopes. He saw her again at a party where she was scrabbling around on the floor searching for a lost contact lens. The incident amused Rich because, at first, he thought she was roaring drunk.

Dispatched to make discreet enquiries, Brook Williams reported that Susan Hunt, wife of the British racing driver, James Hunt, would be delighted to come over for drinks. No, her husband was not with her. Moreover, gossip had it that the couple were not on the best of terms.

Elizabeth was unperturbed. She was used to seeing pretty girls come and go. Just two months into marriage she did not think she had much to worry about.

In February, Rich flew to New York. Elizabeth preceded him by a few days. Susan Hunt followed. Elizabeth flew on to California; to visit her mother, it was said.

Rich's nervousness showed more obviously the closer he came to Broadway. Taking him for the first time to the Plymouth theatre where *Equus* was playing, Robby Lantz recalls him alone on the stage staring into the empty stalls.

'I stood aside and watched knowing that he was wondering if he could recapture his kingdom.'

His biggest fear was the damage he had inflicted on his memory. Had drink robbed him of his capacity to absorb lines? A recent event served to give him some comfort. As he told it:

'I was with Elizabeth in Jerusalem where I said I'd speak at the University. I thought they wanted a seminar, an invigorating informal chat. But when I got there I found I was booked to deliver two hours of poetry, for charity, in front of an audience of a thousand who had paid fifteen dollars a time to hear me. I did the lot from memory including the twenty-third psalm in Hebrew. Apart from a desperate and unnoticed bit of paraphrasing in the middle of some unfamiliar medieval piece, every word fell into its allotted slot like a computer. Ninety-nine out of a hundred. Not bad, eh?'

But there was another story told to me by an actor friend.

'I was in the middle of a *Times* crossword and there was this clue which referred to a quote from *Hamlet*. Rich would know it, I thought; he's done the part hundreds of times. But when I asked him, he floundered and got very annoyed with himself for forgetting what should have been as obvious as his own name.'

The rehearsals for *Equus* gave credence to the second anecdote. Rich floundered hopelessly and it was the practised cast who kept him afloat. It was in fairness, a difficult role to grasp. Peter Shaffer agrees, 'Equus is the most private, the most deeply erotic of all my plays.' The man of reason, Dysart, pitted against the primitive spirit of the boy who, against all reason, blinds six horses can, in the wrong hands, come across as the most dreadful rubbish.

Rich had to get it right. There was no margin for error. Equus was already judged a success and those who had played Dysart – Anthony Perkins and Anthony Hopkins in New York and Alec McCowen in London, had all earned great praise. If Rich bombed he had no one but himself to blame.

He kept up a brave front. With Hilda, who was bold enough to voice doubts, he made a wager.

'I bet you a thousand kisses to one that I will earn a standing ovation at every performance.'

Making the supreme effort to stay cold sober he sought out the company of those on whom he could rely not to press him to 'one little drink'. He spent time with Robby Lantz and Alex Cohen whose families were the regular providers of weekend distractions.

One evening when there was a big party Rich wanted to avoid, he asked Alex, 'Do you mind if I say that Susan and I have a date with you?'

'Fine,' said Alex. 'But who's Susan?'

Rich was incredulous.

'You are naive, aren't you?'

It then dawned on Alex Cohen that the willowy blonde who happened to be staying at the same hotel as Rich was mightily important to the actor. As the couple were seen more frequently together the question came up, did Elizabeth know? And if, yes, why did she not retaliate? But in a sense she did just that by staying in California and by giving Rich the chance to repent. Nothing would have been achieved by her storming into New York to demand an explanation. Meanwhile, he was kept wondering as to what, eventually, she would do.

Came the weekend prior to Rich opening in Equus. As there was still no way in which he could face the critics and get away with it, John Dexter decided on a desperate remedy. He went to Rich on the Friday afternoon to tell him he was on the following day for the Saturday matinee. It was, he calculated, the shock treatment Rich needed to bring out the innate professionalism. No way, he believed, would it be a good performance but at least the critics would not see it. They had the rest of the weekend to smooth over the edges.

When John Dexter broke the news to him, Rich was quiet for a moment.

'Are you sure it's for the best?'

'Quite sure.'

'Hmm. In that case I'd better go off and learn a bit more.'

The matinee audience gave him a good start. After a moan of displeasure at the announcement that Anthony Perkins would not be appearing, the rider that Richard Burton would perform in his stead brought cheers loud enough to be heard in the dressing rooms. Sustained applause greeted Rich's entrance. A buzz went round the stalls: This will be worth seeing.

But it wasn't. Rich gave not so much a bad performance as a non-performance, declared John Dexter. Mumbling incoherently while barely lifting his eyes from the stage, he seemed to be begging, 'Don't look at me; I'm not really here at all.' At the final curtain he had to make do with a smattering of reluctant clapping. The audience filed out in depressed silence.

John Dexter was the first to see Rich in his dressing room.

'Well?' asked Rich.

'It was dreadful. Absolutely bloody dreadful.'

He continued in similar vein for some five minutes. When he emerged he found Robby Lantz and Peter Shaffer waiting outside.

'Now don't go in there undoing all my good work,' he commanded. 'He's got to know how bad he was.'

The two visitors approached cautiously. They found Richard Burton, sunk deep in his chair, enduring the humiliation of defeat. Looking at him then, a deflated mound of a man, it was difficult to imagine he would ever act again.

But John Dexter knew his actor. After a while Rich summoned up that mysterious reserve of energy he kept somewhere. He went back to the Lombardy Hotel and with Susan, rearranged the furniture of his suite to make a fair semblance of the *Equus* set. Then he started work. It took him most of the hours left to him before Monday evening but by the time the critics took their seats Rich knew as much of the play as he was ever likely to know.

It was still not the performance John Dexter wanted.

'There was too much emotion; too much of the pulpit and the pub.'

But it satisfied the audience and the reviewers. The leading New York critics, Walter Kerr and Clive Barnes, were impressed. 'The best work of his life,' enthused Kerr. An 'unabashedly star performance', intoned Barnes. It was, without doubt, his star presence which carried him though. As Robby Lantz reminds us,

'He revitalised not just the play but the whole of Broadway. In what had been a lacklustre season, business picked up all round.'

No wonder the Plymouth management felt justified in putting up seat prices by five dollars for the duration of the Burton run.

The triumphant return of Richard Burton to the Broadway stage afforded one mystery. Where was Elizabeth Taylor? Or rather not, where, because everybody knew she was in California, but why? The story went round that she did not wish to distract attention from the hero of the moment. She would put in an appearance a little later. Meanwhile, she had left a month-old reminder of her presence on Rich's dressing room mirror. It was a message scrawled in eyebrow pencil, 'You're fantastic, love.'

A week after Rich opened in *Equus*, he was telephoned by Elizabeth to be told that she planned coming to New York the following week-end. Rich, Robby Lantz and Aaron Frosch went to Kennedy to meet her. They had two limousines, one for passengers, the other for luggage. But when Elizabeth appeared with Chen Sam at the head of a procession of porters carrying thirty-five cases, not to mention two dogs and a cat, it was evident that their transport arrangements were inadequate. A truck was ordered to bring up the rear.

On the drive into the city Rich was uncharacteristically silent. Robby occupied the time urging Elizabeth not to put in an early appearance in the Plymouth auditorium. 'The audience won't give the actors a chance.'

He suggested instead a visit backstage. Elizabeth said she would come on Monday.

She left it until the second half to arrive at the stage door. Even so, a crowd quickly gathered. She had difficulty getting from her car. While a path was cleared for her, the cheers and shouts of greeting could be heard inside the theatre where, for a minute or so, the noise threatened to overwhelm the dialogue on stage.

Elizabeth made her way to the wings where she was given a seat with a clear view across the set. She could also see into the opposite wings. Sitting there was Susan Hunt.

Afterwards, they all went back to the Lombardy Hotel – Rich, Elizabeth, Susan and Chen Sam. They sat quietly for some time listening to Rich tapping his fingers on the table.

Eventually, Elizabeth asked, 'What is wrong, love?'

And Rich said, 'I want a divorce.'

As Elizabeth left with Chen Sam she murmured, 'It's easy to say now but we should never have remarried.'

Alex Cohen was one of the first to hear the news. He had arranged

217

a party for the following evening to celebrate Elizabeth's forty-fourth birthday. She rang to say she was leaving on the midday plane. Would Alex please issue a statement explaining about the divorce.

Five months later, in Haiti, Rich and Elizabeth were parted for the second and final time. When we talked on the phone, he confessed, 'I know we can't live together and we can't live apart, and I have no idea how the future will unfold except that I can't live on my own.'

# Chapter 17

On 21 August 1976 in Virginia, Rich and Susan were married during a half-day break in the filming of *Exorcist II*.

In the six years they were together I met Susan on perhaps a dozen occasions, starting in Wales when Rich brought her to meet the family and ending, in traumatic circumstances, in London. She struck me as a capable and assertive young lady but one who, coming late to the Burton story, had an awful lot to learn.

She did not stop him drinking but for a time she kept the intake at a modest level. This job alone needed the application of a saint. But she attempted more. She wanted to direct her husband's career, to put him back where she, and others, thought he belonged, at the top of his profession.

The success of *Equus* encouraged her to plan ambitiously. She urged Rich to think of returning to Shakespeare, a notion supported by seasoned observers such as John Barber, of the *Daily Telegraph*. Having witnessed in *Equus* his 'personal victory over his worst self', Barber appealed to Rich to come home to the National Theatre or to the Royal Shakespeare Company where he 'could keep faith with his genius and crown his career'.

But financial uncertainty – the unscrambling from Elizabeth's affairs was starting all over again – made Rich more inclined towards another Broadway moneyspinner. The most unlikely ideas cropped up. Among those he consulted, Frank Hauser was startled by a proposal to direct *Timon of Athens*. 'I told him bluntly,' he recalls, 'I thought the suggestion was preposterous.'

Strongest support came for a Burton assault on *Lear* – 'the big one' to use Rich's epithet. This project went a long way towards realisation. Having agreed to produce, Alex Cohen persuaded Elia Kazan to come out of retirement to prepare a shortened version of the play. Rich talked enthusiastically of the challenge. 'I have to play Lear as a kind of obligation,' he told an interviewer. 'Lear is the only Welshman of any interest that Shakespeare wrote about. Lear, when he lets off steam, when he really lets go, is utterly Welsh.'

But he moved cautiously, always seeking reassurance that the role was still within his powers. I recall a dinner when, out of the blue, he insisted on reciting lengthy extracts from *Lear*. I was enormously impressed – it was always a joy listening to him. But I could not help noticing that one or two others at the table remained grim-faced. Afterwards, I asked what was wrong. 'Didn't you notice? The words were all over the place. He even threw in bits from *Coriolanus*.'

But Rich was not fooling himself. From other conversations I know that he was soon looking for an excuse to back away. Timing, the place, money – there was always a problem. In London the ensemble work of the National and the RSC with their retinues of contract players and directors made him nervous. Would he fit in? Indeed, would they want him? Anyway, the fees were derisory.

In New York, the excuse was the impossible economics of producing the classics on Broadway. First off, Alex Cohen worked out his figures on the basis of eight performances a week including one matinee. Not unreasonably, Rich argued that he could not sustain the necessary level of excellence if he had to appear twice in one day. So the matinee was cut. Then Rich said he could manage only six performances a week. This brought the profit margin dangerously low but with a few economies and a rigorous control on costs, Alex Cohen thought he might just be able to work out a deal.

He brought the good news to Beverly Hills where Rich and Susan were living. He remembers the evening well because arriving late at the restaurant where they had fixed to meet he left his Cadillac on the roadside. Before rushing in he handed his keys to a man he assumed was a commissionaire leaving him with the order, 'Take my car'. The total stranger did just that. Alex never saw the vehicle again. But that was the least of his worries. Having revealed that *Lear* on six performances was, after all, a practical proposition, Rich said he could only do five.

'It was the night,' ruminated Alex, 'that I lost *Lear* and my car.'

When Rich did eventually return to Broadway it was not in Shakespeare at all but in a revival of *Camelot* – a costlier product but one that was far easier to sell.

Meanwhile, there was his reputation as a movie actor to reconstruct. The prize was the role of Dysart in the screen version of *Equus* for which Universal had the rights. Rich faced strong competition of the quality of Jack Nicholson and Marlon Brando and the antipathy of the studio bosses who judged him to be unreliable and, more to the point, virtually uninsurable. Robby Lantz set out to prove otherwise. His tactic was to get Rich into a film, any film, where he could prove he was still capable of holding the cameras. The opportunity came with *Exorcist II*, a formula horror movie guaranteed to appal the critics while bringing a decent return at the box office.

Rich did all that he was required to do. It was a modest performance (the material allowed for nothing more) but it impressed Universal and reminded them of the Burton triumph in the stage production of *Equus*. Opinion shifted strongly in his favour. The part was his.

Rich must have understood the purpose of *Exorcist II* and the strategy that Robby Lantz was pursuing. Yet, curiously, he failed to explain it to Susan who was furious that he had in her words, 'humiliated himself' in such a dreadful movie. She made him promise never to do anything like it again no matter how much money was put up to tempt him. Perhaps Rich was too shamefaced to admit to her that unless he could pull a few tricks out of the bag he might not have any choice.

When *Equus* failed to translate well to the screen (too much realism shifted attention from the emotional conflict at the heart of the story) the sniping from the sidelines intensified. Robby came under attack. So too did Aaron Frosch, not for any apparent misdirection but for holding on too closely to the details of Rich's financial affairs. In what was quite clearly an attempt to take more authority to herself, Susan found a willing ally in Valerie Douglas whose unrivalled knowledge of the Burton career proved a useful source of ammunition.

As the focus of controversy Rich kept strangely quiet. The once eager participant in any verbal punch up now ran away from confrontations, avoided meetings which threatened to touch on sensitive matters and procrastinated on decisions until circumstances compelled him to say yes or no.

A crisis point came with the 1977 Academy Awards dinner. Rich was nominated for best actor for the seventh time, knowing that it was to be a close race with Richard Dreyfus (*The Goodbye Girl*). As his agent, Robby Lantz was slightly surprised not to be invited to sit at the Burtons' table but passed it off as an administrative oversight. Later in the evening he commiserated with Rich on his near miss and received a courteous response.

Early the next morning, Robby had a call.

'I want to see you,' said Rich. 'Now.'

Robby was apologetic. 'That's impossible, I'm afraid. I have a meeting in just a few minutes.'

'Then I must tell you on the phone,' said Rich. 'You're fired.'

Robby took in a deep breath. 'That's entirely understandable. I get you your best part in years on Broadway, I bring you back into films as a high earner. Yes, of course, it's quite natural you should want to fire me.'

Rich broke in.

'It has nothing to do with work. You insulted Bob Wilson. You made a racist remark. I can't have that.'

Robby spoke very carefully.

'If you believe that I, of all people, am capable of racism, then I am sorry for you and I have nothing else to say.' He put down the phone.

They met rarely after that though, ironically, Robby was soon to become agent to Elizabeth Taylor. Rich did make one hamfisted attempt at a reconciliation. When he opened in the revival of *Camelot*, he invited Robby and his wife Shirley to the first night and to dinner after the show. Robby said they would be delighted to come to the theatre but dinner was not on unless he received an apology.

'Let me think about that,' said Rich.

Some time later one of his secretaries rang to tell Robby his first night tickets had been cancelled.

Aaron Frosch was the next to encounter the new regime. Though now frail and sick, Aaron had done more than anyone to provide an essential stability in Rich's otherwise chaotic life. His work was largely financial but his wise counsel went far beyond the scope of the account books. His loyalty to Rich was unquestioned and he expected the same from everyone else on the Burton payroll. He was a tough negotiator and a cautious administrator. Chen Sam remembers the contract she was expected to sign when she was first employed by Rich and Elizabeth.

'There were several pages of closely typed rules and conditions. It was as if I was handing over my entire life.' She refused to comply and Aaron, recognising a kindred will, backed down. But he was not accustomed to defeat. Though ravaged by a debilitating illness the quality of his stewardship never wavered.

I found it almost impossible to believe that Aaron had been dismissed. But Chen Sam was there and saw it happen. In fact, Rich gave her the letter to deliver to Aaron. But forewarned of its contents, she refused. In the end it was taken by one of Aaron's assistants, the man who pushed his wheelchair.

The sourness and suspicion that characterised so many of Rich's affairs extended to his closest relatives. One of the sadnesses of Gwen's later life was the falling out with Rich over Ivor's will. Both the Hampstead house and cottage were in Ivor's name and so became part of his estate. He left them to Gwen with the rider that on her death one of the properties should go to Kate. It was up to her to choose which one she wanted.

But Rich, or whoever spoke for him, argued that Squire's Mount was not Ivor's to leave. The contract of possession remained in force only as long as Ivor was alive. After that the house and cottage should have reverted to the true owner – Richard Burton. It was an argument he lost, but I still wonder what it was that made him do it.

After *Equus*, Rich made a clutch of films starting with an interesting and well constructed piece called *The Medusa Touch*. With Elliott Kastner producing he felt at home with a literate script and a strong supporting cast which included Lee Remick and Harry Andrews. The theme was telekinetics, the mysterious power claimed by some, notably Uri Geller, to make objects move without touching them. Rich played a lawyer who discovers that by sheer force of concentration he can influence people and events. Called variously an intellectual or science fiction thriller in an understandable attempt to avoid the horror movie label, *The Medusa Touch* went down well with critics and audiences.

During filming at Pinewood, I saw a lot of Rich and Susan whose rented house in Windsor was not far from my London base. His back gave him pain but he overcame it, he said, by regular exercise. He claimed not to be drinking though I heard he took in what he called 'an occasional glass of good Burgundy'. His temper was on a yet shorter fuse, if that was possible, and while he clearly delegated a lot to Susan and usually fell in with her way of doing things, he was quick to apportion blame when things went wrong. The strain on Susan was having to watch him all the time.

'If I wasn't his wife, he'd need me as his nurse,' she commented, not without a trace of bitterness.

Her worries were intensified by the fear of what could happen on Rich's next assignment. He was to appear in a big budget adventure story which revived memories of *Where Eagles Dare*. This one was called *The Wild Geese* and was about a bunch of mercenaries who pitch into African politics by rescuing a deposed moderate leader from the hands of a corrupt dictator. The location was a collection of mud huts on the northern veld of South Africa. Rich and Susan had an air-conditioned villa but when he was working he was out in one hundred degree heat.

223

The physical strain over three months was matched by the mental struggle of coping with the film actor's tribulation – the hours of waiting for something to happen; hours which would pass so much more congenially with the help of a little drink.

Rich's co-stars were Richard Harris, whose reputation was of an imbiber of Olympic status and Roger Moore who, having spent his youth as a teetotaller, was now making up for lost time. The producer, Euan Lloyd, was a nervous man.

Happily, Richard Harris was also under doctors' orders. The two actors called a truce for the duration. 'We'll let Roger Moore do the drinking for the three of us,' they agreed. Harris did have one small lapse. When Rich heard of it he sternly admonished his friend. 'You broke your word,' he rumbled. 'Remember, if I start drinking, I'll make Africa burn.'

It was a friendly and good-humoured cast of skilled character actors most of whom knew each other from other pictures. In the capable hands of director Andrew McLaglen who, better than anyone, knew how to deliver the thrills, they threw themselves into this latest caper with all the energy of a (slightly ageing) rugger team.

But the abiding memory was of the infinitely modest Roger Moore whose self-effacing style made him unique among film stars. There was the scene in which Burton, Harris and Moore started with some ten lines each. After the first runthrough, Roger asked for a cut, in his own lines, an almost unheard-of request from any actor. Another runthrough and another suggested cut. A third try and Roger thought it best if he lost all his lines.

'But why?' asked the director. Roger puffed on his long cigar. 'Do you think I want to act against these guys? I'll just sit here and watch them do the work.'

Some time on when it was pointed out to him that he was getting less then his share of star action, he was cheerfully unconcerned.

'I'm not paid to act. I'm paid to turn up.'

With the success of *Wild Geese* confidently anticipated, Rich looked forward to a postbag full of offers. It came, but it was not quite what he had hoped for. Instead of big studio projects with the promise of worldwide sales, he was faced with a selection of modestly financed movies which could turn out to be worthy or worthless. It took him two years to find out. They were worthless.

Three of the four films he made in this period were so far departed from popular appeal, the producers had difficulty in finding distributors. *Absolution*, completed in early 1978, did not actually appear until 1981. Rich played yet another priest who hears the confession of a boy murderer. One of the few critics to give it space dismissed it as 'pretentious melodrama'. A war film called *Breakthrough* (*Sergeant Steiner* in the States) covered its costs but little else (despite the ministrations of Andrew McLaglen).

Then came the extraordinary *Tristan and Isolde*, a costume drama made in Ireland. Rich picked it out as a certain winner. He was wrong. It was one of the dreariest pieces of nonsense in the Burton canon. Rich lost both ways, professionally and financially. He agreed to work exclusively on a percentage which, not surprisingly, failed to materialise.

The run of bad luck came to a merciful end with *Circle for Two* in which the visibly ageing Burton in the guise of a college lecturer was called upon to have an affair with a teenage student (Tatum O'Neal). 'At my age,' he grumbled, 'they should have paid me danger money.'

On and off drink and feeling thoroughly sorry for himself, Rich found consolation at Puerto Vallarta, his favourite home. But memories of Elizabeth intruded – there was even a street named after her – and Susan was not best pleased to be offered up to the locals as a comparison to her predecessor. Susan was younger and, arguably, just as attractive but she was not the star turn. She was, well, just Richard Burton's wife. Casting his mind back to the days of *Cleopatra*, Rich may have felt a hint of what it was like for her.

To further the distance from his past, Rich commissioned a new home at Puerto Vallarta, at a spot higher up the mountain. Susan was told she had a free hand on the design. Getting it just right became something of an obsession with her. Friends were called in to help and advise. One who was particularly solicitous was a near neighbour, Jack Hayward.

At a loss as to what to do next Rich talked wildly of this or that long cherished ambition. *Lear* resurfaced briefly and Rich was to be seen going out to dinner with a copy of the play tucked in his pocket. But he knew he was indulging in a pipe dream. He even thought of retiring.

'But the boredom, Gray. Can you imagine the boredom? It would be a living death.'

I reminded him he had his books – to read and to write.

'Hobbies, just hobbies,' he sighed. 'They're not what I call real work.'

I could not bear to tell him that twenty years earlier it might have been a different story. Watching the occasional glass become the occasional bottle and knowing that he was suffering excruciating bouts of pain with his back and shoulder, I felt a sad premonition that I was witnessing the last chapter in the career of Richard Burton.

Then, out of the blue, there was a call from Alan Jay Lerner. Could Rich still remember the songs from *Camelot*, he asked? Rich thought so. But, why? It was just that producer Mike Merwick was interested in staging a revival. The engagement was for one year with a fortune at the end of it. Was Rich interested? Wasn't he just.

To return to the stage in a role he created twenty years earlier and which he knew backwards was not perhaps the most adventurous move. But it got him off the treadmill of bad to mediocre films, the money was good and Susan approved.

All this he cheerfully conceded. What he was less happy to admit – because deep down it suggested a weakness he tried to deny – was that he had a need for a public show of approval, the standing ovations which had sustained him in his last crisis.

So it happened that producer Mike Merwick was received enthusiastically when he came to Geneva to talk with Rich about his *Camelot* plans. Somewhat to his surprise he left with a firm commitment from Rich to reassume King Arthur's crown.

The show opened in Toronto in June 1980. Rehearsals started a month earlier. Recalling the horrendous problems of the first *Camelot*, the latest team had an easy ride. But it was not entirely without incident. The director, Frank Dunlop, came with a distinguished list of credits which missed out on any experience with musicals. The omission soon became apparent. Called in to advise, Alan Jay Lerner started by urging an immediate replacement of the leading lady. This done he raided his memory for the best fruits of his collaboration with Moss Hart, that complete man of the theatre who had died in 1961.

By the first night, something of the old magic had been recaptured. Though Rich still needed time to work his way back into the role it was noticeable that he brought to King Arthur the older dignity Lerner had always wanted but which had been inevitably missing from the 1960 productions. The sheer poetry of the lyrics, the best element in what was acknowledged as a slight and sentimental story, were perfectly suited to the timbery voice of the mature Burton. He had them crying in the aisles.

The buzz was heard in New York; this is a show to see. Even before opening at the Lincoln Center's State Theater it was a virtual sell-out with advance bookings of over two-and-a-half million dollars, the biggest in Broadway history. The touts did fine business selling tickets at over a hundred dollars a time.

Still, with a nationwide tour to come, the reviews were awaited with the usual trepidation. The opinion of the *New York Times* and the *New York Post* pulled weight throughout the country.

Uncharacteristically, Rich stayed late at the first night party to hear the verdict. Only when the murmur of polite conversation turned to a roar of approval, signifying word had come through of high praise from one of the big name critics, did he feel it was time for bed. He went with the superlatives of Frank Rich to comfort him. 'He remains every inch the King Arthur of our most majestic storybook dreams,' declared the critic whose view from the stalls was rarely expressed with such romantic fervour. He added, 'This actor doesn't merely command the stage, he seems to own it by divine right.'

It was not until the next morning that another, less flattering view emerged. Clive Barnes had evidently left the theatre in unhappy mood. It was, he said, 'a knight to forget'. There was a lot more of this before the full force of his invective was released on the leading actor. Burton, he declared, 'is little more than a burnt-out dummy. His face leathery and unanimated, arms to his sides and his hands are flaccid'.

Hurtful it may have been but Clive Barnes touched on a truth which we all secretly affirmed. Rich was tired; more, he was desperately sick. As early as Toronto he was having trouble with his shoulder and right arm. Called upon to raise a battle sword above his head, he needed a painkiller and the adrenalin of a live performance to show conviction. Knowing what he was going through, Frank Dunlop re-choreographed the duel scenes and gave Rich a light alloy sword to wield about him. Even so, the strain was apparent.

Rich asked Alex Cohen if he had any advice. 'Stay sober,' said Alex. But that is just what Rich did not do. Two weeks in to the New York run he met up with Peter O'Toole. It was early evening two hours before a performance. They had a few drinks. Not many; just enough. When he made it to the theatre, strictly an hour before curtain up, he took some booster painkillers. The mix was lethal. As he went on to the usual tumultuous applause he felt his eyes misting over. He spoke his first words. The sound of his own voice came back to him like a distant echo. He stumbled, recovered and stumbled again. A whisper went round the audience: 'He's drunk.' Halfway through the first act the curtain was brought down. When it went up again Rich's understudy stood in his place.

Next day the story was front page news across the world. In a more reflective mood, Rich might have told himself that if he could attract that sort of publicity, he must still be worth something. Instead, he let loose a torrent of anger which, to those who knew him, meant that he was very frightened indeed. To anyone who was prepared to listen, he protested his innocence: 'I was *not* drunk.' And technically he was right. But there was no escaping the fact that he was living dangerously with a constitution which could no longer be relied upon to sustain his excesses.

After New York, *Camelot* played four weeks in Chicago, three weeks in Dallas, four weeks in Miami Beach, three weeks in New Orleans and twelve weeks in San Francisco. Rich did not miss a single performance. But on the last stretch, in Los Angeles, where the show was booked for a three-month run, he had to admit defeat. He dropped out of the show and into St John's Hospital where he was told he needed major surgery on his spine. He was warned the operation was risky. If it failed he could be paralysed for life. In fact, it was only when the operation was underway that the surgeons fully realised what a bad state he was in. They had virtually to rebuild his vertebrae. One of his doctors told me he could not begin to understand how Rich had managed to hold an audience night after night.

The operation was successful, but not successful enough. After six months in hospital Rich was told that he would find it easier to move about but would have to go carefully. A release from his dependence on painkillers could not be promised.

To convalesce, he retired to Celigny where he was restless and bored in equal measure. When Susan flew off to Puerto Vallarta it was as much to get a break from nursing a temperamental invalid as to check how the new house was coming along. On the phone to me, Rich asked me, 'Is there anything you can think of for me to do? Now I've got time to read, I can't concentrate. I need to be taken out of myself.'

As a matter of fact, there was something I could suggest. I put the idea to my masters at BBC Radio. Coming up was the royal wedding between Prince Charles and Lady Diana Spencer. Brian Tremble, a senior producer, said, 'How would it be if you asked Rich to be the link man for the radio commentary on the ceremony in Westminster Abbey, the procession and the public celebrations?' The response was enthusiastic. It would be quite a coup for outside broadcasting to attract one of the best-known voices in the English language. But would he do it? The effort required in sustaining six hours of live radio was out of all proportion to the modest fee.

I rang to explain all this to Rich. Was he interested?

'Why not come over and talk about it,' he said. 'It can't do any harm.'

I and a BBC colleague flew over to Geneva in mid-June. Rich met us at the airport. I did not expect him to be in top form but the strength of his voice on the telephone had suggested a part-way return to his old vigour. Instead, it seemed to me that he had slipped back. He walked with a slight stoop which was to stay with him for the rest of his life, and he moved slowly. One arm was held tight by his side and there were frequent nervous twists of his head as if he was being slapped by an invisible hand.

Not wanting to sell him the job as an easy option I explained carefully that he would be on air from morning to evening without much chance of a break. 'Not even for a pee.'

'Well, I think we might manage that.'

We were sitting at lunch. Rich ordered wine and poured himself a large glass. Then without touching his drink he seemed to relax a little, leaning back to his chair as if to say, 'There, I can still keep off it, if I want to.'

We talked more about the programme, how much of it would be scripted and how much he would be expected to ad lib.

'Can I say what I like?'

'Within reason,' I said, remembering some of his oratorial heights – and depths.

Rich appeared satisfied.

'Right then,' he boomed. 'It's just a question of money.'

My colleague tightened his lips.

'I know the fee is modest,' he apologised. 'But, as I've explained, it's contractually impossible for the BBC to exceed its pay guide-lines. . . .'

My brother raised a hand. 'I'm not arguing about the sum. It's just the way it's paid. I want it all to go to charity. If I give the details, can you arrange it?'

We both thought the BBC could rise to the challenge. The conversation turned to other matters and when we finished lunch, Rich was well away on stories of past triumphs. As we got up to go I noticed his glass was empty.

For a first time reporter, Rich did a wonderful job on the wedding. When he ran out of script, he extemporised with poetry and prose on regal topics, much of it acquired for a dramatised history of monarchy he had narrated for the BBC four years earlier.

He made only one minor error. Handing over to Wynford Vaughan-Thomas on the processional route, he told listeners they were off to Clarence House when in fact that distinguished commentator was speaking from Buckingham Palace. Those who were closely following their route maps must have wondered what was going on but otherwise the slip passed unnoticed.

When it was all over I joined Rich and Susan for a celebratory dinner at the Dorchester. Both were in cheerful mood though Rich complained volubly at having to rely indefinitely on painkillers to keep him active. He could not imagine how it would be possible ever to appear again on stage in any role that was worthy of him. But there was one exciting screen possibility, a mammoth internationally backed television series on the life of Richard Wagner.

A little to my surprise, Rich had no trouble in identifying with the great German composer. 'I am close to Wagner. I could be Wagner.'

The association escaped me until, at home, I checked out a dictionary of biography. Wagner, I read, 'was apt to arouse either blind adulation or violent antipathy, but seldom indifference. Supremely egotistical and unable to sense when he was wrong, he was capable of somersaults of opinion and conduct which mystified and sometimes antagonised his friends.'

I could see then what Rich meant.

The next day I had a call from Susan. She sounded nervous and distressed.

'Can you come over to the Dorchester? I need some help. Rich is in a bad way.'

Driving from the other side of London I made it in less than an hour. When I went into their suite it was to find Rich slouched in a chair, half dressed, his shirt open. Only his eyes moved. Then he saw me.

'Gray, my brother, Gray. A friend, indeed. Get me a drink, dear brother, will you? Get me a drink, my dear chap.'

I looked at Susan who was pacing up and down, her clenched fists held against her mouth.

'He's been like this all morning,' she babbled. 'He must have started hours ago. We've got a plane to catch today. I'll never get him to the airport like this.'

Rich stirred himself. His voice was a slurred shout.

'Will someone get me a fucking drink?'

I said something banal like, 'Don't you think you've had enough?' which set off a torrent of anger.

'All right,' I said, 'hang on.'

I took a litre bottle of vodka from the drinks tray, went into the bathroom and tipped three fifths of the vodka into the washbasin. Then I refilled the bottle with water. The much diluted Bloody Mary I handed to Rich was enough to keep him quiet.

'It'll take more than the two of us to sober him up,' I told Susan. 'We need someone he'll listen to.'

I rang the first and most obvious candidate to come to mind. Cliff Morgan was BBC's Head of Outside Broadcast on Television but to Rich was better known as 'the finest fly half Wales has ever seen'.

Though not close friends in the ordinary sense, they met whenever the opportunity presented. The conversations were always about rugby. Five years earlier when Cliff had gone into hospital with a heart attack, Rich had insisted on the best treatment.

When Cliff arrived we both talked to Rich, gave him coffee, walked him up and down.

With my arm around him I said in Welsh, 'You know don't you, you're killing yourself?' He replied in English, 'So be it.'

By early afternoon he was just about fit to be taken to the airport. We went in Cliff's car with Susan and Rich in the back. Not much was said on the drive but when we saw them off from the VIP lounge both tried to put on a show of conviviality.

Back in London, Cliff observed gloomily, 'If he goes on like that he won't last very long.'

I said, 'If he goes on like that the marriage won't last another month.'


No sooner was Rich back in the States than he fell ill again, this time with a stomach ulcer. In St John's Hospital the doctors warned him that his liver and kidneys were on the danger list. He was told bluntly to cut down on painkillers and to cut out the drink, otherwise his life was forfeit. Rich said he would try and no doubt he did but his resolution was hampered by Susan's absence in Puerto Vallarta and the knowledge that she was attracted there by more than a zest for property development.

Incredibly, the backers for *Wagner* were prepared to take a risk on him. Seven months was a long haul in the life of a middle aged actor with a poor medical record. More, there was the strain of a punishing schedule – filming in twenty-seven locations in six countries, across Europe and back again.

But against the risk of contracting Burton had to be set the conviction that few actors could give the role the authority it demanded. And unlike some of his possible rivals, Rich came at a reasonable price. One million dollars was not chicken feed but inflation had robbed the figure of its mysticism. For younger Hollywood stars it had more significance as a starting price. For Richard Burton, who had commanded a million-dollar fee twenty years earlier, it was enough to take him to the finishing post. My guess is that, if pushed, he would have accepted a lower offer.

To be Wagner was his compensation for his failure to be Lear. And there was a bonus, the chance to work in such august company. The three white knights of the theatre – Olivier, Gielgud and Richardson –

231

were enticed into playing cameo roles. To overcome delicate questions of precedence, a neat compromise was achieved whereby the three eminent guests appeared together but not with Wagner, thus overcoming any suggestion that they might be playing second fiddle to Richard Burton.

It gave Rich pause for thought when he found that while Olivier was an obviously sick man, Gielgud and Richardson were hale and hearty septuagenarians.

'Do you think I'll last that long?' he asked rhetorically.

The celebrated trio treated him with respect but not, he thought, with affection. He detected a certain condescension. When in reminiscent mood Olivier was heard to murmur, 'We were the best,' he was looking away from Rich.

As *Wagner* got underway in January 1982, Rich was on his own. When the time for Susan to join him in Vienna came and went without word, he knew his marriage was in bad trouble. He sought consolation in the company of other women and of old friends like Ron Berkeley who was in charge of make-up and of Bob Wilson and Brook Williams, his convivial gofers.

But whoever his companions, they had one thing in common – a tolerance for fond stories about Elizabeth Taylor.

For five eventful years Rich and Elizabeth had seen little of each other. Elizabeth had married again (husband number six was Senator John Warner) and divorced again. Her liking for hard liquor had taken a leap. If not quite up to the Burton scale it was enough for her to put on thirty pounds in weight and to qualify for the front cover of Kenneth Auger's *Hollywood Babylon II* – a living symbol of Tinsel Town excess.

But at forty-nine the star still sparkled. Even without the big film roles she could still pull in the crowds. This was made evident by the commercial success of the otherwise undistinguished touring production of *The Little Foxes*. As the villainous Regina she competed valiantly but unsuccessfully against the memory of Bette Davis's film portrayal. No matter, the audiences loved her.

In February, Elizabeth was in London to prepare for her West End debut in *Little Foxes*. Coincidentally, Rich also had a London date, to lead a St David's Day retrospective of Dylan Thomas at the Duke of York's theatre. Elizabeth cabled him an invitation to her fiftieth birthday party. The acceptance came by return.

Before departing Vienna for his long weekend break from filming, Rich was made aware of a thirty-four-year-old production assistant, Sally Hay. She was not the type to stand out in a crowd. She had neither the salary nor the style to make the best of herself. But she was conscientious at her job which required an attention to details and a willingness to rush in to help solve any problem which threatened to interrupt filming. Rich liked to have her around but, off the set, was unable to put a name to her.

Until, that is, one evening in a restaurant with Ron Berkeley, he spotted Sally Hay, alone, at another table. After a few puzzled glances in her direction, he asked Ron, 'Who is that girl?' Ron told him. Whereupon he shouted across the room, 'Hey, Sally, come over here. Help to bring a little joy into a dull life.'

Rich and Sally spent some time together that night. And on subsequent nights.

In London, it was just like old times, in the best and the worst sense. Elizabeth's party, not for once at the Dorchester, was nonetheless a splendid affair. Pictures of Elizabeth alternating between a *Time Magazine* cover and a publicity still of her in a bubble bath, covered every inch of wallspace. As the guest of honour, Rich was suitably attentive to his hostess, hardly leaving her side. To those who asked the inevitable question, he was charmingly enigmatic.

'Elizabeth and I are like a pair of bookends. Other people may come between us but in the end the two of us are still there, opposite each other.'

That was said before Rich got drunk. By midnight he was incapable of much more than incoherent ramblings. The photographers gathered to record the depressing spectacle of Rich being lifted into his car like a helpless invalid.

On Monday evening, he had sufficiently recovered his professional poise to appear at the Duke of York's theatre for the Dylan Thomas reading. Early on in his performance as he waited for the silence after the applause, he was distracted and then thrown by the extraordinary sight of Elizabeth, unannounced, appearing on stage. In front of six hundred witnesses she spoke to him in faultless Welsh, '*Rwyn dy garu di mwy na un arall yn yr holl fyd*' – 'I love you more than anyone in the world.' Rich stared amazed for a moment then gave her a great hug and said, 'Would you mind repeating that?' She did so and made her exit to rapturous applause from the largely Welsh audience. Rich was left rummaging through his script for a way back into the programme while apologising for his confusion.

'You must forgive me. Elizabeth always has this effect on me.'

Elizabeth joined him on stage for the curtain call and backstage for a party. When I saw them off to dinner they were holding hands.

The idyll was brief. Early on Wednesday morning, Elizabeth rang me at home. She skipped the preliminaries.

'I could kill your brother.'

I was half awake.

'Why, what's he done?'

'Don't you read the papers?'

'Elizabeth,' I pleaded, 'I'm not even out of bed yet. I'm not so desperate to catch the headlines.'

'Well, here's one that should interest you. "It Looks Like Love Again" over a picture of me and Richard.'

'Well, what's wrong with that?'

'Nothing, it's what comes afterwards. He's shouted his mouth off about making love to me on the night of my birthday.'

'Oh no.'

'Oh, yes.'

There was not much I could do but sympathise. I urged her not to demand a retraction; it would just fuel the interest of the gossip writers. 'Especially,' I added incautiously, 'if what he says is true.'

'True?' she shouted. 'Did you say true? Of course it's not true. He was too drunk to find his way down the street, let alone into my bedroom.'

The best I could do was to warn Rich of the impending storm. I tracked him down at the Gritti Palace in Venice, the latest stopover in this peripatetic production. But first I got through to Ron Berkeley. I asked, 'What state is he in?' Ron sounded as if he did not want anyone to overhear.

'He must have put away a load of drink. He's spent all day in bed. That means we've lost a day's shooting. Not good news.'

When Rich came on and heard that Elizabeth was gunning for him, I could almost feel the weight of his hangover bearing down yet more heavily.

'Oh God, did I say that? I must have been talking metaphorically.'

'Okay,' I said, 'but don't be surprised when Elizabeth breaks a metaphorical vase over your head.'

Rich did not miss out on any more shooting. For the rest of the film he was a model of punctuality if not, sadly, of sobriety. He relied increasingly on Sally to organise his life. She was only too happy to oblige. When Rich felt pain in his shoulder, she was his masseuse. When he forgot a line, she was there to feed it to him. When he needed someone to tell him he was still in the game, she was ready to comfort and reassure. But Sally had her demands. Her jealousy of Elizabeth was obsessive and she made no attempt to disguise it from Rich. Twice, plans for Rich to fly in to see *The Little Foxes* had to be cancelled at the last moment. The pressure of a tight schedule was the formal excuse but, on location, it was known that Sally pulled every trick she could think of to stop him from coming. At the second disappointment (a cancellation that came so late there was a £600 bill for time the hired Rolls-Royce had to wait at Heathrow), I stood in for Rich by taking Elizabeth to dinner after the show. It was an evening of reminiscences with my guest clearly finding me a poor substitute for the man she really wanted to see. I hesitated to ask the obvious question.

'Go on, say it,' Elizabeth demanded and then, before I could open my mouth, 'You want to know if we'll ever marry again.'

I confessed, the thought had crossed my mind. She was silent for a moment. 'Do you know what he calls me?'

I said I had no idea.

'Instant nostalgia. He says it's because every time he sees me, I bring out in him a longing for home.'

'What does that mean?'

'It means, I don't know if we'll ever marry again. But what I do know is that in the end, every man comes home.'

As they entered the last stretch of Wagner's life story, Sally devoted herself exclusively to Rich. Though still on the production payroll she was no longer a humble PA. Now, she was assistant to Mr Burton. Her rise in the pecking order was clearly noticeable to Cheryl Campbell who had befriended Sally when they first met on location.

'We saw a lot of each other early on and I heard all about her affair with Richard. But after a while she became a different person. She bought herself a fur coat, lost some weight and looked much more glamorous. After that, there was no time for lunches or shopping trips. She stayed close to Richard and held aloof from the rest of us.'

Emotionally washed out and physically in poor shape, Rich allowed himself to be carried along by events. There were few humdinger rows. The pleasure of verbal combat had long since faded. When he felt that Sally was intruding too closely on his life he simply wandered away to spend time with friends or with an accommodating lady.

That he was not too choosy about some of his partners became obvious when the *National Enquirer* in the States and the *News of the World* in the UK gave a prominent splash to the kiss-and-tell story of Judith Chisholm, a pliable young journalist who occupied Rich for a week in Venice. The articles – scrambled reflections on sex and booze – made sad reading. But thankfully they were cut short by the intervention of Ron Berkeley and Bob Wilson. Realising what was happening they confronted Rich, told the girl precisely what they thought of her and then threw her out of the hotel. It was one of the rare occasions when I felt that Sally was entitled to all our sympathy.

Where Sally deserved great credit was in bringing some semblance of order to Rich's life, reviving his confidence and in keeping him away from hard spirits. Wine was another matter. Cheryl Campbell remembers whiling away a rainy morning with Rich when he got through three bottles. Still, when on the completion of *Wagner* he came to London with Sally, he appeared in reasonable shape. Elizabeth was there too, completing her run in *The Little Foxes*. Since there were no further excuses for not seeing the play Rich took Sally to the theatre and afterwards talked with Elizabeth. She asked Rich what he planned to do next. He had no idea. Though he expected *Wagner* to put up his value, the editing of that production was such a mammoth task neither the four-hour cinema version nor the nine-hour television serial could be expected to appear in less than a year. Meanwhile ...

'Meanwhile,' said Elizabeth, 'what do you say to having some fun and making a pile of money on Broadway?'

The idea was to revive *Private Lives*, a 1930 comedy by Noel Coward at his most acidic. To recall the plot was to see immediately how it appealed to Elizabeth and her backers. A divorced couple who love each other venomously book into adjoining honeymoon suites with their new partners. The dialogue read like a case study of the Burton–Taylor partnership. It was like saying to the public, you've read the story in the gossip columns, now see it live on stage.

There were loud voices urging caution. That the stars were at least twenty years too old for their parts was the least of their problems. Neither was strong on acerbic quick fire comedy and without this talent there was a terrible danger of getting all the laughs in the wrong places. It would be so easy for good clean fun to descend into excruciatingly bad taste. Among those who warned of disaster was Robby Lantz, now Elizabeth's agent, who flatly refused to have anything to do with the venture.

But Rich was hooked. As his friend Richard Harris said of him, he could never turn away from a gamble. The more outrageous the risk, the less likely it was that he would take good advice. The time for cool, rational thought – and the regrets – came later.

Early signs were that Elizabeth had made a sound commercial judgement. With bookings solid from Boston to New York the two stars would look forward to a clear $60,000 a week – each.

But what they had to do to earn the money was humiliating beyond belief.

The Boston critics led the assault on what was popularly known as the Dick and Liz show or The Private Lives of Burton and Taylor. The production was said to be shabby, self indulgent and a shrieking self parody. As for the principals, Elizabeth was described as 'a dumpy middle-aged woman with . . . legs too short for her size', and Rich as a 'sick, burned-out dissolute man'. But the audience kept coming to roar their approval at unintentional double entendres. The biggest cheer of the evening went to Elizabeth for her declaration via her character Amanda Prynne that 'Marriage scares me really.'

In New York, the pre-opening publicity was phenomenal and while the reviews were damning there was no let up at the box office. Such was the enthusiasm of the punters to see the two celebrities slug it out in public that a lively trade developed at the interval with those on the way out finding ready buyers for tickets for the second half. A television station asked viewers to phone in and vote whether Liz and Dick should marry again. Out of 3500 votes, seventy-three per cent were in favour of a third try.

Whatever else was said of *Private Lives*, no one could deny it was the show business event of the season.

But on a personal level the old stresses were beginning to reappear. Ex-husband and ex-wife took an almost sadistic – or was it masochistic? – pleasure in provoking jealousy. Rich did nothing to discourage Sally from talking about marriage. With the divorce from Susan now finalised, a reattachment was feasible, but to the extent that Rich was thinking of it as a serious possibility, he might sensibly have dampened the speculation until the end of the run. For her part, Elizabeth made a great show of her consort, the Mexican businessman, Victor Luna, a kindly and unpretentious character who gave every indication of wanting to be elsewhere.

A month after the New York opening, Rich came up against an agonising conflict of interest. He was offered the lead in a film adaptation of Malcolm Lowry's *Under the Volcano*. But John Huston, who was to direct, had to start work in August. This meant Rich backing off *Private Lives* well before the end of the tour. He put the case to Elizabeth. The Lowry role was, he insisted, one that he badly wanted to do. By comparison, *Private Lives* was mere frivolity. But that was not the way Elizabeth saw it. This was her creation Rich was trying to break up. She had not even read *Under the Volcano*. No way was she going to lose her percentage for the sake of an arty film.

Rich agreed to stick to his contract but his anguish at losing the opportunity of working again with John Huston (the part eventually went to Albert Finney) was increased by the embarrassment of the nightly fiasco on stage. He realised now what he had previously ignored, that for Elizabeth the theatre was the sideline to her career whereas for Rich, it was the centre of his existence.

237

Every entrance he made at the Lunt-Fontanne reminded him of the days at that theatre when he had played Hamlet and later, Arthur in *Camelot*. He was still winning the applause but now he felt like a monarch who was wantonly abdicating his kingdom.

'How can I redeem myself?'

The question was asked of Richard Harris who urged his friend to think again about a Broadway production of *King Lear*. But that chance had gone for ever. On the other hand, there was a realistic prospect of returning to Shakespeare in a less demanding role. The previous autumn Rich had been contacted by Anthony Quayle, the actor and director who had given him his great chance at Stratford back in the fifties. Ever restless and eager to try new schemes, Tony Quayle was putting together a touring company, to be known as Compass, to present mainly classical work. A probable London venue for his first production was the Old Vic, recently bought and restored to its former splendour by a Canadian businessman, Ed Mirvish. It seemed only appropriate that the Old Vic should reopen with Shakespeare, that the play should be *The Tempest* which holds the substance of all that Shakespeare believed about the theatre and that the world-weary Prospero should be played by Richard Burton.

The idea was first talked over in any detail at Celigny just before Rich embarked on *Private Lives*. Tony Quayle and Andrew Leigh, the administrator at the Old Vic, flew to Geneva. They were met by a relaxed and confident host who, resplendent in a long scarlet coat, outdressed everyone else at the airport. The business was cleared with hassle. Rich agreed in principle to a touring schedule for the first quarter of 1984, which took him to Leicester, Manchester and London. The possibility was held open of a West End transfer followed by visits to European cities and to New York. Rich did not balk at the niggardly fee (£250 a week in rehearsals rising to £650 a week playing salary in the UK) but asked for thought to be given to a video spinoff. Memories of Nevill Coghill's audacious plan for filming *The Tempest* were vividly revived when Tony Quayle suggested this should be done on location – 'either in the Caribbean or on one of the Greek islands'.

Dinner that night at the Café de la Gare was devoted to reminiscences of great days at Stratford. Rich and Tony Quayle shared the talking. Andrew Leigh and Sally did all the listening.

Just before departing for the States, Rich sent a note to Tony Quayle.

'I am more than merely excited at the thought of coming back home to play my favourite theatre in the world and equally delighted that you will be in charge.'

What happened in New York to make him change his mind? Well, *Private Lives* happened but, on earlier reasoning this should have strengthened his resolve. Sadly, it was not that simple. Losing the gamble on *Private Lives* robbed him of his self-assurance. He no longer believed he could do anything more on stage that was worthwhile. By their inability to give the right advice those close to him reinforced his insecurity and his tendency towards depression. When *The Tempest* and the Old Vic came up in conversation the only reaction from the people who were supposed to represent his interests was incredulity. How could he possibly think of working for peanuts?

Friends and colleagues who understood his problem were not around long enough to give proper weight to their countervailing view. Among those who did try, Richard Harris expressed himself most forcefully, and not just on the way Rich was damaging his career. At the end of what purported to be an alcohol-free dinner at Sardi's, Rich had difficulty in moving.

'Are you ill?' asked Harris.

'No, no. Don't worry. It's just that, for the moment, I can't get up.'

Suspecting more than fatigue, Harris took the head waiter aside.

'What's going on?' he wanted to know.

'It's the coffee,' he was told. 'Every cup he has is laced with brandy.'

Harris stormed back to the table. Sitting opposite Rich was one of his party. Harris tapped him on the shoulder.

'Come outside for a moment, will you? I want a word.'

Their exchange was conducted in a fierce whisper.

'What do you think you're doing to him?' asked Harris. The response was characteristically bland.

'Just giving him a good time.'

'Oh yes,' said Harris. 'You're certainly doing that. And you're doing something else. You bastard. You're killing him.'

When, after several weeks of not hearing from Rich or his agent, Tony Quayle flew to New York for another meeting, he still assumed that an agreement on *The Tempest* could be worked out. But it did not take long for him to discover otherwise. After seeing *Private Lives*, he and Rich went off to a restaurant, one of the busiest and noisiest off Broadway. The suspicion grew that Rich had chosen the place deliberately to forestall questions. The suspicion became a certainty when, on the way back to the hotel, Rich admitted strong opposition in his camp to any thought of going to London. 'But don't worry,' he added quickly. 'Let's talk about it tomorrow.'

At the meeting next day, Tony Quayle was confronted by Valerie Douglas and a sharp young lady who described herself as an agent.

They accused him of going behind their backs to get a deal on the cheap. The way they saw it, he had taken unfair advantage of Rich's good nature. Rich sat listening, not saying a word. Tony Quayle waited for the attack to end. When he was allowed to speak, he observed calmly,

'Then we do not have an agreement.'

'That's about it,' said the girl.

'In that case,' said Quayle, 'I see no point in continuing.'

It was Rich's last chance to play Shakespeare. And he blew it.

Working together in an unsuitable play brought out the worst in Rich and Elizabeth. He resented being made to do what he did not want to do and let his resentment show. His partner found this hard to take. She held doggedly to the view that she deserved something better – like a vote of thanks for earning them both a lot of money. They continued to flirt outrageously on and off stage but their exchanges had a steely edge.

When in late June Elizabeth fell ill and had to drop out of four performances, Rich was not sympathetic. His irritation mounted when Elizabeth announced she had to go away for a few days to recuperate and proposed taking Victor Luna with her. In a mood of angry depression he summoned Ron Berkeley and Bob Wilson to his suite at the Laurent Hotel. He had important news, he told them. He was intending to marry again, immediately. Ron Berkeley urged caution.

'You're only doing this to spite Elizabeth,' he warned.

'Maybe you're right,' said Rich, 'but it doesn't make any difference.'

Shortly afterwards Rich and Sally departed for Las Vegas. They were married on Sunday, 3 July.

He rang me that night and I, not realising the information was in any way confidential, passed on the story to my colleagues at the BBC.

Featuring prominently in the early morning bulletins, news of the marriage was quickly picked up by the rest of the media at home and abroad. Rich came back on to the phone. 'What are you trying to do to me?' he shouted. 'Why couldn't you have kept quiet for a few hours? I wanted a chance to tell Elizabeth. She should have been the first to know.'

Marriage to Sally spelt the end of *Private Lives*. To that extent, at least, Rich got what he wanted. After Washington and Chicago the show ground to a halt in Los Angeles were poor health forced Elizabeth to miss more performances. The Burtons then went off to Haiti where Rich had just bought a new house. They stayed there for two months, taking them through until the end of 1983.

By then *Wagner* had been seen by the critics though it was still

240

waiting for its television premiere. First reactions were generally favourable to Rich though inevitably he was thought to be best in the later episodes when he could act 'with all the appropriate dignity, stature, contradiction and arrogance' of the older Wagner. The problem with this mammoth production was that nobody could think what to do with it. Though visually splendid and with some fine performances, *Wagner* was too weighty and ponderous to justify peak viewing in television or, in its shorter version, a movie distribution beyond the art houses. When the public did eventually get the chance to see what must be counted as one of the outstanding Burton portrayals, the initial excitement had worn off and the response was disappointingly muted.

There was just one film to go. It was produced by Virgin, a new British company founded on the commercial genius of Richard Branson and profits of the pop music industry.

Given the year, a remake of the George Orwell classic, *1984*, seemed entirely appropriate. It had a young director, Michael Radford, and a notable acting talent in John Hurt who was cast as the much persecuted Winston Smith. Now all that was needed was a bankable name to occupy the role of O'Brien, the evilly self-righteous interrogator.

Rich was not first choice. Paul Scofield was asked, so too was Jason Robards. When, among the late starters, Richard Burton was mentioned as a possibility, worried questions were exchanged as to his fitness and his capacity for staying sober. The film had to be finished by mid-year. There was no margin for changing an actor halfway.

But the testimony of *Wagner* was hard to fault. Evidently, Rich could sustain an exacting performance and still win plaudits. And there was the voice, with its hypnotic intonation, so right for the seductive persecutor that Orwell envisaged.

His contract ran from May to July. For most of that time he and Sally stayed at the Dorchester.

'Home again,' he greeted Marjorie Lee.

But it was not at all like old times. Rich looked tired and much older than his fifty-eight years. The pain in his neck and back dogged him all his waking hours and he had trouble lifting either arm above shoulder level. On set for rehearsals he wore a neck brace.

He was still a great raconteur. Some of the stories had worn thin with repetition but the younger people in the production – and nearly all were younger – may not have heard them before. At any rate, they gave every indication of enjoying his company and Rich, for his part, was happy to relax as the convivial elder.

I saw Rich for the last time three weeks before he died. We had dinner, just the two of us. When I arrived at the Dorchester I was

241

waylaid by Brook Williams. 'He's not at his best,' he said. 'You won't overstay your welcome, will you love?'

Rich was in the mood for a heart to heart. We had barely sat down before he was cogitating on the way his life had turned out. Every time he opened a paper he dreaded yet another lament on Richard Burton, the actor who had sacrificed his great talents to booze and the fast life.

'Do you think it's all been a waste?' he asked me.

I reeled off a dozen of his performances which I reckoned were as good as any of his time. 'You've given pleasure to millions of people. How can that be a waste?'

He ignored the question, choosing instead to follow his own thoughts.

'Olivier and Gielgud, they've acted in rubbish. We can't be good for all of the time.'

'But there is a difference,' I reminded him. 'You've spent most of your life on a film set. Olivier and Gielgud have given more to the theatre.'

He laughed.

'You mean, if the rubbish is on film people remember it for longer.'

'Something like that.'

He went serious again.

'Do you know what I heard the other day? That I've never found a part as good as playing the husband of Elizabeth Taylor.'

I skirted that one. 'Do you miss Elizabeth?'

'Of course,' he said. 'All the time. But Elizabeth can't look after me. I need Sally. She takes care of an old man.'

We talked on about Elizabeth. It was his greatest pleasure. At the end of the evening he said to me, 'We've never really split up. And we never will. We're always there when we need each other.'

Leaving the hotel I remembered a visit to Elizabeth's home in Los Angeles. In every room and every corridor there were pictures of Rich. Sometimes whole rows of them.

'He's where I can keep an eye on him,' joked Elizabeth. 'And he'd better believe it.'

If they could not live together in harmony, the bond between them defied all efforts, including their own, to make a clean break. If Rich had lived, I don't doubt they would have tried again to work it out between themselves. Who knows, it might have been a case of third time lucky.

*1984* was the last film but Rich did make one other appearance on screen – a cameo role in *Ellis Island*, a made-for-television film about the European immigrants who poured into America at the turn of the century. It was not the sort of production he would normally have taken on but he had a special reason for making this an exception. His daughter Kate played one of the lead roles. Rich had tried to persuade her, as he said, 'to do something sensible for a living' but when she showed her determination to be an actress, he insisted only that she should go to a decent drama school. After three years at Yale her first big break was a revival of *Present Laughter* in which she made her Broadway debut. Rich was there on the first night to show his pride. With *Ellis Island*, there were not the same opportunities for Kate to prove her talent but she made the best of modest material.

'A chip off the old block,' said Rich with feeling.

The reviews for *1984* came out a month after Rich died. Greeted as 'one of his best appearances on film', the premiere gave the critics their opportunity to pay tribute to one of the great screen personalities. In the best tradition of the movie business, Rich went out in fine style.

## Chapter 18

*E*lizabeth did not come to the memorial service in Wales. There was, I know, pressure from Sally to keep her away but by Sally's own testimony she relented at the last moment, ringing Elizabeth in Los Angeles to say that, after all, the Pontrhydyfen service was open to ex-wives. She made a great show of telling me of her munificent gesture.

'But that gave her much less than twenty-four hours,' I pointed out. 'There was no way she could get to Pontrhydyfen in time.'

'No,' mused Sally, 'I suppose not.'

The Bethel Chapel, solid grey stone set into the hill, was not built for crowds or grand occasions. Normally, a congregation of more than twenty signalled an event of special interest. On Saturday 11 August 1984 over four hundred friends of Richard Burton squeezed inside the building while outside twice that number listened to the service as it echoed over the tannoy and joined in the hymns. It was an unfussy goodbye made all the more effective because of that. No one who was in the chapel is ever likely to forget the simple display of red carnations resting on a Welsh flag beneath the pulpit.

The Minister, Eric Williams, spoke of Rich's love for his homeland.

'He never forgot his roots. He never forgot the rock from which he was hewn.' He went on, 'Richard Burton was a man of genius, a man of generosity; he gave, he shared, he showed tremendous kindness.'

Among hundreds of letters which bore testimony to my brother's capacity for giving was one from a Biafran family who thanked Rich for saving them and many of their tribe from starvation. It would be tedious to list the charities which, at one time or another, were helped by Rich or by Rich and Elizabeth together. But no one has ever

244

quarrelled with the estimate of an annual handout in the region of one million dollars. I cannot help adding, for the sake of all those journalists who maintained the Burtons would do anything for publicity, that neither ever sought an atom of recognition for their generosity.

After the service, the crowds gathered at the Miners Arms and at the rugby club. We sang 'Calon Ian', 'Sospan Fach' and 'Guide Me O'er Thou Great Redeemer'. Eddie Thomas, a celebrated Welsh boxer, gave a solo of 'Bless This House'. The first time I heard him sing it, we were all thirty years younger. Eddie had just won the British Welterweight championship. He went to the ringside radio microphone to prove his voice was as powerful as his punches. Then, as now, there was not a dry eye in the house.

Sally did not stay with the family but she did spend time with us at Hilda and Dai's house. When she left, there was a gathering outside to see her off. On a sudden impulse I led into a chorus of 'Sospan Fach', waving to the onlookers to join in. Sally smiled and held my arm. It was the closest I ever got to her. When the family were talking together that evening, Verdun said, 'It's not right, Rich being buried in Switzerland. This is where he should rest. The plot was all picked out and paid for.'

I went over to him.

'Don't let it trouble you,' I said. 'It doesn't matter where he's buried. His spirit is right here in Wales.'

Ten days after Rich's funeral and eight days after the Welsh memorial service, Elizabeth came to Pontrhydyfen. I picked her up from Swansea airport in a hired car. She was late. A crowd of about a hundred waited patiently and gave her a big cheer when, dressed all in pink, she stepped down from her executive jet. Her only jewellery was a large diamond ring, a gift from Rich.

The plan was for Elizabeth to stay overnight with Hilda and Dai. Inevitably, there was a large reception committee out in the street. As we pulled up at the front door they raised their voices for that best loved of all Welsh songs, 'We'll keep a welcome in the hillside'. Elizabeth smiled her thanks. 'I feel as if I'm home,' she told them.

At dinner that evening with the Jenkins clan, I heard about Elizabeth's belated visit to Celigny, two days earlier.

A hardy group of photographers who had stayed on in expectation of her arrival followed her to the cemetery. When they refused to leave her she went back to her hotel, but returned early the following morning.

'I couldn't help thinking,' she said, almost wistfully, 'it was one of the few occasions ever that Richard and I were alone.'

Elizabeth was naturally sad to have missed the funeral; sad too that apparently there was nothing she could do to convince Sally of her goodwill.

'If we had been at Celigny together,' said Elizabeth, 'I would have been happy to have walked with her hand in hand.'

We all stayed up late going through the vast number of cards and letters which had made our local post office look like Cardiff central. Much of the correspondence was addressed simply to Elizabeth Taylor c/o The Burton Family.

When our guest left the next morning she took with her a painting by Verdun of the house where Rich was born. Today, it has a place of honour in her Los Angeles home.

Three more memorial services were held in the last week of August. The first, at the Wilshire Theater in Beverly Hills, had Richard Harris leading the tributes. In the middle of his address he broke down and had to leave the stage. When he came back he confessed, 'If Rich had seen me a moment ago he would have howled with laughter.'

Of all the tributes to Rich, one of the most touching came from his co-star in *Who's Afraid of Virginia Woolf?*

'There is nothing in my life that comes close to the experience of working with Richard Burton,' declared George Segal. 'We have always known, those of us who act, that he was the best one. He makes us all proud to be actors.'

George Segal cancelled two days' filming to be at the service. Some other big names who had worked closely with Rich were not prepared to take the same trouble. Noting their absences and their reasons (one lady of the screen backed off when she heard that television cameras were not expected) John Huston growled, 'So what's new? We just have a few more candidates for the shit list.'

In New York as in Los Angeles the service ended with Rich singing the title song from *Camelot*, his own sweet dedication to 'one, brief, shining moment'. Pamela Mason had the best line: 'We should feel bad that he has gone, good that he was here.'

Over the Atlantic, invitations went out to some fourteen hundred friends and colleagues of Rich to attend the Church of St Martin-in-the-Fields, just off Trafalgar Square on 30 August. As master of ceremonies, Tim Hardy had first thought of the actors' church in Covent Garden as the obvious choice but changed his mind after talking to Emlyn Williams.

'It'll never do,' said Emlyn. 'Far too small.'

Tim was slightly taken aback.

'Where would you suggest, Emlyn? Westminster Abbey?'

246

'Don't be flippant,' said Emlyn sternly.

Come the day, the press photographers focused their lenses for three women. Elizabeth in black silk came first, arm in arm with Cis. Susan followed, a cockade of red and black flowers at her shoulder. Then Sally, belying her unglamorous image with a close-fitting black dress with a dash of red. She alone of the three wore a veil. Sybil was not there. For her, I guess, it was all too long ago.

The orchestration was impeccable. The only hiccup was the late arrival of John Gielgud who had gone to the wrong church. Flustered and evidently distressed at his failure to be on time, he quickly transformed into a model of composure to read John Donne's *Death Be Not Proud*. A favourite of Rich, he would have loved to have heard that sweet voice ('like an A-string on a violin,' said Tim Hardy).

Hopes of an easier relationship with Sally were disappointed. She objected strongly to Elizabeth sitting with the family in church, a sin of commission for which she blamed Marjorie Lee who had taken on the administration. Having given her time freely and generously Marjorie was upbraided by Sally as if she was a naughty schoolgirl. For thanks, Marjorie had to look elsewhere.

There was more trouble from Sally over the tribute from Emlyn Williams. Why so many references to Elizabeth and none at all for Sally? Well, as a matter of tact, it might have been wise to shift the balance slightly. But if Emlyn was seeking truth in his portrayal of Richard Burton, he got it just about right.

My brother was a star. Many have tried to dissect and analyse that word. But it is enough to say that you know a star when you meet one. He compels attention. Rich did it as a small boy. He went on doing it throughout his life.

Richard Harris said of him, 'If there were twelve elephants on a stage and Rich was there too, you would look at Rich.'

When the script was on his side he could raise it to greatness; when the script was against him he would still give it a touch of distinction.

A wasted life? Only by his own estimation. He was a confused man, often carried along by events because he could not think of any better way of arranging matters. His gifts were a mystery to him; his power, such as it was, frightened him. He made many mistakes but at least he recognised his failures and, to his credit, agonised over them.

There are those who believe Rich should have persevered with his stage career. Perhaps he would have reached the heights. But there was no certainty, as others found to their cost. John Neville, who shared with Rich the glory of the Old Vic, stayed slavishly loyal to the theatre. Whatever happened to him?

Anyway, as Warren Mitchell, a friend of Rich from RAF days, reminded me, 'It's the same old story. We want people to be what we want them to be which is not necessarily what they want for themselves.'

If there was some way of calling him back to judge his own life, I believe that Rich would say that he took his chances and stood by the consequences. He always kept his pride. He was his father's son. He was Richard Jenkins.

As my father would ask outside the Miners Arms on a summer Saturday evening, in the massive stupor of his cups, fixing his stoned eyes on his assembled miner cronies as he drank a toast to the setting sun as it slipped down the wall of the world just beyond Swansea and Mumbles Head:

'*Pwy sydd fel nyni?*'
'*Neb,*' they would answer.
'*Pwy sydd fel fi?*'
'*Neb.*'

'Who is like us?'
'Nobody.'
'Who is like me?'
'Nobody.'

*Cu oedd gennym*

# FALSE
# HEARTS

# FALSE
# HEARTS

# LAURA LAM

**TOR**

A TOM DOHERTY ASSOCIATES BOOK
NEW YORK

FALSE HEARTS

Copyright © 2016 by Laura Lam

A Tor Book
Published by Tom Doherty Associates, LLC
175 Fifth Avenue
New York, NY 10010

www.tor-forge.com

Tor® is a registered trademark of Tom Doherty Associates, LLC.

The Library of Congress Cataloging-in-Publication Data is available upon request.

ISBN 978-0-7653-8205-4 (hardcover)
ISBN 978-1-4668-8574-5 (e-book)

Our books may be purchased in bulk for promotional, educational, or business use. Please contact your local bookseller or the Macmillan Corporate and Premium Sales Department at 1-800-221-7945, extension 5442, or by e-mail at MacmillanSpecialMarkets@macmillan.com.

First U.S. Edition: June 2016

Printed in the United States of America

0  9  8  7  6  5  4  3  2  1

*In memory of my father,*

*Gary Lyle Richardson (1945–2015).*

*You were weird and wonderful, and I'm glad you were able to read an early draft of this before you rejoined the Cycle.*

# ACKNOWLEDGMENTS

As with any book, there are a great many people to thank. This was a fun book to write, but it was a departure from my previous fantasy, so I was nervous. Many people helped me find the confidence to keep going.

Thank you to my agent, Juliet Mushens, for invaluable early feedback, always being in my corner, and being fabulous and amazing. Many thanks also to her incredible assistant, Sarah Manning (not the *Orphan Black* character). To my original acquiring editor, Julie Crisp, and to editor extraordinaire Bella Pagan, as well as Louise Buckley and Lauren Welch. Everyone at Tor, both UK and U.S. (thank you, Marco Palmieri), has been amazing to work with and so enthusiastic about my work—it's been a blast.

I sent this book to so many people over many drafts and received so much great feedback that truly transformed *False Hearts*. Thank you to my husband, Craig, and two of my closest friends, Erica Bretall and Shawn DeMille, who always read my really, really ugly first drafts before I send them out to anyone else. Thank you to my mom and staunch cheerleader, Sally Baxter. Much gratitude to Kim Curran, Amy Alward, Katharine Stubbs, Cassandra Rose Clarke, Wesley Chu, Lorna McKay, Hannah Beresford, Mike Kalar, Jonathan Butcher, Nazia Khatun, Colin Sinclair, Vonny McKay, Lisa McCurrach, Katie Kemp (for neuroscience help specifically), Leah Woods, Justina Ireland, Tristina Wright, and Ann Godridge. Whether you saw the very early drafts or the nearly finished one, I appreciate you taking the time to read and tell me what you thought. Thank you to several sex workers who read scenes about Tila's work and made sure I hadn't unintentionally fallen into any stereotypes. Thank you to Nick Harkaway for the name of Sudice for the company when I asked for suggestions on Twitter. I think that's everyone, but if I forgot someone because my inbox is too disorganized, I'm super sorry and I'll buy you a coffee.

I did a lot of research for this book. The initial idea came from reading an article about Daisy and Violet Hilton and wondering what it would be like to be connected to someone every minute of every day, and how strange it would be if you found out your literal other half had kept something from you. Alice Domurat Dreger's book *One of Us: Conjoined Twins and the Future of Normal* really impacted the twins' view of being conjoined, their relationship to each other, and how they were perceived by the outside world, both within the Hearth and San Francisco. I was also inspired by Lori Lansens's work of fiction *The Girls*. I watched a lot of documentaries and interviews with conjoined twins: *The Twins Who Share a Body, Abby & Brittany, Two Hearts, Bound by Flesh, The Twins Who Share a Brain*, and more. I asked a few twins about their relationships and also observed my twin nephews, Ruben and Kade. For cults, *Last Days* by Adam Nevill and *Whit* by Iain Banks were some fictional influences, as was the film *Martha Marcy May Marlene*, and documentaries such as *Jonestown: The Life and Death of Peoples Temple, Jesus Camp*, and *Cults: Dangerous Devotion* gave me some invaluable insights. I also read numerous articles on various cults. I read *Mapping the Mind* by Rita Carter as a good resource on neuroscience, and I looked at the History Channel's City of the Future's entries for San Francisco, which inspired some aspects of my near-future city. I have a fuller list of resources on my website, if you'd like to learn more.

As ever, thank you to the readers who picked up the book and spent some time with Taema and Tila. You're the reason I can keep doing this.

*False face must hide what the false heart doth know.*

—William Shakespeare, *Macbeth*

# FALSE
# HEARTS

# PROLOGUE

# TAEMA

*San Francisco, California*

This is the first time I have ever been alone.

The first time I have ever woken up to silence and emptiness next to me. The only sounds in the room are the beeping of the heart monitor and my own labored breathing.

It isn't supposed to be like this.

Groggy from the medicine, I raise my hand to hover over the hot wound, throbbing even through the pain of the IV. It is the first time my hand has been able to linger three inches above my own chest. Below my shaking fingers is the deep cut that will heal into a thin seam from just below my collarbone to right above my navel. Beneath the newly grafted skin and reconstructed breasts is a titanium sternum—bulletproof, so they say—and half of my ribs are made of the same substance. Below that metal sternum is my new, false heart. The old heart is gone, cut out and replaced with an upgraded model that will never tire. I can almost imagine I can hear its mechanical ticking.

This is the first time I've ever been lonely.

The doorknob to the recovery room turns. My automated heartbeat doesn't quicken, though the old, fleshy one would have. I still feel the thrum of adrenaline. The door opens, and for the first time, I see my own, moving reflection. My full mirror image. The same brown skin, the mane of curly hair. The same long nose and dark eyes, features hollowed in fear and pain. My twin, Tila.

*Are my knees that knobby?* I ask myself, almost laughing from the ridiculousness of the thought. The drugs still rush through my system, and everything is dreamily gold-tinged.

She's trailing her IV with her. I can barely move, so she shouldn't be up, but Tila doesn't let a small thing like pain stop her. I'm surprised she hasn't triggered the alarms. She probably disabled them—she's always been clever with her hands.

We're not supposed to see each other for a few days, so we grow used to being separate. As usual, she's ignored all the rules and advice and followed her own heart. It is really her *own* heart now. She creeps closer, her bare feet swishing along the floor.

"T?" she whispers.

"T," I answer. We always call each other T when we are alone. I close my eyes, a tear falling down my cheek. *What have we done?*

Painfully, I move over on the bed as best I can. We haven't just come out of surgery, if the date on the wallscreen is correct. They put us in a medical coma for a few days to speed up healing. I find the fact they can do something like that more than a little frightening. Neither of us has ever been to a hospital before this. There aren't any in Mana's Hearth.

Tila slides into the bed. On her chest, in mirror image of mine, is the same wound that will one day become a scar. Beneath her false sternum is another new, false heart. I wonder if they are set to the same rhythm and even now beat together.

Gently, we turn onto our sides, pressing our foreheads

together. Then and only then can we fall back asleep, in the position we have fallen asleep in for the last sixteen years. Now three inches of emptiness separate us, when before there had been nothing, and our heart had beat as one.

# ONE

# TAEMA

*Ten years later*

I'm starting where it all falls apart.

Tila is late for dinner.

We meet twice a week, once at her place and once at mine, though lately it's always been at my apartment in Inner Sunset. She says she's staying late at work, but I never know if that's true. I hate it when she keeps secrets. It used to be that we couldn't.

Outside, fat drops of rain drum against the glass window. The sunset has faded to darkness, a few stars just bright enough to shine through the San Francisco fog. I pace across the living room, peering at the blurred view of the city skyline, the green shimmer of the algae farms in the bay, the lights of the hovercars flying past. I paid a lot extra to have the penthouse for this view, but at the moment it does nothing for me. All I can do is be irritated at my sister.

Back in the kitchen, I push the curls from my face. I use my auditory implants to ping Tila, but there's no response. I turn on the wallscreen, but the moving images and sounds irritate me, and I shut them off. The scar on my chest twinges. It's psychosomatic. There's no way it could actually hurt, not after so many years. I rest my fingertip on the top of the rough line of healed skin. It's been almost a decade to the day since the surgery.

I sigh and set out the food, the time flashing in the corner of my ocular implants until I send it away. Her shift at Zenith supposedly ended over an hour ago. She works at the hostess club at the top of the TransAm Pyramid. Not a bad gig, but not for me. I don't think I'd be as good at pretending.

I've made Tila her favorite curry, adapted from a recipe from the Hearth. I could have ordered it from the replicator in the corner of the kitchen, but I needed the distraction of doing something with my hands. It's time to tell her I quit my job this afternoon, and I accepted a new job offer I couldn't refuse—in China. I don't know if Tila will want to come with me.

Or if she should.

The doorknob turns. I stand and rub my palms along my skirt. Tila flies in, disheveled and wild-eyed. Her short, teal hair is wet and plastered to her skull, contrasting with my brown curls. Her clothes are flashy where mine are plain. Her face is different than mine now too, from trips to the flesh parlors. They're not drastic changes, but we no longer look identical.

It isn't until she rushes to me and clutches the front of my shirt, on either side of my scar, that I realize she's covered in blood. She's wearing a man's coat I don't recognize, and it gapes open, dripping onto the floor. Her light blue dress is splattered red, the rain smearing it into a garish watercolor.

My mind takes a beat to process it. "Are—are you hurt?" I ask, trying to pull back to go for the first aid kit. But if it's that much blood, she might need more than bandages. Fear rushes through me, and I can't seem to catch my breath.

She doesn't answer right away. Her mouth flaps open, and then shuts. She lets go of me, backing away from the door.

"Not my blood. You have to help me, T. Oh God, you *have* to help me."

I tense. *Not my blood.* "If it's not your blood, whose is it?" My breath comes faster, hitching on the inhale. My sister feeds off my fear, grabbing my shirt so hard the fabric rips. "What the hell is going on, Tila?" I ask.

Expressions of fear and guilt flit across her face like shadows. "Please, Taema. Please. I have to get out of the city right now. Both of us do. Hide out somewhere. The Sierras? If only Mana's Hearth would let us claim sanctuary."

Mana's Hearth is exempt from Pacifica jurisdiction. That she would mention *going back*, despite everything that happened ten years ago, and that she wants to bring me too, is what tells me just how serious this is. "Tila, slow down. What have you done?"

"I haven't done anything, Taema. It didn't happen the way they'll say." I can see the whites of her eyes, the tension lines around her mouth. Despite her surgery, her face reminds me too much of that last day in Mana's Hearth when we thought we would die in that redwood forest.

The tips of my hands tingle and my vision swims. "OK. OK." I force myself to try and calm down. "What *haven't* you done?"

Sirens sound outside the high-rise apartment. I startle— you hardly *ever* hear them in San Francisco anymore. They're growing louder.

Tila presses against me. "Oh God, they've found me. Must have tracked my VeriChip. I knew I should have torn it out. Can I hide? There must be somewhere I can hide!"

Her panic is infectious, but I have to be the pragmatic twin she expects. The twin she needs. "No point. All the police will have infrared sensors. If you didn't do this, then it'll be fine, right? They'll take you in for questioning and then let you go." I don't want to be the calm twin. I want to grab her, shake her, demand she tell me what has happened and whose blood she's wearing.

Tila only sobs, resting her hand just below my collarbone, right on my scar. I rest my hand on hers. I can feel the mechanical beating of her heart. Despite our obvious terror, our hearts beat at their same, steady pace.

"It'll be all right, T," I say. "I promise."

She looks at me, dangerous and untamed. I barely recognize her. "You can't promise that, T. You can't promise that at all."

Red and blue lights flash outside the window. A police hovercar floats outside the balcony, rain falling off its sides. The searchlight illuminates the room, paralyzing us in the bright beams. Three police jump down onto the tiny balcony, their boots splashing in the puddles on the concrete. Tila's shaking, burrowing close to my side. I wrap my arm around her, but I'm shivering just as badly.

They open the sliding glass door, but too hard. The glass shatters. Fragments spill into my living room, as if the rain outside has crystallized.

"SFPD!"

"Really, now," I say, looking at the glass and rain scattered across the living room. Fear shifts to anger. "Was that necessary?"

The police look between us. They are all wearing bulletproof Kalar vests over their sleek, dark blue uniforms. Cops almost never wear Kalars, not in this city that prides itself on its lack of crime. The whites of their eyes shimmer in the light with their extra implants.

An Indian-American woman with curly hair tamed in a knot at the nape of her neck clutches her gun, shifting her stance. The other man, white and brown-haired with a face so generically good-looking I'll forget what he looks like as soon as he leaves the room, begins to make a perimeter of my apartment. Perhaps he thinks extra backup is hiding behind the couch. The last man, their leader, is black with a gold tattoo I can't make out peeking over the collar of his uniform. He narrows his eyes at us, focusing on Tila and her teal hair: "Tila Collins?"

She doesn't answer, keeping her head bowed.

He steps forward and grabs her upper arms. For a second, I fear she's going to resist and try to run for it, but then she goes limp.

"What's going on here?" I ask. "She says she hasn't done it, whatever you're after her for."

They ignore me. Gold Tattoo says, "Tila Collins, you are under arrest for murder in the first degree. You have the right to remain silent. Anything you say can and will be used against you."

When was the last time he had to read anyone their Miranda rights?

Gold Tattoo pulls Tila from my grasp. My hands fall useless at my sides. Tila tilts her head up at him and spits in his face.

Gold Tattoo wipes the spittle away, expressionless.

The wind leaves my lungs as the full implications sink in. Murder. There hasn't been a murder by a civilian in San Francisco in years. Not since Pacifica was formed after the United States fractured forty years ago. Not since VeriChips and implants and cameras on every corner.

"Tila?" I ask as Gold Tattoo marches her back to the hover-car, handing her over to Curly Hair. I sound forlorn, lost.

She throws a pleading glance over her shoulder as they push her inside. "Taema!"

Within moments, they are all gone save Gold Tattoo. He towers over me, but he looks so young. He might not be, with flesh parlors everywhere, but it's hard to find him terrifying when it looks like he only learned how to shave yesterday.

A sob lodges in my throat. It's all I can do not to break into pieces in front of this man. One moment, I was annoyed that dinner was growing cold, and now my apartment is a mess and my sister is accused of murder. I can't wrap my head around the word. *Murder*. It's Tila. My sister. I know her better than I know myself.

Don't I?

"Miss Collins?" There might be a hint of concern behind the brusque tone. He's close enough that I can make out his tattoo: a California grizzly bear.

I find my voice. "My sister's just been taken for murder. How do you think I feel?"

He has no answer to that. Within moments, the sirens blare again as they take my sister away from me.

"Who's she meant to have murdered?" I ask, my voice tight. That word again. It's ugly.

"A body of a man was found at Zenith under suspicious circumstances. I can't say anything more."

My hands ball into fists. Gold Tattoo notices the movement, his hand resting on his gun. My lungs burn from holding in the sobs.

He pauses. I realize why he's stayed behind.

"I'm to go in for questioning too? Why didn't you take me with Tila?"

He shifts slightly. "Yes, Miss Collins. We're to take you in as a precaution. You'll be going to the station. Your sister is being taken elsewhere."

"Where?"

"I'm not at liberty to say."

I fold over, trying to take in deep breaths but still hyperventilating.

"Miss Collins."

I hold up a hand. I think of the Hearth, how Mana-ma taught us to control our emotions. *Let the darkness float away. Let in only the light.* I imagine the chapel on the hill at the center of the town, the five-pointed symbol carved on its side, the birdcalls that floated through the open windows on a spring day. Despite my hatred of her, her techniques work.

I stand up, smoothing my features, shaking my head a little from side to side. "Yes. We have the same DNA. You'll want to make sure *I* didn't do it."

He says nothing.

"Am I under arrest?"

"No. You're being detained for questioning. Please grab your things, Miss Collins."

I look around at my apartment. The wet footprints all over the carpet. The shining bits of glass. The food cold on the table, the plates laid out for a meal we will never eat.

I grab my coat and purse.

As he leads me down the stairs, curiosity seems to get the better of him. "I shouldn't ask, but do you really think she didn't do it?"

I pause. I still think he's been waxworked—he's too highly ranked to be any younger than late thirties—but his eyes aren't quite as jaded as a lot of older people masquerading in younger bodies.

My hand snakes toward my sternum again, pressing against the faint seam where they unzipped me and Tila and took us apart a decade ago. Underneath, my mechanical heart beats, beats, beats.

"I know my twin better than anyone else. If she says she didn't do it, then she didn't."

I'm sure I believe it.

Ninety-nine percent sure.

## TWO

# TAEMA

Officer Oloyu, or Gold Tattoo, is all business when we reach the San Francisco Police Headquarters. He has become hard— perhaps on the silent hovercar trip he's changed his mind and decided I must be as guilty as my sister. Or the question in the hallway was an act, and he decided he wouldn't catch the fly with honey. He gazes down at the blank tablet, little more than a white piece of plastic to focus the eyes as he accesses his ocular implant for my file.

He hovers close, almost touching, knowing that it will make me defensive and on edge. Then he strolls to his side of the table, perching on the chair, legs spread wide.

He's offered me a coffee, but it sits in front of me, an oily sheen on top from the artificial creamer, untouched and grow-ing cold. My mouth is dry. All I can think of is Tila. Where have they taken her? What's going through her mind?

Oloyu is the only one in the room. Aren't there usually two, a good cop and a bad one? Granted, all I have to go on is old cop shows they play late at night on the wallscreen.

Oloyu stares at me, unblinking. I can't decide whether or not to be intimidated by him. His splayed body language is aggressive, and it's working—I feel like prey being stalked. Yet his features are still so young, honest and symmetrical. If he really wants to be more frightening in situations like these, perhaps he should make another visit to the flesh parlor.

"When's the last time you saw your sister?" Oloyu asks.

"Almost a week ago," I answer, keeping my voice flat to stop it quavering. I'm also embarrassed to realize it's been that long. I'd invited her over for dinner twice, but she'd claimed she was working both times. I don't have anything to hide, yet I still feel like this is a test I could pass or fail, depending on my answers. Or that I could accidentally incriminate my sister.

*How could you incriminate her?* I ask myself. *She couldn't have done anything. Right?*

"And where do you work?"

I swallow. This is all in my file from when he scanned the VeriChip in my wrist. "Silvercloud Solutions."

Officer Oloyu makes a show of perusing my file on his blank, white tablet. "That's a subset of Sudice, right?"

"Yes." I don't know why he's pretending he doesn't know. Sudice is the biggest company in Pacifica, with offices in San Francisco, Los Angeles, Portland and Honolulu. They supply the drug Zeal to all Pacifica states, and have most tech in the city patented.

"It says here you helped design the VivaFog." Those machines have been my life's work for the past five years: the machines that take energy from the ever-present fog around the bay and relay it to the coastal apartments. We're going to try and expand to the maritime district this year.

"I was one of the team that did, yes," I respond. Why isn't he asking the questions he really wants the answer to? Beneath the table, I press my knees hard to stop them knocking together.

Officer Oloyu isn't saying anything out of order, but everything in his body language screams: *I suspect you, either of murder or accessory to it.* I wish I still had that microexpression overlay

14

downloaded to my ocular implants, but I deleted it months ago. I didn't like what it told me about people.

"That's impressive," Officer Oloyu says. I'm not sure whether or not I sense the underlying subtext I often do from people who know my past: *for someone who grew up in the cult of Mana's Hearth.*

"Thank you," I tell him, meeting his eyes.

"We contacted your employer, but it seems you quit your job today and have plans to leave the country."

"Yes, that's correct. That's been in the works for months. It's not a sudden decision." I feel a flutter of nerves, deep in my stomach. It's a coincidence, but it doesn't look good.

"We're unclear if this is premeditated or a crime of passion."

"I had nothing to do with *this*. Whatever *this* is. And I'm sure my sister didn't, either."

He pauses, considering me. The overhead lighting leaves half his face in shadow. I look down at my stone-cold coffee. I want water, but I don't ask him for it.

"Did your sister seem different at all, the last time you saw her? Distressed in any way?"

"No. She seemed the same as usual. Laughing, joking. We went to an Ethiopian restaurant in the Mission."

His gaze goes distant as he makes a mental note with his implants.

This is my first lie to the police. She seemed thinner, she didn't laugh. She picked at her food, when usually Tila has a voracious appetite. I kept asking her what was wrong, but she said she'd just been working too many late nights at the club. The lie fell from my mouth before I thought about it, and I can't take it back.

They've mapped my brain to see if I'm lying. A model floats above our heads, delicate and transparent, dotted with neuron clusters like stars. Oloyu glances up to check. Between my mechanical heart not growing as excited as a flesh one and my Hearth training, nothing happens. I could lie with impunity. If they map Tila, she can too.

"So nothing unusual over the last few weeks? No signs she was keeping anything from you? You two must be close." Again, I can hear from his tone what he really means: *close enough that if one of you did it, the other would know about it.*

"Closer than you can ever imagine," I say, my voice sharpening with fear. I don't want him to see he's struck a nerve, but by the flint of his eyes, he knows he has. I decide I'm not going to let him scare me, even if terror still rolls in my stomach. Even though I hate the Hearth and all it stands for, another one of Mana-ma's sayings comes to me: *They only have power over you if you let them.*

"Does your sister have any enemies?" Oloyu leans forward. I can't stand anyone that close to me unless it's Tila or someone I know extremely well. But I lean forward on my elbows, right in his face, ignoring the mirrored window behind him and whoever watches me through it. I'm still scared, but I haven't let it paralyze me.

"Everyone *loves* Tila. She can go buy food and make a new friend." That's true. If we take a shuttle somewhere for a holiday, I read, ignoring those around me. Tila will become fast friends with whoever is sitting next to her: an old man with a white beard, a new mother and her squalling baby, and once a Buddhist monk in his saffron robes.

She can make enemies as well: people who don't like her because of her blithe way of speaking, her easy enthusiasm. I'm sure there are probably a few other hostesses at the club who are jealous of her. She can charm clients with a half-lidded glance and she often crows to me about how she receives the lion's share of the tips. Tila seems to know what it is each person wants and reflects that back to them, flirting by acting like one of the ribald men as easily as playing the coquettish minx. Heaven knows where she's learned all that. I sure haven't.

"Nobody at all?" Officer Oloyu presses.

I shake my head. "None that come to mind, no. Sorry I can't be more helpful." I'm not sorry I haven't given them anything to incriminate my sister. Or at least I hope I haven't.

He presses his lips together. "Now then. The question you must be expecting: where were you at 1700 hours this evening?"

"On the way home from work on the MUNI." My voice has stopped shaking, and I feel as though I'm no longer attached to my body. That I'm just a floating head. I have taken full control of my emotions, like Mana-ma always taught us to do in the Hearth.

"Which line do you take?"

"Clement Lot."

"You do understand we'll be checking the cameras."

"I'd expect nothing less."

Officer Oloyu narrows his eyes. At first, he thought he had me. Now, he thinks I'm being secretive, and he's right. But there's not much more he can do without concrete proof, and I'm not giving him anything. Even if there was anything to give.

"Can I have any details of the case, or is it all confidential?" I ask. "Maybe if I understand what's happened I can think of someone who might wish to harm my sister. Whose body did they find? Was it a guest of the club?" I'm desperate for more information. Anything to help piece together what happened tonight. Murder. The word keeps pulsing through my mind, until it doesn't even seem like a word anymore.

"We can't name the victim," Officer Oloyu says. The unspoken: *not to you.*

*Thanks for nothing.* "Right. Well, if you can't tell me anything, and I have nothing to tell you, is there anything else you need? Or can I go home and clean up the mess you made of my apartment?"

"I don't appreciate your tone, Miss Collins," Oloyu says. "You don't seem overly upset by tonight's events."

*Fuck you,* I want to say. *You don't have the first clue how I'm feeling.* Instead, I look at him calmly. "Am I free to go?"

"For now."

"Good." I stand and clutch my purse, and then I bend down and look him in the eye. I'm pleased to see him move back slightly. "I'm not upset because I'm sure she's as much of a victim in this as whoever died tonight." I lean back and pull my collar down. It's a good way to unnerve others. In San Francisco, where everyone has made such an effort to appear flawless, nobody likes to see such obvious signs of imperfection. Tila taught me the trick. For all she changed her face and hair to not look like me, she kept the scar.

Oloyu looks at the scar with a mixture of fascination and embarrassment.

"You can't spend sixteen years with someone, *every* minute of *every* day, and not know if they're capable of murder or not. I'll do *whatever* it takes to clear her name." I push my collar up and walk out. His eyes on my back make the hairs on my neck prickle.

•

Officer Oloyu follows me from the interrogation room to the hovercar, and we rise and fly along the coast of the bay toward my apartment in Inner Sunset. The last thing I want to do is see more of him, and I wonder why a senior policeman is taking the time to chauffeur me back instead of some rookie. I haven't seen any other police officers except for the two who took Tila away—it's almost as if they don't want anyone else to see me.

I ignore Oloyu and stare out the window. It's full night by now, and San Francisco glitters below us. The sight of it helps me forget my anxiety and terror, at least for a moment.

I love this city. It's the complete opposite of Mana's Hearth. In the Hearth, the lake is ink-black at night. In San Francisco, the algae farms make the bay glow green. To my right is Angel Island, and the ruined Alcatraz, the building too decayed by the salt and wind to visit, and the man-made islands where the rich live in their sumptuous houses. The Golden Gate and the Bay Bridge lead toward the city skyline. Billboards advertising Sudice products flash their garish colors: implant upgrades, a new Zeal lounge downtown, the virtual reality center next to Union Square Mall. The car passes between buildings: greenhouse skyscrapers with their lush, forest-like interiors, multilevel apartment towers, most of the windows lit, small silhouettes staring out the windows toward the bay.

Scattered throughout the city are revenants risen from the Earth after the Great Quake of 2055—antiquities of architecture preserved and joined with their modern counterparts in a hybrid of old and new: Coit Tower, the skyscrapers on California Street and near the Embarcadero, the old iconic Ferry Building at the base of the newly built air hangars above and the piers jutting out into the gentle waves of the bay. And there, just coming into sight, the TransAm Pyramid, twice as large as the old Transamerica Pyramid. I can't look away from the glowing top floor, home to Club Zenith.

San Francisco.

Our new home after we'd left the Hearth. At first, we'd hated it. It was too different, too new, and we'd had to learn about its ways while struggling with our newly separated status. Eventually, we'd grown to love it. The freedom it gave us. The opportunities. Now, I fear I'll grow to hate it again.

Officer Oloyu clears his throat. I turn to him, trying to bring something approximating a smile to my face, but it fails.

"I'll tell you a little about the case," he says, grudgingly. "I've been given the go-ahead by my superior."

Why the change? "All right," I say, slowly. The flashing lights of the city play across his face, catching in his eyes.

"You are not permitted to share this information with anyone. Understood?"

"Yes."

"The victim has not been formally identified yet, but another hostess says they called him Vuk. He was tall, muscular, wore a sharp suit. Tipped very well. Spent a lot of time in the Zeal lounge. Tila was one of his favorites."

"Vuk," I say, tasting the name on my lips. The retinal display of my implants tells me the name means "wolf" in Serbo-Croatian. I send the text away. "Why are you telling me this?"

"We want you to come back in tomorrow," he says. The hardness has left him again. I prefer him without it—it doesn't suit him. Too forced.

"Why?"

"You'll see. Please come to the station tomorrow at 0900. Take the MUNI. Come through the back entrance."

"This is not a request?"

"No." We've reached my apartment. He sets the hovercar down on the balcony. I sigh at the sight of my broken sliding glass door. At least the worst of the rain has stopped.

I get out without saying goodbye, stepping into my damp

20

living room. I turn around, watching Oloyu lift the police car away.

"Vuk," I say again. "Who were you?" A rich man, if he frequented the club, who liked to plug into the Zeal virtual world fantasies. I can just see a Sudice billboard for Zeal, flashing through the fog. A woman in a Chair, wires hooked up to her arms and temples, eyes closed, a smile on her face. Above her head, her dreams come to life—she's clad in armour, and fighting a sinuous monster. The billboard blinks again. She's flipping head over feet, wearing a skintight star-spangled uniform, an Olympic athlete. One last blink, and the tagline: *Find your Zeal for life. What will you dream today?*

What were Vuk's dreams when he was plugged into that Chair, and did Tila join him in them?

I look down over the city again, wondering how I'll find out who he was and how he entangled Tila in this mess.

# THREE

# TILA

They've given me an old-fashioned paper notebook to write my last will and testament, with a pencil blunt enough I can't kill myself with it. I'm sure I still could, if I wanted to.

I refused a tablet. I don't want them sneaking and reading this as I write. So here I am, with my paper and pencil. I'm more used to this than most people in the city—out in the Hearth, there are no fancy gadgets and very little technology.

I'm not going to write my last will and testament. What's the point? I don't have much to leave and my only next of kin is Taema, so everything goes to her. I couldn't send any of my stuff to my parents at the Hearth even if I wanted to, since we're apostate and all that.

So I'm just sort of scribbling, seeing what will come out. It passes the time, I guess. There's nothing else to do. The cell is cold and boring, with everything gray and beige, though I do have a window that shows a tiny patch of blue sky. Maybe writing this will distract me, at least a little, from the fact they're going to kill me soon.

There's no point sugar-coating it—it'll happen. My lawyer is halfheartedly trying to put up a defense, buy me more time, but I don't know why he bothers. The trial's in a few weeks. Though can you really call it a trial if there's no jury, just some judge deciding your fate? The government is keeping it all hush-hush. The media aren't meant to know—most of the people here don't even know who I am or what I'm meant to have done. I overheard the guards talking about it. I'm not in a normal prison. They don't even have prisons in San Francisco anymore, there's so little crime. I'm locked away somewhere else, but we didn't travel long so I think I'm still in Northern California. Maybe they took me to the Sierras? The air seems colder and crisper.

If it ever does get out, I wonder if they'll let me read the news feeds. They'll call me all sorts of names. Some will be true. Some won't.

The judge will say I'm a criminal, and then they'll put me in stasis. Freeze me like a popsicle, and then I might as well be dead. That sounds flippant, I know, but that seems to be the only way I can write about it without crying.

Shit, never mind. There's tear stains on the paper now.

Putting people in stasis is Pacifica's answer to capital punishment. They're not killing them, but cryogenically freezing criminals. It happened a lot more in the early days of Pacifica, after the United States split up. Now, maybe only a dozen people, tops, are put into stasis every year. It's only for the really hopeless cases, those who don't respond to Zeal therapy and will never be redeemed. I guess they think I'm unredeemable.

Hardly anyone who goes into stasis comes back out. It does happen—some tireless lawyer will discover someone frozen was actually innocent. They come out of it, disoriented, to find years have passed them by. One woman was taken out after thirty years. Her husband and mother were gone, most of her friends had moved away. She ended up committing suicide, because she felt the rest of her life she got back wasn't worth living.

How would I react if I was frozen and woke up in fifty years to discover Taema was old and frail, or gone entirely?

I don't really have to worry about it, though. People coming out of stasis has only happened a handful of times in forty years. Not good odds.

Then there are the outages. Whole wings of people in stasis losing power, and they die before anyone can fix it. So convenient, right? The government always claims it's an accident. They promise to install a back-up server. Then they never do. One day, I'm pretty sure there'll be an outage on everyone in stasis. Whoops. Away they go.

Thinking about living without Taema has weirded me out. I can't get it out of my head. I'm alone in this cell, and my sister's miles away. I'm still not used to being alone, even ten years after we separated. Tomorrow is our surgery anniversary. Whoo. The first sixteen years of my life were spent looking over my sister's shoulder, or resting cheek-to-cheek with her to look at someone together.

I wonder sometimes if I started on this road as soon as they took the knife to us. She's my better half, Taema. She's the one with the sensible head on her shoulders, who would talk me out of doing stupid shit as kids because she didn't want to be drawn into my trouble. She was usually drawn in anyway, though. It's not like she had much of a choice.

If the news does get out, she'll have to dodge paparazzi drones left and right—how many alleged murderers have an identical twin they were once conjoined with? *And* grew up in that crazy cult in the redwoods across the bay? They'll have a field day. At least she's not here in the cell with me, and she's not going into stasis ~~when~~ if I do, so that's something.

Ugh. I'm almost tempted to crumple this whole thing up and flush it down the toilet. I'm not stupid. Even though this is paper, they can read whatever I write on here and they're going to rake through it with a fine-tooth comb to see what I'm trying to hide. When I'm in the shower or something, they'll sneak in here and read it.

WON'T YOU, ASSHOLES?

It's a waste of time. I might as well tell you now. There's not going to be any confession in here. Don't hold your breath.

The guards just dropped off my food. Boring meals of algae and vat-grown meat. The guards seem to like the look of me. Men always do. Plenty of women as well. But then their eyes drop to my chest, to the white scar against my brown skin, peeking over the collar of my prison uniform. They can't hide their fear at what it represents: that I am only half of who I used to be.

•

I've just been sitting here the last few hours, trying to think of what to write next. It's dusk outside now, and the stars are coming out one by one in that little patch of sky by the window. It reminds me of the fireflies Taema and I used to chase in Mana's Hearth when we were little. We were good at catching them. We walked sideways then, like the lake crabs, but we never slowed each other down. One of us would reach out and sweep the fireflies into jars, take them back to the house to light our bedroom, and let them out a few hours later. I miss those days.

It was after I left the Hearth I learned the fireflies had only recently come to California, introduced to the area a few years after the Great Upheaval. How strange, that if that hadn't happened, those memories wouldn't have existed.

Out there, I think Taema has been trying to help. The lawyer's dropped a couple of hints. Plus, I know her. Obviously. She's not going to sit around, playing with her VivaFog machines, waiting for me to die. Or basically die.

She'll be trying to follow a trail, to piece together what happened. I hope she doesn't, and that the trail goes cold. I don't want her to find out what I did that I shouldn't have, and what I didn't do that I should have. How I lost my innocence while she still has hers—but she might have to lose it, if she wants to save me.

Yep, that's cryptic as hell. But remember: no confessions. Not from me.

Since I'm not going to write my last will and testament, and I'm not going to confess, I figure maybe I'll write a different sort of testament, or a different kind of confession. It won't be a beautiful story. Taema has a way with words, not me. She's the thinker, following the rules, lost in her machines and books. I'm the unpredictable artist, always wanting to do things on the spur of the moment. Guess that's why I'm here now.

I don't even know who I'm writing to. The general masses, maybe, if this somehow leaks to the press. Or maybe I'm writing to my sister.

So this is the story of Taema and me, the life we had. Maybe, while writing it, I'll figure out where it all went wrong.

# FOUR

# TAEMA

The first thing I do when I'm home is turn on the bots to clear up all the broken glass and to dry the carpets. I order a new door from the replicator, which will be ready by the morning, and draw the curtains against the breeze.

Everything's been searched. They haven't trashed the place, but so many things are not quite where they should be, and the whole apartment has the aura of being manhandled.

I turn music up loud in my auditory implants and try to set it to rights. I help the bots clean. I throw out the meal I spent all afternoon making, my appetite gone. I order a Nutri-Paste from the replicator and force the tasteless goop down my throat to keep my blood sugar even. I focus on cleaning with every fiber of my being, the pulse of the beats of scrubbing driving out all thought.

When everything is perfect again, I can no longer deceive myself.

I stand in the middle of my silent, spotless kitchen. My eyes snag on the cookie jar on the counter.

Tila and I have keys to each other's places, of course. Our schedules have always been different—I work the standard nine to three, whereas Tila works nights. When we meet for dinner, it's actually closer to her breakfast. When she first moved out eight months ago, I found it really difficult, and I wasn't good at hiding it. I felt betrayed. When we fight, we know the perfect way to wound the other, but it's like hitting a mirror—the glass cuts us just as deeply.

After that first, terrible fight, she left me an apology note in the cookie jar. Problem is, she eats more cookies than I do, so it took me three or four days to find the note. It worked, and I forgave her, not that I can ever stay mad at her for long. Over the next few weeks, she kept leaving notes in the cookie jar, dropping them off on the way to work for me to find on the way home. They were silly, full of in-jokes and puzzles. Then when she started acting more distant, working more hours at the club, they stopped. I haven't even checked the cookie jar in days.

I open it. There are no cookies, only a few scattered crumbs, but there is a note. I unfold it with trembling fingers.

*T,*
*I'm doing something possibly dangerous tonight.*
*If everything goes well, I'll come here and take this note away*
*before you find it. If you do find this, and you don't know*
*where I am, then everything has gone belly up.*
*And I'm sorry. I'm really sorry.*
*T*

I blink, my eyes unfocused. She has kept something from me. For days? For weeks? For months? Lying to me, doing . . . whatever it is she's been doing, and leaving me in the dark.

I crumple the paper in my hands. I have to get rid of it. If they come back and find it, it'd look beyond incriminating for both of us. I glance around nervously. What's to say they aren't already monitoring me through the wallscreens or my implants? I've heard the rumors that Sudice monitors all implant feeds, and reports crimes to the government.

I incinerate the note over the stove. After it's nothing but ashes, I take ten deep breaths, forcing the fear and pain away. I can almost hear Mana-ma's voice in my ear:

*The world is around you. You can change it. Be the change you want.*

I shake my head, as if her voice is a buzzing fly. I don't want to hear her in my head just now. I had enough of Mana-ma in my head as a child. The woman at the head of the Hearth, pulling her strings, weaving her web, ensnaring us all.

The breaths calm me enough that I can push the hurt, the terror and the panic deep into the back of my mind. I shut down my conscious thoughts, focusing only on the physical. I hold the heels of my hands to my eyes until dark spots dance behind my eyelids. Everything's so jumbled. I've always hated being alone. My thoughts are too loud.

I go to the spare room. It was Tila's before she moved out. It's been searched, but there wasn't much for them to go through. A plain bed, an empty dresser, the closet filled with spare linen. I remember how it used to look when she was here: a rainbow of clothes littering the floor, leaving a trail from the bed to the closet. High-heeled shoes kicked off in a corner. Empty coffee mugs left on bedside drawers caked with dried makeup powder. The police would have been lucky to find anything at all under all the chaos.

I stand there for a moment, looking at the perfectly made bed. The searchers took the time to put it back to rights. I suppose that's polite. Tears prick the corners of my eyes, but I take more deep breaths until they go away. I reach forward and muss it a bit. Tila never made her bed. "What's the point?" she'd say. "You're just going to get right back into it at the end of the day." I used to be the one to make the bed, back in the Hearth, with Tila sighing and occasionally patting down a pillow to keep me happy. I pull the covers back again. Tila's not here.

I go back to the kitchen. I bring up my contacts list on my ocular implants, scrolling through the names. I want to speak to someone, though I don't think I can share anything about what's happened. My gaze pauses on a few exes—David, Simone, Amrit. I used to be so close to them. I almost married David, but then I realized he didn't know how to love and could only keep people at arm's length. Now I have no idea what they are doing. There are no friends I want to tell—most are colleagues. Tila's the one with all the friends. I'm slower to trust and, perhaps like David, I never truly let anyone in. Normally it's Tila I'd turn to, and I can't turn to her now.

I send the names away. I still want to believe this has been some big misunderstanding. I can't pretend, now that I've found that note.

"Tila, what have you done?" I ask the empty room. There, alone in the dark, I realize another lie I told myself.

I'm far less than ninety-nine percent sure she didn't do it.

•

I lie awake all night, trying to piece together everything Tila has told me in the last few weeks; but if she's given me any hints, they don't jump out at me. After I finally stumble from my bed, I'm too tired to even yawn. I project the news from my implants directly onto the white table as I drink coffee, and then I set the coffee down.

There's no headline.

How is there no headline? I scroll through the pages, open other news sources, then another, until several are sprawled out over the white table. Nothing. Nothing about the first violent, brutal homicide in almost eighteen years, committed by a civilian, who also happens to be a former member of a well-known cult? If that's not headline news, I don't know what is.

I can't help but be a little relieved, too. It's taken a long time to make that cup of coffee, to sit down in that seat, to steel myself to look. And there's nothing.

I blink and send the news away.

When the coffee—if it can even be called that, for it's almost caffeine-free and from the replicator—is gone, I have no idea what to do with myself.

I pop a few Rejuvs and curl up on the sofa, a second cup of coffee beside me. I don't read. I don't watch the wallscreen. I stare at the ceiling and clear my mind.

It's no use. The anger still creeps in. My thoughts can only turn to Tila. I imagine her, with her blue, spiky hair, that teasing grin she always wears. It's like she's darting through my cerebrum, laughing. *You can't find me,* she seems to call. *You don't know what I've been up to, do you?*

I fling one of the couch throw pillows across the room. It's an empty, childish gesture.

"Why didn't you tell me?" I yell at the empty room. My voice drops to a whisper. "How can I help you if I don't know what you've done?"

The tears come again, and this time, I let them. They trickle down my cheeks, warm and salty. I don't wipe them away. Memories of us in the Hearth flash through my mind. Going to our secret spot in the woods, whispering to each other for hours. Playing cards with our parents, Tila and I on the same team. Our voices lifted in harmony during sermon. The first time I saw her in that hospital room. She came back to me as soon as she woke up. Those first years after surgery, when we always walked holding hands because we still had to be connected in one way or another. And then the look on her face last night. The stark fear, the whites of her eyes showing. It was as if I didn't know her at all.

This is not a dream. It's too real. And there's no going back.

"Why did you lie to *me*, of all people? What do I do?" I ask the empty room again.

There's no answer.

Until there is: the implant in my ear beeps.

I have a message.

•

I'm back in the SFPD interrogation room. I came in by a back entrance, with my hood up to partly obscure my face.

Officer Oloyu stares at me from across the table. His eyes look tired, though his face doesn't show it. I doubt he's slept, but he's popped a few Rejuvs to keep him going, just like I have.

"Why am I back here?" I ask, ignoring the pleasantries. I have water this time instead of coffee, but I still don't touch it.

"Have you read the news this morning?" Officer Oloyu asks.

"I've noticed what's not in it."

An eyebrow quirks, along with the corner of his mouth. "Quite."

"How did you keep this quiet?"

"Who controls the media bots?" he counters.

Decent point.

"Your sister is out of the news because this is part of something larger. If we're to find out what's really going on, we have to get to the bottom of it before they peg we're onto them."

"Them? Who's them? What does this have to do with me?"

"This has everything to do with you." He takes a breath. "The SFPD have a proposition."

His body language has changed again—palms out, brown eyes calm but firm. He still looks heartbreakingly young.

My hand goes to my chest. I shake my head. "I don't understand. Why do you need me?"

"What do you know about the Ratel?"

"The Ratel?" I echo faintly. They're the main remaining source of crime within the city. The government has been trying to eradicate them for years, but they're tenacious. They intimidate businesses; they have a hand in the property market, and some say within certain branches of the government or Sudice. Like everyone, I've heard the whispers that the Ratel have grown more powerful in recent years, morphing from an annoyance into something more significant and dangerous. I always figured it was just rumor, but looking at Officer Oloyu's face, I'm no longer so sure. What else have they been keeping from the media bots?

Something stirs in my memory. Tila joked about the Ratel a couple of weeks ago. Or I thought it was a joke. I'd reprimanded her for being late to one of our dinners yet again.

"Just ping me if you're going to be late. Obviously I'm not your mother, but you never used to do this," I'd said, turning away from her.

"Oh, relax, T," she responded, with that infuriating tilt of her head and flash of white teeth. "It's not like I'm hanging out with the Ratel. I'm just late."

I remember wondering at the time why she'd even joke about such a thing. I feel sick.

Officer Oloyu is still waiting for a response. "A little," I manage.

"Do you know what they traffic in more than anything else?"

My breath hitches. "Not really." I've never had any dealings with them. I go to work. I come home. I live my life as a law-abiding citizen of San Francisco.

"They traffic in dreams. More specifically, the information from dreams."

"Zeal?" I ask, confused. Sudice own that. I've only plugged into Zeal a few times. It did nothing for me.

"No. Something new. Something different. The next step beyond Zeal. Have you heard of Verve?" He watches me.

I look at him blankly. "Never." What would the next step beyond Zeal be? Zeal enacts fantasies, becoming catharsis for pent-up emotions. People start doing it in their early teens, and it's often a lifelong habit. After they let off steam and come out from their fantasies, the aftereffects are soporific. Any anger or violent urges are suppressed, and if they build up again, the craving for another visit to a Zeal lounge kicks in. Tila and I arrived in San Francisco several years after those our age were hooked, and we never fell into it as much as the others. It's integrated into therapy, into brainloading information. Most people use Zeal every day, in one form or another.

He hesitates, searching my face for signs of falsehood. I fight the urge to squirm.

"There are two reasons Verve is bad news. First, unlike Zeal, there is no comedown. If you enact a violent fantasy, then when you come out, you don't feel sated. If anything, a desire for violence is heightened. If it were widespread, we'd see a very clear upswing in crime. Second, Verve is a way for the Ratel to mine dreams for information. It's like a virus. Once you take it, it locks into your implants. Until the half-life leaves their system, the Ratel can watch what they see, hear what they hear, and even spy on their dreams."

I don't respond right away. This doesn't sound possible. That's advanced technology, and if Sudice or the government haven't already done this, then how have the Ratel?

Unless . . . perhaps they stole it from them? It's not like Officer Oloyu would ever admit something like that happened, not to me.

He's still waiting for me to say something. "OK. That's fascinating, but what does it have to do with me?"

"You and your sister are from Mana's Hearth."

My stomach tightens, and my knees start shaking again. I clench them together, digging my fingertips into my thighs. "Yes. So?"

"Well." He leans back in his chair, considering me again. "Lucid dreamers are immune to being influenced by Verve. They could pump you full of the stuff, and not be able to look through your eyes or listen through your ears."

My breath stops. How could he know about that? "What makes you think I'm a lucid dreamer?"

"Because anyone who leaves Mana's Hearth is."

"Not enough people leave the Hearth for you to confidently make that hypothesis." My science is showing.

"There's enough. And let me guess—you rarely go to Zeal lounges."

"So? Plenty of people don't."

"The drug does nothing for you. Never has. You don't wake up feeling your anger has bled from you, or elated by whatever fantasy you had. Why take the drug when you can lucid dream each night?"

I shrug noncommittally.

"Your skills can help us."

He pauses again. My tongue feels glued to the roof of my mouth.

"You really didn't know what your sister was doing, did you?" Officer Oloyu asks. He sounds almost sorry for me. My anger flares again, but I clamp it down. I want to understand,

and yelling at a police officer won't help me. I hate that he's seen how in the dark I am.

"This murder at Zenith isn't a crime of passion," Officer Oloyu says.

"My sister didn't *murder* anyone." Although if they're right, and Tila's been keeping secrets from me, how would I even know?

"Maybe she murdered this Vuk, maybe she didn't."

I say nothing.

"I am cleared to tell you a little more about him, if you're curious?" He smiles, not waiting for an answer. "He was a representative for an anonymous philanthropist. Or that's who he claimed to be. But we've exposed that for a pack of lies. The cover allowed him entrance to many places he wouldn't otherwise have been permitted. Fundraisers. Exclusive parties. The Zeal room at Zenith."

I look up, searching his face, but I can't read him.

"Vuk wasn't an innocent client, just another regular of the club. He was part of something darker. He was a member of the Ratel. We think perhaps he was trying to replace the Zeal in the back room with Verve. Lots of important people come to that club. If the Ratel could get into their heads . . . think of the secrets they could find, and how lucrative that could be for them."

I can't suppress a shudder. My mind is spinning with this information. "So, what, you think Tila caught him and killed him for it? If so, didn't she do you a service?"

Officer Oloyu shakes his head. "From what we can gather, your sister had an existing relationship with him. Last night was not the first time they'd been seen together. She might even have been working with him."

I can't help it. I laugh, though it's high and nervous. Inside, I'm frozen with terror. I can imagine some things of Tila—but this? Never. "The Ratel. You think Tila—my sister—has some-how become involved with the biggest criminal organization in Pacifica?"

Officer Oloyu shakes his head. "We don't *think* . . . we *know* she is involved with them. There's more than enough evidence to prove it. What we don't know is *why*. Your sister is clever. Whatever she's been up to, she's left very little trace."

"My sister *is* clever. Clever enough to know to stay far away from the Ratel." It doesn't make any sense. Tila, my Tila, in-volved with the underground crime syndicate? There has to be some mistake.

"What makes you think she has anything to do with this? What's she said?" I ask.

"She's not saying much."

I bet she's driving the police up the walls. She knows how to toy with people.

"Can I speak with her?"

He shrugs a little. "She doesn't want to speak with anyone. Even you. Specifically demanded it, actually."

I feel like I've been punched in the stomach. Why the hell wouldn't she want to see me? It's all I've been thinking about since her arrest. If I could just see her, talk to her, clear these doubts—I know I could help her. If she'd let me.

"The man she killed—" Officer Oloyu begins.

"Is accused of killing," I interrupt, my voice razor-sharp.

With a sardonic smile, he tilts his head. "Vuk was a hitman for the Ratel."

My stomach plummets. I take a few sips of the tepid water to give me time to untangle my thoughts. "Was he . . . after Tila?" She could have died yesterday. I hadn't really considered that before now. I swallow, hoping my thoughts aren't flitting across my face. Why would she be a target?

"We don't know if he was actually out for your sister. Our sources say he wasn't on assignment last night, but our sources could be wrong."

"Seems like there's a lot you don't know." I'm testy, but he's still dangling what he really wants from me out of reach, and I'm impatient and frightened.

Officer Oloyu ignores the comment. "Your sister wasn't meant to be working last night. Another hostess, a woman named Leylani, was meant to be manning the Zeal lounge, but she never showed up for work."

I sag a little with relief. "See? Tila could have come into the wrong room at the wrong time, had to defend herself against this Vuk. But do you even know if that could have happened? Is there a murder weapon, and if so, can you link it to her? What about the cameras in the Zeal lounge? You couldn't have found a murder weapon, or she'd be charged rather than just accused. How do you know she has anything to do with this?" The questions fall from my lips, faster and faster, until I'm breathless.

"Funny," Oloyu says. "When we interviewed your sister, she posed the same scenario. Almost verbatim."

I glare at him, but he only stares at me calmly, and then makes a gesture with his fingers. The wallscreen to my left turns on. It's a recording from my interrogation yesterday, my eyes blazing at Officer Oloyu. That angry, I look more like my sister than the woman I see in the mirror every morning. I watch myself snarling at him: *You can't spend sixteen years with someone, every minute of every day, and not know if they're capable of murder or not. I'll do whatever it takes to clear her name.*

He flicks it off. "Do you still mean that?"

My nostrils flare in anger. "Of course I mean it."

Officer Oloyu leans forward. He's smiling, that open, sweet

smile, and it makes me want to hit him. He's glad he's slipped under my skin. "*This* is why we need you, Taema. You understand how she thinks, what she'd do. But there's more than that, isn't there?"

I say nothing.

"She's stumped you. She's managed to keep part of her life secret, and it's burning you up. You want to believe that she hasn't done anything, that she's just as innocent as you want her to be—but she's lied to you, no matter what. That hurts. So. You can help us, and you can find out the truth once and for all. Whatever it is." He leans even closer. "There's not much time. We may have kept the case out of the papers, but she'll still go to trial. And if she's convicted . . ." he trails off.

"They'll put her in stasis," I say. "But then if exculpatory evidence comes to light, she'll be set free?"

"If it's brought to light, yes." He gives an expectant pause.

"What do you want from me?" I whisper.

He sighs and rubs his forehead. "Personally, I don't think your sister killed Vuk. Or if she did, it was an accident or self-defense. She's been working on her own in the Ratel, I'd gamble. And she's grown close."

He's changed his tune since yesterday. "What if she grew *too* close, and they already know she was an infiltrator?"

"No sign of that. What we figure is that the Ratel were after someone else that night in the club, and that assignment was interrupted. They don't know your sister's been taken. We've moved fast and we have kept this a small, tight operation. Only a handful of police officers and higher-ups know who your sister really is. We're keeping her out of the city. This situation gives us a unique opportunity to get close to the Ratel. They haven't infiltrated many people with Verve, but if we don't stop them, it's only a matter of time. The Ratel are a threat against

San Francisco and all of Pacifica. They have to be stopped. So far, your sister has given us some information to work with, but not enough. We need more."

He looks at me, and I begin to suspect what he's about to ask of me. He's read me to the bone. I do want—need—to find out what's going on with my sister. What she hid from me and why. More than that, I need to get her out of prison, as much for me as for her. The thought of going through life separated from her, alone forever . . . I don't think I can face that.

"We can't let your sister out to go back undercover." The corners of his mouth tighten. I think he's holding something back.

"No. You asked her and she refused, didn't she?"

A rueful hint of a smile. "She did. But it would have been a tough sell to my superior, even if she did agree. She was found by the owner of the club, sitting in a pool of blood. That doesn't exactly make her seem like someone who would be easy to work with. She's too much of a liability."

I flinch at that mental image.

"Then there's you."

I swallow, my eyes glued to his face.

"You're intelligent, but you also play by the rules, unlike your sister. You could do this. Infiltrate the Ratel. We believe your sister has already been recruited as one of their lucid dreamers, delving into Verve dreamscapes, monitoring their implant feeds."

"But she hasn't told you that."

"No, but from another source we know her exact position within the Ratel."

"What source?"

He holds up a finger. "We obviously can't tell you that, unless you sign on."

40

"Sign on, and . . . pretend to be my sister?"

"Yes. You'd go undercover into the deepest, darkest under-belly of San Francisco. You'll need to *become* your sister in order to go into the inner circle of the Ratel. This is much bigger than the first civilian murder in years, whether the victim was a hired killer or not. This is a chance for us to learn more about the inner workings of the Ratel, what their plans are, and to stop them from using Verve to access people's secrets. We can learn more about Verve, about who's actually in charge of the Ratel—and then bring them down, once and for all."

I blink at him. Surely the Ratel can't be that much of a threat?

"If you do this, then I've been authorized to let you know that even if your sister did kill Vuk, all charges against her will be dropped. Any crimes you might need to commit as part of the investigation will also be pardoned, within reason. Is that a deal?"

I fight the urge to grab at the opportunity, even as traitorous hope rises within me. I feel sick. Not only at what it is they've suggested Tila has managed to do—for reasons I simply can't comprehend—but also that they now expect me to do the same thing. That I *can* do the same thing.

I am *not* Tila.

"If I was going to do this—how am I supposed to know what to do, or how to infiltrate the Ratel?" I ask.

Oloyu doesn't hesitate. "We can train you and give you the information you need. The skills that will keep you alive. And we'll have a partner for you."

My breath catches. Somehow, the idea of working with a stranger seems even more frightening than working alone.

"I don't even look much like my sister anymore," I say, my voice weak with protest.

"That can be changed."

I raise a hand to my cheek, thinking of scalpels and flesh parlors.

Officer Oloyu interlinks his fingers together, leaning forward, his face starkly earnest. "So, Miss Taema Collins—are you going to join us and save your sister?"

My mouth opens, but I have no idea how to answer.

# FIVE

# TAEMA

They give me one hour to make up my mind. They can't give me any longer. If I'm going to do it, they have to start prepping me right away, so that "Tila" isn't out of circulation too long.

I go to Golden Gate Park, taking the MUNI. No unmarked hovercars anymore—nothing to make me stand out. For this one hour, I am not alone. The SFPD are tracking my VeriChip, watching me through camera drones. I fight the urge to hunch my shoulders, to somehow disappear from their sight. I can't.

I go through the entrance to the glass dome that covers Golden Gate Park. Though evening is lengthening, it's still as bright as early afternoon from the artificial light within. It's always open, even in the dead of night. Tila and I used to come here at midnight for picnics sometimes, watching mothers with day shifts walk their babies in prams, or joggers flitting along the paths, their toned bodies covered in bright neon logos, moving adverts for sports tech. Most people have nano muscle inserts to keep them in shape these days, including me and my sister, though we also take pride in doing it the old-fashioned way, or at least making the odd attempt. I want to take off down the paths, running at full speed until my lungs burn, but I run to stop myself from thinking, and I can't run away from my own mind, not now.

I sit under a willow tree, taking off my shoes and dipping my toes into the water of the lake. It's quiet here, with its false eternal daylight, the wafting scent of flowers and cut grass. I search the news with my ocular implant again for a moment, closing my eyes and letting the words scroll past my darkened eyelids. Still no headline about my sister. There's an article about the mayor of San Francisco and her bid for reelection. She smiles with white teeth from the feed. Sudice says they will announce a new product next week at the tech expo. The city is building more housing and orchard towers to meet rising demand. Nothing in the news about crimes, or the Ratel. I wonder how often they cover up what really happens in this city. If the public doesn't find out about it, has it happened at all?

Endless adverts flash from the corners of my vision. Go on holiday to Dubai, or New Tokyo. Order this mealpack from your replicator tonight. Another Zeal advert flashes and I bring it forward. This one shows a man sleeping calmly, but over his head he's screaming at his boss and walking out, slamming the door behind him. He wakes up, stretching, smiling at the camera. *"I've let it all out,"* he says, his voice tinny in my auditory implants. *"I'm ready to face the day."* A blink and he's in a suit. The same tagline twines above his head: *Find your Zeal for life. What will you dream today?* I send it away, a headache blooming in my temples.

My sister and I surprised people in San Francisco by taking to the implants with ease, considering we were about eleven years behind almost everyone else. The doctors and such never realized how many hours we had already spent learning to control our minds, so that implants were only a small side step.

I sigh and lie down in the grass. I try to pretend I'm sixteen again, in Mana's Hearth, before we ever found that other tablet and learned that everything we thought we knew had been a lie. But it's no use. That daydream won't come. How can it? Tila isn't by my side.

I open my eyes.

I've made up my mind, though it was never really in question. Officer Oloyu knew I'd say yes before he even asked me.

•

I'm to meet my new partner immediately. I don't even go back to SFPD headquarters to give Oloyu my answer; I ping him through my implants.

I'm back on the MUNI. I swipe my VeriChip at the entrance, the fare deducting from my account, and take the elevator underground. I only wait a minute for the train heading toward downtown, and find a seat in the corner. The train pulls away. I cross my legs as the green glow from the underground algae plants passes by. Everyone looks sickly in this light, and my eyes dart to and fro. I keep rubbing my palms over my knees. Who am I meeting? What have I signed up for?

I get off at the McAllister and Pierce stop and walk the few blocks to the address I've been given. It looks like a residential house—one of those sweepingly beautiful, reconstructed Victorian houses, painted in pastel colors. I've always admired them, and when I came into a shocking amount of money for my role in the VivaFog, I debated buying one. But Tila scoffed, thought they looked like gingerbread houses, and so I held off. I wonder now why I let her talk me out of it. It didn't seem important. How many times have I let her decide for me what I really want? Even now, I'm not making my own decisions, not really. This was all started by my sister, without her telling me anything.

I shake my head of the cobwebs of thoughts and climb the

stairs, knocking on the door. It swings open on its own. I step in cautiously, a shiver running down my spine. The door closes behind me. Inside, the hallway is empty. No picture frames on the walls, no flowers, no tables strewn with personal items.

"In the kitchen," a male voice calls.

I walk through, trying to keep my tread firm rather than hesitant. A man leans against the table, arms crossed over his chest. He's muscled, with strong eyebrows, a slightly hooked nose, and scars on his knuckles and forearms that, in this city of image perfectionists, draw my eyes.

"Hello," he says, pleasantly enough.

"Hi," I say hesitantly. It seems very informal after all the interrogation rooms at the police station. The kitchen looks as stark and un-lived-in as the hallway.

"I'm Detective Nazarin," he says, moving toward me and holding out his hand. I take it. His handshake is warm and firm.

"The undercover agent," I say, feeling stupid.

"Yes." He doesn't elaborate. I wonder what he's done as part of the Ratel. What I might have to do, now that I'm joining him. He sees me eye the door nervously. "We're the only ones here."

"I thought there'd be others." A whole team, determined to keep me safe.

"There will be. But not until they're needed. Do you want a drink?"

I do, but I shake my head, clasping my hands into fists. I'm shaking again, and it irritates me, but being here means it's real. It's happening. I'm about to start training with this scarred stranger who could probably snap my neck without breaking a sweat.

"Do you want to go to a room and settle in, or have a tour and get started?"

"I'll get started." It's not like I'd be able to relax here.

He walks ahead of me, his stride sure and powerful.

One room is filled with dozens of wallscreen monitors, showing the street outside and other locations through the city. Others show long streams of code, blinking in the dim light. Empty chairs and desks line up in front of them.

"The rest of the team will mostly be watching us from the SFPD headquarters, but they can be based here occasionally, once we're undercover."

So many screens. There's the outside of the TransAm Pyramid. There's the outside of my apartment building, and Tila's. The police station. Warehouses. Stark skyscrapers.

"Right," I say, for lack of anything better.

He shows me the other rooms. Many of them are empty. There are a few bedrooms, stark as hotels. I throw my bag into one that has a good view of the park. He doesn't show me his room.

The last area of the house is the training room. It's large, with that gym smell of rubber, metal, old sweat and cleaning solution.

To the right is a practice mat, weights and staffs along one wall. My eyes are drawn instead to the brainloading Chair on the right.

He sees the hesitation, his brow drawing down in confusion. "You knew brainloading would be the main component of the training, correct?" he asks. "We don't have time to do it another way. Your file says you used a Chair frequently when you came to San Francisco, to catch up on all you and your sister hadn't learned while at the Hearth."

At the mention of my sister, I suppress a flinch. I'm here because of her. This is all happening because of my twin, but I still miss her with a pain deeper than my scar. I stand unnaturally still, every muscle tense. I force myself to appear unconcerned. I'm annoyed my fear is so obvious. "It's fine," I say, keeping my voice smooth. "I just haven't used one for years, is all."

That machine was one of my first introductions to modern technology after the actual surgery. Upon realizing just how damn ignorant we were, Tila and I had jumped into Chairs willingly enough, brainloading information on history, politics, math, science and anything else that captured our interest. Tila had been more interested in art history and other cultures, whereas I'd been drawn to science.

People were surprised by how easily and quickly we integrated the information. Most people had a fifty percent retention rate. Good, obviously, for hours of information pooled into a brain, and people often finished degrees by age sixteen or seventeen, so we were grossly behind. It didn't take long for us to catch up. From our training with Mana-ma, we had a ninety-five percent retention rate.

It wasn't long before others expressed interest in our abilities, though our background was kept largely under wraps. Tila found a tutor for her art, and I found a mentor to further my education in engineering. Tila grew sick of it all a lot sooner than I did, leaving her mentor in order to do her own art without plugging into the Zealscape. I stayed, and I did well.

After I finished my education, I never touched a Chair again. I hate the feeling of information trickling into my brain. It's like it fills my skull with noise and pushes out who I am. I always woke up after a night of downloading information as tired as when I'd gone to bed, muttering facts to myself as I made coffee. Perhaps it was harder for us because of our high retention rate, or the fact that Zeal is not as pleasurable for us as for others. In any case, I prefer to learn things the way the brain was meant to absorb them.

The Chair by itself is fairly antiquated. As of a few years ago, most people can download information directly into their brain, with extra implants in the hippocampus and frontal cortex. They don't have that in Zeal lounges, but it's the inevitable next step. Neither Tila nor I have those extra implants, and I'm glad they haven't asked me to get them. I'd rather have the Chair.

"You have your room to store your things, but I'm afraid you'll be sleeping here, most of the time," Nazarin says. "Come on, let's go have some coffee. I'll help fill you in on what you can expect over the next few weeks."

Finally. Oloyu hadn't gone into a lot of detail about the day-in day-out plans of being undercover. He didn't know.

He makes the coffee—well, orders it from the replicator—and sets the makings on the table. I've been in his presence over half an hour and I still have no idea what to think of him.

"So. We don't have long to train you," he begins. "Tila works at the Verve lounge a few times a week. We know where she goes and what her shifts are, and we do know how she communicates with them. We can tell them you're ill, which means you can miss one, maybe two shifts, but after that they'll expect you back. I can't have the luxury, so I'll still be working my usual night shifts while you brainload."

"Verve . . . lounge?" I ask.

"That's what she does for them and how she rose so fast through their ranks." He seems frustrated that I'm confused. "Surely Oloyu told you about Verve?"

"Some. That it's different from Zeal, and they need lucid dreamers to mine it. I didn't realize that I'd have to do it so soon. Or that there were lounges for it."

"By the time that happens, you'll be trained and know what to do." His words are so confident I allow myself to believe them, at least a little.

"OK," he continues. "Today, you'll be contacting people with your cover story, and we're going to switch your VeriChip to your sister's. Once that happens, you'll contact your friends to tell them her cover story, and then you'll be able to contact the Ratel. We'll also start your training. It'll be physical, hand-to-hand combat, and weapons, and as much information as you can retain. I'm here every step of the way, and any questions you have, you can ask me."

Despite his harsh features and his scars, his eyes are warm. It steadies me a little more.

"How long have you been undercover?" I ask.

"A little over two years."

That's a long time. If he's deep undercover, that means he might not have been able to contact his close friends and family, and even if he could, he'd have to lie to them day in and day out about what he was really doing with his time.

Like Tila lied to me. And how long will I be doing this? A few days, weeks, months? Years?

I push the thought away, but a worse one follows in its place. "Have you . . . met my sister?"

"I have. Not often, but we were at some of the same parties, and I saw her in passing if I dropped off deliveries at the Verve warehouse."

A strange thought. I feel strangely exposed. "What about . . . the fact we don't look alike?"

"Visiting a flesh parlor will be one of the last steps."

I touch my face. Like everyone else, I've been to flesh parlors and erased a line here, a dimple there. I've never done anything drastic, but I'll have to change my hair, my nose and my cheekbones. Not much, but enough that I won't recognize myself so easily in the mirror. Enough that I'll look like Tila again. "Can I change it back . . . after?"

"There's no reason you can't."

I'm not reassured. I stare at the dregs of my coffee, counting my steady heartbeats.

"Do you feel ready for the first step?" he asks gently.

I look up, pressing my lips together. "Sooner we start, the sooner it's over with."

He gives me a smile, and it transforms his face. His eyes light up, and they crinkle around the corners. I can almost forget the scars hiding beneath the buzz cut of his hair, and the smile puts me a bit more at ease, despite the strangeness of this day.

He gives me my script but leaves me alone to make the calls, saying he's only a ping away if I need him. I thank him, glad he won't be hovering.

One by one, I go through my few friends and colleagues. I'm only amending the story of my life a little—or what was going to be the story of my life, before all this happened. I'm to say I'm going to China earlier than I planned, and Tila's coming with me. Once I change my implant, I'll phone Tila's friends. It'll be my first undercover role: to convince them that I am my sister. I shiver at the thought.

After those first calls are done, it's physical training. Detective Nazarin takes me to the room with the Chair and the gym. He faces me, crossing his arms over his chest. "You have muscle mods, correct?"

I nod. "Enough to keep me toned without having to exercise much." Because I'm lazy.

"Good. That'll help with recovery. Fighting techniques will be part of the information you download, but let's see how you are on your own."

He runs me through a basic diagnostic, figuring out how much weight I can lift or press, how flexible I am, how fast and far I can run. His fingertips rest on the pulse of my neck, taking my resting heart rate. I look up at his dark brows, the scars, the square jawline. He's attractive in a dangerous way.

"Slow resting heart rate," he says.

"They programmed it that way."

He smiles a little, and again it lights the harshness of his face.

I think I do a little better than he expected, which is good, but I can tell he wishes I were stronger than I am. I think of my sister—the muscles on her arms. She claimed it was from dancing with customers at the club, plus a few extra implants. I didn't wonder at the time why she felt the need to be so much stronger. How dangerous are the Ratel—has she needed to physically protect herself?

Nazarin teaches me self-defense moves. I've never taken any kind of combat sport, though I've often wanted to. Tila convinced me to go with her to dance classes instead. Some of the moves I learned in capoeira transfer pretty well, at least.

Overall, though, it's a thoroughly humbling experience. Detective Nazarin doesn't hurt me, but after a while his light blows start to ache. My limbs aren't moving as quickly or as seamlessly as I'd like. Nazarin easily dodges my paltry attempts to attack him.

"You're small and quick. Your best hope is to avoid the blows. If you came up against someone like me in a real fight, you wouldn't stand a chance." He probably weighs about half again what I do, so he has a point. It grates, but I learn.

He's not a bad teacher. He doesn't shout—he tells me what I do wrong, but praises what I do right. As my muscles grow more exhausted, his voice seems to hum near my ear: "Duck, left, back," and I move almost without thinking.

Detective Nazarin calls a stop after three hours. I'm panting, but proud of myself that I kept going and didn't ask for breaks except the odd gulp of water. Nazarin is glazed in perspiration, but strangely, he smells good. Musk and cologne and clean sweat.

"Strong start," he says. "Soon, you'll be better."

Once it's wired into my brain.

"Now," Detective Nazarin says, "it's time for you to legally become Tila, at least for a little while."

•

I have enough time to shower and choke down some vat jerky and dried fruit before Detective Nazarin takes me to meet Dr. Kim Mata, a biohacker working for Sudice, Inc.

We can't go to the Sudice headquarters: they're the parent company of VivaFog and I've already told my co-workers I'll be on a jet to China imminently, and it would compromise Nazarin's cover. But we can't bring Dr. Mata to the safe house. Instead we make our way down to one of her empty properties. She's often hired by the SFPD to do these sorts of jobs, Nazarin says, but she keeps it quiet from Sudice. I'm surprised she's able to.

Time to switch identities.

On the way there I lean against the window, my tired muscles quivering. It feels good, though, like my mind has connected better with my body now that it has that particular buzz of exercise exhaustion. I'll take some Rejuvs when I get back, and between that and my implants, tomorrow my muscles won't even be sore, but I'll be that much stronger.

How much stronger do I have to be? What exactly do they think is going to happen?

We meet Dr. Mata in one of her townhouses by SF State. The walls are pure white and there is no furniture. Dr. Mata is

Japanese-American and tiny, barely coming up to my shoulder, and I'm not the tallest of women. She's also one of the few people in San Francisco who has let herself age, at least a little. There's the barest hint of wrinkles around her eyes and at either side of her mouth. It's refreshing to see a face that looks lived in, evidence of countless smiles reflected on her skin. I estimate she's about forty-five. She has dark hair cut in a bob to the corner of her jaw, and a face that's always on the verge of grinning.

"Can't keep away from me, can you, darling?" she says, dimpling at Detective Nazarin.

"My heart beats only for you, Kim," he responds, deadpan.

She rolls her eyes. I'm amused by their exchange. Dr. Mata is open and friendly, and Detective Nazarin seems more at ease around her. With her easy manner and the way she slouches against the wall, she doesn't strike me as one of the most prominent biohackers in the world and worth a few million credits or more.

"What's it to be this time, sweets?" she asks. Her gaze flicks to me, assessing me from head to toe, before she focuses on the detective again. "Better not be too trying. I have back-to-back meetings all afternoon and if you tire me out, I'll nap through them."

"Identity switch," he says. "This is a sensitive matter. I saw you returned the confidentiality agreement to HQ."

"I'm hurt you don't trust me," she pouts. "When have I ever let you down?"

"Never. I trust you implicitly."

In contrast to their earlier banter, he's serious here, and she feeds off it. Dr. Mata looks at me again. "OK. What's up?"

"Kim, this is Taema Collins. Her sister, Tila Collins, has been accused of murder."

Dr. Mata's eyes widen. "Civilian?"

"Not exactly," he replies. "Tila Collins is implicated with the Ratel. Last night she was caught and accused. You know what I've been doing with myself the last few years."

"Yeah, being an idiot and playing with fire. I've told you time and time again you need to get out of that game."

"You speak sense as always, but I can't. Anyway, I never would have been able to do what I've done without you."

She blows him an air kiss. "Damn right. So you're being taken into protective custody or something?" Dr. Mata asks, addressing me for the first time. "Need a new identity to lie low?"

I shake my head. "Not exactly. Tila and I—we're identical twins, you see."

Her eyebrows rise. She looks between us, and her sharp mind fills in the blanks. "Well. That's a first for me. Switching sisters. You got all the paperwork in order?"

Nazarin nods.

"OK then. Let's get started."

She motions for me to come closer, and I do. She takes hold of my wrist, turning it over. Her hands are cool and dry. "Thank you, Dr. Mata—" I begin.

She waves her free hand. "Call me Kim."

"Kim." She meets my eyes and grins. There aren't a lot of people who smile genuinely in San Francisco. She holds nothing back, and I can't help but return the gesture.

She takes a little electrode from a box in her pocket and fastens it right over the tiny mark where the chip lies under my skin. Her eyes unfocus, and on the blank white tablet in her hand is code only she can see. Before long, she has full access to my identity. I shiver, realizing that if she wanted to she could wreak complete havoc with my life. She senses my nervousness.

"Don't worry, buttercup, your identity is safe with me. You don't have anything I don't already have ten times over. Hmm."

"What?" I ask.

"Your chip wasn't put in at birth. You've only had it for ten years." Her gaze is piercing. I want to look away, but I don't. "And no record before that. How'd that happen?"

"I'm from Mana's Hearth."

"No shit!" she exclaims, her head jerking back. "Really? Your sister, too?"

"Yes. We came here when we were sixteen."

She meets my eyes, still holding my wrist. "Well, before, I thought you were cute and must be at least a bit interesting, to be hanging around with Sugarcube here." She jerks her head at Nazarin. "Now, I find you endlessly fascinating."

I can't help but laugh a little.

"And what's this?" she says, noting the top of my scar.

I pull down the collar of my shirt a few inches. "My sister and I were conjoined until we left."

She whoops. "Now you're officially one of the most interesting people I've ever met. When this is all over, I'm taking you out for a drink. Sound good?"

"All right." I smile, but it fades. I can't help but wonder if I'll even return to a normal life after this.

"Come on, you charmer," Nazarin says. "Can you do the switch?"

She scoffs. "Can I do the switch? That's just insulting."

She cocks her head, sending the projection of code onto the wall.

There we are, up on the screen. All those numbers represent our identities. Me and Tila. Side by side. I wonder what she's thinking about, just now, in her cell. I wish she'd speak to me, and I don't understand why she won't. Nazarin says she chose not to, but what if they aren't letting her speak to me? Hope flares within me at the thought. Or perhaps she thinks by keeping quiet she can protect and shield me from all this. Does she realize I'm caught right in the thick of it?

Dr. Mata waves her fingers, moving code around so quickly I can barely follow. She clicks her tongue against her teeth. "There. Done."

I blink. "That's it?"

"That's it, buttercup. You're now officially your sister, Tila Collins." She takes the electrode off my wrist and rubs the skin with her thumb.

"That's scary, how easily you could do it."

"Don't worry. I'm one of only about three or four people in San Francisco who can do it at all, let alone that quickly. I helped invent VeriChips."

I rub my thumb over the chip, covered by a thin layer of skin. "Well, thank you," I say.

"No prob. But remember, when you're done dipping your toes into danger, come meet me for that drink and I'll reset your own identity."

"I will." I'm not sure if it's an invite for an evening of chat or a date. I don't mind either way.

Kim pats me on the shoulder, and then goes over to Nazarin. "You better not get her hurt, Naz. She's way too innocent for the shit you're about to throw her into."

My stomach flutters. He looks at me, then away. "She'll be fine."

Kim holds out her arms and he gathers her into a bear hug, lifting her off the ground. She whispers something in his ear, but I can't hear it.

"Thanks a million, Kim," Detective Nazarin says. "You ready, Tila?" he asks me.

And now I am Tila, for all intents and purposes. At least legally. But for all that I know my sister better than anyone, I'm not her.

"I'm ready," I say, though I'm not sure I'll ever be.

# SIX

# TILA

The first cracks between us happened long before the surgery, although Taema would never admit it. When we were little, we were two halves of the same coin. We've gone so far from where we were. So far from that long-ago innocence.

Life was simpler in the Hearth, before we knew for certain it was a prison.

Supply ships came to Mana's Hearth every two weeks, and it was always a big deal for us. A glimpse into a world that wasn't ours.

As soon as we heard the distant roar of engines, we'd find somewhere to watch the ship set down. The men and women, dressed in strange uniforms that clung close to their bodies, looked so different from us as they directed the droids to unload the crates.

It was the droids that fascinated Taema—a lot more than they did me. They weren't something we had on the Hearth, of course, and I thought they were freaky. The blocky machines looked roughly like humans with blank faces, but moved with much less grace as they unloaded the crates onto the lawn and then walked back up into the ship and powered down. Just like that. They moved around, and then they looked dead.

They didn't say anything about droids in the Hearth school,

59

but Mom and Dad had told us a little bit about them. Kept stressing that they weren't "sentient." That they didn't have feelings, and were just machines made to do humans' dirty work.

"Why make them look human, then?" I remember asking. Surely having more than two arms would be better for lifting. Taema and I often found our extra limbs handy.

My parents didn't have an answer to that.

We usually stayed out of sight of the supply ships. Obviously the droids didn't care, but the humans from the city stared something awful when they realized we weren't hugging—that we were connected. Say what you like about Mana's Hearth, but at least they treated everyone equally. When we were younger, this one guy from the supply ship came up to us and actually reached out like he was going to touch the spot where our flesh joined, but I bit him. He jumped back and put his finger in his mouth, sucking the blood. Taema didn't even tell me off for it; she was just as mad. After that, it was just easier to stay hidden and watch secretly.

One day, after the ship took off, we noticed they had left something behind on a rock. We shuffled closer. It was a piece of tech. We'd seen them using things like it—it was called a "tablet." It wasn't meant to be left behind. No tech was. The only machines me and Taema had ever seen were the supply ships and the droids, and almost everyone in the village stayed well away when the city folk landed. Sometimes our mom would come and speak to them, relay requests or whatever, but that was it. After the supply ship took off, others would then tiptoe down the hill, performing Purifying rituals with burning sage and whispered prayers, before they could bring themselves to take the supplies back to their homes.

I reached down for the tablet.

"Tila," my sister said. "It's forbidden."

I ignored her, still trying to reach down, but Taema stayed stubbornly straight. I pulled harder, until she grunted in pain, but she didn't budge.

"Come on," I wheedled. "We have to turn it in to Mana-ma, don't we? We can't leave it here." Really, I just wanted to hold it, at least for a moment.

With a reluctant sigh, she leaned forward. I wrapped my hand around the metal and glass.

"You'll get in trouble for touching it with your bare skin," she warned.

"So will you."

"Exactly. I'll have to be Purified along with you, and you know burning sage always makes me cough."

I looked around nervously. How long before people came?

"Let's go to the tree, first," I said.

"So you can look at it?"

I didn't answer.

"It's Impure," she whispered, her brow furrowed.

I started toward the trees and she followed, her legs stiff and straight.

"We shouldn't do this," she kept whispering. "Mana-ma wouldn't like it."

"Mana-ma doesn't need to know."

"She knows everything."

I felt a little bit of guilt, but I squashed it right down.

The tree was our favorite spot in the forest. We went to it whenever we really wanted to hide from everyone else in the Hearth. In the compound it was hard to ever be truly alone, but out in the woods there were only the redwoods and the birds. Our tree was an old, hollowed-out redwood, struck by lightning a long time ago. We shuffled inside, smelling the old smoke and damp greenness of the forest. I loved it there. When we were younger, we'd had tea parties or played cards, whispered secrets, stashed things we didn't want to share. It was our safe space.

I held the tablet in front of me, turning it this way and that. It felt so smooth, hard and cold. It seemed alien.

I found a little button on the side and pressed it, and the screen came to life in vibrant greens, blues and yellows. We both gasped.

How had the people from the city worked it?

I pressed it with my finger.

Words appeared on the screen: *No implants detected. Use manually? Y/N.*

"I'm going to press yes," I said.

"You know you shouldn't. Mana-ma says it's evil."

Sometimes she drove me nuts. "For God's sake. You can't tell me you're not even a little curious."

Taema set her mouth in that stubborn line we both make when we're not budging.

"If God didn't want us to look at it, it wouldn't have been left there," I tried.

"It's a test. That's what Mana-ma would say." She bit her lip. I knew she was curious, almost as curious as me.

"Come on, T," I said, my voice singsong. "We'll just take a quick look, then we'll turn it in to Mana-ma. She never needs to know we took a peek. We'll learn just a little more about the world outside."

We'd spent hours tossing possibilities back and forth about what the rest of the world was like—even if my sister was far more interested in the rules of the Hearth than I was, always quoting the Good Book to me when I broke a rule. When I plucked my eyebrows: *God created us as he wanted us. In his eyes, there are no flaws. To change your body is sacrilege.* When I said I wished we could leave behind the Hearth and go to a city with proper skyscrapers, whatever they were: *God has laid out his plan for us in the glory of nature.* When I complained about going to the meadow with the rest of the Hearth: *One must Meditate to remain Pure and open to God's gifts.* Over and over, even though we both knew it was all an act. Behind closed doors, she wanted to know what the world was like, just as much as I did.

Taema sighed.

I pressed the Y on the tablet.

The screen stayed lit, but neither of us knew how to work it. There was nothing taught about this in the commune. We understood a tiny bit more than others about life outside the Hearth: our parents were (still are?) pretty high up in Mana-ma's inner circle, so they knew plenty and they shared some with us. They weren't meant to and they were sinning by doing so, but they said they wanted us to be prepared, "just in case." So we knew that there were things called wallscreens, and flying hovercars that looked like smaller supply ships. That there were buildings made out of smooth stone called concrete. No matter how hard we tried, though, we couldn't imagine it. Not really. So we weren't *totally* ignorant about the big wide world out there— just mostly. And that chafed me.

I rested the tablet against the inside of the tree. I had no idea what to do next. I tapped it again, but nothing happened. I knew that it was a link to the outside world, that I could learn all I wanted to, but I didn't know how to start.

I tapped it once more, grinding my teeth in frustration.

"Maybe you have to speak to it," Taema said, her voice so small. "I heard them talking to it before."

That was right. They'd say "tablet" first. I kept a finger on the screen. "Tablet. Search," I tried, speaking louder.

A new window opened, showing a blinking box. *Enter search parameters* flashed above it.

I looked to Taema for guidance, but she only shrugged, the movement pulling against the skin of my chest. I rested my face against my sister's, our cheekbones touching. My knees were shaking with excitement. Taema's shook too, but more with fear.

"Should I search for conjoined twins?" I whispered. We'd never seen any others. How did they live in the cities? How many were there?

You might wonder if our condition hurt, or if it was awkward, and the answer is no. It never hurt being attached to Taema. Though I could get so mad at her I could spit—and I had before but then she'd spit back and we'd be staring at each other's spit-covered faces and then usually burst into laughter at the stupidity of it all—I couldn't stomp off. There was no way for either of us to have the last word on anything.

Taema looked resolutely away. "Let's not."

"Why not?"

"Just don't, OK?"

I was tempted to push her, but then we'd have fought and she'd have been even more pigheaded than before. "Fine."

I stared at the tablet again. *Please state your search terms clearly*, the screen reminded us. How did it even do that? Our parents told us about the internet and radio waves, how they floated through the air. Dad said that within the compound, the internet didn't work, but the tech dampeners only worked so far in the forest. If this place was meant to be so Pure, why hadn't Mana-ma stopped service out in the woods, too?

Taema's cheekbone grazed mine. She kept trying to look away but couldn't help herself. Even though we had the whole world at our fingertips, we didn't know what about the world we should learn.

That's it. I'd start with what I did know.

"Tablet. Search for Mana's Hearth," I said.

Information came up immediately: a list of some kind. I touched the first one with my fingertip, tentatively, and more information loaded. I felt Taema turn closer to the screen. She couldn't resist. We read, side by side.

### Mana's Hearth—The Infamous Cult of the San Francisco Bay Area

"What's a cult?" Taema whispered.

I shook my head, confused. "I don't know, but they seem to think it's bad." I read through an origin story of the Hearth, written by someone called Tobias Diaz, which fitted mostly with what Mana-ma had told us in sermon:

Not much is known of the secretive commune set where Muir Woods was once open to the public. The First Mana-ma was Elspeth Foley, a mistress of a prominent politician who was also a member of the Bohemian Grove.

"What's that?" Taema asked. We took a brief break to search for Bohemian Grove. They were a group of rich and powerful politicians who met in the redwoods at Monte Rio once a year to network while pretending they weren't networking. Some of their ceremonies seemed a little similar to what we did in the Hearth, such as the "Cremation of Care," where they burned a large fire to let go of their worries. We did that every summer equinox down in the meadow, though we didn't wear such stupid outfits. After a few false starts, I managed to bring the screen back to the original page we'd been reading.

As a woman, Elspeth Foley had no chance of ever becoming a full member of the Bohemian Grove, and she was not sure if she wanted to. She began her own commune a few years later, and recruited several prominent relatives of the very same Bohemian Grove members who would not accept her. Over the next few decades, she gradually recruited more members and closed them off from society, until, by her death, it could only be considered a cult.

When one Mana-ma perishes, she will have already chosen and groomed her successor. There have now been eight Mana-mas, with the current one in power for the last thirty-five years. They were settled in the Mojave Desert, by Chimney Rock, but after the Great Upheaval they moved to the red-wood grove across the bay from San Francisco.

Mana-mas often have a husband, who is called the Brother, as they are meant to be a Brother to the whole community. They are not actual siblings. The current Mana-ma's Brother died around twenty years ago, though this information is difficult to verify, and she has not taken another.

Many rumors have circulated about day-to-day life in the Hearth. Some say they perform animal or human sacrifice, but that is entirely unsubstantiated. The Hearth does ban any technology invented past 1969, or the Summer of Love. They live the same way that the original Mana-ma lived in the First Hearth. Every Mana-ma has said that the first commune was perfect and it shouldn't change. Their houses have electricity, they play antiquated record players, but there are no computers, and definitely no implants. The Hearth believes that to alter oneself in any way is sacrilege. They avoid modern medicine, relying instead on natural herbs from the earth. No make-up, no flashy fashion, no waxworked features at flesh parlors.

What we do know is that in the decades since the Hearth started, barely anyone has ever left. It is rare for a cult to remain stable for so many years. A decade ago, after complaints of curious people trying to sneak onto the grounds, the government constructed a large artificial swamp around the perimeter, making the former site of Muir Woods technically an island. With several thousand members, the commune is largely self-sufficient, but must order in some supplies from outside. Within the grounds, people will occasionally disappear, and no one knows where they have gone. Some claim that Mana-ma kills them herself, though again, is this only sensationalism?

"The swamp is artificial?" Taema asked.

"*That's* the question you ask after reading that?" I said, incredulous. "This thing accused Mana-ma of being a murderer!"

"That's just another rumor. People don't go missing. They die of natural causes and rejoin the Cycle." She sounded so matter-of-fact, so certain, and I was jealous of her.

"I don't get it, either. People die out there, too, don't they?" I couldn't help but think: what if they didn't? What if out there people lived forever? Did I want that?

We looked through other links about the Hearth, but none of them seemed as close to the truth as that first one. People writing about us wondered how the Hearth was funded, for our "tawdry wares" and "paltry produce" weren't nearly enough to keep us going. Talk about rude. We worked as hard as the others on those stupid quilts and things, and I wouldn't call them tawdry. We helped pick the mushrooms from the greenhouse and send them to the mainland, and it wasn't easy picking for hours on end.

They said that Mana-ma brainwashed us all, twisting our minds to her will, forcing us with drugs until we knew nothing different. I looked at Taema out of the corner of my eye. How nervous she was even being near the tablet, yet unable to look away. I should have believed the Impure technology was evil, too. Why didn't I?

Other sites said that everyone within the Hearth was there because they were twisted and ugly, with missing limbs and scars and other blemishes. I thought of my friends and family, me and my sister. None of us were ugly, were we? Physical beauty was not something we really dwelt on in the Hearth. It wasn't important, as God made us all perfect and we had to only trust in His judgment and continue trying to be the best people we could in this world.

I searched for "flesh parlor" next. They showed before and after photographs of people who had changed their faces. In the after pictures, it was as if they'd erased what truly made them look like . . . themselves. It was all generic, with no defining characteristics.

I swallowed, feeling Taema stiff and hurt beside me. That seemed . . . wrong. Wicked. Like Mana-ma always said about the outside world.

And what would they think of us, out there? What would they do?

Taema and I didn't speak to each other. We read as fast as our eyes could speed across the text, looking up words we didn't recognize, nudging each other gently when we could scroll down.

We spent hours in that tree. Taema said she'd had enough and closed her eyes, going to sleep. But I kept reading and learning, and appreciated that even if she was afraid of it all, she wouldn't rat on me.

So much of it I didn't understand. At first, I didn't want to believe it. I mean, this was all I'd ever known. I wanted to believe that maybe the outside world was lying, making it all up for some reason. For money, probably. Mana-ma said that was all people out there ever wanted. Money and all the evil they could buy with it.

But deep down, I started thinking about all the ways she treated us and the others. All the things she made us do. Outside wasn't perfect. I'd never expected it to be. I couldn't help but wonder if maybe, just maybe, life didn't have to be like it was in the Hearth.

•

I stuck the tablet in the bottom of our bag and slung it across my shoulder. The movement woke my sister. I knew it was dangerous to take it back to camp, but I also didn't want to leave it out here. I didn't know much about technology, obviously. If it rained in here, would the water break it? I knew that could happen with things like the record player.

Taema was quiet as we slunk back to the town center with our rocking gait. My arms were around her waist, and hers were around my shoulders. She felt guilty. Both because she'd let herself be close to something Impure and because she knew that we wouldn't be giving it over to Mana-ma. We wouldn't mention it in Confession. I'd get in trouble, and so would she by default. I'd put her in a shitty situation, and I should have felt worse about it than I did.

After reading those articles, I felt like I was seeing everything with fresh eyes. I'd seen a couple of photos of cities as we searched on that tablet deep within the forest, and they seemed so unfamiliar compared to our trees and single-story houses. But to hear Mana-ma talk about it, San Francisco and the rest of the outside world was a vast cohort (yes, she actually used the word "cohort" in everyday conversation) of corruption, abomination and filth.

Now I knew what so many people out there thought of our church, our town hall, our little houses all in a row. Our tidy allotments, or the fish smoking over an open flame. Nathaniel, a boy our age who was missing a leg, waving a hand to us as he turned the meat.

I tugged my skirt straight. Simple homespun. Taema and I made the dress ourselves—everyone did, but sometimes they swapped or inherited hand-me-downs. Not us, of course.

I shouldn't care what they thought. They seemed more like aliens than other humans.

Yes, I knew what aliens were. My parents had two pulp science fiction paperbacks, smuggled in when they joined the Hearth as teenagers. My parents loved the Hearth and believed in it, but my dad couldn't bear to leave them behind. He found a logic loophole for himself—they were both editions from the Golden Era of sci-fi and therefore pre-1969, and the far-fetched futuristic tech in them was just fantasy. I'd found them a few years ago: *The Stars My Destination* and *The Voyage of the Space Beagle*. Again, Taema had been annoyed at both me and Dad, convinced we should turn them into Mana-ma. Again, my sister had stayed quiet as I read long into the night, turning the crumbling yellow pages delicately. I'd loved escaping to those other worlds and dreaming about life on other planets.

Our planet was this small: 1,000 acres of redwood forest. I couldn't stop thinking about its past, laid out as it was on the tablet. How it used to be somewhere called Muir Woods. How the swamp was created to keep people out.

Or maybe to keep us in.

After we left, Taema and I hardly ever told people in San

Francisco that we grew up in Mana's Hearth. When we did, they usually looked at us the same way the supply ship people did. As if we were unnatural. Aberrant.

I hated that look. It made me feel trapped. Made me want to lash out.

I've written this all down to show what the Hearth was like from the inside. I know you're all as curious as the rest of them. I'll keep telling you about life in the compound, and I won't tell you lies—whether you believe that or not. I can only tell you what it was like ten years ago, since we haven't been back. We're not allowed, even if we wanted to go to that godforsaken place.

On that walk back, tablet well hidden, a few people were milling around the church, waiting for midweek prayer, dressed in shades of cream and brown. A lot of us had brown skin, brown hair, brown eyes. When we first came to San Francisco, we couldn't believe all the color.

I remember I looked up at the church. The five-pointed symbol was carved over the door, painted gold and silver. A light was on in Mana-ma's study. As far as I know, she's still the leader out there, as I haven't heard anything about her dying. She'll probably outlive the apocalypse; she's just that stubborn. The supposed wife of God, according to the Good Book. I used to believe that, I really did. But I'd started losing my faith long before I found that tablet, I think. I can't pinpoint what caused that; just a lot of little things adding up. Guess I was proven right.

Mana-ma would probably be pretty interested in a Confessional from me now, a lot more than she was when I told her I'd stolen some cherries from Leila's allotment. Confession was meant to be one-on-one with Mana-ma, but Taema and I were a two-for-one special. A few times, she asked one of us to cover our ears while the other confessed, but she gave up after a while. We already knew each other's sins, anyway. Obviously.

It's late here in the cell. Earlier today they asked me some questions, some about my sister. I hated every second of it. She's definitely trying to help me, and I don't want her to. What if something happens to her because of me? I thought I was doing the right thing. Now, guilt haunts my every moment. Maybe I fucked everything up beyond repair. Stupid, stupid. So stupid.

I'd rather write about the Hearth. Back then, everything was messed up, but we had each other. We didn't realize how terrible everything was going to become.

Mana-ma would hate that I was writing about all this. She'd be absolutely livid at me for exposing her secrets, but you know what? Fuck her.

I should probably end on some profound note, instead of a swear word. But I told you already: my sister's the one who has a way with words. I have a way of getting things done.

## SEVEN

# TAEMA

After Dr. Mata, we return to the safe house. The sun begins to set. It's been such a long day.

"Meeting Kim for that drink will be fun, if you take her up on it," Nazarin says, "though don't be surprised if she busts out a bottle of real tequila and you wake up with the hangover of your life the next day."

"You speak from experience."

He winced at the memory. "Oh, yes."

I smirk and climb into the hovercar.

I turn to him after we buckle in. "Did she ask me for an evening out, or a date? I couldn't tell."

"She'd probably be open to either." He pauses. "Do you date women?"

"Sometimes. I'm bi."

"Is your sister, too?"

"Yep." I wonder why he asks. It's not as if it's rare in San Francisco.

He looks away and powers up the hovercar, taking off toward the safe house. We don't speak, both gazing at San Francisco and its flashing lights spread out before us, lost in our own thoughts. I lean my head against the window, my eyes fluttering shut as I doze fitfully.

Once we're back in the gingerbread house, it's growing late. I want nothing more than to crawl into bed and pull the covers over me, but Nazarin has to hook me into the Chair for a few hours. Then it'll be time to call Tila's friends—as her—and tell them why I won't be answering their pings for a while.

I sway with exhaustion. All the mental and emotional stress has now compounded with the physical. I pop a few Rejuvs and let Nazarin strap me into the Chair. It brings back memories of my engineering training and waking up with facts and numbers in my head, but not being able to move. I push them away.

I want my sister. I want to hold her close, to tell her everything, to have her tell me it'll be all right. When I'm anxious and my mind moves too quickly, she rubs the back of my neck, easing out the tension, her words soothing in my ear. How many times have I fallen asleep to the sound of her voice?

Tila is not here, and she's the reason I'm doing all this. My whole world has tilted on its axis. Memories of my sister are now tainted by all the lies I know she's told. I didn't see it. How could I not have seen it? How can I ever hope to trust my own judgment again?

"OK," Nazarin says, drawing me from my thoughts, setting the electrodes on my skull and lowering me down. He even draws the blanket over me, which is an oddly touching gesture. I am shivering, but more from unease than cold. Nazarin takes out the needle, prepping the Zeal and melatonin mixture which will help ease the learning. It's a much lower dosage of Zeal than they use in the lounges—just enough to prep the implants to receive the information.

"We're starting you off with general Ratel info," he says. "What we know, so will you. The hierarchy, the main businesses they're involved in, the identities we've managed to scrounge. Some recordings of interrogations, that sort of thing."

After my nap, I'll be a Ratel expert. I wonder if they're going to have to wipe all this information after this investigation is over, but I decide not to ask now. They can take info out almost as easily as putting it in, these days.

"I have to go out tonight after dark, take up my cover," Nazarin says. "But I'll be back by dawn."

"What do you do for them?" I ask.

"This and that," he says. "Mostly I deliver Verve or act as security."

So he saw my sister when he was picking up or dropping off the wares. He's about to go into the place I'll soon join. I close my eyes and hear the whirr as the machine starts. I can hear the low beating of blood through my mechanical heart in my ears.

"I'll wake you up in two hours. I'll just be in the next room doing paperwork."

"All right," I say, already drifting away as the Chair gives off melatonin.

A calm, robotic female voice is the last thing I hear:

*Brainload initializing.*

•

There are two people in the interrogation room.

A man chained to the table looks haggard, like he hasn't slept in days. He has the same shaved scalp, bisected with scars, as Nazarin. Usually, in these informational dreams in the brainload, the person has no sense of self. But I always remember who I am, and that I'm dreaming. The other man, a detective, I guess, stands tall, but he seems tired. His sandy-colored suit is wrinkled, as though he's slept in it.

It's almost like I'm an invisible ghost in the room with them. I can imagine what it looks like to walk around. The scientists who examined Tila and me said that was why we retained so much more—because we could visualize and fit things into patterns more easily than those who couldn't control the recordings. Other people can learn to do it, but because of Manama's training we've been doing it since we were small, even if we didn't realize it at the time.

The recording has been doctored, streamlined so the information can reach my brain efficiently. The man looming over the prisoner is yelling at him, and the prisoner glares back. They shout at each other, their staccato movements jerky. There's a jump, as if something has been cut. The view switches from the standing man leaning toward the prisoner, screaming into his face, to him sitting on the other side of the room, appearing calmer. The prisoner now has a red mark on his cheek. I guess that they've fast-forwarded through the intimidation, which I didn't want to see anyway.

The prisoner seems cowed. "This is how the Ratel works," he says, his voice and eyes flat. They've drugged him, or broken through some other way. "The Ratel's hierarchy is set up like a chess game. The Pawn is the lowest level. They run errands, stand guard, collect extortion money from businesses. Deliver drugs or guns. Drive cars. They do what they're told and hope they make a name for themselves. If they do well, they might get promoted to Knight. Some people directly enter the Ratel at this level, but not many. To become a Knight, you have to prove yourself by committing a . . . worse crime than the ones you have already committed." The man pauses, swallows. He seems haunted.

"What did you do?" the detective asks.

"I had to kill someone," he rasps, and he shuts his eyes.

"Who?"

"It doesn't matter. They were invisible."

The detective frowns. "What –?"

"Do you want to know how the Ratel works or not?" the prisoner interrupts, harsh.

"Go on. Do you want water?"

The prisoner shakes his head. He pauses again, staring down at the table, as if gathering strength. "After that, you can graduate to a Rook or a Bishop, each with subtly different roles in the organization. They're all under the King, of course, but Pawns and Knights hardly ever see him."

"Do you know who the King is?"

"I'm a Knight, so what do you think?"

"That's not a yes or a no."

"It's a no, you dick." The prisoner leans away from the table, the chains of his handcuffs clinking together. He lifts his head in a defiant tilt. "That's all I'm telling you."

The detective opens his mouth to respond, but the scene dissolves.

"Do you know who the King is?"

The question again, asked by a different voice. The faces of the two people in the room are blurred this time, to protect the identities.

"Ensi," the other person whispers, and the word picks up, echoing around the room: *Ensi, Ensi, Ensi.*

"Who is the Queen?" the voice asks. The Queen is the right hand—and like the chess piece, she goes anywhere. Does anything. Including some of the worst crimes in the Ratel. Most of the time, if you're invited to see the Queen alone, you don't leave the room alive. All this information slots into place.

The other blurred face responds: "Malka." It, too, reverberates around the room. That's all they have on the King and Queen. Whispered names or aliases. How they truly function, who's closest to them—the SFPD hasn't cracked any of that. Even after two years, Nazarin has only seen Malka a few times, and has never seen Ensi.

More snippets of interrogations trickle into my mind. I learn names of prominent members of the Ratel, more details about the relationships between the various pieces on the chess board of San Francisco underground crime. The information changes, and I see tables of the same data, laid out logically, so that my brain will process and store it in a subtly different way. This includes maps of suspected Ratel hideouts, possible combination codes or passwords.

Still later, music floats through my brain, the wavelengths undulating through my mind. Here, my brain finally enters REM, and facts still trickle in through the music, deep into the subconscious. Certain nuggets of information will arise if and when I need them.

So many words, so many sounds, so many pieces of a puzzle that I try to fit together. Throughout it all, I wonder: how much of this does Tila already know?

•

"Wake up," Nazarin says, his voice low and soothing.

I open my eyes, and his face is the first sight to greet me. His dark brows are knitted together, studying my face. "How are you feeling?" he asks. He takes off the electrodes and brings the Chair into a seated position.

I press a hand to my temple. "Like an overly damp sponge."

He gives me a humorless half-smile. "I remember that feeling. I made some coffee. Do you want any?"

"Yeah, sounds good." I rise to my feet, steadier than I expect to be.

I follow him into the kitchen, slumping into a chair. I clamp my teeth together to stop the endless litany of facts streaming through my brain from escaping my lips. Within a few hours, the information will settle, but right now, my brain feels like it's in overdrive.

Nazarin pops a Rejuv and sets the steaming cup in front of me. "They put a lot more into you than I've ever seen before in two hours. You sure you feel all right?"

"Fine," I say, trying to sound so. I take a sip of coffee. It's the sanitized San Francisco stuff, nearly caffeine-free, with creamer, but it's warm as it slides down my throat.

"Do you have any questions about what you've learned?" Nazarin asks.

I frown. "I'm still sorting through it. Maybe later."

Nazarin glances at the clock above the replicator. Half past six. "I'll leave you to drink your coffee. But then you should phone Tila's friends. Your first assignment. I have to go." His eyes are a little puffy, despite the Rejuv.

"Right," I mutter, staring into the coffee cup. Nazarin stands, and pauses right before he passes me. For a moment, I wonder if he's going to rest a hand on my shoulder. I think I would have appreciated the gesture. In the end, he sighs and leaves me be.

"Hey," I call after him, and he turns. "How old are you?"

"Twenty-eight." Two years older than me. He probably became a cop at eighteen, a rookie recruit around the time I entered San Francisco. "Why?"

I shrug a shoulder as he leaves. "Just curious."

I drink the coffee slowly, laying out all the recently acquired information in my mind. Between this and my already chaotic anxiety about Tila and about what I'm doing, my brain seems too crowded. I want to scream, to let it all out. I clutch the coffee cup tighter, and then force my fingers to relax. I push the chair away from the table and fold my body into a corner of the room, so that both walls press against my shoulder blades. I breathe in, breathe out, and empty my mind of all extraneous thought.

It's time to phone my sister's friends, as my sister, and tell them I'm going away to China.

I can't do it. It's a simple thing, and the easiest job I'm likely to have undercover, and I can't do it. Sweat breaks out along my skin. So much stress and heartache over the last twenty-four hours has been building, and the dam finally breaks. My mechanical heart thumps rhythmically in my chest against my metal sternum—completely immune to the external factors that would speed or slow a biological version.

*Tila—why did you do this to me? What were you trying to do? To prove?*

My fingertips find the familiar scar as I blink my burning eyes and slow my breathing. I close my eyes, grabbing my emotions and forcing them under control. Even now, I can't escape Mana-ma, but at the moment, I'm glad of her training.

I imagine the fear and the stress as darkness swarming around me to settle on my skin. Then, deep within myself, I kindle a light that starts from my heart and emanates outward, a pure white to eradicate the darkness. My skin is now clean and glows softly, settling in my mind.

"I'm calm," I whisper aloud. And I am. I'm almost giddy with it. A last breath, and I'm back to myself.

I meditate for around ten minutes, the tension leaking out from my neck and shoulders. I float in nothingness, in blackness. All anxiety lifts from my skin, in tiny flurries, like soot in the wind. When I open my eyes, I'm almost giddy from the endorphins. I return to the kitchen table, my breath even and steady. The information has ceased overwhelming me. I'm myself again, more or less.

I learned this from Mana-ma, and part of me feels nervous when I do it. As if just by meditating, I'll somehow fall back into her thrall. But I've . . . *we've* been free of her for years.

I set the pings to audio only. Tila has a lot more friends than I do. It never bothered me before, but looking at the list of names downloaded from my implants and projected onto the kitchen table, I feel like she's left more behind in this world than I have. Her artwork. She collects people, and always remembers faces and names. Though I've made some impact with my VivaFog machines, I only have a small circle of friends, and I couldn't say for certain if I'm closer to them than she is to hers or not.

"Here goes," I mutter, and ping the first name on the list. I have a little thrill of anticipation. I've often wished I could be more like my sister: stronger, braver, so sure of herself, whereas I always questioned myself and my perception of others. I relied on her too much, in many ways. By channeling her, maybe I can start relying on myself.

I start with Diane, the curator of an art gallery nearby. Once, she had an exhibition of Tila's artwork. It was a success and yet after that first and last exhibition, Tila couldn't stand the thought of another gallery opening. She told me they were stealing pieces of her by buying her art. I hadn't understood it: wasn't that the point of making art? You put a little bit of yourself on canvas, or into a sculpture, or onto a page, and then you give or sell it to others so they also enjoy it?

Since then, whatever work she did was never seen by anyone but the two of us. Her paintings are beautiful, and it seems a shame that nobody else shares them, but I respect her decision and the reasons behind it, and so does Diane. They've remained close friends.

"Hey Tils!" Diane says.

"Hey, Di," I say, folding my face into a smile—even if she can't see it, she'll hear it in my voice. I lean on my right elbow, like Tila does. She pitches her voice different from me, a little lower, but aside from that, our inflections are identical. We can still speak at the same time if we want to. It unnerves people when we do it. Diane's speaking, and I focus on her words.

"...You can make it to the gallery this weekend, right? You'll love this new artist. Such dark, fascinating work."

And here we go. "Sorry, Di, I'm gonna be out of town for a while."

"Really? Where?"

"China. Taema's got a job and I'm going with her. Can you believe it?" I strive for Tila's lighter tone.

"Oh, it'll be lovely this time of year. How long are you going?"

"Not sure. I have an open ticket. Might even be a few months."

"Wish I could come! Are you going to get one of those virtual assistants to help you do everything?"

I laugh and say probably not. We chat for a bit. It's not that difficult at all to be my sister. I was worried it would be, with how much she's changed the last few years. I wasn't sure I'd be able to bridge that final gap. Perhaps it was just different hair, a different face, a different job. I can slip into her personality almost as easily as my own. I thought it'd make me feel braver, but it only makes me all the lonelier.

Diane never asks me what's wrong, or if I'm feeling all right. I've masked everything behind Tila's mannerisms. She's brasher, doesn't self-edit before she speaks. Or at least she doesn't appear to, so it makes it seem she has nothing to hide. Though, obviously, she did.

I say farewell to Diane and make my way through the other

names on the list. The only people I don't ping are the friends from Zenith, since Nazarin says we'll be going there soon enough.

When he first proposed that, so soon, I thought he was crazy. But now, as I say goodbye to Tila's last friend on my list, I think it won't be as bad as I fear. Although I have a lot less experience with seeing how the "hostess Tila" acts at work. Her job is a far cry from anything I'm used to doing—the machines I work with don't speak to me, as I'm not in robotics—and I wonder if they'll see straight through me as soon as I set my foot through the door.

After I finish pinging everyone, I lie down in an actual bed in my room and doze.

Nazarin comes for me a few hours later. When he knocks I tell him to enter, forcing myself to sit up. Though he's only slept four hours, he looks refreshed, whereas I'm sure my hair is frizzy and my makeup has smeared halfway down my face. "No rest for the wicked, I'm afraid," he says. "I'm to plug you back in. I'll be going back out again. I'm needed."

I get up, pulling my sweater around my shoulders. "What for?"

"Security for a Verve drop." He sighs. We go downstairs. My feet drag on every step.

"Who are they selling it to?"

He grimaces. "They're bribing a Zeal lounge, one of the shitty, off-grid ones, to spike the Zeal with Verve."

My eyes widen. "Why?"

"I think they're experimenting with it on a wider scale, and using the Zealots as a testing ground."

"Fuck," I say. Zealots are those who become so addicted to Zeal that they spend more of their lives plugged in than out. Sometimes, if their fantasies are too violent or depraved, the government takes an interest, worried that they might pose a threat to society despite Zeal's soporific aftereffects. So some go off-grid and take Zeal in unregulated, horrible dumps. Anything for their dreams. Most of them don't live long, spending so much time within the Zealscape they stop eating and waste away. I've always wondered why the government never cracked down on those illegal Zeal lounges. Now, with a sinking feeling, I wonder if it's because letting them starve is easier and cheaper than stasis.

"I know. They have an orderly there, a lucid dreamer, who will be tasked to see how many dreams he can mine and how quickly. There might be more to it as well, but as a Knight, they don't tell me much, and I can't ask questions. I want to stop it, but I can't."

Because it'd blow his cover. That's another aspect I haven't thought of—how I'll have to see horrible things and let them slide, because to speak up would make me stand out.

I don't want to talk about it any more. "What are you shoving into my brain this time?" I ask in dread.

"We'll give your brain a rest from Ratel info. Some of the data now will be physical fighting techniques. The rest of it . . ." Unease flickers over his features, and I can feel it mirrored in my own. "This . . . might not be easy for you."

"What do you mean?"

"Well, it's to help you with going to Zenith. Help you fit in."

"You interviewed a hostess?"

His eyes flick away from me.

Oh. Shit. I suddenly understand, and I don't know whether to be hopeful or angry. "You spoke to Tila."

He nods. "Yes. She gave us an interview. For you."

He's looking for a reaction, but I keep my face blank and still, despite my insides turning to water. "OK."

"Are you all right with this?"

What does he expect me to say? Of course I'm not all right with this. I'm not remotely all right with any of this. It'll be the first time I've seen my sister since she was literally dragged from my arms by the police. She's the one who hasn't spoken to me since—for if Detective Nazarin was right, she didn't wish to speak to me. After everything I've discovered about her, everything I've learned she's hidden from me, and everything I know I will learn, will she still look like the same Tila I thought I knew?

"It's what needs doing, right?" I say, with a weak, humorless smile. "Have to tie off the loose ends before we really go fishing."

"Yes." Still, he hesitates. "If you don't want to do this, nobody is making you."

"You've changed your tune. What, do you now think I won't be able to do it?" Does he think I'm weak? I don't want him to think me weak.

"No, not at all. I haven't changed my mind in the least. But . . . sometimes, I wish someone had asked me that, the night before I went undercover. Asked me if this was really what I wanted to do, and given me the option to back out, without shame." His head tilts downward. I can't see his eyes.

"Would you have turned it down?"

"I'm not sure."

His words frighten me. "It couldn't be without shame. Not for me," I say, almost gently. "I couldn't leave my sister. I might be terrified of what's going to happen. I might be so angry at her for hiding things from me that if she were here right now, I don't know if I'd hug her or scream at her. But I could never just leave her to freeze. That's not an option."

He meets my eyes. "Good."

Detective Nazarin plugs me into the machine. My eyes grow heavy.

I sleep.

•

Tila's sitting at a table almost identical to the one where I saw all the Ratel people interviewed the last time I was plugged in. It's only been a few days, but I'm shocked at the change in my sister. She seems haggard, and thinner. They've dressed her in a plain, dark blue uniform similar to nursing scrubs. Her short hair is frizzy instead of spiky—prison shampoo, I suppose.

The biggest difference is in her eyes. I've seen it before— she gets the same look when she realizes she has to either start a painting over again or ditch it entirely. The look that screams, *I failed.* It wouldn't matter what I said to her. She couldn't shake that the failure was due to something deep within her. A flaw.

Yet her strength is still there. The bright glint in her eye when she knows she has something the other person wants. I've been on the receiving end of those bright, tormenting eyes before. It could drive me crazy.

Across from her sits Officer Oloyu, the man with the Golden Bear tattoo. I'm half surprised it's not Nazarin for a second; but then, he wouldn't have had time to go see her, wherever she is, interview her, and be back to train me. Oloyu leans forward, but I can tell he's nervous. "Tell me about the Zenith club, please, Miss Collins."

Tila plays with a snag of dry skin next to her fingernail, almost as if she's bored. She recites her litany. "I've worked as a hostess for the last four years. I started in some really shitty clubs, like Gamma Ray. I bounced around a couple of other places, then Sal took me on at Zenith. Right away I knew that was where I wanted to stay."

She leans back in her chair. She has an audience for the first time in days. After all she's put me through, I find it infuriating that she's still putting on a show.

"That's something I didn't realize going in," she continues. "That even though people pay money to go to these clubs, they sometimes still hate you, deep down. Hate that they can't form any genuine connections in real life so they have to pay for you. Or pay for Zeal in the rooms and for you to join in, as they don't have any friends who will link with them. They resent you for it. It can make things plenty awkward, lemme tell you. In Zenith, people are nicer, and really seem to like being around you."

She'd said something similar to me before, but she'd also shrugged, saying that they loved her too. Love, hate, desire, envy, or simple enjoyment of her company. Sometimes all of it wrapped up together.

"And did Vuk hate you?" Officer Oloyu asks.

That stops her. "No, I don't think he did." Her voice is quiet.

"What's the exact specification of your job at Zenith?" Officer Oloyu asks. I can tell he's interested. He's likely never been to a club like Zenith. Not on his salary.

She crosses her arms over her stomach, pulling the fabric tight against her breasts. She knows Oloyu's looking. Her head tilts up, defiant, one corner of her mouth quirked. I know that look, too. "I suppose—I'll never work there again, will I? I've been called a hooker, a whore, a call girl. All that. Whatever. It's not just sex—sex work rarely is, anyway. I'm their fantasy." She smiles, and it lights up her wan face. She has reclaimed many of those terms for herself, telling me the words couldn't hurt her if she did. Maybe she's distancing herself from other types of sex work because she's speaking to a police officer. Even if being a hostess is not illegal, she's still nervous. "These days, so many men and women work all alone, connected to their wallscreens and their small, cramped apartments. They don't seem to understand how to make real friends, or maybe they want some who are a bit less . . . complicated. So they come to clubs like Zenith, where friends, lovers or almost-lovers are all lined up at the ready. There are no expectations, no birthdays to remember or weddings to attend. Connection without attachment. Without strings. Without disappointment.

"So that's what I do. I talk to them. I pour them drinks. I laugh at their jokes. I listen to them. I look them in the eye. Most of the time, that's all they need. They have a nice time, and then they go home to their empty apartments and their wallscreens."

"And if they need more?"

She shifts in her chair, resting her head on one hand. She's positively chatty, now that she's started. She has a rapt audience in Oloyu, and she wants to entertain. "It's usually only high-end business people who have enough money to use Zeal in the club. We're exclusive. Best product, best experience, and all the hosts and hostesses are great actors in the Zealscape. For the clients, it's like a mini-holiday in a really expensive virtual reality hotel. The same host or hostess can plug in the whole time, but only if they want to. They get a bonus. Sometimes if they wake up in between fantasies, they'll have physical sex, but that's only if they want to. Same with sex when in the Zealscape. It's not about the sex. Or again, not only about it. It's to feel close to someone, even if it's just for a little while, but still knowing the next day they can get on with their life without any guilt. And the sex is freely given or not at all, and the client can't complain. They all understand the rules."

And what if they didn't? Would they grow angry? Angry enough to attack Tila?

"And do you stay overnight?" Officer Oloyu asks. He shifts in his chair, probably aroused and uncomfortable with it.

Tila shrugs a shoulder, the movement seamless and elegant. "Sometimes. Not that often. I have to actually like the person. Want to spend more time with them. Most of the time, I'm happy enough just to stay in the bar and chat and laugh with them. It's a good job. Was a good job."

She falters, and her mask slips. There's the vulnerable side of my sister. The side that only I see. Then it flits back up, and she's back to figuring out how she can wrap him around her finger. With a dip of my stomach, I realize I've seen her use that expression on me, too.

Here, in the brainload, I finally let myself think what I've avoided thinking for some time now: *has she used me too?* But at the same time, I wonder if it's like back in the Hearth. Where my own mind couldn't be trusted, and Tila had to spend weeks convincing me that we needed to escape. I shy away from that, unable just now to cope with the guilt of how I once believed in Mana-ma unfalteringly.

"And was your night with Vuk an overnight stay?"

She shakes her head. "No. He liked Leylani for that. I was only a hostess to him." Her eyes slide to the side, and I know she's keeping something back.

"Right. We need a list of all the people you work with, and what they look like. Your file says you're an artist, so perhaps you can draw them?" Oloyu clears his throat.

My sister narrows her eyes. "Is this for Taema?"

Oloyu hesitates, as if he's not sure if he should answer. "This is to help with the investigation."

She fidgets. "And I *have* to do it?"

What is she thinking? It used to be I'd always know. She's hesitating, not jumping to help until she knows all sides, works out her advantage. Altruism is not a trait my sister inherited. Not even for me.

When I'm awake, I don't think such nasty thoughts about her. Why am I so cruel when my body is unconscious?

"You agreed you would," Oloyu continues.

Her mouth twists, but she takes the proffered drawing paper and pencil. She pauses before she draws, tapping the pencil against the table. Why haven't they given her a tablet? Finally, she brings the pencil to paper.

It fast-forwards her drawing, but I stare at her furrowed brow and the way her hair obscures half her face. How many times have I watched her draw?

When she finishes, she holds up the paper. I drift closer, examining the names and the faces. Even sketched in haste, her drawings are beautiful. Dispassionately, Tila gives each name, a short description, and a few key personal details about each person. I feel the information sink into the deep recesses of my brain. As soon as I see these faces in the real world, I'll recognize them.

Officer Oloyu asks her to then sketch and describe the most common clients to frequent the club, especially those she's worked with most often.

At this she finally starts to look concerned. She hides it well enough. But not from me. "This *is* for Taema. You're putting her undercover, aren't you?"

"I'm not at liberty to say."

"When you first took me in, you told me you were putting her in protective custody. You can't do this. Going undercover is too dangerous for her."

I can't help but bristle. She thinks I'm soft.

Oloyu's mouth twists. "Why? Because of what you've done as part of the Ratel?"

She scoffs. "Nice try. No confessions."

"We already know irrefutably you worked with them. There's no need to be coy. So why isn't your sister allowed to go undercover?"

"So she is undercover." Her eyes are bright with triumph.

Oloyu's mouth twists as he bites down a curse.

"Gotcha." Tila smirks and bends over the paper. Again, the strange fast-forwarding as she draws, me unable to turn my "eyes" away from the quick movements of her fingers holding the pencil. Again, the sketches of men and women appear, their names, their habits, their dreams and desires find a place deep within my mind. I won't forget any of them, even though, if I'd been awake, I'd probably forget about a third of the names.

Officer Oloyu asks my sister more questions, ones that I suspect Nazarin has given him. What is the layout of the club? What sort of food is served? Music played? Cocktail menu? Most popular liquor? A lot of it seems unnecessary. I'm only going to be at the club for an hour or two at most, speaking to the owner, Sal, and to Leylani, the girl who was meant to be entertaining Vuk that night. Still, everything goes into my memory bank.

At the beginning my sister fights back, toying with Oloyu and giving flippant answers. Then she seems to tire of the game and gives him the answers he asks for. By the time the questions end, Tila's visibly wilted, her voice hoarse. Officer Oloyu thanks her for her time. But before she leaves, she looks at the camera.

It seems like she's looking right at me.

"I don't need saving, Taema," she says. "You don't *have* to do this for me. And maybe you shouldn't."

I can't read her, and it hurts.

She turns and leaves, the door clanging shut behind her. The scene goes dark.

•

When he returns sometime in the night, Nazarin turns off the brainload long enough for me to have a few hours of real sleep. I wake up to the information having settled better within my mind. I still feel tired, as though I've been doing calculus for hours. Brain gymnastics, Tila always called it.

I've had nightmares about my sister. Over and over, I saw her saying that maybe I shouldn't do this. Drawing away from me, her eyes calculating, weighing me up. Maybe she didn't believe I could be her, do whatever she did. Maybe she didn't trust me, that my mind couldn't handle it.

Even despite her manipulations, her games, I couldn't let her go. I could never let her go into stasis without even trying to set her free. She knows that. So why try to warn me away?

Maybe this is even more dangerous than I thought.

I say nothing as I sip my ersatz coffee in the morning. Despite the nightmares, I haven't changed my mind.

The first thing I have to do is send the Ratel a message. Tila is evidently meant to work a shift at the Verve lounge tonight. Nazarin walks me through it. They have untraceable methods of contact. There's a portal on an untracked website where Ratel members can check in. Nazarin knows the code, and he tells me just what to say. I'll miss two shifts: next Tuesday and Thursday.

A message comes back confirming it, and I sign off. The SFPD have changed my VeriChip to show my location as Tila's apartment whenever I'm at the safe house, so if the Ratel do look up my whereabouts, it won't arouse suspicion. Today is Sunday—by next Tuesday, I'll have to go in. It's not nearly enough time to get through all we need to, but it's all the time we'll get.

I go through more brainloading and more physical practice with Nazarin, honing my body and my mind. They give me facial recognition software, to help me recall the faces Tila told me about in last night's session, as well as another program which will help give me instructions if I do get into a physical altercation. I hope I don't have to use it.

Over Chinese takeout ordered from the replicator, Nazarin tells me more about his experiences in the Ratel, though he skitters away from a lot of the explicit details. After two intensive days, I feel more ready than I ever thought I could in such a short span of time.

It's not enough, though.

I still have to change my face.

•

We go to a flesh parlor out of the city entirely.

It was the easiest way to avoid people who might have known me or Tila. The SFPD, the Ratel, Zenith clients, my co-workers—none of them would bother traveling fifteen miles to change their features when there's a flesh parlor on every doorstep.

We take a hovercar over the Golden Gate Bridge flightpath. It's been over a year since I left the city, unless it was for work. I always mean to explore more, but I've been too busy, usually working on VivaFog machines even on the weekends. When we were younger, Tila and I would take so many day trips from the city. We went up to Monterey, to Santa Cruz, to Berkeley. We'd pack picnics and laze on the beach or in a park, Tila sketching and me reading a book before exploring the shops and the markets. I miss those days.

Nazarin takes us up to Marin, the affluent area where tech workers commute in and out on the underwater high-speed BART. He looks tired. Working for the Ratel by night and training me by day means he's functioning on too little sleep. Rejuvs help, but they're not a substitute for proper sleep. The flesh parlor he's chosen is one of the best in the nation. When the hovercar touches down, my nerves refuse to behave, no matter how much of Mana-ma's training I use.

They're going to change my face.

Not much, but enough. I keep trailing my fingertips along the lines of my brows, my nose, my cheekbones. Nazarin notices but does not say anything. I swallow, putting my hands down. It's not much of a change. And I can always change it back.

We sit in the waiting room. I press my nails so hard into my palms that they leave marks. I'm shaking and I can't seem to stop. Nazarin lifts his hand, pauses as if tempted to take it away, and then rests his hand on top of mine. He gives me a look out of the corner of his eye as if to say: *is this too much? Should I not?* His hand is warm, the palms callused. I can see the small scars, pale against his skin, which is only a little lighter than mine. I put my other hand over his and squeeze, grateful for the comfort, before taking both hands away.

A nurse pokes his head into the hallway, his scrubs white and crisp, and makes eye contact.

"I'll be right here," Nazarin says.

I give a sharp nod. I follow the nurse through the bright, white walls and into a room. There's another Chair within. I've had my fill of these things the last few days. They'll knock me out, and through gene therapy and a scalpel, I'll wake up with a different face.

"The doctor will be with you in a moment," the nurse says,

helping me into the Chair and plugging the wires and electrodes into me. I'm still shaking. He gives me something to calm me, until I feel as if I am floating. I listen to the beeps of the monitors and my mechanical heartbeat. It reminds me of that first day I awoke from surgery.

The door opens. In my addled state, for a moment I wonder if it's Tila, coming in to find me, IV trailing behind her.

It's only the doctor, coming to change my face to molten wax and mold me into my sister. The SFPD doctored the files, to make it seem like "Tila" went back to her original face, and has now changed her mind yet again.

He comes forward and asks if I'm all right. I nod. I'm floating, high above myself. He sends me to sleep, and my last thought is that actually, I don't mind this. My face will change, but I'll look exactly like my sister again.

# EIGHT

# TAEMA

I'm wearing Tila's clothes.

They're nothing like my usual attire—a coverall for scurrying up a VivaFog antenna, listening to its gentle hum as it draws the fog into its whirring machines, or a dress similar to the ones we wore in the Hearth on weekends, plain, comfortable, unremarkable. All the things this dress is not.

I have never cared much for fashion. We both experimented when we first arrived in the city, excited by the freedom of being able to choose our own clothes; of not having to make everything and alter the torsos; of wearing different clothes from one another. We had fun peacocking ourselves and dyeing our hair, having moving tattoos inked on our skin, playing with materials of strange textures and cuts. I soon grew bored of it, erasing the tattoos, letting my hair return to its brown corkscrew curls, giving the fancy clothes away and buying things that felt more familiar.

Tila erased all the tattoos but one, a stylized broken heart on her thigh in a Polynesian style (we are part Samoan, as well as black and white), the two pieces not quite connecting. Doesn't take a psychologist to figure out the symbolism of that. The waxworker gave the same one to me this afternoon, and it twines from my upper thigh down to my knee.

I swallow, tugging the dress down over my hips. It's a slinky number, the skintight material shimmering purple in one light and midnight blue in another. The boots I wear have thin, faux-leather ribbons that wrap around my legs until they reach where the tattoo begins. I've rubbed lotion with small gold specks all over my legs and arms (the tattoo is already completely healed, along with my face; the marvels of modern medicine), and my limbs glow.

My hair is gone, chopped short, the texture changed from curly to straight and the color to bright blue. They've mapped the color to my genes, so I don't have to worry about roots. My nose is shorter and wider, and turns up at the end. My cheekbones are slightly higher, my lips a little fuller, my chin a little pointier. It's subtle, very subtle, but I don't like it. It makes me more conventionally pretty, and more anonymous in this city of perfect faces.

I paint my lips dark purple and outline my eyes in blue. I tip the ends of my eyelashes with silver dust. I have dressed like midnight to go to Zenith. That's me in the mirror, but I can't see myself. Tila looks back at me, but it blurs. Tila. Me. Someone in between. A stranger. I turn away from the reflection.

I slip on a coat and leave the safe house, the door snapping shut behind me. I take the MUNI, like Tila would have. As I enter the station, in the corner of my vision I see Tila's name and the amount of the fare deducted from her account. It's true. I am officially my sister.

I step on the train and it takes off. I stare at the strangers, lit green by the algae of the tunnels. I feel like people are watching me, but perhaps it is merely because I am showing more leg than I usually do, and humans are biologically programmed to stare at bare flesh.

I'm nervous about meeting the owner, Sal, and Leylani. I fear what they will say, what I might find out. I fear I will disappoint Nazarin and be a poor undercover agent. More than that, I fear I will fail to find out what they need to know to free Tila, and she will go into stasis. Or worse, that I'll find out things about her that I'll never be able to forget or forgive. This is the point of no return. For both of us.

I leave at the correct stop and walk along Montgomery Street, the mica in the sidewalk sparkling.

I feel very alone as I look up at the TransAm Pyramid dwarfing the surrounding buildings. It was rebuilt a century ago, based on the original Transamerica Pyramid but twice the size, all glass and quartz-concrete. Evidently in the foundations, echoing the original, there are thousands of dollars' worth of credit chips instead of coins, thrown in for good luck as the concrete was poured over it. I hope I can take a bit of the luck, though evidently it didn't work for my sister.

I take a deep breath and enter the lobby, nodding at the doormen before making my way to the glass elevator.

I have to let Taema fall away again. I have to become Tila.

I'm alone in the elevator—most of the other hosts and hostesses won't arrive until later. I rise above San Francisco, staring down at the sparkling lights in the growing darkness.

"Hey, Echo," the hostess at reception greets me. Too brightly. I fight the urge to narrow my eyes. Does she know? Does everyone know what actually happened in the back room three nights ago? Are they all being bribed a king's ransom to keep quiet, or did the SFPD really manage to keep it under the radar?

I nod to her, and the brainload intel tells me her nickname is Pallua. All the hostesses choose nicknames. Psychological distancing, I guess. I was touched when I found out Tila's was

Echo. Now I'm the echo, a thin replica of Tila. Even my serviceable walk in heels is different from her feline prowl.

Through my VeriChip I'm able to bring up Tila's employee file, but Nazarin had the owner expand my access. I bring up internal communications from the club over the last few days into my ocular implant overlay. Since the incident, nobody's used the back room where the crime scene was. Everyone's been told that a high roller's rented it out for a long, exclusive Zeal trip.

I've been staring blankly into the distance for too long. Pallua looks down at her bright red nails. She's a prototypical hostess—perfect features, perfect body, golden-brown skin, her hair a riot of purple, blue, and green. Tattoos of peacock feathers glow around one shoulder, snaking toward her breasts, which are on display in her low-cut gown.

I wave vaguely, and something stills in the other girl's face. A crease appears in the smooth skin of her forehead, tense lines deepening next to painted lips. She swallows and busies herself with the reception desk. I rub my clammy palms discreetly on my dress, avoiding eye contact with the few other hosts and hostesses who are milling around Zenith waiting for their shifts to start.

"Your client's waiting," Pallua says, her bright smile back in place. "Cute, too."

"Thanks." I smile, hoping it reaches my eyes.

The door to the back room where I'm meant to be seems to stare at me, waiting for me to enter. I pause in front of it, take a deep breath, and the scanner reads my VeriChip, identifying me as Tila.

The door swooshes open. I step through and the dim lights brighten. Detective Nazarin waits for me, perched on a luxury sofa. He must have come in the rear entrance. He looks like a thug in the dark clothing that doesn't quite obscure his shoulder holster.

The room is simple, but everything screams of wealth. I don't look at the round bed in the corner. There's a well-stocked bar, and a wide expanse of polished floorboards and low-pile rugs with abstract designs. Zeal Chairs are parked discreetly in the corner of the room.

Next to him is Sal, the owner of Zenith. He's a tall man, thin and elegant. He wears rings on all his fingers and a dark green suit, the cravat at his neck a vivid blue that matches his eyes. It looks old-fashioned, almost Edwardian, but then Tila said he was like that: picking bits of the past and interweaving them into his look. Sal is one of the few people that Tila genuinely respects. He took a chance on her by taking her on at the club, trained her up, and always treated her well. She spoke of him sometimes, over dinner. He's meant to be fiercely protective of his employees and he prides himself that Zenith has had no scandals, no violence.

Until three days ago. I feel nervous that he knows about the switch between me and my sister. How trustworthy is Sal, really? I asked Nazarin about it earlier, right before I went up to change into Tila's clothes.

"From all we can tell, he's fairly clean," he reassured me. "There's nothing connecting him to the Ratel. There's a chance of course that he's covered his tracks well, but it's a risk we have to take. For an exorbitant sum, he's keeping very quiet."

"Tila told me once that he prides himself on keeping his word," I responded.

Detective Nazarin nodded. "We have to hope that's true."

The door closes behind me. "We thank you for your assistance with this investigation, Mr. Kupka," Detective Nazarin begins.

He waves his arm. "Call me Sal, please. And we all know it's in my best interests as well as yours." He looks me up and down. "My, but you do look just like Tila. It's nice to meet you, Taema."

I incline my head. "It's nice to meet you, too. Tila's spoken well of you."

I notice he doesn't call my sister Echo. The man before me looks polite, and a small smile rests on his face. I glance around the room, swallowing. There's absolutely no trace of a crime scene, but this is the room where it happened. Did Tila sit on that very sofa on the night that tore both our lives apart?

I lean against one of the pillars of the room. It's rude, but I can't bear the thought of sitting down. Why are we meeting in this room, and not the others? I bring up the logs again. Ah. Because all the other rooms in Zenith are booked, and even if Sal wants to help us, he doesn't want to eat into his profit.

I look toward the floor-to-ceiling windows overlooking downtown San Francisco. The bay is tinged its usual phosphorescent green, the lights of the skyscrapers blue and white. Hovercars wink and blink as they weave their way through them.

"So," Nazarin begins, and I turn. "Was Vuk Radke a regular client of Zenith?"

"He'd come maybe once every other month or so," Sal replies. He seems at ease, relaxed. I find that unnerving. A dead client was found in this very room, my sister covered in his blood, and he doesn't seem to mind at all. I swallow.

"Did he often see Tila or Leylani when he was here?"

"Leylani was his favorite hostess."

"Did he stay over when he visited?"

"Every other time. So perhaps three times a year."

"Have you had any dealings with him outside Zenith?"

Sal shrugs a shoulder. "Here and there. I go to charity events. Sometimes he'd be there. We were on friendly enough terms, I'd say." A flicker of emotion on his face: regret.

"Why wasn't Leylani here three nights ago?"

Sal takes a cig out of his breast pocket and sucks on it, the end briefly glaring red. He blows out the mist. "Said she wasn't feeling well and had to cancel her shift."

"Has she missed any work since?"

"No, she came in yesterday. I haven't told her anything about this."

"Can you tell us more about what happened three nights ago?"

*Why am I here?* I want to ask them. I don't want to listen to this. I don't want to hear this slick, shiny-suited man dispassionately explaining the night my sister's life fell apart—and mine, as a side effect. Yet I'm curious, too, and find myself drifting closer. Adrenaline courses through my veins. I force myself to calm down.

"I found her. The room sensed the blood on the floor and it triggered an alarm. My employees are protected—they are never to be harmed. Fantasies like that are reserved for the Zealscape, but even so, we don't allow violent sexual fantasies unless the host or hostess consents to it. Tila was always very clear she was not interested in that, and their engagement that night was not likely to be sexual."

My shoulder muscles are so tense they feel like they could shatter.

"So I was concerned, obviously, and came in personally. There was Vuk on the floor, with Tila sitting next to him, covered in blood."

I close my eyes, but the vision is too vivid. I open my eyes to see Sal's blue ones focused on me, curiously watching my reaction. I release the tension in my body, but cross my arms over my chest.

"Did she say anything to you?" Nazarin asks.

"She did."

I frown, and Nazarin nudges him. "What was it?"

Sal pauses, as if trying to remember. "Ah. Yes. It was something like, 'He is the red one, the fair one, the handsome one. He came from the Earth and now he returns. The faces keep changing.' I had no idea what it meant. And I still don't. I wasn't sure if she actually saw me, or was muttering it to herself. Does it mean anything to you?"

"No. Not yet. Why didn't you tell the police?"

He looks down, slipping the cig into his pocket. "Slipped my mind." Clearly, it hadn't. It reminds me uncomfortably of Tila. I wonder why he's giving it to us now.

I can tell Nazarin wants to play the hard cop, but restrains himself—that wouldn't work with Sal. "What did you do next?"

"Called the police. And it was one of the hardest things I've ever done. I debated letting her go, you know. I don't mind admitting that. Tempted to let her wash herself off and disappear into the night. Dispose of the body. Clean up the blood." He sighs. "But I knew I'd never get away with it, and much as I care for Tila, I didn't care to sacrifice my livelihood for her. So I locked the doors and pinged the police, instructing them to come in the rear entrance and make as little fuss as possible. But then Tila threatened me with the knife, so I let her go. She grabbed Vuk's coat by the door to cover up her blood-soaked dress and escaped out the back. I think Pallua saw something, or realized something was wrong, but she hasn't said anything."

That explains her nervousness around me, at least.

"Is Leylani here tonight?"

"Her shift should start soon, yes. Will you be telling her what happened?"

Nazarin shakes his head. "No, I don't think so. No need. But we'll probably observe her and the other clients briefly before we go home." He nods at me. "She's going to work a shift like you agreed. Try her hand at being her sister for a few hours. Let the other hosts and hostesses know that she's going away to China with her sister. Then she'll be gone."

"But Tila's never returning," Sal says, his voice bland.

"No, I find it unlikely she'd return to your employ, or that you'd let her."

Sal considers me again. "Very well. This will be interesting, I suppose." He tilts his head and points at his eye. "I'll be watching."

He smiles, but I'm not reassured.

"It'll be interesting to see how similar you are to your sister," he continues, standing and making his way to the window as well.

I say nothing. What is there to say?

"We appreciate your cooperation, Sal," Nazarin says, standing.

Sal looks around at the room and sighs. "I'll have to redecorate. I got all the blood out, but the memories are still here. All of this will have to go."

The blood drains from my cheeks. Something terrible happened here last Thursday, but the idea of it all disappearing and being replaced with more bland, expensive furniture is hard to take. The room that changed everything for me will continue to be just another back Zeal lounge in the Zenith nightclub.

"One last thing," Nazarin says. "I recommend you check your Zeal supply." He nods to the Chairs in the corner.

Sal starts. "Why?"

"I can't give details, but we have reason to believe that someone may be responsible for tampering with Zeal in certain lounges. If you find any anomalies, buy fresh stuff. Check it every time."

"We've had people plugged in since Friday morning. Why didn't you tell us this?"

"We only just found out about it. And it's unlikely, but I wanted to warn you to take precautions." I am pretty certain the thought has only just occurred to Nazarin. The lines around his mouth are tight. I wonder if he's thinking about the night he had to provide security to the off-grid lounge. Tila told the SFPD she hadn't been asked to lucid dream within Zenith yet, but it's only a matter of time. Was Vuk sent here to tamper with the supply, and is that why Tila came to blows with him?

"I'll check the Zeal daily myself," Sal says.

"Good. Please let us know if you find anything unusual and send a sample directly to us for testing. No one else." His voice sharpens.

"Of course not," Sal says, all smooth charm.

With a last look out the window at glittering San Francisco sprawling below, the owner of Zenith walks away, and Nazarin and I are left alone.

"Are you OK?" Nazarin asks.

"Yes, I am." It's not a lie: my fingers shake a little, and I really want to get out of this room, but I'm holding it together. Mana-ma's training is in full effect, and I've dampened my emotions enough to function. I ask if he thinks Vuk has tampered with the Zeal here and mixed or replaced it with Verve.

"I don't know. I don't think so, but I'd rather warn Sal than risk the supply being contaminated."

"Right. So am I to stay for the whole six hours of Tila's shift?"

"We'll see how you get on. If you like, we can leave early."

"Are you going to be posing as a client?" I ask.

He pauses and turns to me. "Yes. I'll be watching along with you. It could be someone here knows more than they let on. Pallua, maybe."

I nod. "OK."

He moves close and slings an arm around me, and I start in surprise.

He leans close enough for me to feel the heat from his skin. "We have to sell it, don't we?"

I consider, and then nod, pressing my hip against his, resting my hand against the warm dip in his waist. It feels strange, to be touching a near-stranger like this. It happens so rarely for me, these days. It's also a comfort. I want to lean closer to him, breathe in the scent of his skin.

In the Hearth, there was a lot of touching. Not necessarily sexual—people just touched each other more. Greeted each other with hugs, or casually threw an arm around someone else. Here in San Francisco, people are more reserved. Maybe that's why so many feel the need to come to places like Zenith, where they can pretend the barriers between people are thinner.

I shake my head, patting my shorter hair and trying to gain a bit of composure. The door swooshes open. We sidle through, still touching. Nazarin settles into his role with an ease I envy. He laughs, warm and deep in his throat, his hand lingering on my hipbone. I feel the strong ropes of muscle on his back beneath his shirt. I resist the irrational urge to stroke my hand down his spine.

We make our way through the club, which is busier now. Beautiful men and women with perfect bodies, perfect faces, perfect clothes, laughing their perfect laughs and drinking their perfectly delicious drinks. The minty mist of cigs fills the air, mingling with the flattering blue and purple lighting. There's that *sameness* to so many people in San Francisco and the rest of Pacifica. When anyone can choose to alter their appearance at will, so many tend to go for the same bland, symmetrical features. Now I feel like I'm a little more like them.

I still miss the simplicity of certain aspects of the Hearth. Knowing that if you looked at someone, it was the face and body they were born with, shaped by their experiences. Everyone in San Francisco wears a mask.

Having said that, there's plenty about the Hearth I don't miss one little bit.

We perch at a round table. I access my brainloaded info and lean toward Nazarin to say, "What'll it be to drink?"

"Gin and tonic," he replies.

I go to the bar and order two drinks, which will be added to Nazarin's tab. The bartender's name is Ira, and he smiles at me as he gives me the glasses. We chat for a bit, but Tila didn't give much information beyond his name, so I'm glad when other hosts and hostesses come up with their drink orders.

I take my gin and tonics to the table. It's synthetic, like all alcohol in the city. No damage to the liver, non-addictive, no hangovers. I pass Nazarin his, and we clink our glasses together.

I take a cautious sip and fight the urge to make a face. It lacks the peppery, juniper punch of the true stuff. Not that we had that much of it at sixteen in the Hearth. But at the start of each season, anyone could have a glass or two (or ten, in the case of Mardel) of whatever had been brewed for the celebration. The blueberry vodka from the summer we were fourteen was my favorite.

I wonder if Nazarin's ever tried real alcohol. If he was raised in cities, in this supposed perfection, and if he's ever seen through the pretty illusions to the ugliness beneath. He must have, within the Ratel at least. I shudder.

We keep to ourselves as the bar fills with more attractive people. I match the faces and names to the sketches that I gleaned from Tila through the brainload. Eventually, I spy Leylani. She's tall, with razor-straight dark hair to her waist. She has tanned skin, bright green eyes, and wears small shorts and heels so high my ankles hurt just to look at them. She's obviously with a client, an Afghani woman in a hijab, wearing a long, dark blue dress with bell sleeves.

"Invite her over here," Nazarin mutters under his breath. "Pretend to be Echo, and then eventually find a way to get her on her own. See what you can learn from her, if anything, and then afterward, tell me everything."

I feel a little rush of excitement. After all the fear and uncertainty, the cramming and drilling and brainloading, here I am, about to truly pretend to be my sister to a stranger and start investigating what happened to her. One step closer—hopefully—to setting her free and finding out the truth of what she's done.

I approach Leylani and smile confidently at her. Tila has given me more information about Leylani than any of the other hosts or hostesses—she spoke about her for at least half an hour in the brainloaded conversation, recounting past conversations and what she knew about her. Although Tila was friendly with her co-workers, I don't think she was actually close friends with any of them. I've certainly never met any before. I've never questioned why that was; I assumed she wanted to keep her personal and work life separate. Now I wonder if there was more to it.

It seems like there was always more to it, when it came to my sister.

I smile at Leylani. Below the surface, I'm afraid that she'll immediately realize I'm an imitation of the Echo she knows.

Leylani gives me a hug and a kiss on the cheek. "Echo!" she exclaims. "So good to see you. This is Sarah," she says, introducing her client.

"Won't you join us?" I ask, gesturing to the table where Nazarin lounges. I can see the look of appreciation that Leylani and her client give him. They agree, and follow me to the table. Soon we're joined by others: a host called Boa, and his client, a businessman named Graeme.

At first I'm nervous, but as more time passes and nobody stands up and proclaims me a fake, I gradually relax. I wouldn't say I have fun—drinking SynthGin and chatting with strangers, playing the part of my sister to try and save her life, isn't exactly my idea of a party. However, my confidence that I can pass for Tila is growing, just as Nazarin hoped. When I'm pretending to be my sister, the fear doesn't paralyze me—Tila's confidence seems to seep into me. I sit up straighter, I laugh more, even try my hand at flirting the way I've seen Tila do. While I still feel unsure about my skills at wrapping people around my finger, I can see the effect my new assurance has on others. If Taema was sitting here, awkward and disinterested, it would be a different story—but as Tila, they listen to me, make eye contact, respond and seem to enjoy my company.

When Leylani stands up to go to the ladies' room, I go with her. *Such a cliché*, I think as we totter through the now-crowded club at the top of the TransAm Pyramid, *going to the bathroom to try and bond with another girl.*

Once the door of the employees-only bathroom shuts, Leylani's work smile falls off her face. "Are you all right?" I ask, reaching out and touching her shoulder.

It undoes her. Her face crumples, and she starts to cry. I stare at her, a little lost. What would Tila do? Tila would be warm, both to offer comfort and to gather the information she wanted. I wrap my arms around the young woman, making soothing noises, stroking her silky dark hair. Leylani sobs against my neck, tears falling on my collarbone to trickle to my scar.

"What's wrong?" I ask, rocking her gently back and forth. It feels strange to comfort a stranger, yet I find it calming too. I haven't hugged or touched anyone since they tore Tila from my arms—unless you count sparring with Nazarin or pretending to be his hostess. It seems that I need the close contact almost as much as Leylani does.

"Sorry," she mumbles, pulling away. She wipes her hand across her eyes. "Sorry, sorry, I'm being so silly."

I pass her a plush, pink towel from the railing and she daubs her face and hiccups.

"You're not being silly," I say. "Not at all. Come on, Ley, tell me what's wrong."

Leylani collapses on the settee against a wall, and I perch beside her, hoping nobody else will come in to interrupt us.

"A client's missing, I think," Leylani starts, hesitantly. "I haven't seen him in a few days."

If she's speaking about Vuk, I'll have to tread carefully. "That's not that unusual, right?"

"For most clients, of course not. But . . ."

"He's become more than a client," I finish, my heart sinking. She must see him outside of Zenith, if he only comes here every other month.

"Yeah." She sniffs. "I even went to see him today but no one answered. They say he's gone out of town, but he wouldn't just *leave* without telling me." She turns, her watery green eyes boring into mine. "I've been wanting to talk to you tonight anyway. You saw Vuk on Thursday, didn't you?"

My tongue freezes in my mouth. "Y-yes," I say. The palms of my hands begin to sweat.

She doesn't look away. "Did he seem disappointed that I couldn't come? I really wanted to, but I was . . . really unwell." She looks down and away, and I frown. What is she hiding?

"Yes, he missed you," I say, hoping that was true. The files the police have on Vuk were relatively light, and Tila refused to speak about him. She pretended she'd never met him before, but I knew that was a lie. *Don't think about Tila just now.* "Kept asking about you," I add. "He didn't seem to be interested in my company at all. He—he left early."

Each word hurts to say as she looks at me with such hope. I wonder what Vuk was like. He was meant to work for the Ratel, but that didn't mean he was incapable of kindness. Of love. And now he's gone; supposedly killed by my sister.

"What was wrong with you, on Thursday?" I venture.

"I . . ." She hesitates, but she wants so desperately to tell someone that she blurts her secret in a rush. "I'm pregnant."

I let out my breath in a *whoosh*. "Oh. Wow. Congratulations," I say, my voice flat despite my best efforts, feeling sucker-punched.

"I know you never wanted kids, Echo, but I'm so happy about it. I was going to tell him on Friday, but I haven't been able to find him. I'm so worried. Should I go to the police?"

*The police already know where he is*, I want to say. "I don't know, Leylani. Maybe wait a little longer to see if he shows up. Maybe he had to go on an unexpected business trip, and he'll be back any time now." The lies come surprisingly easy to me, despite my distaste for them. Maybe Tila and I have that in common, after all.

She nods, wiping her eyes. She gives a last sniff and then goes to the mirror to fix her makeup. I sit there silently, waiting for her to finish. When she's done, I give her another hug. She clings close to me.

"It'll be all right," I say to her.

"You can't promise that," she whispers, and I stifle a gasp. It's exactly what Tila said to me on Thursday night.

"No," I say with a sigh, thinking of my sister in jail—with me as her only hope. "I can't promise that at all."

•

When Leylani and I return to the tables, our work faces are back in place. Leylani smiles brightly, kissing Sarah on the cheek before going up to get more drinks. I settle next to Nazarin again, brushing my elbow against his.

He leans close, pressing his hand against my cheek. "Find out anything interesting?" he murmurs in my ear. I smile demurely at him, nodding. He takes another sip of his drink.

We only stay a few more hours, and it exhausts me. I don't know how Tila does it, staying switched "on" for so long, vigilant for every client's needs. I follow the others, offering cigs and drinks. Later on, we dance, Nazarin holding me close, the bass thumping through my metal ribcage, his hands warm on my waist. I speak to Pallua casually, but if she knows anything about what happened on Thursday, she doesn't let it slip.

I've drunk enough SynthGin that by the end of "my" shift, the world is fuzzy around the edges. Sal has told everyone this is Echo's last shift, and I bid everyone sloppy farewells, saying I'll send them pings from China and I'll miss them all. I lean on Nazarin as we take our leave. There are a few raised eyebrows at Echo leaving with a client.

"I hope you've enjoyed your time at Zenith," Pallua says to him as we pass the front counter.

Nazarin reaches into his pocket, grabbing a handful of credits and passing them to her. They disappear into her dress.

"Oh, it's been a cut above," he says to her, slurring his words very slightly, before we saunter out into the night.

•

We take the MUNI back to the safe house. The green light of the tunnels makes me feel ill and I bury my head in Nazarin's shoulder. Whatever his cologne is, it smells nice. He puts his arm around me. Are we still playing a part, or is he genuinely comforting me? I don't know, and in that moment I don't care.

Nazarin has us get off before the safe house stop and take another train too far before we circle back. I have no patience for the circuitous route, but it makes me nervous just the same. Does he really anticipate people trying to follow us? As we trudge up the steps to the pastel Victorian house, I'm exhausted.

When we're inside and Nazarin is making the strongest coffee he can from the replicator, I tell him about Leylani and Vuk. I kick off my heels, leaving them under the table. He's surprised, and a little sad. I suppose it's reassuring to see that even a hardened undercover cop can still feel for a girl who's lost her lover, the father of her child, and doesn't even know he's dead yet. I doubt he felt very sorry for Vuk, though.

The coffee does nothing to wake me up; my eyelids are drooping as I sit at the table. I trudge to the Chair and climb in. I don't even have the energy to clean my teeth or wash the makeup off my face. Nazarin dutifully plugs me in and draws the blanket up over me, and I'm asleep before he leaves the room, to brainload still more information on the Ratel. Instead of dreams it's endless interrogation scenes, reams of numbers, facts and dates settling deep into the folds of my brain.

Flitting behind all the lessons is my never-ending unease. It's almost like I can sense Tila hiding in my mind, just out of sight and reach.

*Do you really think you can find out what happened? Do you really want to know?* she seems to taunt.

And my mind can't answer her.

# NINE

# TILA

That tablet we found didn't last forever, of course. Without charging, something we were unable to do even if we'd known how, the battery only lasted a few months before it died. I felt so sad when the screen went blank for the last time. For a while, I'd had access to a completely different world, and then it was taken away. We were left back in Mana's Hearth, isolated and alone.

Taema even came around. Well, somewhat. She stopped pretending to look away from the tablet, although she never suggested topics to research. We were lucky nobody ever found us with it. We wouldn't have been punished, really, but people would have treated us differently—as if we'd wronged them by showing curiosity about life outside, when life inside was supposed to be so fucking perfect. Disappointment can be worse than anger. They'd also have been wary, wondering what we'd learned. But I knew Mana's Hearth for what it was now, and Taema did too, even if she didn't want to admit it.

It was a prison.

So, you see, this isn't my first time in a cell. I spent the first sixteen years of my life in one, even if it was surrounded by trees and flowers.

I started to notice little things. Then bigger things. How we were kept in the dark about so much. And then there was the Meditation.

I thought it was a normal part of life. That everyone on the outside must do it as well. And some do, but not the way Mana-ma did it. Three times during the week, and then just after Sunday service.

It was always the same. We'd line up, quiet and patient. One by one, we'd each go up to Mana-ma and open our mouths, a little like a Catholic communion. She'd place a small tablet on our tongue. It tasted bitter and earthy. I always wanted to make a face, but forced my features to stay blank like everyone else. The pill dissolved on my tongue, and the world would grow brighter yet hazier at the same time.

We'd lie down in the meadow, or in the church if it was raining. We'd hold hands in one large circle. And we would lucid dream. Mana-ma would guide us through visions so realistic that when I awoke from them, sometimes the real world didn't seem like the true one. The dreams were meant to be calming, with visions of nature.

"A mountain stream," Mana-ma would say, and all of us world work together to create the perfect one.

"A sunrise," she would say next, and the sky of our mind's eye would bloom so bright.

The trouble was that collective dreaming hurt. Every nerve ending would feel as though it were on fire. Tears would leak from all our eyes. We'd cry out as each vision shifted. Yet we still did it. Day after day, week after week. I think she did it to bring us closer together, and because she could. Out there, with no Chairs, no needles, we made our own dreamscapes.

We'd do it on our own, too, without whatever drug she pumped us full of (it wasn't Zeal, I know that much), and it meant we never woke up unable to remember our dreams. It made me and my sister incredible lucid dreamers. I still do it now, especially now that I'm in my cell. I can close my eyes, drift off, and then take off into the sky and fly. It's pretty much the only thing I can ever thank Mana-ma for.

We only had Confession once a week, different days for different people in the Hearth, but it was always just after Meditation. We'd be weak with the comedown and pain and drugs, so we'd tell her everything.

Of course, now the whole ritual seems strange, but at the time it was considered a normal part of our routine. Even with our newly gained knowledge, my sister and I didn't question it too much—until Adam grew sick. Then we couldn't pretend Mana's Hearth was anything other than what it was. What it is.

Adam was born missing the lower half of his left arm, though it never troubled him. I've learned, since escaping the Hearth, that people within are born with a higher chance of disabilities. Like me and Taema. My guess is that it's either because of the bloodline being so intermingled in a small populace, or because the drug Mana-ma gave us for Meditation did something to babies in the womb.

Anyway, Taema and I had both been sweet on Adam. We still hadn't quite figured out how romance would work, with us being conjoined. I guess we thought we'd deal with it when the time came. I think we would have been happy enough sharing Adam, if he liked us.

That might sound odd to some of you, but I don't care. San Francisco has poly relationships aplenty, even if none of them are with conjoined twins. The Hearth would have accepted it just fine.

Adam caught an infection when he was tilling the fields, which most of the men and some of the stronger women took turns with. He cut himself on the plow and didn't wash it properly, or something. It shouldn't have been fatal. If he'd had access to a needle full of magic medicine from the city, he'd have been right as rain in less than an hour. But whatever infection Adam caught was more stubborn than our medicine could handle.

He grew worse, and was moved to the Wellness Cabin. People weren't really allowed to go see him, but Nurse Meadows allowed us to peek in through the window. He was happy to see us. I liked to think he was sweet on us too, but that he liked me best. We brought him some grapes. His leg was all wrapped up and propped up in a sling. He was sweating and pale. I hated to see him like that. But he didn't seem on the brink of death or anything. I figured he'd get better in no time. Just needed some rest.

"How are you feeling?" I remember Taema and I asked at the same time. I hated when we did that. We'd have the exact same tone, timing, everything, as if we were creepy echoes of each other.

Adam smiled weakly at us. "Been better, T-and-T," he said, and we both fought down blushes. I'd always liked the joint nickname, understanding we were two, but also one. And he didn't even know we called each other T when we were alone.

We threw him the grapes, and he tried to catch them in his mouth. He missed, or we missed, more often than they landed in his mouth, and soon the floor of the cabin was littered with green grapes. We collapsed into laughter, clutching our sides.

"You cheered me up and no mistake," he said when we'd run out of grapes. We reached through the window, each of us holding out a hand. He reached out with his one hand and clasped both of ours in it. I remember his skin was so warm. Too warm.

"We'll come visit you every day until you're well," we promised.

But he was gone the next day.

Considering the rudimentary medicine, there weren't actually that many deaths in Mana's Hearth. His was such a shock for Taema and me. We couldn't cope. He was there, and then he wasn't. We'd never see him again. We lay in bed, arms wrapped around each other's shoulders, foreheads pressed against each other, just sobbing. It wasn't fair.

There wasn't a funeral; we didn't really have them in Mana's Hearth. We didn't gather around a corpse and plant it in the ground, or burn it up. I knew they did something with the body, but not exactly what. People mourned, and people would still talk about Adam and others who died and say they missed them; but there'd be no celebration, or wake, or anything like that.

Seems backward too, doesn't it? Looking back now, I see that, but the Hearth doesn't celebrate beginnings or endings. We focused on celebrating the day-to-day life that continued. The passing of seasons had a special meaning for us, but other holidays that lingered on from past religions we had nothing to do with. In the Hearth there were no Christmas trees or Hanukah menorahs.

I tried to convince Taema to get a Christmas tree, the first year we were living in San Francisco, but she didn't want one.

"We're never going to believe in it," she said.

"Does anyone? It's a tree in the living room with pretty lights, and there aren't many Pagans around anymore. Santa Claus and a tree have nothing to do with Jesus. And not a lot of people seem to believe in him here, either."

"Shouldn't we celebrate winter?"

"Why? We don't believe in Mana-ma or her God anymore, either."

She had no answer to that.

Back then, it was almost time to celebrate summer. Taema and I dragged our feet as we made our way to the church, wearing our best dress. It wrapped around our conjoined torso, but we'd taken the time to have it fit around each of our waists. Taema had green ribbon and I had blue. The skirt swished around our legs, edged with hand-stitched lace.

We stood near the back, since the pews were too uncomfortable for us to sit on—the hard wood dug into our sitz bones. We still hadn't gotten over Adam, and we were feeling pretty morose. Nobody even spoke about him—as if he'd shamed us by getting ill enough to die. I looked at the backs of all the heads of the people sitting in the church, and realized a lot of them might not even know that Adam *could* have been saved. And that somehow made his death even sadder.

Adam's death was the first thing that made us really think about leaving. Strange, isn't it? We'd willingly let ourselves be mentally tortured, but that wasn't what made us want to run. It was a boy dying who could have been saved.

Mana-ma was up on the pew at the front of the church. She was the minister, the wife of God, the mayor, everything. She always wore a plain black robe, as if she were mourning all the sin we were surrounded with in the outside world. Everyone in the audience was wearing white with just a little bit of color. Summer was the season of prosperity and warmth—yes, I know, not that it ever really got that cold in winter, compared to, say, Minnesota—and it was a reason to celebrate. The mushroom crops were growing well in the greenhouse and the fields were lush; aside from the small issue of Adam, health was pretty good. No drama. If there ever was anything, it was swept under the rug to be whispered about after lights out.

So we celebrated summer. We sang the old songs, like "Let's

Live for Today," "Everlasting Love" and "Wonderful World, Beautiful People."

None of you reading this will probably have heard of these songs, but I still love them, despite everything. They remind me of the good parts of the Hearth. The bees buzzing, the scent of flowers in the warm breeze, the feel of the water and sand from the lake between my toes. We had a bunch of vinyl, and a record player that they must have replaced part by part over the years. Taema and I sat in our room and listened to the music a lot. I miss music, here in this cold, dark cell.

When we moved to San Francisco, we tracked down a lot of it with some of our early wages, going pale at how much it cost on the original vinyl. So we bought the songs on the modern players, but they didn't sound the same. We still listen to "The Sound of Silence" together, remembering all we've lost.

On the day we celebrated summer, we sang loud and clear, our voices lifting to the rafters, and Mana-ma read from the Good Book.

It was a little different, that particular summer celebration. Mana-ma mentioned Adam. She decided she wanted to say something, so she could. That was the hierarchy; if we were sad and wanted to remember him, we couldn't publicly without her say-so. We couldn't change anything in the Hearth, because we didn't hear the voice of God.

"I know that we do not acknowledge endings often," she said. "Especially at the beginning of such a warm and prosperous season, but God spoke to me last night. He told me that today, we should have a moment to mourn Adam."

There were quiet murmurs in the crowd.

"The loss of Adam reminded me of all the other losses we've had through the years. God told me that they are never truly gone. He wanted me to remind you all that those we have loved

121

have returned to the Cycle, to bloom elsewhere in the universe. Remember that in times of sadness, and remember the light. Every time you see the glory of God and nature, remember that those we loved are still a part of it."

We all bowed our heads for a moment and thought of Adam. Taema and I felt better after that. It was better than pretending it never happened, or never really acknowledging it. Maybe Mana-ma finally realized that.

We went outside and we each rested a hand on the sunflowers now thriving in the summer heat, their yellow faces tilted toward the sky. We thought of Adam.

Afterward, though, we could not escape the meadow and another Meditation. It was the last thing I wanted to do, but there were no excuses granted unless we were ill. We queued, and took our bitter medicine. We lay on our sides. I looked into Taema's eyes. We both already felt the effects of the drugs, our eyes heavy and lidded. Our whole body tingled.

I'm not sure if Mana-ma realized that this was a side effect, but Taema and I were even closer when we took those drugs. I swear I could read her every thought, her every feeling. We all connected, but no one connected more than me and her. It was as if we did become one person. Even Mana-ma noticed.

I sort of wish I could do that again with Taema. It'd be so much easier to explain everything that way, but I'm too afraid of what she would find.

That Meditation was like all the others. Mana-ma's voice rang out, clear and reverberating. The sun beat down on us. We closed our eyes and held hands, and created worlds with our minds inhabited only by us as our bodies stiffened with pain. This time, though, the pain was less, which made the dream sweeter.

It ended up being a turning point. We were all becoming

better at lucid dreaming. The better we were, the less pain we felt. By the time we left the Hearth, Meditation barely hurt at all.

Afterward, it wasn't our day for Confession. As we left the meadow, people paired off. For some, the drug made them incredibly horny afterward. Sex was another way of connecting, a way of expressing God's love, and it was fully supported if all parties were willing. Most marriages were open, though not all. Our parents only had eyes for each other.

Taema and I never did that. We didn't feel ready yet, and no one minded. We wandered through the path into the forest.

The forest was better than any church for me. Nowhere ever felt as holy to me as when Taema and I looked up at those gigantic redwood trees, smelling bark, dirt and leaves, the light filtered through so many shades of green. Mushrooms sprang up beneath the ferns, bright yellow like banana slugs. The sunbeams would catch the swirling motes of dust in the air. Overhead, birds called to each other. I do miss that. In the city there are the skyscrapers of trees, but you know it's manufactured. I miss raw, unfettered nature.

We went to our hollowed-out redwood tree to be surrounded by that perfect smell of charred wood, damp and greenness.

That was when we first felt it.

The irregular jump of our heart in our chests. The painful squeeze. The faintness.

We gasped. We left the tree, and staggered to the forest path. We had to make it back to camp. Our vision blurred and we couldn't breathe. I clutched Taema hard. I was so scared.

"What's wrong?" she wheezed. We could see the roof of the church in the distance. It seemed so far away. "What's happening?" Her head lolled on my shoulder.

"Don't you dare faint on me, Taema," I said, pinching her

cheeks until she squeaked and her eyes opened wide. "If you faint, we're a tortoise on its back. Come on, Taema. Come on."

Somehow, she stayed with me. When we were a little closer to the main town, it felt like we couldn't go any further. We leaned against the fence that lined the path. It was warm, the sun beating down on our hair. I couldn't breathe. Up ahead, we saw a figure. For a second, delirious with pain and lack of oxygen, I thought it was Adam. That he was dead, coming to take us into God's loving arms to begin the Cycle again. But then the figure cleared and I saw that it was Dad. We collapsed, and he started running.

# TEN

# TAEMA

I have a crick in my neck from sleeping in the damn Chair.

I sit up, managing to unplug myself. Again, it looks as though Nazarin turned it off for me a few hours ago, so I could have at least some proper sleep. It's, as ever, not enough.

It's another day of training. Of fighting Nazarin, a quick pause to eat, and then training some more. My muscle mods have responded well to the extra stimuli, and already I can feel that I'm the fastest and strongest I've ever been. After another shower and a giant meal to replenish my energy reserves, I ask Nazarin what we'll be doing today. I crunched the numbers. Tila was arrested Thursday, I agreed to go undercover on Friday, I told the Ratel I'd be missing two shifts on Saturday and I went to Zenith on Sunday. Tila's shifts are Tuesday and Thursday afternoons for two weeks, and then Mondays and Wednesdays the next two. She went to her last Thursday shift before she went to Zenith and everything went to shit. My next shift is next Monday. One week until I'll have to go in as my sister. It doesn't feel like anywhere near enough time, despite how much information I've had crammed into my brain already.

"Today I'm to show you the crime scene," Nazarin says.

That brings me up short. "What?"

"Forensics have finished with it, along with the autopsy.

I had them make a re-creation holograph here. We can view it upstairs."

My eyes rise to the ceiling of their own volition. "Now?"

"Now. If you're ready."

I feel like he's testing me. "All right."

He starts up the stairs and I follow hesitantly. The old wood creaks beneath my feet. At the top, he turns to the right and opens the first door.

"Wait," I say. I suppose I'm not ready. I need a moment. I'm about to see a re-creation of a gruesome crime scene. One that my sister might have created. I've never seen large amounts of blood before. "Will it look . . . real?"

"At first glance, it'll look exactly like the crime scene, down to every last angle and splash, but remember: it's not. It's only a hologram."

A flash of Tila gripping my shirt. *Not my blood.* I rub a hand over my new face, composing myself. "Right. OK." I push open the door and step inside, Nazarin following me.

A transparent plastic bubble lies over most of the open floor, mirroring the one that would have been put over the real scene as soon as the authorities arrived, and just after Tila had apparently fled the scene. A huge bloodstain lies within, wet and glistening, as if it's just been spilled.

I fight down my gag reflex. It is so much blood.

Almost all five liters of it, some of it soaking into the white rug, ruined beyond repair. Just a few days ago, Tila had been in that original room in Zenith, entertaining, joking, flirting, laughing. I can imagine it so clearly now, after being there last night. What happened? What changed?

I want to understand everything—whether she'd known this Vuk she'd attacked, and if so, how, and from where. I move around the bubble, Detective Nazarin watching my every reaction. His brown eyes have flecks of gold in them.

I don't know what he wants me to find—if there is anything to find. There are empty glasses on the replicated coffee table. Most are overturned or shattered, but a wine glass is still upright and unbroken, the imprint of lipstick on its glass. Purple, the same shade I painted my lips last night. I try to remember if it was the same color Tila was wearing on Thursday night. I only saw her for those few moments before they took her away. The make-up, half-smeared across her face by rain, tears and wiped-away blood. It must have been purple lipstick.

"Have they done the autopsy?" I ask.

"Yes. They sent through the report and a possible re-creation. I can show it to you. Are you sure you want to see it?"

I nod, even though watching it is the last thing I want to do.

He takes out his tablet and places it next to him on the sofa. He presses a button and a little holographic display comes up. He could have streamed it right to my implants, but I appreciate him putting it on the tablet instead. It gives me the illusion of distance.

Three-dimensional holograms appear and, unlike the solid-looking crime scene around us, these are as transparent as ghosts.

*Vuk is laughing, knocking back champagne. He has a similar look to Nazarin—bulky and muscular, with short-buzzed hair. But where Nazarin's features are strong, Vuk's are almost delicate, the features too small for his face. He sets down the glasses, chatting with his friends. Tila perches next to him, her legs crossed, as she sips from a wine glass. It's a re-creation from the infrared sensors at Zenith, so their expressions are only the bare minimum—a huge smile or no emotion at all. One by one, the other people leave, until Vuk and Tila are alone.*

*The image wavers. Ostensibly this is where Tila and Vuk speak, but the program does not know what was actually said that night. Normally, the cameras in Zenith would, but in the Zeal lounges, clients can pay extra for privacy. When the image clears again, Tila holds a knife. Vuk turns back to her with the drink and she attacks him. He manages to fend her off. She cuts him in a glancing blow to his wrist, which accounts for the blood splatters to the left of the large bloodstain. She manages to stomp on his instep and her knee flies up between his legs. He crumples, and Tila doesn't hesitate. The knife flashes and goes beneath his ribcage and up, right to his heart. She rips the knife down, widening the wound, and Vuk bleeds out on the floor. She has no expression on her face. She bends down to the coffee table in front of her, driving the knife into the wood.*

The holographic image goes dark.

I'm shivering, despite the perfect temperature of the room. It can't be true. There must be some mistake. The infrared sensors were tampered with. It wasn't actually my sister. It was someone else. Something. I can't believe that Tila would do that, with no hesitation, with such precision and skill. There has to be more to it. There has to. Because if not, then I have no idea who that woman is I just watched kill someone in cold blood.

"That's only one way it could have happened, right?" There's a note of pleading in my voice, and Nazarin looks at me with a hint of pity. I turn away, not wanting to see it.

"Right. From infrared we know there were two people in the room, but their body movements weren't mapped. This is their best guess as to the sequence of events, judging by the wounds, but the order could be off, and we have no context."

I ask myself, in reality, how different could it be? Someone stabbed Vuk and ripped him open that night, and no one else was in the room but my sister. He didn't do it to himself. I push the doubt away. It's too much. I've never been more thankful for Mana-ma's training. "What more can you tell me about Vuk?" I ask. The information I have on him from the police download is scant at best.

"Pretty sure he took out at least one person a week for the Ratel, between his other duties. With all his schmoozing, he could gain access to places many members of the Ratel couldn't. For all that, though they trusted him, I doubt he was in their very inner circle, though he was hoping to be. He'd had a lot of mods and upgrades to his body, according to the autopsy." He pauses to scroll through the medical chart. "Muscle implants and nanobots, almost an entirely new face, a prosthetic hand with skin grafts, new teeth. He even changed the shape of his ears. So whoever he was before, he wanted to make sure we'd never know, not even in death."

I swallow. "Can I . . . go into the crime scene for a closer look?" I ask, my mouth dry.

"Yes." His eyes go distant as he accesses the controls with his ocular implant, and the bubble pops. Carefully tiptoeing around the blood, I ignore the body, as that's not what catches my attention. I look closer at the coffee table.

My fingertips hover over the items on the table.

"Can I move things?" I ask.

"Yeah."

I reach out and move the glass with the lipstick print. I can't feel it. It's like I'm holding air. There's a chip on the rim. It had fallen over, but Tila had put it to rights before she left. Below where the glass was is a hasty carving of five points. Next to it are a few other scratches. The glass falls from my hand and slides back to its original position on the coffee table.

"She didn't stab the coffee table. She carved it," I whisper.

Nazarin looks over the crime scene notes. "They noticed those. Five points. That's the symbol for the Hearth, isn't it?"

"Yes." I haven't seen that simple design in a long time. Why did she leave it here? She hates the Hearth as much as I do.

"We couldn't make any sense of these, though," Nazarin says, nodding toward the dashes and dots, almost like Morse code. "No language or code we could figure out."

I shrug, not wanting to tell him, looking at other things.

"You understand those markings," he says. "I can tell."

I debate lying, and then decide it's pointless. "It's an alphabet Tila and I made up when we were children, so we could write notes to each other nobody else would understand."

"She knew you'd see it." Detective Nazarin scratches the stubble at his chin. The muscles of his bicep flex under his shirt, and I'm reminded of how much larger and stronger than me he is. He's suspicious. And why shouldn't he be?

The fact is, I'm just as flummoxed. Why would Tila leave me a sign? And why *that* as a sign? She had no way to anticipate how all this would play out . . . did she?

I feel sick. I back away from the blood and the scratched coffee table, breathing loudly, and move to the bay window, looking out over the cloudy San Francisco day. The sailboats are coming into port, the hovercars leaving and arriving the Embarcadero to and from their sundry destinations. The sun is setting, and everything glows that soft pink and purple of approaching dusk.

Detective Nazarin glides to my side, silent. I press my forehead against the cool glass of the window. Throughout it all, my mechanical heartbeat has barely quickened. Somewhere out there, Tila is in her cell, and her heartbeat is more or less in time with mine.

"What does it say?" Nazarin asks. He's close to me now, but his voice is gentle, and his breath puffs on the back of my neck, smelling of spearmint. But the gentleness is a ruse— underneath he's all steel.

I could lie. Tell him it means something else, and they'd never be able to follow the path any further. Then I could try and do it on my own. But I wouldn't be able to, would I? If Tila is involved with the Ratel, then I don't know the first thing about how to deal with them.

Nazarin does.

"'MIA,'" I say, still turned to the window. My breath mists the glass. With a fingertip, I write the letters in our secret alphabet.

"And what's that? Missing in Action?"

"It's not a what. It's a who. Mia. The woman who took us in after we left the Hearth."

"Why do you think she wrote that name? Where can we find her?"

I shrug, wrapping my arms around myself. I want to go home and close my eyes and wake up and have everything fixed.

"She's an apostate of the Hearth. Like us. She got Tila into hostessing. Used to be one of the best in the city. But now she's a Zealot. We can find her at the Mirage in the Mission district."

"That's a shithole."

"Yeah. But the Ratel haven't tampered with the Zeal there and replaced it with Verve?" I ask.

"Not that I know. Fuck." He rubs his hand over his shaved head. "If they have, it's dangerous to go there. Someone could be watching."

I say nothing.

"She'll be there now?"

"She's always there."

"Then let's go."

Nazarin accesses his implant, and the crime scene hologram disintegrates into nothing.

·

When people think of Zeal, they don't think of the dark, dingy Zealot lounges. They think of brainloading. They think of the bright, shiny lounges in the nice parts of the city, a place for people to go to let out a little steam and return to the real world, refreshed. They think of the drug that keeps the city largely crime-free, and provides a little fun along the way, all thanks to Sudice, Incorporated. The company I used to work for, along with so many other people in San Francisco. I've never thought before about how many tendrils the company has within the city, and how much the government owes it for its many inventions.

Those dark Zealot lounges, though; those, most of the city tries not to think about, and they do a very good job of forgetting. They don't sit and imagine those who might be the worst criminals, serial killers or rapists or abusers, locked in the Zealscapes, too out of it when they come out to think about anything except plugging in again. The people who go there have dreams so dark they don't dare go to the beautiful lounges. They say the government can't properly eavesdrop on dreams, not in great detail—but not everyone believes that. So they go underground.

Mirage is one of the worst Zealot lounges, and that's where we head in the hope of finding Mia.

Mia. I haven't seen her in a year and a half. She took us in when we left the Hearth. She was like a second mother, or an aunt. We lived with her for years—the only other Hearth apostate, or at least the only one we met. We loved her, and she loved us, but she was always troubled. In and out of the nicer Zealot lounges, but when her Zealscapes became darker, police showed up at our door. She cleaned up her act until she almost seemed like the Mia we knew when we first came to her.

After the last time she relapsed, and disappeared to an off-grid Zealot lounge, both Tila and I washed our hands of her—at least, I thought we both did. It wasn't easy, but I couldn't watch her self-destruct. She turned down all my efforts of help, of therapy, of rehab. There was no going back for her. Not this time.

I still felt guilty about that, but I couldn't help her if she wasn't willing to help herself.

Nazarin thankfully has the night off with the Ratel, though he'll be there all day tomorrow. There's still a chance we could be recognized if the Ratel have visited Mirage before. We're both wearing masks, like a temporary visit to a flesh parlor. They fit perfectly over our features, light enough not to be noticed but enough to trick the camera drones, and we can peel them off when we wish. There's a small chance the orderlies might notice, if they look too close, but so many there are overworked and underpaid, I think we'll be all right. My mask itches.

We take the MUNI down to the Mission district. By the time we arrive, night has fallen. The streets here are full of wavering holographic ads. They assault the senses as we walk down the street: men and women wearing next to nothing, displaying their wares, licking their lips suggestively and calling out to us what they're offering. Loud, tinny music blares from each of them in a cacophony. If anyone still had epilepsy these days, they'd have to avoid this whole neighborhood. I feel the beginnings of a headache flaring at my temples. Shielding my eyes with my hand, I make my way through the glare, Detective Nazarin at my side.

The ads grow darker, more reds and blacks and deep blues. They flicker, leaving the streets in darkness but for the street lights. There's no sense of welcome. The people who come here want only the dreams they're too afraid to dream in a proper Zeal lounge.

Mirage is at the end of the street. An ad of a palm tree in a desert ripples over the front of the building. A stone sphinx wavers in the distance, and as we watch, it opens its mouth and yawns before gazing at us mysteriously. The windows are shuttered. I don't want to enter.

In that building I know there are dozens of people strapped into Chairs, wires poking from their veins, their eyelids twitching as they live out their dreams.

I wonder what causes some people to favor more violent dreams than others. Some say that people who are predisposed to crime have different brains, like damage to the prefrontal cortex. That means that the two hemispheres of the brain can't communicate properly, and aggressive impulses are in overdrive. Ticking time bombs.

I never bought that, but it's the endless question of nature versus nurture. Free will versus predestination.

Sudice developed Zeal at first as a virtual reality game in which to act out fantasies. They discovered the extra benefit by accident, that if people acted out violent urges, when they came out, vicious tendencies were dampened. The neural pathways are reworked, suppressing the amygdala, or the prehistoric "lizard" brain we've had since we crawled out of the ocean. It worked on those with so-called violent brains, and those without. Overall, people were calmer, happier. Perfect citizens. Zeal lounges became all the rage.

Sometimes I wondered what Mana-ma would have to say about all that.

The first time doing Zeal is a rite of passage, one my sister and I missed. When we tried it later, it was anticlimactic. All the dreams seemed but pale echoes of what we saw during Meditation back at the Hearth, or when we closed our eyes each night.

"The government and Sudice are both terrified of Verve, aren't they?" I ask.

"Yes."

"The same drug, but stronger, more powerful, a better high and people wake up not calmer, but angrier. More prone to lash out. San Francisco has peace now, but how peaceful would it be if people weren't kept dampened by Zeal?"

I wonder if I'm pushing too far, saying that. It sounds critical of the government, his employers. Nazarin only smiles sadly. "I don't want to find out, do you?"

I don't say the other thing I've wondered, from all the information I've brainloaded: what happens if the government gets hold of Verve? Dangerous as it is, it lets people see into others' dreams remotely. And what if there's more it can do?

"How did the Ratel develop Verve?" I ask.

"We think it's Ensi himself who designed it. The genesis is from Zeal. He took it and twisted it somehow. The man is a genius."

"And where did he come from?"

"That's the question, isn't it?"

"How deep do the Ratel run?" I ask out loud, more to myself than to Nazarin, but he answers.

"Deep. They've got their little tendrils everywhere. Right now, in a way we're fighting a losing battle. Getting rid of the Ratel completely will likely never happen. What we have to do is have the upper hand, choke off their stronghold before Verve becomes too widespread."

I understand. "And the easiest way to do that is to get to Ensi. Cut off the head."

He gives me a sidelong glance. "Exactly. This is the best chance we have."

A sentence from one of the captured men in my brainloads comes back to me: *There are some who don't agree with Ensi. Some who want him dead.* It had seemed obvious to me—of course every organization has those who resent their leaders. The Hearth taught me that. But now I wonder if there's more. "Unrest?"

"Yeah. That's my primary goal. I'm seeing who might be thinking of causing trouble and gently encouraging them, but in a way they don't suspect me as the cause. Division will make it easier to find a chink in their organization. Not easy, let me tell you."

I rub my temples, the flashing lights of Mirage getting to me. "This keeps getting more and more complicated."

"That's how I've felt ever since I went undercover. The deeper you go, the crazier everything seems to be."

"But you've still never met Ensi."

"No. I'm too much of a Knight. There's an upcoming party they've invited me to, though, this weekend. He's meant to be there. After two years, I might finally meet him."

"I'm not sure how much I'll be able to help with all of this."

"To be honest, a lot of it depends on how far Tila has delved into the inner circle. The fact she rose to working in the Verve lounge so quickly is impressive, but it's difficult to see the bigger picture. Sometimes she seems to be a relatively little fish, despite being a dreamsifter, but other times I suspect she's almost reached upper management."

A shiver runs down my spine, and my flesh breaks out into goosebumps. Tila not only involved with the Ratel, but in deep? Without telling me, without asking for my help. Why has she done this in the first place? What does she hope to gain? Money? Tila's never struck me as greedy, not in that way. What, though, do I really know about her? She's been living a whole different life. I bite back a sob.

"Let's go see what this Mia can tell us, if anything," he says.

"And if she's plugged in, we have to go in? Instead of waiting for her to come out?" That's the part that gives me the biggest pause. I don't want to go into her dreams and see what her deepest, darkest desires are. I had a secondhand view, watching her relapse, and that was awful enough. Zealscapes can be unpredictable—especially, I hear, in these off-grid lounges. For some, they're almost like the real world. For others, they're twisted nightmares. I fear Mia's will be more like the latter.

"Depends on how long she has left. If she has more than twelve hours, we can't wait that long."

"And if we do go into the Zealscape, you think I'll be able to lucid dream," I say, looking nervously at the entrance to Mirage. Most of the time, when people plug into other people's dreams, they're carried along helplessly by the other person's fantasy. They can't really change much. It's why most people do it alone. Nazarin hopes if I can lucid dream I might be able to affect things, at least a little. The problem is, lucid dreaming might not always change the reality in a way you'd like.

"Yes. This serves two purposes. Question Mia in the Zealscape, if we must, and see how you fare within the dreams. I'm certain you'll be able to manipulate things, judging by how you've integrated the brainload."

"Maybe." I'm noncommittal. And frightened. Years of training at the Hearth—it should be easy. I have flashbacks to those shared dreams. I can almost taste the bitterness of the drug as Mana-ma gently placed it on my outstretched tongue.

"Will it hurt?" I ask. I remember so much pain. And mental pain is so much more painful than the physical.

"It hasn't hurt me."

"And you haven't become addicted?" That's another fear. I only tried Zeal once or twice, but it was years ago. What if I've changed since? What if I go into the Zealscape and come out of it to discover my brain is flawed and that I'll want nothing more than to go back in? It's a stupid fear, perhaps. I've seen scans of my own brain. I know all synapses fire normally. That doesn't mean I couldn't still love the violence. That doesn't mean I couldn't grow to need it.

"No," he says. "I'm not addicted. But I think about the Zealscape, sometimes. The power. The freedom. I think anyone who's tasted it does, even if their mind isn't hardwired for violence."

Nazarin's been undercover for a while. I'm sure he's had to commit violence, and not just as a false member of the Ratel. As a detective, he'll have seen things, done things that would be difficult to forget.

"OK," I say, squaring my shoulders. "Let's do this."

My nervousness doesn't fade as we walk toward the door. I've never been in a Zealot lounge, and I've no idea what to expect. I wonder what Mia knows. If anything. I can't help but wonder if Tila wrote Mia's name on the table to send me off the path and keep me out of harm's way. It's the sort of thing she would do.

Nazarin knocks on the door and exchanges words with the guard behind the hatch, a man with a face that's lost a fair number of fistfights in its time. I can't hear what they're saying, but the man looks me up and down, assessing me. Does he think I'm an addicted Zealot? The door opens with a metallic groan.

"Come on," Nazarin says, holding out his hand. With the barest hesitation, I take it and duck inside.

The Zealot lounge is dark, with red lights tracing the path to the back. The front is the waiting room, but dim enough to obscure faces. Zealot lounges do not scan your VeriChip at the door. You pay with actual coins. Anonymity guaranteed.

We wait our turn. Nazarin goes up to the woman behind the bulletproof glass of the counter. She's chewing gum, blowing bubbles and popping them wetly. They murmur through the intercom, too low for me to hear. The addicts near me twitch in the darkness. Their fetid breath floats through the air, their fingers spasm on the fabric of their clothes. A woman leans close to me and smells my neck.

"You're new to this," she whispers. She's lost most of her teeth. Her glazed eyes stare at me above dark bruises.

"First time," I manage, fighting the urge to lean away.

"I don't know whether to be envious or sorry for you," the woman says. She could be my age, but she looks older. Her skin hangs from her wasted muscle. Her hand clutches the coins for her trip.

I lean away from her, wondering what this woman does in her Zeal-fueled dreams. I'm sure if I knew, it'd make the hair on the back of my neck stand on end.

Nazarin returns. "Come on," he says. "We're up."

"It's my turn," the woman says, but weakly, as if all her fight has fled. She stares at the wall. I can feel the other Zealots' eyes on me, even if I can't make out their faces.

"I'll see you in my dreams soon enough," the woman says, her voice distant.

"I don't doubt it," I say, shivering.

I stand, and Nazarin takes my elbow, leading me through the dark.

An orderly is there, wearing a reassuringly white lab coat. It's less comforting when I'm close enough to see it's grimy about the cuffs. "The woman you wish to speak to is in too deep to take her out," he says.

My muscles stiffen.

"How long until she can come up for air?" Nazarin asks.

The orderly's eyes unfocus as he checks his ocular implant. "Fourteen hours at the absolute minimum."

Shit.

"We don't want to wait that long." A sly passing of credits from Nazarin's hands to the white-gloved orderly's.

"Like I say, I can't take her out without killing her, and I doubt you want that."

That's an option? Good God.

"But I can put you guys in a shared dream with a small dose, if you want," the orderly continues. "You'll have to deal with a lot of crossover, but you should be able to speak to her if you really go for it."

I knew this was a likely outcome, but I'd been hoping to avoid it, yet it all has a feeling of inevitability. Deep down, I think I knew I'd have to visit Mia's dreams tonight.

Nazarin senses my dismay and leans close. "The sooner we interrogate her, the sooner we can get to the bottom of this. You can find out what Tila was up to."

*Cheap ploy, Nazarin, but effective.* "Is it dangerous?" I whisper.

"Of course it is. But you'll be fine. You'll be in control."

"You're lying." I follow him down the corridor anyway.

•

Within minutes, I'm strapped into the Chair. It's different from a brainloading Chair. Bulkier. More wires. It feels like a cage.

We're in the same room as Mia, in Chairs on either side of

her. Nazarin paid extra for privacy, so the fourth Chair is empty. I turn to look at Mia. She looks so small, with so many wires poking out of her arms and neck. People who sign up for long trips have to be catheterized. Her mouth is pulled into a faint grimace, showing yellowing teeth. The wrinkles in her brown skin are deeper, the cheekbones more prominent. She's wasting away, like so many Zealots have before her, and so many others will. She doesn't eat enough, doesn't drink enough, and eventually, her body will give up. The government doesn't step in here, though they're meant to care for each and every citizen. How many people truly realize this is what's happening, right under their noses? Why isn't anything being done?

It's a very small percentage of people who become addicted to Zeal on their first try. Those that do come out and are completely changed by what they've seen. What they've done. They can't wait to plug in again and be who they are in their dreams. Real life can cease to have any meaning. If they have money, they fritter away their savings. If they run out, they receive unemployment, and the amount they receive is just enough to keep them in Zealot lounges. They spend enough time in the real world to eat some NutriPaste, perhaps clean themselves, go to the bathroom, and then they're back to their nearest Zealot lounge, huddled in the darkness, waiting for the cold prick of the syringe to send them back to dreamland.

I still can't help fearing I'll like the dreams so much that I become someone who can commit murder. Someone like Tila could be.

*No. Don't think about that.* But that re-creation of a holographic Tila stabbing Vuk, wrenching the blade up into his heart, haunts me just the same.

The orderly puts on a mask. It's just for show—for all of Zeal's dangers, there's no risk of infection, even in a shithole like Mirage. He plugs us into the slots on the wall, starts up the program.

"Ready?" Nazarin asks. Lying supine, his face doesn't look so harsh. His features look almost tender.

"Ready as I'll ever be," I say.

The orderly has connected the wires on our Chairs, so that we'll feed into Mia's program when the drug hits us. Couples and such will do it sometimes, so that they can revel in the Zealscape together. The thought makes me sick. "Sweet dreams," says the orderly.

I feel the prick of the syringe.

Then we're gone.

## ELEVEN

# TAEMA

I don't like the inside of Mia's head.

Everything in the dream world has a soft quality of washed-out gray and muted reds, blues and browns. I'm standing outside a building, gazing up at its broken windows. It's a scaled-down version of the tower complexes in San Francisco, all steel, concrete and glass, five stories tall instead of fifty. The sky is dark, the clouds bruised black, blue and purple. Warm wind blows my hair, and the air smells like a storm is about to break. I'm wearing the mini-dress I wore to Zenith, for some reason, and the straps of leather dig into my legs. I can see, hear and feel everything, but it's dampened in the way of dreams.

"Nazarin?" I call out, but there's no answer.

Up above, the angry, frozen sky rumbles. Rain begins to fall, and my dress is soaked, my hair plastered to my head. Like Tila on Thursday night. Shivering and alone, I go into the house. Mia will be inside. Some part of me feels it.

The lobby of the minuscule apartment complex is empty. Crumpled leaves on the ground crunch beneath my feet. I climb the stairs, following the vague prickle of intuition that leads me to the top floor.

I hear the screams first.

The door opens for me into a barren room as long as the

building. The concrete floor is cracked, the paint on the walls peeling off in layers. Exposed wires hang from the ceiling, and a flickering overhead light casts a harsh light on the two figures before me.

One is Mia. She's strong here, as she no longer is in real life. Her bare arms ripple with muscle, the fitted jumpsuit hugging her full breasts and thighs. Her hair is long, like it was in Mana's Hearth before she left when Tila and I were eight. But she is a long way away from the gentle woman in soft dresses that I recall. This Mia's face is twisted in rage and bloodlust, and she's wielding a scalpel stained with blood.

I shudder, my hand involuntarily going to the scar beneath my dress. Mia's tool falls, and she bends over. My eyes finally rest on the other figure.

It's Mana-ma.

Our former leader has collapsed to the ground. She's alive, breathing hoarsely. The black robe she wears is heavy with blood. On her back, she gapes at the cracked ceiling, her mouth opening and closing. Mia has cut out her tongue. It lies next to her like a dead fish.

I cry out, stumbling away.

Mia pauses in her terrible work, her eyes meeting mine. Her face goes slack in surprise.

"Taema."

I'm dressed as Tila. I have her face, and her tattoo snaking down my thigh. Despite this, Mia still recognizes me.

"Why are you here?" she asks. "You've never been in my dreams before."

That's a comfort, I guess. She's never wanted to kill me. Mia's covered in blood, and the broken shell of a replica of the woman who leads Mana's Hearth cowers beneath her.

"Mia. Something's happened to Tila. I need your help."

"You're . . . not part of the dream?" Mia seems confused.

Mana-ma gives a strangled gasp, more of a high wheeze. Without batting an eyelid, Mia brings down the scalpel into Mana-ma's neck. The colors of the warehouse grow brighter, sharper, until they're hypersaturated. I step back, horrified.

Without realizing what I'm doing, I focus on that mental state I found while in Meditation at the Hearth. The clear, calm stillness. "Stop," I say. Mia's eyes widen, but her hand jerks back, taking the scalpel with her.

"You don't tell me what to do! Don't make me do what I don't want to!" she shrieks.

*Did* I make her do that?

Blood spurts out of Mana-ma, and once the blood—the reddest blood I've ever seen—leaves her body, it turns from scarlet to black. The dark oil rises, covering Mana-ma's corpse, and then the figure collapses into a puddle. It reminds me uncomfortably of the spread of blood of the crime scene re-creation.

The scalpel is still in Mia's hands. I hold up my own hands, spread wide, to look unthreatening. "No, I'm not part of the Zeal," I say. "They couldn't pull you out, so I took a small dose and came in."

Mia shakes her head. "I don't know if I can believe that. They all say they're real when they're not. Either way, you shouldn't have come. You're too innocent for the Zealscape. Especially mine." Her face creases in a grin, and I take another step away. She is utterly transformed from the woman who took us in just after the surgery, when we were weak as kittens and just as innocent in the ways of the world. I remember the way she pushed my hair back from my face, kissed my forehead goodnight. She took us to museums on weekends, patiently explaining so many things to us that we didn't understand. Mia, my second mother in many ways, is looking at me like she wants nothing more than to stick that scalpel in my eye.

She shakes her head again, mystified. "Can't believe a girl who escaped the Hearth would ever step foot somewhere where they mess with your brain. Didn't you have enough?"

"Didn't you?" I counter.

That same sly grin. A gesture at where Mana-ma's corpse had been. "Do you really think I actually escaped the Hearth? It's always here." She taps her temple, and then considers me. "Maybe it's still in you, too."

My breath hitches. I don't want to talk about the Hearth. "Tila's in prison. She's been accused of murder."

That penetrates through her Zeal-fog. "Out there?"

"Yes. Real murder. I'm trying to prove she didn't do it."

I have to cling to the hope that she didn't do it, even if the crime scene re-creation left so little room for doubt.

"So why come here?" Mia asks.

"She . . . wrote your name at the crime scene. She led me straight to you. You tell me why, because I have no idea."

She shrugs, the scalpel flashing in the light. "Don't know."

Even in this twisted dream world, I know she's lying. I can't read her as well as Tila, but we still lived with her for years. I heard her, thrashing in the dark, on the other side of our bedroom wall, unable to forget the Hearth when she closed her eyes. She never told us about her dreams, tried to hide them as long as she could as we adjusted to our new, separate lives. It was because of Mia that Tila and I became halfway productive members of society just before she ceased to be one herself.

"Bullshit," I say.

She cocks her head, but she's unnerved. Her eyes dart to the side, the tip of her tongue snaking over her dry lips.

"Why did she really send me to you?" I ask. Outside the

strange rain grows heavier, thrumming against the window. A flash of green lightning casts Mia in a sickly glow, making her look for a moment like the drug addict she is in the real world.

The black oil bubbles and rises, molding into a new figure. It's Tila.

She's wearing her favorite dress, green like the otherworldly lightning outside, or snake scales. She looks at me and holds out her arm.

"T," she calls. I can feel the steady thump of my mechanical heart beneath my metal breastbone.

"This isn't mine." Mia's voice is harsh. "You're affecting my dream world now. With your own memories and fears."

"How? I don't feel like I'm doing anything." Shared people aren't meant to be able to change the dreamscape much at all if someone has plugged in first. If it's someone else's dream, Zealscapes are meant to be like reading a script, or watching a film on a wallscreen, except with more sensory detail. I didn't concentrate, like I did to have Mia pull the scalpel away. I've never experienced anything like this.

"Fuck if I know. I never share my dreams. I'm always here on my own." She's shifty, though, her shoulders hunched. She's keeping something back. Mia holds out the scalpel. "Take this. Maybe you have to exorcise her."

I can feel her fear spiraling from her, belying her blasé words. She doesn't like that I've changed her dream, much as she didn't like it when I caused her to pull the scalpel out of the Mana-ma apparition.

My fingers close around the blade, but I don't harm Tila. How could I? How could Mia think that I would, even hopped up full of Zeal?

"Tell me why Tila sent me to you," I say.

Mia rocks back on her heels, shaking her head. "Get rid of

her first. You're ruining it. This isn't my *dream!*" Her last word rises to a shriek, the whole room tingeing red with her anger.

The anger infects me. It pulses through me, as insistent and inevitable as my mechanical heartbeat. Mia's not giving me what I want. I need answers.

Tila's apparition gazes at me impassively. I ignore it. The irrational anger bursts and I rush Mia instead, knocking her down. She feels almost insubstantial beneath my hands, as if I see her healthy self but feel the wasted version of her that's plugged into the Chair. I hold the cold scalpel to her throat. Mia swallows, and the blade nicks her neck, a small trickle of blood running down the column of her throat to pool at the hollow of her clavicle.

"Tell me, or I'll make both your dreams and your reality a living nightmare. I'm working with people who can make life very difficult for you." It's a half-bluff, but it's the only card I have.

"You're working with them, too?" she gasps. I press the scalpel slightly harder and she winces. I don't understand how pain translates to her inert body on the gurney, but she's scared, and that's enough.

"Working with who?"

"The Ratel."

"You're working with *them?*" I ask, incredulous.

"N-no!" Her wide eyes dart to Tila's apparition. "*Her.*"

"You think Tila was working with them? Tell me!" The anger still pulses through me, a roiling, dangerous thing. Have I ever been this furious?

"I didn't mean to tell him," Mia whispers. "I didn't want to."

"Tell who what?"

"About Tila. It's my fault." She begins to gasp, almost choking in the intensity of her sobs. I feel a twinge of pity for her, for who she used to be, but I squash it down as low as it'll go. I press the scalpel slightly harder.

"Tila found something out, and I got scared and told him. He'd never have known. All for a steady supply of Verve. I fucking hate myself. I can never escape him. Never escape. Never." After that she can't say anything more, sobbing so much that she hiccups. The drug is also taking a stronger hold, the lucidity fading. Her back arches and her eyes roll up in her head.

"Stay with me, Mia!" I shake her. "How did they give you Verve?"

Her eyes half-focus, and she laughs maniacally. "God, you don't get it, do you? This isn't a Zealscape. Why do you think you could infect my dream and change things so easily? This is Verve."

I rock back. If her Zeal has been spiked by Verve in this lounge, that means the Ratel have been there. Fuck. Fuck. Do they know? Are they coming for us, even now, for mine and Nazarin's bodies, prone and helpless as newborns?

"Why did Tila send me to you, Mia?" I ask again. "Did Tila tell you anything? I need to know. If you care even a little for us, please, *please* tell me, or we're both good as dead."

"She found the link," the figure of Tila says, twisting her torso back and forth, child-like, the green sequins on her dress twinkling. "The link that no one is to know. He is the red one, the fair one, the handsome one. From Earth, and now he goes back to the Earth. Ashes to ashes. Dust to dust. Changing faces like kaleidoscopes." My false sister laughs, high and insane. It's almost exactly what Sal said Tila said in Zenith, just after he found her with Vuk's body.

As I recall the crime scene, it starts to blossom around the figure of my sister. Blood seeps up from the floorboards, the coffee table grows like a mushroom, the broken glass scatters.

The colors are so bright and saturated, the real world seems a pale echo. Tila reaches her hands up to cover her ears, rocking back and forth, her mouth open in a silent scream.

"This is you, too," Mia whispers, watching it with awe.

"Go away!" I shout at the blood and glass. It stays, feeding on my anger.

Nothing happens. The anger and fear threaten to choke me. I have to push them away.

I let out a breath and close my eyes. I try to let go of the urge for violence. I manage to find that small center for self Mana-ma always pushed us toward. I thrust all emotion away. Slowly, so slowly, the crime scene fades and disappears. I feel the briefest flash of triumph before I turn my attention to Mia. I no longer have the same desire to hurt her. Thank God.

"Tila's words make no sense," I tell her. False Tila quoted from the Bible, not Mana-ma's Good Book. Once, that would have offended me. Now I grind my teeth in frustration, gripping Mia's shoulder harder, until if this were reality she'd bruise.

"Who's that man you were talking about?"

Mia starts to shudder. She's taken control of her Vervescape again, but she's unstable and it reflects in the world around us. The ground cracks and shudders. Lightning blasts outside the glass window. Thorned trees grow from the cracks in the concrete, slinking along the ground and up toward the ceiling. The trees bear fruit, but in horror, I realize they're small humans, like thorny mandrakes. They reach their barbed hands toward us, dark mouths open in silent screams. Little red lights pulse from the bottoms of their throats, as red as Mia's anger. I try to push them back, but they're too strong.

The scalpel disappears from my hand, and Mia wriggles away from my grasp. False Tila is trapped by looping roots. She twists and turns, trying to free herself.

"Taema!" Her eyes bore right into me, and I can't help but think that she is my actual sister, here somehow in this nightmare.

The demons grasp Tila, their wooden roots digging into her flesh. Black blood seeps from her wounds. Next to me, Mia cackles. She's euphoric, fully caught in the throes of the drug.

I struggle on the floor to free my sister—even though rationally I know she's not real, I can't leave her. My hands are soon slick with dark blood. Mia attacks the mandrake-demons, plunging knives deep into their bellies until the lights in their throats go out.

The faces of the figures are changing and with a sickening drop of my stomach, I realize that many of them are the faces of the men and women from Mana's Hearth. *Changing faces like kaleidoscopes.* Is this what Mia meant? She still hates so many people there, all these years later. She never told us why she left the Hearth, and it was never spoken of while we were growing up in the redwood grove. We'd thought it rude to ask.

I've seen the darkness that threatened to overwhelm Mia, as she tried to escape Zeal only for its tendrils to delve deep into her again. Now Verve has her in its grasp, and it's worse. Will she wake up, angry and enraged, still thirsting for blood?

Clutching the facsimile of my twin, I can't help but fear that maybe I missed the darkness in her, too. Or in myself, because aren't we the same?

Mia comes back to herself, just a little. "You should thank your sister."

"Why?"

"She's protecting you. Or trying to."

"I don't need protecting." Even though it's a dream, my body reacts as it would in the real world. My ears feel like I'm going through a tunnel at high speed, and my vision darkens to a little point. I am filled with more rage than I've ever felt. I want to hurt Mia with that same, shocking intensity I felt before. My sister came to her, confided in her, and Mia ratted her out to someone. If it's the Ratel, then my cover is blown before it's even begun. If it's not the Ratel, then we have someone else to worry about. Perhaps it was Vuk, and that's why my sister killed him. To keep him silent.

I know nothing.

Because of this broken woman, my sister might die. Maybe she killed, but would she have been put in that situation if Mia had been stronger?

There's still no proof of my sister's innocence or guilt, I have to remind myself. The forensics report was only one way it could have happened. She might have had to defend herself. I still cling to the hope that there was someone else in that room. Somehow. But if she killed to protect me . . . how would I ever be able to accept that? Especially if I can't save her?

My false sister is dead. The blood flows until she's enveloped in the black, oily muck. The demons with the faces of the people we grew up with open their mouths impossibly wide, the coals in their throats glowing as they devour her. Our parents are among them. I see their twisted faces slurping up the muck in euphoric delight.

Screaming, I launch myself up and leap on Mia again. She has another scalpel in her hand. I manage to dodge it, knocking it to the floor. The demons pull on my ankles but I ignore them. My hands are around her throat and I'm squeezing, squeezing, squeezing. Mia gasps, purpling beneath me. I can't calm down enough to try and affect the dream in any other way.

"Lucid dreaming, my ass," I gasp.

If this was a straight Zealscape, I know that if I killed her in the dream, she'd wake up, strapped to the Chair, knocked out of her hallucination. That's dangerous enough. But I have no idea what happens in a Vervescape. What if it's more of a shock to her weakened body, and I kill her in the real world?

I should care. But my hands don't slacken.

Strong hands grip my shoulders, yanking me back. "Let go of her," Nazarin says. "Let go. You've learned all you can from her."

His deep voice snaps me from the iron vise of Verve. My hands jerk from her throat, though a red imprint remains.

"It's the drug," he says. "Happens to everyone who takes it. Everyone has a darker side."

"Zeal or Verve?" I ask.

His brow furrows. "What?"

"This batch has been contaminated. We're in a Vervescape, not Zeal."

"Shit," Nazarin says. "We need to get out of here."

"Where have you been?"

"Mia found a way to trap me in a different part of her dream. It disappeared when she was too distracted to control it anymore."

He means when I was half-strangling her. I flush in shame at what I've done.

Mia has already stopped paying attention to us, like I never interrupted her. Mana-ma has returned, whole and shivering in her black robe. Mia is engrossed in a grisly task involving one of Mana-ma's hands, peeling back the skin and picking out the tendons one by one. Simulacra of the hands that once rested on our heads, giving us benedictions, asking us to purge the darkness within.

"Mia," I say. She looks up, eyes distant.

I gather that stillness within me again. "You don't need to

do this to live. You can be free of it. Try to live your life in the real world again. I loved you so much, and you were so good to us for those years we needed you most. You can be good again."

Her breath hitches. She gives me a long, unblinking stare, and a flash seems to pass between us, before she turns her head back to Mana-ma, her shoulders heaving with silent sobs.

I turn my back on Mia and her phantom, letting Nazarin's hands remain around my shoulders, reassuring in their realness. It's only as we're leaving I notice that Nazarin is also covered in blood, cuts marring the skin of his arms and his left cheek. He's wearing the same dark clothes from Zenith as well, fitted close to the muscles of his chest and narrow waist. He looks dangerous. What nightmares has he endured, over the past few years?

Or what nightmares has he enacted?

We trudge silently down the abandoned corridors of the apartment complex, the dead leaves whispering underfoot. Outside, we look up at the building again, the rain drenching us through. The sky still boils red, blue, black and purple, an endless, wounded expanse. Even though the bloodlust of Verve still sings through my veins, I am comforted by the fact that I can't imagine how anyone would do this willingly.

Nazarin rests his forehead against mine.

"Wake up."

## TWELVE

# TILA

I remember dreaming of trees after we fell.

The redwoods towered above me, the branches criss-crossing like dark lightning against the blue sky. Taema and I were lying on our sides, staring up. There was no birdsong, and barely a rustle of wind. I felt like we were the only two people in the world.

"Are we dead?" I asked my sister.

She leaned close, pressing her forehead against mine. "Not yet."

•

It was our heart.

We'd always known it was weak. There'd been a few scares when we were little. Thinking about it, it's pretty crazy that we had as few health problems as we did, without proper medicine and all that. That day, at the age of sixteen, we had a heart attack.

So then it was us resting in the Wellness Cabin, in the same bed where Adam had been when we threw grapes at him. I hated being in the bed where he had died.

I was so scared that we were going to die too. Taema slept a lot. I think she had less oxygen than me, since I was the bigger twin, just barely. The supposedly stronger one.

I kept wondering if this was the beginning of the end.

It was.

•

I had to stop writing for a bit. The lawyer came to visit me. It's not long until the trial.

I don't trust him. His name is Clive Ranganathan, and he's tall, with dark hair slicked back with too much gel. He's supposed to be a pretty good lawyer, but I can tell he doesn't give a crap about me. He thinks I'm guilty, I can see it, so why would he break a sweat really trying to set me free? It'd be bad for his reputation if he did—every guilty fucker out there would beg for him to take their case before they were hanged by the system. Not that there are many, these days, in the Shining Example of San Francisco.

Not yet, at least.

It's more fun to defend the innocents. Mr. Ranganathan is already slumming it more than he wants to, having to defend someone who might be wrapped up in the Ratel.

He went through his plan and I sort of half listened to him. He nodded his head as he talked, his big hands flipping over his tablet, showing the evidence against me. There's more than last time.

After a bit, I stopped listening altogether. I started humming "A Hazy Shade of Winter." He was offended and left. I don't care. He can't do anything for me. The only person who can save me is Taema. And I still don't know if she's trying to, or if I want her to.

I don't want to write any more about the present. It's depressing, though the past is getting depressing too.

Looking back is almost scarier than looking forward.

•

We felt better after a couple of days of rest and we were able to leave the Wellness Cabin and go home. Our parents were really relieved, to say the least. They cooked us our favorite food that first night: amaranth with vegetables and chicken, baked apples for dessert.

Yes, it was real chicken, not the vat-grown stuff everyone eats in the city. We raised them. Killed them. Ate them.

We were all quiet at the dinner table, not wanting to talk about what we all knew: that it was only going to get worse from here.

We'd known since we were pretty little that we might not live that long. But it was sobering to have to actually face that.

I felt so bad for Mom and Dad, though. They were the best parents you could ask for, really. Some of our friends fought with theirs all the time, but we hardly ever fought with ours. They talked to us as if we were equals, asked us our opinions. Even writing about them right now I'm tearing up like crazy. I miss them most out of everything back in the Hearth. I miss all of us sitting by the fire on cold days, me and Taema sewing clothes, or Taema reading and me chattering away to Dad. Dad and I were closer, and Taema and Mom were closer. Which seems sort of funny, now that I think about it, since obviously we spent the same amount of time with both of them.

I wish they'd have come with us.

They were both so worried for us. It hurt to look at them, as they tried to keep the knowledge that they knew we were dying from their faces. They were bad at it.

•

The next day we had to go to Confession for Mana-ma. We'd already missed a week. Neither of us wanted to go, but then we'd never really enjoyed it. Nobody likes to have to list all the ways they're defective.

Mana-ma didn't preach it that way, though. It's supposed to be exposing who you are fully, both the bad and the good, acknowledging it and then letting it go and moving forward. She seemed more concerned with the bad. Like most people.

Before that treat, we had Meditation. It was our first session since the tablet died. I really didn't want to do it, and I could tell Taema didn't either. Even if we said we were still feeling bad, though, they'd wonder why we were missing it. So off we went.

I remember that Meditation so clearly. Lying in the meadow, the day clear and perfect. California weather through and through.

Almost everyone was already gathered there by the time we huffed and puffed our way down to the dandelion-studded meadow. Mana-ma waited by the path. She rubbed the fingers of her left hand against her thumb, something she did when impatient. Another bitter pill to go down our throats. We felt the "zap" that meant the drug had taken effect. The colors all grew so much brighter.

Dimly, I wondered if we should be taking whatever Mana-ma's drug was, with our heart. Surely our heart could have been an excuse to get out of that day? Then I was so high I didn't care in the least. We stumbled down and joined the ring of people.

Mana-ma stood in the center of the circle, and we all began humming as the drugs took a stronger hold. We reached out for each other as Mana-ma listed the images for us to create in our minds. A butterfly's wings. The petals of a rose. The sky, dark with clouds, fresh rain falling.

There was a flash, pure and bright, that traveled through the ring. The pain that had been lessening with each Meditation returned. We writhed and panted, and I wondered if Mana-ma enjoyed it.

"Yes," I heard Mana-ma say, even though she was speaking so quietly no one should have been able to hear her.

Another flash, and we weren't in the meadow anymore. We were standing in a forest. The trees weren't redwoods like the ones in Muir Woods. The bark was all silver, the leaves blue and purple. The sky roiled a deep green. All the members of the Hearth stood in this weird forest, looking about, confused. In the middle was Mana-ma. Triumphant.

"Mardel," she said. "Come forward."

He came forward, blinking, dazed.

"You have often spoken to me in Confession of your struggle with drink," she said.

Mardel's cheeks, always red from alcohol, flushed deeper. Way to break the sanctity of Confession, Mana-ma.

"I think together, with me as the conduit for God, we can heal you of that urge, here in the sacred wood. Will you permit us to try?" She held out her hand.

Mardel nodded, visibly shaking.

"My flock," Mana-ma said. "God's blessings upon you all. Let us join hands again and think healing thoughts to Mardel. Let him never again crave another drop of drink, so his mind and heart are clear to receive God's love."

We sent him healing urges, yet with so many people, each had a slightly different emphasis and flavor. Some wanted him to also become kinder, less prone to snap. His wife wished he would smile more. Others simply hoped he'd never again crave drinking to excess. I could feel everyone's thoughts, see into their minds. Except for Mana-ma's. She was closed off, wrapped up like her long, black robes.

Another flash. Another burst of pain.

We were back in the meadow.

"Excellent," Mana-ma said, bursting with pride. "I knew it."

She helped Mardel to his feet. "How do you feel, my son?" she asked.

"I feel . . . better," he said, smiling from ear to ear.

"Do you crave vodka?"

"No," he said, surprised. "I don't."

We all cheered.

I hoped that, because of the triumph or whatever the hell we did in the meadow, we wouldn't have to do Confession that day.

No such luck. "We'll celebrate after," she said.

We walked slowly back to the church.

The night before, I had felt our heart flickering, stumbling unevenly as it tried to pump blood to both of us. I wondered how long it'd keep beating. Morbidly, I wondered when it did stop, which of us would die first. Selfishly, I hoped it was me. I didn't want to see Taema without that light in her eyes.

We passed the greenhouses with the mushrooms. We wouldn't be able to help with our chores that afternoon.

We had to wait about half an hour for Confession, slumped against the church wall. There were two people ahead of us. They came out of the Confession room, looking all contemplative. When they saw us, they stopped, rested their hands on our shoulders, and kissed our foreheads. It was meant to be comforting, but I couldn't help but feel they were saying good-bye. *We're not dead yet*, I wanted to yell at them, bashing my fist against their faces to snap them out of it.

Finally, it was our turn. I pressed my forehead against Taema's for a moment.

"T," she whispered.

"T."

It gave us strength.

Mana-ma's Confessional was a tent erected within a secluded

room of the church. It was made of white silk, and within were only low cushions and a low table, in soft pastel colors. Often there was tea if you wanted it. It was meant to be calming, like a shrine to truth and Purity and release. Really, it was more like a hippie psychologist's room.

Mana-ma was perched on her usual cushion, dressed all in black, a stain on the pale colors of the Confessional. She held a cup of tea in her hands. Her eyes crinkled as she smiled at us. She seemed so damn proud. She was still buzzing from her triumph at the meadow.

Mana-ma looked like a mother—warm and generous, with laugh lines about her eyes. She had skin the same brown as us, eyes so dark they almost looked black, her hair in the same tight corkscrews around her face. No, the Hearth's not inbred, but a lot of us are related distantly to each other, or near enough. It was hard to tell what age Mana-ma was—she always looks the same in my memory. Ageless. I used to think she knew everything. She was a Vessel for God, the embodiment of Love.

That was a lie, too.

I remember wondering what the hell she was up to, in that moment before she spoke to us. What was the point of getting us to connect? What was the drug?

"Sit, my children," she said, gesturing.

We had to almost lie down on our sides, resting our cheekbones together so we could both look at her. Taema was nervous—even more nervous than me. I fought the urge to stroke her hair. I had to admit to myself that Taema still believed in Mana-ma, or at least she did a heck of a lot more than I did. She felt guilty knowing she might have to lie, whereas I didn't give a fig.

We'd already lied by omission to Mana-ma, and it hadn't sat well with my sister. We never told her about the tablet. How we

(OK, mostly I) dreamed of the big, wide world and what we'd do if we could ever get to it. We didn't tell her plenty of things. We skittered around the subject of sex and desire, pretending that we couldn't become aroused when so close to each other. That wasn't true.

"I welcome you into the Enclave of the Self," Mana-ma intoned, resting her palms on our foreheads. "Close your eyes and imagine all darkness, all unhappiness, leaving you, leaving only Purity and light."

We dutifully imagined this, breathing in and out, our chests rising and falling in tandem. I imagined I was covered in mud that dried and cracked and flaked off. The flakes scattered around me, whisking about on the wind like when paper has burned to ash. In my mind's eye, I was just me, Taema nowhere around. When I opened my eyes, feeling her warmth, I felt no better, no lighter. Our heart was still weak. We were still dying.

"The darkness cannot flee until you give voice to it. State the nature of it and it can no longer hold any power over you. Confess, and be free. Let the darkness absorb deep into the Earth, so you may leave lighter than when you entered."

I wasn't in the mood for this. I'd believed it all, once upon a time, to a point. I don't know why I was never as completely under Mana-ma's spell as the others, what in me refused to give in. After we found the tablet, something irrefutable had changed in me. I knew this place wasn't where I wanted to be. That Mana-ma might not be the real voice of God. It's a scary thing, when all the beliefs you have shift under your feet like that. I didn't know who to trust, how to feel, if my morals were my morals, or just the Hearth's.

Taema spoke first. I listened to the gentle sound of her voice, my eyes half-closed.

"When our heart hurt," she said, "I didn't think of the Creator, or light, or goodness, like I should have done."

"And what did you think of, my child?"

"I knew my soul could leave, and that I should prepare it since I'd have the time, but all I could think of was the pain, and that I didn't want to die. All was dark and cold. I was scared."

Mana-ma leaned forward. "Did you have a vision? The Creator will sometimes deign to visit one so close to beginning the Cycle again."

"N-no . . ." My sister shook her head, shamefaced, hands clenching. I hated to see how easily Mana-ma could influence Taema's emotions. Not that Taema was weak—far from it—but she was sensitive. Mana-ma made her feel like she had been wrong for no reason.

I had an idea, but I decided to wait my turn as I played it over in my mind.

"What other darkness lives in you, child? Speak it and let it free." I fought the urge to curl my lip and slap her away from us. How had I never seen what a spider she was?

"What else?"

Taema licked her lips. "The Meditation frightened me."

Mana-ma nodded. "I know, my child. God's world is terrifying and vast. But, together, we may access it. This is our purpose. Do not be afraid. This is wondrous. This is transformative. This is divine."

I noticed she danced around saying what it was for.

"I will try," Taema whispered.

"Anything else, my child?"

Taema tried to think of something else. Bless her. She had to dig deep to bring up any darkness. It was all too easy for me to think of dark things, but I'd long since stopped telling Mana-ma about them. Partly because I didn't want Taema to hear what went on in my head. Mostly because I hated the way Mana-ma sucked it all up, reveling in the darkness of her flock.

Taema eventually muttered something about how she dreamed of the world outside, and Mana-ma perked up at that, rearranging herself in her seat, like a cat puffed up at a threat.

"Outside is where no one listens to God—to the birds and the trees and the ways of the world. They think all must bend to their will. They change the land, their bodies, regardless of how the Creator made them, their very souls. They think they can make themselves perfect, spitting in the Creator's face, for my Husband has already made them perfect. Really, they sully all that they touch, and you must never forget that. Now, let that darkness leave the room, never to return."

"Yes, Mana-ma." Taema was all meek, and I wanted to pull my lips back from my teeth and snarl. "That's all, Mana-ma," my twin finished.

Mana-ma waved a bit of smoking sage incense around Taema's head, though of course that made me cough, too. She and Taema hummed the One Note, and my face squished up because it was right against my ear.

Then Mana-ma turned her attention to me.

"Tila, my child," she intoned. "Envision the darkness flowing from you, pooling on the floor, ready to leave and return to the Earth . . ."

I imagined so much flowing out of me that it flooded the room to the Moroccan lamp hanging from the ceiling, but Tila and I floated on it while Mana-ma squatted at the bottom like a sunken stone. A few bubbles burst from below, then all was still. Then the darkness that had been in me carried us away from Mana's Hearth out to the wide world, to San Francisco, dropping us off in Golden Gate Park. The darkness flowed back into me, and I was just like I'd been before.

"Have you completed the visualization?" Mana-ma asked.

I opened my eyes and smiled. "Yes."

"What darkness must you give name to so that it may have no power over you?"

"I thought about dark and pain instead of light and goodness when I thought I would die, too. My soul wouldn't have been Pure."

Mana-ma's eyes lit up. "And did you have a vision?"

"I did."

Taema turned her head. She almost always knew when I was lying. This time she didn't know why.

Mana-ma's eyes shone and she took my hand. Her touch was all cool and clammy. I fought the urge to take my hand and wipe it on my shirt. "Tell me what you saw, my child."

She bought it. I think most people in the outside world think the people at the top of Mana's Hearth know it's all a crock of shit—that they've been shrewd enterprisers since the beginning—but I think Mana-ma *believes*. She believes just as much as, or more than, anyone else in the Hearth. That's why what I did next was just so easy.

"I saw a man I'd never seen before and he was yelling at me to turn back, that what lay before me was only wretchedness. That everything I'd been told was a lie. He even told me who he was."

"Who was he?"

"He called himself the Brother."

Mana-ma paled, rocking back from us. I think I said this before, but the mates of the Mana-ma of each generation were called the Brother. Which is kind of weird, now that I think about it. It was just what they were called, and sort of their role in the community. They were meant to support everyone, even Mana-ma. Because Mana-ma could only really be married to the Creator, for she was his voice.

165

Because of the whole don't-talk-about-the-dead thing, there was no real way for me to recall that name, as far as she knew. The Brother wasn't mentioned in the Good Book, or the sermons, and it was so many years ago now that most people didn't have any reason to mention him, or even think about him much.

Except that little tidbit had slipped into that website about the Hearth, and I overheard our parents once mentioning "the Brother" in passing. I remember thinking it was weird they were talking about a brother in Obvious Capital Letters. So I asked them about it and they told me and Taema, but told me not to tell anyone else about him. I didn't know why they were so nervous about it at the time.

"You heard from the Brother?" Mana-ma asked. Her voice shook. It was the first time I'd ever seen her scared.

I nodded. "He was really upset that I was there. Kept yelling at me to turn back, that there was nothing but darkness and pain beyond. He said the forest was poison."

That was considered bad, if you didn't begin the next Cycle. How else could your soul grow and learn, on our world or another?

"That can't be right," Mana-ma said. She gripped my shoulder, hard. "He wouldn't say that. You're lying. You're lying!"

With difficulty, I shrugged that shoulder, the skin of my chest pulling against Taema's. "I'm just telling you what I saw."

Mana-ma looked deep into my eyes. Whatever she saw there, she didn't like it. She backed away from me. "You're ruining the sanctity of the Confessional by lying within its confines."

I said nothing.

"You are lying. You must be! He can't contact you. There's no way."

I shrugged a shoulder, my skin pulling against Taema's, all

innocent. "Yesterday we connected with each other. Maybe I can connect with those beyond, too." I was just throwing things out there and hoping they'd stick, and I'd struck deep.

She grabbed either side of my head, looking deep into my eyes. Whatever she was looking for, she didn't find it. She let me go.

I didn't register that she'd slapped me until I heard the noise and my cheek stung. Taema gasped, but I stayed silent. Taema's hand clenched mine.

"Get out of here. Get out."

"Don't I have to formally release the darkness?" I asked, still all innocent.

"I don't think the darkness can be released in you," she spat. "Get. Out."

We stood and walked sideways from the room, Mana-ma watching us go.

"What the hell were you doing?" Taema asked as soon as we were out of the church and walking down the dirt road toward home. "What was the point?"

"She does that to us, wrapping us around her finger. I wanted to see if I could do it, too. And I could."

It was easy, and sort of fascinating even if I knew, deep down, it was wrong. Like picking legs off of an insect.

It made me wonder what else I was capable of.

# THIRTEEN

# TAEMA

I wake up completely disoriented.

My mouth feels like cotton wool and my vision is blurry. The room hums with the soft whirr of machinery. I try to move, but there are wires poking from my veins, holding me in place. I panic, not sure where I am. Have I come out of surgery again? My arm tries to move to my scar, but it can't.

"T," I whisper. Where is she?

"Is she OK?" asks a male voice I think I recognize. "It doesn't normally take this long to wake up, does it?"

"It's her mechanical heart. Usually when people are . . . excited in the Zealscape, their heart pumps faster—works through the drug quicker."

I blink, shaking my head. A man leans over me. "You OK, Tila?"

I start at my sister's name, still trying to figure out where I am. I shake my head, but the man gives me a warning look. I squint. He's a detective. Detective Nazarin. I remember. I focus on my breathing, everything coming back to me as the last vestiges of Verve leave my system.

The orderly is taking out the needles from my arm. I shudder as I feel them slip out of my skin. Seems strangely barbaric and old-fashioned, but intravenous is still the best way to administer the drug to make the immersion in the Zeal or Verve world complete. *You must know it wasn't a Zealscape,* I want to say. *How much have the Ratel paid you? Have you contacted them?* If he had, wouldn't they already be here? I feel the aftereffects—a buzzing in my veins, a twitching in my muscles. If it was actually Zeal, my urge to kill and maim would be diminished. I'd feel happy and glowing. Because it's Verve, I feel more keyed up than ever. I keep grinding my teeth together in anger, clenching my hands into fists.

Mia's still deeply dreaming, lying flat on the Chair. Time can go a bit funny on these drugs. It felt like I was only there for an hour at most, but it's been three hours out here. According to the clock on the wallscreen above her head, she still has eleven hours of depravity before she has to wake up and remember what she did in the harsh light of day. Perhaps eighteen hours before she's here again, ready for more. How can she bear to do this, day after day?

The orderly finishes and I get off the Chair, unsteady on my feet.

I lean closer to Mia, and then I swallow hard. I'm almost sure I see the barest hint of bruising around her throat, and another thin mark where the scalpel nicked her. But that can't be possible, can it? I clench my hands into fists deep within my pockets.

Nazarin looks a bit better than I feel, though not by much. He's decidedly green around the gills. I want to ask him what he saw. Were his urges to kill just as strong, and if so, who did he hurt in that shared dream world?

Nazarin tips the white-coated orderly extra, and he responds with an obsequious nod. He opens the door for us and smiles, but to me it seems more of a leer. I squeeze past him, as does Nazarin, and the orderly leads us down the hallway, his perfectly coiffed hair solid as a helmet under the dim lighting. He motions toward the discreet side exit.

I brush off my arms after we leave, as if I can shed all the horror of what I've seen. I'm shaking, even though it's a warm San Francisco night. I let out a breath, my ears perked for an alarm, my eyes to the sky for any unmarked hovercars to take us away. I'm grateful we made the effort to wear masks, and can only hope the orderly didn't lean in close enough in the dim light to see the seams. They're not something that works well in the bright light of day, but are usually reserved for costume parties or nights out on the town.

We walk along beside the garish advertisements of the Mission district. All the smiling, bright men and women seem to be cackling at me.

"We need to talk about what happened," he said. "But not here."

"Back to the safe house?" Though I don't feel comfortable there, between the Chair and seeing that spread of false blood in the upstairs room.

"There's another safe house, closer. Just around the corner. We'll regroup there, then head back to the main one."

He sets off, and I trail him.

•

The extra safe house turns out to be a small apartment, and it's Nazarin's second home. He has one that the Ratel know about, but this is a separate one, not in his name. He'll sometimes meet his superiors here, he explains, since he can never go to the SFPD headquarters. Or he'll come here when he wants privacy, escape. They'll be shutting it down soon, or assigning it to someone else, since he's moved to the new safe house to train me.

Though Nazarin has spent nights here, there's nothing personal about it. It could be a hotel room. It's a studio apartment, though the one room is a decent size. The bed, with cushions against the wall to make it double as a sofa, takes up a corner; a tiny kitchenette takes up a second; a bathroom another (it has a door, at least) and a wardrobe the last corner. A table and chairs are by the window, and he gestures for me to take a seat.

I wonder what his actual apartment looks like, whether there are knickknacks and photographs that would give a glimpse into his life. Tila and I, when we lived together, had a perfect shelf in my entrance hallway to show people just a little bit about us. Holographic images of the two of us, our arms around each other. My engineering degree, and a little glass award I won for my work on VivaFog. A gorgeous, glazed pot Tila made herself and false sunflowers, some of her smaller pieces of artwork, and a glass sculpture a client at Zenith had given her. All of it rested on top of a scarf we bought when we went on holiday together to United Korea. Now it's only my half, photos and engineering accolades, and it doesn't look right.

Nazarin passes me a glass: more SynthGin and tonic. Better than nothing. I shoot it down my throat, grimacing at the subtly wrong taste. I close my eyes, but I keep seeing the screaming mandrakes with the familiar faces. One had looked like Mardel. My eyes snap open.

"Got any more?" I ask.

He takes my cup the three steps to the kitchenette and dutifully pours me more. I drink it down.

"I don't know what you saw, or what you learned," he starts. He's barely touched his drink, swirling it around in the glass. He makes a pretty, if somewhat frightening picture. He's taken off his overtop and wears a tank, the muscles on his arms bulging beneath his brown skin. He has more pale scars crisscrossed along his forearms. The light from the ceiling screen casts part of his face in shadow. He's taken off his shoes, and the sight of his socks—the beginnings of a hole in one big toe—makes him look strangely vulnerable.

"What happened to you? What did you see?" I ask. I feel like he has to tell his side before I can tell mine.

I think Nazarin understands this. He finally downs his drink and then goes to the tiny kitchen for more. Begins to pour a drink, thinks better of it, and brings the entire bottle to the chair with him. I approve of that plan.

"Mia doesn't like men much, does she?" he starts.

"No, she doesn't." More SynthGin splashes into my cup. I think of Mana-ma. "There's plenty of women she hates too."

"When I came in, I was in a prison cell," he says.

I can't help but wonder if it looked anything like the cell my sister is in right now.

"There was no light. I thought maybe the drug hadn't worked and it'd killed me." He smiles ruefully at this, as if it's funny. "I didn't realize it was Verve, though I did think something was off. I haven't taken much of either Zeal or Verve."

*Interesting*, I think, *considering how many people have it as part of their daily lives.*

"Anyway, I realized where I was pretty fast," he says, swigging again. "Found a way out, but then I saw those demon things. They were surrounding the building, like a barricade. Twisted little fuckers."

"Yeah. A lot of them had faces of the people I grew up with."

He shudders. "I fought my way through them but it wasn't pretty. Then the drug hit me pretty hard, and I saw all the people I wouldn't mind dead. That took a while as well." He drains the drink.

"Wait, so you affected the Vervescape too?"

172

He stops at that. "I guess I did."

"You're a lucid dreamer, then, or you could become one." I set down my glass with a *clunk*. "If you can lucid dream, you don't need me." Can I quit? Can I stop this before it's really begun? The hope is painful.

"I'm untrained, and I can't do what you can. I couldn't get rid of these ones. It seemed like they almost killed me. I ended up having to kill them all. Cut them to pieces."

I swallow.

"Most of the people I saw deserved it. A few have been put in jail and then quietly locked up in stasis. Doesn't mean I don't sometimes wish I could have had the honor of actually killing them myself."

"Everyone has a darker side," I whisper, echoing his earlier words.

"That they do. Still, the shared dream should have worked better, even if it was Verve. I should have appeared right with you. I should have guessed that she'd be so strong. She was raised in the Hearth too."

"When she was there, the Meditation stuff wasn't as common," I say, almost distantly.

"Really?" Nazarin leans forward, interested. "When did it really start?"

I stare off, remembering. "Maybe a year or two before Mia left, so like . . . fifteen years ago now? Mana-ma became obsessed with the idea that we could all become one, and when we did, that's when God would speak to her even more clearly. So we trained. Before that, it was more Meditation to clear the mind, not to try and impact anything. But maybe that still gave Mia a foundation to start being able to control the Vervescape."

"And did it work, this Meditation?"

"It did. By the end, we could take a pill and connect into

one large shared dream world populated by every member of the Hearth."

Nazarin's mouth falls open, almost comically. "What was the drug?"

"I don't know. Mana-ma kept her secrets. Maybe it was God, after all." My voice drips with sarcasm.

Nazarin's forehead furrows as he turns over this new piece of information. I'm sure he'll follow it up with the SFPD, but I have a question of my own.

"What would have happened, if Mia had killed me in the dream?" I ask him.

"If she was lucid and knew you weren't a part of the dream? She could have found a way to kill you there that would have been . . . permanent."

"I could have died?" I want to throw my glass at him. "I didn't sign up for death."

His eyes spark at that. "This whole thing started with a death. With your sister killing a Ratel hitman."

"Accused of killing."

He makes a noise deep in his throat. "You still so very sure she didn't do it?"

I say nothing. I'm not sure why I still defend her, when her chances of innocence seem to dwindle the more we follow the clues. If she did kill him, though, I have to cling to the fact that murder and self-defense are two very different things.

"You knew this would be dangerous going in. You knew full well death could always be a possibility, and don't pretend you didn't. You're going into the underworld of San Francisco, Taema, you can't have expected not to get your hands dirty."

I glare at him, and he glares right back.

"Here's how it'll go," I say. "When we do something, you tell me what kind of danger we're facing. Don't just let me barrel into it headfirst without knowing what the hell I'm up against. OK?"

He's the first to look away to take another swig. "Deal. If it's any comfort, I didn't think today would be dangerous. It wouldn't have been if it was Zeal and not Verve, because Zeal is so much more static when you're in someone else's dream."

"What a lovely surprise for us."

"It means we have a problem, though."

"Don't we already have lots of problems?" The SynthGin has made me irritating, but I can't seem to stop the sarcasm.

"If the Ratel have spiked the Zeal with Verve, they're going to try and eavesdrop on the dreams."

Oh God. "And if they have a lucid dreamer see Mia's dreams, then our whole cover is blown."

"Exactly."

"We're screwed then."

"Not necessarily. One: the other Zeal lounge they spiked, the one I was security for? It didn't work. They couldn't get the levels right; no one could mine even a millisecond of a dream. Second: they might not be recording the dreams, but trying to find lucid dreamers based on physiological reactions. That might mean that Mia comes to their attention, but they'll likely discount her because of her ill health."

I can't banish the mental image of Mia sobbing. "She's afraid of someone. She told them about Tila. She could be in contact with the Ratel already."

"Maybe, but if so and if she wanted to sell out your sister, she likely would have already. Third: even if they do manage to record, there will be a backlog of so many dreams. It'll take them time to sift through it all, because they still don't have that many lucid dreamers. That's why Tila was able to rise through the ranks so quickly. So, if the dreams have been recorded, then when you work your first shift at the Verve lounge as Tila, you'll have to erase that one without detection. That won't be easy."

"Nothing is easy." I rub my face. I'm so tired.

"What happened in the dream?" he asks.

He's been wanting to know this since we arrived, but he waited (wisely) until I was drunk enough to talk about it without screaming. Though I'm not drunk enough that I don't realize that's what he's aiming for.

I don't answer right away, but stare out of the window. This second safe house is near the Panhandle, on Fell Street. It looks right onto the thin strip of park connected to the Golden Gate Dome. I can just barely see the tips of Grace Cathedral from between two orchard high-rises. It's quite a pretty view—those pure white towers flanked by fruit trees within glass buildings thirty stories high.

I get to my feet and wobble.

Nazarin leans back in his chair. "You're drunk."

"Very deductive, detective."

"Come on. Tell me what happened to you in there."

I stagger to the little bathroom. "I'll tell you in a second."

I pee and then lean over the tiny sink. I press my palms against my eyes, breathing raggedly. It's late and I feel like shit. I've drunk at least a quarter of the bottle of the fake gin. I'm definitely drunk.

When I come back, Nazarin has a huge glass of water and I gulp it down. I've delayed as long as I can. Time to return to the nightmare world, at least for a little while.

So I tell him everything. I don't leave anything out, and I've got a pretty good memory. I tell him about the mandrake demons, false Mana-ma and Tila, Mia's scalpel. "The drug seemed to pull her in deeper. My sister was there and she started ranting. I guess Mia made that happen? Maybe it's a hint, but mainly she just sounded batshit crazy."

"What'd she say?"

"Something about finding the link and then: 'He is the red one, the fair one, the handsome one. From Earth and now he goes back to the Earth. Ashes to ashes. Dust to dust. Changing faces like kaleidoscopes.'"

"Sounds like the garbled scripture that Tila spouted in Zenith, according to Sal."

"That's what's weird. If Mia was going to give me a hint, shouldn't she have referenced Mana-ma's Good Book? That's what we all have memorized. Mana-ma would show us other holy writ, all sorts of it too: the Torah, the Qur'an, the Book of Mormon, gnostic texts, the works—but out-of-context bits that suited her. Usually she ranted about how they were the warped echoes of the true voice of God, which only she heard. Naturally."

That familiar guilt twists deep in my stomach. For a long time, I'd believed that Mana-ma did hear the true voice of God. That she was the vessel able to bring us salvation. And I'd been so stubborn, so willingly blind, for so long. After Tila and I had left the Hearth, after the last holds of Mana-ma were finally gone from me, we went through a phase of reading all the holy books we could get our hands on. Buddhist texts, ancient Egyptian things (I admit to reading the *Book of the Heavenly Cow* mainly because it had such a great title), Ellen White's Seventh-Day Adventist texts. A lot of stuff from other cults, especially ones formed after Mana's Hearth. The Contours of God. The Green Cabal, which thought that people who saw aliens were actually seeing fairies, and lived in the woods with toadstools for a few decades.

Everything and anything, wondering if maybe we'd find the truth in one of them.

We didn't, but I remember sitting side by side in our little San Francisco apartment in the Inner Sunset, our legs touching and our cheeks pressed against each other as we read, like when we had been connected. I still feel I think best when I'm sitting like that with Tila, feeling the steady beating of her heart in time with mine, and the gentle sound of her breathing. Maybe that's why I've felt so lost: I can't think properly when she's gone. All the good memories with her hurt.

The silence has gone on too long. I can tell he's been watching me as I stare blankly into space.

"So. Let's start looking at what Mia might have meant. It sounds like religious rhetoric, so I'm thinking the Bible," Nazarin says. He blinks and his ocular implant activates the wallscreen, bringing up a version of the King James Bible.

Nazarin taps his thumb against his lips. "Vuk's dead. It could be about him. So I guess that explains the ashes to ashes part. 'For dust thou art, and unto dust shalt thou return.' "

"Ashes to ashes, funk to funky . . . we know that Mia's a junkie!" I sing. The SynthGin has made me silly.

At Nazarin's confused look, I giggle even more. "Never mind. Old song by a man called David Bowie. Sorry." It was from post-1969, so I first listened to it after coming to San Francisco, during my and my sister's self-taught education in music. I clear my throat, try to calm myself. "I have no idea what she meant by 'the red one, the fair one, the handsome one.' "

He searches for quotes relating to *red*. The following appears on the wall:

Isaiah 1:18: Come now, let us reason together, says the Lord: though your sins are like scarlet, they shall be as white as snow; though they are red like crimson, they shall become like wool.

Exodus 28:15: You shall make a breast piece of judgment, in skilled work. In the style of the ephod you shall make it— of gold, blue and purple and scarlet yarns, and fine twined linen shall you make it.

"Mean anything to you?" he asks.

I shake my head. "Nope."

He searches for "the fair one" and the snippet from the Song of Solomon appears:

My beloved spake, and said unto me, Rise up, my love, my fair one, and come away.

I still shake my head. Tila is beloved to me, of course, but the quote doesn't jump out to me in any significant way. Does she want me to come away with her?

He frowns. "I'm sure we'll find out something. There'll be a kink in this trail somewhere."

He tries a general search, not in the Bible, of "the red one, the fair one, the handsome one."

"Got it," Nazarin whispers.

The triliteral Semitic root ADM: red, handsome, fair. And a word from it, "adamah," meaning "ground" or "earth."

"Adam." The word rasps from my throat. My head spins and I lean back on the chair, closing my eyes, hiding my face in my hands.

"The first man? Does that mean anything to you?"

Of course it does. And it has nothing to do with the original Adam from Genesis, the rise of Eve's original sin or the fall of man. It has everything to do with a nice boy with a genuine smile, laughing through the pain as he tried to catch green grapes in his mouth, his left arm a stump on the pillow, his infected foot propped up on the bed. A lifetime ago. A world away across the bay.

"It does. We knew a boy named Adam. But I don't know how the hell he'd have anything to do with this."

"Maybe Mia wanted us to speak to him. Where is he?"

Not opening my eyes, I say, "He's dead. Died ten years ago, in Mana's Hearth. Maybe she meant another Adam. Or she was babbling nonsense hopped up on Zeal or Verve. Fuck, I don't know. I don't know. I can't think about this any more." I take my hands away and reach for the bottle of SynthGin. It only has enough for half a glass.

"Any more?"

He brings out the bottle of SynthTequila. Holds it out to me like an offering.

"That'll do."

•

Our empty SynthTequila glasses sit on the table by the window, glowing silver in the moonlight. Nazarin and I are on the bed. The detective is splayed against the wall, his arms crossed behind his head. His eyes are half-lidded, his lips parted. I'm lying on my side, my head resting on my arm. He makes a pretty picture. In this soft light, he does not look so fierce. I can't see his scars.

Nazarin stretches, his shirt lifting just enough to show the muscled planes of his stomach.

"Do you want another drink?" he asks, his voice quiet.

"No," I say. I sit up, move a little closer. We pause, six inches apart, sizing each other up. We both know what the other wants. What we don't know is if we should cross that line.

The old Taema wouldn't have. The old me would have decided it was too improper, unprofessional. The new me, though? The one who has given up everything, who just nearly killed my foster mother in a dream world? She's a different creature entirely.

Nazarin opens his mouth to say something.

I close the distance between us.

His mouth is warm. His lips part further, his tongue darting against mine, soft and tasting of tequila. His stubble scratches my chin. I pull him against me, and his body is the opposite of his mouth—hard, angular, strong. I roll on top of him, and his lips move from my lips to my neck. I close my eyes, a small smile curling my lips.

I sit up and Nazarin pulls my shirt off of me. His fingers trace their way down my scar before reaching behind me, unclasping my bra. I slide it down my arms, tossing it to the floor before helping him out of his clothes.

We are not slow. We are not gentle. We are not tender. We each take what we want, what we need, yet we do give the other what they desire. It's been almost a year since I broke up with David. It's a long time to be alone. I concentrate entirely on Nazarin and the sensations he gives me, determined to quiet my racing mind.

Afterward, I lie on top of him, my breasts pressed against his muscled chest. From this close, I can see all his scars, crisscrossed against each other. I trace my fingertips along them as he drifts off to sleep, wondering what story lies behind each one.

His heartbeat is in time with mine.

## FOURTEEN

# TAEMA

I wake up curled up against Nazarin's side.

In the harsh light of day, sleeping with my undercover partner doesn't seem like the brightest idea I ever had, even if I am delightfully sore and sated. I ease myself away from him, running my tongue over my dry lips. Synth alcohols don't give you a hangover, but your body still understands on some deep level that you've messed with it. I lean on my knees.

I dreamed of Adam. My first crush. How he used to visit us and stay for dinner. He'd flip through the books in our room, and I'd watch his fingers turn the pages. I'd often wondered if he liked either me or my sister, or both of us. He was so tall, and strong from helping plow the fields for grain. I could picture his face so clearly in my mind, as if I'd just seen him the day before.

Nazarin shifts, curling on his side, turned toward me, his face burrowed into his arm so I can only see the tips of his eyebrows and his buzzed hair. He looks cute, something I still find remarkable in such a large, intimidating man. Images of the previous night flash in my mind, and though they are pleasant memories, I'm nervous about how he'll react when he wakes up. I watch him for a minute, willing my body to feel better, even if nothing exactly hurts. Nazarin's breathing hitches, his brows furrowing. I wonder what his dreams are.

I move to leave the bed and Nazarin stiffens, his arm snaking out to grab my wrist. I cry out in surprise. We freeze. Nazarin meets my eyes, the sleep clearing from them as he remembers what we did. His gaze darts down to my naked torso. He lets go of my wrist and I rub it.

"Sorry," he mumbles. "Light sleeper."

It's more than that. He's someone used to sleeping with one eye open and a gun under his pillow.

I stand, feeling his eyes on me as I slip the cotton dress over myself. I go to the bathroom and shut the door. Looking in the mirror is still a shock. My hopes rise for an instant when I think it's my sister, and then crash when I realize it's only me. My imitation-Tila hair is a wreck. I try to pat the blue spikes into some semblance of order, and give up.

When I come out, he's up and dressed in a tank top and sleep shorts, making coffee in the kitchenette. There's a bulge in his shorts. I feel a shot of desire go through me, culminating between my legs. Even in the light of day, knowing it's a bad idea, I'm more than half tempted to go over, push him against the wall and do it all again. I clear my throat, slide my eyes away, and take the cup when he offers it to me, sipping gratefully.

It's real coffee. The caffeine settles into my system. They haven't outlawed that from the city yet, even though it's stupidly expensive to buy with the extra taxes.

"Good God, Taema, you can drink," Nazarin says, admiringly. "If that was real alcohol, I wouldn't be able to open my eyes today."

Are we pretending last night didn't happen? I play along. It's easier this way. "So you've had the real stuff?" I ask, taking another sip.

"Of course I have. I haven't always lived in this hippie ecotopia."

"Where are you from?" I ask.

"I was born in Turkey, but moved to Dakota when I was eight."

"Ah. Rural boy." I skirt about asking him why he left Turkey. There was a nasty civil war in that area of the world at that time, though it's stable now. Chemicals, bombs and far too many civilian deaths.

"I grew up on a farm. Might have been a little similar to how you were raised, come to think of it."

My mouth twists, my hand hovering to the top of my scar. "Probably not quite like me."

He raises his coffee cup in acknowledgment. His eyes dart down, but I'm not sure if he's looking at the scar or my breasts. I feel the thrum of desire again. *Get it together*, I admonish myself.

"Definitely not," he says, as if echoing my thoughts, but he's still talking about his childhood. "I just have a little more in common with you than someone who grew up surrounded by this." He gestures out the window at the distant skyscrapers. "We had plenty of moonshine out there. Real beer. No one out there would touch synthetic alcohol if their lives depended on it. They pride themselves on swilling the real stuff, even if they're left with skull-splitting hangovers."

He stops and tilts his head, his vision going distant. Seems like we're both plagued with memories this morning. Then I realize he's been pinged. I down the first cup of coffee and pour myself another as he listens to his auditory message.

He shakes his head to clear it and the way he looks at me makes my insides freeze.

"What is it? Is it Tila?"

"No. Not your sister. But Mia is dead."

•

I can't have my answers right away. Nazarin has been called back to the Ratel, and they're still performing the autopsy report. We've returned to the gingerbread safe house, and I'm alone for most of the day. I work out and practice the fight sequences that I've brainloaded. I order a lonely meal from the replicator, barely tasting it. I take a long shower, turning the water up as hot as I can bear, staring at my toes. First, I try to read, then I try to watch something on the wallscreen, but I take nothing in. I end up wandering the empty rooms, staring blankly into space, numb.

Mia is gone. The woman who took me and my sister in. The woman who helped us navigate our brave new world of San Francisco. She was flawed, she was deeply troubled, but she loved us, and we loved her. Now she's gone. I wonder if they told Tila, and what she's thinking, wherever she is.

When Nazarin returns, late that night, he has the autopsy report. He lays the tablet on the kitchen table and we perch next to each other on stools. We still haven't talked properly about what happened, but I don't want to anymore.

"They warned me it's inconclusive," he tells me. "They're not going to incinerate her right away."

I jerk my shoulders up at that. I can't stand the thought of her turned into nothing but ash.

"Sorry. I've been told I can be insensitive in times of loss. When I had a partner, she was usually the one to break any news like this."

"Yeah, you're not being remotely comforting here. Why don't you have a partner anymore?" I can't believe it's never occurred to me to ask. I also don't want to look at the autopsy report just yet, so I'm stalling.

"She died. Not long before I went undercover. Right now, you're the closest to a partner I have." He looks away from me, but there's a tension in his muscles that wasn't there a moment before.

"I'm sorry."

"Yeah. Me too."

"Were you two . . . close?"

He raises an eyebrow. "We weren't fucking, if that's what you mean."

I don't react, though of course, his words make me think about him without his clothes. It's a nice mental image.

"She was actually married to Dr. Mata," he continues. "That's how I met Kim. But yeah, we were close. And she was a damn good detective. We cracked a lot of cases together. Put a lot of bastards away. One got away and killed her."

"Did you catch him?"

"Nah. Asshole got away with it. I ever find out who did it . . . they won't make it to prison." He works his jaw, hesitating, as if deciding whether or not to tell me what's on his mind. "I'm pretty sure it was the Ratel."

Was that why he went undercover? "If they hurt your partner, wouldn't they then know who you were?"

"You're not the only one wearing a false face and using a false name," he says.

I wonder what he used to look like. What his real name is. I'm not sure he'd tell me, so instead I ask: "What was her name?"

He closes his eyes. "Juliane. Juliane Amello."

"Pretty name." I raise my coffee cup, and he taps his with mine. "In memory of Juliane."

He smiles at my sentimentality, and drinks. "We're toasting with the wrong stuff."

"Can you stand the thought of more SynthGin or Synth-Tequila?"

He grimaces, and I laugh. I sober when he glances down at the tablet again. I don't want to see a hollow re-creation of Mia. I don't want to remember the way she was in the Vervescape. I don't want to think about how she might have screwed Tila and me over. I want to preserve her in my mind as the woman she was when we were sixteen and scared, and she protected us.

"Did you find out anything about Mirage?" I ask, stalling further.

"Yeah. I think we're OK. Another Knight told me Mirage was a bust for recording dreams, too, and that the King and Queen were annoyed. They've only managed to do it in small batches, with one or two people, and they want to do it with more people at once."

"How many more?"

Nazarin sighs. "As many as possible. Get them hooked, get them buying straight from them. Money and information flows toward the Ratel. The Ratel becomes the true power in San Francisco."

Hence why the government and Sudice have to squash them before they can't any longer. What would San Francisco be like, if we were all under Ratel control? Even less privacy than now, if not even our dreams were our own.

"Still terrifying that the Ratel are using Zealots as experimental subjects. Have any died from Verve?"

"Plenty."

"Why isn't the government doing more? Surely they could do something to protect them?"

Nazarin's face is impassive. "In this case, it means the

government can watch what they're doing. If the Ratel realizes the government knows, then they'll do something more underground. Maybe take people to experiment on. Zealots are expendable." His mouth tightens.

Expendable. Like Mia.

"They're both as bad as each other in some ways, aren't they?" I say, my stomach roiling. Am I really on the right side? Is there a right side in all of this?

"Be careful what you say," Nazarin says, leaning close to me.

I rest my head in my hands. I want to leave all of this. I want to give up. Everything is too muddled, too confusing; but if I give up, then Tila goes into stasis.

"You ready?" he asks.

I nod, and he presses the button and the hologram pops up like a macabre children's picture book.

It's Mia, alone. She's not connected to the machine, but she's just come off it. The medical information scrolls to the right of her, listing all the physical ways the Zeal and Verve have messed her up. Malnutrition. Kidney disease. Skin abscesses near injection sites. Tooth decay. Jaundice. It's reflected in the hologram—Mia is thin and unhealthy, just as she was the last time I saw her, strapped to the Chair, wires emerging from her arms as she dreamed her nightmares in the Zealot lounge of Mirage. But in this her eyes are open, moving from side to side as she staggers back to the hovel where she lives.

Lived.

I swallow, unable to look away. A dark, shadowy figure comes up behind her. A man, most likely, judging from his height. His face is covered in a dark fabric mask. He grabs Mia around the neck and pulls her to him, whispers something in her ear.

I pause it. "How do they know he whispered to her?" Mia's face is also a lot more detailed and expressive than the re-creation of Tila murdering Vuk had been, and everything is shown from the same angle. I can answer my own question.

"It was caught on camera," Nazarin says.

"Do you think it was the Ratel?"

"I honestly don't know. I hope not. And this isn't their usual MO. If they order a hit, they want you to know it." His jaw works, and he must be thinking of his partner. He presses play again.

Mia's eyes widen at whatever the masked man whispers. "Which lost soul are you?" she asks, loud enough to be heard by the camera.

He doesn't respond except to grab her face in his hands.

"I wanted to try and be good again. I suppose it was always too late." She closes her eyes. "I forgive you."

He breaks her neck. She falls to the ground. The man is gone. Mia is also gone, even if her body remains.

The image goes dark and I turn away. A round, heavy weight of dread and grief sits in my stomach. I cross my arms over my torso and hunch forward.

"I don't want to push you, after just seeing that," Nazarin says, leaning on the counter next to me. He's close, but not too close. Perfectly trained. "I think there's something in here that can help us. What do you think she meant, when she mentioned 'lost souls' just now, and when Tila mentioned changing faces in Mia's dream?"

I lean closer, lowering my voice to a whisper in his ear. I feel him shiver. "Are you sure the government didn't do this?" I ask. "Catch her lucid dreaming because of us, and snuff her before the Ratel found her?" The government being behind this would be marginally better than the Ratel, though still ter-rifying, but the real question simmers behind those words: is it our fault?

He shakes his head. "No. I have access to those records. Whoever this was, it wasn't one of us."

Unless they were off the books and they don't want him to know. That's always a possibility.

I furrow my brow. *Changing faces.* Vuk's autopsy said he'd had lots of plastic surgery. Even changed the shape of his ears. Had she known him, somehow?

*Changing faces like kaleidoscopes.*

A horrible theory blossoms in my head. "Fucking hell."

"What?"

"Turn on the wallscreen."

The blank wall home screen appears in front of us.

"Bring up the list of Vuk's suspected surgeries."

He does, and I stare at them. Sure enough . . .

"Bring up his face."

A photograph of him appears. I look closely, but at first it still seems impossible. The face is totally different.

"Give me the tablet."

He passes it to me and I take the little stylus from the side and start to sketch. I'm a passable artist at best, but I focus on the shape of the eyes, the nose, the wide mouth. I draw him almost smiling, as if we've just thrown a grape at him and missed. I project the drawing of Adam onto the wallscreen, right next to the picture of Vuk. Maybe, just maybe. The jawline is the same. The eyes are the same color—that warm hazel I remem-ber. I close my eyes and imagine that face I'd just seen in the dream. I open my eyes and look at Vuk. Yes. Yes.

"The missing link," I say.

Nazarin catches on right away, which I appreciate. I can't quite articulate my thoughts anyway.

"It'd be difficult, but with enough surgery, Vuk could be this boy, Adam."

I shake my head. I've made the connection, but it still doesn't seem possible. He'd had his left arm reconstructed. Underneath the synthetic skin, it had been as metal as my mechanical heart. "The boy I know was a fetal amputee. His arm ended at the elbow. But Adam *died*."

"Did you ever see the body?"

"N . . . no." There were no funerals in the Hearth.

What did they do with the bodies?

Adam was in the Wellness Cabin that first day, and he seemed ill, but not on the brink of death. And the next day he was gone. "Did he escape, like we did?"

"It's possible." He taps his fingers on the countertop. I think back. Escape for us was hard. Escape for us meant planning. Adam didn't escape. I meet Nazarin's eyes, knowing what he'll say next.

"Or Mana-ma sold him to the Ratel," Nazarin says.

*Which lost soul are you?* Mia asked.

Did that mean there's more than one? Who else did we lose in the Hearth? Who else might be here?

"In the year before I left, at least three teenagers died. A cut that went septic. A flu that wouldn't stop. And then they'd be gone. They were all men." My stomach hurts.

"So you think your Mana-ma might have . . . sold Adam and others to the Ratel?"

"She might. She just might have. It'd mean money to keep us afloat and keep the Hearth solvent. We weren't self-sufficient from trading our makeshift items and selling produce. A lot of us were raised to be pliant, to listen to those in charge. Despite that, though, I can't picture Adam turning into a hitman. And why would she do it? It'd be against the morals she taught us, to sell Hearth folk to the Impure."

Nazarin exhales. "Brainwashing can be very persuasive, if it's done over years. The Ratel might have been able to break him, psychologically. And I don't know. Maybe your Mana-ma wasn't as holy as she led you to believe. In any case, this is circumstantial evidence on top of more circumstantial evidence."

"Stop calling her *my* Mana-ma. She's no such thing." Not anymore. How could I ever have believed in her?

"Sorry. You're right. I'll send the sketch back to the station, see if they can make any matches."

"My drawing might not be good enough. Unfortunately I don't have any photographs."

"We'll see what they say in any case. The drawing's good."

I feel a strange little rush of pleasure at that. "So, if this is all true, then there could be a link between the Hearth and the Ratel. Maybe Tila found that out. And that's why she went after them."

I fight down a rush of nausea. Even if this is why she did it, why didn't she tell me? Why didn't she ask me to help? And if Vuk was actually Adam, why the hell would she kill him? She loved him just as much as I did. Wouldn't she try to help him instead?

Tila was stupid, brash, and left me behind. She never used to leave me in the dust . . . but then, she never used to have a choice in the matter.

I look back at the autopsy and the police report to distract myself from the racing, circular thoughts I have no answer to. As I make sense of the words, I gasp. "Did you see this?" I ask.

Nazarin leans over my shoulder.

It's a report from one of Mia's neighbors, saying she was acting strangely yesterday and this morning.

"Like a totally different person," the woman said. She didn't give her name to the police. "She'd been singing really old songs from the 1960s, said she was giving up Zeal, moving away. She seemed happy, but also sort of manic? I thought she might have still been high, her eyes were so glazed."

"She wanted to quit? This makes things so much sadder," I say, nearly choking with grief.

Nazarin frowns. "Something's weird about it, though. We saw her physical stats. She was really far gone, to change so suddenly."

"Maybe I got through to her."

"What do you mean?"

"In the dreamscape, just before we left, I told her she could be better if she wanted to be. Remember? I told her to try and be good again."

Nazarin's face goes still.

"What is it?"

"Nothing." He gets up and leaves me, confused, at the kitchen table. I can hear him hitting the punching bag in the gym.

About an hour later, he asks if I want to go for a walk, for some fresh air. His eyes dart imperceptibly to the wallscreens.

I agree, put on my coat, and we head out into the night. Nazarin turns on a White Noise, a tiny device the size of a fingernail, which will distort any nearby cameras trying to record our conversation. I wish we could use it in the safe house to speak freely, but the SFPD would wonder at the scrambled readings. We walk along the darkened streets, leaning close. Nazarin has his hand in his pocket, and I know it's curled around a gun.

Whatever he's about to tell me, he doesn't want his employers to know, either.

"I've been developing a theory, over the last few months. I've been trying to find more definitive proof before I go to the SFPD."

"About what?"

"I think Verve does more than simply giving people access to dreams."

I focus on him. The light from the streetlamps plays across his face, casting dark shadows.

"I think," he says, each word heavy and deliberate, "that some lucid dreamers can influence the Vervescapes and change personalities. I think . . . you might have done that to Mia. And I think the government realized that and they killed her, not the Ratel."

I take a few steps, trying to process the information. It doesn't want to process. "Fuck."

"It makes sense. I've seen other Knights or Pawns in the Ratel suddenly change personality completely. They wouldn't seem to know me, even if we'd spoken the day before. Think how dangerous that makes this drug."

"Whether it's in the hands of the Ratel or the government."

"Exactly."

"So you think . . . the Ratel overwrote Adam's personality, and made him Vuk?"

"Yes. I do."

"What does this mean for us?"

"It means we stick to our original plan for the SFPD. It's all we can do."

"If we take the Ratel down, though, then the government will have Verve."

"Yes." He doesn't look happy about it.

"There is no good and evil in this scenario, is there? There's only bad and worse."

We keep walking through the streets for hours. At some point, Nazarin's warm and callused hand takes my own. I don't pull away.

# FIFTEEN

# TILA

I feel sorry for those still left in the Hearth.

I've tried to put the Hearth behind me and to forget as much as possible. But I don't think I can ever forget. Not completely. All those people, following Mana-ma's rules set out in the Good Book, listening to her sermons, their voices rising up in song. Did they really think that by following those rules they'd achieve salvation, and have their pick of next lives in the Cycle?

I never knew how many people were actually happy there, and how many people were just pretending. How many knew the truth of Mana-ma?

Mardel discovered it, in the end. True enough, he stopped drinking alcohol. The problem was, he also stopped drinking everything else.

No one noticed right away. I heard my father comment that Mardel looked weak and wasn't able to pull his weight in the fields, but he put it down to alcohol withdrawal. By the third day, Mardel was badly dehydrated. They tried to make him drink water, but he'd start shaking and spit it out. They managed to force some down him. We tried another Meditation, urging him to drink water rather than alcohol. It didn't quite take, not like the first time. Perhaps our fear lowered efficacy. He lingered a few more days. Then he died.

Mana-ma found a way to spin it. God had simply called him home. I saw it for what it was: a failed experiment. Would she try to change us again in Meditation, and if so, who would she choose next? Would it go wrong?

I didn't want to stick around to find out.

My parents were from San Francisco. They'd joined as idealistic teens and I think, somewhere over the next twenty-odd years, they realized they had made a mistake.

Our mom helped run the accounts and our dad was in some ways Mana-ma's muscle, along with Uncle Tau (not our uncle by blood). They didn't often have to be muscle, thankfully, but if people weren't pulling their weight they'd have a quiet word with them. But they weren't Mana-ma's right-hand men; her most trusted advisors were Kieran, Niran and Daniel.

When we were sixteen, Kieran, Niran and Daniel were aged about twenty-seven to thirty. They're probably still her main muscle. She'd groomed them for the role since they were little. Loyal as watchdogs, and just as scary.

After our heart attack, everyone in the Hearth was very nice to us. We didn't have to do our chores (we couldn't really, anyway, we were so weak). Our friends came by the house a lot and we played cards. Taema and I played on the same team because otherwise it'd be too easy to cheat. Our friends were shy around us, not wanting to meet our eyes. They knew we were probably dying, and it embarrassed them. Made me want to force them to look at us, right in the eyes; but if I'd done that, they probably wouldn't have come back and played cards again.

We'd ask Mom and Dad how much time we had left, but they didn't want to answer. We heard them murmuring at night in the other room, but even though we pressed our ears to the doorjamb, we couldn't hear anything. We knew they were talking about us, though, from the tone. Hushed, worried. Nervous.

We were in bed late one night when I finally asked the question I'd been wondering ever since we had the attack: "They could fix our heart out there, couldn't they?"

Taema was silent for a moment, and then ran her fingers through my hair. I loved it when she did that. I found the faint tickling so comforting. I ran my hand through hers, offering comfort back.

"They could," she said. "But it doesn't matter. Mana-ma won't let us go." Getting past the swamp was difficult, even with a boat. And Mana-ma had eyes everywhere. My sister didn't say it, but I knew what she was thinking: if we got out, we'd be Impure. Despite everything, she still believed a hell of a lot more than I did. It was so frustrating. Couldn't she see how messed up this place was? It made me angry at her.

"Some have made it out," I whispered. "Remember Mia? She left, even though Mana-ma didn't want her to."

"Nobody knows how, or what happened to her."

I was quiet for a bit, feeling the coarse, curly threads of Taema's hair. She could annoy me so much sometimes, but obviously I didn't want to lose her. Death did scare me something fierce. Because it'd be the first time I'd be alone.

I also knew that we had to leave the Hearth, or we didn't have a shot. Taema hadn't wanted to research conjoined twins on the tablet. She was afraid of what we might find—though I didn't understand what exactly she thought that might be. So when she fell asleep and the tablet was still on, I'd researched on my own.

I knew that everyone out there could change how they looked, and that most did. There was very little obesity, few eating disorders, unsightly scars or pockmarks or missing limbs. Everyone was whole. Perfect. And I knew that out there, there were no conjoined twins. I couldn't find any, not anywhere.

Maybe they were all aborted, never even had a chance to live, or "fixed" as soon as they were born.

So even if we did get out, how would people react? It explained the way the people in the supply ships acted around us. Even those grunt monkeys supervising the drones were all beautiful. But getting out still seemed better than sitting here, waiting to die. I knew we only had one chance of getting out, although neither of us wanted to put them in such a tight spot:

"Mom and Dad will know."

## SIXTEEN

# TAEMA

The next day, I'm alone.

Nazarin's gone to the other safe house to check in with his SFPD superiors. He's going to dig into plastic surgery records at a bunch of flesh parlors, to see if Vuk has any official history there. It's useless—if Vuk was actually Adam, then he won't have an official record of even existing, much less getting plastic surgery.

Tomorrow Nazarin has a busy day with the Ratel, as it's not long until Saturday, the night of the party, and there's lots to do. Saturday is the night when he might finally meet Ensi, face to face.

I can't reconcile the image of Adam, that sweet boy, grown up into a hardened killer. Maybe I'm wrong about it all, but I don't think I am. But then, what do I know about people? My sister could be a murderer too, and I can't forget how I acted in Mia's Vervescape.

I can't stand to think about what happened in that twisted nightmare. Ever since we left the Hearth, I've worked hard to fit in: get a good job, buy an apartment, pay my taxes. I don't stand out, except for my scar. I never wanted to be that strange girl who used to live in a cult. In a world obsessed with perfection, I didn't want to be known only for having spent sixteen years as a conjoined twin. My goal has always been to stay out of trouble.

Now I'm headfirst in it.

Nazarin's been undercover this whole time, balancing training me and his work with the Ratel. I don't have long before I'm to go in.

Being alone is forcing me to consider what's going on. I don't have a job. I quit my last one, and turned down going to China. I want nothing more than to sit with numbers and calculations, or fly out over the bay to visit the machines I helped design, and view the city from the top point of a VivaFog. I want to forget about people, and stay with the machines and their cold logic. Maybe after this is all over, I can go back. I hope so.

I have permission to return to my apartment for clothes, so I leave and ping Nazarin with a message of my whereabouts. I take the glowing green MUNI, the ads flashing on the tops of the train. Halfway there, though, I change course; I don't want to go to my place. I get off, take another train, and head for my sister's apartment instead. After all, her clothes fit my cover better than my own.

The door opens at my VivaChip, which makes me realize I would have had to use a key at my own place. Tila's home is a dump, though I'm not sure how much is her usual disarray and how much is from the SFPD searching the place. As I set down my bag, I feel like an intruder, even though I've been here countless times before.

I decide to set things to rights—though it's really an excuse to go through her things, thoroughly and systematically, in case there are any more hints.

Tila stores things in almost the same places I do. Her underwear is in the same drawer, though everything's just thrown in. Her jeans and skirts are likewise crumpled. I take the time to fold them and put them back, arranged by color. I don't find anything but clothes in the drawers or closet, and I take a few to bring back with me to the safe house. My fingers hover over the green dress she likes, but the memories of Mia's mind are too strong, and I leave it on its hanger.

There's nothing but dust under the bed. No gun beneath the pillow, no grenades in the bedside table. What was I expecting?

I give up and sit on her bed, sighing. I snuggle under the cover, missing Tila so much it's a physical ache. I'm angry at her, I'm terrified for her, and I'm a little terrified of her and what she might have done. But I've never gone so long without speaking to her, or seeing her. The blankets even smell like her perfume—lily of the valley. I press my nose into the pillow.

I allow myself to cry about it all. I've kept most of it bottled up close inside, trying to stay strong, to dampen everything through Mana-ma's training; but I can't do it anymore. It hurts too much. It's not pretty tears. I'm keening and sobbing, my nose running almost as much as my eyes. I rock back and forth, clutching the pillow to my chest. I feel like a lost little girl. I don't know how to save Tila. I don't know if I can. I don't know if I will. If I don't figure this out, then my sister will go into stasis. I can't even imagine never seeing her again. I really would be ripped in two.

It takes a long time before I stop crying. I sit up, sniffling, and take a tissue from the box on the bedside table. Beneath the tissue box is Tila's sketchbook. Still sniffling, I take it and rest the book on my knees, flipping through the pages.

She loved to people-watch. She used to say she liked to record the people that surrounded her in her sketchbook. *"It's different than a picture. This is more honest,"* she'd say, bending over the paper to shade in an eyebrow. She never used a tablet, always drawing the way she had at the Hearth, with pen and paper. *"So many people. And we don't really know what makes them tick. So few people we really, truly know in this world. With the rest of them we're just pretending. But when I'm drawing them, I feel like I can find something about them that's real. That maybe they didn't want me to see. Sometimes I feel like I'm pretending with everyone except for you, Taema."*

I turn another page. Here are hosts and hostesses from Zenith—I recognize Pallua, Leylani and a few of the others, either that I saw that night or from the police information brainload. There are a few of her favorite clients—beautiful men and a few women, smiling and holding glasses of champagne. Their names are neatly printed next to them in our alphabet. Nadia. Jeiden. Locke. Men and women with money to burn to stave off their loneliness.

Here are total strangers. People Tila would sketch in cafes and restaurants. I can remember when she drew the old man at the bar down the street—not that he looked that old (hardly anyone in San Francisco does), but you can still tell when someone's over seventy. Something about their eyes.

This man was always there, at the same seat at the bar, with the same glass of SynthScotch, staring into the distance with the withdrawn look that meant he was accessing his ocular implant. We often used to wonder what he was reading or watching, lost in his own little world, not moving except to raise the glass to his lips or lift his finger for a refill. I remember how my twin looked, bent over the sketchbook as she shaded in his features, while I sat across from her sketching out calculations for whatever project I was working on. Companionable silence.

I close my eyes tight, not wanting to cry again. But I don't have any tears left. I make my way through the rest of the house, looking under the sofa cushions, in every kitchen cupboard, all the various nooks and crannies.

In the middle of the kitchen, I stand up, my eyes wide. Why hadn't I remembered?

I *do* know where Tila hides her secrets.

She showed it to me once, not long after she moved in. It was to be her version of the cookie jar, where I could leave her messages if I was passing by. Such a childish game, but I'd appreciated it. Yet in all the months she lived here, I never left her any messages. I kept meaning to, but never did. Hers were always so clever, so thoughtful, and when I tried to think up a return message, they all seemed unbearably dull. She never mentioned the lack of baubles and notes. I never knew if she was hurt by that or not.

I go to her spare bedroom, grunting as I pull back the bed. Another reason I didn't leave messages: it's harder to get to than a cookie jar in the kitchen. Tila was always the more paranoid of us, though, and now I understand why.

I can't see any evidence that the police moved the bed, and the cubbyhole she built behind it seems untouched. I take the key she gave me from my purse and put it into the lock, and the door swings open.

Inside are another sketchbook and a datapod. The pod is only the size of my thumbnail. I want to bring it up on my implants right away, but I'm also afraid of what it may contain.

I open the sketchbook. The first few pages are blank, but near the end, the pages are filled.

The style is looser, more abstract. It's how she draws when she's drawing from memory rather than from a model. These faces, though still beautiful and symmetrical in the way of San Franciscans, are harder. Some have scars or predatory tattoos. Hissing snakes inked around a neck, the fangs of the open mouth framing a cheekbone, the forked tongue tasting the skin. They look like criminals. Their names are written next to them, too. A fair-haired man named Hatchet. A Japanese woman with long, sleek hair named Haruka.

The next page has a more detailed drawing of a man with the too-smooth skin and haunted eyes that mark him as older. He has a luxurious mane of dark curls around his face, high cheekbones and symmetrical features that are purposefully not perfect. The mouth is wide, the nose long and thin. He has a mole just under his left eye, with a tattoo of a crescent moon around it. Next to the sketch is the name in our secret alphabet: Ensi.

Here he is. The King of the Ratel. I lean close, until my nose almost touches the paper. I memorize every detail about him. This is who Tila was after. Who I am now after.

I turn the page. There is Malka, the Queen of the Ratel, supermodel beautiful, dark hair in long ringlets around her face, a quizzical smile on her face. A few pages later, among other hardened-looking criminals, is an unmistakable sketch of Nazarin. He looks crueler here, his eyes shadowed by his brow, the scars on his head sharper. His sketch is detailed. She'd drawn this from life. The name next to him is "Skel."

Nazarin himself has told me he's met her a time or two before, so it shouldn't surprise me that he's there with the other members of the Ratel, but it's still so strange to see a sketch of him done by my sister. There's a familiarity to the drawing that gives me pause.

I close the sketchbook and go to the kitchen. I log into my messages on the wallscreen. I want to turn something on and zone out and forget about my life, at least for a few moments.

Of course, it's Tila's account on the screen, not mine, because my VeriChip is under her identity. It makes me wonder:

did they change Tila's chip too, and, legally, is it Taema who's in prison and Tila's who's free? Or is she a non-person at the moment?

I shake my head. Curiosity gets the better of me and I delve into her inbox with the same systematic ruthlessness as her apartment. Everything is squeaky clean, nothing stands out. I enable the motion sensors and flick my hands, bringing up her remote storage. I go through each folder, taking my time. I grab a glass of Synthehol white wine, knocking it down far quicker than I should. I stop once I feel a little fuzzy around the edges, numbing the pain.

It takes me a long time to go through my sister's files. I look through all the photos, many of us together, smiling identical smiles. I spend a lot of time looking at the ones from our trip around the world. I got a big return on the initial investment in VivaFog when it was officially bought by the city, and I used some of the money to take three months off work and take Tila with me around the world. We went absolutely everywhere: Jakarta, New Cairo, New Tokyo, Auckland . . . so many places with such vivid memories. No country we were remotely interested in went unvisited. It changed both of us, seeing things so far outside of our limited realm of the Hearth and San Francisco. So many different ways to live.

Nothing suspicious is there. That's because it'll all be in the datapod.

I finally pick it up again. Such a small thing, nestled into the palm of my hand, the swirling designs on the metal like a seashell. I sigh, and put it in my ear.

The datapod connects to my auditory implants and begins to download information directly to my ocular ones. I focus on the white expanse of the table. The information within is for my eyes alone.

A folder called "Eko" flashes before me, a misspelling of her Zenith name. Within are some files with gibberish titles. I pour another glass of the ersatz wine and drain half of it, and then open the top file.

The first file is an invitation to a party, and my eyebrows rise in surprise. It's the same one Nazarin is going to on Saturday. Did he know Tila had an invitation? It's at the Xanadu. A reclusive millionaire named Alex Kynon is said to own the historic building, rebuilt perfectly after the Great Quake to mirror Frank Lloyd Wright's original design. I've never heard of a party, or anyone going there. I also never realized whoever owned it was tied up with the Ratel, but considering how secretive they are, I suppose that's not too surprising.

I open up the second file. I suck in my breath. I open more, reading through them quickly.

I've struck gold.

It's Tila's notes on the Ratel, all written in our hidden alphabet and scanned, the originals destroyed. Tears prick my eyes as I read them. Yes, it's proof she was working with them, but more than that: it's proof she was really working against them. She'd hidden the notes in a place I knew about—if I'd come to leave a message and found these, would she have told me everything? I hide all the files in an encrypted subfolder, deep within my implants. I thank whatever fate or stars aligned that I found these before I went back in. These notes might just save my life.

I sift through more of Tila's notes in my mind's eye. I come across something that makes me both furious and shamed:

*There's a delivery boy/security Knight I'm going to use to get closer to Verve,* she wrote, about four months ago. *His name is Skel. There's a party tonight. I'll turn on the charm and get him to take me back to his. After, I'll convince him to introduce me to Malka, and then I can prove I can lucid dream.* I force down a flush.

The doorbell rings. I jerk in surprise. Hurriedly, I finish hiding the files in my implants and take the datapod out of my ear.

"Coming!" I call as I run to the guest room, stash the sketchbook and the pod in the cubby hole, and push the bed back into place. A few days ago, this would have winded me. Thank you, gym practice and muscle mods.

I peer through the peephole. It's Nazarin. I take a breath, composing myself.

I open the door and Nazarin pushes past me, closing the door behind him.

"Why are you here rather than your place, like you said?" he asks.

I look around, shrugging. It's a way to avoid meeting his eyes. "I realized I hadn't been here since it all went down. And I needed more clothes."

"Let's head back to the safe house. We have your VeriChip putting a false signal here most of the time, in case the Ratel decide to track you, but you actually being here has messed with it."

"There's cameras there, right? In the wallscreens?"

"Yeah?" His forehead crinkles in confusion.

"Not here?"

A beat as Nazarin accesses his implants to scan the apartment. "No."

"Then we should speak here for a moment."

Nazarin opens his mouth to ask why, but I hold up my hand, cutting him off. My anger over what I discovered in the notes crystallizes to a fury just as strong as I felt in Mia's dream world. I lead him to the living room.

"How well do you really know my sister, *Skel*?" I ask. I had hoped I'd somehow been wrong, or read the notes wrong, but his sheepish face shows I'm right. My gut twists. "Spill, and you better not tell me a word of a lie, or I'm out." It's an empty threat, but I still cross my arms. "You haven't just met her once or twice."

He swallows, looking down and away. "I have only met her a few times. I just didn't clarify what . . . happened during one of them." He licks his lips, trying to figure out what to say.

I pour another glass of SynthWine, but don't drink it. I've had enough, but at least it's something to do with my hands. Anger bubbles inside me. No one trusts me to have all the information. The decisions I've made without knowing the full story . . .

"I first met her a few months ago. She was at one of the parties for Knights, Rooks and Pawns. I thought she was a young hopeful, trying to get into the Ratel, get a taste of power by latching onto a powerful member. She had a way of drawing the eye. I guess she would, being a hostess and all."

He stares into space. He's still standing in the middle of the kitchen. He takes the chair across from me, its legs screeching softly against the linoleum.

I say nothing, letting him find the words. "Near the end of the party, we were both pretty drunk. Real alcohol at those things, and neither of us were used to it. Whatever she'd been there for, she hadn't found it. But she took a shine to me. I didn't understand why. It's not like I was important. She asked me to go to a hotel with her."

I feel like I've been punched. I should have seen it, guessed it. I try not to think about his hands on my waist when we danced at Zenith. I try not to think about how he took off my clothes, so expertly. How well he seemed to know my body.

Tila got to him first. She always gets there first. And if he was attracted to me, it wasn't actually for me. It was because I look like her. In a surge of paranoia, I wonder if my sister slept with any of my exes. David? Simone? I shake my head. The constant lies are getting to me, and I'm not even undercover yet.

I pick up my glass, the wine within sloshing. I set it to the side.

It's always weird, when Tila or I meet someone the other has been sleeping with. It's knowing that this other person, this stranger, has a pretty good idea what you look like naked, even if they haven't slept with you. It's the worry that they'll look at one the same way they look at the other.

This is so much worse than any of those other times.

"I didn't go with her," Nazarin says, calmly. I look up, confused.

"I was tempted, but I went home alone. In the end, I knew that sleeping with her was a bad idea. My orders were clear: not to become involved with anyone in the Ratel. Yet she stuck in my mind."

"Did she try to get you to do anything?" I ask carefully. I don't want to tip him off that I have her notes. I'm not sure whether or not to believe him. Tila always gets what she wants, when she puts her mind to it. I can't remember a time anyone rebuffed her advances. If people were to choose between us, they'd be almost certain to choose Tila.

"Yeah. Later, she asked me to introduce her to Malka."

"The Queen."

He inclines his head. "At that point, I hadn't met her, or even seen her, so I couldn't give her what she wanted. She didn't bother with me again after that."

That sounds like Tila. Slyly, I bring up my notes again. She never definitively said she slept with him. After that one entry, her focus shifted to other topics. She mentioned her frustration, and that she was having difficulties seeing Malka, but "Skel" wasn't mentioned again. He could be telling the truth. I hope he is.

"When I saw the murder charge, saw her picture, and discovered she had a twin, I realized I could figure out what she was up to. At first it was curiosity. When I learned she was working in the Verve lounge as a lucid dreamer, I figured she's in deep—deep enough that nobody could follow her."

"Except me."

"Yes. Except you."

He's run out of words. I sip the wine. No, I gulp it. "Why didn't you tell me about this? Especially before you slept with me?" I ask once the glass is empty. I'm trying not to think of them together.

"Nothing happened. She's not the only one in the Ratel who's tried to sleep with me." He shrugs. "I don't know your sister. I can't pretend I do. For what it's worth, I don't think she'd have killed without a reason."

"She didn't kill anyone."

"As I've said, are you still so sure of that? Or are you saying it out of habit now?"

I glance down at the empty glass. "You still should have told me."

"You're right."

I meet his eyes. "No fight? No protests?"

"No. You are entirely right. I shouldn't hold anything back, even if it doesn't seem important to me at the time. It might prove to be. I'm sorry." His body language is open. He seems sincere. I feel like I can't trust my own judgment in anything, anymore. Tila's fucked with my head.

"That's twice you've not told me things I needed to know," I say.

Nazarin stares at me, somber. "I wanted to sleep with you. Not your sister."

My breath catches. He had cut to the heart of what was bothering me. I look away. I see the framed holophoto of me and Tila, arms around each other and smiling. We look so young, so happy. I feel like I've aged about twenty years in less than a week. I thought I knew her better than anyone. "Still probably not the best idea to sleep with your undercover partner," I say. "Did you, uh, mention that to your superior?"

His face goes still. "No, I didn't. If I did, they might throw me off the case, despite all the inroads I've made. Conflict of interest. They'd put someone else on, and starting all over again means they probably wouldn't be able to help your sister."

The careful way he chooses his words makes me tired. "Relax. I'm not going to tell the SFPD." A horrible thought occurs to me. "Does the other safe house have cameras?"

"God, no. Don't worry."

I let out a breath.

"It might not have been the best idea, what we did," he says gently. "I don't regret a moment of it, though." He hesitates, glancing up at me. "Do you?"

I can't help it—the smallest smile hooks to my cheeks before it disappears. "No. I don't. But I don't think it should happen again. Not while we're doing this."

He nods. "That's fair."

I stand up, hold out my hand. "So. You'll tell me everything. I may not be an actual member of the Ratel, but I'm not stupid. I'm your best chance of figuring out what's really going on in the Ratel. Stop trying to protect me or cover your own ass, or you'll get us both killed."

He stands and takes my hand in a warm grasp. "I promise," he says.

I look at him for a long time. He doesn't look away. He wants to kiss me. I want to kiss him, but only our hands touch.

I'm still confused and a little jealous, but I push it away until I'm calm and steady.

It's a new start. We're partners.

•

I'm getting sick of the safe house. It's not home.

Nazarin tells me about the party, and that he wishes he could somehow add my name to the guest list, as starting there versus at the Verve lounge would be easier. The look on his face when I tell him Tila has an invitation too and I should probably go with him is priceless.

I've hidden all her notes, but I bring up the invitation onto the wallscreen. I tell him I found it in her hard drive. It's a white lie, and pretty rich considering I just made him promise to be honest with me in all things. I can't mention the other files, though. I haven't had a chance to translate them all yet, and there could be something incriminating in them. She's my sister. I get first look. If I find anything useful, I'll tell him.

I give him the sketch of Ensi to take back to headquarters, as well. He shakes his head in amazement. "This is what he looks like? Do you know how long we've been trying to find this out? This alone will help us so much."

*Good*, I think. Maybe that'll make it easier for the government to let my sister go. Regardless of what she might have done.

That night I'm strapped into the Chair yet again, to download more confidential information on the Ratel from the SFPD. Since I've been undercover, I haven't seen another cop except in these scenes. But they're there. They'll be ringed around the Xanadu, hidden, supposedly lending whatever support they can, with another few stationed at the safe house. Though I know as well as Nazarin that if we're truly in trouble at that party, they're unlikely to go in and blow the SFPD's cover. We have until Saturday to prepare me as much as possible.

We'll be on our own.

The next day is Thursday. One week since my life turned upside down. It doesn't seem possible. Nazarin is away for most of the day with more Ratel activities. More security. More drop-offs of Verve, to other Zealot lounges.

I wonder how far he goes when he's undercover. How deeply does he play his role? Does he hurt people? His actions do, at the very least. By his delivering a weapon of a vial of Verve, someone will be harmed or killed. Soon, I'll see what he does firsthand.

Soon, I might have to do some of it myself.

Will I be able to? I've prided myself on following the letter of the law since I left the Hearth and arrived in San Francisco. The crimes I may commit while undercover are sanctioned by the government, but I can't help but fear they'll find some legal loophole afterward. What if they don't honor their side of the arrangement, and keep Tila locked up? Or throw me in with her? I know Verve's secret. Will they want to cover up its true purpose?

I have a little ammunition in that regard that I'm keeping close. A week ago, I never would have considered these mercenary thoughts.

I read through Tila's notes. I sit cross-legged on the floor, tilting my head back, eyes closed. I've read them so many times by now. They have so many things I need, like details of the relationships and hierarchies between the various members of the Ratel. There are smaller things, too, like what people like to drink, or their favorite foods—side effects of her training as a hostess. Tila recounts crimes she's witnessed: people picking up packages full of Verve. Information gleaned from dreams. I know what businesses have Ratel members integrated into every level, gathering insider information to their advantage or bullying the owners to give them protection money. Some of this information is incriminating to the government. I know a few high-ranking officials who have tried Verve. A few members of Sudice as well. This is what I'll keep close, to protect myself and Tila when this is all over.

Tila has written her suppositions about Verve—how if it becomes widespread, the Ratel could essentially create an army to do their bidding. The government, or Sudice, wouldn't stand a chance. She also wonders what would happen if it fell into government hands. *San Francisco sure can look beautiful*, she writes, *but it's corrupt to the core with the Ratel and a government not much better. It's all infested, like termites in rotting wood.*

Her notes also seem to echo what Nazarin said outside Mirage—that there is unrest within the ranks of the Ratel. She mentions a young man who's risen quickly through the ranks but still seems discontented:

*Leo. White-blond hair. Black eyes. Has realized how much Ensi keeps at the top end and how little the others are rewarded. Can't be sure if he'll actually do anything about it yet. He's cautious and methodical, but still a bit of an upstart. I figure he's going to get himself killed sooner rather than later, before he can actually make any trouble. One to watch. Could be an ally.*

215

There had been a drawing of him, too, in her sketchbook. Serious, intense.

"Oh, Tila," I murmur aloud. She is in deep. She's been doing this for months. And she'd come to my apartment, pretending she was only a hostess at Zenith. I should be hurt. I should be angry. It's as if I've moved through that, to the other side. Now I'm only sad, disappointed, and still deeply afraid.

All day I read the notes, until I have everything memorized. I take breaks to practice in the gym using the virtual reality overlay, dodging imaginary foes, aiming imaginary weapons. I brainload as much as I can on hacking into implants and hiding information within them, with the hope that the government will not discover what I have hidden.

Thursday melts to Friday. Nazarin stumbles in close to dawn, and I wake slightly as he turns off my Chair. It's only later that day I manage to build up my courage to tell him something in the notes I have to mention before we go to the party.

"I'm going to be Tested tomorrow at Xanadu," I tell him over coffee.

He's slept perhaps three hours, and looks drawn and haggard. At my words, he glances up sharply. "What makes you say something like that?"

"I've, um, found Tila's notes at her place." I give him handwritten, printed-out translations. I've left out the information about the government and Sudice, for our later protection, and a few other things where I didn't understand what they meant and feared they could be dangerous. Everything else is there, and our handwriting is similar enough he doesn't question it.

Nazarin reads the notes right there. I sip my coffee, watching his bowed head, the way the light through the bay window highlights his cheekbones. When he's finished, he holds his head in his hands. "Shit. This changes everything."

We prepare even more intensely. There's a hint of desperation in the detective—he doesn't turn off the brainload to let me have uninterrupted REM. There's no time. Nazarin trains me, and my muscles grow stronger. I can run faster. The SFPD sends still more information to my brain. Out there in the city, my friends are going on with their lives, and so are Tila's.

I meet the team who will be watching us from outside Xanadu. It's only four people, because they're still containing how many within the SFPD know about Tila and me. I recognize the Indian-American officer who helped bring us in that first, awful night. Her name is Officer Jina Shareef. Her handshake is firm. Officer Oloyu is there, though he's only helping part-time. The rest of the time, he's up wherever they're holding my sister. I want to ask him how she's faring, but I'm afraid of the answer. The other two have worked on undercover operations, including with Nazarin, many times. Their names are Detective Lucas and Detective Tan. Both have the large, blocky look of bodyguards, and of men who know how to use a gun. The officers will be watching surveillance, and all four will be posted near the Xanadu, a hovercar at the ready if we need a quick escape.

The morning of the party, I read through the notes one last time. I don't think there's anything more for me to learn from them. The puzzle pieces have fallen into place.

All we know of the Test is it's another lucid dreaming assessment, perhaps to let Tila into the next level of the Verve lounge. No one knows what the Test exactly entails. Not Nazarin. Not the SFPD. Not Tila, though I expect she had some inklings that never made it onto the pages. We've done all we can.

But we won't know if it's enough until I pass or fail.

Tila was after Ensi. The leader of the Ratel. Though I still don't see why, or how she could ever have thought she could take him down. All I can do is get closer to the quarry at the party in Xanadu.

# SEVENTEEN

# TAEMA

The Xanadu is just off Union Square.

I wonder who the billionaire Alex Kynon really is, for it's a pseudonym wrapped in many layers of bureaucratic red tape and obfuscation.

I've wandered through Union Square so many times, especially around Christmas. Tila and I would always come here to see the lights. The giant Christmas tree in the center, the man-made ice rink where people zipped to and fro on old-fashioned ice skates. The city tries to trap the past like an insect in amber. It doesn't really succeed in capturing a sense of what it must have felt like—not with those hypermodern fashions the men and women wear as they bustle about, actually shopping in person for the sheer nostalgia of it, droids following behind carrying their wares—but I do appreciate the effort.

Nazarin and I discussed our plan over and over before I left. We'll take different MUNI trains, arriving at Union Square at different times from different directions. We'll enter the party nearly together, though. Tila and Skel have been seen flirting with each other at previous parties, so we can act friendly, but won't linger together too much. Nazarin is hoping to network, and speak to one of the discontented members of the Ratel, try to become closer to him. He tells me the name, keeping his promise not to hold anything back: it's Leo, the man that Tila wrote about in her notes.

My objective is to do the Test, try not to die, and find out what happens at the next level of the Ratel.

No big deal.

Nazarin appears on my right. I'm waiting for him beneath the pillar of the Dewey Memorial. Far above him, the young woman balances on one toe, holding her wreath and trident.

He pauses. "You look nice."

"Thanks." He saw me leave with my coat, but I have it unbuttoned in the warm evening. I must have tried on all the clothes I'd taken from Tila's place three times before I decided on an outfit. In the end I chose a form-fitting silver zip-up catsuit that covers me from neck to wrists to built-in heels. According to Tila's notes, I'm meant to attract attention at these things. Here's hoping no one misses me, looking like a human-shaped disco ball from space.

"Have you ever been here before?" I ask, jerking my head in the direction of the Xanadu.

"No."

"And you think both the King and Queen will be there?"

"They're meant to be."

Ensi is the named leader of the Ratel, but if the chess analogy is to be carried on, the Queen is the most important player. She's the one who does the dirty work and takes out the other pieces, if need be. I recall Tila's sketch of her, the beautiful woman with long dark hair, a sardonic smile and a cruel glint to her eye.

"OK," Nazarin says. "It's nearly time."

"Right."

He reaches out and grips my shoulder. "We're in this together. You've prepared for this as much as you can. You can do this."

"You have more faith in me than I do."

A short smile. "I have no doubt you can do this. You're tough as nails."

His words hearten me, as they are meant to. I watch him walk away, counting in my head.

Then I follow him, my silver heels clicking along the sidewalk.

It doesn't take long to arrive at the gates. The whole block used to be high-end stores, but now it is all a private residence. I didn't know this before the SFPD told me in the brainload. The average civilian wouldn't. Distribution of wealth isn't as uneven as before the Great Upheaval. Most people make enough to live comfortably, poverty is erased in all but the worst of the Zealots, and though citizens can order vast amounts of goods from the replicator, all can be recycled back. There are still obscenely wealthy people in this city but they tend to keep a lower profile than, say, those in Hollywood, where status and ranking have more pull. Having far, far more money than you need is seen as wasteful.

Nazarin walks through the gates. I approach a minute later, projecting Tila's invitation from my ocular implant onto a little wallscreen to the left. The door opens with a *snick*, and I walk in.

In front of us is the large, faux brick building, now made of bomb-proof, acid-proof material. We walk through to the second gate, a replica of the original Art Deco iron arched gate, topped by four rings of brick. Like many buildings, it was destroyed in the Great Quake and rebuilt to be larger than the previous plans. The original building was a store, and now it is a mansion.

Nazarin—no, Skel, he is *Skel* now—lingers enough that we almost walk into the darkened tunnel at the same time. He

221

does not turn back or acknowledge me, but I'm thankful for his nearness.

I take a steadying breath. I am about to enter the same building as the Ratel King and Queen. It's what I've prepared for. I am now, for all intents and purposes, my sister: a lucid dreamer for a Verve lounge for the biggest mob in the city. None of it seems real. I can't really be doing this. Still, I place one foot in front of the other, moving closer to whatever is to come.

The tunnel fills with soft lights of green, blue, and purple, and a light fog drifts at waist height, scented with lilacs.

"In Xanadu did Kubla Khan a stately pleasure-dome decree," I whisper.

Nazarin stiffens and almost turns back in confusion. I guess he's never read Coleridge.

We enter, still staggered, and the droids take our coats. I shed that outer layer like a carapace, wearing only my silver, shining second skin. Nazarin passes over his gun. No weapons at parties. Nazarin's eyes slide over me, but I ignore him, staring upward, unable to stop myself from gaping.

The whole ceiling is open, showing the stars and moon above. It's made from the finest bulletproof glass. Despite the seriousness of the situation I can't help but be transported by the beauty of it. The main ballroom has a re-creation of the original spiral staircase along its edges but much larger, like the inside of a shell, perfect circles cut out of the sides, like the holes in an abalone. The walls are creamy white, lights tingeing the smooth plaster green and blue. Twining, living vines hang from the ceiling, framing an enormous organic chandelier suspended above the dance floor, twinkling with emeralds and other jewels among the leaves. Elephants drink from a palm-framed water hole, and birds fly overhead. They're all mechanical, their eyes cameras for security posted in the next room, available to come in at a moment's notice if needed.

There aren't as many people here as I would have thought, but everyone looks so sleek and stylish, they nearly put Zenith to shame. Yet they are obviously dangerous too, marked with moving tattoos and wearing their scars proudly. A few dance to music, twining their bodies together, skin pressed against skin. Others huddle together, murmuring among themselves, while some wander from group to group, hovering here to say a few words before fluttering onward, like butterflies sipping nectar from each cluster. Despite their prettiness, I cannot forget the venom they all have the ability to spread. More lines of that poem come to me:

> And there were gardens bright with sinuous rills,
> Where blossomed many an incense-bearing tree;
> And here were forests ancient as the hills,
> Enfolding sunny spots of greenery.

I straighten my shoulders and put on Tila's sultry smile. I let her personality settle over mine. I'm Tila. I'm confident and strong. I'm unafraid. A droid leaves the bar nestled at the back and passes by, offering me a glass of champagne. I take a sip and almost choke. It's real champagne—nothing remotely synth about it. The liquid burns slightly, and my taste buds tingle, the bubbles popping against my tongue.

I recognize some of the faces from Tila's sketches. I stay calm—my eyes flicker over them quickly, but I don't see the King and Queen of the Ratel.

Nazarin leaves me, mingling with others before returning. He greets me, giving me one of those small hugs you give people you don't know very well. "Something's not right," he whispers in my ear. "Be careful."

Before I can ask him more questions, he disappears, and I'm taken aback. I know we can't be seen too much together, but surely if Tila flirted with him at a previous party, we could take up the same cover again. How can he just leave me here on my own, with what I'm about to face?

Some of the familiar faces from Tila's sketchbook come to greet me, and I smile and kiss them on the cheeks, greeting them by name, all too aware that the hands gently resting on my shoulders have killed people. All these polite guests are hardened criminals, many with hits under their belts. It's almost like I can feel the ghosts, a press of the invisible, cold corpses these people are responsible for, crowding the room with the revelers.

I shake my head, which feels fuzzy. I eye the scented fog in suspicion—have they put something in it, like the way they release extra pheromones in the casinos? Was there something in that glass of champagne—real champagne!—I drank far too quickly?

I have to keep my wits about me.

I understand a lot more than I did before, but there are still so many gaps. Tila came into the Ratel from a different direction than Nazarin. She may have run errands briefly, but as soon as she proved that she could lucid dream, she worked her way in deeper without going through the official steps. Until now. She's close enough that they want her to do something more important for them, if she just passes this Test. If I just pass the Test.

I force myself to stay calm, to smile at the guests as if nothing is bothering me.

What did the Ratel think, when Vuk disappeared? Do they think he went rogue, or do they know that something happened to him? Tila wasn't supposed to be working that night, but surely someone at the club noticed her. Sal saw her. Did he change his colors and decide to turn her in to the Ratel? There is a chance that this is all an elaborate trap. Nazarin said that the hitman, that Adam-turned-Vuk, wasn't after her. I'm not sure if I still believe that.

I look around for Nazarin again, my mouth dry. I drink more champagne to wet it, though the bubbles are going to my head already. It all just seems so very, very stupid. We're here with essentially no backup because any type of surveillance would be instantly recognized by the scanners we passed at the gate. There's plenty of cops seconds away if we can manage to call them, but the odds of that in here are next to nothing—all signals are blocked.

I'm beginning to panic, sweating beneath the silver fabric. Where is Nazarin? He wouldn't leave me, would he? I keep saying hello to strangers, fudging conversations, my mind working in overtime not to step in the wrong place. Nobody mentions a thing about the Ratel. They comment on the decor, how amazing this building is, the champagne, the salty caviar blintzes. I want to scream.

*Be Tila. She'd know how to react. None of this would faze her.*

The party wears on. My cheeks ache from the effort of appearing cheerful and flirtatious, uncaring and unaware of the precariousness of my situation. I dance with people. I sip more champagne, nibble at the decadent treats. There's still no Nazarin. I can't help but feel he's thrown me to the wolves. The shiny, silvery distraction.

Nazarin finally returns. He has a pretty man next to him, who's flirting shamelessly, and he's flirting in turn with considerable skill. I feel an unwelcome flare of annoyance at the display. With a start, I recognize the other person: he's Leo, the young man Tila mentioned in her notes. The potential ally. I make my way toward them.

"Good evening. Great party, right?" I sound inane.

Nazarin gestures to me. "Leo, I believe you've met Tila."

"How could I ever forget?" he says, taking my hand and kissing the back of it.

I wonder what sort of impression Tila made.

Leo seems composed, but his eyes keep darting about the room. Perhaps he's uncomfortable with eye contact. He moves with the grace of someone who knows how to fight.

He meets my eyes. "The party's only just getting started, isn't it? Lots more entertainment to come, I'm sure."

I smile, though something makes me uneasy. Nazarin narrows his eyes at Leo.

"Leo," Nazarin says. "You'll have to excuse us, but I want to steal Tila for a dance."

Leo smiles. "Of course. I might have to steal her after, if you don't mind that is," he says to me. Smooth. Very smooth.

"That'd be lovely," I say, thinking it would be no such thing. "Excuse me, I'm going to find another drink, first." Nazarin reaches out to touch my elbow. He wants to tell me something, but there's no way he can. The crowd is thicker than at the start of the evening. Too many ears to overhear a whisper. Ocular and auditory implants have been blocked by tech dampeners.

Nazarin's eyes follow me as I take another flute of champagne I will not drink from a droid servant.

I turn around and a woman stands right before me, flanked by two guards. She looks me up and down, smiling in recognition. She knows me and has seen me before.

And I recognize her, though it takes me a moment to realize who she is, with her hair up.

It's Malka. The Queen of the Ratel.

She has the tightness around her eyes that speaks of facelifts. Her brows are high and arched, her full lips curl at the edges. She has skin of a deep brown, her hair in a slick updo, with a web of metal and crystals holding the hair in place.

"Tila," Malka says. She reeks of power. The two bodyguards at her sides are droids, their blank faces twisting from side to side for danger.

I smile blankly in return, my mind running in frantic circles. I glance at Nazarin and his eyes are wide, locked on me.

"The Khan of Xanadu is ready to see you now. It's time to Test your mettle."

I blink quickly, then put another inane grin on my face. "Wonderful. I've been looking forward to it."

She laughs, low and throaty, rubbing the fingers of one hand against the fleshy base of her thumb. "I wouldn't be, if I were you. Come along, little canary."

Malka takes my arm and leads me through the crowd. She stops as people greet her, introducing me. I watch other people's reactions, the awe and fear she inspires in them.

People notice me at her side, and wonder why I've been so favored. Why has she come to get me herself? How well does she know me? Tila's notes didn't tell me much about her. I'm lost.

"Come," Malka says. "We musn't be late."

All my nerve endings seem to freeze. Malka takes my arm, unlocking me, and I follow her toward the spiral ramp. I chance a look over my shoulder and Nazarin's staring at me, barely concealed panic in his eyes. Leo is speaking to him, but he doesn't seem to hear. He wanted to tell me something, but now it's too late. I try to smile at him, but I can't. I turn away and walk up the stairs.

I don't have a choice.

Nobody is up on this level. The clear glass of the ceiling seems almost close enough to touch. Up here, little rooms helix off around the huge circle in the center, a maze of little hidden nooks and crannies. I peek over the banister down at the revelers below. Nobody looks up except for Nazarin. I nod at him, try to smile.

I feel strangely detached. Deep down, I'm aware I should be more scared about this. But it feels . . . inevitable. I'm following Tila's breadcrumbs, seeing if they lead to the ginger-bread house and the hungry witch.

The Queen opens a door. I can't see anything inside but another dark, curving hallway.

"Put these on." She passes me a small white box. I open it. Inside are small electrodes. She helps me attach them to my temples, the back of my neck, my heart. There's a thin pair of dark glasses. I put them on, feeling silly.

"These will track your physical responses," she says.

"All right." I wonder if my mechanical heart will impact anything. They'll know of it, I'm sure. They know everything; except, hopefully, that I have changed my face and taken my sister's place.

"There. Now. Go down to the end of the hallway and turn left."

I lick my lips. "Any advice?" I ask, striving for a light tone. Desperate as I am, she's my only point of contact and I'll take any help I can get—even if it's from the devil herself. I sense she appreciates that I've asked her.

She leans close, and she smells of jasmine and expensive makeup. "Don't speak unless ordered. Don't lie. Don't look away. Don't let us down."

She looks into my eyes, deep and searching, as if she knows

228

all my sins. After a moment, she leans back. I don't know what she found. With a twirl of turquoise silk, she is gone.

I've never been more confused. My head hurts, and I'm still dizzy. There must be something in the fog in that room downstairs. I should be tempted to throw myself out that window, climb down, jump the impossibly high fence, and make a break for freedom. How would Tila feel, if it was still her walking down this hallway to this Test? If she'd never come across Vuk, if he'd never ended up dead, then she'd be here, right now, and I'd never know. My head feels unattached to my body, like it's floating down this darkened hallway.

I turn to the left as instructed, and push open the door.

I'm the last person to arrive. In the room are four chairs. The other three are occupied. One is a girl with bright crimson hair down to her waist, dressed in black trousers and a glittering top. A man with a tuft of blond hair and black eyeliner wearing a red suit, with a tattoo of a tarantula on the back of his hand, sits in the middle. The man next to him has dark green hair and is dressed in black leather. It goes without saying that they're all beautiful.

I sit in the last chair, crossing my legs to stop them from shaking.

The room is completely blank. White walls, white chairs, white floors. I open my mouth, but then I remember what Malka said. *Don't speak.* My mouth snaps shut. I grind my teeth together. The drug from downstairs might be wearing off. I'm petrified.

There's a flash in the corner of my vision, a small beep in my ear. I have a message. Judging by the way the others grow still, they've received it, too. The white wall in front of me seems to undulate in waves. I can feel the little electrodes buzzing against my skin.

"You are here because you have done well. You have served and done all I've asked of you." The voice is disguised—it echoes, distorting strangely in my mind. "You have made it to a level that few can claim to reach."

It wasn't me. I did none of it. *How did you get here, Tila?* I want to ask.

"Now, for the moment, do nothing. Just watch. And listen."

*Don't look away.*

Images flow onto the blank wall, so quickly I barely register one before the next flicks into my field of vision. A praying mantis. The inside of a cat's mouth. The glowing algae of the bay. The aftermath of a battle. Blood splattering on white walls. A decomposing corpse. A little girl in pigtails, holding a teddy bear by an arm. Ink blots, like in old psychological tests. Nature. War. Humanity. Over and over again.

Sounds come with them—from soft birdcalls to shrill shrieks and sirens. Smells appear too, and some are nice: cinnamon, the green smell of broken pine needles and the scent of crushed apples. Others are putrid: rotten fish, decomposing flesh, the oniony smell of unwashed bodies.

The man with the blond quiff bends forward and throws up onto the white floor. I glance at him but then fix my eyes to the wall.

*Don't look away.*

I don't know what this means. What it's meant to test. Am I passing or failing?

The images go on for what feels like a long time. I clutch the sides of the chair. My stomach roils, but I clamp down tight on my tongue. I won't throw up. Soon, someone else pukes, but still I don't look away. I think it might be the red-haired girl.

The images cease. All returns to pure whiteness. I sag against my chair in relief. The room smells of acidic vomit and new sweat tinged with old fear.

"Now," says the distorted voice in our minds. "Stand."

We stand. I allow myself to look at the others. The other girl has vomit smudged in her red hair. The blond man's hair is in disarray. The green-haired man seems relatively unruffled. I wonder what I look like to them.

"Now, face each other. Tila, look at the man with green hair."

I almost start at being addressed by this stranger. This is the oddest test I've ever taken. I don't understand the rules. I don't know the score. I haven't studied, as Tila's notes stopped right before I needed the cheat sheet most.

The voice changes slightly. Still modulated, but more familiar. "Study your opponent's face, Tila. Memorize every line."

I look at him, and he looks at me. I see a man, but only barely. He can't be much older than twenty. I think he's half-Chinese and half-Mexican, or something along those lines. I wonder what awful things he's done to get this far.

"Good. Now look at the man with blond hair."

I look, and as I turn my head, I see the red woman and the green man have done the same. As soon as we're all looking, the blond man crumples. Blood pours from his nose, his ears, his eyes. He's dead.

"He failed," the voice whispers in our minds.

*Fuck,* I think. I should think more. Feel more. I can't—all I can concentrate on is making sure that it's not me next.

"Look forward."

We stare at the screens again. More images flash, even quicker this time, so that I couldn't explain them even if I wanted to. I hear retching beside me. Why do they affect them more than me? My stomach hurts, my head hurts, and I feel pressure behind my eyes, but I'm still looking.

*Don't look away.*

The voice starts asking me questions. I'm to blink once for yes and twice for no. The man doesn't ask me about what I—Tila—have done for the Ratel. Instead they're hypothetical questions. Some are difficult: *Would you kill your childhood pet for X sum of money? Would you risk your life to save a drowning child? What about a drowning person who wronged you?* Some are beyond asinine: *If there were ice cream and sprinkles on that white coffee table right now, would you add the sprinkles?*

I answer them all without thinking too hard. There are hidden layers and messages in this, impacting us all in ways we can't anticipate. Feints and jabs before hooks and crosses. I don't even try to outsmart them. There's no way to.

The scarlet-haired girl goes next. Falls right out of her chair. Her red hair perfectly matches the blood.

*This is insane*, I think distantly. *This is absolutely insane.* I wonder if I'll be the next person to die.

Maybe this is all a trap. These are people hopeful of moving up in the Ratel, and maybe the King already knows that we're not worthy. He's here to catch us in lies, pick us off one by one. Perhaps it's his idea of sport.

Maybe he wants to discover whether we've betrayed him before he kills us.

The green man is nervous, sweat dripping down his temples. I'm surprisingly calm. I must look unafraid to him, and that makes me feel braver. I stand, staring at him. His pupils behind the darkened glasses dilate as he listens to his own instruction. Then he rushes me.

He grabs my arm, hard enough to stop the blood flow. I try to jerk out of his grip but he only holds on tighter. The man's face is red, twisted with rage.

He means to kill me.

"Kill him," the voice whispers in my mind. "Or be killed."

I stomp on his insole, the way Nazarin taught me. The sharp stiletto of my heel presses on his foot and I'm sure I hear something snap. He cries out and I twist my arm, breaking free.

He rushes me again, but this time I see it coming. Nazarin's training serves me well enough, but I won't be able to avoid him forever. He's much bigger than me, and much, much angrier. I look for a weapon and grab the nearest chair, stepping over the body of the blond man. I bring up the chair and swing it at him, trying to frighten him off, and then I hold it close to me like a lion-tamer against a rabid man with a mane of green hair. The signal to my implants is blocked—the voice and images are silent in my head, including the self-defense programs for the implants. I'm left to fend for myself.

He attacks me and I smash him with the chair, grunting with the effort. He barely staggers, and then reaches out and grabs the chair so hard that I have to release it.

"Stop it!" I bellow at him, even though I'm not supposed to speak. He gives a shout, more of a roar, and hits me hard on my shoulder and I drop. I cry out and roll out of the way just before he brings the chair down again, and it shatters into splinters. I grab a broken leg, sharpened to a point. Snarling, enraged as I was in Mia's Vervescape, I thrust up.

Blood spurts from the wound, drenching my hands. The green-haired man sputters. He no longer looks angry. He looks scared, and hurt.

"Oh God," I say, over and over again. "Oh God. Oh God. Oh God."

He falls right on top of me, driving the splinter of wood deeper into himself. His blood seeps onto me. I push him away. He's so heavy. I crawl away and throw up, retching until there's nothing left. When I'm done I sit back on my heels, wrapping my arms around my knees and shaking. I'm surrounded by three dead bodies, splatters of blood and sick marring the perfect white of the room.

Now, even if Tila hadn't killed Vuk, I've killed someone. I'm no longer the woman I was a week ago. I'm no longer an engineer and someone who follows the rules. I'm a murderer. I say it out loud. "I'm a murderer." I almost choke on the words, but I force myself to say it again. "I'm a murderer." My throat is raw from vomiting and screaming. I want to curl up and disappear.

I close my eyes tight. My heart is still beating far too calmly. I tear the glasses from my face and throw them across the room, ripping the electrodes from my body by touch.

"Open your eyes," a man's voice says.

I obey. The room is now completely empty but for the cooling pile of my own vomit beside me. There's no red woman, blond man or green man. It's as if they never existed. They never did.

Instead, in front of me is Ensi.

The leader of the Ratel.

He's tall, leanly muscled, with skin a little darker than mine and close-cropped, curly hair. It had been longer in Tila's sketch. He wears a collarless blue silk shirt and black trousers, and looks almost like a priest.

He holds out his hand. "Up you come. Time to talk."

I take his hand.

# EIGHTEEN

# TILA

I didn't know how to approach Mom and Dad about escaping the Hearth. Neither did Taema.

*Hey, Mom. Hey, Dad. Can you ignore all your beliefs and help us abandon you?*

They hadn't been born in the Hearth, though. They knew the world outside—or at least they had known it, thirty or so years ago. They were the only ones who could get us out.

We were going to die soon if we didn't do something. We felt tired all the time, and our ankles had swollen so much we had to wear old shoes of Mom's, and her shoes were ugly. We never wanted to eat. I'd wake up in the night and Taema's breath would be all hitchy. Sometimes she'd even stop breathing and I'd hold my own breath until she started up again.

I could feel our heart thumping beneath our skin all the time, like it was a fish trying to jump from the surface of the lake. Every day, it was getting harder to do basic things. Mom had to help dress us. Dad, embarrassingly, had to help bathe us because Mom wasn't strong enough to haul us up. Now we had even less privacy.

So after dinner one night, we confronted them. They were doing the dishes, Dad washing and Mom drying them and putting them away, humming to themselves. They were still very much in love with each other. Still are, I hope, though I haven't seen them in a decade. Seemed a shame to ruin the nice moment.

We'd agreed that I'd do the talking. We knew some hard things would have to be said, and Taema wasn't up to it. Her fingers were digging into my ribcage and she was shaking. I was nervous too, but in this I was the stronger twin. I wasn't afraid of saying things to our parents that might make them cry, if it meant we'd get what we wanted. Needed. A lifeline.

"We don't want to die," I started, cutting right to the chase.

Our parents stopped humming.

Dad turned off the water carefully. "What, Tila?" Even though he'd been facing the other way, he knew it was me. He and Mom came through and sat on the couch across from us. My mom pushed her curly hair back over her shoulder. My dad worried his lower lip with his teeth the way he did when he was nervous. Their faces were tight, trying to keep any emotion from sneaking out.

"We don't want to die," I repeated. "And we don't have to, if we can leave the Hearth and get to the city. Can you help us do that?" I kept the emotion out of my own voice.

Mom's face crumpled, and Dad put his arm around her. "My girls," he said, his voice breaking. "I wish we could. But no one leaves the Hearth."

"Mia did. We remember."

It'd been hushed up, but even as children we heard the rumors. I'd forgotten about them until we started thinking of leaving. She'd left. On purpose. No one ever found out how she'd escaped.

Our parents looked away.

"Please. You have to help us . . . we're dead if we stay."

"If you escape . . ." our mother whispered, "you'd be apostate.

You'd be damned. Surrounded by all that technology . . . all the Impure . . ."

Next to me, Taema flinched. "That's true," I said. It wasn't worth telling them we—I, at least—didn't believe in the tenets of the faith anymore. Damn, they'd been so brainwashed in the last sixteen years, with Mana-ma battering away at their brains like the rest of us. Could I even break through? I pushed on ahead.

"We'd rather be alive and damned than dead and saved. Please. We don't want to die."

Though for me, it was more that I didn't want Taema to die. I knew more than her. I knew if we did get out and found a doctor to fix our heart, there was a chance we wouldn't both survive. Of course there was. Medicine out there was really advanced, but it wasn't infallible. I just had to hope that if death took one of us, it took me and not her.

Dad pressed his lips together as he thought.

Shit, I miss them so much. They were good parents. They did their best by us. Even then, when they knew that if they helped us they'd never see us again, they still risked their jobs and their faith to help us.

"What about smuggling them out in the supply ships?" Dad asked Mom. "We could hide them . . ."

She shook her head. "Mana-ma would find out that way, as so little goes back out."

"Even if we bribe them?"

"With what? Hand-stitched quilts? Those few credits we have from thirty years ago are worthless now."

"What goes out to the city? Just blankets and apples and stuff, right?"

Our mother looked uncomfortable. Next to me, Taema rested her head on my shoulder. She was especially tired today.

"Yes," Mom said. "Plus several boxes I'm not allowed to open. If they get paid for any of it, I never see the money. Mana-ma packs those boxes herself, so there's no way to sneak you out in those."

"Doesn't that . . . worry you? That she's sending stuff out and you have no idea what it is?"

"She must be doing God's will in one way or another." My mother did not sound convinced as she gave us a tremulous smile. Dad looked worried.

"You're both doubting her, aren't you? At least a little bit."

Taema's head rose from my shoulder as she stared at them.

"We'd never . . ." Mom trailed off, unable to complete the lie.

"The closer we get to the top," Dad whispered, "the more we see. The more we aren't able to unsee."

He wouldn't elaborate more than that. This conversation was going very differently than how I'd thought it would.

"We'd have to go behind Mana-ma," Dad said. "It won't be easy."

"Can you do it?" I asked.

They looked at us as though we were crazy for asking. "Of course."

"Will you come with us?"

A pause. My parents exchanged a glance. "We can't. It'd be too hard to sneak all of us out. We can do more good here."

I lost it then and started crying. So did Taema. Mom and Dad came and put their arms around us. Nothing would ever be the same as before our heart attack. Or before we found that tablet and realized that there was a whole world out there, and this one was fucked. Maybe, even if our heart hadn't been weak, we would still have tried to escape. I'd like to think we would have. Somehow.

Taema finally spoke up. "Thank you," she whispered.

They kept their arms around us, kissing the tops of our heads.

Our heart kept skittering in our ribcage. If they were going to save us, they would have to do it soon. If they were going to be able to do it at all.

•

The worst part was waiting.

I was never very good at waiting. I'd rather barrel in head first and figure it out later.

Our parents were formulating a plan, but didn't tell us the exact details. They said it'd be safer that way. It made Taema and me feel guilty and confused—what would Mana-ma do to them, or us, if she found out we were trying to leave? I imagine she'd been furious when she found out that Mia left. None of us were meant to speak of her, in any case; just like nobody spoke about the Brother.

It was hard going through day-to-day life when we could barely move. We started sleeping more and eating less. We needed canes to support us when we did try to walk.

It was terrible.

When we were feeling stronger we'd walk through the path in the woods until we reached the swamp. The air smelled thick and fetid, cutting through the scent of crushed pine needles. There were no boats on the island, for no one ever needed to leave, at least according to Mana-ma.

We ran our hands along the ferns, their leaves tickling our hands. We wanted to leave the confines of the Hearth more than anything, but we were also so scared.

"What do you think it'll be like?" Taema asked. She always asked that when we were alone. Now that we'd decided, and even though deep down the crisis of faith was getting to her, I could tell she was daydreaming about it all the time so that she didn't have to focus on the here and now. I kept wanting to pretend it was perfect on the other side, that we'd have wonderful new lives. The problem was, I've always been too much of a cynic to believe in happily ever after.

"It'll be the best," I reassured her. "We can do anything we want. A whole fresh start. The world is our oyster!"

"What does that even mean?"

"No idea. It was in one of your books I borrowed."

She laughed weakly. Up overhead, the supply ship flew for its first drop in three months.

Taema shifted uncomfortably next to me, pulling on our shared skin. "Should we go see it?"

I shook my head. I didn't want to risk anyone seeing us hanging around there this time.

The last time.

# NINETEEN

# TAEMA

"Tila," Ensi, the leader of the Ratel, says with a smile. Like so many in San Francisco, he looks hardly older than thirty, but I'm sure he must be at least ten years older or more. Perhaps significantly more.

He's not quite as classically handsome as many men I've seen in the city—most likely intentionally. The crescent moon tattoo by his eye glows slightly green.

I'm still shaking. "What's going on?"

"I Tested you."

"The others . . . they weren't real?"

"No. Mere images projected from those electrodes and your ocular implants."

"I haven't killed anyone," I whisper. I can't believe how relieved I feel. I'm light-headed with it.

"Have you not?" He smiles in a way that makes me wonder, with a sickening feeling, if he knows about Tila and Vuk already. If he knows *everything*.

I force myself to appear calm and collected, like I haven't just completely lost it in that white room. But how was that possible? It seemed so real. Not even virtual reality games were that realistic. Only the Zealscape. I shudder. "Did you drug me?"

"A little."

"What with?" The thought of being drugged without my permission or knowledge is unnerving, to say the least.

"A Verve derivative." My breath catches. That derivative doesn't need a Chair. I feel invaded.

He smiles, as if amused by my distress. "If he had been a real person, you would likely have killed him just the same."

I feel very cold. "Did I pass your Test?"

He smiles. "You did. You didn't hesitate to do what's necessary. Many who move up the ranks traditionally would have come across this situation in different ways. Your situation is . . . unique. After all, we're already well acquainted, aren't we? This was really just a formality." He moves closer to me and holds out his arms, expecting me to go into them, as I have before. Or so he thinks.

Oh. Shit.

What if this is a trap? If I pretend to recognize that closeness, am I caught, or is it the other way around? The questions whizz through my mind, as quickly as possible. I don't have long, so I choose, praying that I'm right.

I step into his arms. "Ensi," I murmur.

The arms wrap around me, strong and muscular. He's a head taller than me, and rests his lips on the top of my head. It's strangely tender. I'm shaking, but hopefully he thinks it's from the aftermath of the Test rather than the fact I'm terrified of him.

I'd thought my sister had met him before, or at least seen him, close enough to sketch him well. Now it seems my sister's done significantly more than that.

Goddammit, Tila. She couldn't just infiltrate the Ratel, she had to go and sleep with the leader of it? There was no mention of it in her notes. This makes everything about ten times harder.

Or it might make things easier, depending how I play it. My mind whirrs, scheming and plotting just like my sister's would have.

"So what now?" I ask, smiling, although I'm hoping that he doesn't expect me to jump into bed with him anytime soon. I may be able to fake Tila, but I'm not sure I'm *that* good an actress.

He smiles, full of secrets. I look at his hands, long and thin. With a twitch of his little finger, he could order my death. He's responsible for so much misery. Yet he's still oozing charisma as he holds my upper shoulder, and I feel caught in his trap and angry that there's no easy way out of this.

Shiny, silvery bait.

He leads me out of the white room into another across the hall. Here, everything is comfortingly modern. The room is warm, decorated in oranges and browns. I perch on a chair, crossing my legs and folding my arms. It's a defensive body posture, but I can't help but try to barricade myself against him.

I have two options: I can plead illness and hope he lets me leave and go home. Or I can be Tila.

She's done this. She's trapped him with all her grace and sex appeal. She's someone who stops at nothing to get what she wants. I could do the same and ride this out and see what happens.

As soon as I make the decision that this is what I'm going to do, I relax.

I slouch back, leaning on an elbow. The man sitting across from me is more powerful than the mayor of San Francisco, and maybe even the president of Pacifica.

Out of the corner of my eye I think I spy a spot of blood on my silver jumpsuit, but it's just a play of the light from the false fireplace. I blink, willing the memory of the bloodbath, the bodies, away, but the smell of my own vomit still lingers. *It wasn't real. It wasn't real.* I really wouldn't mind some mouth-wash.

"So, now that I've passed your Test, what happens next?" I ask, my voice teasing. I can't be scared. Tila never seemed scared, no matter how difficult things were. She seemed so calm when we ran away from the Hearth. Her strength was what got us out of there. Without her I wouldn't have made it. Now it's my turn to rescue her.

Ensi pours two glasses of what looks like whiskey and passes it to me. I drink it, more to get rid of the lingering taste of vomit in my mouth than anything else. Of course, it's not Synth. I don't know enough about whiskey to guess at the type, but I'm sure it's one of the most expensive to be found in San Francisco.

I'm trying my hardest to be Tila. But I'm on such thin ice. I have no idea how well they know each other. If he references anything specific, a past conversation or event, I'm doomed. I'm so very aware that the likelihood of me exposing myself as a fraud rises the longer we speak.

So. I'm going to have to get him to stop talking. The best way to get him to stop talking is probably to sleep with him. I look at him under lowered lashes. Physically, he doesn't repulse me, quite the opposite. From growing up in the Hearth, I've always thought of sex as a conversation or a connection. In this case, it's a tool I can use, and I'm fully aware of that. I can't say that sleeping with the head of the Ratel was how I expected this evening to end.

Goddammit, Tila.

"Now, you're in," Ensi says. "You help me, I help you, and all of San Francisco is at your fingertips."

I force myself to smile, as if that's all I've ever wanted. Really,

I'd rather grab a nearby candlestick, bash him over the head and run away. Evidently I'm capable of it. I flinch at the violent urge. Did the Verve or the Test change me? I finish the drink and set the glass on the little table by the sofa.

"You caught my eye when we first met," he says, standing and drifting closer to one of the paintings on the wall. I join him, my mind still spinning. Where did they meet? When? "You put yourself to any task I asked of you with a single-mindedness few possess. You've proved yourself at the Verve lounge, these last few weeks. I have no doubt you'll be an asset to us."

He has a way of speaking that seems familiar. Didactic—that's what it is. Expansive, confident, the way Mana-ma would deliver a sermon. His voice draws me in close. I try to resist his spell. I wonder if there are still remnants of the drug in my system, or if he exudes some sort of pheromone that I can't resist, either manufactured or natural, that makes me want to open to him like a flower. I close my eyes and call on Mana-ma's training, imagining a bright light cleansing my whole body. When I open my eyes, I feel in control of myself, cold and calculating.

"When do we start?" I ask.

"Soon enough. Tonight, though, is a celebration. Don't worry about business for now." He moves closer, holds out his hand. "Shall we dance?"

I take his hand, warm and soft. No manual labor for him. "Shouldn't we go downstairs, where the music is?"

With a flick of his eyes, the same music that plays downstairs flows through unseen speakers. "Much as I'd like to, I can't go down to join in. Not just yet." He smiles to himself, as if he's told an amusing joke. I shiver.

His hand moves around my waist, slipping on the silver fabric. It reminds me of when I danced with Nazarin, and I flinch from that memory. I put my arms up around his neck. He's six inches taller than me, even with my heels. We move in time to the music.

"Ah, little Tila," he says. "What a relief. After that Test I know all about you."

His words are ominous rather than reassuring. I look into his eyes as he dances. I can't see any sign that he doesn't think I'm Tila, but I'm still nervous. We're similar, my sister and I, but our personalities are not identical. I'm also sure the Ratel have looked up Tila's file and know she has a twin, and I have to hope they know the twin is meant to have a different face.

We dance to the music, soft and steady. It's almost hypnotic. Ensi knows just where to put his feet, just how to move. Before long, he bends his head down to kiss me, and I open my mouth to his. His mouth is warm and sweet, tasting of spices and whiskey. He's surprisingly gentle for the crime lord of the city, yet firm. He wants me. And he expects to get me.

It occurs to me again that I still have time to change my mind. Draw away and shake my head and smile, reach for some whiskey. I could say I was unwell or on my period. I don't. I'm choosing to kiss him.

There are several things that keep me kissing him. One: sex is a way to get to understand him better, to see him in a state of vulnerability. Two: these are his personal chambers, or one set of them. I'm pretty sure Alex Kynon is actually one of his (several) aliases. There could be something in here I need. There are wallscreens. I've brainloaded a lot of information on hacking during the last few days. If he trusts me, it will make it all the easier for me to get what I need from him. Three: he's a good kisser and I'm surprisingly into it. Four: it's what Tila would do.

It's risky, though. For all I'm close with my sister, we're not close enough that I know exactly how she has sex. I have to hope we're similar enough. Another thought of Nazarin and Tila together. Such strange, inverted parallels. *Stop. Nothing happened. Let that go. Focus on the here and now.*

His arms move lower, and I can feel the strength in his fingertips. Perhaps I enjoy the danger. Perhaps I'm more like Tila than I thought.

He picks me up, presses me against him. His hair tickles my face. I wrap my arms and legs around him and he carries me to the sofa.

The music trails away, forgotten. He pushes me into the soft velvet. I kiss him fiercely. His fingers run through my short, blue hair. I dance my fingers along the skin of his neck, unbuttoning his shirt. He helps me, shrugging off his coat and pulling his shirt over his head. He has a swimmer's body, with hardly any fat to speak of, his abs a rippled six-pack. I touch his skin, and he shivers.

A little notebook peeks out of his jacket, and attached to it, I see a small datapod. I half-lid my eyes as I study it. I want it. It's important enough he keeps it on him at all times in the inside pocket of his jacket, where no one can get it.

He soon distracts me, at least somewhat, from the thought of the little paper book. His lips move from mine, down to my neck. I arch against him, my nerves on fire. The adrenaline of the recent Test is still pumping through my body. I pull him against me, nipping his neck with my teeth.

Those long, nimble fingers work at the zipper at the hollow of my neck. Within moments, I'm exposed to him from neck to navel. He traces the scar down my sternum with his fingertip. It reminds me uncomfortably of Nazarin.

His fingertip moves from the scar to circle my left breast, teasing the nipple until it stands upright. He bends his head and I stare up at the ceiling, gasping slightly.

*Bang.*

We both start. His head jerks up, and I squirm to a sitting position.

The sound came from downstairs. It sounded like a gunshot. People scream.

"Was that—?" I start, but then my question is answered by an outpouring of screams, more gunshots, and the stampede of fleeing footfalls.

He jumps away, reaching into a cabinet under the alcohol bar and drawing out a weapon and a bulletproof Kalar jumpsuit. I have a feeling they are hidden in every room. What that means cuts through the fear for a moment: this is a man who always expects an attack.

Ensi wriggles from the remainder of his clothes, his lithe body catching the light before he covers it with the black fabric. He hefts the gun, not quite pointing it at me.

"Were you the distraction?" he asks me. There's a tightness to his voice. Is he hurt by the possibility? How close are he and my sister? "Do you know who's down there?"

"No." I don't have to feign surprise.

A long pause.

"No," I repeat, meeting his eyes, willing him to believe it. "I have no idea what's going on. But I'm scared shitless." I'm shivering, folding in, covering my naked torso with my arms.

The tension bleeds from his shoulders. "Stay here." He starts to leave, then turns back, grabs another gun and tosses it to me.

I catch it, holding the gun like it's a snake that will bite me. I've had training through brainloads, and done a gun simulation, but I've not touched a real one. I wonder whether Tila is experienced with guns. Two weeks ago I would have sworn to anyone that she'd never even touched one. Not now.

Ensi gives me a last look and shakes his head before he pulls the bulletproof hood up, until every part of him is protected and obscured by the Kalar.

I want to ask what's going on, but he's already gone.

I stay there for roughly half a minute, listening to screams and gunshots, before I realize that standing there and doing nothing is not an option. I go to the cabinet, my body confused by the whiplash of fear, arousal, and fear again.

There are another few bulletproof jumpsuits hidden in the cupboard, so I shimmy out of my silver outfit and trade it for a black Kalar, pulling it up over my face. I can see through it just fine, and I feel safer.

Like earlier when I went down the corridor to the Test, I have the sensation that I'm just a floating head attached to my body. That this is not me or my life that I'm living, but someone else's. Not Tila—more like, this is all a dream or a movie, and I'll wake up, or the credits will roll.

But they won't. This is me. I'm dressed in a Kalar suit. I've just kissed the leader of the Ratel. I've committed criminal acts, thinking they were real. It was all me. But I'm also not the same girl that set out curry on the table, waiting for her sister to come home from work so she could tell her about that exciting job in China. I don't know who I am anymore.

And I have no time to figure that out.

I grab my gun and turn it over, trying to figure out how it works. I press the button and it turns on, humming slightly. It's not a laser and has actual bullets, but it's more complicated than the hunting guns we had at Mana's Hearth.

I want to test a shot but the room is too pretty to destroy. I have to hope my virtual training is enough.

Before I leave the room, I remember Ensi's jacket. I duck down and take out the notebook. The Kalar suit will hide my fingerprints. I unzip the suit enough to free my face. Will scanning work? I turn on my ocular implants. As long as I don't try to upload it yet, I can scan the notebook. I turn each page, running my eyes along the text. Each shot downstairs makes me flinch. I want to help, but I have to finish this, first.

The notebook is his personal schedule and diary. It's all in a code of scribbled acronyms, and I can only hope I can find a way to decipher it. When I finish, I pick up the datapod dangling from the bookmark. I set it to my ear, but, of course, it's locked, and I don't have time to even attempt to break the encryption. I set everything back in his pocket and arrange his jacket just as I found it.

I leave the room, peeking out into the darkened hallway. All the sounds of the melee are from the ground floor, the ballroom. I grit my teeth against the screams of pain and fear.

My mind spins. Who can it be? Is it the police? Is this why Nazarin snuck off? *Was* I actually the distraction against Ensi? I swear, if that man has lied to me yet again, I'll harness my new penchant for violence and use this gun to shoot him in the leg. Or between the legs. I'll decide when the time comes.

If he's not responsible for this, then that means Nazarin is in just as much danger as I am. More, if he's still down there in the ballroom.

I reach the top of the staircase. Bits of the banister are riddled with bullets. I peek over the edge. The guests are rounded up in one corner. The grand, green chandelier has been shot down, leaves and emeralds strewn along the floor. There are a few casualties scattered on the floor, sprawled out with legs akimbo, red mixing with the green. I swallow hard, memories of the vision of Ensi's Test fresh in my mind. Of seeing Mia killed in the hologram. The death in Mia's dream world. The crime scene in Zenith. Death and blood is following my every move.

*Focus, Taema. Focus or death will catch you, too.*

A bullet whizzes by my ear and I duck down. At least the other side doesn't have lasers, or we wouldn't stand a chance. I look over the banister again, taking the safety off the gun. There are about twenty people in dark blue Kalar suits, holding weapons. Enough to overwhelm the guards, though dismantling the security must have been a bitch. I see security people and droids scattered on the floor, the droids spilling wires, the people spilling blood. I try reaching out through my implants to contact the police, but that signal's still blocked. We have two members of our team just outside. Did they hear the shots? If so, is there anything they can actually do?

A suited figure fires another warning shot to gain people's attention. He has a rapt audience.

"The King of the Ratel has lost his power," the man says. Who is it? For a moment, I fear it's Nazarin; but the detective is at the back of the huddled former revelers. I let out my held breath. He's crouched low, poised to pounce, his eyes not moving from the main man with the gun. Is this what he's been planning? Nazarin said he was trying to sow unrest within the Ratel. From the shocked look on his face, though, I'm not sure he expected rebellion so soon.

"I've taken control of the biggest Verve drop the Ratel has ever done. I've taken control of the biggest arms smuggle. You can see the result right here." He holds up the bulky gun. His voice radiates with pride. "Ensi is so used to his routine that he's weak. It'll all crumble, having an old man like him at the helm. He makes too many deals with the other side. Getting soft."

Where is Ensi? While I was upstairs, has he already been executed? Would I care?

I crouch and move down the ramp. At one of the circular

cut-outs, I peer out again. Part of me wants to hide upstairs. The masked leader takes a string of men and women and lines them up against the white, curved wall. Even though most of the partiers are hardened criminals, not all of them are, and I think the masked man chose at least some of the business associates under Ratel control. People unafraid to get their hands dirty in crooked deals, but who've never before had guns pointed at their faces. A man pisses himself, the dark strain spreading down his trousers. Another woman shakes so badly she can barely stand. Malka has also been chosen for the line-up, but she does not look afraid. She stands tall, like the Queen she is.

"Here is the court of the Ratel, gathered for their party," the masked man says. "Think of me as your jester for the evening, providing the entertainment to you peons. Do you realize that for every tiny bit of money you get, the King gets over one hundred times more?"

He walks closer to the men and women lined up along the wall. "But for you, I'm not your jester. I'm your executioner." He raises his gun and points it at the first woman. As soon as he aims, someone lets out a wail. The man is startled and lets out the shot, and the woman crumples. I shudder, hidden behind the curving white wall of the ramp. I can't tell if she's been hit or not.

Ensi—I'm pretty sure it's Ensi—emerges from the shadows, knocking the gun from the leader's hand. Nazarin, seeing that the situation has changed, jumps over a frightened member of the Ratel and grabs the gun out of another of the masked men's hands. The rest of the Ratel realize the tide has turned and follow suit, wrestling the weapons from the other side's grasp. A few more shots fire, but they all go wide.

A masked man or woman falls to the ground, the gun skittering across the floor, the person grabbling for it. Nobody else has noticed yet. After an agonizing moment of indecision, I dash from my hiding place and jump on top of the figure, holding my gun against the temple, praying I don't have to fire. Nazarin sees me, but masked as I am, he thinks I'm one of the insurgents. I hold up my hand and call out "Wait!" He starts, recognizing my voice, and I pull off my hood, shaking the hair out of my face. Nazarin looks stricken. I nod at him.

It's not over that easily. There's a riot of people fighting, and guns blaring. More people fall. The perfect white walls are singed.

Only a few people in Kalar suits have fallen—bullets have to hit the right area of the body at the perfect angle to do any damage. But even in my Kalar suit, I don't feel safe. A fair number of Ratel revelers have died. Blood smears the white floors. I clutch the gun against his forehead, but I don't fire. I turn off the fear, watching everything with a sort of detached fascination. It's that, or start screaming and never stop.

Ensi wades through it all, the bullets bouncing off his suit, wrestling the ringleader behind it all to the ground and ripping off his hood. It's the young man I met at the beginning of the party: little more than a boy, with white-blond hair and black eyes. Leo.

My eyes dart to Nazarin. His mouth has twisted, and I can't guess his thoughts. I'm still not sure he anticipated the coup.

Leo tries to say something, but Ensi doesn't give him the chance. The King of the Ratel takes the gun, holds it to the younger man's head, and fires. The boy goes limp, his head nothing but a mass of blood, bone and brain tissue. Ensi is splattered with gore. I stare at him, not blinking, until my eyes burn.

Ensi pulls off the hoods of all the other masked men and

women who dared to rise up against him. Then he calls out a few other names. The Ratel Pawns and Knights bring the people forward. Nazarin holds one of the named men's arms behind his back.

"You really thought I didn't know exactly what you were trying to do?" Ensi asks.

He shoots the first person.

I flinch.

"You really thought that, in my own house, I wouldn't sniff a rat?"

He shoots the next person.

"This is my house. You are mine."

Another shot. Another fall.

"You should have learned this long ago. Most of you have."

*Bang.*

"You cannot cross me and hope to live."

*Bang.*

"Reward me with loyalty, and I will reward you."

*Bang.*

"Cross me, and reap the consequences."

All the men and women are dead, to join the other corpses on the ground.

"It's simple, really." He smiles at us all.

I look at all the bodies on the floor, numb. It feels like a warning. He'll find out about me. And he'll kill me. He's walking toward me. Is he about to shoot me in the head?

He aims the gun. I squeeze my eyes shut. Better not to see it coming.

The gunshot is so loud my ears ring.

I'm not dead.

I open my eyes. Ensi has shot the man I captured. The blood spreads across the floor, a slow red tide. A woman's cry-

ing, screaming, and I wish she'd shut up. More lines from the
poem return to me. The paradise of Xanadu is ruined.

> *Then reached the caverns measureless to man*
> *And sank in tumult to a lifeless ocean.*
> *And 'mid this tumult Kubla heard from far*
> *Ancestral voices prophesying war!*

Nazarin has a spray of blood on the left side of his face.
He stands straight, at attention, his expression blank as a
soldier's.

Ensi stops in front of him. "Thank you," he says. "Skel,
isn't it?"

"That's right, sir."

"You saved a lot of lives tonight. You'll be rewarded. Speak
to Malka about it."

"Thank you, sir." I almost wonder if Nazarin will salute.

Ensi looks around at the silent party. "Let this be a lesson
to you all."

Does his gaze flick to me? A shiver runs down my spine.
He comes toward me, the gun still in his hand, and I steel
myself. He's going to kill me. Shoot me in the head. Even if
I wasn't involved with this uprising, if he knew about that, he
must know about me.

He looks down at me with something very like tenderness.
"You didn't stay."

"I couldn't."

He stares at the man I captured. The man that's now a
corpse, though not by my hand. "Good job."

"Thank you."

For a moment, I wonder if he's going to hold out his
hand, and lead me back upstairs. The blood has washed the
last vestiges of the drug from my system, and I've scanned

the notebook. I have no desire to go back up there. Then Ensi turns, his head down.

"Malka," he says.

She comes forward, to his side. I can't tell if they're romantically linked, but their bond, whatever it is, is deep. The King and the Queen walk away from the ballroom, side by side, leaving the carnage behind them.

# TWENTY

# TAEMA

I dream that I went with Ensi, and I awaken in a silken bed.

The sun streams through the window. Ensi lies next to me, fast asleep, his arm thrown over his eyes against the light. His face is clean of blood, like the events of the night before never happened. But they did. And this, right here, is the man who did them.

His other arm is around me and, trapped in his embrace, I can't stop thinking about all the dead bodies. The fact that I had taken a gun and gone down there, something I never thought I'd do. I still feel like I'm changing and morphing. I'm becoming more like Tila, but I'm turning into someone else I don't recognize, either, and perhaps someone I don't like.

I turn and watch him, sleeping peacefully. I look at his torso, chiseled by modern medicine. What would he look like now if he couldn't alter himself? Would that taut skin sag against a growing paunch? Would I recognize his face, with its lines that show the type of life he chose to live?

He opens his eyes, and his eyes are black pits. His mouth stretches wide, and deep within his throat is a glowing, pulsing light.

"Are you strong enough to kill me?" he asks, his voice crackling like a flame. "Do you really have what it takes?"

•

I jerk awake, for real this time.

I'm in the room in the safe house where I store my things, but where I hardly ever sleep. It's my first brainload-free night in over a week.

I ease out of the bed, my sore muscles stretching. I have a bruise on my side, where a bullet grazed the Kalar suit. If I hadn't been wearing it, the bullet would have killed me. I rub my sore muscles and stagger into the shower to wash off the sweat and the imaginary scent of blood that still clings to my nostrils.

After I've scalded myself, I go down to the kitchen, ordering strong, real coffee from the replicator despite its warning that caffeine is bad for me. I load it with cream and sugar, to boot.

Nazarin isn't here. He's gone to report in to the Ratel, receive his reward for helping with the fight. I want to ask him if that was his plan all along. I thought he wanted to foster unrest. So why, when unrest presented itself in a very real way, did he decide to help Ensi instead?

Using every security measure I can think of, I bring Ensi's scanned notebook to my implants.

His handwriting is almost impossible to read, so tall and slanted. Each appointment is only a few letters and a time, perhaps a first name. Last night's entry was only "XNDU," presumably shorthand for Xanadu. There's nothing over the next few days, but Wednesday has an entry: "D/O. MM." I flip through the rest of the pages, wondering who the names are. On the last page of the book are various scribbled notes. Up in a corner, I spy "MM." Next to it is a phone number, strange enough in itself, and it brings me up short.

I recognize it.

It's the number for the emergency line at Mana's Hearth.

I looked it up, after we left, after the surgery. When, despite everything, I was homesick. So many times over the years, I had turned on my implants, ready to input the number. I wanted to see if my parents were all right. If the Hearth was all right. I was too afraid, and I never pinged.

My throat tightens with unshed tears. It's not totally unexpected, but it's still a shock. We knew there might be a link between the Ratel and the Hearth when we discovered Vuk was Adam. We still don't know what the connection is, exactly. Is Mana-ma sending people to the Ratel, and if so, why, and to what purpose? Is Mana-ma working with Ensi? That means interacting with someone Impure, and having a connection with the world she always taught us was evil.

I flip back to Wednesday's entry. D/O. Drop off. Sure enough, Wednesday is the 15th—the date Tila and I used to look forward to. The date that the supply ship would come from the far-off shiny city of San Francisco. I guess, even ten years later, it hasn't changed.

MM stands for Mana-ma.

"Fuck," I whisper, wondering if I'm reading the signs wrong. Maybe I'm just seeing what I want to see. I flip through the calendar. Every two or three months, right on the 15th, there's an entry with "D/O. MM."

Why? When I lived there, people didn't die more than once or twice a year. Has Mana-ma started making more disappear? Or is there something else the Hearth has that Ensi and the Ratel want? The hairs on my forearms stand up straight. I'm still missing something.

What?

How long has this been going on, whatever it is? At least ten years. That's when Adam disappeared. I have a feeling it's been longer.

I take a deep breath. Nazarin comes into the kitchen and I send everything away, hiding the scans deep within my implants again.

He nods at me in greeting and grabs the SynthGin. It's early in the day.

"Did it go badly?"

He pours liquid into the glass, bringing over a second one for me. "No. I've been promoted. He's going to Test me, make sure I'm trustworthy. It'll be different to yours, as he's not using me for lucid dreaming, but I imagine it'll be along the same lines. I guess we're celebrating that somehow things didn't totally go to shit last night."

"Did you know what was going to happen?" I ask him.

He takes a swig. "No. I knew Leo was going to try something, but I thought he was months away from actually doing it. I guess he didn't trust me enough to include me in his plans."

"If he had, would you have sided with him?" If he had, would the end result have been different?

"No. Too dangerous. If there'd been even a hint I was involved, I'd be as dead as the others."

"Right." I sip the SynthGin. "Did you know Tila is sleeping with Ensi?"

"She's his canary?" he asks. "No. I most definitely did not know that." His eyes ask the question I don't answer.

I take another gulp. "What does that mean, to be his canary? Malka called me that, too."

"Tila is—you are—his newest pet. His newest toy. He'll play with you for a time, like a cat with a canary."

"Then, what, he'll eat me? Is that what he does with the others?"

"Sometimes. If they displease him. If not, he lets them fly away, and then finds another."

"Right. He's been with her before. Tila. I got the feeling it'd been more than once. He seemed to . . . care."

Again, the question with his eyes. I sigh. "I didn't sleep with him. I almost did but we were . . . interrupted by gunfire."

"Right." He takes another sip. "How did the Test go?"

"It was horrible," I say. "If you're going to be Tested, I shouldn't tell you about it."

If he knew it wasn't real, it'd alter the readings to the electrodes. And, in any case, the Test for him could be completely different from mine.

"And if I fail, I'm stuck as a Knight or a Pawn for good." Or worse. Nazarin's heard of the odd Pawn or Knight disappearing after their Test.

We're silent. I slosh more drink in the cup. I'm drinking too much. Before all this, I hardly ever touched the stuff. At least my liver will be safe. Whoo.

"So what does the SFPD want our next step to be?"

"I take the Test. We keep playing our roles. Kim's been perfecting something she thinks can help us gather evidence."

I let out a slow breath. "How soon do you think she'd be able to do this?"

Nazarin perks up. "Why?"

"Because there's going to be a drop in a few days." I project the scanned pages of Ensi's notebook onto the wallscreen. He squints.

"I have no idea what any of this means."

I walk him through what I found in the planner. He also has no idea what the link between the Hearth and the Ratel could be, beyond inheriting occasional men and women without identities that Ensi can brainwash into working for them.

"We still don't definitively know if that's what they did," I say, thinking of Adam, the way he'd smile more on one side than the other. The way he loved to play with the younger children, and how he loved to go swimming in the lakes with the others, turning back to wave at us as we watched from the shore, unable to join him. He'd never harm another person.

*Everyone has a darker side.*

I still think there must be more to it than that. Adam was sixteen when he supposedly died. How could he change that completely? I suppose being torn from everything you've grown up with could do that. I remember how confused Tila and I felt. How it was like we were drifting, unanchored, in this strange new world we knew nothing about. Is that enough?

"Verve," Nazarin says. "He's rewriting personalities."

Rewriting personalities. I still don't know if I believe I changed Mia in any way in the Vervescape. Maybe it was only my words that got through to her, rather than a deeper sort of push. Imagine not remembering who you were. Becoming exactly what Ensi wanted you to be. A weapon. An assassin. A tool.

The only reason he didn't do it to me in the Test is because it doesn't work on lucid dreamers.

"You can't do the Test," I say.

Nazarin's eyebrows lift. "You think he'll change me."

"Of course he will. Your loyalty doesn't matter if it's not completely guaranteed. He can make sure you never dare to cross him." I think of the Zealot lounges where he experimented. "I worry he might have found a way to reprogram people on a wider scale via Zealot lounges by now. He'd start with his own people and then cast his net wider, wouldn't he?"

"That's what my superior says. He has other sources in other areas. We are certain he can expect them to amass an attack sooner rather than later."

"We still haven't been able to get any coverage. All recording devices were dampened in Xanadu, and they're dampened in the Verve lounge. We can't pin anything on him, even though we saw him gun down insurgents and splatter us with the blood." I look up at the wallscreen. "Does the notebook help?"

"It's a start, but not enough. They're too carefully intertwined for us to barrel in now. Ensi will disappear, along with the Verve, and it'll still trickle its way to the masses. We need concrete proof we can show the public, to turn everything against him. A few scanned pages with some acronyms won't do that." Nazarin licks his lips. "That's where this new tech from Kim comes in. It might record, even if we're somewhere the signal's jammed. It's dangerous, but it might work."

"I don't understand," I say. Nazarin is animated, driven. It should scare me, but it doesn't. It's infectious. My fingernails trace across my scar.

If we succeed, we'll take down the biggest mob in the city. The government and Sudice will be in our debt. That's not what I care about; it's a side effect.

*I'm going to find out what you were up to, Tila. Once and for all.*

# TWENTY-ONE

# TILA

Do you know why they really built that swamp around the Hearth? I mean, the "why" is pretty obvious, I suppose—to keep some people on one side of it and everyone else on the other—but there were events that led up to it.

I can't tell you everything about them because I don't know that much. I've managed to gather bits and pieces over the years, but I still don't understand how they all fit together.

I'm going to tell it like a story, try and sensationalize it, fill in some gaps. You know when they have documentaries and then the camera goes all fuzzy and golden-tinged if it's a reenactment of a good event, and dark and dreary if it's bad? This is the dark and dreary kind, and I guess I'm the dramatic voiceover.

First, here's roughly how Mana-ma tells the story when she's lecturing about the evils of the Impure. I'm sure she's told this story dozens of times in sermon:

**Mana-ma's Cautionary Tale**

One night around twenty years ago now—let's say it was dark and stormy, because what else could it be?—a man from the Impure outside world snuck into the Hearth. In those days, there was just a fence rather than a swamp. There were signs everywhere saying that the fence was charged, but it was a lie. We didn't want to be surrounded by the new generator that would have been used. Surrounded by an Impure circle, the Hearth would feel just that much more trapped. Makes no sense, if you ask me, since the Hearth was already surrounded by, you know, the entire Impure world.

So this bogeyman came into the Hearth from San Francisco, creeping and sneaking his way closer to the main settlement. Mana-ma took great delight in explaining how horrible he looked, with green hair and metal studs, moving tattoos and Impure clothing, none of it made from good cotton, silk or leather.

Why did he come? Let's see . . . perhaps he ran out of money and thought he'd be able to steal from us. (That would have been a failure—we didn't have anything worth anything, except some vintage stuff in not-too-good condition. Well, at least that's what I thought at the time.) Mana-ma said he thought he'd be able to get away with a crime more easily here. And that was maybe true, but she left out how low crime in the evil, Impure world really was, which would have made a few people wonder if it was really that bad if it was so safe.

This bogeyman came right into the center of the Hearth and stole a young girl from her own home. He drugged her and dragged her, kicking and screaming (evidently not loud enough to wake anyone up), into the forest. Under the silent redwood trees he had his way with her, holding a knife to her throat and saying if she screamed that he'd give her another smile. So he hurt her and she stayed quiet. Just as she was about to give up and scream so he would kill her (because people would some-how hear that scream), a brave member of the Hearth came to her rescue.

This upstanding member of the Hearth fought off the

intruder and the miscreant was slain. Though the girl was obviously traumatized by events, through the help of the Hearth she was able to release the darkness the man had planted within her, at least for a time. Later, the darkness took hold of her again and nothing could be done for her.

"This tragedy is why we must remain separate," Mana-ma would cry, holding her arm up high at the pulpit. "This is what we seek to prevent. For the Impure can poison the minds of the Pure, and we must guard that untainted spark within us all."

It was always that sort of lesson—that the Impure would blemish us all and we were the last true humans, unaltered, unsullied.

The thing is: that's not remotely what happened.

**The Real Story**

The man who came to the Hearth came to rescue the girl, not hurt her.

A gap in the story is, I have no idea how he knew her. Perhaps they met in the forest: her on one side of the former chain-link fence around the border, and him on the other. I could imagine the romance developing—putting their fingers through the metal wires and touching for the first time.

Eventually, the girl wanted to escape and they came up with a plan. When she didn't stick to it, he grew worried. Thoughts swirled through his head: maybe her parents kept her in, or she even changed her mind at the last minute.

So he came into the Hearth, worried, not wanting to leave without her. She'd told him where she lived, and he peeked in her window.

He was seen.

The Hearth would automatically recognize someone not of

their own, especially this boy in his synthetic clothing, bright green hair, moving tattoos on his knuckles.

They grabbed him, dragged him to the main chapel. Mana-ma had been roused from bed. I can imagine her, hair wild around her face, wearing her dark robes like a witch. The boy was nervous, probably a bit sheepish. Thought if he apologized and left, it'd all be OK.

Instead, they didn't let him go.

He was thrown into one of the empty rooms that nobody used. They managed to get out of him who he was and why he was there. Then they went and got the girl.

The girl had planned to go. Her parents had caught her leaving with a small rucksack under her arm and locked her in her room. They were the ones to alert the watch, who had found the boy. The girl was more scared than the boy. She didn't like the blank looks on their faces. They could be thinking anything.

Mana-ma was incensed. This boy had infringed on them, slipped past the toll roads, the infrequent park wardens, the fence, to come into the inner sanctum of the Hearth itself. The whole place would have to be Purified to prevent his presence from poisoning everything. The girl was sobbing, but the boy didn't say anything. He knew crying wouldn't solve anything when they'd already made up their minds.

They were all up all night, or at least all of them except the boy. He died at sunrise.

They didn't kill him quickly. Mana-ma did most of it, with only her three trusted right-hand men. (Importantly, my parents weren't involved. I think they learned about this after, and it was what put the biggest dent in their faith.) One restrained the boy and the other the girl. Throughout it all, Mana-ma lectured about the sins of evil and darkness, all while she tortured a boy to death in front of the girl who loved him. She used a scalpel, and she was delicate and dedicated in her work. The room was soundproof, so nobody else heard the screams.

They took the body of the boy away when the sun had crept over the tops of the redwood trees, but they weren't done with the girl. Mana-ma used every trick in the book to brainwash and manipulate her. Before long, she believed it was her fault, that the boy was evil, that Mana-ma had saved her. Yet she was dead inside, walking around like a zombie, unable to feel happiness or sadness.

The spell didn't last forever. Eventually, Mana-ma stopped paying such close attention to the girl. There were other things on Mana-ma's mind besides a follower she thought had been dealt with. The girl started thinking again. Started waking up. And one night, deep in the dark when the moon was just a little sliver in the sky, she escaped and climbed over the chain-link fence, making her way to San Francisco, where the Hearth could not catch her.

When Mana-ma realized a member of her flock had fled, she was even angrier. That's when the swamp was created. She said it was to protect us from those outside who would want to hurt us. It's really to keep everyone inside.

•

These were the people Taema and I were raised with.

These were the people we were trying to escape from, naive and unaware of what we were really dealing with.

You must be wondering where I learned this story, if we didn't know it when we left. Or perhaps you've already figured it out.

The girl in the story was Mia, the woman who took us in after we left. The woman who saved us before she damned me.

# TWENTY-TWO

# TAEMA

We've come to see Kim again.

We haven't gone back to that empty safe house; instead, we're going to her home. She seems nervous as she opens the door and ushers us inside. She's been sworn to secrecy. At the moment, not even Sudice is meant to know what she's about to do to us. If they find out she's lied, even if it's on behalf of the SFPD, she could easily lose her job.

Nazarin knew, without a doubt, that she'd do it. His former partner, Juliane Amello, had been her partner as well. Her wife. She died, and Kim wants answers, too. Or at least retribution.

"Well, no point wasting time in pointless pleasantries or offering you a cup of tea," she says. "Might as well come through to the lab."

We follow. I had forgotten how tiny Kim is. At the safe house, she wore a simple suit, but now she's wearing something made of strips of fabric in all the colors of the rainbow, and it billows behind her as she walks.

Her home is large and sumptuous. As she's one of the most talented biohackers in the world, this doesn't surprise me. What does surprise me is how cluttered it is. On the way here, Nazarin told me that Kim collects old memorabilia, specifically from the twentieth and twenty-first centuries, before the Great Upheaval. I think he told me so I wouldn't be quite so taken aback when I saw it all.

Most of the cheesy knickknacks from the past have been recycled by now, but Kim hunts down the remaining ones and probably pays a lot of money for the lurid plastic and metal figurines that seem to stare at us as we walk through the lounge. Superheroes and celebrities I don't recognize, cartoon animals with eyes far too large for their faces. It all seems strangely alien to me as someone who grew up in the Hearth. There, nothing was made by robots or replicators and toys were hand-carved and took weeks to make. Here, in San Francisco, so much was ordered and then recycled the next day. Clothes worn once, plates made of compostable material. Cherishing things from the past was rare. I mean, what in the world was Hello Kitty?

"Like 'em?" Kim asks, noticing my stare. "I got the biggest collection on the West Coast."

"They're . . . interesting," I say.

She laughs. "Yeah, it's tacky as hell, but I don't care. A girl's gotta have a hobby." She was serious when she let us in, but now she's striving for lightness. It's forced. Underneath she's as scared as we are.

At the end of the hall, Kim presses her fingertip to the sensor and the door slides open. We step through into her lab.

Though the lab is small, it's fitted with the best equipment, stuff I would have killed to have in my lab at Silvercloud Solutions. The Chair bolted to the floor in the middle of the room reminds me uncomfortably of the Zealot lounge.

"All right, who's going first?" she asks.

"Me," Nazarin says, to my relief. He sits in the Chair, and Kim straps him in.

"I don't know why I'm doing this," she mutters to herself.

"Yes, you do."

"Don't kid yourself, babe," she says, pinching his cheek. "You're not my type."

She winks at me and I smile a little.

"OK, then. You want to prove to yourself you can do it. I've appealed to your professional pride."

"That's a bit closer, but you forget, I've done this before."

"I guess that's a comfort," Nazarin says. "You won't leave me blind and deaf."

"Most likely not."

Neither of them mentions Juliane. I have the feeling they rarely speak about her, even though she's a shared link between them. Too painful for them both. Better to banter and tease, even when they're both terrified.

"Now shut up," she says, without rancor. "I have to concentrate."

He dutifully shuts up as Kim attaches the last of the wires. It is almost exactly the same set-up as at the Zeal lounge, and I say so.

"Where do you think they got the idea for it, buttercup?" she asks. "Who do you think helped develop Zeal, if not the biohackers? Grade A Sudice merchandise right from the start."

It's rather obvious now that I think about it, but I know nobody who did Zeal, except Mia. My throat twinges as I think of her. She didn't have a funeral, and even if she had, no one would have come.

Kim turns on the screen on the table next to the Chair, her quick fingers dancing as she brings up the various controls. It only strikes me now how dangerous this all is.

Kim is going to hack into Nazarin's brain.

"Does it hurt?" I ask. Switching my identity had been easy

and painless. This isn't a chip in a wrist. Implants are wired right into your brain.

"It won't be pleasant, I'm sorry to say." She fills a syringe with unidentified liquid. "Why do you think we don't have our implants set to record as standard? Be able to keep our memories and replay them in their entirety whenever we want?"

"No idea."

"We're not meant to remember every little thing. If we were, that's what our brains would do. They're not meant to store so much. They can be overwhelmed. Even brainloading is too much for many. Not every brain can do it. But non-stop recording? I am part of a Sudice project that works on it." She pauses, looking haunted. "Some subjects end up going crazy, and some brains shut down. Aneurysms. Strokes. Poof. Gone." She snaps her fingers. "So it will probably be nixed pretty soon. Most of us involved in the project are glad it hasn't been easy, to tell the truth. You know why?"

I shake my head.

"It makes people vulnerable. People already try to hack into implants all the time—send adverts and things. Imagine hacking into your very being. Your very self."

I lick my lips. And what would the government do with that power?

"The government are trying," she says, echoing my thoughts. "Boy, are they trying. They fund all our research, and it isn't cheap. If brain recording worked better, you can bet your bottom dollar that we'd all be recording, all the time. I mean, surveillance is old as time."

She drifts off, fiddling with something, and then sets the code to process. "Anyway, it's been abandoned for widespread use now, until they can figure out how not to fry people. Maybe at some point we'll crack it fully. Until then, I developed a way to turn it on for anyone, at least for a little while. A back door."

A back door into my brain. "Do you have to . . . use it often?" Forced brain recording. It sounds barbaric.

"Very rarely." Her eyes go distant and blank. I swallow. I wonder what she's had to see, had to do, but I don't ask. Easier to think of her as a brilliant, eccentric woman with a penchant for nicknames and bobblehead figurines.

She shakes her head, coming out of it. "Not many people know about brain recording. You didn't for sure, did you, tulip?" Kim asks Nazarin. He's lying back in the seat, his eyes half-lidded. Whatever Kim gave him, he's relaxed and high.

"Educated guess."

"Smart boy," she says fondly. His eyes flutter and he's out cold.

Kim sighs. "Here we go."

"Wait," I say. "You're really not calming me down here. Are we going to go insane or die?"

She meets my eyes. "I'm very good at this. Yes, there's still a chance. Nazarin understands the risks, and he wants to do it. Do you? You have a choice."

"Give . . . give me a minute."

"Sure. You can see what happens with Nazarin. Then decide." She looks down at Nazarin, runs her hand over the rough stubble of his head, and then presses a button on the Chair.

Nazarin goes rigid. Sweat beads on his skin almost immediately, leaving tracks down his temples. Kim frowns at one of the wallscreens, her fingers dancing over a projected keyboard as she studies code that means nothing to me, for all my courses in software engineering. With a flick of her wrist, a map of Nazarin's mind appears, floating over her head like a nebula.

Kim zooms in on the occipital lobe and the auditory cortex first. I remember when people first mentioned implants to me, I thought they were just one machine, firmly glued somehow to the brain. Really, there's a main receiver and dozens, hundreds of little implants scattered through the brain. They call it neural dust. Microscopic little computers, no thicker than a human hair, all taking the data from the brain and feeding in data from the outside world.

Nazarin has more implants than me. "What are those?" I ask, pointing at the various other parts of his brain also speckled with neural dust.

She frowns as she concentrates, changing the view to focus on the tiny machines. "They put them in when he went undercover. Extra receivers for brainloads. Implants to help memory in the hippocampus, extra occipital lobe implants to help retention and processing. There's more in the brain stem and cerebellum to aid with coordination—you'll notice he's not clumsy, and very fast when he needs to be. So they're there, and they help, but they don't record the way you two need the brain to record. It makes this tricky, though. There's a lot of little bits of metal in his head. Now stop talking."

I snap my mouth shut. Kim's barely blinking. Her fingers gesture as she imparts code to the tiny metal specks in Nazarin's brain.

Machines beep—Nazarin's heartbeat speeds up, warning alarms ping. Nazarin arches on his Chair, his mouth open in a silent scream. He jerks as if he's having a seizure, spittle flying from his mouth. The veins in his neck stand out.

His heart flatlines.

"Shit, shit, shit!" Kim's fingers fly faster.

"What's happening?" I have my hands over my mouth. I dart forward but Kim snarls at me to stay back. Nazarin is already turning grayish. His eyes are open and bulging, their whites red with burst capillaries.

"Shut up!" Kim takes another syringe and stabs it into his heart. I watch, unable to think, unable to speak.

I don't want him to die.

Nazarin's heart starts again, and he gasps, his breathing hoarse.

"Oh, thank Christ." Kim slumps against a counter. "I told them, I fucking told them not to ask me to put in so many!"

Nazarin's eyes are still open and staring. "Is he OK?" I ask.

The skin around Kim's eyes and mouth is tight. She doesn't answer. My mouth goes dry. I stay quiet, watching her work, clasping my hands together and whispering incoherently. It isn't a prayer, not really, but maybe it's a whisper to the universe, a hope that things will somehow work out all right.

Three minutes pass, but it feels like three hours. Kim nods, and the map of Nazarin's brain disappears. Nazarin slumps against the seat, his eyes closed again, breathing through his mouth. He seems calmer, but he's still dripping with sweat and twitching. Kim injects him with another syringe, this time in the shoulder, and the frantic beating of his heart slows. After another minute, his eyelids flutter.

He sits up slowly. "I feel like I've been hit by a hovercar."

"You nearly said hi to Saint Peter. You have too many bugs in your brain. As soon as this op's done, come to me. I'll get them out."

"I like 'em."

Her eyes go distant again. "No. Get them out. I spend my life doing this, but sometimes I wonder if we're doing too much to our brains too fast. The more I find out about the mind, the more I realize I don't know and probably never will."

She presses the bridge of her nose with her fingers. "That was too close, sweet pea."

Nazarin reaches out and puts a hand on her shoulder. "I'm OK, Kim. I'm OK."

Kim gives him a hug, clutching his broad back. There's something between them. Nothing romantic. It's that sort of friendship where the term "friend" doesn't seem strong enough.

She pats him on the cheek. Her eyes shine with tears. "Your vitals are all good. You'll need some eye drops to heal the whites of your eyes—you look a fright."

She unhooks him from the machine. He stands up, but his knees are shaking. He leans against a metal bench of the lab, looking at me from under shadowed brows.

Kim motions to me. "It's your turn now, Taema. If you still want to. I can understand if you don't, after all that."

This is the last thing I want to do. She sees it in my face. I look to Nazarin, but his gaze is inscrutable. He's not weighing in. It's up to me.

It's another risk, but I've taken so many risks. For a moment, I do wonder if this is one risk too many. If this is my limit, and I can't do any more.

I can do more. For Tila. For me.

Can we find what we need? Record proof that Ensi is the head of the Ratel? Find out where he stores Verve and what his plan is, and stop it in time? It feels impossible.

"It'll be OK," Kim says.

Tila's words come to my lips again. "You can't promise that."

"No, I can't. You're right. Your implants are newer than his, and you have far fewer. Your heart functions on its own software so it'll stay steady. I'll have less trouble getting your implants to behave. That I can promise."

Nazarin's gaze is steady. His breathing returns to normal. He gulps a glass of water. I can tell what he's thinking, it's so clear on his face. *We've come so far . . .*

I close my eyes and clear my mind, a small Meditation. I bow my head down to my chest. I block out all sound, all sight. I focus on the soft whisper of my breath. In. Out. In. Out.

*I can do this.*

I sit in the Chair. Kim straps me in tight, and prepares another syringe.

She gives me a kiss on my cheek. She smells of antiseptic and artificial cherries. "See you soon, sweetness," she says, and sticks the syringe in my arm.

## TWENTY-THREE

# TAEMA

My senses scramble. I float in space, but sight is sound and sound is touch and all is strange and beautiful. I feel butterfly wings on my taste buds and fireworks of feathers explode on the backs of my eyelids. Heartbeats pulse against me, crashing waves sending me bouncing against the soft red walls of my own skull. I feel the flashes as the neural dust within my mind sparkles, changing, merging into what I need it to be.

Memories fire at me, without warning, without prompting. I'm six, eating roasted butternut squash, laughing with Tila as Mom tells us a story over dinner. I'm ten, reading as Tila sleeps beside me. I'm seven, and we've fallen by the lake. I've scraped my hip, the pain blooming as though it's just happened. We're trying to drag ourselves upright but we keep slipping in the mud. Tila's panting next to me, and above the birds call. She looks at me, and her eyes are deep and as familiar as my own.

"It'll be OK," she says.

"You can't promise that," I say, and I'm out of the memory, back in the Technicolor of my mind. A weird, fractured bit of a memory floats to me. That first moment I saw Tila after the surgery. Standing, unattached. Her own person. Yet as soon as she could, she'd come back to me. She's threaded through my mind. Everywhere I turn, there she is. Tila. My Tila. I see her and I realize: neither of us is the good twin. Not anymore. We never were. Tila is simply my other half. Not my better half. Not my worse half.

Then everything goes dark.

It's quiet, and warm.

I wonder if I'm dead. The same thing, perhaps, has happened to me as happened to Nazarin. Maybe I'm flatlining on that chair in the lab. I can't feel my body.

I float there, not thinking, just existing. It's . . . nice. I don't feel afraid. I don't worry about anyone. Not Nazarin. Not Ensi. Not my sister. Not myself.

Being dead isn't so bad.

During our binge on religious texts once we were free of the Hearth, I remember reading a paper that argued we don't have souls. We're nothing but neural pathways and electric pulses, fatty white and gray matter. Once the organ that houses thought dies, there's nothing left. Nothing drifts up to heaven or down to hell. Floating there, in the dim dark, I'm not sure if the author's right or not.

I felt something similar to this when our heart failed at the Hearth. I remember darkness coming, but I was too afraid to embrace it. I ran away. I never saw that light at the end of the tunnel, like they say. Tila said she saw it, in Confession with Mana-ma. At the time I thought she was lying, but maybe she wasn't as afraid as I was. Maybe she spent some time in this quiet place.

I feel the edges of myself slipping away. I imagine my body disintegrating. My skin sloughs away, my veins lift from my muscles, spiraling out into infinity. My muscles unravel into thin tendrils. Just my bones are left, and even they begin to break down, scattering like snow. I'm now just my mind, my metal sternum, my mechanical heart.

As those start to leave me, light returns. It's as if the stars have turned on again. There's a moment where I hover. The pieces of me are scattered all around. I can bring them to me again, knit it all together and go back.

For a moment, I don't know if I want to. Maybe I should let it all fade away.

I remember Tila. How she looked in that surgery room as she put her arms around me and fell asleep. The fear on her face as she clutched me in our apartment a few days ago, terrified and desperate. If I go into that darkness, I go alone.

I pull myself together and return to the real, cruel, painful world.

•

It's bright.

I should hurt. A migraine aura should warble at the edges of my vision. My skin should be rubbed raw and bloody, my lungs charred, my muscles tender. It's like a Synth non-hangover. Somewhere, down deep, your body knows you did something dangerous.

"It went well," Kim says.

"It . . . was meant to be like that?" I ask, faint.

"What was it like?" Kim tilts her head in curiosity.

"Memories came out of nowhere and my senses went confused, and then it was all dark and quiet. I thought I'd died."

Kim's eyebrows rise at that. "Nope, all vital signs were fine. Your brainwaves did drop off at the end there, but not enough to alarm me."

"The brain is weird," I mutter.

Kim laughs. "You can say that again."

"So how does it work?" I ask. I don't feel any different. "Is it recording now?"

"No. It's pretty easy. You can do it now. I've linked it to a certain place on your body. I stimulated a particular nerve cluster in your brain, and the code can read it. You press it three times, once a second or so, and it starts. Another three, and it stops. Makes it harder to accidentally interrupt if you're bumped. Here." She walks over to Nazarin. "I was tempted to wire it somewhere a little . . . private . . . to make this moment funnier. I didn't. Aren't you impressed with my restraint, my parakeet?"

"Very," Nazarin says, deadpan. His skin is still a little gray. Kim takes Nazarin's hand and makes him put his index finger to his throat and has him press once, twice, three times in the hollow between his clavicle. He looks exactly the same to me. No little red recording lights in his eyes or ears, not that I expected it.

"How do you feel?" Kim asks, peering at him, holding a hand to his forehead, checking his pulse.

"A bit weird. I have a headache, feel queasy. Does that pass?"

"Probably not, but if that's all you're feeling that's a good sign. It's taken, and your brain's reacting as well as it can to the extra stimuli. Try not to record for more than five minutes at once. Otherwise side effects might worsen."

He nods, his brow creasing.

"OK, so I'll jabber a bit so you can see how this works when we play it back. Walk around the room and look at things a little."

Nazarin does so, peering at the lab instruments. He looks at Kim and she does a little twirl, and then he comes and peers at me. I feel strangely vulnerable, knowing that soon I'll see myself through his eyes.

"So, just do this to stop it?" He presses the hollow of his throat three times again.

"Yep, that's all done."

The crease between his brows eases. "I feel better now."

"Good. Come on, let's get out of the lab. Better wallscreen in the lounge."

I'm not sad to leave that lab behind. I'm fairly sure it's going to give me nightmares. We settle onto the sofas in the living room. I take my shoes off and tuck my feet up on the sofa, wrapping my arms around my legs. It's a childish sort of body language, but I got into the habit after the surgery and it makes me feel more grounded, feeling something pressed against my chest. I'm so tired. I want to go to sleep for at least twelve hours.

Kim passes us glasses of water and we sip as she brings up her interface.

"It'll still send even if we're somewhere all signals are blocked?" I ask

"They won't be completely blocked, of course. The Ratel can communicate with each other on their own frequency, but they're well protected against any sort of outside tampering. I can use a subfrequency they won't suspect. There might be a bit of a delay, but it should get through to me soon enough. I've had Sudice send to one of my secure drives just now. Nobody can get into it but me, so whatever you find will be safe."

Perhaps too safe. I like Kim and I've had no reason to distrust her, but she suddenly has a lot of power over us. She could turn us in, pretend we forced her to neurohack us. She could take whatever we record and hold it to ransom, or delete it.

Nazarin sees my hesitation. He doesn't say anything, but reaches over and takes my hand and squeezes it. *Don't worry,* he seems to say. I wish I could feel as confident.

Kim must have noticed our exchange, but she chooses to ignore it. She logs into the drive and there it is. A little file of two minutes of Nazarin's life. She opens it.

It's a strange echo. It's the words Kim just said, that I just heard, but from a different viewpoint. It's the lab from the vantage point of Nazarin's extra height. I can hear all the sounds of the lab—the ticking of some of the instruments, Kim's voice, the shuffle of Nazarin's feet as he explores. He looks at the lab equipment, and it's like there's cameras behind both of his eyes. But at the same time, it's different from an image from an actual camera. Like the difference between Zeal and Verve. It seems more familiar. More intimate. Like I have become him.

Kim turns around, and then I see myself. He looks down on me a little. I look up at him. Even though it's meant to be just a straight recording, some feelings and thoughts creep in somehow, and I can feel it. I can't tell what exactly the emotion is . . .

I look away, and the video ends.

"It's weird," Nazarin says. "It's in my mind with that same clarity. None of my other memories are like that. I remember everything. And when I remember, I get a little headache again. It's far stronger than the memories assisted with my other implants, and I thought those were good."

"Yep. That's why you shouldn't do it more than you have to. OK, Taema, your turn. Have to make sure it works for you, too," Kim says.

I dutifully press the hollow of my throat three times. Nothing really changes, except the slightest sharpening of focus, a pressure at my temples, a clenching of nausea in my stomach. It's not too bad, though. I can ignore it. I circle the room, peering at all of her various collectibles from the previous few centuries. I only recognize a few of them—that

283

one's Superman, resting an arm on Batman, who looks rather grumpy.

Nazarin and Kim murmur to each other behind me. I turn on the ball of my foot, twirling around, wanting to see the same blur on the wallscreen. It's a heady feeling, knowing that everything I'm seeing and hearing is permanent. Even if I forget it in the depths of my brain, though evidently that's unlikely, I could relive it all in perfect detail. Someone else could experience this little slice of my life. Anyone. Even centuries from now, all of this could be gone, but if that file somehow survived, someone could be me for five minutes.

I feel a jolt of weirdness as I recall that Nazarin, with his implants, probably remembers every detail of his encounter with me better than I do. I try not to think about it. If my emotions right now bleed through my perception, what will they think of a flash of panic? I force myself to calm, tapping the hollow of my throat again to turn it off. That same feeling of focus dissipates. My headache and nausea fade.

They play my video. Nazarin glances at me during that surge of emotion. It feels strange, experiencing that same echo again, almost like I'd gone back in time to a few moments ago. How the hell does all that bleed through? It's disconcerting, for sure.

"Well, it's a job well done for me," Kim says, eyes narrowed in satisfaction.

"Thanks, Kim," Nazarin says. "Really. Thank you."

She waves a hand. "For you, anything." Then she pauses. "I want to give you one last thing before you go, Taema. For Ensi."

"What?" Nazarin asks. Kim doesn't answer right away, but takes out a box from her pocket and opens it. Inside is a little white strip.

"This will mold around your tooth and harden. I can link

it to your brain through a nerve in your gum. If you think a trigger word, then you can bite down and break it."

"And why would I break it?" I ask.

"It'll bleed a liquid. It won't affect you—it's exempt to your DNA—but it'll affect Ensi. Kiss him. Dose him. This will do the rest."

"What is it, Kim?" Nazarin asks, wary.

She doesn't directly answer him. "You realize what he'll do to either of you if you're captured. How he . . . disposes of those who have particularly displeased him." Her voice grows thick. "What he probably did to Juliane."

Nazarin's lips thin in pain. "Yes."

"Promise me you'll do this, Taema." She looks at me, deep into me. "You're the only one who can get close enough. Even if you catch him red-handed, he has so many people in his pocket—judges, politicians—that he'll find another way to weasel out, or ways to hand over the Ratel to his successor without a hitch. Or send out Verve to the whole city, let it tear itself apart. I wouldn't put it past him. This. This is the real way to get him once and for all."

"I don't understand what's going on," I say. "I can't promise until I understand what it is you want to put in me."

Kim explains what it will do, and she also explains, in great detail, how Ensi disposes of those who displease him. I very nearly puke on her expensive shag carpet.

We return to the lab. Memories fire in my brain again. They all feature Tila. I have to remember I'm doing this, risking myself, for her.

She's going to owe me so much when I save her life. She's going to have to do a lot to make up for all I've gone through. As Kim works her magic, I wonder why I'm not angrier at my sister. For all the lies, for what she's put me through. And though I still don't fully understand why she decided to go into the Ratel in the first place, I have to believe that she did what she thought was best. For both of us. And I have to finish what she started.

Though she will owe me the truth. All of it.

Afterward, I still feel woozy. My tooth doesn't feel any different. But it's there. Third molar from the back on the left-hand side of my mouth. I keep thinking the trigger word, but Kim's given me some tips to try and push it from my mind unless I need it. She recommends chewing with the other side of my mouth, just in case. And if it breaks by accident, Kim says it won't harm me. I have to go back and get another one. If I can.

By the door, she pauses, and then gives us both kisses on the cheek. "Safe travels. I'm trusting you two to get the bastard, one way or another. And I know you will." We walk out of the door. I look at her and Kim smiles, but it doesn't reach her eyes. Those are dark with remembered grief and anger.

"Taema," she says. "I still want that drink and chat when this is all over and done with."

"Yes." I wonder if I'll bring my sister. If I'll be able to. If I'll want to.

# TWENTY-FOUR

# TILA

The trial's going to be soon. My lawyer said so today when he came to visit. He didn't give me any false hope, so I guess that's something. It's better than him saying I actually have a chance of staying unfrozen for longer than a week.

I've had this notebook open in my lap for hours, just staring at it. I debated continuing the story, but I figured I should write at least a little about what it feels like to know that I'm about to die.

Well, go into stasis. It's basically the same thing.

I'm not afraid of the actual trial. I just have to stand there and stare straight ahead. I can pretend I'm somewhere else. They're still not letting the media in on it, so I won't be livestreamed into almost every home and head in San Francisco. I guess that's something. I'll still be recorded. At some point, they'll let it out. The whole world will see me, a murderess in a city that prides itself on murder being a thing of the past. Never mind that murder happens in this city all the time, just quiet and unseen. The Zealots. The Ratel. The Ratel's victims. So many deaths.

I'm not afraid of the trial. I'm afraid of what happens after.

I keep looking at my hands. All the whorls and wrinkles in them. The almost-invisible bump of the VeriChip, just to the right of the vein under the skin of my wrist, like blue lightning. I have a mole in the crook of my elbow. Taema has one there, too. I keep looking at these little details that make me Tila because I realize that soon, they'll all be frozen in time. The blood won't pump through my veins anymore—it'll be all congealed and disgusting. My fingers will lie still. My skin will turn gray. And then, if the power of that wing fails and defrosts us—a few days after they freeze me, a few years, it's all the same—they'll burn up the dead corpse into nothing. My bones, my skin, my brain, everything will be gone. I'll just be dust.

Right now there are two of us, but soon there'll only be one. Taema will probably be better off without me, but I can't help thinking she'll also be all alone.

.

The supply ship came for its scheduled drop and we made our way to where it would land. Taema and I watched it fly over-head. It cut through the air so smoothly, a bird diving underwater to catch a fish. We went to watch it all happen, like so many times before.

But this time was different.

Dad oversaw everything, ordering men where to program the droids to put the boxes coming off of the ship. Mom came to sign off on all the shipments and deliveries. And there, just around the side, there was a box or two going on the ship. I'd seen that happen before, but I'd always assumed that it was the blankets and trinkets we made to sell in the city for people who liked that crap. Things that had been made by human hands in-stead of robot ones or replicators. Now I know that it was a hell of a lot more than that, but back then I had no idea.

The woman Mom was speaking to earnestly shook her hand. There was something hidden in her palm, which my mom took. After the woman went away, Mom put it in her pocket. She looked guilty, and worried. I knew it had something to do with us.

"What do you think it is?" Taema asked me.

"We'll find out soon enough."

We did.

That night after dinner, Mom and Dad drew the curtains and asked us to sit at the kitchen table. They wiped off the worn wood with antiseptic. They took out a little package and unwrapped it. Little silver squares fell onto the table, glinting in the buzzing electrical light overhead. I knew they were whatever the woman had given my mom that afternoon.

"What are they?" I asked.

"VeriChips. For identification. Made out to Taema and Tila Collins," Dad said.

"Our last name is Amner," Taema said.

Because the VeriChips had our real first names, it meant that Mana-ma would be able to find us more easily, if she really wanted to, after we escaped. After losing everything else, we couldn't stand the thought of having to call each other false names, too. We didn't think there was anything she'd be able to do to us once we escaped. Once we arrived, we kept our past hidden, kept our noses clean. We thought it was enough.

(We were stupid.)

Mom and Dad got out the medical supplies. They were going to put the VeriChips in now, since we'd leave on the next supply ship out. Mom arranged it with that same woman, who was in charge of the ship. I don't know how—we wouldn't have had anything to bribe her with. Maybe she appealed to her conscience or something.

Mom did it. She swabbed our right wrists and numbed the area with some ice. It didn't do much for the pain, but we didn't cry out as she used a scalpel to cut the skin and slot in the ID chip. She told us everyone in the cities outside had VeriChips. They were important. She closed the wound with a tiny stitch and wrapped it. It was autumn so it was getting a little colder, and she ordered us to wear long sleeves and not show anyone the bandages while we were healing. There might be a small scar, but we could get it erased once we were in San Francisco with a bit of our first paycheck. I remember wondering what a paycheck was, and how I would receive one.

Mom and Dad spent several hours that night telling us all the outdated information they knew about San Francisco and the outside world that the Hearth hadn't taught us. Even though Taema and I had already learned some of it from our contraband tablet (still hidden under our mattress), we were both totally overwhelmed. It was so much information that we couldn't take it all in. Mom and Dad were desperate to try and give us as much of a head start as possible, so we didn't say anything and just listened.

That night we lay forehead to forehead on the bed, looking at the bandages on our wrists.

"We're already Impure, I guess," Taema whispered. She looked so young, so vulnerable, and I hated that I must have looked the same way.

"The Pure and Impure stuff is bullshit, Taema."

Her mouth twisted. She knew that on some level, but she couldn't help her gut reaction. That the technology she'd been taught was evil her whole life was now implanted under her skin. "It's really happening, isn't it?"

"Once we're gone, we'll never come back," I said, and I felt both triumphant and a little sad. For all Mana-ma and the Hearth's philosophy weren't for us anymore—especially me—it was the only place we knew. Our friends were here. Our parents. Our whole way of life. Through that tablet, we'd only had a little peek into the window of the Real World. Everything was going to change.

We fell asleep that night knowing our time in the Hearth was coming to an end.

# TWENTY-FIVE

# TAEMA

It's time for my shift in the Verve lounge in a warehouse down by the docks. The reminder came through on my implant, on an untraceable line. This week, Tila's shifts are Monday and Wednesday.

Nazarin's on security duty. They're trying to arrange his Test, and he's bending over backward trying to find excuses for it to be delayed until after the drop.

As I take the MUNI through the glowing green tunnels, I can't stop thinking about the Test. All the images that flashed before my eyes, the smells, the confusion. The simulated murder that had seemed so real. Murder. The word that seemed so ugly when I first heard it, but now I've acted out homicidal violence in two simulations. I'm about to dive back into another Vervescape, and who knows what or who I will find there.

Once I'm at the warehouse, I force myself to push the macabre thoughts from my mind. I have to focus on being Tila again, one of the newest lucid dreamers in the Ratel. A Rook.

The outside of the warehouse is boring, blocky concrete. A faded sign once proclaimed "Geary Hovered Automobiles," but it's faded and tagged with moving graffiti. A stylized bunny holds knives and does a cartwheel above the old image of a hovercar, over and over again.

Malka opens the door before I can even knock. I can't help it; I start and take a step back in alarm. She narrows her eyes and smiles at me. She's wearing a long dress of artful folds, like a Grecian tunic.

"Hello, canary," she greets me. "Come on in."

I cross the threshold.

Inside, I expect it to be as dilapidated as the outside, but instead it's bright and fresh as a hospital room.

Malka leads me down the long hallway. Her heels click on the tiles, her hips swishing back and forth. She glances over at me. "I'm glad you're feeling recovered. We've missed you, the past few shifts. Could have used your expertise. Now you're all Tested, though, we can trust you with more than the menial dreams, canary girl."

Like Kim, she seems to be fond of nicknames, but there the similarity ends. Kim is warm and genuine, and everything about Malka is carefully engineered. She gives a throaty laugh and stops by a door. It opens with a soft exhalation of air. "In you go. Think of this as part two of your Test. What can you do with a juicier dream?"

I step in, my palms damp with nerves. Inside is a Chair, far smoother and sleeker than the ones in Mirage, or even in the training room at the safe house. A man lies down, strapped in. He doesn't seem to be there against his will. Next to him is a second, empty Chair.

I look closer and jerk with surprise.

"Thought you'd recognize him," Malka says, smiling. If I'm the canary, she's the cat with the cream.

"This is . . . Mr. Mantel." The owner of Sudice, Inc. One of the most powerful people in the world. He was technically my boss's boss's boss's boss. I've only seen him from afar a handful of times in my years working for Silvercloud. It's so incongruous, seeing him plugged into a Chair in this secret Verve lounge run by the Ratel. Does the government know?

I put my hand up to my necklace, pretending to fiddle with it. While Malka gazes down at the man's supine form, I press the hollow of my throat. One. Two. Three.

I swallow against the nausea and the migraine.

"You see why trust is important to us," Malka says smoothly. "No one else may know that he comes here. And no one will learn of it, will they?" The tip of her tongue darts out to wet her red lips.

"Of course not." My breathing is shallow. I force myself to fill my lungs. It doesn't help. I still feel as though I can't breathe.

*Hold it together, Taema. Hold it together.*

"Are you all right?" Malka asks with false concern.

"Fine," I say with a little half-smile. "Just . . . amazed to meet the man in person. So to speak. I'm to . . . go in?" I eye the second Chair.

"Yes. You observe the dreams, I observe you, and we see how you do. Another Test, as I said, yet this one is not quite so . . . complicated."

I give a strangled approximation of a laugh. "Let's hope I do as well."

"Yes. Let's hope."

The halfhearted smile slips from my face.

The room is soundproof. Outside in the hallway, dozens of people must walk by, but I can't hear any of them. It's as if this room is all that exists, and the only sounds are the short susurrations of the machine, and the faint sounds of three humans' breaths.

"What do you want me to suggest to him?"

"Nothing this time. Just observe. You don't want him to notice you."

"All right." I turn off the brain recording. I'm not sure if it'll work in the Vervescape, and Kim told me not to use it for too long.

She plugs me in, prepping syringes. If they can do it Chairless, like they did with my Test, why go through the steps here? Perhaps it's still in process, or the level Ensi dosed me with was too low. I hadn't even realized I was on it.

"Night, night," Malka says from above me.

I float away.

•

Mr. Mantel's dream is grainy. Small flecks of white float along my vision like static. I focus on making myself invisible as a ghost. *I'm not here*, I try to tell the dream. *Don't notice me. I'm just another speck.*

The static parts, the dream clearing. The colors brighten until it's as vivid as Mia's dreamscape. Mr. Mantel has a woman tied up on a bed in a penthouse apartment. It's Sharon Roux. The woman is the mayor of San Francisco.

She's as naked as he is, their clothes scattered around the room. Fresh bruises paint her legs and upper arms. Nowhere they'd show in her suit. I furrow my brow, until I see her smiling. She wants the restraints, and he wants to restrain her.

He crawls on top of her again, beginning anew. He hurts her, she cries out, she smiles, he smiles. It's different from the Zealscape. He's not killing her. There's no blood. No oily muck. No monsters. They're both enjoying themselves with pleasure and pain.

It seems to me like he's reliving a memory. Verve can enhance memories, so you relive them in glorious hyper-saturated color. It's a strange sensation, to watch someone having sex, knowing that you're strapped into a Chair and another woman is monitoring your physical sensors. I don't look away, though. I'm doing my duty and observing everything, in the hope I notice what Malka wants me to.

Why has Mr. Mantel chosen this memory to relive? What is he enhancing? How will he be when he wakes up? Angrier? Ready to come back again tomorrow? And what will the Ratel suggest to him? There are so many options. To take a deal that will profit the mob. To hold back a patent or push forward another? Or they could overwrite his personality completely, and make him into whatever they want. If they have the main man of the most powerful company in the world as their puppet, think what they could do. Control the top of Sudice through Mr. Mantel, and control the bottom by sending violent, hungry Zealots, reprogrammed by Verve, into the fray. Topple the structure and make what they want of it.

After what seems like hours, Mr. Mantel and Mayor Roux have finished. Mantel unwraps her restraints and they sprawl across silken sheets.

Pillow talk. Time to focus. I shift closer, keeping to the shadows. Neither of them notices me. Even in the dream world, my temples throb and my stomach feels as though I've swallowed rocks, despite the fact that I turned off the brain recording.

Mantel and Roux lie next to each other, but don't quite touch. I can't tell if they love each other or are using each other. Maybe both.

"It's getting out of hand," Roux says, staring up at the ceiling. Static dances across her face. Strands of dark hair cling to her glistening forehead.

"What is?" Mantel asks, folding his hands behind his neck.

"The Ratel situation. Do you know how much of my time it's taking up these days?"

"I can only imagine."

She bares her teeth. "They have to be stopped, Mantel. It's your pharmaceuticals they've twisted."

"You think I don't realize that? I don't see how they can be stopped."

"Yeah, yet it means the criminal bastards are out on the streets. There was a robbery last week. From a civilian. We had to cover it up. But I don't think we'll be able to do that much longer. And what if there's a murder? We'll have riots. This is a delicate balance, and I don't want it to fall in the Ratel's favor."

"We're trying to find a countermeasure, but it's taking time."

"We don't have time." Roux sits up, the bed sheet falling to pool at her waist. Her large breasts defy gravity, thanks to the wonders of flesh parlors. I don't feel Mantel's emotions like I did when Kim played Nazarin's memories, but it seems somehow linked. How else can these drugged dreams be so clear, if they aren't somehow messing with implants?

Everything's connected.

"If you still had Veli, then you'd have a cure by now." I have no idea who or what Veli is. The name hasn't been mentioned in Tila's notes, or in the SFPD's brainloading.

"You don't know that. And he was an imposter. Some little upstart my father plucked from one of his pet projects." Mantel's brow draws down. Almost against his will, an image flickers on the wall of a younger man with a strong jaw and angry eyes. It disappears almost immediately, until I'm not sure if I really saw it at all.

"He was a genius and you were a jealous little boy." She sounds bored, as if she's said this to him many times before. She swings her legs over the bed and begins to pull on her stockings.

"Be careful, Roux." Mantel's voice simmers in anger.

She looks over her shoulder at him. "I always am."

The dream shifts. Another woman enters the room, and I don't recognize her. Mr. Mantel looks over his shoulder in my direction, and I worry he sees me as everything fades away. His dream continues, but I leave.

I wake up in the Chair, Malka watching me, unblinking. In the Chair across from me, Mr. Mantel has a hard-on. I avert my gaze.

Malka folds her hands over her knees. "Well, what did you notice?"

I think through it, replaying the conversation over in my mind.

*"Be careful, Roux." Mantel's voice simmers in anger.*

*She looks over her shoulder at him. "I always am."*

"Roux knows that Mantel's not to be trusted."

"What makes you say that?"

"She doesn't give him any specifics. She hints that she's doing things to bring the Ratel down, but that's all. She chides him about letting Veli go . . ." Here I falter. "Who is he?"

"He's the man who truly invented Zeal. Mantel ousted him from Sudice and put a hit on him, so they say." She raises an eyebrow. "Veli hasn't been seen since, in any case. What else did you notice?"

"The government still wants to take us down," I say, though even pretending to be a part of the Ratel sets my teeth on edge, "but we already knew that."

Malka smiles. "Good girl."

"I'm right?"

"On the right track, in any case." She stands, and I mimic the smooth movement. "We already knew you were a fine dreamsifter. We'll up the stakes a little next time. You'll have grown more used to his dreams by then, and will be able to make one little suggestion."

"Of what?" I ask, my stomach twisting in dread as I give her a plastic smile.

"Next time is time enough." She leans back. "I had my doubts, but I think Ensi was right about you."

What a backhanded compliment. I stretch my plastic smile. "Thank you."

"Don't thank me just yet," she says. She drifts closer, puts her hand on my face. I force myself not to stiffen. "I have to show you what happens to little birds who chirp. Just in case."

She takes my hand and leads me from the room. I take a last look at Mantel before the door closes. He's panting, low, animalistic, rhythmic. Lost in the throes of Verve, where sex is better, and even memories of threats make you smile.

•

Another soundproof room. Outside the door, Malka takes a sword in a sheath from a hook on the wall with a familiarity that terrifies me. I play with my necklace, turning the brain recording on again.

Inside the room is another face I recognize from Tila's sketchbook. A woman named Nuala. She's small, dainty. She has pale skin and her hair is a lilac and gunmetal gray. She looks like a pixie from a fantasy film.

She looks terrified.

"Hello, Nuala," Malka says, as if they're about to have tea. "How nice to see you."

Malka unsheathes the sword. It looks ancient. Nuala squeaks and pushes herself back in the corner, as if that could make any sort of difference. Whatever's about to happen won't be pretty, and I won't be able to do anything to stop it. I clamp down tight on my emotions. The only way to get through this is to be a robot. My knees are still shaking.

"Nuala, this is Tila. Your replacement. Tell her your crime."

Nuala bows her head. I stare at the straight parting of her hair. Every muscle in my back is so tight I fear if I move, they'll break.

"I squeaked," she whispers.

"Yes, you did. And who to?"

"The police." Another whisper.

If anything, my muscles go tighter. She knows. She has to. I'm not a replacement at all. The Queen is going to kill both of us in this soundproof room and nobody will hear our screams. I force myself to stay quiet, my breathing even. My mechanical heartbeat thrums, steady and strong. I still have the headache and the fist of nausea in my stomach. All of this is recording. Even if I die, Kim will get this. Hopefully.

"That you did."

Malka hefts the sword.

"I prefer to do this the old-fashioned way," Malka says conversationally. "This is from the twelfth century. Beautiful, isn't it?"

It is, in a horrific way. The metal blade is scratched with time, but its edges are still sharp. Emeralds embellish the hilt.

Nuala is crying. "Please," she says. "Please."

It's a useless plea. Malka drifts closer, the light overhead catching on the blade. She's stalking her prey. Nuala pushes back into the wall as hard as she can and starts screaming for help. Nobody can hear her but me, and I clasp my hands over my ears. My resolve breaks and I hear the rough sobs from my throat. I want to shield Nuala with my body, but I know it won't protect her. And I'm too much of a coward. I'm not Tila. Tila would rush Malka and disarm her, consequences be damned.

"Don't you dare close your eyes, Tila," Malka says, her words almost singsong. "You need to understand just how imperative it is to keep your goddam little mouth shut."

I open my eyes wide, afraid to blink. *Don't look away.*

Nuala keeps screaming, a high banshee wail. Malka presses the point of the blade through the hollow of her throat. Nuala's screams cut short.

Blood stains the white uniform, falling in a crimson tide down her front. It was quick, at least. No torture. No scalpels like in Mia's dream.

Malka draws the sword out, wiping the blood off with the end of Nuala's tunic. The girl's eyes stare straight ahead, still shining with tears. Her beautiful hair is matted with blood. Malka looks down, and all the anger has fled from her face. She looks serene, as if she's come out of the dreamscape, wiped clean of her bloodlust, at least for a time.

"Now you see what happens if you cross us."

"Did I not already see that at Xanadu?" I whisper. I wish this could be a Verve hallucination like the original Test, but it's not.

"Nothing like a repeat lesson to drive it home." She comes closer to me, until I can smell her perfume under the iron tang of blood. It smells of incense, dark and smoky. She pauses scant inches from me. I can see each perfect pore in her face, the glitter of her eyeshadow.

She's close enough to kiss me. I feel the tip of my tongue touch the false-crowned molar. It's meant for Ensi, but would it harm her, too?

"And I don't know if I trust you," she murmurs. "See, I liked Nuala. This, this was the kindest way. If you betray us, you won't be so lucky.

"I'm not sure what he sees in you, or what he wants from you. Whatever it is, he'll get it, little canary," she whispers to me. "At the moment you're interesting. He's still figuring out what he really wants from you. And, once he gets it, you'll be obsolete. If I were you, I'd make sure I was useful elsewhere, and prove myself trustworthy. To him. And especially to me. Or else you'll find you'll never flee your cage."

She stays that way, almost nose to nose, staring into me. I worry that she can see everything—my treachery, my fear.

After a moment, an age, she pulls away, putting the sword back in its sheath, like an avenging Valkyrie. I don't want to be against her, because I fear I'd have no chance.

She smiles at me as if she knows this, and then she leaves. I press the hollow of my throat three times, try not to look at the corpse of Nuala, and trail after her.

•

Back at the safe house, I can't stop shaking.

I don't cry, but I want to. So I sit in the living room, wrapped in a blanket, simply shivering. Nazarin sits next to me. I've told him everything that happened. We've transferred both of our recordings to Kim's server. We told her not to watch them. I didn't want her to see that girl murdered. It might remind her of what happened to her wife, just because she came too close to her quarry on what seemed to be just one more case.

"Do you know who Veli is?" I ask. Something about Malka's body language made me think it was important.

"No. I'll ask my superior, see if he knows anything."

We trail off again. Nazarin's eyes go distant and he pings his superior. His fingers dance as he types in the air. I lean against him, his arm warm against mine. It helps ground me. My eyes drift closed, and despite everything that's happened, I doze.

A time later, Nazarin gently shakes me awake.

"What is it?" I ask. My brain is fuzzy. Memories of Nuala come back, and I want to vomit.

"My superior looked up the name, but it was classified. Even for him."

"Shit. Really?"

"Yes. He's gained access now, though, and he can share it with us."

"All right."

Nazarin gets up and brings back two glasses of water. I gulp mine down. He takes a breath. "Veli was once CEO of Sudice, Inc.," Nazarin says. "Veli Carrera. Alex Mantel's father, Peter Mantel, and Carrera started Sudice. They created Zeal. After Peter died, Alex ousted Carrera, wanting Sudice to be a family-run affair. Carrera didn't take it well. Alex thought it was dangerous to leave Carrera . . . untethered, and so he tried to kill him, hiring a hitman, probably hired from the Ratel. But Veli Carrera escaped and found his way into the mob. He changed his face so that no one would find him. The SFPD think that he worked his way up from the bottom and became . . . Ensi."

I let that sink in. "So Ensi is the man who helped invent Zeal in the first place. It explains why he was able to fabricate Verve. He has the technical foundation. It also explains why he's interested in weakening Zeal's hold on the city and replacing it with Verve. They can break down the city, and hurt Sudice in the process."

"Exactly."

"So many layers and secrets."

"I told you. The further undercover you go, the more there seem to be."

We lapse into silence.

"I think he might be coming up with a form of Verve that

doesn't need a Chair and implants," I say carefully. "He dosed me with Verve, I think, before the Test."

"Easier to dose large numbers of people that way, or in places they don't expect." Nazarin rubs his face.

"He'll be able to peek into everyone's heads at will. No secrets. Not from him."

"Exactly." Nazarin sighs. "One good thing, I suppose. Ensi's asked me to be his bodyguard. That drop from the Hearth? I'm going to be right there by his side, with a perfect view to record everything." He taps his temple.

"One good thing, good being relative," I say. "After the drop, I think we need to duck out. This is growing too dangerous."

"I agree completely. If we can find out what the Hearth is delivering, prove Ensi is receiving illicit material, and that Alex Mantel is involved, that's enough that we can bring the force of the law down on the Ratel. We're not needed after that."

"Just until the drop," I say, in almost a sigh.

"Just until then."

Then it's over.

•

Monday ends. Tuesday passes in a blur of last-minute preparation and too little sleep. Then it's Wednesday. The drop will happen at midnight.

Nazarin will be there, guarding the King. I'll be on my own, trying to move close enough to watch and record from another angle. Nazarin said I didn't have to go, that he could do it alone; but I can't back out now, not when we're so very close to the end. If there's anything connected to the Hearth, I'm the best person to figure out what it is and who's behind it on the other side of the bay.

Yesterday was a long day. I didn't have to go to the Verve

lounge, at least, and with luck, I'll never have to set foot there again. It was more training, more last-minute information. I picked through the information on Veli Carrera, or Ensi in a previous life, wondering what he was like back then. Sudice betrayed him, but he didn't have to turn to crime. Yet he did.

Now it's Wednesday. The last night of having to do this.

No more watching people's Verve dreams. No more pretending to be Tila and losing more of the Taema I used to be each day. No more putting myself in danger.

That's the plan.

The King of the Ratel doesn't often get his hands dirty, but it seems he'll attend this drop personally. It's clever that Ensi stays out of things as much as possible. Nazarin has seen so many crimes over the past year in his time with the Ratel; but it's always other people. If they were arrested, nothing would really change. They'd be replaced the next day, and Ratel business would continue as usual. We still only have proof of Malka killing someone. We don't have direct proof of Ensi doing anything illegal. Hopefully, in fifteen minutes, we will.

The pier appears abandoned, but the Ratel own it, and no one trespasses. The cranes, built in water, tower over us like strange mechanical beasts. Dotted around the pier are reinforced docks, stacked with rusting cargo bins. I'm hidden behind one, dressed in a black Kalar suit. I've been here half an hour, waiting and watching; Nazarin gave me a gun, now tucked into the small of my back. The air is cold, and I shiver. The green glow of the algae in the water lends everything a sickly tinge, but it's enough light for me to see.

They haven't arrived yet. I worry that I've messed up and read the notebook wrong, or that Ensi changed it at the last moment and Nazarin couldn't tell me.

Off to my right is movement. There they are. I push the

hollow of my throat three times. The headache returns, worse than it was at the Verve lounge. I nearly throw up the scant meal I had a few hours earlier. I bend over, breathing hard, before I peer out around the crate. It's a man, tall and muscle-bound, patrolling the perimeter. There's Nazarin, standing next to other muscle-bound men. Waiting. The men begin to patrol. I press myself into the shadows.

I can see Ensi's profile, his hair in disarray from the wind. He's standing with just one or two other people. The lights of the ships pulse overhead as they slip into the Ferry Building. Ensi's body language is impatient.

There it is.

A ship that looks almost identical to the supply ships that came once a month to Mana's Hearth drops down, its engines flaring. The light illuminates Ensi's face in the green fog. He's smiling to himself.

I'm so focused on him that I don't notice that a bodyguard by Ensi's side has gone missing.

By the time I feel the prick of the needle in my neck, it's too late.

All grows dark.

# TWENTY-SIX

# TAEMA

I wake up groggy and hurting. I'm strapped into a Chair, like the ones I've seen in the Ratel warehouse the last few days, unable to move.

Nazarin is in another Chair next to me, but he's still out cold.

Unlike the bulky Chairs of the safe house and Zeal and Verve lounges, these have no wires. There are only little electrodes resting against my skin, like during the Test. The Chair is little more than a prop and a way to restrain me.

Ensi sits across from me, legs crossed, eyes staring into the distance as he reads something on his feed. When he sees me move my head, he gives me his full attention.

His face is smooth as still water, his gaze frigid. As if he's never met me before, never danced with me, never unzipped that catsuit. I'm intensely grateful I didn't end up needing to sleep with him, so there is not that extra layer of guilt and betrayal.

"Good evening," Ensi says, as if we're sitting across from each other at a dinner party. His mannerisms are similar to Malka's. Unfailingly polite, even as they're about to commit cold-blooded murder.

I say nothing.

"You and your sister are cute, you know that?" he says. "Thinking you're so clever, sniffing around my business. That I wouldn't know exactly what you're doing at all times. You really think that notebook was left in my pocket by chance? Silly, silly girl."

I'm an idiot. If he knew about an uprising like he did at Xanadu . . . there, he even let them make their display, sacrificing a few people, his own people, before he crushed it and summarily executed everyone involved. He played with us, him the leonine cat and us the little mice.

"How long have you known?" I manage, my voice hoarse.

"As soon as Tila came snooping a few months ago." I close my eyes. "I knew her right away. I even fed her some clues, knowing she wouldn't be able to resist trying to solve the mystery."

My mouth is so dry. I lick my lips. "You know who we are."

"Of course I do. You're the only two to make it out of the Hearth on your own terms in years. I've kept tabs on you. You proved more interesting than I thought."

"Who the hell are you?" I ask. "What do you have to do with the Hearth?"

He smiles. "I don't owe you any explanations. In fact, I quite enjoy the idea of you working so very, very hard to find out the answers and then never getting them." He sighs. "I'll humor you. I did find Tila amusing, at first. Trying to find out everything she could. For a long time, she went nowhere, and I enjoyed her struggle. I decided to toy with her more, seducing her even as she thought she was seducing me. Then, to my surprise, she actually found something useful that she could use against me. And I couldn't have that, now, could I?"

"So you sent Vuk after her. Or, should I say, you sent Adam after her." The words feel acrid on my tongue. I feel my face twist in disgust and horror. Images of the crime scene swim in my vision. So much blood.

"Ah, I see you found that piece of the puzzle. She'd realized who he was, so it seemed fitting he should be her downfall. Of course, the plan did not go perfectly." His mouth flattens in anger.

My implants are still recording everything we're saying, even if they're not broadcasting to Kim right away. It's been over five minutes, and I have to hope the side effects don't kill me. I've gotten enough to hang him with, and I have a feeling he's only about to give me more.

I concentrate on my mind, trying to focus inward. I can't tell if it's sending or not. And even if it is, then our location's probably blocked as well. We're trapped.

Stupid. Stupid, stupid.

"You know why your sister did it, don't you?" Ensi asks. "Tell me you at least figured that out."

"Did what?" I ask, my mouth dry.

"Killed him. Your sister did do it. Her hand held the knife that went right into his heart." He pauses, just for a moment, reveling. "She did it for you."

I hear a ringing in my ears.

"She realized that if she was found out, then I'd come after you to get her to do what I want. I'm still not entirely sure what happened that night at Zenith. She did something to Vuk before she killed him. His mind went haywire, broke through the Verve programming, which I didn't think was possible."

I can't breathe. I don't want to believe him, but why lie now, when he's about to kill me?

"What's your link to the Hearth?" I ask again. I want—I need—to know.

He only shakes his head.

I want to snarl at him, but I won't give him the satisfaction. "What are you planning to do?" My voice is even, cool. I'm proud of that.

"To you?" He picks up a syringe of Verve. "I'm going to plug you in, but I've programmed this Vervescape a little differently. It's extra potent, and not a mix you'd find in any lounge." I swallow. He's the man who invented both Zeal and Verve. He can do almost anything he wants, for he knows the code and the pharmacology better than anyone alive.

He considers the syringe. "Who else but me could reprogram personalities and brain chemistries? Who else could take timid, shy Adam and turn him into Adam, a killer on command?

"I've programmed this particular world here so that instead of you enacting the violence, the violence is enacted against you. Your own personal little hell. It's how I execute those who really disappoint me. And, Taema, for all your cleverness, you've disappointed me." He gestures to his right and I see a third empty Chair. "I'll be joining you."

He's going to torture me. I think of Mia and her scalpel. False Mana-ma's soundless, tongueless, painful scream. It's as if I'm made of stone. I want to scream, cry, piss myself, laugh hysterically, but I can't do a thing.

I turn my head. Nazarin's awake, his open eyes locked on me. I can't contact Nazarin through my implants because of the blocked signal. I try my restraints, but they're stuck fast.

Ensi reaches down and pushes up the sleeve of my Kalar suit, revealing the bare skin. He runs his finger down the exposed flesh. I shiver.

"It's such a shame," he says. "If I'd found you both right when you left the Hearth, your lives could have been so very different. You slipped past too quickly, already within the system as soon as you arrived in the city. When I did find you, I let you be. Why? Curiosity, I suppose—what would two girls who escaped the Hearth choose to do with their new lives? You went through engineering school. I was at your graduation ceremony, though you never saw me." My skin prickles. "Tila grew into her art, and had that gallery show. I went to that, too. I even bought one of her paintings."

Were we experiments to him? He watched us, to see what we'd do. The gallery showing was so long ago. Did my sister realize Ensi had bought one of her paintings? Does she feel he has a piece of her? Did she know he's been keeping tabs on us for years?

"Which painting?" I ask, still avoiding looking at Nazarin. I think he's worked his way out of a restraint. But how can he get out of the rest? If he reaches around, Ensi will notice.

Just keep him talking. He wants to talk, even if he says he doesn't. I should be more scared, but I must be in shock, using the Hearth training to drive the fear away, at least a little. I'm grateful for it. It means I can think, I can speak. I can try to survive.

"The quasi-self-portrait."

I know the one he means. It's a woman who looks nothing like us, but her shadow falls out behind her, separate, but connected. She'd painted it in all the colors of the rainbow, yet for all the crazy hues, it was so realistic. My sister had called it *The Kaleidoscope Woman*. I'd been sad when it sold, but she'd said she couldn't turn down the price. I feel sick that he has it.

I swallow. We're alone, but I have no doubt that dozens of guards are posted outside this room, wherever it is.

Ensi stretches his arms over his head. "Now, fascinating as this conversation has been, it's time for us to be getting on, isn't it?" He aligns the needle against the crook of my elbow, poised over the vein. The electrodes begin to buzz, tightening against my skin. The fear I'd banished rushes back. I stare at the ceiling, and that white expanse may be the last thing I see. How boring.

Ensi leans closer to me. This is my only chance. I think the trigger word: "sweetpea." I bite the seal on the tooth. A liquid spreads into my mouth, and I lock my throat. I'll kiss him if I can, and if I can't, I'll spray it into his face.

"I didn't see you partnering up with a detective. And I didn't peg him until he waltzed into that party with you, so I give him credit for that. A good detective—but not smart enough to quit while he was ahead. I'll tell you one thing before you go, my dear," he whispers. "You want to know who I am, but I'm a little disappointed you haven't figured it out."

He presses his lips to mine. I open my mouth, as if gasping, and he presses his tongue into mine. The tasteless liquid spreads into him. There. It's done. I can only hope it's enough.

He presses the plunger on the syringe and the drug begins to work.

"I'm the Brother," he whispers as my mind starts to go.

Everything that happens next is a blur. Nazarin bounds up from his chair and knocks Ensi back.

My mind burns. I'm still conscious—barely—because Ensi hasn't started the program. It takes all my strength to raise my head a few inches. Ensi is manipulating the fight with Nazarin so he inches closer to the controls. I try to warn Nazarin, but my mouth won't open. Ensi's hand snakes back and the program begins. Soon, I'll be trapped in a dream.

The King of the Ratel knocks Nazarin against the wall. He slumps over, his battered brain out cold again.

With the last of my consciousness, I see Ensi strap Nazarin

in the Chair and begin the program, then strap himself into another, starting his own sequence.

He's grinning like a hunter going in for the kill.

And then we're gone.

# TWENTY-SEVEN

# TILA

We really thought we'd succeeded.

The month had passed without any problems. We went to school, we did the chores we could do, we listened to sermons, we did the Meditation and we did our best not to stand out at all. Mom and Dad did their jobs. We tried to act both positive and remorseful at the thought that we would be reentering the Cycle again soon. Our health continued to worsen, and our main fear was that we'd die before we could escape.

We should have been more afraid of Mana-ma.

The morning the supply ship was due to come, we'd gone into the forest to hide near where it would land. It was slow going—we had trouble walking and had to use canes, stopping to rest every few steps. We left before most of the Hearth was awake and kept under cover of the trees, hoping that nobody would see us. We didn't bring anything with us except a bit of food—no clothes, no trinkets, no journals. I think that hurt Taema more than me. She wanted to bring at least one book. I decided then and there that if we survived and got jobs in San Francisco, I'd buy her all the books I could with my first paycheck.

We waited there in the shade all morning, eating the snacks

Mom and Dad had packed us. We wouldn't have long once Dad gave the signal.

"Are Mom and Dad going to get into trouble if Mana-ma realizes they helped us?" Taema asked. She hadn't asked the question before, though it must have been on her mind as much as mine.

"Probably, but it shouldn't be too bad. Mana-ma loves them, and maybe she won't find out. Maybe they'll think we went off to die in the woods and then animals ate us."

"That's gross, Tila."

"What? I'd rather be eaten by a fox or a bear then buried in the ground and then eaten by worms. You're going to be eaten either way."

I was trying to distract her, though I wasn't doing a very good job. I thought Mom and Dad would get in big trouble if Mana-ma found out they helped us escape. I didn't think their lives would be in danger or anything, though. I didn't know the full story of Mia and her lost lover back then. If I had, I might have been too scared to risk Mom and Dad by running away.

Even to save our lives.

"Maybe we shouldn't do this," Taema says. "I . . . can't help feeling it's wrong. That out there we'll lose ourselves."

I pressed my cheek against hers, then reached around and stroked her hair. "If we stay, we die. I don't want you to die."

Her breath hitched. "I don't want you to die, either. Maybe it's better to be damned by Impure things than be dead."

I shook my head, pushing down my anger that, despite everything, she could still believe in the tenets of the Hearth.

The ship came down, all silver and chrome and the blue fire of its engines. It was so different from anything in the Hearth. So smooth and sleek and futuristic. I remember thinking how strange it would be to be surrounded by a world where every-thing looked so flawless like that.

The hatch opened and the worker drones went about their business like ants, crawling out of the belly of the beast, lugging crates to be set onto the grass. Once the ship left, the people from the Hearth would slink down the hill and take their essential supplies back to the buildings, trying to have as little contact with the Impure as possible.

"So fucking hypocritical," I said out loud.

"What is?"

"All that bullshit about the Impure. Yet they still take regular orders of things they can't make. Never really thought about it before. The Hearth has plenty of Impure stuff that we all use. Light bulbs. Some of the cleaning stuff. Metalwork. We can't make a lot of that here. It's all over, but we pretend we're all Pure and untouched by the outside world. So stupid."

A pause, and then: "Yeah. It is." It was the first time she had really agreed with me out loud. Usually when I ranted about the evils of the Hearth she stayed pretty quiet, tacitly agreeing but not really saying anything out loud that could be considered anti-Hearth. It had always annoyed me. Now, she sounded so sad that I felt guilty for all my ranting. I also felt justified.

"It's almost time," I whispered, wrapping my arms about her. She rested her chin on my shoulder.

"Everything will be different now," she whispered against my neck.

"It'll be better."

"Maybe." She pulled away, and I could see the dark circles under her eyes, the yellow undertone to her skin, how thin she'd grown. I looked exactly the same. We felt especially weak that day. The excitement of freedom was overworking our already weakened heart.

"Taema?" I murmured, shaking her shoulder. She slumped, and I fell to the ground with her. I clutched her to me, taking deep breaths, forcing myself to stay calm, because I couldn't stress the heart any further. Her arms were slack against mine. I wrapped my own arms around her and rocked us like we were children, resting my face against her slack skin.

"Stay with me, Taema," I said over and over, careless of who might hear us above. I could feel her inhaling and exhaling against me and tears ran down my face. If she died, I'd be glad that I'd be following her a few minutes later. It wouldn't be fair if this was the end, just as we were about to escape.

I looked up into Mana-ma's face.

She squatted over us, her dark robes billowing.

"And just where do you think you're going?" she asked.

My mind spun, but there was no good excuse I could give—of course there wasn't. I decided to say nothing, and glared at her.

She looked at us, taking in Taema's head lolling against my shoulder. I could tell what she was thinking: she'd already lost us. She knew that during our last Confession, when I fucked with her and freaked her out.

"You might as well let us go," I said. "You can say we died in the forest."

"But what if I let you go and you find a way to survive?"

"I guess that's a risk you take. We're not doing so hot right now, anyway." I sucked in a breath. "Do you want us to die?"

"I want you to follow God's plan. If you weren't meant to die, your heart wouldn't be failing."

"Maybe God wants us to leave your godforsaken Hearth and go to the city."

She leaned down, close to me. There was no one around.

Her ageless face gazed down at us. Would she raise her arm in benediction, or would the hand hold a knife?

317

"It didn't have to be like this," she said. "It all could have been different."

"Well, this is how it is. So what are you going to do?" I glared up at her. "The power's in your hands, I guess. You going to kill us here? Do nothing for a few minutes? That's all it'll take." Already my vision was wobbling, going dim. My chest hurt, and my fingers were numb. I wanted her to go away and leave me to die in peace.

"You want to go out into the Impure world?" She sneered down at me. "Very well. I'll let you go. You can never return. Never contact your parents or your friends. You're cut off from here in every possible way. I know that the big, wide world out there will chew you up and spit you out, until you wish you could come crawling back. But you can't. You're apostate. You're dead to the Hearth."

"You done?" I asked wearily.

She glared at me for a long time before she finally moved away, her robe whispering against the forest floor. She turned her back on us and made her way through the forest to her Hearth. She'd made her point. We couldn't hide things from her, even if we tried. Our choice was final.

I spat in the direction she had taken.

I looked up toward the spaceship. We heard the low whistle of an owl—Dad's signal. Oh God. If Mana-ma knew about our escape, would she hurt my parents for helping us?

I tried to move, but Taema was so heavy, and I was so weak. We weren't far. I could see the ship through the redwood trees. A little door came down, but as much as I tried to move toward it, I was too weak. Our heart beat so loudly it seemed to be the only sound in the world.

I collapsed against the dirt, defeated. So close and yet so far.

I heard a clicking, whirring sound.

With my fading vision, I looked up into the face of one of the droid supervisors, her machine at her side. "You're the ones we're meant to pick up?"

I managed to nod.

"Shit," she muttered, and then she hauled us up by the shoulders and dragged us toward the ship, the droid assisting her. I watched our legs trail through the dirt. She kept under the cover of trees, looking around nervously. I didn't have the breath to tell her that she didn't need to bother, that Mana-ma had already found us and let us go, at least for now.

She put us in the ship and closed the hatch behind us. All sound cut off, and we were in a hallway. Everything was made of metal. I'd never seen that before. Looking up, we could see the metal crosshatches, the boots of people walking past and the wheels of droids.

"I'll get the medic," our savior said, and took off at a jog. All fell silent and then I heard the low roar of the engine. I hadn't expected it to echo all around us, from all directions at once. And I could tell when it left the ground.

"We're flying!" I whispered to Taema. But she couldn't respond.

I slumped on the floor, my arms around her, tears running down my face. "Please," I kept gasping. "Please." I actually prayed. Prayed to a God. Not Mana-ma's. My own idea of a God, one who wasn't a total asshole.

A group of people came running down the metal hallway. About five or six, their footsteps and voices echoing all around me. I was barely conscious. For a moment, when the unfamiliar faces peered down at us, I wondered if they were going to toss us out like so much junk. But my first experience with those from the outside world after we'd actually left the Hearth was kindness.

They'd never seen conjoined twins, and they looked at us with a mixture of awe and fear. They touched us gently, as if afraid they'd break us. I was almost all gone by then, but I still remember those soft fingers laying us down in the sick bay. I could see a gray fog with vague shapes and hear distorted sounds, but that's it.

A mask was put over my face and I could breathe better. My vision cleared, but I still felt so very weak. I wrapped my arms around Taema and closed my eyes, pressing my face against her neck.

The last thought I had before I fell unconscious was that I really, really didn't want us to die. Not when we were so close to that big, wide world out there.

# TWENTY-EIGHT

# TAEMA

Something is wrong.

Or, at least, it's not what Ensi had planned. I see the tall, towering redwoods of the Hearth. The sky is full of rainclouds, and the luminescent green fog of the bay floats through the air. I smell sea salt and old smoke. It is more vivid than anything I've ever experienced.

It's almost exactly like that shared dream forest my sister and I visited along with everyone else in the Hearth after we took the little pill from Mana-ma's hand.

I'm not bound. Neither is Nazarin. I don't see Ensi. This isn't where we were meant to end up. This definitely isn't where Ensi would send us to torture us. This is too . . . peaceful.

"Were you able to dose him with what Kim gave you?" Nazarin asks.

I nod.

He looks around, and then glances at his hand. He frowns. I blink, and a gun appears in his hand.

"It worked. That tooth was full of nanites that worked their way deep into his implants and biochemistry."

I take a shuddering breath. "How did Kim learn to do this?"

"Sudice's labs and a brilliant brain."

We start walking through the woods, cautiously. We don't see Ensi, but he'll be here, somewhere.

"How'd you meet Kim?" I ask, keeping my voice low. "Through Juliane?" We both scout our surroundings, but I want to focus on something other than the fact I could die at any moment.

"I met Kim the first time the SFPD hooked me up with her to put in my memory mods. She met Juliane the same day. Juliane and she hit it off right away, started dating. Then they married, and they were one of those married couples that just worked. You saw them both together and you could only hope to have something like that someday. We both helped each other heal when we lost Juliane. I think if we hadn't had the other person to lean on, we might have both been broken by it."

We reach a break in the trees and a small clearing. The forest has shifted into an alien landscape. The sky is somehow night and day at the same time; shafts of sunlight-moonlight make the now silver bark of the dream redwoods shine, and the needles are turquoise and vermilion. Even the soil is tinged blue and purple. I listen for birds, but all is silent and still.

"I told the SFPD that they should use Kim to help me in my undercover op," Nazarin continues. "She's the reason I haven't been caught and killed before now. She wants Ensi taken down just as much as I do. Maybe more. I loved Juliane, but my love can't compare to Kim's. Not even close."

We've passed through the other side of the clearing, and the forest towers over us once again. I feel so small, so insignificant. It's as if Nazarin and I are the only people in this Technicolor twilight world.

"Kim knew even if we got proof that it'd never be enough.

She's been developing that false tooth for a long time. Used us, in a way, I guess, though I can't blame her. I would have done the same in a heartbeat."

*Like you used me.* The unspoken words hover between us, almost a presence. I can't really blame him, either. It was my choice, too.

My nerves are on edge. I keep waiting for the world to turn dark and ugly. For the mandrake demons to grow from the ground and reach for me, for the sky to burn, for Ensi to appear with a scalpel, pin me down and cut me open.

"So we should be able to manipulate this place? Even you, though you're not a trained lucid dreamer?" I concentrate, and make a knife appear in my hand. It seems solid and I feel better holding it. It was far easier than when I was in Mia's dream world, or even Alex Mantel's.

I remember Kim telling me about the nanites after she'd fixed my tooth: *This will hack into Ensi. Once you dose him, he'll have little control over the dreamscapes he creates. When he goes in to take his pleasure and revenge against someone, he goes in deep, leaves nothing back. If he dies in one of his creations, he'll be brain-dead.*

It was supposed to be a long con. Eventually someone would realize they could affect the dreamscape, fight back and get rid of him for us. I doubt she expected him to go in so soon after he'd dosed, bringing us with him.

"What happens if we kill him while we're still in here?" I ask.

"Kim never said."

"Well, shit."

"Yeah. Guess we'll find out."

I feel like something should have happened by now. The cyber forest is eerie, but not as frightening as Mia's demons with the faces of people I grew up with. It's such a strange echo of Mana's Hearth.

I crane my head and peer through the branches up at the violet sky. Where is Ensi hiding? Does he know we're here?

I start to recognize the tree formations. I grab Nazarin and lead him to the left, to the thin track through the forest that my sister and I have taken so many times. But the redwood forest I grew up with is merged with the dream forest of mercury-dipped trees and their vibrant needles.

I stop. There's the hollowed-out tree that Taema and I used to go to when we wanted to get away from everything. Perfectly rendered in the code of this corrupted dream world. Where we went just after we found the tablet. Where we found out the world outside was vaster than we had ever dreamed.

There is a tiny pinprick of light in the middle of the darkness.

"We have to go inside," I say, my voice small and far away.

Nazarin doesn't question me. He follows me as I move closer, crouching on my hands and knees and crawling inside. Sure enough, it's like *Alice in Wonderland*.

I take Nazarin's hand and we fall down the rabbit hole together.

•

Ah. Here's the nightmare.

The phosphorescent green fog is here, too, but this is a swamp rather than a forest. It is a re-creation of the barrier around the Hearth that no one was meant to cross. It smells of bilge water and sulfur, of decomposing plants and bodies.

In front of us is a boat. We step into it, and it begins to move. Things swim in the deep—creatures with white teeth, scales and long, slithering tails.

"It's like we're crossing the river Styx to the underworld," I mutter.

"As long as there's not a three-headed dog." Nazarin is alert, watching for any threat. Unconsciously, I move a bit closer to him.

As the ship takes us through the swamp, large opalescent bubbles shimmer ahead of us, resting on the water. We're heading straight for one, and there's no way to steer. Nazarin wraps his arms around me, as if he could protect me if it was dangerous. I wrap my arms around him, just as tight. We slip through the barrier, and it feels greasy against my skin.

We're in a memory.

Zeal and Verve. Dream worlds and heightened memories.

I'm no longer looking at the scene through my own eyes. Ensi is young, perhaps twelve years old. The memory is from his point of view. Like when we played the recording in Kim's lounge, we can sense some of his experiences and emotions.

He's in the Hearth. I recognize the view of the lake from the cabin window. He's playing with a little girl, and it's Mana-ma. They're playing marbles, and Mana-ma's tongue sticks out of the side of her mouth as she flicks one marble toward another. They hit each other with a click. "See?" she says. "You have to have a plan, to figure out the next move."

Ensi takes his turn, scanning the marbles. Flick. Click.

"Good," she says, smiling at him, and Ensi beams back.

The boat moves through to the other side of the bubble and we're out, but not for long. We enter another memory. Ensi's older now, perhaps late teens or early twenties. He's standing behind the pulpit as Mana-ma lectures, her face rapturous as she turns it toward the stained glass of the church. The Brother stares ahead, thinking about God, and a higher power. If His will is really what Mana-ma proposed.

The sermon ends, and the Brother follows Mana-ma. They go to the Confession room. Mana-ma sets out a chessboard, and they play as they usually do, but the Brother isn't in the mood for strategy.

"I don't see why I should leave you. Isn't my work for God here?"

Mana-ma rearranges her robes about herself. She's only recently taken up the title from her predecessor. She must be about the same age in this memory as my sister and I are now.

"God spoke to me. This is the way to do His will. You have a brilliant mind. You are interested in the sciences, but you've learned all you can here. You are meant to go on this journey into the unholy land, and bring glory to us. I am not sure exactly how, but He has told me you will find your way. You have my full support, and my faith in you."

Ensi moves his pawn forward. Mana-ma captures it.

I have a feeling Ensi programmed this world, a personal Vervescape separate from where he torments his victims. A place to categorize his memories, but now they're bleeding into each other, his past and his present colliding.

As Ensi's memories merge, Nazarin and I are thrown into slivers of his life. After coming to San Francisco, he looks into a mirror after shaving. He isn't as beautiful then. His nose is bigger, his hair not as full, his chin a little weaker. He is Veli Carrera, the man I saw projected on the wall in Mantel's Vervescape. He doesn't like this world, how loud and strange and Impure it is. He presses the razor against his wrist. He wants to go back to the redwoods, and back to Mana-ma. At the same time, the lure of knowledge calls him, and he knows he can continue God's work here, and make his Mana-ma proud. Reluctantly, he takes the razor away.

I want to know how he went from under her thumb to being the true, unseen hand that rules San Francisco.

With another shuddering lurch, the boat sails through the next memory.

Mana-ma is in Ensi's apartment. I startle to see her not in the Hearth. They move toward each other, resting foreheads close. Ensi looks as he does now, and Mana-ma looks a little older than I remember. It is a more recent memory.

She has brought him more mushrooms from the Hearth. He takes them, handling the bag as though it's precious.

"We'll need more, if we're to do what we desire," Ensi says.

"We're growing greenhouses full. You'll have as much as you need."

"And the government does not suspect?"

"No. They take their regular shipments for Zeal. We are but one of many suppliers. They respect our privacy, finally. They have stopped sending in their observers once a year to make sure we are toeing the line. They do not look too closely."

"Are you ready?" Ensi asks.

Mana-ma looks up at him, and in that moment, I know their relationship has shifted over the years. Mana-ma was once stronger than him, leading him, but now they are equals in their twisted journey, whatever it may be.

He brings her through to the next room. His apartment is humble, despite the masses of wealth he must hold. Simple wooden furniture, woven rugs that look like the ones we made in the Hearth. No technology, except for two Chairs. One is empty and the other one holds Malka.

"This is her?"

"Yes. It took a lot of doing, but we managed to steal her from stasis. She's not been woken. She is Godless, she has no soul, and thus she can be your avatar."

"My avatar," she echoes.

"Yes. Whenever you wish to be by my side, I can bring you forth, in this body, projected through Verve. When we are finished, you will return to your body."

"And this girl?"

"She remains in stasis, her consciousness never woken."

She hesitates, her hand rising to her collarbone. I can't remember ever seeing her look uncertain.

"I know it pains you to do this," Ensi says. "But it means we can be close together, in a way."

"You know I never wish to be apart. How did you think of this idea?"

"I dreamed it. Perhaps God chose to whisper to me, just this once." He smiles, and does not notice the way Mana-ma's eyes flash. "I believe the initial idea stemmed from the twins, Taema and Tila."

Mana-ma's mouth curls. "So they survived? They are in this city?"

"Yes. I lost track of them for a time, but with my resources, I was able to find them again."

"What will you do with them?"

"Nothing, for now. At the right time, we will know what to do. Come now, my love."

Mana-ma plugs into the Chair. Ensi runs a program, and connects Mana-ma to Malka. I watch through Ensi's eyes as his fingers tap the code, as he watches their responses, the way their eyes twitch beneath their lids.

Mana-ma's eyes still. Malka's eyes open.

"How do you feel?" Ensi asks.

"Reborn," Malka says, and her face twists into that chill smile I saw just before she killed a girl with a sword.

They rest foreheads together again.

I come out of the memory like I'm coming up for air. Nazarin and I gape at each other, but there's no time to speak before we collide with other memories. I experience more of the fractured life of Ensi. From the shards, I piece together more of the picture. Ensi is almost sixty, which must be Mana-ma's age as well. She looks younger, but it could be genetics rather than a hypocritical visit to a flesh parlor in the city.

Ensi left the Hearth with Mana-ma's blessing, coming to San Francisco with the plan they had stitched together. He was found on the streets and given a VeriChip and a place in a home for youth, choosing the name Veli Carrera. Seeing his obvious interest in science, the home encouraged him to brainload, and he did so well, he soon had a degree. He researched local scientists and decided Mantel would be his mentor, and he found a way to come to his attention.

He thrived, and Mantel helped him flourish. Mantel had no son, but a few years later, one arrived. The CEO of Sudice still treated "Veli Carrera" as a son, and when Veli earned it, Mantel passed the company to him rather than to his biological son.

Memories of the lab, of using the mushrooms Mana-ma sent from the Hearth to distill and create Zeal. Brainloading more information than it seems he can bear, shuddering at the feeling of electrodes and wires against his skin, so different from the simple ways of the Hearth. He wouldn't have done it, he couldn't have done it, if he hadn't loved Mana-ma so deeply.

Throughout all the memories is the stink of the swamp, the threat of things swimming beneath the surface.

Ensi, as Carrera, was there through the run-out of Zeal, but as new product after new product was shot down by the government, he grew increasingly annoyed. His and Mana-ma's plan was delayed. Zeal kept the crime low, which kept the city happy enough. Ensi did not share his ideas for another drug, one that could change personalities to make citizens more tractable.

Then Ensi lost it all. Mantel's son ousted him. Ensi was cut loose, and he was making new plans when he discovered that Mantel's son's hatred ran deep enough for murder. I saw fragments of him killing the hitman sent to find him, hiding in the streets, the many surgeries in back-end flesh parlors, and then deciding to enter the very group hired to kill him. He started as the lowest Pawn, but strategy had been drilled into him since he was young.

I hate experiencing what he did to become head of the Ratel. He killed so many people through his favorite method: torture by dreams. He experimented on Zeal until it split and became the drug he truly wanted: Verve. I have to live through those pockets of horror and pain: the fate I would be experiencing right now, if not for Kim and her code. A fate I might still face. Where is the real Ensi? I feel him in here, somewhere.

We've reached the end of the memories. We have passed through the swamp, and up ahead is the Hearth. He never left it, not truly. It's always in his head, too. I remember Mia tapping her temple. None of us ever truly left, did we?

Nazarin and I reach the end of the muck, climbing out and setting foot on solid ground.

It's a short walk to the town. It's similar to how I remember it, though there are fewer houses, as the Brother left decades before my sister and I did. It even smells the same, like redwoods, earth, the sulfur of the swamp, the chimney smoke from the houses.

"Where is this?" Nazarin asks.

"Home," I say, not sure if the answer is truth or a lie.

The green mist thins, wisping around our ankles. I catch Nazarin's hand. It feels like I'm really touching him, even though in reality he's a few feet away from me, strapped to his Chair. But my brain sends an impulse, and so Nazarin's skin seems warm.

The brain is so very capable of lying to itself.

We walk through the pathways, the sky still the same twilight. Most of the flowers in the gardens are closed, their little heads nodded in sleep.

"It's peaceful," Nazarin says. "This is very strange."

"It's his fortress," I reply. "The quietest corner of the mind. He created it in the image of the Hearth. Perhaps he knows something's wrong with the code."

"So he's come here to hide."

"I think so."

"Where?"

I think of the memory where he felt safest. "The chapel."

We turn a corner of a path, and there it is. It's an innocuous building, made of wood and painted white. My memories of the place blend with Ensi's. We spent so many hours within its interior growing up. So many hours of Confession, of sermons, singing and whispering and praying. I once loved going into that building. Tila was always more suspicious than me of Mana-ma and the whole Hearth's creed. For most of my young life, though, I was a believer.

The illusion around us is cracking. The acrid smell of the swamp returns despite the fact it's no longer in sight, the green fog thicker. Fractal swirls of black mar the clear blue sky of early morning. The atmosphere is no longer peaceful, but expectant. The Hearth is abandoned, but I swear the place is holding its breath.

A light flickers in the chapel. We walk up the steps, lined with smooth, white stones. To either side of the path, the world continues to crumble, the images glimmering at the corner of my vision. The doors loom before us. Nazarin reaches forward and pulls them open.

Inside, it's dark but for a candle flame. As we enter, it brightens.

Ensi stands at the altar where Mana-ma always preaches. He's looking up at the window. It's almost as if he's waiting for someone.

Water has leaked in. I splash through shallow puddles toward him. I have no idea what to do, what to expect. We have no weapons. Once I stopped concentrating on that knife, it ceased to exist again. I try to imagine it, bring it into being. It starts to appear—it's the same as the murder weapon from the autopsy report at Zenith, the one Tila may have used—but as soon as I almost have a solid grasp on it, it disappears again. The same happens to Nazarin and his gun. The pews shake, as if in an earthquake.

"What have you done?" Ensi asks. He looks almost as he does in the real world, except he's pale and shaking. There are more lines on his face, ghosts of the one he would wear if he hadn't waxworked his features. Still, he moves out from the altar to face us, staggering a little, but standing strong.

"I injected you with a virus. When you kissed me."

"What does it do?" He sounds calculating, rather than afraid. He's used to being a victor. He won't give up so easily. The ground shakes again, rumbling, and dust falls from the rafters.

"It's eating your world. Gobbling it up byte by byte. When it's all gone, you're finished." I don't know if that's true, but it sounds good. I guess Kim didn't plan it as a long con, after all. Makes sense. Why take the risk that he'd discover it and destroy the code?

His eyes glint. "Then I can take you with me."

Ensi moves toward us, smooth and deadly. A long blade appears in his right hand. He jumps over the shallow steps of the altar, water splashing around his feet. The blade is a replica of the one his Queen—I still can't process that Malka is Mana-ma in another body—used to kill Nuala. The chapel creaks with another violent shudder.

He lunges for me first. I dodge the blade by inches and jump onto the nearest pew to escape. Ensi grabs my ankle and I fall flat, knocking my cheekbone against the wooden pew. Pain flares like a flame, and my breath leaves my lungs in a rush. I taste blood. He drags me toward him and I scrabble away desperately. Far away, my body in the Chair will have begun to bleed as well, I'm sure of it.

I kick back and his grasp weakens. I kick again, pain flaring in my ankle as I hit his torso. Ensi grunts in pain. Gasping, I turn toward him. Nazarin and Ensi roll on the ground, snarling. Nazarin manages to free an arm and punches Ensi, his knuckles glancing along the other man's cheekbone.

I try to stand, but the chapel shudders. The world seems to fill with warm, dark green muck, like in Mia's dream. I don't know if it's Kim's code, my fear, or Ensi's.

The mud laps at my ankles, my knees, my hips. It rises over my head. If I breathe in, the muck will coat my lungs. I can't see Ensi or Nazarin, but I feel them, close, struggling against the collapsing dream.

I close my eyes, think of all my Meditation training. I push and push, and let go.

# TWENTY-NINE

# TAEMA

The green muck disappears, leaving dregs of dried mud. I fall to the ground, landing on my injured ankle. I hiss in pain, drenched and cold, spots wobbling in my vision.

The dream is still broken. The chapel still shakes and flickers, except where I focus my eyes. Nazarin and Ensi still fight, both of their faces bloody and beginning to bruise. My head pounds.

I hold on to a pew for support and move toward them, biting down on my lip to keep from screaming in pain.

I can't move forward another step. It's as if I've met an invisible barrier I can't cross. Ensi hits Nazarin again, and his head jerks back before he falls to the floor. Ensi's eyes flash to me, the corner of his mouth curling in triumph. Like me, he has found a measure of control in this broken world. He knows I can't come any closer. He moves toward me. I struggle, but I'm stuck fast.

"This is my mind. My dream. Your lucid dreaming may be impressive, but you can never hope to be as strong as me. Whatever you've done to the code, I can fix it. This night may have had an unnerving start, but I can still have fun with you and your pet detective. I can still hear my little canary sing so sweetly."

The chapel isn't wavering as much. It's almost as if it's repairing itself. Was this all a ploy, somehow? A trap within a trap?

It can't be. Ensi is still nervous, licking his lips, his eyes darting from side to side. He furrows his brow, and the blade that he conjured earlier is back. It's his weapon of choice, like Mia with her scalpel and Malka with her sword. The steel gleams.

Ensi comes closer, until he is scant millimeters from me. He brings up the knife and holds it against my throat. He nicks it, and I wince at the pain. Blood trickles down my neck.

I look to Nazarin, but he can't help me. What does it mean to be unconscious in an unreal world?

*Think, think, think.* I try to remember all I learned while in Mia's Verve world, and when I experienced Ensi's earlier Test.

If I kill him in here, maybe I can defeat him. If I can kill him.

My first experience in Mia's dream, I managed to make the crime scene go away, even if I couldn't do anything else. And although the Test scared me, I passed.

I can lucid dream, too.

I focus on building my own barrier. I put all my terror into it. The barrier grows over Ensi's, pushing the knife back from my throat. Ensi's face twists into a snarl. What will unnerve him most? What will give me the upper hand?

I focus. I have the barest bones of a plan, but it's my best chance. My only chance. The air around Ensi ripples, like I've thrown a rock in a still pond.

"I know who you are," I say. "I know your dreams and desires. I know what you've done."

I imagine Ensi wearing the face he was born with. I imagine Ensi as a young child. I imagine him as the man who has just joined the Ratel, hungry for revenge and power. The three acts of his life: child, Brother, King.

The true Ensi drops the knife. It disappears before it hits the ground. He feels the dream warping, wrenching away from his control.

The air vibrates with energy, and green, crackling lightning flashes overhead. A bolt comes down and hits me, and I scream as it sears my skin. Where it struck my shoulder, fractal burns appear, snaking down my arm like tree branches. The energy travels through me.

Three more bolts of lightning hit the floor of the chapel, creating rents in the fabric of the dream. The sulfur smell of the swamp returns, mingling with the ozone scent of lightning and thunder. The holes in the dream widen.

Child. Brother. King.

I bring forth the three versions of Ensi from the dreams. Ensi, a small boy of eight, his arms spindly. Ensi as the Brother, about to leave the Hearth. Ensi as he looks now, just after he killed a man and left the persona of Veli Carrera behind. None of the three do anything. They stand, waiting for my instruction.

The King of the Ratel looks at his past selves in fear. I take the threads of the dream in my mind. I have no idea what I'm doing. I am only instinct, a result of Mana-ma's training.

The knife appears in my hand again, cold and reassuring, but I no longer need it. I send the three simulacra toward Ensi. He backs away, pressing against the chapel wall. He's gone gray, beads of sweat on his forehead. He glances at me, then away, as if he can't stand to meet my eyes. He's not the leader of the Ratel, the man who's tortured many men and women to death, been responsible for many more. He slides down the wall, landing hard. He's a frightened man, a broken man, huddled with his arms around his knees, completely unable to face himself.

The three versions of him open their mouths wide. Red light pours from their throats, and then the same green muck emerges. Ensi closes his eyes, scrabbling for his own threads of lucid dreaming. Some of the muck pushes away, but I redouble my efforts.

The child, the Brother, and the King wrap their arms around the true Ensi. The green liquid covers them all, until it forms a perfect sphere. Another bubble of memory, sealing the King of the Ratel within.

The chapel ceases shaking. The lightning fades.

I go to Nazarin. He's awoken, and watched the whole thing.

"What do we do now?" I ask. "How do we leave?"

"You do it," Nazarin says. He sits up slowly, coughing. One eye has swollen shut.

"Yes." I gather the remnants of the shattered dream around us. I press my forehead against his. "Wake up."

•

I open my eyes, and then close them immediately against the brightness. Everything hurts. My entire body feels as though it's been charred. I wheeze, my tired lungs struggling to take in oxygen.

"Nazarin?" I croak.

"Taema."

I almost cry in relief.

"Is this real?" I'm so afraid that we haven't escaped. That we've been launched into another memory, another subset of Ensi's mind. I open my eyes again, ignoring the pain of the light.

We're in the room Ensi took us to after he captured us on the pier. I'm strapped into the Chair, the bindings pressed tight against my arms, my torso, my forehead.

I hear rustling and just manage to turn my head. Nazarin

pulls himself upright, struggling from his bonds. He rips the electrodes from his skin. The mechanical sound of his heartbeat on the monitor flatlines. Mine still beeps, steady despite the lingering fear.

I turn my head in the other direction. Ensi is strapped into his own Chair. His body is still alive, but the line on the monitor showing his brain function barely moves at all.

I did that.

Nazarin limps over and begins to untie me. His face isn't as swollen as it was in the dream world, but it's livid with bruises. Tracks of blood have dried from his nose, his ears and even the corner of his eyes. The whites of those eyes are red with broken capillaries, but his gaze is clear.

"Nazarin," I whisper.

He leans close to take the strap off my chest. "I never told you my real name, did I?"

"No."

"It's Aziz. Aziz Keskin."

"Aziz," I echo, tasting the name on my tongue. He smiles at me. I smile back. After all that has happened, we're able to smile at each other. He helps me sit up. I peel the electrodes off and throw them away, then lean against him, my head spinning. My ankle hurts. He wraps his arms around me, holding me close. I can feel his heartbeat. We both smell of sweat and blood and fear.

"Let's get the fuck out of here," I say.

"I couldn't agree with you more."

We stand, leaning on each other. We look down at the fallen King of the Ratel.

"Should we kill him?" I ask. I feel nothing at the prospect of it. I already killed him off, bit by bit. Now, it would be more or less getting rid of the shell.

"I want to. I really want to." He turns from Ensi. "Let's not cross that line. I think we've avenged enough today."

We start to hobble toward the door. Our guns are hidden in a cupboard, and Nazarin passes me one. We keep them in our hands, at the ready. My tongue keeps niggling at the molar, now missing its strip and the virus. My mouth tastes of iron.

Nazarin opens the door, darting his head out and back, gun held up by his ear. "It's clear."

We leave that awful room behind, staggering against the walls. We don't seem to have any lasting damage, but my brain still feels . . . confused. Senses still don't seem anchored to this plane of reality. My brain is still recording, but I don't turn it off yet, despite the headache. I guess I can handle it better than Kim's subjects. I swear, the white of the walls tastes like lemons. The squeak of our shoes against the floor feels like fear. I can't trust what I see. Only Nazarin feels real. Aziz.

We're so disoriented, so very focused on getting out into the fresh air, away from this place of terror, that we don't think about alarms. As soon as we open the outer door, high, piercing wails sound. It's too much for my raw, mixed senses. I clap my hands over my ears, screaming, adding to the cacophony. Nazarin cries out too, but recovers before me. He takes my arm. The King of the Ratel had not taken us far. We're still on the pier. I can even see the cranes where Ensi and his men were earlier that night, the storage crate we hid behind.

There are the men that had been with Ensi. Standing guard. With them is Malka. The Queen.

Mana-ma, wearing a poor soul's body.

She wasn't there before we went in. Ensi must have sent notice. Was she on her way? Was she going to join us in the dream world, and visit one of the missing members of her flock? Or did she only come when things went wrong? Is her true body lying supine back in the Hearth?

Malka, or Mana-ma, is the first to see us. She raises her head and meets my eyes, and I can read her expression: *You've failed this Test.* She wishes it was me, her, and her sword in a soundproof room.

She yells a warning, and the men run toward us.

"You've got to be kidding me," is all I can think to say, staring at them. I'm so tired.

Nazarin takes my hand, pulling me with him behind the nearest crate. He shoots over the top of the crate and ducks down. There's a distant cry of pain. Nazarin shoots again. No cry of pain. I can only seem to stare at the gun in my hand. A bullet ricochets against the metal of the crate with a crack that seems to hover in my vision, a riot of yellow, red and orange. It's beautiful.

My sister's voice is in my head: *Get your gun, T. You have to get your gun.*

I'm imagining it, but it's comforting to hear just the same. The gun still lies in my numb fingers. More shots fire. I can barely see. My head is splitting. There is a ringing in my ears, like tinnitus. Another shot. Where is Nazarin? Is he all right?

I clutch the gun to my chest, and the cold metal grounds me. Nazarin is next to me. A bullet has grazed his forehead; his Kalar suit didn't have a hood. Blood pours down the side of his face, but it hasn't stopped him. He shoots and dodges, shoots and moves. Another bullet hits him, and he falls. I can only hope it's the force of the bullet that felled him, not that it's breached the not-always-infallible Kalar.

*Shit, shit, shit, shit.* I can't tell if I'm thinking it or saying it out loud. Gunshots still pepper the storage crates. I unlock the safety of the gun and put my finger on the trigger. My hand shakes.

I peek over the crate, and then dart back. There's only one person left: Mana-ma. It's fitting. Her against me.

I gather the last of my strength and bravery and stand up from behind the barrier. I try to gather my senses together to make sense of the world again. I fire off shots, my vision still blurry enough that I'm not sure if I'm aiming at her. The shots focus me.

The first few miss, but then a bullet hits her in the arm. She folds forward. She's wearing a Kalar suit, but I've still hurt her. I aim again, and hear the crack of her gun. I squeeze the trigger and start to move back behind the crate. Everything slows. Mana-ma crumples, the bullet hole over her third eye beginning to weep.

I watch, almost disinterestedly, as the bullet she fired hits me straight in the chest. It does not puncture the suit, but I feel the impact against my metal sternum. My mechanical heartbeat slows.

Then stops.

# THIRTY

# TILA

I don't remember actually arriving in San Francisco.

Taema and I were out cold, but we woke up in the ambulance hovercar. The attendants pulled back the window screen, and even though I felt the worst I'd ever felt in my life, I remember how beautiful San Francisco looked the very first time I saw it. The sun was just setting, and it was like seeing a whole new planet, alien and strange. Tall buildings full of people, others full of trees, cars flying through the sky, bridges linking the lands across the water. It was so *big*. I knew billions of people lived out here in the world, but it was still something else, this city where over a million people lived, flying and seeing straight out to the horizon, tiny people walking down below. This new world seemed infinite.

At the hospital, they stabilized us and Taema woke up. I started crying when she did. I was so scared that she wouldn't.

The doctor who spoke to us had the same mild confusion about us as the rest of the people out here. We were so lucky, though. He knew our VeriChips were brand new, and he later quietly found someone who would be able to advise us about claiming sanctuary from Mana's Hearth and make our identities real.

He was one of the most attractive men I'd ever seen. I

342

hadn't grown used to how everyone was perfect in the city yet. I kept doing double takes as we went down the corridors of the hospital on our way here. It almost made me wonder if there were no humans in the city, and everyone was a robot. There were differences in height and some in weight (though nobody was too thin or too overweight), but everyone had unnaturally symmetrical features.

The doctor kept staring at where we were conjoined, but I guess he'd have reason to, considering what he was proposing. Everything we saw was new and strange. So shiny. I didn't know how to describe any of it or what any of it was called. I missed my parents and wished they were here with us. Mana-ma must have realized what they'd done. How would she punish them?

"You have to go into surgery immediately," the doctor said, cutting right to the heart of it (ha, ha). When he spoke, I kept getting distracted by the pretty curve of his lips, the way the blond stubble was just beginning to come in on his cheeks.

"What will you do?" Taema asked, evidently less blinded by his beauty.

A flash of emotion crossed the doctor's face. Discomfort? It was gone before I could tell.

"How much do you know about life in San Francisco?" he asked.

I remember thinking it was a strange sort of thing to start with. I thought he'd talk about the intricacies of whatever he was going to do to us. Though it's not like I knew what doctors did. I'd never met one before.

"Only a little," I said.

"Well," he began. "I have read up on where you've come from. It must feel almost as if you've traveled into the future."

It sort of did, though I hadn't really thought of it like that. We hadn't seen enough of this new future yet.

343

We nodded noncommittally.

"There are no cases like yours anymore," he said, and I could tell he was choosing his words with care. "The fact that you've survived in relatively good health as thoracopagus twins with rudimentary medical care is extraordinary. You therefore have a choice to make. We can operate and fix you, but the team I'm working with wish to separate you. Two separate hearts. Two separate bodies."

I felt what little blood there was left in my face rush away. Separated? Of course we'd thought about it, but we'd never considered it a real possibility. My feelings were all tangled.

"The way San Francisco is now, you would perhaps find it very ... challenging to remain together. People would not be cruel, necessarily, but you'd be stared at wherever you went. It would be difficult. Very difficult. I tried to convince them to let you stay together, if you choose, but they wouldn't agree to it. And I can't do it alone, not even with the help of drones. I'll leave you to discuss, but there isn't much time. We need to operate, and soon."

He nodded at us and left, closing the door behind him.

"We have to do it," Taema said.

"I don't think we *have* to do anything."

"The team won't operate if we opt to stay together. They just won't do it. But they won't let us die, either. That doctor made it seem like a choice, but I don't think it's really a choice at all." She saw through it all.

"Do you want to separate?" I asked her.

"I don't know. Not really. Or I wish we had more time to decide. We don't. I do know I want us both to live."

She made it sound so simple. "OK then."

"Yeah?" She seemed as scared as I was.

We sat in silence, holding hands, until the doctor returned.

We told him our decision. He seemed relieved—he could pretend it was our choice instead of taking it away from us.

The doctor explained what they'd do to us—give us new, mechanical hearts, restructure our sternums and part of our ribs and chest (despite everything, I still remember being excited by the thought of finally having proper boobs), straighten my spine because it was a little crooked. We didn't have time to process it much, because they hauled us into surgery right away, put us under, and then I woke up alone.

I remember that part so clearly. I spoke about it with Taema, sometimes. How very wrong it'd seemed, to wake up and not have anyone else in the room. How alien. I couldn't take the silence, so I'd worked myself out of the foreign machines and found my way to her.

We always find our way to each other. The first thing I did when I woke up from the surgery was find my other half.

This time, Taema will find her way back to me.

# THIRTY-ONE

# TAEMA

When I wake up, I think I'm in the Chair.

I thrash against the covers, crying out. The machines around me beep. I have the fuzzy, floating feeling associated with pain medicine. I realize that I'm not in a Zeal or brainload Chair, but I still can't place it. Hospital? The last time I was in a hospital was ten years ago, when I woke up alone for the first time in my life.

I'm alone again.

Screens surround the bed, all of them showing different parts of me—my steady heartbeat, my blood pressure, my brain activity. An IV stands sentry beside me, pumping nutrition and fluids into my veins. I can't sit up. I'm too weak. What happened?

I was shot.

My hand rises, hovering over my chest. I have bandages. I remember the bloom of pain, shooting straight through me, more painful than being hit by dream lightning.

I'm alive, though. That's something.

With difficulty, I manage to sit up. Moving triggers an alarm and a nurse droid comes in, topping up my medicine before going away.

I curse the droid as my eyes grow heavy again. I sleep.

•

The next time I wake up, I'm not alone.

Nazarin sleeps in the chair next to me, scrunched up awkwardly. His name is Aziz, but it's hard to break the habit. I feel much better this time. More awake, more alive.

There's a bunch of flowers on the nightstand next to my bed. Little white roses. I take one out of the vase and flick the stem at him. The water droplets splash him and he jolts awake.

"Hi," I say, managing a weak smile.

"Hey," he answers. His bruises are almost gone.

I try to sit up. Nazarin helps me and then passes me a cup of water, and I sip gratefully.

"Tila?" I ask.

"She's been given a full pardon. It's all still out of the press. You're not being held for any crimes committed while undercover."

"She'll be free?" My voice quavers.

"Yes. She'll be transferred and released tomorrow. You did it. You freed her."

I laugh, though it sounds hollow and weak. "I did it." My sister is safe. Safe. I fall back against the pillow. It hurts. "What's my prognosis?"

"The doctor will fill you in on the jargon and everything, but I can tell you what I know. You were shot in the chest. It didn't penetrate the Kalar suit much, but the impact of the bullet against your metal sternum messed with your heart and broke the skin. They had to repair and restart it. You flatlined. You'll have another scar, unless you want to erase it."

He snuck it in there, among the other stuff. *You flatlined*. I died. My fingertips graze the bandages. "Can I unwrap it?" I ask.

He shrugs. "Probably not yet."

347

"When can I go home?" I want to go home and sleep. I want it to be tomorrow, when my sister is free.

"Soon, I expect. Let me call for the doctor."

"Wait. One thing first."

"What?"

"Tell them to send down the waxworker. Get them to give me back my face."

•

We're silent as the hovercar takes us to my apartment. Not the safe house. My real, actual apartment, where I haven't been since they asked me to become my sister. My fingers trace my features. My nose is back to its usual shape, my cheekbones a little lower, my cheeks a little fuller. My hair is still short, but it's curly again and no longer blue. Even my old face in the mirror doesn't look familiar anymore.

I look out the window at San Francisco. It's foggy today, making everything look soft and dreamy. The algae tinges the gray with green. It reminds me of the world in Ensi's head, and I look away.

Nazarin helps me up to the flat. He seems to have recovered much quicker than I have, though he wasn't shot in the chest, so I suppose that makes sense.

I collapse on my sofa. It feels like I haven't been here in so long. A different person has come home than the one who left. It's going to take a long time for me to make sense of what happened in my head. I wonder if I'll ever be able to fully trust my own mind again.

"Give me some SynthGin, will you? It's in the cupboard to the left of the fridge."

He dutifully pours two glasses and comes to sit next to me on the sofa.

"Fill me in," I say.

Nazarin's voice is soothing. I take a long gulp of gin and close my eyes, listening. Ensi's body is still alive, but he's brain-dead. The government plans to put his body into stasis all the same. The Ratel has crumbled somewhat at the loss of its King and Queen. The government is breaking up the rest.

"They'll find Verve," I say.

"Yes, though Sudice is arguing that Veli Carrera began his research in their labs, and is trying to patent it. We've one saving grace, though: they're not exactly sure how to re-create it. It seems only Ensi knew the recipe."

"How?"

"It's what the drop was. Mana-ma grew a mushroom at the Hearth. I expect it's the same ingredient she used to dose you before Meditation. She processed it as much as she could there, and Ensi personally put the final touches on it once it arrived in the city."

I sigh. "It's only a matter of time before they figure out how it works." I'm not sure if I'm talking about Sudice or the government. Does it make a difference? "Have we really helped anything?" If Verve goes to market, the violent after-urges removed, it remains a way to make people more tractable.

"It won't be that easy for them. Someone might have leaked a medical report detailing the true effects of Verve to the entire city."

"Kim?"

He only smiles in response.

So things are not fixed. It is not a happily ever after. We can hope the Ratel stays scattered, and there's a glimmer of hope that Verve won't be released to the city from another's hands. A glimmer of hope. That's all.

"I suppose that's enough for now," I manage. "What's next for you, then, now that your undercover op is finished?"

"I've asked for a leave of absence."

I manage a smile. "A well-deserved break."

He sighs. "I don't know if I want to go back."

I understand. At the moment, I can't imagine going back to engineering. I feel too shattered to be a functioning cog in society.

I drain my glass and look down at the bandages beneath the collar of my shirt.

"I haven't seen the full extent of the damage yet," I say.

I begin to unbutton my shirt. Nazarin stands up. "Do you want me to go?"

"No. Stay."

I slide the dress off of my shoulders. I suck in a breath, looking at the fractal marks from being struck by phantom lightning in the dream world. The red has already faded to white, stark against the brown of my skin. It shouldn't be there, but it is. My mind thought it was hit by lightning, and the body obliged.

"They can erase it," Nazarin says.

"I don't want them to." It's beautiful, in its own way. And it'll always remind me that I was strong when I needed to be.

He stands again, moving closer. He raises a finger, hovers it over my skin. I meet his eyes and his fingers rest, lightly, on the fractal marks. He traces the swirling branches of the scars.

"It's like trees. Or blood vessels. I've never seen anything like it."

I don't reply. His touch makes me feel grounded and alive. It cuts through the dregs of the pain medicine. My whole body tingles.

I start to unwind the bandages across my chest. I'm afraid

to see what's underneath. The last of the bandages fall away. Nazarin and I both look down. Between my bare breasts is a new scar, just to the left of the one that bisects me from collarbone to navel. It's healed cleanly. It looks a little like a star.

Nazarin presses the scar gently with his fingertip. "Will you keep this, too?"

"Yes."

I look up at him. His eyes are soft.

I want to ask him, but I'm not sure how. "Is Tila—?"

"No. Only you."

We stop speaking after that. I've wanted to have him again since our ill-considered night, and now there are no barriers. He pulls me to him, and my body presses against his. I melt into him, and he melts into me. We kiss, my fingertips running along the short buzz of his hair. He wraps his hands around my waist and lifts me off the ground. I wrap my legs around him.

We fall into the sofa, tasting each other. After we came out of Ensi's mind, my senses were confused, and Nazarin was the only thing that made sense. It's the same again. His skin, warm and firm, giving beneath my touch. The feel of his breath on my neck. The flicker of a tongue along the pulse of my throat.

My fingers unbutton his shirt, sliding it off of him. I run my hands along the firm muscles of his back, over the fading bruises. He's kept all his scars. His skin shows a life lived with danger—a shallow slash along the ribs, little nicks along his arms. I kiss each one.

I nip his skin with my teeth, and he pulls me up and crushes my mouth to his, holding my tongue between his teeth, just hard enough to hurt. I run my fingernails along his upper arms and he gasps against my mouth.

We shed the last of our clothes to mingle on the floor. I still feel weak, but Nazarin holds me. He moves into me, and

I draw him closer, as if our flesh could blend. The only sounds are the soft gasps of our breathing, the sound of our skin sliding against the fabric of the sofa. We move together. I roll on top of him. I kiss him as we move, faster and faster. We are the closest two people can be without being conjoined.

I shudder against him, my eyes shut tight, focused on that point deep within. I keep my mouth against his as we finish, loving the sound of his moan of release thrumming through me.

I lie on top of him, our limbs entangled, his heartbeat racing against the skin of my chest. My limbs grow lax and tingling with the ebb of desire. All thought has left me, and for the first time since this all began, I feel at peace.

Later, when we are in bed, I breathe in, long and deep, resting my lips against the top of Nazarin's skull. My fingers toy idly with the sheet. There's something about someone asleep next to you, vulnerable and breathing softly, that's so comforting.

It's not long until dawn. In a few hours, I'll see my sister again. I set out to free her, and I did.

I'm terrified. She's the person I know better than anyone else possibly could. All these people I see every day, they couldn't understand my relationship with Tila. How for so many years we were two people, yet we were the same. We couldn't hide from each other. All our strengths, all our weaknesses. We knew it all.

She kept all this from me. If she hadn't been caught, if Vuk hadn't attacked her, would she ever have told me?

She would never have been able to keep those secrets from me if we were still connected. Perhaps we should have fought the doctors harder. Claimed religious reasons—they wouldn't have been able to argue with that. But we didn't know that then. We were so young. So very innocent, compared to how we are now.

I want to let go of the anger, but I can't. Tila killed someone. She killed him to protect herself, and to protect me. I can't blame her for that. I don't think I ever did.

It's easy to take a life. We're such delicate creatures. Nazarin slumbers on, and my thoughts continue to circle. Thoughts of death, and blood, and wondering what will happen tomorrow, when I see my sister for the first time since they dragged her away from me.

Part of me wonders if I still want to see her.

## THIRTY-TWO

# TILA

I've been moved back from the prison in the Sierras (or wherever it was) to a holding cell in San Francisco. The guards told me I'm getting out in a few hours. So this will be the end of my testimony, which is good, I guess, because the notebook is almost full anyway. I still can't believe it, though I should know better than to ever underestimate Taema.

I've tried to tidy myself up a bit, but the girl in the mirror still looks like shit. Circles under my eyes, and my hair frizzy thanks to the cheap prison shampoo. Now I'm sitting here on the uncomfortable bed, alternately writing in here and looking out through that tiny window at the blue sky.

I'm scared to see Taema, after all this. Will she blame me? Will she be hurt at all I kept from her, even if it was to try and protect her? I don't know.

I've decided to spend my last moments in jail writing out what really happened. I'm taking this notebook out with me, and nobody else will read what I write in here now except my sister.

T:

I've made mistakes. I thought I'd be protecting you by not involving you, but now . . . I know that you were shot. You're going to be OK, but still. You were shot because of me. I put you in danger because I didn't want you to realize what I'd be willing to do to find out the truth. If I'd told you from the start, if we'd done this together, it would have worked out so differently.

How are we going to move on from this?

This is what happened. Here are your answers, T.

I first stumbled onto the whole Ratel business by accident. Mia met Adam in a Zealot lounge. He recognized her, but she didn't know who he was. They met up a few times. He tried to get her off the drugs, and they bonded enough that he told her who he really was. She ran, moved house, changed as much as she could, terrified that he was sent from Mana-ma to kill her. Remember when she upped and moved halfway across the city and took a few trips to the flesh parlors? That's when it was. Maybe he really was after her, too. I don't know.

She didn't tell me eveything at once. I was curious from the start. Someone from the Hearth who had changed their face? Who? When she told me it was Adam, that he was alive and working for the Ratel, then I knew I couldn't walk away. I tried to, but it burned at me.

It didn't take long for me to figure out that Vuk was a hitman for the Ratel, so that to even look into this meant capital-D Danger. I still couldn't leave it alone, though, especially when he walked into Zenith. I watched him for months, whenever he came in, though I didn't get too close. He didn't recognize me because I'd waxworked myself (that's why I did it, T: for your protection, not because I didn't want us to look the same anymore). I had blue hair, and you don't expect to see one half of a pair of conjoined twins from your former cult in an exclusive club in San Francisco.

That's what I thought at first, anyway. Until I realized the

Ratel had changed him. Overwritten his personality with what they wanted. Someone who could kill in cold blood, to order.

He fell in love with Leylani while I watched. When I saw that, I thought: if he can still fall in love, maybe they haven't made him disappear completely. Maybe there's still a little bit of Adam in there. I asked Mia, but all she told me in her Zeal-addled state was, "He is the red one, the fair one, the handsome one. He came from the Earth and now he returns. The faces keep changing." She said it over and over, until it freaked me out enough that I left her in her Zealot hovel.

It wouldn't surprise me if she did sell me out in the end for more Verve, but I can't prove it. Never will, now that she's gone.

I knew it was risky to speak to Vuk, so I didn't, at first. I kept my ear to the ground, and I heard that the Ratel were looking for lucid dreamers. It seemed too good to be true. No matter how much I tried, though, I didn't know how to get the Ratel's attention.

So I spoke to Vuk.

I didn't tell him I knew who he was. I told him only that I was the best lucid dreamer in the city, and his boss should speak to me at his earliest convenience. He said nothing and left the club early. I thought maybe he'd come back and kill me, and there would go that plan before it had even begun.

Instead, he came back a few nights later, and told me I had to prove it. We plugged into the Zeal Chairs. He'd swapped the drug with Verve without telling me. I followed all his instructions, moving through the dream world, making it do what I wanted. I liked that feeling of power, but I was also terrified of ending up like Mia.

Vuk was the one who got me into the Ratel. I started working for them, and it didn't take me long to become a dreamsifter in the Verve lounge. I met Ensi. One thing led to another. The closer I kept to him, the sooner I could learn secrets. How had the Ratel found Adam? How was Mana-ma linked to it all?

Eventually, I realized the best way to find out would be to speak to Vuk himself. I was going to get out of the Ratel after I did. Never go back. Go with you to China. Yeah, I knew you had that job before you told me. Saw the letter on the wallscreen at your place while you were in the bathroom. I peeked. Sorry. If I went, I thought I'd change my name, change my face again. I thought it'd be enough. I don't think it would have been, really. I can be so damn dim sometimes.

So I went to Zenith that night as usual. I'd met Leylani for coffee the day before and given her something that would make her a bit sick. Nothing to harm the baby or anything (I figured out she was pregnant, with all the running to the bathroom she did), but enough that she wouldn't be able to come in to work. I cozied up to Sal, saying I'd cover for Leylani that night. And I did. Vuk was in with a group of people. He didn't notice me any more than usual. He knew I worked for the Ratel, but otherwise we didn't interact. He was sad, wishing Leylani was there.

Eventually, most of the other partiers left, going to the main bar, and I managed to catch him.

"Adam."

He flinched. "Come again?"

"Adam, it's me. Tila. From the Hearth. I know I look a little different, but it's me."

He shook his head, as though batting away flies. "Don't know what you're talking about."

I moved closer. "You do. Some part of you remembers. Taema and Tila. T-and-T. We came to visit you. We brought green grapes."

His face twitched. His body shook. It was like he was having a war with himself. I stayed close, keeping my eyes on him.

He fell down on his knees, his hands rising to his temples. His mouth opened in a horrible, silent scream. I went to him and clasped my hands on his wrists.

"Adam," I said again.

At that, his entire body went rigid and he started convulsing, like he was having some sort of fit. Then he went completely limp. I thought he was dead. I wondered what would happen if someone opened the door in Zenith right then and saw him dead—they'd blame me.

Funny I worried about that then. Considering.

I pressed my fingers to his throat and he was still alive. I sat with him, holding his hand. It was his metallic one, though it felt just like cooling human flesh. I kept looking down at his face, trying to find the skinny boy I'd had a crush on in that blocky body, those different features. It really drove home how completely someone can change.

After a while he started groaning. I waited for him to wake up, and when he did and saw my face, he started crying. "Tila," he said. "I remember you."

"Hi, Adam," I said.

He really looked at me and his eyes popped. "Where's your sister?"

"They separated us."

I started to say something else, but his body devolved into spasms again. "Adam?" I asked, scared.

Spittle began flying from his mouth, and I really thought he was going to die.

When he could speak again, he clasped my hand. "I'm going to lose it, to go back to who I am now. I'll want to kill you. I'll think you're a threat." He clutched me closer. "When I go back,

I'll have to tell him everything. About you, about your sister. I won't be able to stop it." Another shudder. "It's who he made me to be."

His eyes rolled up in his head. His eyes focused on me. Sharpened. "You're a threat."

I scrambled back, knocking over a bunch of the glasses and breaking them. Adam-turned-Vuk stood up and started coming for me. He took out a knife from his inner jacket pocket. I picked up a broken shard of glass but I knew, I knew it wouldn't do a damn thing.

Adam-turned-Vuk's face was twisted with pain. "I don't want to do this, Tila. I don't want to. I'm tired. I don't want to go back to the man who made me into this." Every word was a struggle.

It took me a moment to realize what he was saying.

"Do it," he said. Every muscle was straining. He held out the knife, and I thought he was going to kill me. But instead he dropped it, and it landed on the floor within reach.

"Don't have . . . long," he gasped. He juddered again, knocking over more of the furniture.

I hesitated. I didn't want to. But then he said, "If he finds out about you, he'll find out about your sister. He'll—" another shudder—"hurt her to get to you."

That decided it.

Of course that decided it.

It wasn't as easy as that. He didn't lie still and let me kill him. His programming took over. His hunter's instincts. I took a swing and he blocked it, so I only cut his wrist. He grabbed me and I twisted back, stomping on his foot and then kicking up between his legs. He wheezed, dropped to his knees. I knew I couldn't hesitate. If I did, I would die.

I had a lucky strike. It went right into the upper part of his stomach, and I thrust up, and I think I hit him in the heart.

He fell down almost immediately. But he wasn't quite dead. He met my eyes and I didn't look away until he was gone.

I remember the blood was warm and sticky. That everything smelled of red, rusty iron. I felt angry, like I'd been trapped. I slammed the knife into the coffee table and it stood there, quivering.

The puddle of blood got bigger.

The blood must have triggered an alarm or something. Sal came in, and it was the first time I ever saw him shocked by anything.

I knew I should say something to him, but I was really out of it. I ended up parroting Mia's words: "He is the red one, the fair one, the handsome one. He came from the Earth and now he returns. The faces keep changing."

That definitely freaked him out. He snapped his fingers in front of my face until I could look up at him. It was hard to focus.

"Why?" he asked me. I blinked like I was waking up from a nightmare.

I told him. Not everything, but a little. That Vuk was a hitman for the Ratel and he'd asked me to kill him to free him. Sal, bless him, believed me right away. Barely even blinked before he was thinking of a way to fix it. Mostly to help himself, but still, he wasn't a totally selfish bastard, either.

"They'll be sending the Ratel here. The only way you won't die tonight is if you get out of here right now. Go home, get your things, and then go. I'm trusting you. Go straight there."

So I followed his advice. Before I ran away, I felt like I needed to . . . I don't know. Leave my mark. I scratched the sign of the Hearth, sad because I knew I'd never figure out exactly how everything was connected. Then I wrote Mia's name in our alphabet. She was the only person who knew I was undercover. If the Ratel got me before I made it home, then I knew you could ask her, Taema, and at least have a few answers.

I started going home, but then I changed course and went to you. Sal ended up phoning the police after all, though, and they tracked my VeriChip and came and found me.

I wish I'd done it differently. Ripped the VeriChip out of my wrist, made you do the same, and we could have disappeared before they could find us. I don't know where we would have gone, or what we could have done, but it would have been better than all this mess.

You know everything that happened after that. I think you even know more than me now.

They were supposed to put you into protective custody. That's what they told me they were gonna do, just after they took me, when I said you were in trouble, too. That Mia might have sold me out to the Ratel so my cover was blown. But instead, they made you become me, and you got put in just as much danger.

Bunch of fucking bastards.

I'm sorry, T. I made a huge mess out of everything. And, as usual, you found a way to fix it. But that's not fair. It's not fair on you at all.

I am so nervous. I almost want to stay here, so I don't have to face you. I only scratched at the edges of the Ratel. I'm afraid to learn your full story. It's going to be painful to listen to it. But I will.

The guard just came and told me it's time to go. I asked him for five more minutes. Five more minutes of scribbling crazily, the muscles in my hands cramping, as I try to figure out how to end this.

I guess I'll be trite—it's not like what I've written is good. Maybe I'll get you to help me write it into something properly resembling a story, if you're still speaking to me after all of this.

So this isn't an end but a beginning. This morning, I thought I was going to be frozen solid and put in a freezer with other frozen humans. Now, I find out I have my whole life ahead of me again. You are the one that brought down Mana-ma and broke up the Ratel. Maybe Adam's story can be told, along with all the other men and women whose memories were stolen. I heard Mia was killed, and I'm sure it was another one of Ensi's poor creations. Changing faces like kaleidoscopes.

Maybe we can see our parents for the first time in a decade. Go back to the Hearth, walk through the forest. Listen to the birds. We could swim in the lake for the first time.

I don't think we'll really change anything in the long run. But I've always been pessimistic. You've been the one with all the hope.

So, this is my new chance. My clean slate. All thanks to you. As soon as I finish this, I'll tuck my notebook into my pocket, give my lipstick a touch-up, walk out of this shithole and look you right in the eye.

# THIRTY-THREE

# TAEMA

I'm too afraid to go into the building where Tila's being held, so I wait outside. It's quiet, this time of day. People mill to and fro, heading to the MUNI or their offices and homes. They don't spare me a second glance. They don't know what I did and what I helped prevent, or at least delay. I hope they never find out.

The SFPD will send someone to the Hearth, to see how they're faring. They received an emergency phone call from our old cult. Mana-ma was found dead the next morning, tangled in her bed sheets, electrodes attached to her head. I've asked if they can send Nazarin, and if I (and maybe Tila) can go with him. We're not banned from the Hearth anymore, and I want to see my parents. I *need* to go back. Both of us do.

It's a cool day, even though it's late spring. It's the famous uncertain San Francisco weather. I'm wearing a scarf and a hat, my hands deep in my pockets. Nazarin isn't here. I came alone.

The door opens, and my breath hitches, but it's not her. A man in a suit walks down the steps and past me, not even glancing in my direction. I rub the palms of my hands against my thighs.

I turn away from the door for a moment, taking in the view

of the gunmetal gray of the water, the graceful arches of the bridges. The islands, half-hidden in the mist. Boats are out on the bay, gliding slowly through the white breaks, occasionally calling out softly to each other. It all seems so peaceful. I turn back.

There she is.

Tila stands on the top step. She's already caught sight of me, and her body is stiffly uncertain. Security drones circle her head like bees before drifting away to continue their perimeter check. She hesitates, and then begins to walk down the stairs.

It's so very strange, watching her come to me. She's no longer my reflection, now that I've changed my hair and my features back, but we're more different from each other now than ever before. I have two scars she doesn't have, and that's only the physical ones.

My sister stops a few paces away. We don't speak. She looks a little thinner. She glances down, takes something from her coat pocket. It's a notebook.

"Here. I wrote this, when I was inside. It was sort of a good-bye to you, I guess. When I thought I was going to freeze."

I take it from her, not touching her fingers. I swallow. My mouth is so dry.

"It's not very good, but it . . . explains a lot of it," she says. "I'll tell you the rest."

"I know some of the rest," I say quietly.

"Some of it was curiosity, but in the end it was all to protect you. Even if I did a monumentally bad job at it." She pauses, ducking her head to the side. "They told me you were shot. Did it hurt?"

I give her a half-smile. "Like a bitch. But not as much as getting struck by lightning when I was in Ensi's head."

"What—?"

"Come on," I say. "Let's go home. Figure it all out. And then move on from here. Any more secrets I should know about?" I'm only half jesting.

"I don't think so." With a strangled sob, she throws herself into my arms. I wrap mine about her, resting my head on her shoulder. We're both shaking. I hold her so tight, like I'll never let her go. We have a lot to work out. To get beyond. To heal from. But we will. We have to.

We stand together, forehead to forehead, chest to chest, our scars aligning, and beneath our bones our mechanical hearts beat, beat, beat.